BLOOD OATH

THE COMPLETE SERIES

J.A. CARTER

Blood Oath: The Complete Series

Published by J.A. Carter

Copyright © 2023 by J.A. Carter

www.authorjacarter.com

ALSO BY J.A. CARTER

Blood Oath Series

Bound in Crimson

Tempted by Fire

Entangled in Scarlet

Fated in Ruby

Unraveled by Desire

Raptured by Eternity

Join my mailing list at https://www.authorjacarter.com/newsletter-sign-up to be the first to know about new books and get access to reader exclusives!

To listen to the Spotify playlist while you read, scan the QR code!

BOUND IN CRIMSON

ONE

There are four vampires in my living room.

The space is blanketed in darkness save for the dim light cast against the aged hardwood floor from the one window in the room. It's closed—painted shut by the previous tenant—but the chirp of a car horn in the distance still rings through the silence.

None of them move. One leans against the exposed brick wall near my flat-screen, while the others occupy the light gray L-shaped couch I saved up for months to afford.

Do they think I can't see them? Surely they can hear the thundering heartbeats in my chest.

I stand frozen in the entryway, my key still in the lock. My eyes shift to the clock on the stove in my kitchen. It's almost one in the morning. Tonight has already been long, full of studying at the campus library, but the pit in my stomach tells me it's about to get a lot fucking worse.

My right leg shifts back.

"Don't run."

That smooth, deep, siren-like voice tries to trick my brain into keeping my feet anchored in place, but I know better. I whirl around, dropping my book bag in the doorway as I bolt for the bank of elevators at the end of the hall.

My heart slams against my chest in time with my white Doc Martens hitting the polished floor with each stride.

"Calla."

I swallow a yelp, turning to look over my shoulder as I keep running, only to find the hallway empty.

I slide to a halt and slam my fist against the elevator button, throwing myself inside the second it slides open. It's only once the door has shut that I let out a shaky breath. I inhale slowly, fighting the urge to scream until my throat is raw.

This can't be happening. Not yet.

Pressing the button for the lobby, I fall back against the wall, my eyes burning with exhaustion. Panic floods in when I realize what a terribly stupid move that was. They'll head straight for the lobby. I chew my lip for a second and press the button to the sixth floor. The elevator descends as the numbers count down *10, 9, 8, 7, 6* and it slows to a stop. The soft *ding* makes me push off the wall and step out into the quiet hallway.

I have no idea what the hell I'm doing. All I know is that I can't go back to the fifteenth floor and I can't go to the lobby. I'm trapped.

Unless...

They likely took the stairs down to the lobby and are waiting for the elevator—and my dumb ass.

I walk toward the door to the stairwell. I can take that down to the parking garage and slip out onto the street from there.

The door slams shut behind me, echoing off the concrete walls and stairs. I grip the cold metal railing as I race down the flights, noting the floor number painted in bright yellow on the wall at each landing.

My deep brown hair clings to the back of my neck. I suck in a shallow breath as my feet hit the landing on the second floor and the door to the hallway flies open.

I don't have time to scream. In the time it takes me to blink, I'm against the wall. Hands grip my shoulders, pressing my back into the concrete. My dull brown gaze flies up and collides with swirling silver irises.

I immediately turn feral. I fight against his grip, kicking and scratching at his chest with my chipped emerald fingernails. It doesn't faze him. And when I open my mouth to scream, he quickly clamps his hand over it before I can make a sound.

He exhales slowly. "Atlas told you not to run." His voice is low, tinged with amusement. He's enjoying this.

It takes every ounce of strength I have to rip his hand away from my mouth. He returns that hand to my shoulder, tightening his hold on me.

"I don't give a shit. Let go of me," I say through my teeth, trying to escape his grip as my heavy breathing makes the world spin around me.

He cocks his head, and his dark brown hair falls into his face. "If I do that, you'll run again." The twitch of his lips has me thinking that's exactly what he wants. *They love the chase.*

"I'll scream," I warn, shoving against him again. I'm no match for his strength, though knowing that doesn't convince me to stop. If anything, it makes me fight harder. It's what has kept me motivated every single morning to wake at the crack of dawn and spend at least an hour at the gym. Training regularly to build my strength for this exact moment. I've managed a bit of muscle on my sadly curve-free figure but compared to these guys, I'm tiny. I was kidding myself that I'd stand a chance against a vampire—let alone four. Years of training, and it was all for nothing. My stomach plummets at the thought; I'm not ready to admit it.

"You will," he agrees, "though it'll be my name before it's anything else." The vampire in front of me pushes me back, lowering his face to mine. "But by all means, give it a shot." He knows as well as I do it won't get me anywhere.

"Who the fuck are you?" I growl instead, ignoring the way his words made my heart race. It's a dumb question, but if I can keep him talking maybe I can buy myself some time to figure a way out of this mess.

The guy smirks, a subtle twist of his lips that would make the purest of angels desire sin. "You know who I am. You ran because you know exactly who we are."

I grit my teeth when his fingers flex against my bare shoulders. It doesn't hurt, but his proximity is making my knees shake. Though that could also be from sprinting down the stairs. "I ran because it's the middle of the night and you broke into my apartment."

Those silver eyes snare me without effort and sparkle. "Calla, Calla, Calla."

I scowl when he tuts his tongue, and swallow the bile rising in my throat. "Stop saying my name."

He grins. "Are you going to play nice if I step away now?"

"That depends," I say, "if you consider me punching you in the face playing nice."

He whistles softly. "You're going to be quite the handful, aren't you?"

That catches my attention, and I stiffen.

"Kade, that's enough." The voice comes from above, and my head turns in time to see another silver-eyed guy walking down the concrete stairs toward us. This one isn't as muscular as the guy holding me against the wall—Kade apparently—and he has wavy copper hair with strands that appear pure gold in this light. It's a mess of waves that I can't stop staring at.

"Relax, Gabriel. She's fine. Aren't you, Calla?" He hooks my chin with his finger and turns my gaze back to him. The moment our eyes meet, a pleasant warmth floods through me, washing away the tension in my muscles.

I nod without a single thought. Of course, I'm fine. I can't even remember what I could have possibly been upset about.

Kade smiles, and I find myself smiling back... until he blinks, severing the glamour.

I stare at him for several seconds, horrified by my complete loss of control, and then I lose my shit. Tension grips me again as my eyes narrow, and I curl my fingers against my palms. "You fucking pr—"

Gabriel pulls me away from him before I can start throwing fists. "All right, angel, let's go."

In the brief moment he lets go of my arm, I duck under his and run. My grip on the railing slips from the dampness of my palm, but I manage to grab it again before falling. I make it to the next landing and collide with Gabriel's chest.

My head whips back toward the level above where he'd just been, and I shake my head as I struggle to catch my breath.

"Stop running," he says in a voice so soft, so gentle, I pause. He isn't glamouring me.

I take a step away, and I'm about to tell him where he can go when my back hits a solid wall of muscle. I turn to find Kade grinning at me, and my eyes burn with angry tears.

There's no way out.

"Calla." Gabriel's smooth voice makes me look back at him.

I shake my head, cursing myself as one awful word leaks from my lips. "Please."

"Oh, come on," Kade says, wrapping his arm around my shoulders and holding me against his side. "Don't start begging now. I much prefer your sharp tongue."

My brows knit as anger crackles through me once more, and I grit my teeth. "Fuck you," I seethe, shoving away from him.

Gabriel steps in, placing his hand at the small of my back, guiding me toward the hallway. The warmth of his hand surprises me, though I'm not sure why, and all of a sudden, it doesn't matter. We're moving out of the stairwell, back into the hallway to the elevator bank.

"See? That's much better," Kade says from behind us, and I inhale slowly to keep myself from launching at him again. Theoretically, I know it won't get me anywhere, but that sure as hell doesn't mean I'm restrained enough to ignore the urge.

We get into the elevator, and Gabriel presses the button to my floor as the door slides shut, then he leans against the wood-paneled wall. He rakes his fingers through those copper curls, and my eyes roam over him, taking in his formal appearance. Dark slacks and a starch white collared shirt make him look as if he came here from some sort of business meeting. Especially compared to the distressed jeans and the T-shirt that is barely containing Kade's insane muscles. Gabriel looks to be a few years older than him, though both have at least a century on me. Despite that—and the reason they're here—I can't help but notice how attractive they are. Would I prefer to not have them in my life? Of course. Perhaps if we'd met in a bar instead of my apartment in the middle of the night, I might've let them buy me a drink. But that isn't our circumstance.

I'd like to think I can chalk up my physical attraction toward them to their vampiric allure. All humans are drawn to it despite—for the majority of the population—being oblivious to the existence of vampires, so how could I possibly think I'd be immune?

I stare at the stubble along Kade's defined jaw, watching as a muscle feathers along it. Despite his outward amusement to the situation, he's tense too. And if that doesn't put me on edge even more... *What the hell does he have to be worried about?*

Kade hums under his breath—a Pink Floyd song, I think—as the elevator ascends, and my jaw is clenched so hard my molars are throbbing by the time we step off on the fifteenth floor. When we reach my apartment, Kade opens the door and walks in as if he owns the place. I follow him inside with Gabriel behind me and faintly notice my book bag is hung on the hook next to my jacket. Someone has turned on the light above my kitchen island as well as the few lamps around my living room, blanketing the relatively small space in warm light.

The other two guys are still sitting on my couch. Waiting. They knew Kade and Gabriel would have no issues returning with me, and I hate that.

Kade walks over and drops onto the end of the couch. It's unsettling how comfortable he seems in my apartment. Like maybe this isn't his first time here… A chill runs through me, and I push the thought away. I can't think about that now.

"Calla Montgomery," a new voice says, and another of the guys gets off the couch and walks toward me.

My breath halts as I take him in. He's dressed in black from head to toe in wrinkle-free pants and a button-up shirt that makes him look as if he's about to attend a charity banquet. His hair is a deep brown, cropped on the sides and slightly longer on top, but styled expertly, not a piece out of place. His face is all sharp angles, paired with dark brows and thick lashes. He's tall and built like Kade, and definitely not the kind of person you'd want to meet in a dark alley—or anywhere for that matter. My body tenses, recognizing the vampire before me as a predator. Everything about him warns me away and pulls me closer in the same breath. It's a contradiction that makes my head spin. He's different than the others. I don't know why or what it is about him that makes me realize it, but there's something about him… I reel my thoughts in. Now is *not* the time to debate this.

I press my lips together for a moment. "If I say you have the wrong person, will you leave?"

Kade chuckles from the couch, but the guy standing in front of me doesn't so much as crack a smile.

He watches me thoughtfully for a moment, those silver eyes darkening and slicing right through me. "You understand why we're here." It isn't a question.

"Of course she knows, Atlas," Gabriel chimes in.

"For me," I say anyway. My voice is flat, emotionless.

"Are you afraid?"

I almost laugh at the audacity of his question. "No. No, I'm super thrilled to have four strangers in my apartment for the sole reason of stealing my future." I clamp my mouth shut as stiffness ripples through my muscles, but it's too late. The words are out there.

Out of nowhere, the fourth guy appears in front of me, making me jump back in surprise. His hair is white, but what really catches my attention are the black ink tattoos covering his arms and what I can see of his chest from the black V-neck he's wearing. Vines of differing sizes wind around his left arm with thorns spaced along them and incredibly detailed roses, shaded in such a way they appear as if they're on fire. I've always wanted a tattoo, but I'm not sure what. That, and the idea of undergoing that amount of pain on purpose... I don't really understand it. Though I get the feeling that'd change after my first one.

"Perhaps not the *sole* reason," the tattooed vampire muses, and my eyes snap to his face just as his smoldering gaze trails the length of my body.

Heat floods my cheeks, and I stare at him, wide-eyed. I want to look away, to run far, but I have nowhere to go. I won't make it past these guys—I need to be smarter, which likely means I need them to think I've given up. At least for now.

"Don't freak the poor girl out, Lex," Kade says, pulling himself off the couch and approaching the small group we've made in the middle of my apartment.

My stomach feels heavy as my gaze bounces around the room. I bite the inside of my cheek to keep from saying something that definitely won't help my situation.

I shouldn't be in this mess.

These guys—these *vampires*—are here because my ancestors promised them the first-born female of their bloodline in exchange for saving their lives. To help them out of some shady, very much illegal business deal they got wrapped up in on Wall Street. Long story short, they sacrificed my life to save themselves, sealing the fate of an unborn girl before she even had a chance.

You'd think that might deter my great-grandparents or my grandparents or even my parents from having children. But no. In my mom's defense, she didn't know about the deal the Montgomery family made with the vampires until she was pregnant. My father kept it from her and prayed—like his father and grandfather did before him—that the child would be a boy.

When the doctor told my parents I was a girl, they were heartbroken. My mom was beside herself with anger—toward my dad and the cruelty of the fate her family had been given. They wanted to protect me, of course, but how were a couple of humans supposed to fight four hundred-or-so-year-old vampires? Any possibility would've been laughable at best. That's the problem with blood oaths. We are bonded on a level I'll never be able to outrun. Though that certainly isn't going to stop me from trying.

I moved to Washington, D.C. from New York City three years ago, just shy of my twentieth birthday. I took a couple of years off after high school to travel the Pacific Northwest—and had the time of my life experiencing new places—before moving here to start my undergrad in Sociology at Georgetown University, courtesy of the guilt money my parents send to pay my tuition and rent. It's an unspoken agreement. They wire money into my account, and I live with knowing my own family sacrificed my freedom—and most likely my life—to these assholes.

Sociology piqued my interest after taking a very basic course in high school, and when it came time to decide the path for my future— even with how bleak I knew it would be—something in my gut told me this was the right choice. I'm almost halfway through my major and that hasn't changed—even though everything else about my life is about to now.

"We'll give you a few minutes to pack a bag," Atlas says, moving toward the kitchen and snatching a bright green apple from the bowl on the island. My best friend Brighton and I took a pottery class last year, and that uneven, lumpy bowl was my creation. Art in that form clearly isn't my forte. Atlas takes a loud bite and leans against the counter.

I watch him with a renewed sense of bitterness. "I'm not going anywhere with you. Not only am I pissed you showed up here in the middle of the fucking night, I'm in university. It's the first week of March—I can't just leave halfway through the term."

"That's what you're concerned about?" Lex asks with a sharp laugh, arching a dark brow at me. His brows are an odd contrast to his fair skin and white hair. "Humans truly are silly creatures."

Of course it's not my main concern, considering they are actively upending my life and I have absolutely no idea what's going to happen when we leave this place, but if I let any of that in even for a moment, I'm going to lose it. So I don't. Instead, I snap, "You might be concerned too if you were forking out sixty grand a year." He doesn't know it's not coming out of my pocket.

He shrugs. "You don't want to pack a bag, fine. I'll do it."

Before I can protest, he's gone in a blur of movement, causing a burst of air to blow my hair across my face. I tuck the dark brown waves back over my shoulder and glance around the room.

Kade grins at me when my gaze reaches him. "He's gonna go through your panty drawer."

I shake my head as exhaustion pulls at me. Evidently, the adrenaline is wearing off. "I don't care."

"We should go," Gabriel says from the couch, drumming his fingers along the back of it. "Calla's had a long night."

"Calla can speak for herself," I say in a sharp tone, though he's not wrong. I was tired when I left the campus library with Brighton. If my nerves weren't fried, I'd have likely passed out on the floor by now.

What I wouldn't give to open my eyes and realize all of this was a nightmare. No such luck. The vampires that broke into my apartment to kidnap me are very real, and I am very screwed.

When Kade steps toward me, my eyes narrow, and I immediately step back... right into Atlas's chest. *When did he move from the kitchen?*

I'm in no position to fight these guys, but my muscles tense as if I'm going to anyway.

Atlas snakes his arm around my waist before I can move. "Don't make this harder," he warns in a low voice, his lips brushing the shell of my ear.

I shiver, then try to drive my elbow back to get him to let go, but it does nothing but exert energy I'm already in low supply of.

"Calla." His voice makes me freeze, and I squeeze my eyes shut. If this bastard thinks he's going to glamour me into compliance, he's got another thing coming.

I clench my fists tighter. "Let go of me."

"You don't need to keep fighting." With his free hand, he wraps his fingers around my throat, pushing gently until the back of my head rests against his chest.

The tension leaves my muscles, and I stop trying to break free of his hold. *What the fuck?*

"That's better," he murmurs against my hair, and his fingers slip away from my throat.

Confusion floods through me as I open my eyes to find Kade and Gabriel watching me. "W-what? No..."

Gabriel offers a faint smile. "Glamour works in different ways, angel. For vampires like Atlas, skin-to-skin contact is just as powerful as eye contact."

I shake my head as annoyance flickers through me. "That's not fair."

I think I feel a rumble of laughter against my back.

Lex walks down the hall from my bedroom, a duffle bag slung over his shoulder. His eyes shift between us, and he arches a brow. "We good?" Then he focuses on me. "Don't worry, I grabbed the pretty lace ones." He pats the side of the bag and winks at me.

"I'm going to kill you," I say in a low voice in an attempt to mask my shame; the fight in me is gone. "All of you." I pull away from Atlas, and he lets me. I walk to the door, grabbing my jacket and book bag off the hook before leaving my apartment. When I realize that I may never return, a pit of dread builds a home in my stomach.

TWO

They live in a fucking mansion in the Palisades. Because *of course* their house is in one of the most expensive neighborhoods in Washington.

It's at least three stories high and built into a hill, I realize as the Escalade slows to pull into the paved driveway. The light from inside gives the exterior a soft glow. Stone stairs lead up to the front door, and the massive exterior is made of glass and dark wood panels. The driveway is surrounded by a stone wall that frames the professionally maintained shrubbery and grass and is built taller to fit the height of the wood-paneled garage door. Tall trees surround the property, but not enough to block the curb appeal.

If it wasn't my very own prison, I might actually appreciate its luxury.

Atlas presses a button on the dash, opening the door, and we drive into an unnecessarily huge garage. The door closes soundlessly behind us as Atlas pulls into an empty spot between two other wildly expensive-looking cars. I'm vaguely aware when he kills the engine and the car doors start opening. The cold air seeps inside with the heat no longer blowing, and I shiver, tugging my jacket tighter around me as I peer around the garage from inside the quiet vehicle.

Being surrounded by concrete walls makes me want to bolt. It certainly doesn't help the sensation of being trapped, making it feel as if someone is standing on my chest. Even with the bright track lighting across the ceiling, the walls threaten to close in on me any second.

"Calla."

I flinch before turning to find my door open and Atlas standing there waiting for me to get out. I don't want to. My gaze drops to my lap where my hands are clenched into fists, and I let loose a faint sigh.

The passenger side door slams shut, and I jump, looking up in time to see the back of Kade's head before he disappears into the house with Lex not far behind him, my duffle bag slung over his shoulder.

I unbuckle my belt and reach down to grab my book bag off the floor, gripping it so tight my nails bite into my palm. I focus on that discomfort as I get out of the car to follow Atlas and Gabriel inside, my shoes echoing faintly on the concrete floor.

The shrill chirp of the car locking makes my pulse race, and I press my lips together when Gabriel rests his hand against my lower back.

"You're okay," he says and reaches past me to open the frosted glass door.

I walk into the house and am immediately greeted by warmth and a faint smell of lemon. This place is straight out of a Pottery Barn catalog. The walls at the back of the house are made entirely of floor-to-ceiling windows, which I imagine look absolutely stunning in daylight. The pool reflects the moonlight outside, and though I'm completely out of my element here, I can't help the twinge of excitement that flickers through me. *I've never lived anywhere with a pool.*

My eyes travel around the room, taking in the open-concept space. The furniture is... interesting. Nothing matches, yet somehow it works. There's a long maroon couch with a glass coffee table in front of it, stacked with books, and a few olive green and taupe chairs that complete the sitting area.

Beyond that is the kitchen. The counters are made up of two gray marble slab islands with a sink and stovetop built in. Dark wood cabinets provide storage below and match the tall cabinets built into the wall adjacent to the islands. The double oven built into the wall of cabinets looks professional enough to be in a Michelin star restaurant.

"You don't need to stand by the door," Kade says, leaning against one of the counters.

I blink, barely noticing that Gabriel is still at my side. "This place is ridiculous," I mumble, still taking it all in. Though I wouldn't mind taking advantage of that kitchen to make cookies or pastries. Maybe a cheesecake or some tarts. Baking has always been a hobby of mine, something to distract me when school gets overly stressful. Plus, I have an insane sweet tooth. There's hardly ever a time the cookie jar on the counter in my kitchen is empty.

Next to the kitchen is a full dining set with enough seating to fit a small army. It is also surrounded by windows.

"Evidently, sunlight isn't a concern," I comment in an absent tone as I walk further into the room.

"That's right," Lex confirms, dropping onto the couch and grabbing a book from the coffee table. He cracks it open as he kicks his feet up, then props a pillow under his head. "We don't burn... or sparkle, in case you were wondering."

I wasn't.

"I'll take you to your room and show you around on the way," Gabriel says from beside me.

"I don't need a tour of my glorified prison cell," I snap without a thought. As tired and defeated as I am, that fiery anger still rages on in me.

Lex whistles from behind his book, and it makes me want to throw something at him.

"You can have anything you want here," Kade says, pushing away from the counter to walk closer. My back stiffens in response to his proximity, but I don't move. "Anything at all. I certainly don't think you would receive the same in prison."

A muscle twitches in my jaw, a subtle reminder that if I continue clenching it this hard, I'm going to end up with a migraine. "I *want* to go home." My voice takes on a defiant tone, to which Kade smirks at.

"I do enjoy your sharp tongue."

"Fuck off, Kade," Lex says in a light tone without looking up from his book. "Give the girl a chance to get in the door before you start tormenting her."

Kade keeps his silver gaze on me a moment longer before sauntering away.

Atlas is gone too, I notice. I'm not sure when he disappeared—I was probably too enraptured by this insane house to pick up on his departure. I'm not sure what I was expecting—a stone castle in the middle of nowhere perhaps?—but a modern, mostly glass mansion wasn't it.

I lift my book bag onto my shoulder and sigh. "Let's go," I say, waiting for Gabriel to show me the way.

He leads me to a wide hallway off of the kitchen that I hadn't seen when we first walked in. The high ceilings leave ample room for the painted canvases hung on the otherwise plain white walls, and pot lights cast a golden glow down the hall. It leads to a second, more formal living room with a floor-to-ceiling fireplace and skylights. The dark gray furniture in this room all matches and appears to be more for show, not as though it's actually comfortable to sit on.

I follow Gabriel around a corner to a set of double doors. He opens one and gestures for me to walk in ahead of him. When I hesitate, he offers a faint smile that makes something flutter in my chest. Instead of trying to figure out what in the hell that is, I walk inside, and my mouth drops open.

This bedroom is in the corner of the house, so both outside walls are floor-to-ceiling windows that look out into the forest along the property. There's nothing but darkness to see right now, but I have a feeling the view during the day is nothing to scoff at. The queen bed faces the windows, and in the corner of the room is a gray lounge chair that matches the bedding, a gold free-standing lamp, and a small glass table with a vase of fresh white orchids.

They know my favorite flower.

A chill runs down my spine, and I hug my jacket closer as I'm reminded that these guys know way more about me than I know about them.

"It's pretty plain," Gabriel says. "If you want anything to personalize the space, let me know and I'll have it delivered. And there's a library in Atlas's office if you're looking for something to read. I know you enjoy books."

I bite the inside of my cheek, nodding silently. While I'm definitely curious about the aforementioned library, Gabriel knowing one of my favorite hobbies is yet another reminder of my current circumstances. I've always loved to read, though. And while I haven't had much time for reading anything aside from textbooks and assignments, that passion has stayed with me.

"There's a bathroom around there," Gabriel says softly, pointing toward the break in the wall on the far side of the bed.

I set my book bag down next to where Lex left my duffle at the end of the bed and walk around to the wide-open bathroom. There looks to be a door that will slide across for privacy, and not only does it have his and hers vanities with sinks on opposite sides of the room, but two showers as well—and a soaker tub in between them.

My hand flies to my mouth when I catch my reflection in the mirror. I look like shit. Pale complexion, dark under-eye circles, and smeared eyeliner. Fair enough; I look as awful as I feel. Not to mention, my hair is a tangle of dark brown waves that could definitely use a wash; dry shampoo only lasts so long.

"Do you need a minute?"

I startle at the sound of Gabriel's voice and turn toward him. What I need is to get the hell out of here. Instead, I say, "Several."

He watches me for a moment before nodding toward a cabinet next to the vanity on the left. "There are towels and about a hundred different soaps and conditioners in there."

I arch a brow at him.

Gabriel shakes his head, but there's a fondness in his voice when he says, "Kade takes hair care very seriously."

Perhaps if the circumstances that landed me in this moment with Gabriel were different, I would smile.

He gives me one last look before heading out of the room. It's only once I hear the bedroom door click shut that I let out a breath. The next one gets caught in my throat, and I rush over to the shower and turn it on in hopes of covering the sound of the sob that tears its way up my throat. Tears spring in my eyes, and while I'm surprised at the sudden onslaught, I don't fight them back. I will let myself cry behind closed doors, but I will never let them see.

I strip out of my clothes, leaving them in a pile on the shiny marble floor, and step under the hot spray of water. My chin quivers as tears mix with water on my face, and I run my fingers through my hair until it's wet enough to lather with the glass bottle of eucalyptus and mint scented shampoo. *Stupid fancy soap.*

I scrub until my skin is an angry red, and by the time I'm rinsing the conditioner out of my hair, my belly aches and my temples are pounding. All I want to do is close my eyes and forget this entire night ever happened.

I have to get out of here.

My heavy limbs disagree, but it doesn't stop me from stepping out of the shower, leaving the water running, and quickly drying off. I wrap the towel around me and tiptoe into the bedroom to grab my duffel bag. I tear through it until I find a pair of leggings and a heavy beige sweater. I get changed as fast as I can and towel dry my hair enough I won't catch a cold the minute I step outside.

I grab my book bag with my cell phone and wallet and shove my feet into my shoes. My mind is going a million miles an hour, and I am very aware that what I'm about to attempt is ridiculously stupid, but I refuse to accept this as my reality—being stolen away from everything I love and for what? To be turned into a slave to four vampires? Nausea ripples through me, making my jaw clench as bile rises in my throat. I swallow hard and square my shoulders. I need to at least *try* to escape.

I shoulder my bag and go to the window near the bathroom. It takes up the entirety of the wall, but there's also a window panel that opens enough to get out—which is exactly what I do. I hold my breath as I unlatch the lock and push the panel open. I peek down and cringe. It's still a few feet, but much better than it could've been if they'd stuck me in a bedroom on the second or third floor.

Their mistake.

I climb out, my breath fogging the air in front of me as the cold knocks the wind out of my lungs. I suck in a deep breath and dart toward the line of trees along the side of the house which, to my benefit, is made of actual walls instead of windows.

My heart rattles in my chest as I sprint through the forest, tripping over fallen branches here and there, but managing to catch my balance before eating the ground each time. When I finally reach the road, I don't stop. I follow the asphalt until it meets the main road, then I pull my phone out and order a ride, choosing a meeting place a short distance away so I can keep moving.

I round the corner and see the license plate of my driver. I run the rest of the way down the sidewalk and throw myself into the back of the car, my chest heaving with every breath.

"You okay there, hon?" Leanne, my five-star driver asks, eyeing me from the rearview mirror. She has dark corkscrew curls that reach her shoulders, and she's wearing one of those puffy jackets in a bright yellow color. I can't really make out her expression in the dark, but her tone is kind.

"Yes," I force out. "Please just drive."

When she reads my address aloud to confirm the drop-off, my pulse races. I'd put in my home address just to get picked up.

"No," I say quickly. "I can't go there."

She frowns at me. "Are you sure you're all right? Should I call the police?"

I choke on a desperate laugh. *Unless the police can arrest four vampires for taking what they believe to be rightfully theirs based on a century-old blood oath, you'd be wasting a call, Leanne.*

"Hon?"

"No," I repeat. "I'm fine. Just head toward Pennsylvania Ave."

"I'm supposed to get an address," she says.

"I'll pay you whatever you want. In cash."

She doesn't hesitate this time. We pull away from the curb, heading toward the interstate, and I can't help but feel as though I'm fighting a losing battle.

THREE

The streets of Washington are quiet, unlike the pounding in my chest. My head is spinning and my forehead is damp with sweat. I have no idea what I'm doing, and every second I don't figure it out, I'm losing what little ground I managed to gain on these guys.

The driver keeps looking at me in the rearview mirror; I'm freaking her out.

I'm also putting her in danger. Who knows what the guys will do if they find me with another person?

Panic spikes as I reach for the door handle. "Let me off here," I say, quickly pulling a fifty-dollar bill out of my bag.

She pulls over and hits the brakes as I toss the bill at her. "Wait—"

"Thanks," I mutter, getting out of the car and slamming the door shut before I take off down the street.

My chest is tight as my heart pounds in time with my shoes hitting the pavement. My lungs sting from the exertion and the cold air, but I don't stop. I clutch the phone in my hand, and before I'm even aware of what I'm doing, I've dialed Brighton's number. I chew my lip as the line rings and rings... and rings. Finally, there's a click, and my stomach sinks.

"Calla! Where the hell are you?" Brighton shouts, and I immediately pull the phone away from my ear. Music blares in the background, and I cringe.

I've stopped running so I'm not too out of breath to speak, but I'm still moving at a fast pace. I need to put as much distance between me and them as I can. "Brighton… can you hear me?"

"Hello?" She's still shouting. "Hang on! I'm going outside!" A minute later, the music quiets and the line is silent. "Shit, okay. What's up, lady?"

"I need a favor." A car honks in the distance, and I jump, whipping my head around to find the street and sidewalk behind me empty. I start walking faster.

"At almost two in the morning?" she asks with a short laugh. "What are you up to? Oh god, please don't tell me you went home to keep studying and you want me to bring you caffeine."

"I need your credit card," I blurt. If I use mine, I have to assume they'll track it. But maybe if I go to a building filled with people, I can hide for a short time. It's dangerous to stop, knowing they could come for me, but I need to rest, to come up with a better plan than just running until I can't any longer. If things had gone the way I'd imagined when thinking of this awful moment, I would've killed those vampires before I had an opportunity to know their names. It was a naive thought, and I hate that it was my only real strategy, because now I'm pretty well screwed. "Actually, I need you to book me a room at the Four Seasons."

"Uhhh." Her voice cracks. "Calla—"

"Please, Bri. I can't explain anything right now, but I need a place."

"Why don't you crash at mine? I'll be home soon, and we can talk about what's going on."

"No," I say quickly. I can't lead them to her. I'm not about to put my best friend in the path of four vampires who are likely pretty pissed I gave them the slip in their own home. "Please just get me a room."

There's a short pause before Brighton says, "Calla, you know I'm here for you no matter what. If you're in trouble—"

I cut her off, rushing to say, "I don't have time to fill you in." I'm not even sure what the hell I'd tell her, anyway.

She sighs. "Hang on."

I stay on the line for a couple of minutes, nibbling on the pad of my thumb as I peek over my shoulder every ten seconds. Waiting for them to come after me, to find me.

"Calla?"

My pulse jackhammers momentarily. "Yeah, I'm here."

"The suite is booked under my name for as long as you need. I sent the confirmation to your email. If there are any issues, call me."

I let out a breath. "Thank you, Brighton. Seriously. I owe you."

"Just... whatever is going on, please be careful. And promise you'll fill me in as soon as you can?"

"I'll talk to you soon," I say, disconnecting before I tell her another lie. Honestly, I'm not sure when I'll speak to her next. I just need to make it somewhere safe so I can figure out my next move.

Do Atlas, Kade, Gabriel, and Lex already know I'm gone? I think it's safe to say yes. Can they track me to the hotel? There's a good chance of that if my theory of hiding among a bunch of other people is wrong, which it very likely could be. But if I can barricade myself in a room just long enough to come up with a less awful plan than run and hide, then maybe—just maybe—I can get myself out of this.

The first thing I do when I get into the suite is lock the door and shove the heavy coffee table against it before checking the windows. I'm on the top floor, so it's a little ridiculous, but I do it anyway. Anything to feel a semblance of safety—of control.

I kick off my shoes and pace the fancy room, my stocking feet padding soundlessly across the dark wood floor. I'm not sure what made Brighton spring for a suite with a full living room and dining area, but I'm not going to complain. Considering she knows as well as I do that it'd take me all semester to pay her back for this, and she did it without asking a million questions that I can't answer right now. Though, knowing Brighton as well as I do, she didn't think twice about dropping this kind of money. I suppose that comes with being as well-off as her family is.

I pull in slow, deep breaths, trying to wrack my brain for a plan that isn't absolutely insane. I pull my phone out and scroll through my contacts. My finger hovers over my mom's number, but I shake my head and sigh, tossing the phone onto the marble dining table. As sympathetic to my plight as she may be, there isn't a thing she can do. And my dad... The man isn't brave—or stupid—enough to go against the vampires his great-grandparents sealed my fate with.

I briefly consider what would happen if I went back to New York, but it's pointless. Even if my parents wanted to protect me, two humans against four vampires wouldn't stand a chance. And as much as I resent my family—my father mostly—for this life, I couldn't do that to them.

After I've changed out of my clothes and wrapped myself in the plush bathrobe, I pull my hair into a messy bun on the top of my head and brush my teeth using the complimentary disposable brush I found in the bathroom. All the while trying to avoid my reflection in the mirror.

I rinse out my mouth and exhale slowly before walking out of the bathroom.

A scream tears its way up my throat when my eyes land on Atlas, lounging in the wingback chair in the corner of the bedroom. Something in me—survival instincts maybe—kicks in, and I race toward the door. The table I had pushed in front of it is back where it was when I arrived. *What the hell?* I barely get the door open an inch before Atlas reaches past me and slams it shut. He grabs me by the shoulders and turns me around to face him. My back hits the closed door, and I immediately start fighting him.

"You want to do this again?" he asks with a subtle head tilt.

"Fuck you," I snap, but cease shoving at his chest for a moment to catch my breath.

His eyes roam my face before dropping to my chest where my robe has fallen open. His gaze freezes there, and the air leaves my lungs.

"Kade wanted to come get you," he says in a low voice, his eyes hooded. He's so close I could count his dark lashes. You know, if I wasn't preoccupied with trying to get away from him.

I swallow past the dryness in my throat. "So why are *you* here then?" I force out.

"Be glad it's me, Calla." His eyes finally lift back to my face as he reaches forward and closes my robe. "He was keen on punishing you for running away."

I wet my lips, tipping my head back against the door so I can meet his gaze. "And you?"

He shakes his head. "What I'd like to do to you..."

"You're going to kill me," I say in a flat voice. It's the only conclusion I've come to. No matter what happens, these men will be my end.

Atlas blinks at me. His eyes are dark but there's something else in them. He looks tired. "I'm not here to kill you."

"Doesn't mean it won't happen," I say, my throat suddenly thick with emotion. "You may not even mean to do it—any of you—but it will happen."

His expression remains impassive. "You're so convinced we're monsters."

"Aren't you?" I whisper.

He purses his lips in thought for a moment. "Perhaps to some." He leans in and brushes his fingers along my cheek. "But not you."

My jaw clenches against his hand as confusion floods through me. "Then let me go," I plead, holding his gaze. "Tell the others you couldn't find me. I'll get on a plane and—"

He drops his hand, and my skin tingles where he was touching. "We will find you wherever you run. When are you going to realize that?"

I grab the front of his shirt without thinking, wrinkling the soft cotton material between my fingers. "Why? What could you possibly want from me? You've essentially ruined my life, stolen my future, and for what?"

He peers down at where I'm white-knuckling his shirt before meeting my gaze again. "We've waited a long time for you, Calla."

I shake my head, my brows tugging together. "That doesn't answer my question."

"It's not a simple one."

A shiver runs through me, and I swallow hard when I catch a flash of his elongated canines. "You're going to feed on me," I say, my voice barely above a whisper. What else could they want me for besides a personal human vending machine?

His eyes shift between mine, but he doesn't miss a beat. "Yes." Again he leans in until his lips are next to my ear, his breath tickling the skin below my earlobe. "What's more, you'll enjoy every second of it."

I suck in a breath when he presses his mouth to the pulse at my neck. His tongue darts out and flicks against my skin, and my head swims. I grip his shirt tighter, though I'm not sure if it's to pull him closer or shove him away. His proximity—and ridiculously powerful pheromones—are messing with my head something fierce, and I despise that they affect me so much even though I want to kill him. Because that's the only way I can see out of this—it's either me or them.

Then Atlas steps back, and I let go. A flush creeps across my cheeks, and I look away, suddenly embarrassed by the heat pooling in my belly.

I quickly walk toward the sitting area, wanting to put some distance between us so I can think clearly.

"You shouldn't be embarrassed about your response to me. Or feel shy about what your body desires, for that matter," Atlas says, following me and lowering himself into one of the chairs.

"I have no idea what you're talking about," I lie. "I'm sleep-deprived, that's all."

"With how tightly wound you are, I'd say you're more than *sleep-deprived*."

I choke on a forced laugh. "You don't know anything about me."

Those silver eyes pierce right through me. "Care to make a bet on that?"

"Not a chance," I say around a yawn.

"Because you know you're wrong."

"Oh yeah?" I cross my arms, leaning against the back of the chair. "What do you know about me, Atlas?"

He's out of his chair and leaning over mine in the time it takes me to blink. I suck in a short breath as he grips the armrests and leans in until his nose is an inch from mine. I'm not sure I'll ever get used to the incredible speed these vampires possess.

"You think we haven't spent years getting to know you?" His breath tickles my cheek, and I force myself to hold his gaze. "That we haven't memorized everything about your life while we waited for the right moment to—"

"Ruin it?" I interject with a bitter tone.

His eyes seem to darken, and he lowers his voice. "You think I don't know how to set your body off like a fucking firecracker with a single touch?" There's a challenge in his voice that has my pulse pounding beneath my flushed skin.

Boldness grips me, and I say, "Then why haven't you?"

He stares at me for a long moment without saying anything, and then he murmurs, "Because Kade called first dibs on your pussy."

Those words feel like ice water being dumped on me, effectively murdering the fluttering in my stomach.

I scowl and shove him away. "Asshole."

Atlas straightens and walks toward the door. "Get some sleep. You'll be returning to our place tomorrow. And Calla," he says, pausing to look at me over his shoulder, "don't run again. It won't be me coming to get you next time, and Kade isn't nearly as patient as I am."

I stare straight ahead until the door clicks shut behind him. And then a rush of tears blurs my vision as I stand and walk into the bedroom, crawling into the massive bed. Exhaustion clings to every part of me, which is the only thing that allows sleep to pull me under.

I dream of razor-sharp teeth. Blood everywhere. A pounding in my chest and... a throbbing between my thighs.

My eyes fly open to a dark room, and for a moment, I forget. A fleeting, peaceful moment before it's all ripped away and reality settles in once again.

I shoot up in the bed, clutching my chest as it all comes rushing back.

"Good morning."

I yelp before slapping a hand over my mouth. My head whips toward the voice, and when my eyes meet Kade's silver ones, I scramble off the bed, Atlas's voice ringing in my head.

Kade called first dibs on your pussy.

I back away from the bed, keeping my eyes on him. He leans back against the headboard, stretching his black jean-clad legs out on the white duvet. My breath catches when he flicks his tongue along his bottom lip before smirking.

"Kade," I whisper, my voice shakier than I'd like. I clear my throat. "What are you doing here? What time is it?" I glance toward the window. The sunrise is barely skimming the sky, so it can't be much later than six.

I shift my gaze back to the bed, but he's not there. The hair on the back of my neck sticks up, and I hold my breath. "Kade..."

"Turn around." His voice makes me freeze; he's right behind me. He's not glamouring me, but I do what he says anyway.

I stare at his chest as the seconds tick past. Finally, I force my gaze to his face. He's clean-shaven today and smells annoyingly good. Like peppermint and expensive cologne, as if he took a shower before coming here. And his dark brown waves are tousled stylishly and frame his face in a way that makes him look as if he should be on a runway during New York Fashion Week instead of in this hotel room with me.

His lips curl into a grin. "Good morning," he says again, reaching forward and capturing a piece of hair that escaped my bun while I slept. He twirls it around his finger, before tucking it behind my ear. My skin tingles where he touches, but I don't move away.

"Hi," I say in a quiet voice.

"Hi," he echoes with a sparkle in his eyes. "How did you sleep?"

"Does it matter?"

Kade frowns briefly. "Of course." His eyes flick between mine, evaluating. "You're exhausted." He looks past me toward the bed. "You should go back to sleep for a while."

"I'm fine," I say automatically.

He stares at me as silence stretches between us. "Calla—"

"Don't," I cut him off. "You came here to drag me back to that house. Let's just go." I take a step toward the door, but Kade wraps his fingers around my wrist and pulls me back. Before I know what's happening, he presses a soft kiss against my cheek.

I blink at him as warmth fills my face. "What was that for?"

He shrugs. "I wanted to do that when I crawled into bed next to you an hour ago, but I figured it would be better to wait until you were awake."

"Kidnapping is completely fine, but you draw the line at kissing while the other person is unconscious? Good to know."

Kade chuckles, sliding his fingers through mine and tracing his thumb back and forth across my skin. "Yes, I'd very much like for you to be awake while I ravish you." He licks his lips, leaning closer. "I think you'd like that too."

I'm shaking my head, but my body is saying something else entirely.

"Say it," he taunts. "Tell me you don't want it."

I narrow my eyes at him and try to pull my hand away, but he grips it tighter.

"Tell me, Calla."

"And if I don't?" I challenge. I have no idea what's come over me, but every nerve ending in my body wants Kade's attention. Craves it. It's dangerous and is likely going to get me killed, but I can't deny the way it excites me. *Screw my body for betraying me.* The rational part of me understands that mostly has to do with the lure a vampire has over humans, which is typically how they capture their prey. But it's more difficult than I expected to ignore it. Maybe because there's a part of me that knows this whole thing would be easier if I just... let it happen. If only my stubborn nature could accept that.

He pulls me forward into his chest and clasps the side of my neck with his other hand, using his thumb to hold my jaw and keep me in place. "If you don't," he says slowly, "I'm going to make you come on my fingers. Then with my tongue. And then, if you're a good girl, I might give you my cock."

My eyes pop wide. I'm not a virgin by any means. I fooled around with a couple of different guys my first year of university, but I'm certainly not used to... *this*.

Kade smirks at my response—or lack thereof. "Let me take care of you," he murmurs, brushing his nose along mine.

My heart is in my throat as I lean into him until our lips touch. Once. Twice. I close my eyes and press my mouth against his fully. Kade slips his hand away from my neck and pulls my hair out of the messy bun. Dark brown waves cascade over my shoulders, and he buries his fingers in them, tilting my head back slightly to deepen the kiss. I grip the front of his shirt, my heart racing as I remember that the only thing keeping Kade from my body is the bathrobe I fell asleep in.

Without warning, he slips the hand he had entwined with mine free and slides it into my robe. When his fingers brush the skin above my belly button, I gasp into his mouth. They slide up between my breasts, opening the front of the robe wider as he parts my lips with his tongue. Our lips move against each other while he cups my breast, using his thumb and finger to roll my nipple into a hard pebble.

I groan against his lips. "Kade..."

He breaks the kiss, pinching my nipple as he leans back just enough to look me in the eyes. His eyes are filled with liquid fire, hooded and glimmering with the promise of so much pleasure it's making my knees weak. He holds my gaze as he trails his hand back down my chest to my stomach and then lower. I hold my breath as his fingers dance across my skin, slowing to a stop when he reaches the apex of my thighs.

My breathing turns shallow as he tilts my head to the side and presses his mouth against my neck. And when his fingers start moving between my legs, my head swims with lust.

He traces my lips and drags a single finger up the length of my slit before dipping into me.

I bite my lip hard to keep from moaning.

"Fuck," Kade growls against my skin. "I want to drive my cock into you so hard you won't be able to walk." He bites my neck playfully, his fangs retracted so he doesn't break the skin. "But I'm going to take it slow and enjoy how fucking amazing you feel against my fingers." His thumb lands on my clit, and I gasp. He moves it in slow circles, teasing while he pushes his finger inside me.

"Oh my god," I breathe, grabbing his shoulder to steady myself.

"You're already so wet for me." He kisses up my neck and along my jaw until our mouths meet once again.

"Shut up," I pant against his lips as he adds a second finger and applies pressure to my clit until I'm seeing stars.

Kade grabs my free hand and presses it against his crotch. "It's only fair, considering you've got me rock solid."

I sigh into his mouth as heat ripples through me and kiss him harder, palming the front of his pants until he growls.

In a blur of motion, he lifts me up and carries me to the bed without removing his fingers from between my thighs. My head hits the soft duvet, and Kade leans over me, continuing his ministrations while I writhe beneath him. His teeth scrape the delicate skin at my throat, and my heart slams against my ribcage.

When he hits a particularly sensitive spot inside me, my hips vault off the mattress. He pulls back and smirks before pinning me to the bed with his arm over my waist. I roll my hips, urging him to go deeper, and he quickly obliges, picking up speed as he pumps in and out of me.

My eyes roll back and I grip the sheets on either side of me as my body climbs to new heights of ecstasy.

"Keep going," I say breathlessly.

Kade closes his mouth around my neck, nipping and sucking, swirling his tongue against my skin. My nerves short-circuit. *Fuck.* I want him to bite me.

I tilt my head to the side, providing the invitation as my body vibrates beneath him. "Kade." My voice trembles with a twisted mix of fear and desire. I'm afraid to want this.

He responds by curling his fingers inside me, hitting a new spot that feels so fucking good. I whimper, lifting my hips as much as I can to push him deeper.

"Oh fuck," I moan.

"Come for me," he murmurs against my neck, circling my clit harder, faster.

His words launch me off the edge, and a wickedly powerful orgasm whips through me like a wildfire of pleasure.

"That's it," he purrs, sliding his hand up my chest to wrap his fingers around my throat. "Ride my fingers."

I roll my hips, groaning as he holds his fingers still inside me as I move against them.

"Good girl," he praises, then kisses me hard as I ride the aftershocks of my orgasm. He slides his fingers out slowly, making me shiver and jump when he flicks my clit with a devilish grin on his lips.

When he pulls back and licks his fingers, my stomach pools with heat. *Holy shit.* I'm still catching my breath, but my body already wants more of him. One orgasm from Kade, and I feel as though it would be dangerously easy to become addicted.

And that really doesn't bode well for my escape.

FOUR

We head back to the house once I get dressed. I didn't bring any of my clothes when I took off last night, so I'm stuck wearing the deep blue dress Kade brought me. I slip into the bathroom to get changed and pull on black stockings before grabbing my book bag and leaving the suite with Kade.

I still have no idea how I'm going to explain last night to Brighton, but that's the least of my problems right now.

The ride back to the house is quiet, and when we walk inside, Lex and Gabriel are waiting in the living room. *Great.*

Lex has his nose in a book but glances up when the door to the garage closes behind us. "Look what we have here. Little girl lost found her way home," he says with a wink in my direction.

I shake my head. "What?"

"Perhaps we should get you a leash."

His playful tone grinds on my nerves, and my pulse ticks faster. "Perhaps you should—"

"Coffee is fresh," Gabriel cuts in as he stands from the couch and walks toward the kitchen. "Calla?"

My gaze follows him across the space that looks even more massive in daylight. "Yeah," I finally say, choosing to ignore Lex completely.

In the kitchen, Gabriel hands me a steaming mug of coffee. "You drink it black, right?"

I nod. "Um, thanks." Taking a small sip, I almost moan at the taste.

Of course, their coffee is amazing. I shouldn't be bitter about it. If anything, I suppose I should be grateful. I'm stuck here for the foreseeable future, but at least the coffee's good.

Out of nowhere, I find myself asking, "Why am I here?"

Gabriel leans against the counter. "You belong to us, Calla."

I swallow my immediate snarky retort and instead ask, "To what end?"

Lex lowers his book and glances over at us. "Yours, I suppose," he answers with a wink—he does that a lot.

My stomach churns as panic creeps in, making my muscles feel heavy.

"The agreement becomes void upon your natural death," Gabriel says. "We also have the option to terminate it."

Which will never happen. The words are implied. So my life, whatever future I might have seen for myself, is effectively over.

"Don't look so hopeless, angel," Gabriel says, and I glance at him to find his eyes filled with... compassion? No, that must be a trick. He offers a faint smile before leaving me standing in the kitchen by myself. He disappears around the corner, and I hear faint footsteps climb the stairs to the second level I haven't seen yet. I guess Gabriel has no desire to finish giving me a tour of the house.

I jump when Lex tosses the book onto the coffee table and gets up, coming into the kitchen. When he starts pulling food out of the fridge, I slide out of the way.

As Lex cooks breakfast, the house fills with the savory aroma of eggs and bacon, and despite my desire to flee this place, my stomach rumbles. Because I'm human and need food to survive—and I'm freaking starving.

Kade pulls a barstool over from the dining room and sits at one of the kitchen islands as he scrolls through his phone. I try to ignore it when I feel his eyes on me, but I can't shake the memory of his touch.

I take a long drink of my coffee and walk to the fridge. I pull out a plastic container of strawberries and blueberries, turning to the sink to rinse them off.

Lex flips the sizzling bacon and glances in my direction. "Hungry?"

I nod, plopping a blueberry in my mouth. "So you guys eat human food then."

Kade chuckles, setting his phone on the counter. "Yes, Calla. We eat like normal people. Well, most of us. Only born vampires don't need human food to survive—just blood."

"So turned vampires can survive on either?"

"We need both," Lex chimes in, cracking an egg into a frying pan before scrambling it with the spatula in his hand.

"Are all of you turned then?"

Lex and Kade exchange a glance that I almost miss.

"What? Is that some sort of secret?"

Before either can answer, Atlas walks in from the back of the house. Apparently one of the windows is actually a door that I hadn't noticed last night.

His hair is damp and the front of his light gray shirt is darkened with sweat. It dawns on me at that moment I didn't work out this morning. It's the first time in... I can't even recall how long that I missed one. The thought makes me frown, and I take another sip of coffee.

Atlas stops at the counter and grabs a strawberry from the container in front of me. His gaze lands on me, holds for a moment, and then shifts to where Kade is scrolling through his phone again. His brow arches briefly as if he *knows* what we did at the hotel this morning, and my cheeks fill with heat. I try to cover my face by taking another sip of coffee, but the moment passes without comment, and relief pours through me as he leaves the kitchen.

I'm not sure what causes me to set my mug down and go after him up the staircase to the second level, but I do. Yeah, I'm hungry, but I need answers more than I need food right now.

I follow the brightly lit hallway, taking in the abstract art hung along the white walls until I find an open door near the end. Either Atlas didn't hear me come after him, or he didn't bother to wait for me to catch up.

My breath halts when I step into the last room at the end of the hall —the only door slightly open—and find Atlas completely naked. Every inch of his golden-toned body looks as if it's been etched by gods, which is about as infuriating as it is attractive. I can't help but let my gaze wander...

"Shit, sorry." I whip around so I'm no longer looking at it—*him*. Instead, I try to focus on the room. The dark gray walls, blank of any art or other decor. The entire room actually is very plain. It suits him.

"Did you need something?" His voice is level, as if he's unbothered by my barging into his room and him being on display.

"Uh, yeah. I mean not right now, while you're... I just... I have questions."

"Calla." His voice is closer. "You don't need to hide."

I slowly turn around, forcing my gaze level with his. The heat from his body makes me want to retreat, but I keep still. "I—"

"Have questions. That you need to think very hard before you ask, because you may not be prepared for the answers."

I cross my arms, glancing past him toward the giant four-poster bed in the corner of the room. It's a mountain of black pillows and sheets that look silk from where I'm standing, and I can't help but imagine what I might feel like to—*no*. I need to focus. I look back at Atlas. "I deserve to know what's going on."

"That's not what I said."

I arch a brow. "Then what are you saying?"

"That it would be a lot easier if you kept those questions to yourself."

"Easier for *you*," I remark in a snippy tone. I may be stuck here, but that doesn't mean I'm going to sit quietly.

"For you too, I'd suspect," he muses. "Now, if you don't mind, I'd like to shower."

"I do mind," I snap, surprising myself. I'm sick of the aloof act from him.

"Are you planning to join me then?" His expression is smooth, serious. "You can ask all the questions you want."

I stare at him. I have to assume he's being serious because that's the only side I've seen to this guy, but I can't bring myself to say yes.

Atlas shrugs. "Lost your chance." He walks across the room and slides open a frosted glass door to an en suite bathroom. A moment later, the shower turns on, and I walk out of the room with a knot in my stomach.

Backtracking, I return to the kitchen, though I am definitely not hungry anymore. I stop at the fridge and grab a bottle of water, downing half of it before I close the door and look to where Lex and Kade are sitting in the dining room, devouring plates full of bacon and eggs. When I approach the table and drop into an empty seat, they both turn to look at me, and a frown tugs at my lips when I realize they heard the conversation between Atlas and me.

"Where's Gabriel?" I ask to quickly fill the silence.

"He left for work," Lex says, gulping down a glass of orange juice.

I nod, reaching for the dish of strawberries because I know I should put something in my stomach. I bite into one and ask, "What does he do?" My tone is curious, though it's mostly for show. They seem to know everything about me, and I'm going to have to figure them out if I have any chance at making it through this *arrangement* alive.

Kade shrugs, then with a smirk says, "I don't actually know."

Lex rolls his eyes and tosses a blueberry in his mouth. "That's because you don't pay attention to anything."

"That's not true." His smirk grows as he turns his attention to me. "Isn't that right, Calla?"

I glare at him. "You did not just say that."

His smirk remains. "Oh, come on."

"You should eat something."

I jump at the sound of Atlas's voice behind me. He pulls out the chair next to me and sits before scooping a pile of scrambled eggs onto the plate in front of me.

"Lex ate all the bacon," Kade comments, pulling his phone out.

Atlas ignores him, angling himself toward me. "Eat."

"Fuck off," I shoot back. "I'm not a child."

A muscle feathers along his jaw and a drop of water falls from a strand of hair in his face, wetting the front of his light gray T-shirt. He catches my gaze, and my mouth goes dry. "You're going to eat what I put on your plate and you're not going to argue with me about it. Understood?"

I'm nodding before I can stop myself. Except, I wouldn't be able to stop myself if I tried. *Fucking glamour.* I pick up the fork next to my plate and start eating.

After a few minutes of eating in silence, I glance toward Lex. "Do the rest of you have jobs?"

Lex nods. "I'm a kindergarten teacher."

I almost choke on my eggs when my head whips toward him—only to find him smirking at me. "Funny," I deadpan.

"Hey. I'm great with kids."

"That's terrifying to even think about," I mutter, returning my gaze to the plate in front of me.

"He works for me," Atlas says in a smooth voice before taking a drink of his coffee.

"Best boss ever," Lex remarks dryly, but Atlas's expression doesn't change.

"Doing what?" It's a simple question, but it has the potential to unlock a door to the past I'm not sure I'm really ready to open. Because whatever they do is tied to the reason I'm stuck here. To this day, I don't know how they saved my great-great-grandfather, just that whatever went down in New York could easily have cost him everything, including his life. When you're dealing with shady businesspeople, nothing is off the table.

"Boring communications shit," Lex answers, and I decide to leave it at that. For now.

"I'm a model," Kade chimes in, "though you could probably have guessed that."

I arch a brow at him. "And a humble one at that." My sarcastic tone seems to please him because he's grinning even as he continues to scroll on his phone. "Seriously, though. What do you guys do all day when you're not kidnapping university students?"

Lex snorts. "We typically travel a lot for work. Between Washington and New York City mostly."

"Right," I say, "and what exactly does that entail?" I ask before adding, "If I'm going to be here a while, I think it's fair that I get to know something about you guys."

"What about us makes you think we're fair?" Kade challenges, flicking his gaze in my direction.

"I just... Fine. Tell me something else then. Anything."

"We built this house," Lex says. "Atlas designed it."

My eyes widen. "Wow." I can't help but sound impressed—I am.

"Yep. It's a pretty fancy prison, don't you think?"

I shoot him a glare, but choose not to respond to that comment and instead say, "So Atlas designs stuff. What do you like to do?"

Lex shrugs. "I like pain."

I blink at him. "I don't..." My eyes go to his tattoos; I have to assume that's what he's talking about because the alternatives are just too creepy to consider. "Oh. That's... cool."

"Do you have any tattoos?" Kade asks.

I'm still admiring Lex's when I say, "Pretty sure you know that I don't."

Kade chuckles. "Fair point, though if they were on your back..." He trails off, and I roll my eyes.

"I don't have any tattoos," I reply in a firm voice.

Atlas remains silent through the whole exchange, drinking his coffee as if the rest of us aren't even there.

When I finish the food on my plate, I down a glass of orange juice and push my chair back. "Do I need to ask permission to leave the table, or do I still have *some* free will around here?" I direct the question at Atlas—he seems to be the one the others look to—and hold my chin high when he glances at me.

"Watch it," he warns.

I cross my arms. "You four have been watching me for god knows how long. You'd think you would have learned enough about me to know I'm not going to make this easy for you. You want a quiet, complacent human to boss around and bite?" I shiver at the last part, but quickly continue, "You chose the wrong person."

Lex rolls his eyes. "Well, we didn't just *pick* you."

I get up and step away from the table, very aware of the three pairs of eyes on me. "Yeah, well, you still chose to take me. I'm betting there was nothing in that agreement you made with my family that forced you to ruin my life, and yet here we are."

"You're being narrow-minded," Kade says in an agitated tone. "Have you considered that this arrangement could be a good thing?"

I belt out a laugh. "Don't fucking kid yourself. This *arrangement* is a death sentence. Four vampires and a single human in one house? Wonder how that's going to turn out." Maybe I haven't looked at it that way before, but the moment the bitter words leave my lips, my pulse spikes, and I'm moving backward.

"Calla—" Atlas starts.

"No." My voice cracks, and I cringe inwardly. "I... need to study." I need something *normal*.

Before they can say anything more, I grab my book bag and hurry out of the room. I don't stop until I'm in the bedroom Gabriel showed me to last night, with the door shut and locked. It's an almost laughable notion, that a simple lock could keep them out, but I do it anyway.

I glance toward the bed, kicking off my Docs near the door before I get into it. The sheets are so soft it makes me angry. I'm aware the feeling is a little ridiculous, but I can't shake it. I don't want to feel comfortable here—I want to leave.

With a heavy sigh, I lean against the massive collection of pillows at the headboard and pull out my textbooks. I toss the empty bag to the end of the bed and sigh to the empty room before cracking open my sociology book. I'm probably not in the right headspace to study, but at this point, I'll try just about anything to keep my mind off my very fucked up reality—for as long as I can.

CHAPTER

FIVE

By mid-afternoon, I'm tired of being cooped up in the bedroom—as fancy as it is—so I take my textbook outside and sit by the pool.

Being the beginning of March means the air is still cold, but I don't mind it. The sky is clear and the sun is shining, reflecting some heat off the pool, while the breeze is clearing my head and, surprisingly, allowing me to focus on the words in front of me. I can pretend, at least for a few fleeting moments, that I'm not a prisoner here.

I uncap my pen and underline a section of the text, jotting down a quick note in the margin.

My gaze lifts when Gabriel walks around the side of the house from the front. I press my lips together as I take him in, dressed impeccably in a navy suit, though his tie is pulled away from the collar of his white dress shirt and he's carrying the jacket over his arm. His copper hair gleams in the sun as he approaches, offering me a smile, and lowers himself onto the lounge chair next to me.

"How's it going?" He glances at the textbook in my lap. "Doing a little light reading, I see."

"Studying," I tell him, though he probably guessed that. "How was work? You're not secretly the President or something, are you?"

Gabriel laughs. "Where did you get that idea?"

I shrug, clicking my pen. "We are in Washington, and look at you."

"A lot of people wear suits here," he points out. "You're right in that I do work in politics."

"Do you work for the White House?"

His silver eyes sparkle with amusement. "I can't talk a lot about what I do for security reasons, but no, I don't work at the White House."

"That's a shame. I binged *Scandal* for a third time last semester. It's one of my favorites."

He nods as if he's following along, but then says, "That's a television show?"

I bite my tongue to keep from spilling about the entire show because we'd be sitting here all day, and instead say, "Uh, yeah."

Gabriel seems to pick up that I'm not going to elaborate and looks back at my textbook, tilting his head to read the cover. "Are you enjoying your program?"

"Some of it is pretty dry, but overall I am. My gut tells me I made the right choice going into sociology. Not that I have any idea of what I'll do when I graduate." My chest tightens at the thought. I don't even know what's going to happen tomorrow let alone two years from now. *If I'll even make it to graduation.*

"What made you pick Georgetown?"

"Honestly, the city. My mom took me on a trip here when I was in high school, and I sort of fell in love with it. So when it came time to start applying to schools, Georgetown was my top pick. I knew I couldn't stay in New York"—I also knew it wouldn't have mattered where I went, they would have tracked me down—"and I'm happy this is where I ended up." I frown. "I mean Washington, not *here* specifically."

He smiles faintly. "I knew what you meant, angel."

I nod, then take the lull in conversation to change the topic. "You know, the others aren't very forthcoming with information," I tell him, glancing at my lap. "You all know everything about me, but the moment I start asking questions..." I shake my head and turn toward him. "I don't want to be here. That isn't news. But the least you could do is tell me what's going to happen to me and *why* I'm here, because the fact that you all own me isn't an explanation."

"I understand you want to know, and there will be a time when things will become clear and make sense." The *but not right now* is left unsaid, which almost makes it worse.

"I'm not a pet, Gabriel," I snap. "I'm not just along for the ride. I have a life and friends, and I'm not going to just fall in line and play house with a bunch of vampires." My pulse ticks faster as I catch my breath from that little outburst.

He nods, standing from the lounge chair. "I'll speak with the others." He steps back, but before walking away he drapes his jacket over my shoulders.

I open my mouth, but no words come out. I'm overwhelmed by a woodsy citrus scent with a hint of fabric softener. My lips start to form a smile before I can stop myself, so it's a good thing Gabriel is already walking through the door to the house.

I finish reading and annotating one chapter and yawn. I close the cover and set it on the end of the lounge chair before swinging my legs over the side to stand. The super-fancy coffee maker in the kitchen is calling my name like a siren; I could use a boost of caffeine.

The door to the house opens before I can get up, and Kade walks out—in bright red swim shorts.

I arch a brow at him as he approaches, his bare feet soundless against the concrete. "You're not..." I trail off, glancing toward the pool. "It's March! You're going to freeze."

He stops at the back of my chair, leaning against it as he grins down at me. "It's a heated pool, Calla. Why do you think it's still open?"

"Okay, but—" I don't get a chance to finish my sentence before Kade walks past me and dives into the water.

I jump back when the water splashes, shaking my head at him. *Crazy bastard.*

Kade swims laps around the pool while I attempt to continue studying. It quickly becomes futile. I've read the same line at least three times, but the words aren't sticking. Not when I can feel the weight of Kade's gaze on me. With a sigh, I close my textbook and pull Gabriel's jacket off my shoulders, draping it over the back of the lounge chair before I stand. Inching toward the pool, I lock eyes with Kade.

"You coming in?" He asks, treading in place near the middle of the pool, water dripping onto his face.

"Not a chance," I say, my stockings reaching the edge of the concrete as the breeze blows my hair across my face. I tuck the rogue strands behind my ear and crouch.

Kade swims a little closer. "So you're just going to watch?"

"Like you've been watching me this whole time?" I challenge, sitting cross-legged, the dark blue fabric of my dress gathering in my lap.

He smirks. "I could pull you in here faster than you could blink."

My eyes narrow, and I freeze. "I'll kill you."

"Hmm," he hums, wading closer, "you've said that once before."

I nod. "And I meant it both times."

He tilts his head. "Now why would you want to do that when we have so much fun?" He grips the ledge of the pool on either side of me, and my breath gets lodged in my throat.

"I'm not getting in the pool, Kade." There's an edge in my tone. *Don't you dare*, it warns.

He licks the water from his lips, and they curl into a slow grin. "Do you trust me?"

"Absolutely not," I say without missing a beat.

His grin widens as he stands, the pool shallow enough here that his upper half is above water. He wraps his hands around my ankles, murmuring, "You're a smart girl, Calla."

I bite into my bottom lip, my eyes dropping to where his fingers are warming my skin through my stockings. "What are you...? My stockings—"

"Will dry," he says, uncrossing my ankles and pulling my legs over the ledge. Before I can make a sound, they're submerged in the surprisingly warm water almost to my knees. His hands slide up my thighs, pushing my dress up to my waist.

I watch with bated breath, unable to move as the breeze in the air reaches the delicate skin between my legs, protected by nothing but the thin mesh of my stockings.

Kade snares my gaze, his fingers dancing across the inside of my thighs, higher and higher, until his thumb brushes my folds, and I suck in a sharp breath.

I can't believe this is the second time in two days he's touched me like this—or that I haven't stopped him.

He traces the line of my slit through the stockings, quickening my pulse at the promise of so much more in his eyes.

"What are you going to do?" I ask breathlessly, a flush creeping across my chest as my face floods with warmth. My eyes scan the yard quickly, but we're not close enough to any other house for a neighbor to see. But I'm still worried about getting caught.

"You wanted a distraction." His thumb brushes back and forth, making it difficult for me to focus on his words. "That's why you're out here, avoiding the others with your nose in a textbook."

"I..." My voice trails off when his thumb circles my clit. Fuck, it feels so good.

"Let me distract you."

My head is spinning, hazy with lust and racing with panic. They're battling it out when I meet his gaze and the world narrows on this moment. I feel centered, yet in control of my body, so I know he's not messing with my mind.

I swallow past the dryness in my throat, and the moment I nod, he tears a gaping hole in my stockings. I gasp as the cool air assaults my bare thighs and the warmth between them. "I liked those," I mumble.

Kade peers up at me through thick lashes, only made darker by the water clung in them. "There are about a hundred identical pairs in your closet."

I nod absently, because he's no longer looking at my face. His gaze is locked between my legs as he grips my thighs and spreads them open at an agonizingly slow pace. He's teasing me, and I'm already vibrating with need. I hate my body for betraying me so quickly, but when Kade lowers his face and presses his mouth against the inside of my thigh, those bitter thoughts scatter. His tongue swirls expertly against my skin, a promise of what's to come, and I lift my hand to his head, running my fingers through his wet hair as my head tips back and he gets closer to my core. The sun is peeking through the trees, warming my face, and my lips part in a silent gasp at the first swipe of his tongue along my slit. I'm spread wide open for him and it has my heart pounding almost painfully in my chest. He takes his time, each pass of his tongue lazy yet practiced. I can't get enough. My breathing quickens and my hips jerk off the concrete.

Kade pauses, glancing up at me. "Keep still," he orders in a deep voice.

I catch my bottom lip between my teeth, nodding.

He returns his attention to my pussy and continues his slow torture of winding me up until I'm biting my tongue so hard to keep from moaning I'm afraid I'll slice right through it any second.

His tongue swirls around my clit before his lips close around it and he starts sucking.

I see fucking stars.

Moaning loud, I grip the back of his head, holding him there or just holding on for dear life, I'm not even sure. I don't give a shit at this point, so long as he keeps going. "Kade," I breathe his name, my voice trembling with pleasure, and he presses his tongue flat against my clit.

Without warning, he plunges two fingers inside me, and I cry out, fisting his hair. It only spurs him on, and now he's sucking hard and pulsing his fingers deep in my pussy, curling them in the most delicious way.

My other hand flexes against the concrete behind me, and when my hips lift, Kade hums against my clit. He pauses his thrusts but holds his fingers in me, which has me trying to move against him in an attempt to keep the friction building. "If I have to hold you down, that pretty little dress of yours is going to get wet." He nips the skin above my clit, and I jump in response, shivering at the warning in his voice.

I have nothing intelligent to offer, so I keep my mouth shut and continue circling my hips, urging him to move his fingers again.

"Wanton little thing, you are," he purrs, kissing my pussy softly before his fingers finally start thrusting again. He moves them slowly, pulling almost all the way out before pushing into me again and again.

My chest rises and falls fast, and I can't catch my breath. Kade takes me even higher, sucking hard on my clit as his fingers hit that sweet spot inside over and over, hard and fast. I race toward the edge and fall right over, crying out my release as I come around his fingers. He laps at the over-sensitive skin as I ride the aftershocks of my orgasm and catch my breath.

"Fucking hell," I mumble almost incoherently and pull my hand out of his hair, pressing it against my pounding chest.

"I'll take that as a compliment." His voice is laced with arrogance, but I'm so doped up with pleasure, I couldn't care less. I've had boyfriends go down on me in the past, but no one as skilled as Kade. He can be smug all he wants, I'm the one who benefited from it.

I inch back from the edge of the pool and pull what's left of my stockings off, dropping them in a sopping pile of material next to me.

Kade chuckles, ducking under the water for a brief moment before coming back up and running his hand through his hair. It looks good slicked back, showing off the sharp angles of his cheekbones and jaw—and I am definitely staring.

I turn my gaze away, looking toward the house, and freeze when I see Gabriel standing in the window. I whip back around to look at Kade. "How long has he been standing there?"

Kade arches a brow and looks past me. He smirks when his eyes land on Gabriel. "Hmm, from the look on his face, I'd say long enough."

"What does that mean?" I ask, my voice pitching higher.

He licks his lips, eyes on me again. "He's jealous."

"Jealous," I echo, shaking my head. *Gabriel wants me too?*

Kade must see something in my expression, because he nods. "Don't look so shocked, Calla," he says in a teasing tone, but I'm already scrambling up and grabbing my things. I hurry inside, my jaw clenched tight as I pass Gabriel and practically throw his jacket at him.

He grabs my wrist and pulls me around to face him. "Angel—"

"Let go of me." I attempt to free myself instantly, but he holds me easily.

With no effort, he slides two fingers under my chin and forces me to meet his gaze. "Why are you running from me?"

I blink at him, because I figured it was pretty obvious. "I don't... I didn't know you were standing there. If I had—"

"You wouldn't have let Kade devour you?" Those silver irises flick across my face, waiting for an answer.

"No," I force out, my cheeks flaming, and I don't know if that's true.

"You have no reason to be embarrassed." His low voice is stern but gentle. "So don't be."

"Great, I'm cured," I say under my breath, tugging my arm back, and his lip curls into a smile as he frees me from his grasp.

I don't stick around after that. Retreating to the bedroom my things are in, I close the door and change out of the dress that's still damp near the hemline. I drape it over the tub for now, not sure I want to go searching for the laundry room, and put on my favorite maroon Georgetown hoodie and black yoga pants. I'm not here to impress these assholes.

I grab my book bag and rummage through it for my phone, which is probably dead by now. I owe Brighton a lot more than a text, but that's really all I can offer her at this point. When I can't find my phone, I huff out a sigh. *Did I leave it at the hotel?* No, I remember slipping it into my bag. Anger simmers in me. They definitely took it.

I drop my bag on the end of the bed and walk out of the room, heading directly for Atlas.

After coming up empty on the second floor, I venture up to the third, peeking in a couple of plain, undecorated bedrooms that look as if they could be hotel rooms, before finding a room with double frosted glass doors at the end of the hall. My bare feet are cold against the hard marble floor, and I walk into the room without knocking.

The room is full of windows—not shocking at this point. The amount of natural light in this place has to be some sort of vampire joke, especially considering they built the house. I barely register the rest of the tidy room before my eyes land on Atlas, standing behind a raised black desk, typing on a laptop.

He doesn't glance up from his screen until I'm standing right in front of it. "What?" he asks, his voice distant; I've interrupted something.

"I want my phone." I manage a level tone, but my back is rigid. "My friends are going to wonder why I'm not responding to messages. That's not me." My mind immediately goes to Brighton. She's probably freaking out, wondering what the hell happened to me last night.

"The friend who booked your suite at the Four Seasons?" he inquires.

I cross my arms. "I don't see why that matters." No way I'm going to let them near Brighton. "You can't expect to keep me locked up in here with zero communication with the outside world." My tone sharpens with each word. "Give me my fucking phone."

Atlas moves with speed my eyes can't track, and he's in front of me, glaring hard. "You are in no position to demand anything."

My eyes narrow as his breath stirs the hair at my temple. The faint scent of citrus tickles my nose, as if he'd just eaten an orange before I stormed in.

"I am not a dog," I snap, jabbing at his chest. "I will not sit and stay and do whatever just because you wish it."

His expression darkens, and he grips my hip, pushing me back into the desk. My breath halts at the flash of his fangs. "Shall we test that?"

A muscle ticks in my jaw, and I gnash my teeth together. "Sure, go ahead and glamour me to be your little puppet, because it's the only way I'll sit quietly." My tone is confident, but the truth is, I'm terrified he'll do it.

There's a low rumble in his chest, a growl. His eyes narrow on me, and I grip the desk to do something with my hands. "You are far more stubborn than I expected," he murmurs.

I blink at his admission. "What the hell *did* you expect?" I ask, incredulous. "I'm being held against my will because of something I had absolutely nothing to do with. You lot won't tell me a single thing about what's going to happen, and I'm just expected to sit by and be cool with it? Fuck that."

Atlas leans in until we're practically nose-to-nose and says, "You'd better get cool with it, Calla, and fast."

My hand brushes against something cold and metal, and before I know what's happening, I wrap my fingers around it and ram my arm forward with all the strength I've built over years of weight training.

Holy shit. I just stabbed him.

I pull my hand back in a flash, but the end of what appears to be a letter opener sticks out of his stomach.

Atlas glances down for a moment, then looks at me, his mouth set in a tight line. He slowly removes the blade, which is dripping blood on the wood floor at our feet. He doesn't seem to care and drops the letter opener on the desk before lifting his shirt to reveal the wound is sealing itself.

"That wasn't very nice." His voice is low, hard.

My mouth is dry as I back away. I make it a couple of steps before my back collides with a solid wall of muscle, and I whip around to find Lex smirking at me.

"You can't kill us," he says, nodding toward Atlas. "Not easily anyway, and you're wasting your energy trying."

"What would you suggest I do instead?" I snap back and instantly regret it when he arches a brow at me, as if I should know what his response would be.

I shake my head. "I want to know what the hell is going on around here. Why did you take me just to keep me in the dark? What's in this for you?"

Gabriel chooses that moment to slip into the room, glancing between the three of us, his gaze not missing a single detail—including the blood on the floor and desk. His eyes land on me, and he frowns. "You should be careful with your words, angel. Don't ask questions you're not ready to hear the answers to."

Despite the kindness he's shown me, I scowl at him. "What the fuck is that supposed to mean?"

"You want to know why we took you?" Lex says, almost sneering at me. "We were going to kill you. Your entire family, actually—what's left of it. We don't do loose ends."

The blood drains from my face as the world tilts around me. Death by vampire is how I figured I'd go for as long as I've known of their existence, but to hear my deepest fears confirmed out loud makes me want to vomit.

"We still might," he adds with a wink, "if you choose to continue misbehaving."

My stomach clenches as panic erupts in my chest. I want to leave, to put as much space between me and them as geographically possible, but Gabriel and Lex are blocking my path to the door, my escape route. Behind that thick wall of fear, though, is a burst of excitement. These guys want me—either to kill or fuck—and so long as the latter desire outweighs the former, I get to remain alive. And if I'm being honest, the danger—the knowledge that they can take anything from me at any moment—is wickedly arousing, and I hate myself for wanting it.

Lex steps closer, his fangs descending from his gums. "Why do I think you're going to continue testing us?" He cocks his head to the side while Gabriel leans in the doorway, observing the exchange. "You're curious," he says, again moving closer. He's a mere foot away now, and I can't stop staring at his fangs. "You can't stop thinking about what we're going to do with you."

I open my mouth to shoot that down, but I can't make the words form on my lips.

"You want it as much as we do, don't you?" He reaches for my face, but something in me clicks on and I flinch back, then take off out of the room, brushing past Gabriel on my way through the door. He doesn't try to stop me this time.

Back in my room, I close the door and fall back against it, clutching my chest.

What the hell am I doing?

My heart beats hard and fast, and much lower, my center throbs. There's a part of me, no matter how small, that wants them. I crave the danger they offer, the fear that sparks deep inside when I test their limits. But will I survive when their control breaks?

I wonder if I can request a TV for my prison cell.

As I lay in the bed staring at the ceiling, I wish I could turn on *Scandal* and forget all about the vampires that own me, and instead focus on the crazy, twisted life of Olivia Pope.

A soft knock at the door turns my head toward it. I consider ignoring the sound, but they own the place. Whoever is on the other side could just as easily walk right in.

"Calla." Gabriel's voice is muffled through the door. "Can I come in?"

I purse my lips. He's asking permission? "Yeah," I finally say, and the door opens a moment later.

Gabriel walks in and closes the door behind him. "You doing okay?" he asks, approaching the bed.

I sit up, shrugging. "Sure."

He stares at me knowingly.

"Why are you so nice to me?" I ask in a low voice, pulling the black fleece throw blanket through my fingers. I keep my head down, focusing on the soft material in my hands.

Gabriel sits on the edge of the bed, keeping a comfortable enough distance. "Why shouldn't I be?" Of course, he had to go and turn the question back on me.

I look up at him. "Uh, maybe because you're holding me hostage?" I offer wryly. "Seriously, though. You're making it very difficult to hate you, which is necessary for me because—"

"Because you can't admit you might actually enjoy being here?"

"I... That doesn't matter. I *shouldn't* be here, and I sure as hell shouldn't enjoy it."

He nods thoughtfully. "Why not?"

I stare at him and am quickly reminded of how easy it is to get lost in his silver gaze, glamour or no. "Are you kidding?"

"You don't *want* to want it, that doesn't mean you shouldn't."

I arch a brow, and my stomach knots. This conversation is very quickly going off the rails into *what the fuck* town. "You're really going to sit there and try to talk me into being totally okay with being, what, a sex slave to four vampires? A human juice box for all of you?"

His lips twitch. "I enjoy your humor. I recognize it's a defense mechanism, but enjoy it nonetheless." He pats my leg when I blow out a breath. "Give it a chance."

"'It.' Being a captive to a house of vampires."

He nods. "The sooner you accept it, the better it will be for you, angel. You have my word."

I roll my bottom lip between my teeth, battling with the voice of reason in my head, which is screaming at me to keep fighting. But at this moment, with Gabriel looking at me like I'm the only person on the planet, I lose the strength to deny my desires. A little distraction might do me some good, anyway.

"Calla—"

"I want you to kiss me," I whisper, looking up at him as my heart rate kicks up.

He shifts closer until we're a breath apart. His hand cups the side of my face, and I lean into his touch. I feel safe with Gabriel, though I can't for the life of me decipher why. I'm also not going to question it. Instead, I bring my mouth to his and close my eyes as our lips brush. Slow and soft. Gabriel is gentle with me, as if I'm moments away from shattering apart. It's... sweet.

Gabriel slides his arm around my back and pulls me forward until I'm pressed against him. My arms drape over his shoulders as he tips my head back, deepening the kiss. When his tongue darts out, my lips part to let him in. He makes a sound at the back of his throat, and the muscles in his arm tense around my back. Without warning, one of his fangs slices into my lip.

I pull back in a flash, and a drop of warmth rolls down my chin. I lick it away quickly, but Gabriel's eyes are locked on my mouth. My heart hammers in my chest as I slowly reach up and touch his lips with my finger. He opens his mouth enough for me to see his razor-sharp teeth, and I poke his fang with my finger, gasping softly when it breaks the skin and a bright red bead of blood appears. I stick my finger in my mouth and suck gently, watching as Gabriel's jaw locks.

I lean in again, hesitantly pressing my mouth against his. When he kisses me back, I know the exact moment when he tastes my blood. His entire body stiffens, and he inhales sharply through his nose. He sucks my bottom lip into his mouth, trying to taste more, but I'm quickly made aware it isn't enough when he pulls back and stares at me with liquid silver eyes.

"You want to bite me." My voice trembles.

His eyes dance across my face as if to gauge my reaction it that. My belly swirls with nerves and excitement. I'm scared to bare myself to him, but tempted by the throbbing between my legs.

"Calla," he murmurs, gripping my hip with one hand and sliding the other up my arm to cup the side of my face.

"Will it hurt?" I ask softly.

When he smiles, the tips of his fangs show, making my pulse jump. "It can, but not like this."

I frown, swallowing hard. "What do you mean?"

"When a human offers themselves to a vampire, the bite can be pleasurable—euphoric even. Vampires can also glamour humans to feel that way if the vampire chooses. Otherwise, if the human is being forced, the pain can be excruciating."

I nod absently, a shiver running down my spine at the thought.

"I would never force you to do anything you don't want to do," he says in a hushed voice, his thumb grazing my cheek. And I might be the most naive person on the planet, but I believe him.

Gabriel presses his lips against my forehead in a gentle kiss, and my eyes close. Despite my racing heart, I force my muscle to relax and tilt my head to the side. Gabriel leans in, moving the hair away from my neck.

I expect him to hesitate, to ease into it. Instead, there's a flash of sharp pain that steals my breath—a brutal reminder that Gabriel is a vampire, a monster, and I have absolutely no power here—and then warmth floods through me. The pain is over in a matter of seconds, replaced with sensations I never could have imagined. The pull of his mouth at my throat has me throbbing in seconds as I lean into him, gripping the front of his shirt as he drinks deeply.

Every nerve ending in my body flares to life. My skin tingles and warms, and I feel as if I'm floating on a cloud. It's suddenly very difficult to remember why I don't want to be here, and I press my lips together to keep from moaning out loud.

Gabriel pulls back slowly, lapping at my neck for a few moments before kissing my cheek. Before either of us can speak, the door opens and Lex slips inside, closing it behind him. His eyes shift between us, and when he opens his mouth, his fangs glint in the light.

"I thought I smelled something sweet," he purrs, coming closer.

My head is light and hazy. "I taste sweet?" I ask without looking at Gabriel.

"You taste absolutely exquisite," he murmurs in my ear.

Lex crosses his arms, and my eyes go to his tattoos. "So that's what you kids are up to in here."

"Jealous?" I taunt, then clamp my mouth shut, because *where the hell did that come from?*

Lex smirks. "Fuck yes."

I inch back toward the headboard, and both vampires watch my every movement, making my heart race. I can clearly see which direction this is going in, and part of me wants it so much it's embarrassing. The other part, though, the rational one, isn't sure what to make of the situation. I feel safe with Gabriel, and as much of a wild card as Lex seems to me, the two of them together balance out my nerves. Of course the idea of that is beyond bizarre, but I've quickly come to the conclusion that my knowledge of vampires is detrimentally limited. I wasn't expecting the pull I feel toward them, and while I'm not sure if that has more to do with the blood oath or their vampiric lure, it's something I'm unable to ignore—or resist.

"Stay with us now, angel," Gabriel says in a soft tone, snagging my attention.

I take a deep breath and nod. "I'm here."

In the space of a heartbeat, Lex is at my side, leaning over the bed and tilting my face toward him with a gentle finger under my chin. "If you thought Kade was good, you have no idea what you're in for."

My eyes widen. "I think he'd disagree," I breathe. I don't have a chance to overanalyze this scenario, which is probably a good thing, because I am so out of my element it's not even funny.

"Hmm," Lex hums, leaning in until our noses touch, "allow me to prove him very wrong." In a flash, he grabs my hips and pulls me down so my head rests on the pile of pillows at the headboard. I wet my lips, pressing them together as he slides his hands down my thighs. He keeps his eyes locked on my face, making my cheeks flush, and Gabriel moves up the bed and leans in to kiss my neck. He nuzzles my skin with his nose, inhaling deeply.

Lex trails his fingers back up my legs and curls them around the waistband of my yoga pants. He flashes a wicked smirk in my direction before slowly dragging my pants down my thighs. His eyes flash with something dark when he realizes I'm not wearing panties, and my breath catches in my throat. He looks about two seconds away from devouring me whole, and I probably wouldn't mind it.

He tugs my pants off the rest of the way, tossing them behind him before dropping his lips to my left ankle. He moves achingly slow, peppering feather-light kisses against my skin every inch or so until he reaches my knee, and then he does the same thing on the other side.

I'm vibrating with anticipation, and a pulse of excitement bursts through me when Gabriel's fangs scrape my neck, not breaking the skin but tempting me with the promise of pleasure. He slides in behind me and pulls me against his chest, wrapping his warm arms around me.

I catch my bottom lip between my teeth, tilting my head to the side just enough that I can still watch Lex as his tongue darts out to lick the inside of my thigh. Heat rises in my chest and pools in my belly when he lifts his gaze to mine for a brief moment before his face disappears between my legs.

My entire world narrows on the feel of his tongue against my pussy. I grip the sheets on either side of me, and Gabriel grabs my hands, entwining our fingers and squeezing gently. He sucks gently on my neck, teasing me to the point of insanity. I can't bring myself to ask him to bite me, though I'm not sure why.

Lex pulls back with a hooded gaze, looking between Gabriel and me. "Bite her," he says in a husky tone, and my stomach clenches with excitement. Vampires aren't mind readers—that I know of—so Lex must've seen something in my gaze that showed him exactly what I wanted.

Gabriel's fangs sink into the same spot in my throat as Lex spears me with his tongue. I cry out, holding Gabriel's hands in a death grip that he probably barely feels.

Lex leans back, pulling his tongue out. "Spread your legs wider," he orders, and I comply way too fast. Clearly, I've decided to throw inhibitions out the window tonight. This situation really doesn't leave room for them, anyway.

"Good girl," he praises, flicking my clit with his thumb as he dives back between my legs, thrusting harder and faster until my head spins and I'm gasping for air.

Between the sensations of Gabriel drinking from my neck and Lex devouring me with his mouth, I topple over the edge and shatter apart, my pussy walls clenching hard and my hips jerking off the bed. My moans fill the room, and I couldn't care less if the entire house hears my release.

Lex removes his tongue, circling my clit and making me jump as my chest heaves. Gabriel licks the wound on my neck until it stops bleeding, and my skin tingles in response.

"Fucking hell," I mutter under my breath. My heartbeat pounds in my throat, and I'm so spent I can barely open my eyes.

"Don't worry," Lex says, patting my knee, "I won't tell Kade you enjoyed me better."

I try to scowl, but it comes out more like a purr, and my eyes won't even open now. "What does this mean?" I ask in a tired voice.

"What does what mean, angel?" Gabriel asks.

"You drinking from me," I whisper. It's probably something I should've asked *before* he bit me, but hindsight and all that.

"We're all already connected by blood, so this doesn't change anything."

Lex traces slow circles along my thigh. "Blood sharing on the other hand..."

I press my lips together and pry my eyes open to look at him. "Blood sharing?"

"If we drank from each other at the same time, it creates a sort of connection," Gabriel explains. "It's temporary and wears off after a few days, but can be very powerful the first time you experience it. You'd be able to sense me as much as I can sense you after drinking your blood. We would feel each other's emotions, and it would also draw us together in the sense that being apart would be unpleasant."

"Oh." The thought of drinking blood makes my stomach churn. I'm not squeamish by any means, but drinking blood? Hell to the no. And being connected to any one of these guys on that level seems like a very dangerous thing. The blood oath connection they have to me is invasive enough.

The corner of Lex's mouth kicks up. "It can also be very fun," he points out, shooting me yet another wink as he gets off the bed and heads toward the door.

I yawn. "Where are you going?"

Lex pauses in the doorway. "You're about to pass out, and I've got some shit to do. Sweet dreams, Calla." He closes the door behind him as I yawn again and rest my head against Gabriel's chest. He hasn't made a move to leave, so I decide to get comfortable with him there.

He smooths a hand over my hair, and my breathing evens out. Before long, I drift off, vaguely registering a blanket being pulled over my bare legs. Sleep drags me under fast, and I don't fight it.

SEVEN

Sun streaks through the windows when I pry my eyes open for the first time in what feels like days. My muscles are tight, not painfully so, but certainly enough for me to notice.

Shit. How long did I sleep?

I dreamed of Gabriel and Lex, playing my body like an instrument they'd had an eternity of practice to master and making me explode with the most intense orgasm I've ever experienced. Not to mention, I never could have imagined what being bitten would feel like, but if it felt that good in my dreams, could it be that good in reality?

I sit up, stretching my legs out and yawning as I peek around the quiet space. My eyes land on my yoga pants in a pile on the floor, and I pause. "What the fu..." My voice trails off. *No. There's no way.* I lift a shaky hand to my neck, and when my fingers brush over two puncture marks, I suck in a sharp breath. I squeeze my eyes shut as last night's very real events come rushing back in a flash of fangs and pleasure.

I let Gabriel bite me. More than that, I *liked* it. Way too damn much.

And Lex...

"Oh my god," I whisper to the empty room, prying my eyes open again. I... I can't believe I allowed that to happen. Hell, that I asked for it. I wanted a distraction, and those guys sure knew how to deliver.

Reality crashes down on me like an emotional hangover, and I want nothing more than to pull the blankets over my face and pretend last night didn't happen.

I need to find a way out of this stupid arrangement—preferably before my traitorous body tricks me into wanting to stay.

I pull myself out of bed and get in the shower, turning the dial until the heat of the water fills the room with steam. I wash my hair, then cover it in a generous amount of conditioner, leaving it in while I lather my body with a rose-scented scrub, flinching when some of the soap gets in the bite mark on my neck. I tip my head back to rinse it, then finish showering quickly before shutting off the water and stepping out into the warm haze. My toes wiggle against the plush bathmat as I grab a white terrycloth robe and pull it on.

Standing in front of the steam-covered mirror, I wipe my hand across it and lean in to inspect the small holes in my neck. I poke at them gently. The skin is tender, but it doesn't look so bad. I figure attempting to cover it up with makeup will only amuse my new vampire roommates, so I elect to cover it with my hair instead. No need to put it on display. No doubt the entire house smelled my blood the moment Gabriel's fangs pierced my skin.

I shiver at the memory, biting my lip as heat pools low in my belly and my clit pulses. I scowl at myself. I need to get my shit together.

Walking through the bathroom into the ridiculously massive closet, I stop short, and my brows pull together. Someone has filled the room with clothes. I pad across the marble floor, trailing my fingers along the muted, neutral colors. Everything is incredibly soft, and I bet stupid expensive.

They essentially bought you, a voice in the back of my mind says. *Might as well let them buy you some nice clothes.*

As much as I want to argue that, I can't stop myself from pulling a beige turtleneck sweater off one of the gold hangers. I purse my lips at it before setting it on the cushion-top ottoman in the middle of the room. *Too obvious.*

I settle on a black tank top with a heavy knit beige cardigan overtop and gray leggings. After scowling at the copious amounts of lingerie, I pick a matching black lace bra and panty set and get changed before combing my fingers through my hair and walking downstairs, my nerves as jittery as if I'd had several cups of coffee.

The guys are all here. Lex and Atlas are sitting on the couch in the living room with some news station on the TV built into the wall next to the door leading to the garage, Kade is in the kitchen making coffee, and Gabriel is sitting at the dining table reading something on a tablet.

I pause in the doorway of the hallway, glancing around the room at each of them. Gabriel meets my gaze first, setting the tablet on the table in front of him.

Taking a deep breath, I step into the room and clear my throat. "I have something to say," I announce.

Kade leans against the counter, wearing nothing but black joggers that sit dangerously low on his hips. His hair is damp and messy as if he haphazardly towel-dried it after a swim or shower. He takes a drink from his mug, while Lex turns down the volume on the TV and he and Atlas walk into the kitchen. Atlas is already dressed for the day in a black collared button-up and slacks, where Lex looks as if he's ready for a workout in a white muscle shirt that shows off his tattoos and gray sweatpants that leave little to the imagination in the groin area.

Nope, I scold myself. I have to focus.

"What is it?" Gabriel speaks up, remaining at the table, though I have his full attention. He's wearing a plain navy blue T-shirt, which has me assuming he isn't going to work today, and considering it's a Sunday, I suppose that makes sense.

I bite the inside of my cheek, panicking now that I have the opportunity to speak. Swallowing hard, I finally say, "My ancestors made a deal with the four of you a long time ago that decided the fate of my future before I was even born." I leave the bitterness out of my tone, though it lives on in me, because I'd just be talking in circles forever about how unfair it is that a bunch of men chose what would happen to me and I never had a say. There's no sense wasting my breath at this point.

I look from one vampire to the next until my gaze finally lands on Atlas. "I want to make a deal of my own."

Atlas tilts his head, regarding me curiously.

"What kind of deal?" Kade asks.

I keep my eyes on Atlas. "I won't try to kill you—again. I'll stay here," I swallow and force out, "willingly, for however long I'm obligated."

"In return for what exactly?" Gabriel asks.

"We could easily make you do that regardless," Lex adds with a quick wink.

I ignore him despite the fact that he's right. "I want to finish school. It's important to me. From there, I'm not sure, but I would like the option to renegotiate when the time comes."

"Renegotiate," Kade echoes, and I look at him this time before he continues, "what makes you think you have any leg to stand on to negotiate in the first place?"

My eyes narrow slightly. "The fact you haven't killed me."

"It's been two days," he says, a dangerous glint in his silver eyes. "Don't rush me."

I cross my arms over my chest. "You won't scare me into compliance, and I can't imagine a glamoured human would make for much entertainment, so don't bother with that threat again." I don't direct the second half to Kade, but to all of them.

Gabriel finishes off the glass of orange juice that had been sitting in front of him, then sighs.

Before he can speak, I say, "I'm not asking for much. If anything, my continuing to go to school would be good for you guys. You wouldn't have to figure out how to explain why I'm suddenly nowhere to be found after paying thousands of dollars to attend classes."

Kade and Atlas exchange a glance, and the latter vampire shrugs. Annoyance flickers through me, but I shove it down. I can't let my attitude or sharp tongue get in the way of potential partial freedom.

"Fine," Atlas says at last, and my heart skips a beat. I had been prepared to beg, though I'm relieved it didn't come to that. "There will be rules," he adds. "You will remain living here while you complete your degree."

"What about my apartment?"

"I've terminated your lease," Lex says.

I turn to him, arching a brow. "What are you talking about? How?"

"Lex owns the building you were living in," Kade chimes in.

My eyes go wide. "You what?" I demand.

Lex shrugs. "I have many investment properties. It's good business."

"I don't..." I shake my head. "This just keeps getting more fucked up." I rake my fingers through my hair, and Kade's eyes go to my neck. I quickly remember the marks there and pull my hair around to cover them again, but it's too late. He's seen them. His eyes meet mine and glimmer with heat. It makes me want to back away, but I keep my feet planted in place, counting on him not chomping down on my neck in the middle of the kitchen, though he looks as though he would like to do nothing more.

"You're lucky we are granting you any freedom," Kade points out, flicking his tongue along his bottom lip, and my breath catches at the glint of his fangs in the light from the window across the room.

I keep my mouth shut that time.

"I'll have the rest of your things brought here over the next few days." Lex's words are final. There's no negotiating this term, it seems.

I nod reluctantly. "Any other rules?" I'm unable to hide the agitation in my voice now, and Kade's expression darkens, though the smirk on his lips contradicts it.

"You will be held under glamour to come and go from your classes as we direct."

My mouth goes dry. The thought of being glamoured close to every day makes my stomach flip unpleasantly. "Why?" I force out. "You don't trust me not to run again?"

"Exactly," Lex says, looking rather amused at the thought. "I, for one, wouldn't mind chasing you, but the others aren't always in the mood to play."

My stomach is a pit of anxiety, but I say, "Fine. If that's what it takes to get out of this house for a few hours, I'll do it."

"You won't notice the glamour is in place unless you try to disobey it," Gabriel says, getting up from the table and carrying his empty glass to the sink, then leans against the counter. He's trying to make me feel better about the idea of them controlling me, I think, but it doesn't help the weight pushing down on my chest.

"Okay," I say in a low voice. "I'm assuming the lot of you already have my class schedule?"

Atlas inclines his head in a subtle nod. It doesn't surprise me at this point. It's just another reminder of how little control I've always had over my own life. Perhaps one day I'll be able to come to terms with it more easily, but for now, I'm reserved to wallow in it.

Kade leaves the room and returns in under a minute. He stops in front of me and holds his hand out. I glance down and find a shiny new phone in his palm. Arching a brow, I gingerly take it from him.

"Our numbers are programmed into it already," Lex says.

"So are your parents'," Gabriel adds.

I look up and frown at him. "I haven't—" I stop myself. They don't need to know I've barely spoken to them in months. Maybe I should tell them Atlas, Kade, Lex, and Gabriel found me, but it's pointless. We both knew it was coming and that there was nothing we—or anyone else—could have done to stop it. Telling them I'm here now won't change a thing. "Thanks for the phone," I finally say, dropping it into the pocket of my cardigan and making a quick mental note to shoot Brighton a text to let her know I'm alive.

"You may want to block Kade's number," Lex says with a snicker. "Unless you enjoy unsolicited dick pics."

Kade's deep laugh fills the room. "Please. As if they would be unsolicited."

I roll my eyes, though I'm secretly grateful for the ease in tension. "Thanks for the heads up," I tell Lex, then slip around Kade to walk to the coffee machine. I tap my fingers against the counter, looking it over. The shitty coffee machine at my apartment had maybe three buttons. This one has a touch screen with so many options it's making me nervous I'll break the damn thing trying to make a simple cup of coffee.

"Can I make you something?" Gabriel leans against the counter, watching me.

I shake my head. "I should probably figure out how to use it, considering I'm going to be here for the foreseeable future."

His responding smile makes his eyes sparkle, and something tugs at my chest. I shove the sensation away, doing my best to ignore it as he reaches into the cupboard above the machine and pulls down a mug, holding it out to me.

I take it, murmuring a soft "thanks" as I set it under the machine's spout. After a few failed attempts at navigating the system under Gabriel's silent supervision, I finally figure it out, and the aroma of freshly brewed coffee fills the kitchen, making me sigh happily.

My future may be bleak, but at least there's coffee.

EIGHT

I've never been so happy for a Monday morning in my entire life.

I get up and into a steaming hot shower without snoozing my alarm. I stop in the closet and grab blindly, dressing in a pair of black high-waisted pants and a turquoise blouse. I tuck it into the pants and slide on a pair of plain black flats before grabbing my book bag and my phone off the charger on the nightstand.

The kitchen smells faintly of cologne and coffee but is empty when I walk in. A burst of hope lights in my chest that I might be able to slip out without having to—

"Good morning." Kade's voice in my ear makes me jump and spin around to find him smirking at me.

"Do you have to do that?" I grumble.

His eyes glimmer with amusement. "I enjoy the little noises you make when I sneak up on you."

I don't offer a response to that. Anything I could say would only encourage his annoying as fuck behavior, and I have to deal with it enough already. "Where are the others?" I ask instead.

Kade thrusts his fingers through his messy hair and shrugs. "I think Gabriel left for work. Lex is probably still sleeping, the lazy bastard, and Altas usually runs in the morning."

I nod. "I, uh, have brunch with Brighton at Kafe Leopold in a bit."

He tilts his head. "Really? I don't remember discussing that yesterday."

My molars grind, and I force my tone level when I say, "It's a weekly tradition we have. If I don't show up, she'll know something's wrong."

"Hmm," he hums, pursing his lips. "Fine." He reaches out and taps the tip of my nose before I can move away. "You better behave."

I roll my eyes. "Touché."

He catches my gaze, and the swirling silver traps me in place. "And once your class is finished this afternoon, you'll come back here."

Jaw clenched, I nod. "I'll come back here."

Kade blinks, severing the glamour, and grins. "Good. You don't want to be late. Gabriel mentioned something about making lasagna for dinner."

I arch a brow at him. "You know, for vampires, I've only seen you eat human food since I've been here."

"That's not entirely true, now is it?" He points at the side of my neck, and my cheeks flood with warmth.

"That's not what I meant." I pull my hair forward and make sure Gabriel's bite mark is covered, making a mental note to apply some concealer before I leave the house. "I guess I expected to find the fridge stocked with blood or something."

Kade presses his lips together against a smile. "We have a separate fridge for that. You're not our first human house guest, and, well, it would get awkward rather quickly if someone opened the fridge and found bags of blood."

"Yeah, fair point," I comment.

"You want a ride to brunch?" he asks.

"I'm good." Showing up to meet Brighton with Kade behind the wheel would not go over well, and I already have a ton of explaining to do. I adjust the bag on my shoulder and step around Kade. "Thanks though. I'll see you later." I walk out of the kitchen and slip into the bathroom on the main level to cover up the marks on my neck. My handiwork isn't flawless, but so long as I keep my hair down, it should be fine. I should probably also pick up a few fashionable scarves, because if I have to bet, this won't be the last time I need to cover my neck. I shiver at the thought, recalling the pleasure that came along with Gabriel's bite.

Kade has disappeared when I walk back out of the bathroom. I pull my phone out and order an Uber, walking to the front of the house to wait outside. The front door has a keypad that allows me to lock it, though I realize once I've done that I don't have the code to get back in.

The sun is shining today, making the cold wind somewhat tolerable. My car arrives a few minutes later, and the driver is quiet on the short ride to Kafe Leopold, which has been mine and Brighton's regular Monday brunch spot for over a year now. It's close to campus and the menu is great.

I thank the driver as I get out of the car, and the moment I shut the door, Brighton rushes over to me. Her usually calm and kind hazel eyes are wide and filled with barely restrained panic. Of course her golden eyeshadow and perfectly-winged eyeliner are flawless, as is the rest of her outfit, no doubt all brand name pieces I wouldn't dream of buying myself. I tend to feel a little plain standing next to my best friend sometimes, but that has absolutely nothing to do with her, really. She's been the most supportive person in my life since we met last year as freshmen. Looking at her, you might think she'd be stuck-up, with her Michael Kors tote bag and black tweed Chanel jacket, but she's the complete opposite. She'd do anything to help anybody without a second thought.

"What in the ever-loving fuck happened to you the other night?" Brighton demands, grabbing my arm and pulling me toward the building.

"Hello to you too," I say, trying to ease her panic before it morphs into full-blown hysteria.

She lets go of me as her eyes narrow. "Calla, I'm serious. You need to tell me what happened. Your *I'm fine, will explain everything soon* text from a new number was less than convincing." Her strawberry blonde hair blows across her face in the wind, and I immediately grab for my hair to make sure it's still covering my neck.

"I know," I tell her, glancing around as a few people pass us on the sidewalk. She deserves to know, I'm just not sure how or what exactly to tell her.

"I tried to get in contact with you all weekend," she continues. "I called and texted about a million times, went by your apartment, I even called your parents."

I freeze. "You what?"

She huffs out a breath. "I know you're not super close with them, I just—I was freaked, Calla. Anyway, your mom said she was going to get in contact with you. I was going to follow up with her today and call the police if she hadn't heard from you, but then I got your hella cryptic message."

My stomach sinks. If my mom tried texting or calling my phone after the guys took it... I never got her message. "She tried to contact me?"

Brighton nods. "After you called me Friday night, something felt off. So, yeah. I'm gonna need you to—"

"I'll pay you back for the suite at the Four Seasons," I rush to say. The last thing I want is for her to think I'm taking advantage of her seemingly endless supply of money.

Her brows raise, and she frowns. "Calla, I don't give a shit about the money. Let's just go inside and talk over some cherry scones and lattes. I need some sugar."

I catch my bottom lip between my teeth, glancing toward the busy restaurant. "I'm really not that hungry. Maybe we could just go for a walk along the waterfront before class?"

She hesitates, then nods. "Yeah, okay." Her tone is gentle, but concern underlies her words.

It's a short walk to the water, and I hug my jacket closer as the cold breeze coming off the Potomac River sends a shiver down my spine. The boardwalk along the river is almost empty, which is good considering what I'm going to tell Brighton... just as soon as I can come up with the words to explain the crazy that is my life. Being honest about what happened may not be the smartest thing, but Brighton is my closest friend, she's my family, and I trust her completely.

We pass a middle-aged man jogging with his golden retriever in the opposite direction before Brighton says, "Please start talking, Cal. You're freaking me out."

"Sorry," I mumble, "I just... This is going to sound insane. I'm very aware of that."

She stops walking, and her brows inch closer. "Oookay. So not making me feel any better."

I sigh heavily and glance around to make sure we're out of earshot to anyone who could potentially overhear me. "What I'm about to tell you needs to stay between us, okay? I mean it. You can't tell anyone, it's really important for you to know that." I wipe my palms against my thighs as my heart thumps in my chest.

"I swear," she promises in a firm tone, though her voice wavers slightly; she looks as scared as I feel. "Please just tell me."

"Friday night when I got home from the library, there were four guys in my apartment. They were there for me."

Her eyes go wide, and I hold up my hand when she opens her mouth to freak out at me.

I press my lips together for a moment. "I should back up and start at the beginning."

"The beginning," she echoes breathlessly, and I can see the panic in the rapid rise and fall of her chest.

"You know my family is from New York City, that I moved here from there to go to school. Well, a long time ago—like, way before I was born—my family was involved with some really shady stuff on Wall Street."

Brighton shakes her head. "What, like insider trading?" she asks, and before I can answer, she continues, "What does that have to do with you? Or these guys that you're saying broke into your apartment? I don't—"

"I'm getting there," I assure her, "but you need some background information or this is *really* going to sound crazy." It's going to regardless, but context might be something of a benefit when she attempts to rationalize what I'm telling her.

"Keep talking," she says, crossing her arms over her chest.

"The business my family was involved in was dangerous enough their lives were threatened by some very powerful people. These guys, they helped my great-great-grandfather out of the deal. In exchange, I..." I swallow to try and get rid of the dryness in my throat, but it barely makes a difference. "I was promised to them, as the first-born daughter of the Montgomery bloodline."

She blinks at me. Her hands fall to her sides, and she just keeps shaking her head as if she's trying to figure out what I said, as if I spoke in a different language and she's struggling to interpret it.

"Bri?" I ask softly, watching her face closely.

Her eyes meet mine. "Hang on. You said these guys made a deal with your family before you were born and then they showed up at your apartment the other night?"

My stomach sinks. "Y-yes. They, um..." I lower my voice as dread coils in my chest, making it hard to breathe. "They're vampires."

Brighton chokes on a laugh. She keeps laughing until her eyes are glassy with tears, and I stand there and wait until the sound dies away. "Holy shit. You're being serious right now."

I nod. "Trust me, Bri, I wish I was kidding."

She doesn't meet my gaze, and her face has drained of color. "This isn't possible. Calla, what you're saying—"

"I know." I reach for her, grabbing her wrists, and she finally looks at me again. "I told you it would sound insane," I remind her.

She shakes her head again, and I can't imagine what's going through her thoughts right now. "I can't... This doesn't..." She presses her hand against her chest. "Son of a bitch, I can't breathe."

My eyes sting with tears, and I immediately wish I hadn't said anything, or that'd I'd come up with a better scenario I could give her. I'd be lying, but at least she wouldn't look absolutely petrified right now. I had years of knowing about the existence of vampires before they showed up in my life. I'm dropping this all in Brighton's lap without any warning. Her response is completely warranted. I just wish there was something I could do to make it easier on her.

"Look at me," I say firmly, tightening my grip on her wrists until she does. "I'm so sorry. You shouldn't have to know this, but I... I needed my best friend."

She blinks quickly, as if she's trying to fight back tears. "Calla, I don't know what to do with this." Her chin quivers, and she whispers, "Vampires aren't real." It sounds as if she's trying to convince herself, and it makes me feel even worse.

I bite my lip to keep it from trembling. "They are," I tell her, wishing more than anything in the world that I was lying. "I don't know how populated the world is, but I know at least four of them."

When she blinks, a tear rolls down her cheek, but she makes no move to pull her hands back and wipe it away. She swallows hard. "W-why is this happening?"

"I'm so sorry," I repeat, because what else is there to say at this point?

Her lips turn down. "It doesn't make any sense," she says in a low voice. "Why... I mean how did this happen?"

I already told her why and how it happened, but I tell her again. I wouldn't be surprised if I triggered a shock response in her, so having to repeat myself is the least I can do, even though saying the words again only tightens the knot in my stomach.

She sniffles, straightening as her fear seems to shift toward anger. "They can't do this to you. We have to tell someone! I can talk to my grandfather. He's in with a lot of the high-level security guards in the city." She twists her wrist in my grasp and grabs ahold of me. "People can't own other people, Calla."

My temples ache with tension and bitterness fills my next words. "These aren't people."

"Ouch. Now that's not a very kind thing to say about someone."

I go stiff as a board at the sound of Lex's voice behind me, and Brighton's eyes almost pop out of her face.

Son of a bitch.

I squeeze Brighton's wrists until her terror-filled eyes flick back to me, and then I mouth one word: *run*. I let go of her and turn to face Lex, expecting to find a pissed-off vampire glaring at me.

Instead, he grins, and his voice is almost teasing when he says, "You're in big trouble."

A muscle ticks in my jaw as a dangerous mix of fear and anger flares in me. "I—" My voice cuts off at the sound of a scared gasp, and I whirl around to find Brighton made it about ten feet away before Kade blocked her path. *Where the fuck did he come from?*

Kade wraps his hands around Brighton's shoulders, snaring her gaze, and panic bursts like a firecracker in my chest.

"Don't you dare," I snarl at him, stepping toward them, but Lex snakes an arm around my waist and hauls me back. I whip my head around to make sure no one is paying attention, but there are even fewer people around and none close enough to see what's happening.

"Chill out, Calla," he says in my ear.

I slam my elbow back, trying to catch him in the stomach, but it does nothing. "Let me go," I demand through my teeth, all the while watching Kade speak softly to my best friend, her hazel eyes glazed over as he glamours her. "Kade, stop!" I pull against Lex's grip, but all it does is make my stomach hurt.

He ignores me and continues talking to Brighton. She nods along, and when she smiles, my posture goes rigid. I stop fighting. This was a huge mistake. I shouldn't have told her out in the open, I should have—

Kade turns his face toward me, and Brighton's gaze follows. He's still speaking to her, though I can't make out his words, and she's still nodding. Finally, he lets go of her shoulders, and she turns to walk in the opposite direction. Doesn't say a word to me, just keeps walking away without so much as a glance back.

Lex pulls his arm from around my waist as Kade approaches, and I stalk forward, closing the rest of the distance between us in a few angry strides.

"What the fuck was that?" I snap at him.

His silver eyes narrow. "That, Calla, was me correcting your mistake." His words are clipped. "And I believe the words you're looking for are *thank you*."

"How about *fuck you*?" I shoot back, clenching my hands into fists to stop myself from trying to punch his stupid face.

"Oh, we both know you don't have a problem with that," he taunts, his lips twisting into a smirk.

I ignore that, glancing around to make sure we're still out of earshot to the people around us. The foot traffic has picked up slightly, but no one is close enough to overhear when I say, "What did you say to her?"

Kade cocks his head to the side. "I told her you moved out of your apartment to live with a family friend. I also helped her remember her morning a bit differently than how it went down. You see, we don't particularly like when certain people know about our... lifestyle."

Lex snorts from behind me.

"Certain people? She's my best friend, Kade. You can't isolate me from the people I care about just because—"

"Yes, we can," he interrupts. "You know why? Because when you run your mouth to people that can use the knowledge of what we are in very dangerous ways—"

"Kade," Lex cuts in, and there's a warning in his voice.

"What the hell are you talking about?" I demand. "Brighton wouldn't tell anyone." Considering she said we should go to her grandfather for help, that's not entirely true, but if I asked, she would keep it secret.

"Not a risk we're willing to take," Kade says, his eyes trained on me.

"So, what? You followed me from the house?"

"Yep. Good thing, too. I guess we didn't think we had to tell you to keep our little arrangement to yourself."

I gape at him, incredulous. "Our *arrangement*." Shaking my head, I continue, "You can't just... This isn't... I don't need a fucking babysitter."

"Clearly you do," Lex chimes in from behind me.

"Shut up," I snap over my shoulder before facing Kade again. "This is ridiculous, I—"

"Agreed," he says, cutting me off.

I shoot him a glare. "You have no idea how much I hate you right now."

Kade steps closer, filling my personal space with mint and the crisp scent of his cologne as he lowers his mouth to my ear. "And yet, I bet you'd still come all over my fingers. Again."

I open my mouth to fire back a venomous retort, but my breath catches in my throat. *Fucking bastard.*

Lex clears his throat. "All right, you two. Calla needs to get to class."

Kade moves away slowly, his gaze fixed on my mouth for a long moment before his eyes lift to mine, glimmering with a challenge. "We'd better get going then."

I finally find my voice and say, "We?"

"Uh-huh. You've made it perfectly clear you can't handle the freedom we so graciously offered you, so I'm going to accompany you to this afternoon's lecture."

"The hell you are," I snap angrily. The cool temperature and breeze coming off the water are no longer making me cold. The fire in my veins has made sweat dot my brow.

"Either Kade goes with you," Lex says, "or you're not going at all."

My gaze swings between the two vampires on either side of me. "You have got to be kidding me."

"Nope," Kade says, popping the 'p' with a shit-eating grin curling his lips. "And don't think I'll let you copy my notes."

It takes everything in me not to take a shot at pushing him into the river.

We walk in silence most of the way to campus until my stomach grumbles. I hadn't been hungry when I met up with Brighton, and as upset as I still am, I can't deny the pang of emptiness in my stomach.

Kade casts a sideways glance in my direction and arches a brow. "I heard that. We can stop at the Starbucks on M Street."

"I'm fine," I mutter, picking up my pace.

He catches my arm and pulls me back before pushing me against the side of a building, almost making me drop my book bag. "What you did was incredibly stupid."

My gaze whips around to make sure no one is looking, because this can't look very good, but we're on one of the quiet side streets; there's no one in sight. I scowl at him. "And what you did was incredibly invasive and wrong."

A muscle feathers along his jaw, and he shakes his head slowly, as if he's trying to control himself. "You have no fucking clue, Calla. None."

"And whose fault is that?" I fire back.

His silver eyes flare with anger, and he moves closer, pressing me into the cold brick. "You do something like that again, and you'll never see the outside of our house again. Understand?"

I glare at him. "You know, I thought you were the fun one and Atlas was the high-handed asshole." I tilt my chin up to meet his gaze and lower my voice. "I don't much like this look on you."

For a moment, he says nothing. His grip on my shoulders remains, and he just stares into my eyes. "No?" he finally whispers. "You prefer the look of me between your legs, don't you?"

My stomach clenches as his eyes drop to my mouth. "Honestly? Yeah." No sense in lying now. "And considering we can't do that here, I guess we better just go to class."

Still, he doesn't move. His gaze is locked on my lips, and it takes everything in me not to lick them, to beg him to kiss me. Because as pissed as I am about what happened with Brighton, I can't deny the way my body wants him. His exhale stirs the hair at my temple.

"Hmm." He steps back and waits for me to start walking before he falls into step beside me.

After a quick stop for food and caffeine, we get to campus and slip inside the lecture hall just as Professor Fischer opens her laptop at the front of the room. Some higher power must be looking out for me today, because there are still open seats in the corner of the room by the exit. I quickly take one of them and drag Kade down into the one next to me. The lights flick off, drowning the room in darkness as Fischer gestures to the projector screen behind her and starts talking about this week's reading.

I pull out my notebook and struggle with the little wooden table folded against the side of the theatre-style chair until it finally comes out, creaking as I secure it into place. Clicking my pen open, I do my best to pretend Kade isn't here and focus on the lecture.

It works... for about five minutes.

I can feel his eyes on me even in the dark, and his cologne is clouding my brain; he smells annoyingly good. The last thing I need is a distraction from my schoolwork, but evidently, my body didn't get the memo. I press my thighs together to sate the throbbing between them, and my cheeks burn when Kade chuckles under his breath.

Fucking vampire senses.

"Shut up," I hiss, keeping my eyes on the screen. The words could be in German for all I can tell at this point. My pulse is thunder beneath my skin, and it jackhammers when Kade reaches over and slides his hand up my leg. I suddenly wish I'd worn a dress today instead of high-waisted pants, because as much as I should push his hand away, I want nothing more than to press it against my core.

"Shh..." His lips are at my ear, and my eyes flutter shut.

"You can't," I whisper unevenly.

"I can," he says, and I can hear the smirk in his voice, "but you need to keep quiet."

I wet my lips, then press them together and open my legs a little. My heartbeat is in my throat, and I'm gripping the wooden arms of the chair as if I'm on a rollercoaster that's about to drop.

Kade flicks his tongue against the skin below my ear, and my breath catches as my eyes fly open. I force them to stay on the screen at the front of the room, though I haven't a clue what Fischer is talking about. Kade's fingers trail along the inside of my thigh, and I curse the universe for the existence of pants. He presses his lips against my neck, kissing and sucking gently, and when his hand cups me through my pants, the air halts in my lungs, and I clench my jaw to keep from making a sound.

"Good girl," he murmurs against my skin, pressing his thumb over my clit as his other fingers rub up and down and then in circles until my breathing quickens. My chest rises and falls quickly, and I desperately want his fingers inside me. He might be able to make me come this way, but it will feel so much better if he is actually *in* my pants.

"Kade," I whisper breathlessly, struggling to keep my eyes on the presentation.

His fingers stop moving and he says, "I know what you want."

I nod, finally looking at him to find his gaze filled with lust. A reflection of mine, I'm sure. "We should go." I can't remember the last time I left a lecture early, but I'm more than willing right now.

The corner of his mouth curls up, and he pulls his hand back, resting it in his lap and drumming his fingers against his thigh. "You wanted to go to school," he says, turning attention to the front of the room.

My mouth drops open, and I stare at him. "Are you serious right now?"

His smirk widens, but he doesn't look at me. "Shh, Calla. I'm trying to focus on the lecture."

I narrow my eyes and close my legs. "I hate you," I grumble, crossing my arms.

His soft chuckle is the only response I get.

After the longest lecture of my life, we stop at my apartment to pick up a few of my things.

I walk around the space and already miss it. I don't want to give it up. The coffee might be a million times better at the house, but this place... it was mine.

"Lex arranged for the movers to pick up the rest of your things tomorrow," Kade says, leaning against the kitchen counter.

I nod absently, grabbing a few books off the coffee table and sliding them into my bag. I walk down the short hall and grab a few extra toiletries out of the bathroom, then stop in my bedroom. The twinkle lights on the wall my bed is up against are still on. I've never appreciated how small and cozy this space was until now. Now that I have to go back to a ridiculously fancy mansion full of vampires and play house.

I drop onto the end of the bed with a heavy sigh and stare at the wall. I covered it with pictures—mostly polaroids from Brighton's camera—from parties over the last couple of years. There's also a bunch of pictures from my travels before school started, and even a few from when I lived in New York City.

"Calla?" Kade's voice floats down the hall.

I get up and swallow hard, clearing my throat and blinking back the sting of tears that took me off guard. "Yeah, I'm almost ready." It's a total lie. I'm not ready to leave this behind.

Kade leans in the doorway, his eyes on me. A muscle ticks in his jaw as he frowns, and then he glances at the wall of photos. "You're quite the photographer," he comments, pushing away from the doorframe and walking into the room to get a closer look.

"Memories fade," I say, "photos are forever."

He plucks one from the wall, and I peek over his shoulder to see which one he took. It's a polaroid of me and Brighton at the Lincoln Memorial last summer. Her arm is draped over my shoulder, and she's kissing my cheek. We're both wearing these cheap, bright pink sunglasses we bought from a street vendor, and I'm grinning so hard it hurt my cheeks.

A pang of guilt weighs on my chest for what happened to Brighton this morning. Even though she doesn't remember it, *I* know it happened.

I snatch the photo from him and slide it into my back pocket. "Let's just go," I mumble, heading for the hallway.

"I'm sorry."

His words make me stop. My brows knit as I turn around and look at him. His expression is hard to decipher, but it's free of the usual arrogance or amusement I'm used to seeing.

"For this morning. Your friend—"

"I really don't want to talk about this." Especially if he's going to be an asshole about it again.

"She can't know about us," he says in an even voice, though it's not filled with the same harsh tone as this morning. He almost sounds... sympathetic?

I nod without meeting his gaze. "She's all I have," I say, though I'm not sure why. He must know how important she is to me, considering all of them have been watching me for god knows how long. Still, I keep talking. "Growing up—well, in the years after my parents told me what was going to happen to me—I was careful about who I spent time with and who I let in. I decided very quickly that it wouldn't be fair to any friends I would possibly make if I just disappeared one day. I also didn't know what the four of you planned to do to anyone I was associated with, so I couldn't risk it. Brighton..." I trail off, shaking my head. "I tried to push her away. I was a total bitch, actually, when we met, because I liked her so much. Right from the start."

"For what it's worth, she seems like a good friend."

"She's one of the best people I've ever met. Her family, they have money and power, which in this city can be a dangerous combination, but you'd never know she had that kind of privilege. She's the kind of person who'd empty her wallet for someone struggling with homelessness and always make sure the people around her are okay." I can't help the smile that touches my lips. "She would go to war for me." I look at Kade. "And she'd sure as hell kick your ass if she knew the truth."

A ghost of a smile graces his lips. "I don't doubt that for a second." He steps toward me. "I'm not saying you can't be friends with her, Calla, you just can't tell her about the existence of vampires. People don't tend to take that very well."

"Yeah, I get it." There's an edge to my voice now. I get to keep my best friend, but I can't tell her about the biggest, most life-changing thing that will ever happen to me. No biggie, right?

"What does her family do?" he asks, glancing back toward the wall of photos.

I have to give him a little credit, I guess, that he's at least pretending to show genuine interest in my life—what it was before they waltzed into it a few days ago. "Um, I'm not totally sure. Honestly,

I don't even think Brighton knows. Her parents own their own company and it has something to do with environmental stuff." I shrug. "I'm into social sciences, not bio and chem."

He chuckles. "Fair enough."

"Oh, and her grandfather is a senator." I'm pretty sure that's where most of their money comes from.

Kade turns back to me. "That's interesting."

"Sure, if you think politics is interesting."

"Don't you?" He tilts his head. "At least the kind on television, right?" His voice takes on a teasing lilt, and I scrunch up my nose. I'd told Gabriel about my love of *Scandal*, but evidently, Kade had overheard. That, or it was already something the lot of them knew about me, anyway.

"You're making fun of me."

The corner of his mouth kicks up. "Maybe a little."

"Don't knock it until you try it," I tell him.

He holds his hands up. "All right, all right. Maybe I'll give it a shot." He moves closer again. "Are you ready to go?"

I only nod, because I don't trust my voice not to crack. I don't want to leave, not again. Especially when I won't be back here again. The weight of that crashes down on me and panic surfaces in a rush, making my chest tight. I spin away and hurry out of the room, sucking in air and forcing it into my lungs as I try to focus on something, *anything* else.

Kade appears in front of me, and I jump back, gasping in surprise.

"Fucking vampire mojo," I grumble, still catching my breath as I meet his gaze.

"Look at me," he orders in that voice that latches on to the deepest parts of me and forces compliance. "You're okay. Take a deep breath and let it out slowly. The tightness in your chest will ease in a minute. Just keep breathing for me, okay?" He poses it as a question, though his glamour is making me do exactly as he says.

After a few deep breaths in and out, I'm feeling much better. My head is clear, and I don't feel the immediate need to run away from everything.

Kade steps in and holds my chin between his thumb and forefinger. "You are the most beautiful human I've laid eyes on, you know that?"

I lick my lips without thinking about it. "You don't have to keep trying to distract me," I murmur. "I'm fine."

He leans in until his lips are mere inches from mine. "I'm not," he says, his voice filled with sincerity. "I'm being selfish, actually."

"How so?"

He slides his fingers along my jaw to cup the side of my neck and tips my head back with his thumb under my chin so I'm looking into his eyes again. "Because all I've been thinking about since that boring as fuck lecture was how badly I want to devour you again."

My eyes widen slightly. Perhaps I should be used to his forwardness by now, but he still manages to catch me off guard when he says things like that. Things that make my heart race and my core clench with need.

He presses his lips against my temple and sighs. "Tell me no." His words make me shiver as he rests his other hand against my hip.

"Will you stop if I do?" I whisper, and the throbbing between my legs really hopes he doesn't.

There's a stretch of silence.

"No." His lips crash down on mine, and he grips my hips, hauling me against him. I close my eyes as he devours my mouth, and wrap my arms around his neck, clinging to him so tightly he can probably feel my heart pounding against my chest.

Kade kisses me until my head spins, until I'm breaking away to fill my lungs with air.

"We should go," I manage in between breaths, and put some distance between us. "I was supposed to go back to the house right after class, remember?"

He rolls his eyes, grinning. "And you are. We just took a little detour." He picks up the bag I dropped on the floor at some point—I hadn't even realized—and shoulders it.

We walk out of my apartment, and the sound of the door closing echoes down the hallway.

Back at the house, Lex and Gabriel are gone. I take my bag to my room and stop in the bathroom to freshen up before wandering around a bit. I've got some time to kill before dinner, and while I probably should review the online notes from today's lecture, it's the farthest thing from my mind.

I freeze in the hallway to Atlas's office when the sound of shouting reaches me. Frowning, I step closer once, twice, then once more until

I'm standing outside the closed door. I can only make out every few words; it's as if he's walking—pacing more likely—closer to the door, but turning and marching away midway through his sentence.

"... By next week... what needs to be done... come down there myself and... I don't care how... Dante is not—"

Suddenly, I'm being pulled away from the door. A hand clamps over my mouth before I can scream, and when Kade's cologne wafts under my nose, I pull his hand away and whirl on him.

"What the fuck?" I hiss.

"Listening in on conversations you're not meant to be a part of is rude," he says, shaking his head at me as if I'm a child in need of scolding.

"Maybe if you weren't keeping me in the dark about, you know, *everything*, I wouldn't have to stoop to eavesdropping." I cross my arms over my chest and scowl at him. "Besides, I didn't mean to overhear anything. I was just looking for something to do to kill the time before the others get home for dinner."

Kade arches a brow at me. "I could give you several far more entertaining ideas than listening to Atlas blast someone."

"Oh, I'm sure," I remark dryly.

My head whips back toward the office door when Atlas shouts something, and a second later, the sound of shattering glass comes from behind the door.

"Ah, fuck," Kade mutters, stepping around me and knocking on the door before opening it slowly. "What's up, brother?"

Before he can say anything, I push past Kade and walk into the room.

Atlas stares at me for a moment before glancing toward Kade. "It's fine," he says in a low, gravelly voice.

"It didn't sound fine."

He moves in a blur and appears in front of me, so close the tops of his shoes touch mine. "And what exactly do you think you heard, Calla?" His voice is dark, venomous, and the flash of his fangs makes me stiffen.

I want nothing more than to move away, but I won't give him the satisfaction of making me back down. I also can't ignore that something about him, the darkness in him, draws me in. I want to test his limits. To see just how far I can push him before his control snaps. Clearly, my self-preservation hops on a train straight to crazy town when it comes to Atlas.

"She didn't hear anything," Kade says from behind me.

Atlas is still glowering at me. "Is that so?"

I hold my head high and my shoulders back. "You could tell me now," I offer.

Kade chuckles before exiting the room, the only indication that he left being the click of the door closing behind him.

Atlas purses his lips. "Oh, could I?" His tone is condescending. "I don't see that happening."

"And what exactly *do* you see happening?" I ask in a clipped voice, echoing his words.

He grabs my chin; it's not gentle the way Kade did earlier, and yet, my heart is still racing with anticipation. *What the fuck is wrong with me?*

"What's your angle?" I push, making no attempt to free myself from his grip. "There has to be some bigger reason you're keeping me here and alive. And I don't believe for a second that it's just to fuck and feed on me."

His eyes narrow ever so slightly, and he leans closer. His lips barely brush mine when he speaks. "Did it ever occur to you that maybe you should just be glad we're keeping you alive?"

I hold his gaze. "That's not good enough."

There's a flash of surprise in those bright silver eyes, but it's gone as quick as it came. He drops my chin and steps back. "Fine. You may come in handy with certain... business acquisitions."

I shake my head, clenching my hands into fists at my sides as annoyance fills me. "What the hell does that even mean?"

He shrugs. "Whatever I need it to."

I grit my teeth. "You are such an asshole."

Atlas says nothing to that. The second I trick myself into thinking I'm making a bit of progress here, I'm brutally reminded just how wrong I am when Atlas opens his mouth.

"Who is Dante?" I ask, watching him closely for any flicker of a response.

His jaw tightens before he exhales a dark, humorless laugh. "I thought you didn't hear anything."

I shrug and ask another question. "Is he a vampire?"

Atlas hesitates. His brows furrow as he seems to consider his answer. "Yes."

"You seemed angry on the phone. Why?"

He shakes his head. "Game over, Calla."

"Why?" I push.

"It's not your concern," he growls in my face.

I stand my ground. "I don't believe you. Otherwise, you wouldn't be so fucking uptight right now."

"I do not care what you believe. Now if you don't mind, I need to—"

"I do mind, actually," I cut him off in a sharp tone.

His lips press into a tight line, and he grabs my shoulder, holding me in an unbreakable grip as he drags me to the door. Ripping it open, he all but shoves me into the hallway and slams it in my face. It all happens too fast for me to have any reaction until we're separated by a thick pane of frosted glass.

I slam my fist against the door. "Asshole!" I storm back down the hallway, knowing I'm not going to get anywhere with Atlas. Gabriel, though, I might have a shot getting *something* out of. He seems to have a soft spot for me, and I am not above using that to get some information. Desperate times and all.

Walking back to my room, I close the door behind me. I pull out my phone and open a new message. I'm not sure what brings me to do it, but I start typing a message to my mom.

It's Calla. I have a new number. And a new address—with roommates.

I chew my bottom lip, reading the message over and over, debating on whether or not I want to send it. She knows they came for me based on what Brighton told me. With a sigh, I hit send and drop onto the end of my bed, staring at the ceiling until my eyes start staying closed longer with each blink. I'm dozing off when my ringtone blares, startling me awake and upright as I reach for my phone. I swipe across the screen three times before I manage to answer the call without checking the number.

"Hello?"

"Oh, my sweet Calla. It's so good to hear your voice."

"Hi, Mom." My voice cracks, and I pull the phone away from my ear and clear my throat before bringing it back and saying, "What's going on? Why are you calling me?"

She sniffles, and I can hear the pain in her voice when she says, "Your father is here, too."

My stomach drops and my grip on my phone tightens. "Why are you calling?" I ask again, swallowing the lump that has gathered in my throat.

"I needed to hear your voice. After Brighton got in touch with us, I tried to reach you. I even looked into booking a flight there but... We're so sorry, Calla," Mom cries.

Dad clears his throat, and his voice is gruff. "We wish there was something we could do. If we could save you—"

"Please," I cut in, my chin wobbling as I fight back tears. "There isn't... You can't. You never could." This conversation is a perfectly painful example of why I've barely spoken to either of my parents since I graduated high school. As much as they can't handle the guilt over the deal my dad's family made, I can't deal with listening to them apologize. And it's only made worse by the fact my mom had no idea about the blood oath until it was too late. It was never her fault, and the guilt she carries makes me want to scream. It makes me want to hate my dad for keeping it from her, but even after all these years—even after being taken by vampires—I can't hate him. He's... he's my dad.

"How are you?" Mom asks in a quiet voice. "I mean, are you... Have they hurt you?"

I swallow the lump in my throat. "No. I'm okay, Mom."

She chokes on a sound of relief, and I squeeze my eyes shut.

"I have to go. I..." It takes me a few beats before I can speak again. "Please don't worry about me." I want to tell her not to call me again. That it's too hard to hear her voice—and dad's—but I can't bring myself to do it.

"I'm so sorry." She cries harder. "We love you so much, baby."

I shake my head, though they can't see it. "I love you." I end the call, and the phone slips out of my hand onto the bed. Tears slip down my cheeks, and the pressure in my chest from holding them back so long threatens to burst. I struggle to swallow the sob lodged in my throat. I choke on it, grabbing blindly for a pillow to muffle the sound. I cry into it, unable to hold back any longer. My shoulders shake and my head pounds, but that pain dulls in comparison to the agony of having my heart cleaved in two.

CHAPTER

TEN

The smell of spices and tomatoes reaches me before I step into the kitchen a couple of hours later, where I find Gabriel cooking ground beef in a skillet on the stovetop.

"Calla," he greets in a low voice. It seems... off. Not kind or gentle like I'm used to. He must have gotten home a while ago, because he's wearing dark gray sweatpants and a black V-neck. There's no chance he wore that to work.

"Hey," I say, "I didn't know you were home."

He nods, smiling at me over his shoulder as he keeps stirring the meat, but his usually bright eyes are dull.

"Are you... um, okay?"

Gabriel sets the wooden spoon on the counter and turns to face me. "I'm glad to be home," he says in lieu of a real answer. "How was your day?"

I exhale heavily, leaning against the counter, and steal a mouthful of shredded cheese. I sprinkle it into my mouth and ask, "Did you talk to Kade?"

He arches a brow. "No?"

"My day was fine," I say, forcing a cheery tone.

He sighs, pinching the bridge of his nose. "What did Kade do?"

"Nothing." I wave him off. "Never mind. Tell me about your day."

He gives me a knowing look. "Let's both agree not to talk about our days and make dinner instead. Sound good?"

I nod, coming around the counter. "I talked to my parents," I blurt, then press my lips together. *Where did that come from?* I shouldn't have said anything. This is something I should be talking to Brighton about. If I *could* talk to her about it...

"You did?" Gabriel asks; I have his full attention. "What happened?"

I run my fingers through my hair to have something to do with my hands and watch the ground beef sizzling in the skillet. "Not much of anything. They asked how I was, and my mom got all emotional and apologized. As if any of this is her fault." I pause. "I wanted to tell them not to call again, but I couldn't do it."

He frowns. "Calla—"

"*What*, Gabriel?" My voice comes out harsher than I was expecting. I swallow past the lump in my throat. "Should I have told them everything was great and invited them to come visit?"

His gaze softens. "I'm sure your relationship with them is complicated."

"Yeah," I say without meeting his gaze. *Which is partially your fault,* I don't add, though part of me wants to.

Gabriel glances toward the counter where his phone is vibrating. "Excuse me. I need to take this." He picks it up and answers in a hushed voice. His expression darkens, and he looks at me for a fleeting moment before leaving the room.

So much for getting any information from Gabriel. I sigh to the empty room. I'll have to try after dinner.

Approaching the stovetop built into the island, I pick up the wooden spoon and start pushing around the meat, hoping Gabriel will return in enough time to finish cooking, because it is definitely not my forte.

"Something smells delicious."

I jump a little, turning my head to look over my shoulder, and see Lex walking into the room, grinning softly as he rakes his fingers through his white hair only for it to flop back across his forehead.

"I thought Gabriel was cooking," he comments, walking closer and leaning against the counter next to me.

"He was," I say. "Someone called him, and he left looking all weird and tense." I force a nonchalant shrug. "I have no idea what I'm doing, by the way. You should probably take over if you want this to be edible."

Lex presses his lips together against a smile and comes up behind me. His arm brushes my side as he reaches for the spoon and keeps stirring. His chest is against my back, but I don't move away.

"What did you do today?" I ask to fill the silence and to distract myself from wanting to lean back into Lex. He smells of citrus and spice, a perfect fall evening, and it makes me want to wrap myself in it —in *him*.

He switches the burner off and drops his hand to my hip. "Nothing exciting." His voice is low in my ear, his lips close enough his breath tickles the shell of my ear.

I shiver, fighting the urge to close my eyes. "Same here," I lie. That lecture was the most exciting one I've attended all semester.

"Oh yeah?" he asks, then presses his lips against the skin just below my ear. His tongue flicks out, and I hold my breath.

"Lex..." I whisper.

"I want to fuck you against the counter," he murmurs, and my stomach clenches. "I'd lay you down on the marble and spread those lovely thighs of yours. I'd have you screaming so fast you wouldn't have a chance to be embarrassed that the entire house could hear you moan my name. Though I do enjoy that beautiful pink your cheeks go when you blush."

The heat in my belly spreads lower, making my core throb with desire. My pulse kicks up and it quickly becomes hard to swallow.

"What do you think?" he asks, nipping my earlobe. Without warning, he turns me around and presses me into the counter next to the stovetop. "There's that blush I enjoy," he says with a wink.

I bite my lip, my eyes flicking between his as I lift my hand to his chest, running my fingers upward slowly. His black sweater is soft to the touch; I have the fleeting idea to steal it for myself, though I have a feeling he'd remove it pretty easily if I asked right now. I inhale slowly, overwhelmed by his scent now that I'm facing him. I lean up on my tiptoes and brush my lips across his. "I have no idea what I'm doing." I repeat the words, though I'm no longer talking about cooking.

"You're doing just fine," he says in a low voice, kissing the corner of my mouth, coaxing me to keep going.

I thread my fingers together behind his neck and lean in until we're pressed against each other. I kiss him again, longer and deeper, my heart hammering in my chest. My eyes close as Lex deepens the kiss, his tongue darting out to tease my lips until they part to let him in. I gasp into his mouth when he presses his lower half into me and his erection finds the throbbing between my legs.

"Fuck," he growls against my lips, kissing me harder.

My head spins, and I feel light enough to float away. I grind against him, desperate to ease the ache at my core, but I can't get him close enough to do much besides feed the friction there.

"Calla." There's a warning in his voice.

I ignore it. "Just... kiss me," I plead, gripping the hair at the back of his neck.

He tips my head back and seals his lips over mine once more. We move together as if we've known each other for years, completely in sync. And when his fangs extend and slice into my bottom lip, I don't pull away.

Lex makes a deep sound at the back of his throat and tightens his grip on me, holding on as if he's trying to control himself.

I should be afraid, but my head is so hazy with lust, the thought doesn't have a chance to manifest enough to invite fear in.

Our kisses become quicker, more frantic, until Lex finally rips his mouth away from mine.

I blink my eyes open as I'm catching my breath and find him licking my blood off his lips, his fangs still fully extended and stained in red.

Holy fuck that was hot.

I lick the rest of the blood from my lips, which tingle at the touch.

"Do you want to know what you taste like?" Lex asks, running his thumb along his bottom lip.

My heart falters, and I open my mouth to respond, but nothing comes out. "I..."

He grins. "Everyone tastes a little different. You... taste like the warmth of the sun on your face after a long, dark winter."

"That's poetic," I mutter, heat rising in my cheeks.

His eyes hold mine as he shrugs. "Ask Gabriel what you taste like to him next time."

I choke on a laugh. "Yeah, I'm not going to do that."

That earns me another grin. "You also taste a little like strawberries and coffee."

I blink at him. "Are you serious?"

He nods. "As a white ash stake to the heart."

I arch a brow, making a mental note of that. You know, just in case. "Plain old wood won't do it?"

Lex pauses, seeming to consider his next sentence before he says, "No. Has to be white ash. Lucky for us, it's pretty rare."

"Huh. And that's the only way to kill a vampire?"

"Subtle," he murmurs, tutting his tongue. "You think I'm going to stand here and tell you how to kill me"

I prop my hands on my hips. "Haven't you already?"

The corner of his mouth kicks up; he isn't concerned. "You're very sneaky. Distracting me with your lips and your blood—"

"Hey, *you* bit *me*," I remind him.

"Yeah, I did. After *you* kissed *me*," he shoots back in a teasing tone.

"Whatever," I grumble halfheartedly, but before I can say anything else, Gabriel returns, and I catch his gaze. "Everything okay?" I ask.

He nods, offering me a smile. "Just something at work. Nothing you need to be concerned about."

I press my lips together, nodding, though I'm not sure I fully believe him.

"Fire them," Lex says, leaning against the counter.

Gabriel arches a brow at him. "Helpful as always, Lex. Thank you very much."

"Anytime." He winks.

Gabriel finishes dinner while I pretty much try to stay out of the way and just watch.

An hour later, the five of us are sitting around the table eating the most delicious lasagna I've ever tasted. I stuff my face with carbs, savoring the garlic bread Gabriel made to go with the lasagna and hating myself for how much I'm enjoying it. I almost forgot for a moment what circumstances led me here. Almost.

I take a long drink of water, glancing around the table. The guys are mostly quiet. Kade is scrolling on his phone, and Gabriel is speaking softly to Atlas, who is nodding along. Before my gaze reaches Lex, I freeze at the feel of his fingers trailing up my leg. Shooting him a look, I press my lips together as my cheeks flush. *He isn't going to...*

Lex's fingers slide between my legs and rub slow, firm circles against my center, over my joggers.

My jaw clenches so hard I can't open my mouth. I bite my tongue to keep from making a sound and fight the urge to push against his fingers.

I clear my throat and suck in a breath, flushing hotly when Kade peers over at me. *Shit.*

"You good?" he asks, arching a brow.

"I... Yeah, I'm fine," I manage to say before dropping my gaze to my plate. It takes everything in me to pick up my fork and lift it to my mouth, as if Lex isn't teasing me under the table.

When he pulls his fingers away, my stomach drops, either from relief or disappointment, I'm not even sure at this point. And then he slips them past the waistband of my joggers, and I see red. His lips twist into a satisfied smirk when he realizes I'm not wearing any panties, and he wastes no time, parting my folds and slipping inside in seconds.

Fuck. Me.

I squeeze my thighs together, cursing silently and gripping my fork tighter.

"Calla?" Gabriel's voice cuts through the haze of pleasure, and my head snaps up to look at him.

"Huh? Sorry, pardon?" I mumble.

He watches me for a moment that seems to stretch into forever, while Lex continues stroking me. "Are you not enjoying it?" he asks, pointing to the barely eaten lasagna that I've been pushing around my plate.

"Oh, no I definitely... am enjoying it."

Lex snickers beside me, slipping his finger out and circling my clit.

I manage to shove his hand away without being too obvious about it and return my attention to my plate. "It's really good, Gabriel," I tell him with a smile. "You'll have to teach me how to cook, because I pretty much tap out after instant noodles or those frozen meals you cook in the microwave."

Kade sucks in a breath and laughs. "I think you've traumatized him."

"What?" I say, chewing my lip. "Sorry, I just... I'm not good at cooking."

Gabriel's expression is priceless—it's as if I've just insulted his ancestors or something.

I arch a brow at Gabriel. "You going to live?"

His lips finally curve into that smile I've come to be rather fond of. "I'm going to teach you, because this is simply unacceptable."

I smile a little, then lift a piece of lasagna to my mouth and chew. "Deal."

I'm cleaning up after dinner when Lex slides in behind me, circling his arm around my waist and tugging me back against him.

"Come with me," he says, his lips brushing the shell of my ear and making me squirm and turn in his grasp.

My eyes flick between his, which are glimmering with what I can only describe as excitement, though there's underlying darkness in them too. I've come to realize that's just his normal look, though—a little wild. "Where?"

The corner of his mouth kicks up. "My favorite place."

I arch a brow. "Not really a helpful answer, Lex."

He leans in, lifting his other hand and using his pinky finger to move a few rogue pieces of hair away from my face. I hold my breath— and his gaze—until he says, "I have an appointment with my tattoo artist. I want you to come."

A burst of excitement flares in my belly, and I can't help the smile that forms on my lips. I'm more than happy to get out of this house for a while, and I've never been inside a tattoo parlor. "Yeah, okay."

Before I know what he's doing, he dips his face and kisses my cheek, then steps back. "Meet me in the garage in half an hour."

I retreat to my room and change into a warmer shirt, adding a denim jacket, and tug on my Doc Martens. After pulling a comb through my hair, I twist it into a messy bun on the top of my head and grab my phone from the table beside my bed on my way out of the room.

Lex is leaning against the wall beside the garage door when I walk into the living room, and there's a little bounce in my step as I approach, which he picks up on and grins.

"Remember what I said," Kade says from the couch, and I turn my head to look at him. I haven't even noticed him sprawled there on his phone. "If you're going to get my name in a heart, I want it to be atomi- cally correct." He's talking to Lex, who rolls his eyes in response. Kade's gaze shifts to me. "And what's our girl getting?"

Our girl.

Those words make my pulse jump, and I shake my head. "I'm just going to watch."

His eyes sparkle with mischief. "Watching can be fun."

It's my turn to roll my eyes as I turn back to Lex, and he opens the garage door, gesturing for me to walk ahead of him. I step into the concrete room and peer around at the collection of high-end cars.

"Pick one," Lex says, pausing at the wall with a board of key fobs.

I purse my lips, trailing my gaze over the selection before pointing to the sleek black Tesla.

"Good choice." He grabs a key, and I follow him to the car. He opens the passenger side, and I slide in. Moving too fast for my eyes to track, he gets behind the wheel and starts the engine. The car runs silently as we drive out of the garage, the door opening then closing behind us.

It's dark and unseasonably chilly outside as we drive toward downtown. The street lights cast a golden glow on the road, and the headlights from cars going the opposite direction make me squint. "Isn't it kind of late for a tattoo shop to be open?"

Lex flicks the blinker on and switches lanes to pass a car. "My artist, Scarlett, runs her own place and works by appointment only."

"And she has appointments after ten o'clock at night?" I peer out the window, watching the buildings and trees go by. "Wait." I turn my head in his direction. "Is she a vampire?"

Lex laughs. "Nah. She's just a kickass artist who makes her own schedule, which is lucky for me."

"Does she know about you?"

"What about me?" he asks in an amused tone. He knows exactly what I mean, so I shoot him a look, and he says, "Yes, she knows I'm a big, bad creature of the night." He laughs. "She's glamoured to keep my secret."

I nod. "Did she do the vines and roses on your arm?"

"Yep. She's done all of my ink in the last fifteen years or so. Being immortal means having to find a new artist every handful of decades."

"Wouldn't it be easier just to turn one of them?" I ask without thinking. Of course that would mean taking their life away from them, but Lex and the others have already proven they're not above that. Case in point: me.

"Turning someone into a vampire isn't a small thing, Calla," Lex says, pulling off one of the downtown streets. We drive down a narrow alley between two buildings, barely big enough for his car. He slows to a stop where the alley opens up to a courtyard near the back of the buildings and kills the engine.

I catch my bottom lip between my teeth and pull at a loose thread on my shirt. "Will you tell me how it's done?"

"Why?" His voice has a lilt of amusement to it. "Are you thinking of joining the eternity club?"

My mouth goes dry, and I immediately shake my head. "I just... I was curious is all."

Lex drums his fingers against the steering wheel. "It's a process. There's a venom in our bite that needs to be coursing through your veins—along with our blood—when you die. You'd awaken weak and vulnerable, but once you drank human blood, you'd be stronger and faster than ever before. The first feed has to be directly from the vein, and a newbie vampire needs to drink so much blood to complete the transition that the human rarely survives."

My stomach clenches with unease. "That's intense," I say in a quiet voice, wiping my palms against my pants before glancing toward the brick building with a flickering neon red TATTOO sign in the window. "We should probably go in."

Lex watches me for a moment, his expression calculating, before he nods and gets out of the car. A second later, he opens my door and offers his hand. I take it and get out, and we walk across the dingy, dark courtyard to a large metal door. Lex bangs his fist against it a few times before opening it and ushering me inside.

My senses are overwhelmed by the sharp scent of antiseptic, which I guess is a good thing. The place is clean at least. I stay close to Lex but look around the small space. The walls are a deep red and mostly covered in tattoo sketches of all different sizes, some in color and others done in black ink. The floor is checkered tiles, and there's a brown couch directly to my right, under the window with the neon sign. Old rock music fills the room, and the fluorescent lighting along the exposed ceiling dims and brightens every few seconds.

A curvy woman with a blond pixie cut who looks to be in her late thirties based on the faint wrinkles around her eyes and mouth pushes aside a black curtain and steps into the room. She's wearing a black Rolling Stones T-shirt, ripped jeans, and white Doc Martens. "Lexington, you beautiful bastard, it's good to see you."

Lexington?

I arch a brow at him. "Is that your real name?"

He rolls his eyes, but his lips are curled into a grin. "Nope, but she's about to hold a needle against my skin, so she can call me whatever the hell she wants." Lex steps forward and pulls the woman into a hug. "What's new, Scar?" he asks, stepping back.

She shrugs, reaching behind an old wood counter, and the music quiets. "Not a damn thing." Her pale blue eyes slide to me, and I can't help but admire the dark purple makeup look she's rocking. "Who's this? You don't usually bring anyone when you come to visit me."

I force a smile, but something in my chest tightens at her words, and I'm not sure what to make of that. "I'm Calla. It's, um, nice to meet you."

She purses her bright red lips. "Hmm, okay, Calla." She looks me over. "You got any ink?"

"No," I tell her, "though I've always wanted to get something. I'm just not sure what."

She nods before turning her attention back to Lex. "Give me ten minutes. I'm almost set up."

"Thanks, Scar."

Scarlett disappears behind the curtain again, and I walk around the room, looking over the artwork on the walls. It's mostly skulls, flowers, and quotes, but mixed in are some more unique pieces with animals and languages I can't read. Scarlett is undeniably talented. No wonder Lex comes here.

Before long, she returns and leads us back to a small room with more art covering the walls and a black leather chair that reminds me of one you'd see in a dental office. There's a stool on wheels where Scarlett sits, pulling a tray over as Lex drops into the chair and swings his legs onto it.

I lean against the wall instead of taking the other rolling stool and watch the two of them chat softly as Scarlett pulls on black gloves. She preps the needle and picks up what I gather is a stencil, and Lex pulls his shirt off, flipping it over the back of the chair.

My eyes drop to his lean abs and end up stuck there. I swallow hard and press my lips together, forcing myself to tear my gaze away and instead focus on Scarlett as she presses the stencil to the left side of Lex's collarbone. She peels it away a moment later, leaving a black outline of vines that look as if they'll connect to the design that trails up his arm and over his shoulder. She hands him a mirror, and he nods at her before handing it back.

The buzz of the tattoo gun fills the room, and Lex grins at me.

"What?" I say.

"You don't need to stand all the way over there." He pats the stool next to him.

"I'm good." I'm curious about tattoos, sure, but I don't need to see the needle piercing his skin over and over at close range.

He pouts. "What if I want to hold your hand?"

Scarlett snorts.

"I think you'll live," I remark dryly.

Lex winks at me. "You think?"

I roll my eyes and push away from the wall, walking over and dropping onto the stool. "Baby," I mutter, slapping my hand onto the chair, palm up.

He slides his fingers through mine as Scarlett leans over and lowers the tattoo gun to his skin. The bastard doesn't even flinch. In fact, he inhales slowly and smiles as if he's at peace, and I faintly recall him saying that he enjoys pain. His thumb traces back and forth against my hand, and I watch that instead of the ink being permanently etched into his skin.

"So your thing is tattoos, Gabriel's is cooking, Kade's is… his hair, probably, and Atlas's is being the grumpiest person alive or undead or whatever." I panic and my gaze flies toward Scarlett before I remember what Lex said about glamouring her.

He chuckles. "You're mostly right."

I tilt my head. "What, Kade's thing isn't his hair?"

"No, you're definitely right about that. Atlas on the other hand…" Lex trails off, and I'm holding my breath waiting for him to give me some information that will help me make sense of the broody as hell vampire. "He was born to a very powerful vampire family a long, long time ago. There are certain expectations he's had to live with that would put a strain on anyone."

So Atlas wasn't turned, he was born a vampire. "Is that why the rest of you look up to him?"

"We respect him," Lex explains, holding my gaze as if Scarlett isn't in the room with us. "For many reasons. One of which being, for me at least, that he turned me. There's a special bond between a vampire and their sire. He doesn't control me, but he doesn't have to. I would do anything for him—we all would. And I see that look on your face, but before you say anything, you should know that he would do the same for us."

"Okay," I finally say. "But you're the only one he turned?"

Lex nods. "He saved my life. I was living in Brooklyn at the time, driving into the city for work. I left the office long after dark following a meeting that had run late one night and hit a whiteout storm. I was in a head-on collision and was minutes away from death when Atlas found me. He was driving in the opposite direction and saw the crash. I don't remember that night, just waking up several days later in Atlas's home on the Upper East Side with the most excruciating burning in my throat."

I swallow hard, my heart pounding in my chest. "I… I'm sorry that happened to you."

A flicker of surprise passes over his usually sharp features, softening the gray in his eyes. "Don't be," he says, squeezing my hand, "I'm not."

I wet my lips, nodding. "And what about the others? How did they become vampires?"

Lex glances over to Scarlett as she finishes tracing one of the thorns before turning his gaze back to me. "Kade was a vampire when Atlas and I met him shortly after I turned. He was going through some shit that he never really elaborated on, but he helped me get a handle on my bloodlust. I wasn't ready for the constant urge to rip into people's throats, so it was quite the adjustment."

"You still don't know how he became a vampire?"

He shakes his head. "And before you ask, I don't know about Gabriel either. It's not exactly something we talk about."

"Why not?" I ask, pulling my hand free from his and resting it in my lap.

He shrugs, and Scarlett snaps, "Don't move."

"Sorry, Scar." He clears his throat, then says to me, "Gabriel is a fairly private person, in case you hadn't noticed." The corner of his mouth kicks up. "I think it's just naturally ingrained in him for some reason."

I nod, feeling as if I've gotten to know my vampire housemates a little better—finally. I still have so many questions, most of which pertain to me and my future, but I suppose this is a start.

An hour later, Scarlett is bandaging Lex's new ink. She makes quick work of cleaning up her station and shrugs on a jacket. "I'm late for another appointment," she says, tossing a key at Lex, which he catches easily. "Lock up on your way out?"

"Sure thing."

She pushes through the curtain and disappears before I can say goodbye.

Lex makes no move to put his shirt back on and instead pokes at the bandage across his collarbone.

"Did it hurt?"

"I've felt worse," he answers. "It goes numb after a while."

"Oh."

He catches my chin and tilts my head up so we're at eye level. "I could give you one."

My pulse jackhammers. "What?" I squeak. "No way. Absolutely not."

Lex's deep laugher fills the small room, and he traces the line of my jaw with his thumb. "I'm fully trained, Calla. I just don't ink myself."

I narrow my eyes and pull back instinctively, making his hand fall onto the armrest of the chair. "You're not getting anywhere near me with a tattoo gun, so don't even think about it."

"All right, all right," he concedes, grinning. "You know what I thought about while Scarlett was stabbing me a thousand times?"

"Oh, please do tell."

He lowers his voice and leans toward me, so close I can count the freckles across his cheeks and nose. "I thought about how badly I wanted to get you alone. How I would pin you to this chair and spread those gorgeous thighs of yours. How I would fuck you hard and fast, pounding your pussy until you screamed so loud anyone close enough to hear would think *you* were getting stabbed."

My voice is gone. I stare at him, at the glimmer of power in his wild eyes, and I can't bring myself to speak. Without thinking, I press my thighs together and lick the dryness from my lips. My breathing has gone shallow and my heart is beating in my throat.

"Come here," he says in a low voice.

I hesitate, but the look in his eyes paired with the insane fluttering in my stomach pushes me to move. I stand and swing my leg over the chair, straddling him as he grips my hips and settles me into his lap. I grab his shoulders to steady myself, and my breath catches when I feel him pressed against my core. I shift up slightly, and Lex groans in response, his fingers digging into my hips.

He trails his hands along my arms, then pushes my jacket off my shoulders. I lean back to pull it off the rest of the way and toss it behind me. Without warning, Lex tugs me forward, and I fall against his chest, pressing my hands into the chair on either side of him. His lips find mine in an instant, and he kisses me slowly, taking his time to explore the way my lips move with his as my eyes close of their own volition. His tongue darts out, and my lips part in a moan as he grips my hips again, grinding me against the hard thickness between his legs. His tongue sweeps into my mouth, dancing with mine as he tilts his head to deepen the kiss. I move my hips in slow circles, making my heart pound in my chest almost perfectly in time with the throbbing at the apex of my thighs.

Lex manages to move from underneath me and flip me onto my back, stealing the air from my lungs as I gasp in surprise. He traps me between his legs, his knees pressing into the chair on either side of me, and dives for my neck, kissing, licking, and sucking until my skin tingles. His fangs extend and scrape along my skin, gentle enough they don't slice into my throat but instead send a delicious shiver down my spine.

I reach between us and palm the front of his pants, desperate to feel him. When he groans, I pull his mouth back to mine and kiss him hard, telling him exactly what I want. I pop the button on his pants and tug the zipper down, pulling his cock out and running my hand down the shaft slowly.

"Calla," he growls against my lips.

I wrap my fingers around his velvet-soft length, moving my hand up and down at a lazy pace while our lips remain locked in a battle for control.

He pulls back, staring into my eyes as I continue to pump my hand on his cock. "You feel so good," he says in a husky tone, his gaze filled with liquid silver.

My cheeks feel hot and my pulse is pounding beneath my skin, but I don't stop. I pick up the pace, experimenting with my grip just a little, and Lex tips his head back, closing his eyes as his chest rises and falls faster.

"Don't you dare stop," he demands.

I grin, though he isn't looking at me. I move faster, then slow down, driving him crazy each time I switch paces.

"Christ," he grounds out, grabbing my hand and pulling it away from his cock. He traps both of my wrists above my head and presses his other hand against my stomach, sliding it past the waistband of my pants and finding the heat at my core. He pushes two fingers in easily, flicking my clit with his thumb. "You're a mess," he says in my ear, making me shiver. "I fucking love it." He nips my earlobe before pressing his lips to the pulse at my throat.

I suck in a breath and moan when he hits a particularly sensitive spot inside me. I tug on my wrists, wanting to touch him, but his grip is unforgiving. "Lex," I grumble, tugging again.

He kisses me chastely, pumping his fingers slowly and then picking up the pace as I did to him. "Yes, Calla?"

"How long are you going to keep—" My words break off as a wave of pleasure crashes over me, igniting an orgasm that vaults my hips off the chair as my pussy clenches around his fingers. *Holy shit*.

Lex smirks at me, fangs and all, and pulls his fingers out. He releases my wrists and curls his fingers around the waistband of my pants, tugging them along with my panties down to my knees.

Anticipation builds in my chest as I track his every move, and when he lines his cock up with my entrance, it takes everything in me not to thrust my hips and take him inside me.

He teases me, tracing my pussy lips with the blunt head of his cock, dipping inside a little more with each pass, until he seals his mouth over mine and thrusts all the way in.

I moan against his lips, squeezing my eyes shut as he pulls back and drives back into me. Once, twice, and then a third time. He slows his pace after that, letting me catch my breath as his lips move to my neck. I tense beneath him when his fangs sink into my skin, and I whimper as the sharp, split-second of pain morphs into warm, hazy pleasure. I melt, holding him against me and pushing my fingers through his hair as he drinks deeply and rolls his hips, hitting a spot so deep, I see stars behind my eyelids.

His pace quickens as he pulls away from my neck, licking the puncture marks until they stop bleeding. "You are my new favorite taste." He brushes his lips against mine in a whisper of a kiss, and his words make my chest tighten with a foreign sensation that I have no time to decipher.

I open my eyes to meet his gaze, and the second I do, another orgasm rips through me, stealing my breath as I grind my hips against him, reveling in the friction between us.

"That a girl," Lex murmurs, slowing his thrusts, but continues moving inside me as I come down from my euphoric high. "Catch your breath, because I'm not done with you yet."

That sparks something in me, and I lift my hips to urge him on. Evidently, I'm not done with him either.

His thrusts become fast and hard, until he pulls out completely and flips me over. "Wrap your arms around the chair," he orders, spreading my legs as I move to obey him. He takes me from behind, making my pussy clench around him, and I gasp when hits even deeper inside me at this angle.

"Lex," I breathe, and I'm not sure if it's a prayer or a curse at this point.

He pounds into me, breathing harder. "Hold on."

My entire world narrows on the sensations flooding through me, and everything comes crashing down at once. I cry out with my third release, and Lex grunts, stiffening inside me as his own climax reaches a crescendo. He pulls out and we end up curled against one another, our labored breathing filling the small room with heat and the smell of sex.

Lex rests his forehead against mine, brushing his fingers along my cheek. "You good?" he checks.

I only nod, because I'm not sure my voice will work at this point. I softly trace the outline of his new bandage with my finger before meeting his gaze.

He licks his lips, then grins at me. "That is officially my favorite tattoo."

ELEVEN

When we return to the house, I slip away to my bathroom and start filling the soaker tub with water. I need something to clear my head, and a hot bath filled with oils and bubbles seems like the perfect fix. I'm still going to talk to Gabriel, but I need some time to myself first.

I get undressed, dropping my clothes on the marble floor, then step into the tub and ease myself into the soapy, spearmint and eucalyptus scented water.

The room is hazy with steam, and I sigh, closing my eyes and leaning my head back against the plush cushion. My core aches from the extra time Lex and I spent at the tattoo shop, but it's a pleasant ache. One of satisfaction and one I very much want to experience again.

It's only once I've completely relaxed, the tension literally melting out of my body, that the thought smacks me in the face.

I don't really hate it here.

As much as I should—as much as I *want* to, I don't. I can't pinpoint when it happened, but I don't have the immediate urge to attempt an escape the moment I'm alone. I've only been here four days, so that's a little—or a lot—embarrassing, but maybe it's the part of me that knows it's useless to run. They'll find me and drag me back here and it will all be for nothing.

I guess I should be grateful they're allowing me some semblance of normal in letting me continue to go to class, even after what happened with Brighton this morning.

Now, I just need to find out *why*. There are so many whys, and the more I think about it and try to figure them out, the more my head spins and pounds with tension.

"Calla?" Gabriel's voice floats in from the bedroom, and my body flushes with heat. It could be from the temperature of the water, but the safer bet would be that it's what Gabriel's voice does to me.

"In here," I call without thinking, pressing my lips together. Oddly enough, I'm not nervous about him seeing me naked.

He steps into the room and his eyes immediately find me. "That looks relaxing." His gaze trails along the length of my soapy body as he wets his lips. Evidently, he's not concerned about subtlety.

I close my eyes, feeling warmer under his gaze. "Hmm, it is really nice."

His shoes make little sound as he walks closer, and I open my eyes, turning my head just as he kneels at the side of the tub. The sight has me biting my lip as his eyes flick between mine.

"Did—" I clear my throat. "Did you need something?"

The corner of his mouth lifts and he hooks his finger under my chin, tilting my head up a little. "Seeing you like this is exactly what I need."

I lift my hand out of the water and run it up his chest until I reach his neck, where I curl my fingers and pull him closer. "Kiss me?" I whisper.

His mouth covers mine in an instant, soft but hungry. Our lips battle for control, and I tug at the hair at the back of his neck as one of his hands grips the side of the tub and the other slips under the water. I gasp into his mouth when he pinches my nipple, and he chuckles softly.

I pull back a little, trailing my lips along his jaw. "I'm sorry you were upset before dinner," I murmur, kissing the corner of his mouth. "You can talk to me, you know."

His fingers slide down my chest, and my breath hitches when he reaches my navel. "You're sweet," he says in a soft voice. "I don't need to burden you with these things."

"I know that," I assure him, "but you can, is what I'm saying."

He kisses the tip of my nose and smiles at me. "Thank you."

I mirror his smile, blushing hotly when his fingers delve lower until they brush my mound. "Gabriel..."

His gaze is locked on mine. "Tell me what you need, angel."

"You," I breathe, my chest rising and falling a little quicker now. "Just... you."

He holds my gaze as he pushes two fingers inside me, stealing the breath from my lungs when he curls them and rubs my clit with his thumb. "Relax," he murmurs, and I breathe out slowly, forcing my muscles to unclench. "That's it."

I open my legs as wide as I can in the tub and moan. "Why do I get the feeling this is a distraction for you as much as it is for me?"

"Don't worry about me," he says, picking up the pace as he leans in and presses his lips to the side of my neck.

I tilt my head slightly, an invitation, but he just keeps kissing and sucking playfully. "I do, though," I murmur, and while my motive for the conversation isn't that, I do still care about him. I open my mouth to speak, but all that comes out is another moan when he hits a sensitive spot. He grins against my skin, his tongue darting out to flick along my neck as he rubs that same spot over and over, driving me to new heights of pleasure, to the point I almost forget what I'm trying to do.

"I just don't like seeing you upset," I say in a quiet voice, arching my hips to push his fingers deeper.

He circles my clit with his thumb, again increasing the speed of his fingers. "Calla—"

I'm close. My nerves are vibrating with energy, and the pressure building between my legs is going to explode any second.

"Does it have to do with me being here? With all the secrets?"

Gabriel pulls away from my neck, and his fingers still inside of me. "What?" His eyes search my face, and I fight the urge to look away, as if I've been caught doing something wrong.

"I..."

He pulls his fingers out and shifts back. "What are you asking me? Truly?" His forehead is creased and his jaw is set tight. I don't like this look on him. Even more, I don't like that I'm the reason he's looking at me like that.

"N-nothing. I want to make sure you're okay. You've been looking out for me, and—"

"And you thought I would share the information you haven't been able to gather on your own."

"No," I lie, "I... Never mind."

Silence stretches between us, and I no longer feel all warm and fuzzy. I cross my arms to cover my breasts, wanting to get out of the water.

"What do you want to know?" His voice is low, flat. It's not unkind, but it also doesn't hold its usual warmth that I've grown accustomed to and that has been known to bring me comfort.

I glance around the luxurious space, biting the inside of my cheek. This could be my only opportunity to get some information, but the way he's looking at me has made me unable to grasp the questions I want to ask.

Gabriel exhales heavily and stands. "Next time you want to use me, I'd prefer you be upfront about it." He walks out of the bathroom without another word, and I'm equal parts shocked and embarrassed at the sting of tears in my eyes.

After the epic failure that left me without answers, I'm glad to be on campus all day. Between back-to-back classes and a study session after lunch, my day is full of normal, human things. Time away from the house—and the guys—will do me good. I need to clear my head and refocus so I can make a plan—a *better* plan than last night—to figure this shit out.

Brighton meets me at the coffee cart we frequent on campus in between my second lecture and our study session. We're in different programs but find that studying together keeps us both focused better. We deemed this particular coffee cart as our favorite last year. It's cheaper than Starbucks and pretty much tastes the same. Plus, it's right on campus, so it gets extra points for easy access.

"I got your favorite," she says cheerily, holding up a black paper cup.

I shoot her a grin as I reach for the peppermint mocha and take a sip, sighing in content as warmth floods through me. "This is why I love you."

She snorts, tossing her strawberry blond waves over her shoulder, and takes a drink from her iced latte. Brighton is of the opinion that iced coffee is for all year round, even if there's snow on the ground, which we're not far past. She's bundled up in an emerald peacoat with rosy cheeks from the cold wind, but even still, you won't see her ordering a hot latte. "How was class?" she asks.

I shrug as we start walking along the cobblestone path toward the campus library. "Same old," I tell her, feeling a little uncomfortable chatting normally after what happened yesterday. She doesn't remember, of course, but I do.

Brighton nods. "Oh hey, sorry I had to miss brunch yesterday. I had the worst headache when I got up."

I wave her off, ignoring the pit of guilt in my stomach. "No need to apologize."

"I guess I can't party as hard as we did in first year," she says, winking at me.

I laugh, taking another sip of my drink. "Guess not."

We meet up with a few other friends and get to studying. I'm bouncing between my Sociological Theory textbook, reading and making notes on the legal pad next to me, and the assigned articles for my Law and Society class. It doesn't take long for me to get immersed in my studies, and even the sound of conversation around me becomes white noise.

When I reach the end of my last article, I close my book and cap my pen, sighing. I rub my eyes and glance around the library. Most of the students have packed up and left, including everyone at our table besides Brighton and me. I hadn't even noticed when the others left us.

"Damn," I mumble, checking my phone for the time. We've been working for almost four hours. The sky is getting dark outside, making the space feel cozy compared to the wind blowing the trees across campus.

"You went to this whole other place," Brighton teases without glancing up from her phone. She's scrolling on Instagram with her textbook open in front of her. "Anyway," she says, slipping her phone into her bag before flipping her book closed, "we should get going."

I nod and pack up my things before we head out of the library.

"I'm parked across campus," she says as we push through the double doors outside. "You want a ride?"

The wind knocks the air out of me, and I hug my jacket closer. "Oh, that's okay, I—"

"Calla."

I freeze at the sound of Atlas's voice and turn around to find him leaning against the building. He's wearing a black coat with a high collar, and that paired with the rest of his outfit and the annoyingly handsome way his hair is styled makes him look like he just walked off the set of a GQ magazine shoot.

My jaw clenches tight as he pushes off the building and walks toward us.

"Who is that?" Brighton asks in a whisper, her eyes wide and filled with curiosity.

"Nobody," I say quickly, turning to stand in front of her and put my back to him. "Listen, I—"

Brighton sidesteps me and closes the rest of the distance between us and Atlas. I whip around as she puts on that charming smile of hers and sticks her hand out. "Hi," she says cheerily, "I'm Brighton, Calla's B-F-F."

Just when I think I might see Atlas smile for the first time, he only nods, reaching out to shake Brighton's hand.

"Erm, okay," she says, pulling her hand back and flicking an awkward glance at me before saying, "Calla's never mentioned you before."

I step in quickly. "Uh, yeah. Atlas is a... family friend." The words taste bitter on my tongue. "He just recently moved here, and I've been showing him around a bit." Lying to my best friend is just the cherry on this giant crap cake.

The curiosity in her gaze quickly turns to interest as she looks between us. "That's cool," she says, shooting me a wink that I think is supposed to be sneaky but is definitely not missed by the vampire standing in front of us. Brighton turns her attention to Atlas. "So if you're new here, that means you probably don't know about the St. Patrick's Day party this weekend."

He arches a brow, pursing his lips. "No, I don't."

She perks up even more at that, practically batting her lashes at him. If I wasn't so annoyed at Atlas showing up here and ambushing me with Brighton, I would almost think it was funny. "You definitely need to come. Calla and I go every year. It's a fucking blast."

I open my mouth to tell her that I don't really feel like going this year, but before I can get the words out, Atlas speaks up.

"Sounds fun. I'll be there."

I blink at him in surprise. Since I met Atlas last week, he hasn't seemed like the social type, even among the guys. He'll contribute to some conversations, sure, but he doesn't go out of his way to initiate them. Most of the time, he fits the broody and quiet persona to a T. My eyes narrow; he has to be up to something, or this is just another way to show his control over me.

Atlas shifts his attention to me. "Are you ready to go?"

"Sure," I answer, glancing at Brighton. "I'll talk to you tomorrow?"

"Uh-huh," she says, her tone suggestive as she looks back and forth between Atlas and me.

I shake my head at her before she starts walking across the lawn toward the other side of campus, leaving me to turn and face Atlas.

"Your friend is very... enthusiastic."

I cross my arms, glaring at him. "What the hell was that?"

He cocks his head to the side, watching me. "What was what, Calla?" He sounds irritated by my question, but I'm the one with a reason to be pissed off.

"You showing up here," I say, shaking my head. "Kade messed with her head to make her forget me telling her about you, then you—"

"Her knowing I exist is far off from her knowing you are living with a house full of vampires." His condescending tone makes me scowl.

"Whatever. Let's just go."

I half-expect him to say something more that will only add fuel to the fire in my chest, but he just nods and starts walking. I follow him to the parking lot without a word and get into his Escalade, which looks wildly out of place in the student parking lot. I get in the passenger seat and tuck my bag between my legs, staring out the windshield as Atlas starts the car and drives out of the lot.

"Am I to expect a vampire chauffeur every day, or...?"

"It's dark, and I didn't want you taking a cab," is all he says.

My brows knit, because his words almost make it sound as if he cares about my safety. "Okay," I finally say. "Well, I don't have class tomorrow, so you don't have to worry about picking me up."

"I know."

I press my lips together, frowning at his detached tone. "Right."

Atlas turns onto one of the main roads, tapping his fingers against the steering wheel. "Are you hungry? Gabriel and Kade are out for the night, and Lex already ate, so we can stop somewhere."

"Oh, um, I'm okay." The ball of nerves in my stomach from Atlas and Brighton meeting effectively ruined my appetite. "I mean, unless you're hungry?"

He casts me a sideways glance. "I'm always hungry, but I'm afraid a Chick-fil-A drive-thru won't satisfy my cravings."

Heat floods my cheeks, and I try to ignore the meaning behind his words, but I can't deny the way my pulse races at the thought of him... *Nope. Don't go there.* "I don't know, their waffle fries are pretty good." Despite the upset from earlier, my stomach grumbles.

He exhales on a laugh. "I thought you weren't hungry."

I shrug, though he's focusing on the road now. "I'll eat when we get back to the house. I'm sure there's some leftover lasagna. Gabriel made enough to feed an army."

Atlas nods. "He does that. It makes him feel like he's taking care of his family."

"He's a good guy," I say without hesitation. It's a truth I believe wholeheartedly, which makes me feel a tinge of guilt over what I tried to do last night.

It's as if Atlas is able to read my mind, because he says, "You should try apologizing to him. He cares about you, so I'm sure he'll be forgiving."

My stomach drops. "You know?"

"I'm surprised you resorted to seduction for information so quickly," he says, answering my question with a jab that makes me not want to look at him. *Asshole.*

I inhale slowly before replying, "Well, the four of you don't exactly make it easy to get information otherwise."

"Hmm, and how did your tactic work out?" he asks, turning off the main road onto our street.

"Go to hell," I shoot back, unbuckling my belt the second we pull into the driveway.

Atlas pulls into a spot in the garage, shifting the car into park, and when I open the door, he moves faster than my eyes can follow and pulls it shut.

"Wha—"

"You will know what we want you to know, when we want you to know it." His voice is low, threatening, and his face is so close I feel the warmth of his breath on my cheek.

Instead of backing down, I blurt, "What if I can help?" When he arches a brow, I add, "I mean, if I can—if I help you with whatever 'business acquisitions' you're talking about, will you let me out of this damn contract?"

He leans back a little, his arm still braced on the console between us, and glances out the windshield. I wait, but he doesn't say anything.

"I'm not going to be a slave my entire life," I snap, breaking the silence, and Atlas looks my way again. "If that's all you want me for, you may as well kill me now because I'm not going to be complacent." My heart pounds against my chest almost painfully as I wait for him to respond. I'm fully expecting him to threaten to *make* me complacent, which is a very real possibility, but again, he says nothing. *Fuck this.*

I push the door open and climb out of the Escalade before storming into the house, and I don't stop moving until I'm on the other side of my bedroom door. I collapse against it, my breathing shallow.

At this point, I've played all my cards. Whatever game this is, I have most definitely lost.

TWELVE

The following morning, I wake with a weight on my chest that has me feeling anxious and cagey. Going from working out daily to not working out in almost a week has taken a toll on me physically and mentally. I need to move, to exert some energy.

I tie my hair up and change into a matching black sports bra and high-waisted legging set before shoving my feet into my running shoes and grabbing my phone off the charger on the table beside the bed.

It's barely after seven, so I grab a heavy gray sweater from the closet, tugging it on over my head, then search my book bag until I find my wireless headphones.

After sticking them in my ears, I pocket my phone and jog downstairs to leave for a run around the neighborhood. If I'm lucky, none of the guys will be awake yet, or will have already left for work.

No such luck.

Gabriel is sitting at the kitchen counter, sipping an espresso while reading from his tablet.

My eyes quickly shift to the window... where it's pouring rain outside. When the hell did that start? The forecast didn't call for rain.

"Morning," I say in a small voice as I open the fridge and grab a bottle of water.

"Morning," he echoes softly. "Were you planning to go for a run?"

I close the fridge and nod, uncapping the bottle. "It's just rain."

"It's also freezing out." He sets his tablet on the counter. "Why don't you check out the gym here instead?"

I freeze with the water bottle halfway to my lips. "You guys have a gym? Why is this the first I'm hearing of it?"

"You didn't ask," he offers.

I frown at that. "Okay. Where is it?"

"It's above the garage." He nods toward the door we came in when I first arrived last week. "There's a door to the stairwell that leads up to it."

My heart races with excitement. If I'd known they had workout equipment, I would've been using it every day since I got here. I screw the lid back on my water bottle and make my way toward the garage. Pausing, I turn back toward the kitchen. "Thanks, Gabriel. And, um, about last night... I-I'm sorry." The words are out of my mouth before I can stop them. The apology is genuine, but it tastes sour on my tongue and I'm not sure why.

He nods, smiling a little before picking his tablet back up.

A bit of the weight on my chest over last night eases as I make my way toward the garage. I jog up the stairs after finding the door easily enough and stop dead at the top of the landing when my eyes land on a bare-chested Atlas. My mouth goes dry, and the water bottle almost slips out of my hand as I openly gawk at him.

He either hasn't noticed me yet—doubtful—or he's ignoring me and choosing to focus on the massive amount of weight he's benching. It has to be at least two hundred pounds, which leads my mind to wander... He could lift *me*. Parts of me like the thought of that way too much.

Atlas returns the barbell to the rack and sits up. "Are you planning to stand there and watch me the entire time?" He swings his leg over the bench and looks at me. His hair is falling into his face, the ends damp with sweat. He pushes it back and stands, arching a brow at me as he closes the distance between us.

It takes far more effort than I care to admit to pull my gaze from his chiseled stomach and meet his silver gaze. "I..." I clear my throat and try again. "I was going to go for a run, but it's raining and cold."

He nods. "Cardio machines are back there." He jerks his thumb behind him, and for the first time since I stepped into the room, I take a look around.

For a home gym, the space is impressive. It doesn't surprise me at this point, and in this case, I'm practically giddy over how fancy it is.

The wall across the room is made of windows where the different cardio machines are lined up, looking out to the side of the property that's filled with trees. There's a treadmill, an elliptical, and one of those ridiculously expensive spin bikes with the giant screen attached.

I walk around a bit, the padded floor soft under my running shoes. The other walls are a muted gray, and track lighting runs along the ceiling. The room is cold, which is preferable when working up a sweat. I pass by a mini-fridge against the wall next to the bench press Atlas was using and set my water bottle on it as I continue around the room. It's a simple layout: cardio machines and stretching mats at one end and weight racks and benches at the other. There's plenty of open space in the center of the room and mirrors on the wall adjacent to the door I came in through.

"What do you usually do?"

I jump at the sound of Atlas's voice so close to my ear and whip around to face him, taking a healthy step back before looking up at him. "Cardio to warm up," I tell him, "and then weight lifting until I can barely walk or lift my arms."

He purses his lips. "And you did this—"

"Every day," I answer.

I'm not sure why I'm surprised at how impressed he looks, but it makes me press my lips together against a smile.

"I, uh... I've been training vigorously since the day my parents told me about the agreement." I laugh humorlessly. "As if I could somehow fight my way out of it." Shaking my head as heat floods my cheeks, I add, "I don't know why I'm telling you this."

Atlas steps closer, and I can feel the heat radiating from him. Before he can say anything, though, I speak again.

"I was willing to fight for my freedom. To train and work hard every single day so that..." I shake my head again, mostly at myself. "Forget it."

"Calla—"

"The moment I stepped into my apartment the night you came for me, I knew. No amount of training would have been enough."

"Your dedication to protecting yourself is admirable."

I shrug. "My family certainly wasn't going to." They *couldn't.* Because how exactly do you prevent four vampires from taking what they believe to be entitled to?

His gaze holds. "What's your reason for training now?"

Another shrug. "Maybe I'm going to stab you again," I offer, "gotta keep my strength up."

I'm kidding—mostly—but when he doesn't so much as crack a smile, I cringe inwardly.

"Fine. It's a... release. It feels good to push my body, to test the limits of my endurance." It can also be a really good distraction, which, these days, could most definitely come in handy.

Atlas nods as if he understands what I'm feeling, as if he's felt it too. "Fight me."

I scratch the back of my neck, suddenly feeling a hell of a lot more self-conscious having my hair pulled up off my neck with his silver eyes trained on my every movement. "Huh?" I must've heard him wrong. Surely, he isn't saying—

"Fight. Me." He repeats the words slowly. Pointedly. Then adds, "No weapons."

That stirs something in me, and I cross my arms over my chest. "Fine." There aren't any weapons in my sightline anyway. I meet his gaze and say, "No vampire mojo."

He presses his lips into a thin line. Ha. He's trying not to smile. "You think I need that?"

I tilt my head back and forth. "I don't know. Seems pretty convenient that you can touch or look at your opponent and make them do whatever you say. It's kind of cheating if you think about it." My tone is slightly mocking; I'm baiting him. A dangerous game, but it makes my stomach swirl with excitement.

One second I'm staring into his eyes, and the next I'm looking at the ceiling, my back pressed against the mat with the air knocked out of me.

I suck in a breath and grumble, "Cheater."

Atlas hovers over me, holding himself up with one hand, while the other has both of my wrists trapped above my head. My heart is pounding in my chest, and the heat pooling much lower gives away that I don't particularly dislike the position I'm in. Damn him.

He stands, pulling me up with him in a blur of motion. The room spins for a second before my vision rights itself, and I launch myself at him without hesitation. My fist connects with his jaw, and I just barely manage to duck under his arm when he grabs for me again. I spin around and kick hard, catching him in the back. He stumbles forward a couple of steps before rolling his shoulders back and turning to face me.

"You've got strength behind you. That's good."

I exhale a breathy laugh. "For what exactly?"

He advances again, this time without using his preternatural speed. Even still, he catches me off guard and pushes me back until I collide with the wall next to the bench press. Atlas traps my wrists against the wall above my head and slowly leans in until the tip of his nose grazes mine.

"Being a human in our world is very dangerous," he says in a low voice, though I don't think he's threatening me.

I lift my knee, trying to catch him between the legs, but he manages to turn fast enough that I hit his thigh instead. I attempt to pull my wrists free, but it's useless. I can train all I want, I'll never have the strength to overpower a vampire. "What's your point, Atlas?"

His eyes flare with something I haven't seen from him before—lust. The fire there makes my breath catch, and when he leans back enough for me to see his face and drags his tongue along his bottom lip, I can't keep my eyes from going there. "You're safe here," he says, his voice barely above a whisper. "From outside dangers, at least."

I swallow hard. "Not from you?"

His eyes darken, and when he opens his mouth to respond, his fangs flash. Warmth pools in my belly at the thought of him pressing into me and sinking his teeth into my neck.

His jaw snaps shut, clenching sharply before he says, "Don't look at me like that." There's a warning in his voice that I choose to ignore.

"Like what?" I push.

His upper lip curls, and he leans in once more, his chest brushing mine as he speaks low into my ear. "Like you want me to take you right here against this wall. With my fangs and my cock."

Heat flares in my cheeks, and I close my eyes, my pulse ticking faster, like a bomb about to detonate. "What do *you* want?" I ask in a soft voice, pressing my thighs together, trying to ease the ache throbbing between them.

He laughs darkly. "What I want, Calla..." His lips graze my jaw and his grip on my wrists tightens. "You wouldn't survive it."

His words should terrify me. I should be using every bit of strength I have to fight him off and run away.

Instead, I turn my head and press my lips against his cheek.

He blinks at me in surprise.

"I'm not as breakable as you think," I tell him, "and I don't think you're as vicious as you'd like me to believe."

Those silver eyes narrow ever so slightly. "Are you sure you'd like to take a gamble on that?"

I shrug. "What do I have to lose? Truly?"

His expression softens, and he frees my wrists, though he doesn't move away. He snags my chin, tilting my head back to meet his gaze. "You are not at all what I was expecting," he admits.

Arching a brow, I ask, "What *were* you expecting?"

He purses his lips. "Fear."

Huh. I guess my bravado is better than I thought.

"Do... do you want me to fear you?"

"Yes." There is no hesitation in his response.

A shiver runs through me, and I lick the dryness from my lips seconds before his fingers side from my chin to wrap around my throat. He isn't squeezing, but he's using enough pressure to keep me against the wall.

"I want to tear into your throat and devour your blood. I want to see the moment you realize you are completely powerless against me. And more than anything, I want to feel that delicious moment of surrender when the last ounce of fight leaves your body and you give yourself to me."

Holy fucking shit.

I am completely frozen. I couldn't move even if he didn't have his fingers wrapped around my throat. My heart is pounding against my ribcage, desperate to escape. I've never been so scared and excited in my life, and if I had to bet, that's written all over my face.

Atlas's thumb brushes along my jaw, slow and gentle. "You should go." His voice is hard, reserved.

I blink at him, unable to form words. Part of me is tempted to push him further, to test his resolve and challenge his words, but apparently there's a thread of self-preservation left in me, because when he lets me go and steps away, I hurry for the door and don't stop moving until I'm locked in the bathroom connected to my room.

I stare at my reflection. My cheeks and chest are flushed, and I'm breathing hard, as if I've just finished the run I wanted to go on this morning.

I press my hand over my heart and count the rapid beats until they slow to a normal pace, then I shake my head at my reflection.

"I am so screwed."

THIRTEEN

Two days later, my mind is still reeling from my encounter with Atlas. I've steered clear of him around the house, using the gym above the garage late at night or when I know he's gone for a while.

I'd like to think it's because I'm scared of the vampire, but really, I'm scared of what I want him to do to me. Everything he said the other day has me all twisted up inside.

I increase the speed of the treadmill and turn up my music, running in time with the beat.

My phone buzzes with messages—Brighton's been texting me since I got out of class a few hours ago—but I ignore them, focusing on the rhythm of my shoes hitting the treadmill.

I groan and stop the machine when my music cuts off from an incoming call. I answer it on speakerphone. "Brighton you have got to chill," I say in between breaths.

"Jesus, Cal. What are you doing?" Her voice teases at innuendo, and I roll my eyes, reaching for my water.

"I was *trying* to work out," I say, downing half the bottle.

"What are you wearing tonight?"

"Huh?" I ask, wiping the sweat from my forehead with the back of my hand.

"The St. Patrick's Day party?" She sighs. "I've been texting you about it all afternoon."

"I know," I grumble.

"It's tonight."

"So?"

"What do you mean *so*?" she whines. "Aren't you going to bring that hottie friend of yours? Because if you're not interested, I sure as hell am."

I cringe. When it comes to Atlas, I have no idea what I am. Dangerously attracted to him? Definitely. Scared of what that means? Hell to the yes. I shake my head, though Brighton can't see me. "Yeah, I don't think I'm going to go."

She laughs. "You're cute. I'm ordering an Uber and picking you up at nine."

My stomach drops. Kade said he'd told her that I moved, but I really don't want to be put in a position where she starts asking questions about it that I can't answer. "No," I say quickly. "I mean, I'll just meet you there. Can you text me the address?"

"Ugh, you're going to show up with a hot piece of ass, and I'll be arriving solo."

"And ready to prowl," I tease, getting off the treadmill. I didn't finish my workout, but I'm quickly losing the motivation to exert myself right now.

"You know it." There's yelling in the background, but I can't make out the words. "Shit," she grumbles, "I gotta go, babe. I'll see you later."

I frown, grabbing my water bottle to take back in the house. "Hang on. Is everything okay?"

"Oh yeah, just the usual super-fun family drama. Nothing I can't handle. And by handle, I mean ignore."

"I'm sorry, Bri," I say softly.

"This shit makes me understand your decision to leave New York on a whole other level."

Of course she doesn't know the whole truth, just that I left after irreconcilable differences with my family. That was putting it lightly, but without getting into the gritty details, which included the four vampires I'm now stuck living with, it was really the best I could do.

"Can I do anything?"

"You already are. I'll see you tonight!" With that, she disconnects the call, and I jump when my music starts blaring again. I turn it down and head down the stairs, through the garage—Atlas's black Escalade is in its spot—and back into the house.

I stop in the kitchen to find something to eat. It's not quite late enough for dinner, but I need something to hold me over until then, because my stomach won't stop grumbling.

I search through the fridge and pantry and settle on a bright green apple with crunchy peanut butter and some tortilla chips. Sitting at the kitchen counter munching on my snacks, I scroll through this week's discussion thread for my Urban Studies class on my phone, adding a few comments under my classmates' posts.

I'm washing my dishes when Lex walks in from the garage, whistling what I think is an Eminem song. He shoots me a wink as he approaches, then leans against the counter. "Atlas tells me we're going to a party tonight."

I close the dishwasher and spin around to look at him. "What?" Shaking my head, I say, "No way. I'm not going to show up to a college party with an entourage of vampires. It's not happening."

He grins. "You going to tell that to Atlas?"

My jaw clenches, and I roll my eyes. "I'll—"

"Tell me what?"

I clamp my mouth shut when his voice reaches me, and turn to look at him. He's arching a brow, waiting for me to answer.

"Calla doesn't want us crashing her party," Lex says, and I don't have to look at him to know he's grinning.

"It's bad enough *you're* coming," I tell Atlas. "How do you think it's going to look if I show up with all of you?"

"Uh, it's going to look like you're the luckiest woman in this fucking city," Kade chimes in as he struts into the room.

Where did he come from?

"This is ridiculous," I grumble.

Lex slides his arm around my waist and pulls me against his side, pressing his lips to my ear. "Come on," he murmurs, "it'll be fun."

I'm leaning into him before I can stop myself. "I don't believe that for a second," I say in a low voice.

"I'll make you a deal." He rests his chin on the top of my head. "You don't make a fuss about tonight, and Atlas will do whatever your heart desires."

My stomach clenches at the thought of having the typically stoic vampire at *my* mercy. I can't bring myself to look at him, though he must hear the sound of my pulse racing beneath my flushed skin.

Kade chuckles. "Can I get in on that?"

Atlas rolls his eyes. "Not in your lifetime."

"You little liar," Kade shoots back, eyes glimmering with amusement.

My interest is officially piqued. I shiver at the thought of Kade having his way with Atlas as he did me. Or would Atlas overpower him and take control?

"Fine," I say, refocusing and shifting away from Lex. He lets me, of course, otherwise I wouldn't be able to move. "But you guys better act fucking normal."

Lex grins when he realizes I directed that last bit at him.

"I'm going to shower," I say with a sigh and walk toward the hallway to my bedroom.

"Want some company?" Kade calls after me.

"Not even a little bit," I say automatically without turning back.

"I'm surrounded by liars." His voice carries to me as I close the bedroom door.

***

Arriving at the address Brighton texted me a few hours ago, my Docs crunch against the gravel driveway when I slide out of the backseat of the Escalade. I adjust the knee-length, silk emerald dress that rode up my thighs during the drive across the city. I shiver at the chill in the air and wrap my arms around myself as the guys get out of the car. I'm vibrating with nervous energy and can barely wait to get inside and get a drink in my hand.

Kade, Lex, Gabriel, and Atlas don't exactly exude subtlety. They're wildly attractive and intimidating, and showing up with the four of them flanking me has my heart pounding like a jackhammer. People are going to stare and whisper and make assumptions. Brighton will have a million questions that I won't be able to answer.

"Relax, angel," Gabriel says in my ear.

I force a smile. "I'm fine. Let's just get this over with."

Kade rolls his eyes from my other side. "So dramatic. It's a party, not an execution."

Music booms from the farmhouse at the end of the driveway, the heavy bass making the ground vibrate. Twinkle lights are strung across the front porch, and the air is filled with a heady combination of pot smoke and booze.

I shoot Brighton a quick text to let her know I'm here as the five of us approach the house. I'm not even sure who lives here; the St. Patrick's Day party changes location every year. Not that it matters. There are so many people here, most of which are complete strangers to me and to each other.

The second we step inside, I'm sucked into the chaotic atmosphere. Students are dancing and singing at the top of their lungs to pop music that blares from a couple of massive speakers in what I would assume is normally a living room off to the right of the entryway. There are green balloons and streamers hung everywhere, and most of the party-goers are either dressed in green like me, or have on hats or different bright green headpieces.

I turn to tell the guys that I'm going to find Brighton—and a drink —only to find that Lex and Kade have already disappeared into the crowd. Part of me is relieved I won't have to explain them to my best friend, but another part of me is nervous they're loose in a house full of people.

Atlas lingers slightly behind me to the left, glancing around the crowd of people and looking wholly disinterested by the entire event.

I bite my tongue to keep from telling him that he should have stayed home. My head turns toward Gabriel when he places his hand against my lower back.

He leans in, grazing the shell of my ear with his lips and sending a shiver down my spine. "Drink?"

I fight the urge to lean into him and close my eyes. Everything about Gabriel makes me want to wrap myself in him, and I'm still trying to figure that out. "Sure," I say, "anything is fine."

"I don't think there will be much of a variety at a frat party," Atlas chimes in, glancing at me from where he's leaning against the wall.

I prop my hands on my hips. "You look like someone's dad who's about to bust in and break up the party," I tell him, "just so you know."

His eyes narrow, and my stomach dips in response. "And shall I tell you what you look like in that dress?" There's a thinly veiled challenge in his tone, one I can't help but take the bait for.

"Please do."

Atlas pushes away from the wall and closes the short distance between us. I stand my ground, but my pulse races when I realize that Gabriel slipped away to get our drinks.

He couldn't save you from me, anyway, the dark expression on Atlas's face says.

Before I have a chance to react, Atlas manages to back me up against the wall next to the living room. We're tucked into an alcove between the other room and a staircase. To any onlooker, it would likely appear as if we're a couple trying to find a more private spot, but the race in my pulse tells a different story.

"You're nervous," he says in a low voice, dipping his face so his lips are close to my ear. "Do I make you nervous, Calla?"

I close my eyes as my name rolls off his tongue, and my head tips back against the wall. I want to open my mouth and tell him no, but he'll know I'm lying the second the word leaves my lips. Instead, I turn my face away, exposing my neck. I wore my hair in dark brown curls, pulled away from my face in a high pony. Was it to taunt the guys while we're here tonight? There's a pretty good chance.

I swallow hard, wishing Gabriel would hurry back with that drink. "You make me a lot of things."

Atlas presses closer, and heat floods through me at the hard contact of his body against mine. His hands are flat against the wall on either side of me; I'm caged in with nowhere to go. "What about right now?"

I turn my head to meet his gaze and lose myself in the inhuman color of his irises. I guess they could be mistaken for a really light shade of blue, but not up this close. "Right now..." I echo, feeling bold even as the alarm bells blare in my head. "Right now, you make me want to find the first empty room in this house and let you make me forget why I should hate you."

He tilts his head to the side, staring into my eyes, and I have the fleeting thought that he's about to kiss me. My stomach swirls with nerves and excitement, and the heat between my legs is a pulsing reminder of what my body desperately desires.

I catch a glimpse of Gabriel over Atlas's shoulder and my stomach clenches at the thought of the three of us.

"Not here," Atlas finally says.

When he moves back, my stomach drops, and I try to hide the disappointment weighing heavy in my chest by smiling at Gabriel and taking the red Solo cup he hands me.

"It's some sort of hard lemonade," he tells me, handing a cup to Atlas before taking a drink from the remaining one in his hand.

"Have you seen the others?" I ask, sipping the drink. I grimace at the sharp tang of vodka. Clearly, whoever mixed this went heavy on the booze. Oh well, it's free, and I'm really hoping it'll help me get through this party. "They aren't, like, eating the psychology majors or anything, are they?"

Gabriel grins from behind his cup. "They're in the backyard playing beer pong with some people. Kade's pissed because he's no good at it, and Lex is having the time of his life beating Kade."

Atlas sighs, but I think I almost catch a ghost of a smile on his lips for a second.

"Callaaaaaaa!"

I move around Atlas and find Brighton swaying her hips, dancing through the growing crowd in the hallway to get to us. She throws her arms around me, and her drink slops over the side of her cup, splashing a bit on the hardwood floor at our feet.

"Damn, Bri. Did you drink an entire keg already?" I tease as she pulls back. Her hazel eyes pop with bright green sparkly eyeshadow that has left bits of glitter across her cheekbones, and she smells of her favorite Chanel perfume and hairspray. The black cocktail dress she's wearing is a second skin, but it looks freaking hot on her.

"I'm so glad you're here," she shouts over the music, smacking a kiss to my cheek and, I'm sure, leaving a bright red lipstick stain behind. "Jason was supposed to meet me here, but I'm pretty sure he's bailing. Something about a big test next week." She waves her free hand around as if she doesn't really care why he's not here, just that he isn't. "Whatever. It doesn't—" Her eyes land on Atlas and her lips break into a wide grin. "Hello again, handsome."

He nods at her. "Brighton. Nice to see you again."

Brighton glances back at me and arches a brow as if asking, *what's his deal?*

I take a gulp of my drink, cringing a bit as the vodka burns all the way to my stomach.

Gabriel steps up beside Atlas and offers Brighton a kind smile, his eyes twinkling with warmth. Ugh, I hate how effortlessly charismatic he is.

"Oh, hello," she says, her gaze flicking between the guys. "Another friend of yours, Cal?"

"I'm Gabriel," he says, "It's nice to meet you, Brighton."

Her eyes widen. "Shit, girl," she says to me, as if the guys can't hear her.

I press my lips together. "Gabriel is a friend, yes," I finally answer.

She turns her attention back to Gabriel. "Well, any friend of Calla's is a friend of mine." She sticks out her hand, and Gabriel takes it, shaking gently.

The music in the other room changes, and Brighton cheers, spilling her drink again as she grabs my wrist and drags me into the thick of hot, writhing bodies who have turned the living room into a dance floor. It's dark and hazy from sweat and smoke and smells heavily of too many types of cologne and alcohol—and definitely body odor.

I finish the rest of my drink while dancing to a few songs, and Brighton disappears to refill our cups. Another handful of songs, and I've finished another drink, the second one even stronger than the first. Feeling a little more at ease, my hips move smoothly to the beat. I close my eyes and lose myself in the music and warmth of being surrounded by so many people. It allows me to forget who I am, which these days, is a blessing.

My heart rate kicks up when a hand touches my hip, and I spin around expecting a familiar face, but stare in surprise when I find myself looking into the eyes of a stranger.

The guy has black hair, cropped close to his face, bushy eyebrows, and vibrant green eyes. He flashes me a warm smile and leans in to speak in my ear over the music. "I'm Wyatt," he says.

I return the smile, still swaying my hips in time with the song blaring through the room. "Calla." I catch Brighton's grin over Wyatt's shoulder before she wiggles her fingers at me and disappears into the crowd.

He nods, dancing closer, and I get a whiff of tequila and cheap drugstore body spray. "It's nice to meet you, Calla."

"Yeah, you too." I have to shout as the song gets louder going into the chorus.

Wyatt steps in and hesitates before placing his hands on my hips as we move together to the music. I lift my arms and drape them over his shoulders, careful not to spill any of my drink on him, and smile at the way his cheeks flush when I move closer.

"You go to Georgetown?" I ask him, taking another drink from my cup.

He nods, adjusting his grip on my hips. "Third-year economics."

We lean in each time the other speaks, and I find myself enjoying his company.

"That sounds—" My voice cuts off the moment my gaze connects with Lex's across the room. His eyes are wild, filled with silver fire, and my stomach drops. *Shit.* This isn't going to go over well.

Before I can send Wyatt away, Lex parts the crowd and appears to my right.

"Lex—"

"Hands off," he growls at Wyatt, shoving him away from me without hesitation.

Wyatt stumbles back, throwing a confused look my way before scowling at Lex. "What the hell, bro?"

"Bro?" Lex echoes mockingly, his jaw tightening.

A few people glance at us, and panic clamps down on my chest. The last thing I want is to cause a scene.

"Look," Wyatt stammers, "I didn't know she—"

"She's mine," Lex growls. "Now get the fuck out of here."

Shock fills Wyatt's face, and I send him what I hope is an apologetic look before he shakes his head and walks off.

I turn to Lex, down the rest of my drink, and snap, "What the fuck was that?"

His eyes narrow sharply as he steps in, putting us nose-to-nose. "I was going to ask you the same thing."

"I was dancing," I hiss. "You had no right—"

Lex grabs my hips and spins me around, pulling me back against his chest. His lips are at my ear when he says in a deep voice, "You. Are. Ours. Get that through your head."

I try to drive my elbow into his ribs with no success. To anyone looking, it likely appears as if we're dancing closely. "You're insane."

He chuckles, his breath on my neck shooting a shiver down my spine. "I think you like it."

My body heats, and I grit my teeth, wanting to argue that. But I can't, because there's a part of me, no matter how small, that does enjoy it.

I guess I'm a little insane too.

"I thought you were outside with Kade," I grumble, trying to shift the conversation into safer territory.

"Kade is a sore loser. Plus I get bored easily, and humans are annoying."

I roll my eyes. "So you came in here to annoy me." My voice is flat.

The song changes again, and the room erupts in cheers and hollers as more people fill the makeshift dance floor.

"Let me go," I say firmly, "I need a drink."

"Hmm." Lex's lips brush my neck, followed by a gentle, teasing pass of his fangs. "Me too."

I freeze, and my heart slams against my ribcage. I wouldn't put it past Lex to sink his fangs into me in the middle of a room full of witnesses, which is exactly why I say, "Don't you dare."

Lex sucks playfully, his tongue darting out to swirl against my skin, sending heat directly to my core. He knows exactly what he's doing to me as I squirm in his grasp. He leans away just enough to say, "I'm going to let go in a minute, despite knowing that you'd much rather I take you upstairs and fuck you so hard everyone here would be jealous." He nips my earlobe. "You better behave the rest of the evening, or I will start draining these annoying little humans." He turns me around to face him and captures my chin, forcing my gaze to his. "Understand?"

My jaw clenches in his grip, and I narrow my eyes. I have no doubt he'd follow through with that threat, but would the others let him get away with it? I'd like to think not, considering the importance of keeping their existence as vampires discreet, but I really don't know. "Yes," I force out.

"Good girl," he says with a wink. He leans in and presses a kiss to my forehead before dancing through the crowd toward the backyard.

I'm suddenly feeling much too sober. I weave through the crowd of people and grab another drink from the kitchen, sipping on it while I survey the faces around me, some of which I vaguely recognize, but most of which I've never seen before. Finally, I track down Brighton, dancing near the massive but unlit fireplace in the living room.

"Hey!" she hollers, throwing her arm around my shoulder. "I saw you with that super blond dude. You guys were practically fucking over there. What's the deal with that?"

I take a gulp of my drink. "He's..." I trail off, shaking my head, because I have no idea how to explain to Brighton who Lex is. "Just another friend."

She arches a brow at me, setting her empty cup on the wood mantel above the fireplace. "You've had a lot of *friends* show up recently."

"Yeah, I know. They all, um, came here together." I swallow another mouthful of a drink that is definitely way more vodka than it is lemonade.

"Are you going to tell me who they really are?" Brighton asks in between songs, and I falter. She continues, "They watch you like they'll rip anyone limb from limb if they even dare to look at you the wrong way. And blondie scared off that other guy pretty damn quick."

After downing the rest of my drink, I say, "I told you who they are." I can't help the little giggle that slips from my lips. "Don't worry about them." I glance down at my cup and frown. "I'm empty. You want a refill?"

She nods, grabbing her cup and handing it to me. "Thanks, babe."

"Be right back." I weave back through the crowd as the room seems to tilt and find my way into the kitchen where I fill our cups, leaving enough room so they won't spill while we're dancing.

"Having fun?" Kade's voice in my ear makes me shiver and turn to face him, my cheeks and chest flushed.

"Hmm." I take a drink before setting both cups on a nearby table. "Probably more than you. I heard Lex kicked your ass at beer pong."

He opens his mouth as his eyes narrow, and I can't help the grin that curls my lips. "Bastard," he grumbles under his breath.

I lean up and kiss him softly. He tastes like beer, and the smell of his cologne tickles my nose. "It's okay. We can't all be good at everything."

He peers down at me, curiosity and amusement making his eyes appear lighter. "You're a little drunk, huh?"

I lift my hand and hold my thumb and finger apart to show him *a little bit*. "It was the only way tonight wasn't going to be a complete train wreck."

He shrugs. "We aren't that bad, Calla. Surely, you believe that to some degree."

I frown at him, swallowing another mouthful of hard lemonade. "I don't want to talk about this. So either shut up and dance with me or leave me alone." I grab my drink, down the rest of it, and leave the cup behind, taking Brighton's and heading toward the living room. Kade follows, shaking his head at me, and the smirk on his lips makes my stomach flip flop.

Before I can step into the living room, Kade circles my waist and pulls me to him, pressing his lips against my hair. "You've got me wrapped around your finger, you know that?"

My pulse spikes, and I set Brighton's drink on the closest surface before wrapping my arms around Kade's neck. I lean up in the same moment he dips his face closer, and our lips crash together. We battle for control—I grip the back of his hair and his hands cup my ass, hauling me against him. His erection presses into my core, and I gasp into his mouth. He breaks the kiss and drags his lips along my jaw. When he reaches my neck, I tilt my head, exposing it to him as my heart pounds. The room falls away, and it's only the two of us and his mouth on me. His fangs scrape slowly across my skin, making the hair at the back of my neck stand straight with anticipation of his bite.

"Kade," I breathe, practically clinging to him.

His tongue darts out, and I hold my breath. The music pounds in my ear, but it feels as if I'm hearing it from underwater. I don't want to be here anymore. I want *him*.

He trails kisses up and across my jaw again until his mouth presses to the corner of mine. "Later," he promises, as if reading my mind.

"*Now*," I push, tightening my grip on him.

"Easy, angel," Gabriel says from behind me.

I pull away from Kade and freeze when my gaze lands on where Atlas is speaking to Brighton across the room. The lemonade suddenly feels heavy in my stomach as I watch Bri's confused expression. She looks alert and, well, not glamoured, but whatever Atlas is saying to her is—

"... Calla."

I shake my head, pulling my gaze away from my best friend and... whatever Atlas is to me. I'll press him later about what he was talking to her about. For now, I turn back to Kade and Gabriel. "Huh?"

"Are you ready to leave?"

I pull my phone out and squint at the bright screen. We've been here for nearly three hours. It passed in a blur of alcohol, dancing, and handsy vampires—and now my head is pounding. "Yeah," I say.

Lex chooses that moment to appear and hands me another cup. "Water," he says with his signature wink. "Drink up. Atlas will kill you if you puke in his car."

I scowl at that but sip on the water anyway.

Gabriel catches Atlas's gaze and nods to him, and the three of us walk around the edge of the room, meeting him in the hallway.

"You're leaving?" Brighton asks, frowning.

Nodding, I hand Lex the water and pull Brighton into a hug. "You want a lift home?"

"Nah, I've still got some party in me." Her eyes roam over to the group of guys waiting for me. Something shifts in her gaze, but I can't put my finger on it before it's gone. "I'll call you tomorrow." With that, she dances back into the crowd.

I finish the water on the way to the car, the cool air making me more aware and less nauseous.

"You good?" Lex checks, his eyes flicking across my face, studying it to see for himself.

I shoot him a sarcastic thumbs-up. "I'm so good."

Kade chuckles from beside me and throws his arm around my shoulders. The gravel crunches under our feet and the dark, crisp air fills with fog with each exhale.

Atlas unlocks the Escalade, and we pile in, him and Gabriel in the front, and me, Lex, and Kade in the back.

I tip my head back against the seat, then end up leaning into Kade. He lifts his hand and pets my hair soothingly, and I close my eyes, humming softly at the sensation of his touch. I slide my hand across my lap until I reach Lex's, then entwine my fingers through his. He traces slow circles on the back of my hand.

"Calla," Lex murmurs.

"Lex," I say back.

"Open your legs."

My pulse ticks faster, and I pry my eyes open to find him staring at me with liquid silver eyes. He wets his lips, and the breath halts in my lungs. The ache between my legs from before announces itself once more, and my chest rises and falls quicker as Kade reaches for one leg while Lex reaches for the other, and the two of them slowly spread them open.

I watch, completely enraptured, as Lex slides his hand under the emerald fabric of my dress. I suck in a sharp breath when his fingers reach the heat between my legs.

He smirks at Kade. "You owe me fifty bucks."

"What the fuck?" My voice is uneven and breathy.

The rumble of Kade's laugher vibrates against my back. "No panties," he whispers in my ear, and I press my lips together.

Lex drags a single digit along my slit, and my legs widen, desperate for his touch. He pulls back, tutting his tongue, and I narrow my eyes at him. His gaze holds mine as he trails his finger along the inside of my right thigh and then my left.

"You're teasing her," Kade says. "Her heart is about to beat out of her chest and attack you."

I nod in agreement, trying to push closer to Lex, but he pulls his hand back just as I manage to get his fingers to brush my mound. "Fuck you," I grumble.

Lex tilts his head, a bit of white hair falling into his face. "Hmm, only if you're a good girl."

My cheeks fill with heat as Kade wraps his arms around my middle, sliding his hands along the front of my dress. I'm hyperaware of every inch of me he's touching. I'm so focused on his hands now, that when Lex plunges his finger into my pussy, I cry out in surprise. The shocked sound quickly turns into one of pleasure as he curls his finger and massages my tight walls.

Kade reaches up and pinches my nipples through my dress, and they stiffen into hard peaks under his ministrations.

Lex thrusts a few times before holding his finger inside my hot tunnel. His thumb grazes my clit, and I jump in the seat, pushing his finger in deeper.

"Holy shit," I gasp.

"You want more?" Lex asks, searching my gaze as he drags his tongue over his bottom lip.

"Yes," I say immediately.

He arches a brow. "Yes, what?"

I narrow my eyes. "Yes *please*."

He smiles. "Good girl."

Kade presses his lips against the side of my neck and I tilt my head to give him better access, biting the inside of my cheek to keep from moaning loudly as Lex adds a second finger and continues thrusting slowly. He circles my clit hard and fast with his thumb, and it doesn't take me long to reach the edge.

I'm panting hard, and when I look up, my eyes meet Gabriel's gaze in the rearview mirror. The lust that darkens his eyes sends me over the edge. I clamp down hard on Lex's fingers and cry out my release, whimpering when Kade's fangs sink into my neck. I ride Lex's fingers, circling my hips as much as I can in the backseat, all the while holding Gabriel's gaze from the front seat.

My head spins, either from the blood Kade is drinking from me, or the intense waves of pleasure crashing through me, I don't really care. I've never felt this way, never knew I *could* feel this way.

Lex pulls his fingers out slowly, and my gaze finally moves away from Gabriel, just in time to watch Lex lick his fingers clean. My eyes widen, and Kade pulls away from my neck, dragging his tongue along the puncture marks to stop them from bleeding.

I steal a glance at Atlas when his growl rumbles through the car. His gaze is focused on the road, but his knuckles are white, holding the steering wheel in a death grip. Smugness fills me at his rigid posture, and my lips curl into a sleepy smile. *He's jealous.*

I yawn, my brain foggy from sensory overload, and fall back against the seat, holding onto both Kade and Lex. Minutes later, my eyes flutter shut, and I feel more content than I have in days.

I'm in some in-between state of sleep and consciousness when we pull into the garage. I slip in and out but am vaguely aware of being carried in Gabriel's arms. The plush warmth of my bed envelopes me a few minutes later, and I slip into the darkness once more.

FOURTEEN

The smell of bacon and coffee lures me out of bed and into the kitchen the next day. I peek down at my PJs; someone must've taken off my dress last night, because now I'm wearing a black T-shirt that barely reaches my knees.

There's a glass of orange juice and a bottle of ibuprofen on the counter. I pop a couple and swallow them down with some juice.

"Morning," Gabriel says from the stove where he's flipping the bacon in a sizzling pan.

I lift my hand in a pathetic wave, still not fully awake. I shuffle over to the coffee maker and press a bunch of buttons until, eventually, I end up with an Americano. I sit at the kitchen table, nursing my steaming mug, and stare out at the pool. The water is even, unmoving. There isn't much of a breeze today, but it still looks chilly out.

"How did you sleep?"

"Dead to the world," I reply, sipping the strong coffee and sighing happily as the steam warms my face, making my nose tingle. "Where are the others?"

"Kade and Lex are still asleep, and Atlas is out for a run."

I glance outside again. I could handle a workout. Sweat out the rest of the lethargy clinging to my muscles. "Has he been gone long?"

"About an hour." He flips the bacon onto a plate and sets it on the table. "Eat. You'll feel better."

I lift my mug to my lips. "I'm all set."

He stands in front of me. "Coffee is not food, angel," he says dryly.

I pout. "Let me live my life."

He pushes the bacon closer. "Don't make me tell you again." The authority in his voice has me reaching for a piece of bacon without hesitation.

I take a bite and chew slowly. It tastes freaking amazing, because of course it does. "Thanks, Gabriel." I shoot him a small smile. "You're always looking out for me." I glance at my lap. "I'm assuming you changed my clothes last night?"

He nods when I look back up at him. "You can keep my shirt. I like the way it looks on you."

My smile morphs into a grin. "Good. I was going to keep it anyway. It's super comfy."

The corner of his mouth curls, and he snags a piece of bacon off the plate, biting half of it off. "You like your eggs poached, right?"

I nod, figuring there's no point in arguing about eating breakfast. "You don't need to cook for me, though. I can make, well, not much, but still."

He chews the other half of his piece of bacon and swallows. "I enjoy taking care of you."

I blink at him in surprise, taking another sip of my Americano. "I can't imagine when the four of you made that deal with my ancestors that you did so expecting to put me to bed and cook me breakfast."

He pauses, scratching the shadow of stubble at his jaw. He's usually clean-shaven, but I like this slightly disheveled look on him. "Perhaps not," he says softly. "Regardless, I'm happy to do it."

I decide there's not much else to say. I tried to subtly get some information, and it didn't necessarily backfire like it did the other night, but I'm still no further ahead when it comes to information.

After breakfast, I sneak upstairs and change into bright purple leggings and a matching cropped workout top. I grab a bottle of water on my way to the gym and flick the lights and ceiling fans on when I get inside. I warm up for a few minutes on the treadmill before approaching the heavy punching bag hanging from a thick beam across the ceiling. I've never been much into boxing, but the building pressure in my chest tells me it might do me some good to punch something over and over to exert some frustrated energy.

The first time my fist connects with the bag, a grin splits across my lips. *This is fun.* I stick my wireless headphones in and turn the music way up, losing myself in the beat as my body moves instinctively, punching and kicking the bag until my chest is heaving with shallow breaths and my heart is pounding so hard it feels moments away from breaking free from my ribcage.

I turn to grab my water bottle off the floor and yelp when I find Atlas leaning against the wall, watching me. I rip my headphones out as I struggle to catch my breath. "What... are you... doing?"

"Your form is pathetic," he says, pushing away from the wall and walking closer.

I drop my headphones next to my water bottle and cross my arms. "Gee, thanks for the unsolicited critique."

He stops a few feet away, his jaw tight. When he opens his mouth to speak, his fangs are extended. "You're bleeding."

The color drains from my face, and I step back, only to hit the punching bag. I glance down at my hands and see that my knuckles are an angry red, raw and throbbing with pain. My left knuckle is split open in one place, which is where the blood is coming from. I didn't feel it until now. I cover the injury with my other hand and press my lips together.

Atlas swallows visibly, not moving an inch as he keeps his eyes on me. His fangs retract after a tense moment, and he seems to relax a little. "I'm sorry. I haven't had an opportunity to feed in a couple of days."

I nod, because what else am I supposed to do?

He steps closer again, effectively swallowing what little distance I'd been able to put between us. Without a word, he picks up my injured hand, cradling my wrist gently.

"It's fine," I mumble.

"I can heal it," he says in a low voice, his fangs extending again.

I stiffen and try to pull my hand back, but he holds it tighter. "I—"

"Relax, Calla. I'm not going to hurt you. You're doing a good enough job of that yourself."

"I'll just wrap it up. It's fine," I repeat, my pulse racing beneath my skin; surely he can feel it against his palm.

"You live with four vampires who all want a taste of you. Are you sure that's what you want to do?"

I chew the inside of my cheek. "F-fine."

Atlas nods, then lifts his other hand to his mouth. He quickly bites into the skin of his palm, and dark red blood pools in his hand. "Drink," he says.

Panic seizes me, and I try to pull away again. I have no idea what I thought he was going to do to heal me, but I wasn't prepared for *this*.

"Calla—"

"No," I croak, my heart pounding in my ears. "I can't. That's not... No."

He sighs. "It will heal your injury."

My voice shakes when I say, "I'm telling you, I can't." I'm not trying to be difficult, but the thought of drinking his blood has sweat dotting my brow and my heart beating quicker than it should.

"Let me help you?" His voice is softer than I've heard it before. It makes me pause. Do I trust him? Hell to the no, but there's also something telling me he's being decent here, and I should let him.

"Okay," I finally say, cringing at how weak my voice comes out.

His grip on my wrist softens, and he traces his thumb back and forth across my skin. When he speaks again, his voice is a warm caress that I instantly get lost in. "You're going to drink from me, and it's going to make you better. You don't need to panic or be ashamed. Allow yourself to enjoy it." He leans down so his lips are close to my ear. "Drink, Calla."

I move without hesitation, cradling his hand in my less injured one. I bring it to my lips, and he tips it back. Copper warmth pours into my mouth and explodes across my tastebuds. My eyes close on their own, and I step in closer, closing my lips around the puncture marks in his hand. I swallow greedily, shocked at how electrifying the sensation of drinking blood is. Energy zips through me, and I open my eyes as I pull back, sucking in a short breath. My eyes drop to where Atlas is holding onto my hand, and I gape at the sight of completely healed skin. It's not even tinged red. It's as if it hadn't happened at all.

"Holy shit," I breathe.

He lets go and steps back, watching me closely. "Take a minute. Vampire blood can be overwhelming for humans, especially that of a born immortal."

I squint at him, the light above us suddenly much brighter than it was a few minutes ago. The buzz of electricity echoes in my ears. "A born immortal?"

"As opposed to a turned one," he explains. "The others were turned. I, however, was born a vampire."

Right. I knew that. "Is that why you can glamour people differently?"

"Yes."

"What else makes you different?"

He arches a brow. "Not much else, really. I'm faster and stronger, harder to kill, and don't need human food to survive. But you already knew that part."

I nod, cringing when a wave of dizziness rushes over me, and I sway, reaching out blindly.

Atlas catches me, steadying me in his arms. "Easy," he murmurs.

My cheek presses against the soft fabric of his shirt, and I glance up at him. There's a brief moment where I think I see concern in his silver gaze, but it's gone as quick as it came. "Thank you," I whisper.

"You're welcome."

The room has stopped spinning, but I don't move away. Being close to him like this makes me feel... powerful. I don't know what it is. Maybe it's his blood running through my veins, but I feel connected to him in a way that I haven't been with the others.

"Tell me," I blurt.

His dark brows knit as he peers down at me. "Tell you what?"

I lick the dryness from my lips, then press them together for a moment before saying, "What you're going to do with me."

He exhales a deep breath, stirring the hair at my temple. "Calla..." There's a warning in his voice.

"Please." I put as much force into that one word as I can. "Atlas, I can't stand living with not knowing. If you're going to kill me, just please—"

He cups my cheeks, tilting my head back so I'm looking into his eyes. "Slow down. Breathe. No one is going to hurt you. Killing you would be pointless. A waste of an asset."

My stomach sinks. Maybe I should be relieved by that, but there's a part of me that is hurt by his words. Not to mention being wildly confused by them, considering I have no idea what I could possibly do for them that would make me an asset, especially when they won't tell me a fucking thing. Living in the dark is chipping away at my sanity.

I huff out a sigh. "What would you do in my position? Would you just accept being kept in the dark and given scraps of pretty useless information every now and then?" When he opens his mouth to respond, I keep talking. "I mean, what's the point, Atlas? Really? Be honest with me, please. If I'm just a human plaything for the lot of you, at least let me know. I'm grateful you've had the decency to let me continue my studies—mostly because it gives me something to do that isn't sitting around here wondering what's going to happen tomorrow, but—"

My words are cut off when the sound of shouting from inside the house reaches us. Atlas's brows furrow and his jaw tightens, making my stomach churn nervously.

The shouting gets louder. There are at least three different voices, all sharp and filled with venom, but I can't hear exact words, just noise.

I frown at Atlas. "What's going on?"

"Nothing you need to worry about," he says without looking my way.

Frustration overpowers my nerves, and I take a couple of steps toward the door to the garage that will take me into the house. "Fine, then I guess I'll go see for myself."

His eyes flash with anger, and he moves in a blur of darkness, appearing in front of me in the space of a heartbeat. "The hell you will." He's a solid wall of muscle and supernatural strength, but I refuse to back down.

"Move," I snap at him.

He merely arches a brow.

I scowl. "Atlas, *move*."

"Make me," he taunts, knowing full well that isn't possible. Bastard.

My eyes narrow sharply as the shouting inside continues, and I cross my arms. "I'm fucking sick of the secrets."

"I don't give a shit, Calla. You're not going in there."

"You can't just—"

A door slams, making the house shake from the force, and I jump, my heart leaping into my throat. The shouting has stopped and the house is eerily silent.

"Fine," he says, "go ahead."

I glare at him and storm away, jogging down the stairs and through the garage into the house. By the time I close the door behind me, it's only Lex and Gabriel in the living room, talking in hushed voices. They glance over at me when I walk in, and Gabriel smiles warmly, as if whatever just had them shouting didn't happen.

"Will someone please explain what just happened? Because—"

The garage door opens, and Atlas struts in, his expression dark as he looks between the others. He heard the conversation that happened before I came in.

"Because he won't tell me a damn thing," I finish, jerking my thumb back at Atlas.

Lex smirks. "Nothing we can't handle, which means you don't need to worry about it."

Pressure builds in my chest, and I clench my jaw hard. The desire to scream rips through me, and Gabriel must see that on my face because he catches my attention and nods, offering me a look that says, *I understand your frustration*. His gaze drops to my hands, and he frowns. "You were bleeding."

Shit. I quickly wipe my hands on my leggings. "I'm fine," I assure him. *Physically, at least*, I fight the urge to add.

"Go take a shower," Atlas says in a low voice from beside me. "All any of us can smell is your blood."

My throat goes dry, and I flick a subtle glance between Lex and Gabriel. "Sorry," I mumble.

Lex's responding laugh is a deep, rich sound that booms through the room. "You don't need to apologize for bleeding, you silly little human. We are capable of controlling ourselves."

"Speak for yourself," Kade says, walking into the room. His silver eyes are dark with hunger and something else, and I shift away from him.

I swallow hard. "Tell me what's going on, then I'll take a damn shower."

Lex seems highly amused by my ultimatum, still smirking as he perches on the arm of the couch. Gabriel stands next to him and sighs, shifting his attention to Atlas.

"We can talk about it later," Atlas says.

"Bullshit," I snap. I'm not leaving this room until I get *something*.

His brows lift, and he crosses his arms over his chest. Thick cords of vein pop when he flexes his arms, and I hate that I notice that before forcing myself to look back at his face. Which, let's face it, is just as nice to look at. *Fuck me*.

"Calla—" Gabriel starts.

"No," I cut him off in a sharp tone. "I'm not going anywhere until you..." My voice trails off as I catch movement out of my peripheral.

Kade walks toward me at a normal pace, and my brows pinch together as he gets closer. I retreat a step, only to have my back collide with Atlas's chest.

"What—"

Kade smirks. "You're getting in the shower whether you like it or not. I'll throw you over my shoulder if you don't care to walk there yourself."

Atlas gives me a push toward Kade, and in the time it takes me to blink, he has me over his shoulder.

"What the fuck," I holler. "Let me down!"

He slaps my ass, and I yelp in surprise. Beating my fists into his back as he walks through the house to the bathroom connected to the room I've been sleeping in, my breathing quickly becomes labored.

"You need to settle down," he says, his voice filled with amusement. The motherfucker is enjoying this.

I try kicking him, but it does nothing. "Kade, I swear to god, if you don't—"

He sets me on the marble floor, but before I can move, he pins me to the wall beside the doorway, his fingers wrapped around my throat, firm but not so tight I can't breathe. "Keep talking," he warns, flashing his fangs, "and I'll fuck you against this wall until you can't speak."

All the words in my vocabulary are suddenly gone. I stare at him, my heart pounding against my chest so hard I can feel it in my ears. Heat rises in my cheeks and pools low in my belly.

Kade's lips curl into a slow smirk. "Though that might be exactly what you want." He tilts his head, looking into my eyes. "Is that what you want, Calla?"

My lips part, but I don't speak—I can't. Instead, I shake my head. *I'm a fucking liar.*

He leans in, taking up my entire world. "Deny it all you want." His nose grazes mine, and he braces his free hand on the wall beside my head. "Your body won't lie about what it craves."

Kade's lips crash down on mine, and I moan into his mouth, succumbing to everything I hate.

K ade lifts me, and I instinctively wrap my legs around his waist as we move toward the shower. His lips are soft against mine, and he kisses me slowly, coaxing my mouth open so he can slide his tongue in and graze mine. He manages to turn on the shower without breaking the kiss or dropping me, and the bathroom fills with steam as we lose ourselves in each other.

I pull back enough to take a breath and say, "I don't know about you, but I don't usually shower clothed."

He smirks, leaning back in to place a chaste kiss against my mouth. "No?" He sets me down and tugs his shirt off over his head in a quick motion, dropping it in a pile on the floor. Not a minute later, his bottoms join it, leaving him completely bared to me.

I can't stop my eyes from wandering. From his broad chest and chiseled abs to the long, thick—

"My face is up here," he says in a dry tone.

I lift my gaze, but surprisingly, I'm not embarrassed. I was openly gawking at him, because yeah, he's sexy as hell. He knows it too. I lick my lips, pressing them together. The room is becoming hazier by the minute, and warmth clings to my skin.

Kade steps closer. "Lift your arms." When I comply, he peels my sports bra off over my head, adding it to the pile of his clothes. When his eyes fall to my breasts, I move to cover myself, but he easily catches my wrists and holds me open to him. "Don't hide from me," he says in a smooth voice.

I chew my bottom lip as my cheeks burn, and Kade lifts my arms, draping them over his shoulders before dipping his face and sealing his mouth over mine in a feverish kiss that has my head spinning in a matter of seconds. My breasts press against his bare chest, and the friction makes my nipples stiffen into hard peaks, begging to be touched. I moan into his mouth, and he grips my hips, tugging me harder against him. The heat between my legs pulses, and I break the kiss to pull off my leggings, leaving us both naked and devouring each other with our eyes.

Kade backs me up until I'm standing under the hot spray of water, and I close my eyes when he grips my chin, tilting my head back to kiss me again. My lips move against his, and I trail my fingers up the tight muscles of his stomach as the water cascades down on us. He uses his other hand to palm my breast, pinching my nipple and making me gasp against his lips. I arch my back, pushing my breast into his hand as I kiss him harder. He forces his tongue into my mouth in the same moment his hand switches sides, delivering the same delicious ministrations to my other breast. My pulse kicks up when he presses his lower half into me, his hard shaft brushing the sensitive skin between my legs. I've never ached for someone like this. The tension building is almost painful in its intensity.

I nip at his lower lip, and he groans in response, pulling back for a short moment before burying his face in the crook of my neck. His lips trail along my skin, and when his fangs extend and scrape across the spot where my shoulder meets my neck, my breath catches. I'm not sure what I want more—for him to fuck me or bite me. If I'm honest with myself, I want both—preferably at the same time.

Kade's fingers trail down my stomach, making my skin tingle, and stops just shy of my entrance. My breathing quickens in anticipation, but he doesn't move. Hours pass, or maybe it's only seconds.

"Kade…" My voice is gravelly, filled with lust, and it only makes my heart beat faster.

"Hmm?" His tongue darts out and swirls against my skin.

"Do *something*," I practically growl.

He pulls back and meets my gaze. "Tell me what you want."

My lips part before I snap my mouth shut. Finally, I say, "You know what I want."

Kade nods. "I want to hear you say it."

I narrow my eyes at him as water drips from his hair down his face. "Fuck. Me."

He smirks, pressing one hand against the shower wall as he leans in. "Come on, Calla. You can do better than that." He grips his thick length in his fist and teases my opening, dragging the tip of his cock along my slit. He lowers his voice and speaks into my ear. "Use your words and tell me exactly what you want me to do to you." He leans back, flicking his tongue along his bottom lip.

I nod, tipping my head back against the shower tile and holding his gaze. "I... I want you to pin me against this wall and drive your cock inside me." His eyes are liquid silver as I continue, my heart hammering in my chest. "I want you... to fuck me so hard I can't hold myself up, and right before I'm about to collapse... I want you to sink your fangs into my neck and drink from me while I come around your cock."

Kade stiffens against my entrance. "Fucking hell," he growls.

"Is that descriptive enough for you?" I ask, tilting my head.

His eyes are dark and hooded as he pushes his tip inside me half an inch. "Yes, Calla," he says in a low voice, slowly moving in deeper.

I press my lips together, my eyes flicking between his as my breath halts. I grit my teeth at the discomfort, my body not accustomed to someone so large.

"You need to relax," Kade says, holding himself barely inside of me. The muscles in his arms are tight; he's holding himself back from driving into me.

I struggle to find my voice as I widen my stance a bit. "I'm trying." I take a deep breath, and the tension in my lower body eases slightly. "Keep going," I tell him.

He pushes in a little more and reaches between us, circling my clit with his thumb. "You're so fucking tight," he says, leaning in and pressing his forehead to mine. "I love it."

At his words, a rush of warmth spreads through me, and I arch my back, pushing him in deeper.

"There we go," he murmurs, peppering kisses along my jaw, "just a little more."

He stands still, letting me move at my own pace, spearing myself on his cock until, eventually, he's completely inside me. He gives me a minute to adjust, playing lazily with my clit until my breathing quickens, then he pulls out almost all the way before thrusting back in, stealing my breath.

"Holy shit," I gasp.

Kade grins. "I'll take that as a compliment."

I roll my eyes. "Even when you're fucking me, you are insufferable."

He thrusts harder, a challenging glint in his eyes.

Clenching around him, I grab the back of his neck and pull him to me, sealing my mouth over his. At least if we're kissing, he can't ruin this by talking. Our mouths move together as Kade thrusts into me, deep and slow, and then faster. He brings me to the edge several times, easing off just as the delicious pressure builds to new heights.

I growl against his lips, meeting his thrusts, but he shoves me back against the shower wall and holds me there so I can't move my hips, and continues his languid pace.

His mouth moves from my lips to my neck, kissing and sucking playfully. "Do you want to come?" he murmurs, tracing the shell of my ear with his lips.

My pulse spikes as he holds himself still inside me. "Yes," I ground out.

He rolls his hips, pushing in deeper and hitting a particularly sensitive spot. "Yes, what?"

"What, you're going to make me beg for it now?"

"Hmm, no. But you would if I asked, and we both know it." He thrusts hard and fast, making me gasp in surprise. I hold onto his shoulders to keep myself upright, and my moans fill the steamy room as he pounds into me over and over. The tension builds, and when Kade finds my clit with his fingers, I come undone. I clench around him in the same moment he sinks his fangs into my neck, drinking deeply as he continues thrusting into me.

I cry out, and he catches me when my legs give out. His cock pulses inside me, and my skin tingles with pleasure. I keep my eyes closed as I catch my breath, only opening them when he pulls out of me and backs us into the stream of water. He pulls away from my neck and lets the water wash away the blood before he sets me on the stone bench on the other side of the shower. I'm eye level with his cock, and when I reach for it, he turns to the side and captures my chin between his fingers, tilting my head back so I'm looking at his face.

"But you didn't—"

"That wasn't about me." His eyes take a quick scan of my body. "Can you stand?" He releases my chin and holds his hands out to me.

I take them, allowing him to help me get up. He kisses me softly, slowly, and then he reaches behind me for the shampoo bottle. I'm a little stunned, so when he squirts shampoo onto his hand and turns me around to start washing my hair, I say nothing. I let Kade take care of me, and it's... really fucking nice.

***

The five of us sit down for dinner, and the kitchen is filled with the savory aroma of roast and potatoes—one of my favorite meals. It's no coincidence, I'm sure. These guys did their homework.

I sit beside Atlas, with Kade and Lex across from me and Gabriel at the head of the table. Reaching for the water pitcher, I meet Gabriel's gaze and say, "Are we going to talk about what happened earlier, or what?" I pour myself some water before returning the pitcher to its spot in the middle of the table. When Gabriel doesn't answer and instead glances toward Atlas, my gaze follows. Everything seems to lead to Atlas. I watch his reaction, but his expression is, as always, infuriatingly impassive.

He sighs audibly and glances around the table at the rest of the guys before settling his gaze on me. His eyes are dark and his jaw is set tight. The nerves in my stomach are knots of unease with little flickers of excitement, because despite the tension hanging in the air, it seems as if I'm *finally* going to get some answers. It's about damn time.

"Calla," Gabriel says, pulling my attention away from Atlas. "There's a vampire in New York who is looking for you."

I blink at him, then shake my head. Clearly I misheard him, because that makes no sense. "I don't understand," I say in a quiet voice. The nerves in my stomach have turned to concrete.

He frowns. "There's a lot to it, but we aren't the only vampires your family was associated with years ago. This particular vampire was involved in the business deal we helped your ancestor out of."

"What's that got to do with me? From what I've been told, the oath was only made between my family and the four of you."

"That's right," Atlas says. "There's no merit to Dante's claim to you, but that doesn't eliminate the threat. He wants something to make up for losing out on that deal. He wants your blood in exchange for what he lost. He also has a bone to pick with us for some shit that went down decades ago, but that really isn't what's important here."

Claim to me? My eyes widen at the vaguely familiar name, recalling the phone call I'd overheard Atlas on when that name came up. "And this vampire—Dante—he was here earlier?"

"No," Kade cuts in. "That was Marcel. The arguing you heard was the result of the less than ideal information he provided us."

"Marcel?" I ask, my brows knitting.

"He's an informant of ours," Gabriel explains, taking a sip from his glass that is filled with dark red liquid too thick to be wine.

Kade stabs his piece of roast, slicing a piece off and biting it off his fork. "Apparently Dante has been sniffing around a few of our buildings in the city since word spread that we fulfilled the oath." He swallows and adds, "Guess he figured we'd be keeping you there."

Instead of asking any number of other, far more important questions, I say, "You have properties in New York too?" It hardly matters, and I'm not even sure why I asked.

Lex shrugs. "Real estate is a good investment." It's the same thing he told me when I discovered he owned the building I'd been living in.

I nod absently. "So what exactly does this mean?" Part of me is glad they're finally telling me what's going on, but knowing there's a vampire out there looking for me makes me miss the ignorance of being kept in the dark just a little bit. I try to shake the chill that seems to have settled in my bones, but it's not going anywhere. I swallow past the lump in my throat and push a potato around my plate, chewing my bottom lip.

I glance across the table when Lex murmurs my name.

"We're not going to let anything happen to you while you're with us," he says with what I'm sure is meant to be an encouraging wink, but it doesn't help the pressure building in my chest.

I stare at him for a moment. "That's your plan? Guard me twenty-four seven? I have school and a life I built before the four of you came around and screwed it up. This is insane, I—" I push away from the table and stand. "I didn't sign up for any of this." I blink back the sudden urge to cry. From fear or frustration—or a combination of both—I'm not entirely sure.

Atlas touches my arm, and my world narrows on him. "Sit down," he says in a silky voice.

My body complies while my mind screams profanities at being overpowered by vampiric glamour. I scowl when he pulls his hand back. "I'm allowed to be upset."

"Of course you are," Atlas agrees. "What you're not allowed to do is run away from us."

"Certainly not before hearing our kick-ass plan to ensure your safety," Lex says focusing on his plate as he drowns his roast in gravy, as if we're not talking about how to protect me from an immortal who wants me dead because my family was the reason—at least in part—that he didn't get what he wanted all those years ago.

I take a deep breath, exhaling a heavy sigh. "Okay, fine." I glance around the table. "What's your brilliant idea?"

SIXTEEN

It's been two weeks since I found out about the vampire named Dante who wants to kill me.

According to the guys, they've sent Dante on a wild-goose chase looking for me. I suppose it helps that they have property all over the United States—but it's only a matter of time before Dante comes to Washington.

"You're distracted today."

I blink until Atlas's face comes into focus. His silver eyes are tired, and he hasn't shaved in enough days that he's grown a bit of a beard. I don't hate it, I decide as I stare at it for a moment. "Sorry," I mumble, lifting my arms into the defensive stance we've been practicing over the last week. Since finding out about Dante, I've been adamant about training daily again despite what Lex said about me being safe while I'm with them. Evidently all I needed to reignite the fire in me to protect myself against the supernatural was a threat against my life by one of them. "I'm good."

"I could have killed you a dozen different ways in the time you were spacing out," he says flatly.

I roll my eyes. "You sure know how to cheer a girl up, Atlas. Has anyone ever told you that?"

His expression doesn't change. "No."

"Shocking," I mutter dryly.

He cocks his head to the side. "You want to keep running your mouth at me, or do you want to train?"

I prop my hands on my hips. "Hmm... Option C, all of the above?"

Atlas shrugs. "If you're prepared to defend yourself with witty comebacks, I won't waste my time with you in here." He turns his back on me, heading for the door.

I grit my teeth. "Wait."

He keeps walking.

"Atlas!"

He stops, keeping his back to me.

I storm over to him, and right as I'm about to launch into a maneuver *he* taught me, he turns, causing me to collide with his solid chest.

"Sloppy," he chastises, steadying me. Instead of letting go, he hauls me against him.

I grip his forearms, my mouth suddenly dry. "Wh-what are you doing?"

He leans down until our lips are barely an inch apart. "Fight me off."

Excitement swirls in my stomach and heat gathers south of there. I lick the dryness from my lips and take a steadying breath. "How do you suggest I do that?" I ask in a low voice, hyperaware of the race in my pulse.

"I don't care how, Calla. Figure it out."

I frown. "Anything I do, you'll see it coming. Any maneuver will be too slow to be effective and certainly won't be strong enough."

He nods. "Do it anyway. You might surprise yourself—or your opponent, which is the important part. It will buy you time to run, which is why you've been doing that every day too. The faster and longer you can run, the better chance you have at—"

"Not having my throat ripped out? Yeah, I got that."

His grip on my hips tightens as a muscle feathers along his jaw. "That's not going to happen."

I tilt my head, searching his face for *anything*. "Would that upset you?" I ask.

Atlas blinks at me. "What?"

"My death," I say simply.

He narrows his eyes ever so slightly, barely enough to notice. But I do. "You're not going to die."

"First off, that's incorrect. I'm human—I will die. And second, that's not what I asked you."

He pushes me backward, keeping his grip on me, and my back hits the wall. "What would you like to hear me say, Calla?" he says in a low voice.

I swallow hard, forcing myself to hold his intense gaze. "I want you to answer my question. It's not a hard one."

His jaw works as his eyes dance across my face. "I don't wish to see you dead, no."

I press my lips together against a smile despite the restless beat of my heart in my chest. "Now how hard was that?"

Atlas drags one hand up my side, his fingers skimming over my arm and leaving goose bumps in their wake. He wraps his fingers around the side of my neck, using his thumb under my chin to tilt my head back against the wall. His gaze makes me freeze. Despite what he just said, I can't tell if he's about to kiss me or tear into my throat himself.

"Tell me to walk away," he says gruffly, the space between his brows creased with tension.

I reach for him, sliding my hands up his chest. "No." My voice is soft, barely above a whisper.

Surprise flickers across his features. "Calla—"

"I don't want you to leave," I tell him. "I want you to kiss me." Things with Atlas are noticeably different than with the others. More intense in a way I couldn't have expected. But I crave him nonetheless. I could continue denying it, but that hasn't gotten me anywhere thus far, so what's the point?

His thumb moves slowly along my jaw. "This is a dangerous path we're heading down," he warns, but he doesn't move away.

"Nothing about my life is safe these days," I offer. "It never was."

He shakes his head. "This is different."

"How?" I push.

"Because of *you*," he says. "You're human."

"And you're a vampire," I say plainly. "Now that we've cleared that up—"

"I don't want to rip you apart," he snaps. "Before when I said you wouldn't survive the things I want to do to you, that wasn't a lie, Calla."

I stand there silently, because what the hell am I supposed to say to that? Should I admit that I'm curious, that an incredibly reckless part of me wants to try it—whatever *it* is—anyway? Yeah, probably not.

"Don't," he warns, clearly seeing something on my face that gave away my thoughts.

I pull his hand away from my face and hold it between both of mine. "You're not going to break me."

He laughs darkly on a harsh exhale. "You have no idea what I could do to you."

"You're right, I don't. But you're not going to scare me away. You're stuck with me as much as I'm stuck with you, so we may as well make the best of it."

"You have three other guys walking around this house who are more than willing to see to whatever you need and desire."

I nod. "And they do so quite well. But I want *you.*"

Atlas pulls his hand free and slams it against the wall next to my head. "You're playing with fire." His voice makes me shiver and his grip on my hip tightens, warming my skin through my joggers.

"Then burn me," I breathe, grabbing the front of his shirt and tugging him to me.

His nose grazes mine, and the moment his lips brush mine, my eyes flutter shut, and I melt into him. He kisses me painfully slow, his entire body tense with restraint.

I slide my hands up his chest and wrap them around his neck. "Relax," I murmur against his lips. I'm surprised when he actually does, leaning into me and deepening the kiss as his tongue flicks out and traces my lips. My heart thumps loudly in my chest, and I lose myself in the kiss. So much so, that I don't hear the bounding footsteps up the stairs from the garage.

Atlas pulls away from me, and over his shoulder, I see Lex come toward us. I'm expecting some lewd comment about him walking in on us, so when he says nothing, I know something's up.

"Calla, go back to the house," Atlas says.

I whirl on him. "I want to know what's going on."

"And if you need to know, you will," he says pointedly. "Now go back to the house."

"I... Fine." I walk across the room, passing Lex without a word, and jog down the stairs into the garage. The concrete space is cold, making me shiver as I let myself into the house, where Kade and Gabriel are sitting in the living room.

Gabriel glances up from his phone when I close the door behind me, then stands, offering me a warm smile. "Can I make you something for lunch?"

I shake my head. "You can tell me what's going on, though. Lex came upstairs to talk to Atlas, and I got sent in here." I thought I was making progress when it came to being kept in the dark, but the universe is apparently set on proving me wrong.

"They have some things to figure out," Kade says from where he's lounging on the couch, scrolling on his phone. He seems far less concerned than Lex, but it doesn't make me feel better.

"Does this have something to do with that vampire from New York?" My stomach drops as the panic that's been living in my chest for too long now spikes, making my pulse race. "Does he know I'm here?"

Gabriel closes the distance between us in a blur of movement and cups my face in his hands. His grip is warm and gentle. "Take a breath, angel. You're safe. Dante doesn't know where you are."

"He doesn't?" I hate how weak my voice sounds.

Gabriel shakes his head. "What's going on has nothing to do with him. You don't need to worry about it." His eyes shift between mine. "Okay? You have my word." He lets his hands fall back to his sides, but his gaze remains locked with mine.

"Okay," I finally say. "But if Dante is still looking for me, do you think he'll go after my parents?" Despite the strained relationship I've had with them over the years, the thought of them being in danger because of what happened long before I was born—even though that's the very position I'm in—makes my chest feel suffocatingly tight.

"Your parents are safe," Kade says, setting his phone on the coffee table and swinging his legs over the side of the couch as he moves into a sitting position. "Dante is interested in you—and fucking with us— he doesn't care about your mom and dad. He knows you're not with them and, if he's done his research, he likely figures using them to get to you wouldn't be very effective."

He would be wrong about that. They're still my parents. If they were in danger, I would do whatever was necessary to ensure their safety.

Nausea rolls through me like a vicious, unforgiving wave. I feel like a pawn now more than ever, and that makes me want to scream. I swallow the lump in my throat and straighten my shoulders, holding my chin up.

The garage door opens, and Atlas and Lex walk inside. Lex comes over to me, his expression less severe than it was when he interrupted us in the gym, and slings his arm around my shoulders. He leans in pressing a kiss to the side of my head.

"I should take a shower," I announce. I don't really need to—I didn't get much of a chance to work up a sweat in the gym—but it's a good excuse to get out of this room.

Lex lets me go, and I feel the guys' eyes on me as I walk out of the room. My head is spinning by the time I get to the bedroom and lock the door. I fall back against it, closing my eyes and pressing a hand to my forehead.

I've been here for almost a month now. While I'm not immediately terrified for my life when it comes to the four vampires in the other room, there's still something in my gut that tells me I can't entirely trust them. There's still so much I don't know, so many secrets that are being kept from me for god knows what reason. And despite knowing in my heart that there's no chance I'm getting out of this, there's still a part of me that wants to run, to choose my own fate for once.

I stand in the shower long after I've washed my hair and body, letting the hot water mix with the silent, frustrated tears rolling down my cheeks.

I'm so far out of my element now, I don't even remember what it feels like to have control.

SEVENTEEN

When I return to the living room after changing into a hoodie and leggings, I frown at the empty room. The sun is shining through the floor-to-ceiling windows, but the wind is hollowing through the trees outside. Mother Nature is as restless as I am today, it seems.

I stand at the window with my arms wrapped around myself, watching the branches sway and drop leaves into the pool.

The sound of the coffee maker catches my attention, and I glance toward the kitchen to find Kade leaning against the counter watching me.

"Where did everyone go?" I ask, walking into the kitchen.

"Lex and Atlas left while you were in the shower." He hands me a steaming cup of coffee, and I take it, wrapping my fingers around the warmth.

"Thanks," I murmur, taking a small sip. "Where did they go?"

He grabs another mug from the cupboard above his head and sets it under the spout of the coffee maker. "They'll explain when they return."

I set my coffee on the counter. "Or you could just tell me now." There's an edge to my voice that isn't lost on Kade.

His expression is serious when he turns back to me. "I could," he says, "but I'm not going to."

My jaw clenches. "Why not?" I push. "Does this have something to do with Dante?" Gabriel has said it didn't, but that seems unlikely now that Atlas and Lex have taken off. "I deserve to know if something—"

"It has nothing to do with that," he cuts me off, removing his mug from the machine and adding an obscene amount of sugar and a splash of cream. "We're monitoring that situation, and once there's something to know, you'll know it."

"Fine," I huff out, tracing the rim of my mug with my finger. "Then what's this about?"

"Atlas will explain when he returns," Kade repeats.

I narrow my eyes. "And when will that be?"

He shrugs. "Tomorrow maybe."

"Maybe?" I echo, shaking my head and prompting him to offer a more certain answer.

"Hmm." He takes a sip of his coffee. "Don't you have homework or something you should be doing?"

My brows raise. "What are you, my dad?"

He smirks. "Didn't realize you had a daddy kink, Calla. Good to know."

Heat flares in my cheeks. "I don't," I rush to say.

"Hey, I'm not judging. There's no shame in it. A lot of people with strained parental relationships later experience—"

"Please stop talking." I close my eyes, pressing my fingers against my temples in an attempt to ease the tension there.

Kade chuckles. "Lighten up, Calla. I'm just teasing." He reaches over and taps the tip of my nose with his finger. I attempt to bat his hand away, but it's already back at his side before I can catch it. *Stupid vampire speed.*

The next morning, Lex and Atlas haven't returned.

I get ready for class as normal despite the pit in my stomach and meet Brighton for brunch at our regular spot. Kade doesn't accompany me to class but assured me before I left the house that I was safe, that they have people looking out for me.

I sit at the back of the lecture hall and try to focus, but I'm finding it increasingly difficult to see the importance of this class when my life seems more and more like a rollercoaster I'll never be able to get off.

Gabriel has gone to work when I return to the house later in the afternoon. I wander around until I find myself standing in Kade's doorway. He's laying on top of the black sheets on his massive bed, his head near the end, with his eyes closed. His expression is soft, peaceful. I can't stop looking at him like this. The sight of him so relaxed eases the tension in my chest ever so slightly. If he's not concerned about everything going on, that should make me feel better, right?

"Are you going to continue to stand there staring at me, or would you like to come in?" he asks without looking my way or even opening his eyes.

I chew my bottom lip, stepping into his bedroom after a moment of hesitation. Glancing around, surprise flickers through me, though I'm not sure why. I guess I didn't expect his room to be so... neat and tidy? Kade has always given off a bit of chaotic energy, so I kind of figured his personal space would reflect that. But nope, the walls are a neutral taupe with long, dark curtains covering the windows across the room. There are small round tables on either side of the bed with matching, exposed bulb lamps. On the other side of the room, twin doors lead to what I imagine are a bathroom and closet, and that's the extent of Kade's bedroom. No art on the walls or decor around the room. It's... I don't know, a little sad? It makes me want to drag his ass to Target and spruce the space up.

"Everything okay?" I ask, slowly approaching the bed.

His chest rises and falls deeply as he exhales a heavy breath. "Just peachy. How was class?"

I press my lips together. "Dull compared to some I've been to."

While his eyes remain closed, his lips twist into a smirk. "I bet."

I walk closer, stopping a few feet from his bed as he opens his eyes, then swings his legs over the side of the bed and sits up, gazing up at me through dark lashes. His eyes look more black than silver in this lighting, but they are mesmerizing all the same. "Come here."

I move toward him without conscious thought, stopping when I'm standing before him.

He lifts his hands to my hips, resting them there for a moment before pulling me onto his lap. I gasp, grabbing his arms to steady myself, and settle into his lap.

"What are you doing?" I ask in a quiet voice, my pulse kicking up at his hooded gaze.

"Nothing you don't want me to," he says, nuzzling my neck and making me shiver with anticipation. His lips drag along my skin, peppering kisses in their wake.

I lean into him, pressing my breasts into his chest as I tilt my head to give him better access to my neck. My pulse pounds beneath my skin, waiting for the sharp sting of his fangs in my neck, but it doesn't come. I shouldn't be disappointed by that, and yet...

"I can't stop thinking about fucking you," he says, his breath hot on my skin. "The way you felt wrapped around my cock... I'll never get tired of it."

"So fuck me," I offer, shivering at the thought of having him inside me again.

He chuckles deeply and leans back to meet my gaze. "You know, I figured you'd say that."

"So cocky," I murmur, running my fingers through the hair at the back of his neck and gripping it as I start grinding against him.

His grip on my hips tightens and his eyes narrow. "You're asking for me to flip you onto my bed and fuck you until you're screaming my name."

"Big talk," I taunt, bearing down and putting pressure on his groin, circling my hips against him.

He groans, tipping his head back. "Fuck, that feels good."

My core clenches with need, throbbing at his words. I keep going, the sight of him like this pushing me to move a little faster. "Mmm," I purr, closing my eyes as I continue to grind against him. He hardens against me, pressing into the heat between my legs. I lean down and touch my lips to his in a whisper of a kiss before moving my mouth to his ear. "I want you inside me."

With that, he makes good on his threat to flip me onto the bed. From one second to the next, my back is pressed into the mattress, and I'm staring up at him as he leans over me, his unruly dark brown hair falling into his eyes.

"Happy to oblige," he says with a devilish grin.

"You know, I figured you'd say that," I echo his words.

He seals his mouth over mine, kissing me slow and deep as I run my fingers up his chest, lifting his shirt to expose the tight muscle underneath.

"Will Gabriel be home soon?" I murmur against his lips.

He nips my bottom one. "Should be. You want him to join us?"

My heart races at that, because hell yes I do, but I don't want to stop and wait for him either. "Maybe next time." I kiss him again. "Have you heard anything from the others?" Another kiss. "Where are they?"

His mouth freezes against mine. "Calla," he says in a low voice, leaning back and bracing himself with his hips on either side of me, holding me down. His eyes search mine for a moment, and he tilts his head. "I would've thought you'd be a little more creative than this."

I frown, gripping the sheets on either side of me. "What do you mean?"

"Trying to seduce me for information." He tsks, shaking his head. "I'm disappointed."

"Seriously?" I laugh and reach for him, but he moves too fast, grabbing my wrists and pinning them above my head with one hand. "Kade—"

"Nope," he says, cutting me off, though he doesn't genuinely seem mad. "You're going to keep nice and quiet for me now." He lets go of my wrists just long enough to pull my shirt off before trapping them against the mountain of pillows at my head. His eyes drop to my breasts, and he uses his free hand to trail an agonizingly slow path from my collarbone to the lace of my bra. He licks his lips before unclasping the bra from the front. My breasts spill out, my nipples stiffening at the cool air. Kade makes quick work of palming one, and when he lowers his mouth to the other, my back arches off the bed. He pushes me back down, swirling his tongue around my nipple before sucking it hard.

I gasp sharply. "Kade."

He pulls back and glares at me with dark eyes. "Quiet," he reminds.

I pull my bottom lip into my mouth, chewing it to keep myself from speaking again, and nod.

He drops his mouth to my other breast, giving it the same attention, while his hand slides down my stomach, making my breath hitch when he reaches the waistband of my jeans. He pops the button easily, pulling the zipper down so slow, I have to grit my teeth from scowling at him. He's teasing me on purpose. There's not a damn thing I can do that won't result in him stopping what is making my body come alive, and we both know it.

Kade pulls his mouth off my breast and kisses down my stomach, making my skin tingle at his every touch. He nips my hipbone, making me lift off the bed. He lets go of my wrists, giving me a stern look that says, *keep them there,* and I obey. His fingers curl around the waistband of my jeans, and he pulls them down with my panties to just below my knees, baring my center to his hungry gaze.

My heart slams against my ribcage as he lowers his mouth to my navel, pressing a feather-light kiss there before moving lower, kissing the inside of each of my thighs before dragging his tongue along my slit. My cheeks fill with heat as I watch him between my legs, and I grip the pillows at my head when his lips close around my clit. He sucks gently, making my head spin. I close my eyes, lifting my hips to push his face closer, but he flattens his arm across my waist, holding me down as his tongue dives inside, devouring me completely.

I suck in a breath, and I can't stop the moan that escapes my lips. He plunges in and out of me with his tongue, bringing me new levels of pleasure. And when he uses his fingers to spread me wider for him, my eyes shut of their own accord, my chest rising and falling fast with shallow, labored breaths.

Kade brings me to the edge with his mouth. Licking and sucking until I explode, clenching around him and squeezing his face between my thighs, desperate to hold him there.

As I come down from my earth-shattering orgasm, Kade tugs his shirt off, tossing it behind him before sliding off the bed and tugging his pants down. His cock springs free, and my eyes immediately go to it. *Fuck.* I'm not sure I'll ever get used to its size. I certainly won't get tired of it.

He crawls over me again, positioning himself at my entrance. He drags the head of his cock along my slit and presses hard against my clit, making me gasp. "You're ready for more already, aren't you?"

I open my mouth, then clamp it shut, nodding instead. I lean up and reach for him, pulling his mouth down to mine and kissing him hard, putting all of my desire into it so he knows just how ready I am, just how badly I want him.

His lips move against mine as he spears me with his cock, groaning against my lips. The muscles in my thighs clench at the invasion, but I wrap my legs around him and force him in deeper. He kisses me long and slow, pushing until he's inside me to the hilt. He holds still for a moment, giving me time to adjust to him before he starts moving in slow, small thrusts. His lips leave mine, kissing along my jaw until he reaches my neck. His tongue finds my pulse, and his lips close around it, sucking playfully.

My head spins, and I lift my hips to meet his thrusts as they get faster and deeper. I'm racing to the edge once more, and when Kade's mouth finds the sensitive spot between my shoulder and neck and he sinks his fangs into my skin, I cry out, clenching around his cock. His thrusts quickly become harsh and quick. His mouth seals over mine, and the taste of copper fills my senses. I kiss him back, clinging to him as he pounds into me. A few more thrusts and he stiffens, releasing inside me as my tight inner walls squeeze him.

I break the kiss as he pulls out of me, both of us breathing hard. Warmth leaks out of me, and Kade uses the sheet beneath us to clean me up. I swallow past the dryness in my throat, watching him in a haze of pleasure.

"Guess I'll be doing laundry today," he says with a smirk, falling onto his back beside me.

My lips curl into a sated grin as I stare at the ceiling. Sweat clings to my skin, and my heart is slowly coming down to a normal pace. I sigh contentedly, and Kade chuckles in response. I slide my hand along the silk sheet until it finds his, then entwine our fingers, giving him a quick squeeze before I pull away and force myself to get up. I slide my legs over the side of the bed and plant my feet on the hardwood, giving myself a second before standing. My muscles shake in protest, but I manage to stay upright. I collect my clothes and walk backward to the door, Kade's eyes on me.

"Where are you running off to?"

"The shower," I say, "and then, unfortunately, I need to study. Which is far less exciting than this was."

He props his hands behind his head. "You could just forget studying, and we could do that again."

I press my lips together, warmth spreading through me at the offer. It sounds a hell of a lot better than my assigned reading for this week, but there are more important things I need to do before Lex and Atlas get back—and not knowing when that will be definitely puts me at a disadvantage. "Maybe later? Could be a nice reward for getting through my homework."

"I feel so used," Kade says in a teasing tone.

I hold my clothes to my chest and shake my head at him. "I think you'll live," I say before turning and walking out of his bedroom, closing the door behind me. I let out a heavy breath and hurry to the bathroom connected to my room where I take the quickest shower of my life.

Once I've towel-dried my hair and gotten dressed, I leave my room and walk down the hall toward the stairs leading to the second floor. I hear Kade's voice coming from his room. It sounds as if he's on the phone, though his tone is calm, so I don't bother trying to overhear. I don't have any time to waste.

I hurry toward Atlas's office. Something tells me that if I'm going to find answers, this will be the place. He spends most of his time in here, always behind closed doors, so this has been—and probably will be—my only opportunity to snoop. My hand freezes halfway to the door-knob. I shake it out, shoving down my nerves the tinge of guilt I have for the invasion, and slowly open the door. I slip inside, closing it behind me as gently as I can. When it clicks into place, I whip around and cross the room in a few hurried strides, reminding myself that Atlas and the rest of the guys know virtually everything about my life, and not because I chose to share it with them. I'm not saying the whole tit for tat in this situation is right, but my ever-growing need to figure this whole thing out overpowers the weight of my guilt.

My stomach sinks when I realize Atlas took his laptop with him. I shouldn't be surprised, and honestly, the odds of me being able to guess his password to get into it would have been pretty much nil anyway.

I walk toward the wall of bookshelves and skim them. Most of the books are non-fiction, business-related tomes. There are a few shelves filled with some of the classics—first editions, no doubt—but nothing that will offer me any clarity on what's going on.

I try the filing cabinets on the other side of the room, but they're all locked. I grit my teeth, scowling at myself. As much as I want to believe I wasn't putting so much hope in this search revealing the guys' plans, I can't help the heavy blanket of disappointment draped over my shoulders.

Walking back to the desk, I thumb through a few stacks of loose paper. It's mostly bills and some junk mail. There's a copy of my class schedule, my signed apartment lease, and some credit card statements that go a couple of years back. A few weeks ago that would creep me the fuck out. But now? It's just a drop in the bucket.

Sighing heavily, I drop into Atlas's ridiculously comfy leather chair. I spin around and glance out the window at the trees along the prop-erty for a few minutes. When I turn back, I grab the edge of the desk, my gaze catching the letterhead at the top of a piece of paper sticking out from under a bill for pool maintenance.

Ellis Industries.

"What the...?"

Why does Atlas have something with Brighton's family's business on it?

I pull the paper free and scan it, my heart in my throat as I realize what it is. A stock register. But why... why would Atlas buy stocks in an environmental company? My head spins, and I shake it, trying to clear the jumbled thoughts all trying to come through at once.

Holy shit. Not only does he have stock in the company, he's a majority shareholder. He may as well own the damn thing.

The paper falls from my hand and floats onto the desk. I stare at it, trying to make sense of this, but I can't figure it out. I press my hands against the desk calendar and frown at its unevenness. I lift the calendar and find a file folder. Pulling it out, I flip it open and gasp, the air leaving my lungs in a vicious *whoosh*. I'm staring at a photo of Brighton and me at brunch, but my hair is significantly shorter. This picture was from last year.

My heart pounds as I flip to the next page. And the next. More photos of Brighton and me. Then some with just Brighton. *Surveillance photos*, I realize after a handful of them, and my stomach roils. Her class and work schedules are next, along with call and text logs, email chains, and bank statements dating back before I even met her. But why would they be tracking Brighton before she was even part of my life? It doesn't make sense.

I press my fist against my mouth, my vision blurring with hot tears as my head spins with so many questions I can't think. Pushing the chair back, I stand on shaky legs, and the folder slips out of my hand, the papers spilling onto the floor. I don't bother picking them up. I'm already heading for the door.

CHAPTER

EIGHTEEN

I pace the length of my bedroom, gripping my phone in my hand so tight my knuckles are white. I rake my fingers through my hair, messing up the already frizzy waves.

I've texted Brighton five times in the last thirty seconds.

Brighton, we need to talk.

I have to tell you some crazy things that won't make much sense, but I promise I'm telling the truth.

Please answer me. I'm freaking out over here.

Where are you? I'll come to you.

Brighton?!?!

My heart lurches when the text bubbles appear in our conversation, and I chew my thumbnail as I wait for her reply.

Jesus, Cal. What the fuck is going on? I'm at home.

I let out a relieved breath.

Stay there, I type, *I'm on my way.*

Pocketing my phone, I stop in the kitchen and leave a quick note that will hopefully, if nothing else, buy some time.

Studying on campus with friends. Please don't be creepy and show up uninvited. Be back later. xx, C

My chin trembles as I drop the pen beside the notepad and walk toward the front door, slipping out and closing it quietly behind me. I couldn't hear Kade on the phone when I rushed back to my room after

159

discovering the stalker folder Atlas had on Brighton, so I can only hope he's passed out in his bedroom.

I desperately want to pack a bag and hightail it out of town with Brighton, but I can't. That would lead the guys right to her, and I couldn't do that. I have no idea why they're interested in Brighton or her family, but my gut tells me I need to warn her. They haven't done anything yet that I know of, but that doesn't mean they aren't planning something.

I can't help but wonder what Brighton knows. She's never expressed interest in her family's company before—or in politics. How is the Ellis family connected to Atlas? Do they know one of their shareholders is a vampire? In my search for answers, I only ended up with more head-spinning questions.

My stomach twists into knots as I order an Uber and jog down the street to the main road to catch it. I can't risk waiting at the house for Sylvie—who has a 5-star driver rating and can't wait to help me to my destination, apparently—to pick me up there.

Once I'm in the back of the car heading toward Brighton's apartment, I finally take a deep breath, letting it out slowly in an attempt to calm my racing heart. I have no idea how Brighton will react to what I'm going to tell her, though if her response to me telling her about vampires almost a month ago is any indication, it's going to take a while to get through to her.

"How's the temperature back there, sweetie?" Sylvie asks, glancing at me through the rearview mirror.

"Fine, thanks," I say, staring out the window as my knee bounces.

"Oh, good! There's a bottle of water in the cup holder if you're thirsty."

I force a smile as my response, and when she opens her mouth again, I add, "Sorry, I'm just not really in the mood to chat."

She nods and says nothing for the rest of the drive. I feel bad, but I can't think about anything else right now. I'll be sure to tip her generously and leave a good rating when I get out.

When we pull up outside Brighton's building, I unbuckle my belt and thank her for the ride. I get out, shutting the door as I step onto the sidewalk. The cold air whips through my hair, chilling my cheeks and making me shiver and tug my jacket tighter.

Sylvie pulls away, speeding down the empty street, and I slide my phone out of my pocket to text Brighton so she can let me into her building.

I type, *I'm here*, but before I can hit send, I'm grabbed from behind, and my phone goes flying, smashing against the concrete. I don't have a chance to yell as I'm dragged from the sidewalk, down the space between Brighton's building at the one next to hers. I try to scream, but the hand clamped over my mouth muffles the sound, and the next thing I know, I'm being shoved into the back of a black SUV. My head smacks one of the tinted windows, making me cry out in pain as my vision blurs from the impact.

Finally, my vision rights itself, and I find myself staring into an unfamiliar silver gaze.

I blink hard, my heart slamming against my ribcage as dread coils in my stomach, and my voice cracks as I say, "Dante?"

"Sleep."

Awareness creeps in as I pry my eyes open, and the first thing I see is a massive fireplace with crackling flames. Soft jazz music fills the space along with the faint scent of lavender. I try to look around without moving or alerting my captor that I'm awake.

I quickly come to the conclusion that I've been brought to a fancy penthouse. I'm sprawled on a couch next to a coffee table where a large candle is burning, which is likely where the lavender scent is coming from. The windows on either side of the fireplace show a darkening sky outside and are draped in heavy gray curtains.

Holding my breath, I peek over the back of the couch and exhale when I don't see the vampire that grabbed me off the street.

My pulse spikes. *He found me.* And the guys won't know I'm in trouble because I lied about where I was going. Not that I want to be around any of them right now, but if the alternative is the psycho vampire that's been hunting me because of some ridiculous claim he believes to have over me, I'll take the evil I somewhat know over the one I don't at all.

Either way, things really aren't looking good for me.

I crawl off the couch, tiptoeing around the large, open room. Everything is neutral tones, mostly white with gray accents, and a little feminine. On the other side of the couch is a long dining table with chairs on one side and a bench on the other. There's an ornate mirror hung on the wall behind the table, making the space appear even bigger, and a crystal chandelier hung above it. I fight the urge to scoff at all of it. I've gotten used to fancy living quarters living with the guys, but this is next-level.

"I'm glad to see you're finally awake."

My stomach plummets, and I whirl around to find the vampire who grabbed me off the street. His black hair is slicked back, accentuating the sharp angles of his sun-kissed face. He's dressed as if he just came from a business meeting, in a navy collared button-up, black slacks, and shiny black dress shoes. He's staring at me with a glint of interest in his eyes that makes me want to vomit all over the marble floor at my feet.

He tilts his head, sensing my discomfort, and a slow smile curls his lips. "It's nice to finally meet you, Calla."

I swallow the lump in my throat. "I'm sure you can understand why the feeling isn't mutual," I force out. "Dante."

He chuckles deeply and steps toward me.

I reel back, bumping into the bench at the dining table. "W-what do you want from me?"

Dante sighs. "Must we discuss that right now? I'd would much rather enjoy some time together first. You've captured the attention of some very powerful vampires, Calla. Color me intrigued."

My eyes narrow. "Jealous much?"

"What is it about you that convinced them to let you live?" he muses aloud.

I clench my jaw to keep from saying something I might regret. Which is becoming more difficult every time this guy opens his mouth. "Why exactly do you want me dead?" I ask instead.

"An eye for an eye," he says. "It's nothing personal. You see, I got screwed over when those boys of yours intervened in my business all those years ago."

I blink at that, faintly wondering how old the vampire in front of me is. He appears older than the guys, which I imagine would be determined by the age he was when he was turned—if he was turned. In human years, he looks to be in his mid-thirties. Vampire years, though? I don't want to think about it. "Your *business* that could've cost my ancestor his life."

He shrugs. "We all make choices. He made the decision to go into business with certain people, and instead of facing the consequences of that, he got bailed out."

I cross my arms over my chest and straighten my posture in an attempt to trick myself into believing I'm not terrified of this guy. "He's dead," I say flatly. "Why should I have to face the consequences of something I wasn't even involved in?"

Dante purses his lips before they twist into a smirk. "You try that one with Atlas?" He shakes his head before allowing me an opportunity to respond. "How about Gabriel? He's always had a soft spot for beautiful humans."

My stomach twists painfully at his words. I don't want to think about Gabriel—or any of the guys—with another human.

Wait, what?

When did *that* happen?

Despite the confusion and fear surrounding what I found in Atlas's office, the thought of never seeing them again and finding out the truth makes my eyes burn. As much as I've tried to fight what I feel about being with them, they've taken care of me since arriving in my life like a hurricane. Whatever is going on with them and Brighton's family, I want to be around long enough to find out what it is.

"So what," I say, "you'll feel better about what you lost after killing me?"

He cocks his head to the side, staring at me. "Do you know what I lost?"

"Whatever it is, you're of the opinion that my life is worth less, so I really don't care."

"Hmm, you're a feisty one, aren't you?" His eyes glimmer with what I can only describe as hunger, and it makes me want to run far away. "Perhaps I should keep you around a while. I think you and I could be good friends, Calla."

"Are you offering me a choice between your company and immediate death? Because if you're going to kill me anyway, I think I'd prefer you do it now."

Amusement colors his features, and he laughs. "Kade must get a kick out of your fire."

I roll my eyes. "Your issue is with them. Why don't you take it up, you know, *with them*?"

The humor in his eyes morphs into something darker, something that triggers an alarm in my head. *I need to get out of here now or I'm not going to.*

"Oh, I intend to. When I deliver your cold, lifeless body to their doorstep."

Nausea rolls through me in a vicious wave, and I inch backward.

"How theatrical of you." I force an uninterested tone despite Dante being able to hear the erratic heartbeat in my chest.

He appears right in front of me before I have the chance to register any movement. He wraps his fingers around my throat and tugs me forward, flashing his fangs as a sharp gasp escapes my lips. I've got nowhere to go. When he opens his mouth and his fangs extend, my breath gets caught in my throat.

"Please don't." My voice cracks, and I cringe inwardly. The thought of having his fangs in my neck brings tears to my eyes and makes bile rise in my throat.

His chest rises and falls deeply with an inaudible sigh. "I could make it so much better than what you've experienced. You have no idea, little human." He tips his head back slightly to look into my eyes. "There's no reason for your death to be painful."

I shake my head as much as I can in his grip. "Dante, please don't do this."

His fanged smirk makes my stomach feel as if it's filled with rocks as he leans in slowly. I'm frozen in place, stunned by fear and weighed down by the knowledge that there's no chance I can escape him. No one knows where I am; I don't even know how long I've been here. The only shot I have at making it out of this alive is if Brighton contacted one of the guys after I didn't show up. They could track me here— wherever *here* is.

Dante pulls me out of my thoughts, grabbing my hip with his free hand and digging his fingers into my skin. I yelp in surprise, and the sound quickly turns to that of pain when he sinks his teeth into my neck. I try weakly to push him away, shame and terror rippling through me as the pull of my blood leaving my body fills me with dread.

This is nothing like what I experienced with the guys. This is the worst thing I've ever felt.

"Please," I whimper, silent tears slipping free and wetting my cheeks even as I keep my eyes closed. The room no longer smells of lavender, but the strong, copper scent of my blood as it spills down my neck, staining the front of my shirt.

He doesn't stop; his teeth are like a hundred needles in my neck, ripping and devouring me in the most grotesque way I ever could have imagined. Worse, actually. This feeling, this horrific pain is nothing I could have anticipated or prepared for. My head spins, and I force my eyes open, only to find the world darkening around the edges of my vision. I open my mouth to scream, a final effort with the minuscule amount of strength I have left, but before the sound tears from my lips, Dante goes rigid against me. He makes a choking sound as he pulls away from my neck and stumbles to the side, reaching for his heart—or where it should be.

Instead there's a gaping hole in his chest and blood soaking through his dress shirt.

His mouth opens in a silent scream, his fangs covered in my blood, and then he collapses onto the floor, revealing the most stunning woman I have ever seen... who just so happens to be holding Dante's heart in a perfectly manicured hand.

I stumble back a step into the table bench, and it's the only thing that keeps me upright. My eyes go wide, and if my jaw wasn't locked, I would probably scream. I lift my hand to my neck, covering the puncture marks as they continue to drip blood down the front of my shirt. My chin wobbles, and I swallow hard, desperate to keep it together. The panic in my chest is making it hard to breathe, and I can't look away from the vacant-eyed vampire between us. *He's dead.* I should feel relieved, and a part of me definitely does, but I have to fight the dark ripple of sadness and remind myself that he was going to kill me. Dante was going to drain my blood even as I begged him to stop, then drop me on a doorstep all because of a deal that went sideways over a hundred years ago.

The woman tosses Dante's heart at his feet, and it lands with a sickeningly wet *thud*. "Such a waste," she says with a sigh, shaking her head. Her hair is so blond it's almost white and reaches past her breasts. Her silver eyes are shadowed with dark liner and she has lashes any woman would kill for. Her lips are dark red and pressed in a tight line as I stare at her.

"I... um, th-thank you," I whisper as the blood seeps through my fingers, leaving a trail of crimson along my pale skin, and I cringe.

The elegant woman bends—the white floor-length dress she's wearing pooling around her feet—and rips a length of Dante's shirt from his body, rising as she uses it to clean his blood from her hand. "Do not thank me, Calla." She drops the blood-soaked scrap of shirt onto the floor. "Dante's ill-mannered, silly little excuse for revenge is not the reason you were brought here."

Confusion floods through me as I grip the table behind me, quickly joined by intense dizziness from losing so much blood, and I frown at the woman who I believed was *saving* my life.

She smiles at me, the light from the chandelier above the table catching her fangs.

I choke on a scream as the woman shoots forward with vampiric speed, and her sharp silver gaze is the last thing I see before my world goes dark.

TEMPTED
BY
FIRE

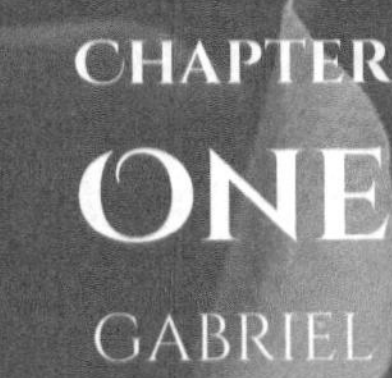

CHAPTER

ONE

GABRIEL

I don't consider myself a particularly violent person.

Despite being a vampire, that has never been my nature. But the moment I knew Calla was gone, an unfamiliar sensation sparked deep in my chest. Something dark and vicious. It threatens to replace the taste of her on my lips. Her sweet skin and rich blood. Two memories I'd never wish to part with.

A quick search of the house—the paper scattered on the floor in Atlas's office and the obvious decoy note in the kitchen—told us all we needed to know.

Calla had run.

What it didn't explain was why none of us could sense her anymore.

I'd been at work planning a new campaign for our senate candidate when the connection fizzled out. Like blowing out a candle in a dark room, quickly fading smoke is the only remnant of the flame that once burned brightly inside. One moment she was there, and the next, I couldn't feel her at all. Where there was once a vibrating orb of warmth in my chest—the connection each of us has to her blood—was replaced by a cold emptiness that made me shudder.

Before I could contact any of the guys, Kade called me, confirming what I already knew—something had happened to Calla. Not long after, Brighton Ellis reached out looking for her, saying that she was waiting for Calla to come over but she never showed up.

While Atlas and Lex got on a flight back to the city from JFK in New York, Kade and I started searching. We couldn't locate Calla, but we were able to track her phone to where it was left on the sidewalk outside of Brighton's apartment building, the screen shattered.

Kade had stared at it for a long stretch of silence, focused on the fragmented background image of Calla and Brighton with their arms around each other as they smiled at the camera, with the Washington Monument in the background. I wanted to comfort him. Kade's like a brother to me, and he was there through some of my worst years. While he doesn't know the extent of the darkness in me, he never let me go through that shit alone.

I took the phone from his hands, and the hardness in his eyes as he looked at me did nothing but fuel the fire in my chest to get our girl back.

After a brief conversation, Brighton showed us the texts she'd received from Calla.

Brighton, we need to talk.

I have to tell you some crazy things that won't make much sense, but I promise I'm telling the truth.

Please answer me. I'm freaking out over here.

Where are you? I'll come to you.

Brighton?!?!

"I don't understand," Brighton told us, wrapping her arms around herself as her hazel eyes shifted back and forth between us. "She was so panicked, then she just stopped responding to me and never showed up. I... I didn't know who else to call. Calla's family is in New York, and you guys seem to be close to her, and I... I have to admit, I'm freaking out."

Kade and I exchanged a quick glance before he glamoured her to delete everything and forget Calla had texted her. The last thing we needed was the Ellis family sticking their noses into this. We had enough to deal with when it came to them as it was. *Damn vampire hunters...*

"Gabe, did you hear what I said?"

Marcel's deep voice pulls me back to the present, to the sitting room of his Manhattan townhouse. The narrow rooms with tall ceilings are decorated with art pieces he's collected over the years. The space is accented with dark blues and grays, glossy hardwood floors, with the smell of leather furniture and crisp citrus candles, which he seems to have burning in every room. It's a bit overwhelming for my senses, but I do my best to ignore the dull ache it's creating in my temples.

I blink at our informant, one of the few people we trust outside the four of us, then force a nod. "Apologies," I mutter.

He rakes a hand through his mop of golden blond hair and sighs. "I get it, man. You're worried about her. But it's only been a week, and—"

"Just tell me what you know, Marcel," I cut him off.

He offers a curt nod, not at all thrown off by my cool tone. "First thing's first. There have been no further developments where Dante is concerned."

My upper lip curls at the mention of him—the vampire who believes he has some claim to what is *ours* because he got screwed out of a job when Calla's ancestor agreed to our protection in exchange for her.

"The guy has gone radio silent," Marcel continues. "I had a friend check out some of the places he's been known to frequent, but he hasn't been around in a while. It's safe to say he's not in New York."

A muscle ticks along my jaw, and I grip the armrest tighter. "Then where the hell is he?" The words taste bitter on my tongue, like drinking stale blood.

Marcel just stares at me, his silver eyes dark, focused. We're both thinking the same thing—the bastard went to Washington. "Let's think about this," he says in a level voice, drumming his fingers against his jean-clad thigh. "We know Dante. He's into the whole pomp and circumstance. If he took Calla, don't you think you'd know about it by now? For the sole reason that the jackass doesn't know how to keep his mouth shut. He'd want to brag, to shove it in your faces that he took something from you."

Some*one*—not some*thing*. My eyes narrow, though I don't bother voicing the anger burning in my chest; Marcel's intentions are not malicious. Instead, I scratch the copper stubble along my jaw to hide how tightly it's clenched. I haven't bothered shaving in days, and it's starting to irritate my skin. "That doesn't explain the break in the connection," I point out in a gruff voice. "Unless she—"

"No," Marcel says over me, shaking his head. "Do you believe she's dead, Gabriel?"

My throat constricts, and I frown at the difficulty I find when trying to swallow. "No." I don't believe it—I refuse to.

"Right. Then there's another explanation we haven't considered yet. Blood oaths are tricky things. You guys knew that when you entered into it all those years ago." He flicks his wrist back and forth. "Witches and their spells."

My eyes widen as a thought hits me with the speed of a train. "A spell," I say. "Wherever Calla is could have a spell blocking our connection to her."

Marcel purses his lips. "It's possible."

Not only is it possible, it's a far better alternative than what's got my stomach in painful knots. What has kept all of us up every night since she disappeared.

"I don't suppose you have a witch handy?"

"Wouldn't matter anyway, considering the only witch that could undo the block is the one who put it in place."

I slam my fist down on the armrest. "What am I supposed to do with that?" I growl without looking in Marcel's direction. I don't direct the question at him because I don't expect him to have an answer, though I really wish he did.

I scrub a hand down my face and sigh.

Why did you have to run, angel?

"I mean this with the utmost respect and only mention it out of concern for your wellbeing. You look like absolute shit. You're not going to be able to help Calla if you end up passing out from exhaustion or snapping and getting caught chowing down on a human because you're starving. You need to take care of yourself." His voice is stern but laced with worry.

I manage a weak smile. "Your concern is noted and appreciated."

"And ignored," he remarks dryly, shaking his head before he pins me with a level stare. "I'm serious, Gabriel. I don't know her much at all, but I can't see her wanting you—or the others for that matter—to get to a point where you're not giving yourself basic necessities because it could take away from potentially finding her. You're no good to her like this, okay? So smarten up."

My hands curl around the armrests, making the wood groan under my grip. He's right.

"Listen, I know you want to get back to Washington, but I think you should stay tonight. Take a break from everything and refocus. I know of a place that has voluntary feeders on standby. I'll text you the address. Go and replenish your strength." He nods, his voice stern but kind as he says, "Take care of yourself, Gabe."

I rise from the chair at the same moment Marcel stands, finding it in me to smile at him. "Thank you, Marcel. You know we appreciate the work you do for us, but you constantly go above and beyond to show how much you care. It doesn't go unnoticed, I hope you know that."

He shoots me a grin, and we walk through the main level, the aged hardwood creaking under our steps as we near the front door.

Marcel slaps me on the back as he opens the door for me. "Keep me posted. You know where I am if you need anything."

"Thank you," I tell him again, stepping out into the bitter afternoon air.

"Gabriel," Marcel calls, causing me to turn back. "You're going to find her."

I nod, jogging down the concrete steps in front of his townhouse to the sidewalk, where the wind picks up, the cold air making my cheeks tingle.

We *are* going to find her.

And then whoever is behind taking her from us will live to regret the decision... until we slaughter them.

TWO

The pressure in my temples makes it hard to open my eyes. Painful even. Like jackhammers pounding into my head at every angle. I manage to pry them open slowly, immediately squinting at the lamp casting light across my face. Blinking hard in an attempt to clear the blur spattered across my vision, I turn away from the light, groaning as my muscles protest the sudden movement.

I have the fleeting thought that I'm dead, but I quickly dispel it. If I was dead, surely it wouldn't hurt so damn much.

When I attempt to sit up, I grit my teeth against the ache in my back. I haven't felt this awful since I got the flu in freshman year, and Brighton ended up having to take care of me as if I was a child.

Brighton.

Holy shit.

I'd been heading for her apartment when Dante grabbed me off the sidewalk. I needed to warn her, to tell her what I found in Atlas's office. She needs to know they're following her, that something in her family's company is connected to them.

My eyes go wide as they dart around the unfamiliar, dark bedroom. The haze in my head evaporates, replaced by panic, making my chest tighten as I press my shaking palm against the warmth of my skin over my heart.

Frowning, I peer down at the black silk slip I'm wearing, and my pulse races. My stomach twists into knots, making the possibility of puking on these lavish, no doubt expensive sheets very real.

Everything comes back at once, making my head spin and my eyes prick with hot tears. This overwhelming sense of dread is like nothing I've experienced before. Just when I thought I was starting to get a grip on all of this vampire blood oath shit, the rug has been pulled out from under me.

All the secrets, Atlas being involved in Ellis Industries, the creepy surveillance photos of Brighton... Then being ambushed outside of her apartment by Dante.

My heart beats hard against my chest as the memories flood in. The fear that overtook me when I realized Dante had found me. The indescribable pain I felt when he sank his fangs into my neck.

I suck in a shallow breath and lift my fingers to the spot he bit me, and when they graze smooth skin, I press my lips together. It's... healed. Which means one of two things—someone used vampire blood to heal me, or I've been here long enough for it to heal on its own. The former makes my stomach roil, but the latter makes me just as nauseous with panic.

Squeezing my eyes shut at the tingling sensation along my neck, I can't stop the scene from playing out in my head. The flash of his fangs, the sickening feeling of him drawing the blood out of me, and the woman killing him right in front of me. The memory of the sound of his heart thumping against the floor makes bile rise in my throat, and I swallow hard, unable to open my eyes as I relive the fuzzy moments after Dante was killed. The angelically attractive vampire cleaning the blood from her hand as if it was nothing but a mere inconvenience to her.

I press my fingers against the thrumming of pain in my temples. My shallow breathing quickens as I recall the woman's words.

"Dante's ill-mannered, silly little excuse for revenge is not the reason you were brought here."

What the hell am I doing here? And who is the vampire behind it?

Once I've managed to pull myself into a sitting position, I let out a breath and slowly swing my legs over the side of the bed. I take my time trying to stand, worried I'll fall over the second I'm upright. Sure enough, when I stand, the world tilts around me, and it takes a long moment to regain my balance. My head is light and fuzzy, as if I haven't eaten or drank any water in days. I've never felt this weak. I keep my eyes trained on the massive window in front of me. It's dark outside, but that could mean anything. It's possible I've been here for hours or days. There's no way to tell. I've been here long enough for someone to dress me. Shuddering at the thought, I take a tentative step toward the window. My legs are a little shaky as if I'd run a long distance without warming up, but they're sturdy enough for me to make it to the window. I press my hands against the cold glass, peering down to the street below. I have to be at least twenty stories up, possibly higher. *Too high to jump.* The sidewalk is empty and the street is mostly quiet, save for a couple of cars, their headlights casting a faint glow on the asphalt.

I turn back to the room and lean against the windowsill, watching the flickering flames in the massive black marble fireplace against the wall farthest from me. My head is full of questions, and not knowing if I'll be alive long enough to get the answers makes my breath catch in my throat.

My thoughts quickly go to the guys. For some reason, they must not know where I am, otherwise they'd be here. They would have come for me by now. Atlas would be lecturing me about leaving the house with Dante on the loose, Lex would be ready to kill whoever's behind this whole thing, Kade would be making inappropriate and mostly unhelpful commentary, and Gabriel... he would just want to make sure I was okay. As conflicted as part of me still feels about them, I wish they were here.

I shake my head. I can't think about my confusing emotions toward the vampires who claimed me right now. I need to figure out what the hell is going on here. That woman... Who the hell is she? And what could she possibly want me for? If she was going to kill me, she's had plenty of opportunities, so there has to be another reason. And honestly, that scares me more than her wanting me dead. Because death is easy. Whatever this is... I'm terrified to find out.

Making my way around the dim room, my eyes adjust to the warm light coming from the lamp next to the four-poster bed I'd been sleeping in. Everything about the space is elegant. Dark wood accents and deep, rich reds and browns. The large crimson afghan rug beneath my bare feet is plush, with an intricate design woven through it.

I find myself standing in front of a closed dark wood door. My hand hovers over the knob, fingers shaking.

Before I can push myself to wrap my fingers around the brass and turn it, the door opens from the other side, and I stumble back, my heart slamming against my ribcage.

I squint hard until the vampire in front of me comes into focus, looking as stunningly elegant as she had in the moments before she—

"You're awake," she says in a smooth voice, the corners of her lips curved slightly upward. "Good."

How long was I asleep?

How long have I been here?

These are the questions I should be asking. Instead, my legs shift back on their own, moving me away from the woman as she watches me with a curious glint in her bright silver eyes. After stepping into the room, leaving the door open, she clasps her hands behind her back. The way she exudes ease and power in equal measure has my heart beating like the wings of a hummingbird. I don't want to be afraid; I shouldn't show this vampire the fear that sings in my veins, but the weakness in my body makes it difficult to keep up my bravado. She can likely see right through it.

"Who are you?" I finally ask once I'm sure my voice won't waver or crack.

She flashes a brilliant, snow-white smile. Her teeth look too perfect, too straight and white to be real. Veneers, I'd guess. "My name is Selene. I apologize, I should have introduced myself the other night."

The other night?

Selene's eyes trail over me, and I fight the urge to look away. Her scrutiny is a heavy weight that makes my skin tingle uncomfortably. Probably because I know she can snuff me out with a simple flick of her wrist if she wants. She's no longer wearing the flowing white dress, which confirms my suspicion that some time has passed since I was brought here. Instead, she's wearing a tight-fitting plum dress with a sharp V-shaped neckline and a hem that just barely reaches her knees, plus some seriously impressive heels. She towers over me, which really doesn't help how intimidated I am by her.

She tilts her head to the side ever so slightly. "You and I have much to discuss, Calla."

My chest tightens. I have no idea who this woman is, so the idea of having anything to talk about doesn't make much sense to me. But if a conversation with her is going to give me the answer to why I'm here—as much as I'm dreading finding out—I should just get it over with. "I—"

"Perhaps we can chat once you've had a chance to clean yourself up and have something to eat."

As much as I desperately want and need both of those things, I cross my arms over my chest, trying to appear more confident than I feel in this scrap of black lace and silk in front of a stranger who is most likely over a century older than me and, you know, supernatural. "I think we should talk now."

The vampire arches a perfectly shaped brow. "You can barely stand upright but you wish to refuse my offer in order to keep some semblance of control? Very well." Selene walks across the room at an unhurried pace, her strides confident and graceful. She lowers herself into one of the red velvet wingback chairs in front of the fireplace, crossing one leg over the other and resting her hands in her lap. She stares at the flames crackling in front of her, and a small smile touches her rose-colored lips. "What is it you'd like to know, Calla?"

I stare at Selene for a few seconds, finding myself wondering why she lit the fireplace in this room she's keeping me in. I find it hard to believe it's for my comfort, considering she knocked me out cold when we met. Is she trying to trick me into trusting her? Hesitantly, I make my way to the chair across from her. Lowering myself into it, the silk glides easily along the velvet. I grip the armrests, too tight at first, before I remember I'm trying to appear less freaked out than I currently am. I force my fingers to relax as my eyes flick between Selene and the light emanating from the fireplace. "I have a lot of questions," I start, dragging my gaze back to her. "How long have I been here?" I ask first.

She tips her head to the side. "A few days, give or take."

"Three or four?" I press, my pulse kicking up.

Arching a brow, her tone is mocking when she asks, "That's your main concern? What, do you have somewhere else to be, Calla?"

Um, yeah. Literally anywhere else. I want to say it, but I'm so out of my element here, I bite my tongue and keep my mouth shut.

Selene rolls her eyes. "Relax. There can't be anything that important in your mundane life you could've missed in the last week. You've been fed and taken care of until I was ready to have this conversation with you. I even healed Dante's little..." She points toward my neck, and I shudder at her confirmation that I'd been fed vampire blood.

A million follow up questions race around my head. I don't remember anything from the last week that I've been here, which likely means she's been glamouring me. Despite the swirling urge in my stomach to purge whatever food she's forced me to eat, I need to know why I'm here. "You said..." My voice trails off as the memory from the night I was brought here threatens to replay in my head. I clear my throat and try again. "You said Dante wasn't the reason I was brought here, so I'm left to wonder, to assume, the reason is you."

Selene nods, tapping her fingers against her knee as she regards me thoughtfully. She offers a ghost of a smile that does nothing to ease the knots in my stomach. "Yes, well, I had to get a look at you for myself."

Shaking my head, I ask, "Why? Why do you care about me at all?"

Her eyes take on a light of amusement. "*Care* is a strong word. Call it a mild fascination."

I frown. "That still doesn't answer my question."

"Why," she echoes, pursing her lips for a moment. "We have a mutual friend, you and I."

A mutual friend.

My back stiffens against the chair, and I sit up straighter. The only possibility would be one of the guys.

Selene nods. "You're putting it together," she observes.

"I'm really not," I disagree. "You know about the blood oath, that I can guess, but that doesn't explain why you had me grabbed off the street."

"Those boys of yours kept you locked up tight for a while," she muses, glancing toward the flames. The light dances across her flawless complexion as she continues, "I'll admit, I was a little surprised when Dante reached out and let me know you were with him. I truly didn't think he'd manage to get to you, not with those vampires' determination to keep you safe."

"*Safe* is a strong word," I echo her previous sentiment without thinking.

She laughs, a soft, melodic sound that floats through the air and makes my cheeks heat. "You're alive, aren't you?"

"I'm a prisoner—again," I point out. "The secrets continue to pile up, and I'm left with more questions than answers."

"Allow me to answer one then. You're wondering which of those gorgeous vampires you've been bound to is tied to me."

I nod, because I really can't figure it out. I can't see it being Atlas; in a way, the two seem too alike. Lex, I think, would be too eccentric, and Kade... well, maybe Kade. He's been known to surprise me on occasion. Or Gabriel. I wholeheartedly believe he could be friends with anyone. Despite what brought us together, I have no doubt that Gabriel's heart is good. He's kind and compassionate, and fuck, I *miss* him.

"Gabriel and I go way back," Selene reveals, leaning against the back of the chair as she lifts a hand to her long white-blond hair, fingering one of the curls and smiling to herself as if she's reliving a fond memory of the two of them.

It twists something in my gut, and I clench my jaw, wanting to look away. Instead, I ask, "How do you know Gabriel?"

Her eyes meet mine, and her next words make the blood in my veins turn to ice.

"I'm the one who turned him."

CHAPTER

THREE

GABRIEL

New York City is one of my favorite places in the United States, but walking down the sidewalk with brownstones on either side of the car-lined street brings me little joy when the only thing on my mind is the fiery human I'm finding it alarmingly difficult to be apart from.

I'm heading toward the subway station when my phone buzzes in the pocket of my black windbreaker. I pull it out in a flash, hoping for an update from Washington, but my stomach sinks when I realize that isn't what it is. Instead, I'm looking at a message from Fallon, one of the vampires I met during my stint living in Manhattan almost forty years ago.

Heard you were around. Jase and I are heading out for drinks. Let's meet.

I stop walking and move out of the way of foot traffic.

Hey, Fal. I'm not in the city long. Maybe next time?

Her response comes less than a minute later. *Don't make me drag your ass out. I'm sending you the address of this new place we found last week. It's super casual, so you'd better not be in a suit. See you in an hour!*

I sigh into the air, fogging it with my breath. It's unseasonably chilly for April, and I've never been one to enjoy the cold. *Fine*, I type back, *but I can't stay long.*

She sends back an eye-roll emoji, then adds, *Looking forward to seeing you too, Gabe.*

As much as the Manhattan social scene isn't something I'm in the mood for right now, this could be a good opportunity to catch up with Fallon and Jase and see if they've heard anything about Dante or the hunters in the tristate area. Marcel does an excellent job keeping his ear to the ground, but it's always good to keep tabs elsewhere. Finding Calla is the priority, but unfortunately, we can't forget about the ever-growing organization of people whose goal is to eradicate our kind.

The place Marcel sent me to is essentially a glamorous feeder den. From the pristine white brick exterior, it looks like a private, luxury spa, but the mouth-watering scent of blood overwhelms my senses the moment I round the corner and before I even spot the building.

Stepping inside, I'm immediately enveloped in warmth. I'm glad to be out of the cold, but the atmosphere here has unease coiling in my stomach. It isn't my first time in a place like this—not by far. I spent the first full year after I turned in a haze of bloodlust and feeder dens, though most of those places weren't nearly as nice as this.

The space smells of sandalwood and citrus mixed with some kind of oil—a heady herbal aroma that does little to ease the ache in my temples.

I walk further into the bright, patron-free room, my shoes silent on the polished dark wood floor. The décor is simple yet warm, welcoming. To one side is a set of gray plush couches around a glass coffee table with lit candles flickering atop it, and to the other is—

A soft gasp from behind the white and gold marble reception desk snags my attention, and I glance at the pale, black-haired girl who is staring at me with wide, olive-green eyes.

Sometimes I forget how well-known we are among the vampires. Though this girl—who can't be older than twenty—is entirely human. The wall behind her is made of light-colored rocks and has a water feature built in. It's meant to be relaxing, I'm sure, but the trickling sound is grinding on my nerves. I'm more on edge than normal—a quick feeding should take care of that, at least a bit. I won't be myself again until we have Calla back, but until then, Marcel is right. I need to take care of my basic necessities.

"H-hi," the girl stammers, a blush tingeing her cheeks pink as she pushes the dark-rimmed glasses up the bridge of her nose. "Mr. Simmons, it's such an honor to have you visit our facility."

I offer a polite smile. I'm not in the mood for pleasantries, but this girl doesn't deserve to be exposed to the wrath living just below the surface. My jaw clenches as my gaze flicks to the vein in her neck, pulsing with the rampant beat of her heart. I swallow hard, struggling to ignore the pressure building in my gums.

"Thank you," I force out, dropping my gaze to the shiny metal name tag attached to her white blouse, "Emerson."

Her blush deepens, and she quickly turns her attention to the tablet in her hand. "If you'd like to follow me, we have a VIP room ready for you." She steps out from behind the counter and opens a set of frosted glass doors, her heels clicking softly on the wood floor that seems to carry throughout the place.

I follow her down a hallway with closed doors lining both sides. The air is filled with essential oils and warmth, but through that, I pick up on the sharp, metallic scent. The reason I'm here—blood.

"Marcel let me know you might be coming by," Emerson says, stealing a glance at me over her shoulder as we continue toward the end of the hall to another set of glass doors. "We don't always have, um, staff on-site for the... treatment you'll be getting, but I was able to call someone in."

I nod as soft piano music plays overhead, seemingly from a speaker in the ceiling, though I can't see it through the collection of chandeliers that line the hallway.

We stop in front of the doors, and I say, "It's much appreciated."

"No problem at all." She pulls out a badge and taps it against a panel in the wall. It gives a soft *beep* and a lock clicks. Emerson opens the door, and I grab it, holding it for her to walk ahead. "Thank you," she says, blushing again.

My lips twitch. If this girl knew how old I was... Though perhaps she's intrigued by it. Not many humans know of our kind, but of the ones who do—even though they're mostly glamoured—can't help but be curious. Some even want to be turned. This isn't a life I would wish on anyone, but it's hard to deter someone who desperately desires eternity.

She walks into the room, the lights turning on automatically. It's a small, inviting space, set up like a living room with the same dark floors from the rest of the building and pale gray walls. Emerson walks toward the plush couch against the wall across the room and straightens one of the black throw pillows.

"Make yourself comfortable, and I will send Jackie in right away."

I shrug off my jacket, hanging it on one of the hooks next to the door. "Excellent," I say, meeting her gaze. "Thank you for your assistance."

She catches her lip between her teeth and nods, her pulse ticking unevenly, then offers a wide smile. "Oh, of course! Please let me know if there's anything else I can do to make your visit more pleasant."

Nodding, my lips curl into a hint of a smile as I turn away from her, walking toward the sitting area. The air is filled with the faint scent of lavender and vanilla, and my shoes make barely any sound on the soft beige area rug on the floor.

The door clicks shut as I lower myself onto the couch and let out a slow breath. This place is a little much for me, but coming recommended by Marcel, I know it's good. Plus, I need to feed. It may as well be from a willing human who is being compensated for her... donation instead of some unsuspecting human off the street. The act of feeding was something I used to enjoy. I relished in the feeling of overtaking my prey, bending them to my will, and taking their life force to make myself stronger.

A shudder ripples through me, and I blink hard. That was a very long time ago. I was a different person then, under the thumb of the monster who created me. She was also the first woman I ever loved.

I growl low in my throat, shoving away those thoughts and clenching my jaw before I realize a small red-headed woman has slipped into the room.

Her wide brown eyes flit around, and she stammers, "I'm sorry. Should I come back?"

"No." I force my expression to soften. "Please come in. I apologize. It's been..." I stop myself, then repeat, "Please come in."

She closes the door and approaches slowly. I see the hesitation in her gaze and the uneven beat of her heart. She's wearing light gray scrubs as if she's about to give me a massage.

I shift closer to the edge of the couch, resting my hands casually in my lap. "Have you done this before?" I ask, attempting to put the young woman, Jackie, I recall the receptionist mentioning, at ease. It's been too long since I fed, and all I want to do is tear into her throat, but I can control myself. I can make this experience enjoyable for her.

The tension in her shoulders fades a little, and she smiles. "Oh, yes. I've been in the service of vampires for many years."

That has my brows lifting. She doesn't look much older than Emerson. "How many years?" I ask as she walks around the glass coffee table in front of the couch and sits next to me, angling her body toward mine.

"You think I'm too young," she says with a smile. Her pulse has returned to a normal pace; she's becoming more relaxed around me.

I lean against the back of the couch, resting my arm along it as I turn to face her as well. "How old *are* you?"

She purses her lips. "How old are *you*?"

A surprised laugh escapes me. "Ah, come on. I asked you first."

It's her turn to laugh. "Really? That's what you're going with?"

I shrug. "Guess."

"Based on your comeback, I'd say you can't be much older than twenty-five." Her voice takes on a flirtatious tone, and the predator in me latches on to it before I can stop myself. I might have the self-control to keep myself from killing her, but playing into this game we've started is another story.

"Hmm. Take that and multiply it by five and you'll be a little closer." I shift toward her, snaring her gaze. Her breath hitches before I say, "Your turn."

Her eyes stay locked on mine. "I'm twenty-seven." She collects the hair from her neck, pulling it over her shoulder. "But people have always thought I was younger." She shrugs. "Must have something to do with my genes. Anyway..." She moves closer and turns her head, exposing her throat. "Whenever you're ready."

The moment my eyes land on the pulse in her neck, my fangs spring forward and my throat burns so intensely, I'm reaching for her, sliding my arm around her narrow waist and pulling her closer in a matter of seconds. My nose grazes her neck first, making her shiver against me, and I inhale before sinking my fangs into her carotid artery. Blood flows into my mouth, the hot, metallic taste exploding on my tongue. My eyes close, and I drink deeply, warmth trickling through me as I regain my strength. Her heartbeat slows, and she leans into me more, but I don't stop. She moans, and the sound goes right to my cock.

My eyes fly open, and I pull away from her, standing and wiping my mouth with the back of my hand. I've had more than enough for now, anyway.

She slumps against the back of the couch, her eyelids fluttering as blood runs down the side of her neck. Shit. I should have healed the bite marks. Too late. I'm already backing toward the door, grabbing my jacket and shrugging it on. I reach for the door handle, but stop myself, letting out a ragged breath before walking back to the couch. I pull

Jackie forward and drag my tongue along the small puncture marks, sealing them. When I pull back, her eyes are still closed and her lips are curved into a content smile. She's been at this a while, which likely means she's addicted to this feeling. The headiness, the feeling of floating... I remember it all too well.

I lift my hand to her face, tucking a bit of her hair behind her ear. "Take care," I murmur before heading for the door again. This time, I don't hesitate. I leave the room, closing the door behind me.

Luckily, Emerson isn't at the desk when I walk through the reception area, so I slip back outside without further interaction with her.

My strides are hurried. I'm not sure where I'm going, but I need to keep moving. I haven't been that affected by a feed in a long time. On the precipice of losing control—and being aroused by it. I could have done anything to that girl, and she would have let me—my venom would've made her think she *wanted* it, even if she truly didn't.

I pick up my pace, weaving through people on the sidewalk. If the street weren't so busy, I would have used my vampire speed to get the hell out of here by now.

Trying to blend in among the humans can really be a pain in the ass sometimes.

FOUR

CALLA

"I can see by the look on your face that wasn't the answer you were expecting." Selene's voice is laced with amusement as she leans back, keeping her eyes on me.

I stare at her, unable to make my lips move to form a word let alone a sentence to respond. This woman turned Gabriel into a vampire. Even the guys don't know about how Gabriel came into his immortality—Lex had told me that much the night I went with him to the tattoo shop—and I'm sitting across from her.

"No," I finally say, quickly licking my lips to combat the dryness.

She nods. "I turned Gabriel, siring him to me for the duration of our immortal lives. Mind you, our connection runs far deeper than the silly little blood oath you've wound up in."

Is... is she *bragging?*

I'm so fucking confused.

"H-how long ago was that?" I ask.

She presses a shiny, manicured finger to her lips in thought. "Hmm... It's hard to say. Time is a little different once you become a vampire, Calla. Years and decades are mere blips of time when you live forever. Surely you've considered that by now."

The knots in my stomach tighten. "Considered living forever? Not really. I'm just trying to make it to graduation." School is the least of my concerns considering my current situation, but still.

Her lips twitch. "You *are* a naive one, aren't you?"

"Why am I here?" I blurt, shifting in the chair and glancing around. "Where is *here*, anyway? Clearly you have some way of blocking the connection between me and them, otherwise they would have come for me by now, and you would be dead."

I have to believe that. If they knew where I was, they would be here. There has to be a reason—something that is keeping them away. The only vulnerability I'm aware of is white ash, though I don't know if it can be used to block a vampire's tracking capability. If so, maybe this place has it in the walls, making it impossible for them to find me. That would mean their adversity to white ash is stronger than their connection to my blood. But I truly have no idea. I can barely think straight at this point.

The hint of a smile fades from Selene's lips, though her tone is still light. "Is that right?"

Fear and anger go to war in my chest, kicking up my pulse as the fire crackles in the fireplace next to me, making my cheeks and chest flushed. "Why am I here?" I ask again.

"I was curious about you," she says simply, as if the reasoning behind my kidnapping should be obvious. "You're involved in Gabriel's life, so naturally, it was important for us to meet." She smooths her hands down the front of her dress, not that there was a single wrinkle in it to begin with. Selene seems like the type to have her clothes dry cleaned and steamed prior to wearing. "I had a friend of mine put a protective barrier around my property to ensure the two of us wouldn't be interrupted by your entourage of vampires."

My brows tug together, and I choose to skip over the whole *protective barrier* thing. I don't think I have the mental capacity to dive into *that* right now. "You don't get a piece of me just because he does and you're his sire or whatever." I shake my head and add dryly, "This isn't a pyramid scheme."

When she smiles at me this time, I get a flash of her fangs. "Perhaps not, but I am prepared to offer you a deal. One I think you'll be very interested in hearing."

"What are you talking about?" I pick at the skin around my thumbnail, avoiding her sharp silver eyes. The weight in my gut tells me I'm not ready to hear what she's offering, but I don't see that I have much of a choice.

"Don't worry," she says in a smooth voice, "this is very simple and straightforward."

I force myself to meet her gaze. "What do you want?"

Selene's lips curl into a slow smile. "I want Gabriel."

My stomach plummets, and I feel as if my ribcage is closing in tighter by the second. I clench my jaw, fighting the urge to snap at Selene, despite knowing full well I wouldn't stand a chance against her. I wasn't expecting to feel so... possessive over Gabriel. But the thought of this woman getting her claws in him makes me want to scream.

"What does that have to do with me?" I ask in a strained voice. I need to tread lightly, choose my words carefully. If her response to Dante is any indication, this woman doesn't give a shit about others' lives.

"Gabriel cares very deeply for you." Her tone makes it clear she isn't sure why. "If anyone can help me get him back, I would imagine you'd be the one."

"Get him back," I echo, desperately trying to find my way through her web of history with Gabriel. "What... what happened after you turned him?" There's a reason they aren't together anymore, and considering whatever it is wasn't something he would tell the guys he sees as brothers, it has to be pretty twisted. And she wants me to help send him back to her.

"That's ancient history. What matters now is us finding our way back to each other."

"Is this the part where you tell me you love him?" I ask, an edge to my voice.

Gabriel made it very clear from the night we met that I belonged to him and the others. That shit is a two-way street, and I'm not about to let this vampire screw with that. Yeah, I'm pissed as hell at all the guys for keeping me in the dark for so long, and they're going to hear about it plenty once we're together. But this woman trying to lay claim to Gabriel has my hackles standing straight.

"Something like that," she muses, continuing to twirl a curl around her finger as her eyes flick between mine. "You see, having a sire means many things. One of which is that when Gabriel is close it makes me stronger. Especially when I'm drinking his blood."

Vampires feed on other vampires?

"So you want him because he can give you more power?" I ask, my stomach twisting painfully. Selene doesn't care about Gabriel, not really—she cares about what he can do for her.

Those silver eyes narrow at me. "Before you refuse," she says in a smooth voice, "don't you wish to know what I could give you in return?"

I shake my head automatically. Whatever she could offer would never be enough for me to trick Gabriel into returning to this... this monster. I can't help the flare of protectiveness rippling through me. This whole thing would be so much easier if I didn't care about the vampires who tore into my life over a month ago and ripped everything apart. Damn them for making me give a shit.

"Hmm." A sly grin spreads across her lips, making my breath hitch. "Not even if I told you I have the power to break the blood oath you're trapped in? To free you from the vampires' claim to you? Think about it, Calla. You could have your life back, could have a future that *you* choose."

I grit my teeth, willing the sudden burn of tears back. *Do not cry in front of this bitch.* Before I can stop myself, I ask, "How would that even work?"

Selene slides her hands along the armrests on either side of her, flicking her tongue along her bottom lip. "As you can imagine, I've been around a long time. I've curated certain relationships with very powerful people in my world. Over the decades, I've grown quite close with the York clan. Now, you may not know just how important a vampire Atlas is, but the Yorks are infamous—practically royalty in the vampire world."

My eyes go wide. "I don't... What does that have to do with the blood oath?"

She grants me a polite, albeit strained smile. "What are the terms of your vow to them, Calla?"

"Um, I'm basically stuck with them until I die."

She curls her fingers over the edge of the chair, her nail polish shining in the firelight. "Or?"

I blink at her, and then it hits me. "Or until they allow me to sever the contract. But that's—"

"Never going to happen?" she offers. "Why don't you leave that up to me?"

"What are you going to do?" I curse inwardly at my words; it sounds as if I've already accepted her offer.

"Atlas's parents owe me a favor from many, many years ago. I think it's time I collect." The corner of her mouth lifts into an amused smile. "And the others will follow him. Gabriel, maybe not, but that won't be a problem. I'll force his hand if I must."

"You can do that?" I ask in a quiet voice, my pulse kicking up.

She chuckles. "I can glamour Gabriel as easily as I can glamour you."

I shake my head. "Then why haven't you?"

The glimmer in her eyes remains. "Where's the fun in that? I'll get what I want in the end, but that doesn't mean it has to be quick or boringly easy. I enjoy a challenge."

I grit my teeth against the bile rising in my throat at her words. My thoughts are spinning, going a million miles a minute as I try to wrap my mind around all of this. "You would do all of this just to get Gabriel back? Even if he wants nothing to do with you? Is the power really worth it?"

Selene inhales and exhales slowly, regarding me with a smooth expression. "Our world is changing," she says in a deeper tone, "and only those strong enough to stand against their enemies will make it out alive."

"So all of this is just about power," I say, "You couldn't care less about Gabriel." The twist of jealousy I felt earlier quickly morphs into anger. I don't want this woman anywhere near Gabriel.

She inclines her head slightly. "Just," she echoes with a laugh. "You underestimate the importance of that power, Calla. But of course you do. You know nothing about the world you've been forced into." She offers me a thoughtful glance. "So allow me to help free you of it."

I want to open my mouth and tell her to go to hell. That I'd never consider what she's offering even for a second. But I'd be lying. I have no idea how she expects me to get Gabriel to return to her—not to mention, the thought of doing that makes me want to keel over and vomit the nothingness in my stomach. Try as I might, I can't deny that the idea of being in control of my future is enticing. Dangerously so.

"Why now?" I ask.

She exhales slowly, as if I'm testing her patience. "The threat against our kind continues to grow stronger every day. I'm doing what I must to ensure my own survival." A cruel, suggestive smile paints her lips. "Plus, you've been with Gabriel, haven't you?" She doesn't wait for me to answer before she rises from her chair. "Take your time and consider what I've offered you, Calla." She walks toward the door without turning back, but she does add, "In the meantime, you need to eat and regain some strength. I'll have the housekeeper bring something up shortly."

The door clicks shut behind her, and a shiver crawls through me despite the warmth emanating from the fireplace. Alone with nothing but the soft crackle of flames next to me, my mind takes a dive back to being brought here. I try desperately to think through each minute, everything that happened from being grabbed off the street, all the way to the moment everything went dark. Bile rises in my throat at the horrific, blood-chilling memory of Dante's unforgiving grip on me. The way he taunted me before sinking his teeth into my throat and drinking my blood.

I swallow hard, shaking my head in an attempt to shove the memory of sharp pain away. It's not one that will soon fade. That's if it ever does.

As much as I've wanted to escape my fate of being tied to the vampires, the idea of selling Gabriel out, forcing him to return to his sire makes my stomach roil. Of all people, he doesn't deserve that.

Blinking back the sudden onslaught of tears, I press my fist to my lips, struggling to hold back the sound.

I can't do it.

It isn't me... and I don't want to be the type of person that would cause another pain for the purpose of their own gain. The way Gabriel came into my life doesn't matter, not in this sense.

As much as I want my life back—and the idea of freedom and a real future, one that *I* choose—I can't destroy someone else's life to achieve that.

I still don't trust the guys, and I haven't a clue what Brighton's family is involved in that links them to the vampires I'm bound to, but I am hellbent on figuring it out.

Which pretty much leaves me with only one option: I need to figure out a way to get the hell away from here. Preferably alive.

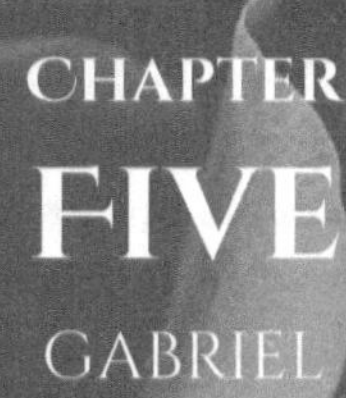

CHAPTER

FIVE

GABRIEL

I arrive at the address Fallon sent and find what appears to be a small dive bar. Getting out of the town car, I step onto the sidewalk and shut the door. The music inside isn't blaring, but it's loud enough to hear when the old, stained glass door opens ahead of me as a group of patrons with whiskey on their breath leave the green brick building.

I walk inside when the doorway is clear, and the sound of Fallon's excited squeal catches my attention immediately. I turn toward it and have less than a second to prepare myself for her to throw her arms around my neck, hugging me as if I'd just returned from war. It *has* been a while since I visited.

The floral scent of her perfume overwhelms me as I wrap my arms around her narrow waist and hug her tightly, pressing a chaste kiss to her cheek when she pulls back. "Fallon," I greet with an easy smile. "Long time no see."

She punches my arm. "Yeah, no kidding. Jerk."

Jase approaches from behind her, shaking his head and grinning at me, flashing a bit of fang. "Long time indeed. You look like shit."

"You know, people keep telling me that," I mutter as the two lead me to the booth they secured near the back of the room. The bar is crowded with mostly middle-aged people. This place certainly isn't a popular hangout spot for the students in the city. Most of the people here are at least fifty years old.

I slide into the booth, glancing around the dark space. The walls are wood panels, covered in curling and ripped rock band posters. The scent of smoke and liquor hangs heavy in the air, and though I don't see anyone actively smoking, nicotine clings to their clothes.

"What brings you to the city?" Jase asks.

I turn my attention back to my friends as they sip on their beers, waiting for me to answer. "It's sort of a long story."

"Such a shame we aren't immortal," Fallon remarks dryly with a mocking sigh, sticking her tongue out at me when I roll my eyes. She ties her bright red corkscrew curls back and dumps a handful of peanuts into her mouth. The black tank top she's wearing is barely containing her breasts, much to the delight of the men at the bar. Not that she notices.

"Something's wrong," Jase says, his voice serious as he looks at me.

I press my lips together for a moment, debating how I should start. "We fulfilled the blood oath."

He shoves a hand through his obsidian-colored hair. "Shit, bro. When did that happen?"

"A month ago."

He nods. "How did it go?"

I exhale on a laugh. "About as well as we expected. Calla knew about the deal her family made with us, but she didn't know when we were coming. She was pretty pissed."

Fallon arches a brow. "I mean, fair enough, Gabe. I'd be pissed too, and I actually like you. The others mind you..."

I just shake my head at her. She and Kade had a fling a few decades ago that ended with her burning his favorite jacket. I never asked, and neither brought it up. "Anyway, we were trying to keep her away from all of the hunter shit we're dealing with, but as you can imagine, after having her future dictated by an ancestor before she was born, and her life now controlled by the vampires she was bound to, she wasn't much of a fan of being kept in the dark."

"Can you blame her?" Jase asks, setting his pint down on the wooden table. There's sticky residue covering it, as if they don't clean them very well—or at all.

"Of course not. And when Dante started sniffing around for her, we had to tell her about him. Well, some of it. She knows he was involved with the business her family was in here and that he was seeking revenge against her for what went down."

Fallon scoffs. "He went after that poor girl because he got screwed out of some money."

"Some money," Jase echoes, downing the rest of his drink. "Last time I checked, twenty million dollars isn't just *some money*, my love."

She rolls her eyes. "Whatever. That shit has nothing to do with—what's her name again?"

"Calla," I say. Her name on my lips makes my chest tighten.

Fallon nods. "So what's going on now?"

My jaw clenches. "She's gone."

Her eyes widen. "Gone. What do you mean gone? I thought the blood oath connected you to her?"

"Something's blocking it. Marcel thinks it's a barrier spell."

"Fucking witches," Jase mutters under his breath.

Vampires and witches have never gotten along very well. Centuries of bad blood between the species has gone unresolved. It's not something I intend to add to my list of problems, but if I found out a witch helped keep Calla from us...

"So what, you think Dante took her?"

I rehash the conversation I had with Marcel, and they agree that Dante's insufferable personality would make it near impossible for him to go without bragging about his conquest if he'd been the one to take Calla.

"You two haven't heard anything from him lately?" I check, just to make sure.

"Nah," Fallon says, tracing her finger along the rim of her glass. She stops, flicking her gaze to mine. "Nothing about Dante, and I'm not sure this is really something you ought to be worrying about right now on top of everything else, but I did hear of Selene showing up around Greenwich a month or so ago. Before that, she hadn't been in the city for years that I know of."

"She was sniffing around looking for you," Jase adds. "When she found out you were living in Washington with your friends, she left New York pretty fast."

My hands clench into fists as a shiver rips through me at the mention of my sire. The sounds of the room around us—the glasses clinking and people talking over the rock music playing—fade in and out as my chest constricts, making my pulse race.

Selene could have used our sire connection to find me once she got to Washington, though trying to track me from New York may not have worked. Distance, from what I've learned, can make tracking through the sire connection difficult.

Sweat dots my brow and upper lip as my eyes bounce between my friends. They know very little about the woman who turned me and the relationship I had with her, which is how it will remain. Not even my brothers know of the horror that was the first year of my life as a vampire. My memories are filled with bloodshed, thoughtless killing, and depraved sex with the monster I believed I loved. Who I naively thought loved me in return, which was her reason for gifting me eternal life.

How wrong I'd been.

Selene wanted nothing but power. Control. Over me and the other vampires she turned. She would never admit to building an army, but that's exactly what we were. She sired us to stay with her, made us believe we were some kind of family.

It took me a long time to figure out that we were being manipulated. By then, I'd killed so many people... I could never forgive myself for the monster I'd become. I did the only thing I could do—I left her.

That was over a century ago, but to this day, I can't get rid of the dark, sickening feel of her claws dug into my chest, my very soul.

Ice shoots through my veins and my back stiffens against the plastic booth. I can't explain the sensations racing through me; I have to get out of here. I need to get home.

"Gabriel—"

My voice shakes as I force out, "It's her."

Jase's dark brows pull together. "What are you talking about, Gabe?"

"She took her," I say through gritted teeth. My gums throb as my fangs threaten to extend and cut through them.

Fallon sucks in a breath, frowning at me from across the table. "You think Selene has Calla?"

I shake my head, a low growl rumbling through my chest. "I *know* she does."

My friends exchange a wary glance as I get out of the booth and head for the door without saying goodbye. Son of a bitch—I should have figured it out sooner. Anger rips through me like a vicious wave, and I fight the urge to put my fist through one of the brick exteriors I pass along the sidewalk.

I pull my phone out of my pocket as I hail a cab, not having enough time to wait for my town car. Getting in the back, I bark at the driver to head to the airstrip I flew into a couple of days ago. He pulls away from the curb with a silent nod, and I don't bother buckling my seatbelt as I scroll through my contacts and select Atlas's name.

"Gabriel." Atlas's voice is low, tired. We're all exhausted, barely sleeping these days. Every waking hour is important; *we have to find her.*

"I know who has her."

There's a beat of silence on the other end, and then, "Who?"

I close my eyes, struggling to focus on Atlas instead of the growing pressure in my chest. "The woman who turned me," I say through gritted teeth, low enough the driver can't overhear my words.

"Why the fuck would your sire take Calla?"

My grip on the phone tightens, threatening to snap the thing in half if I'm not careful. I let out a slow breath, finally prying my eyes open. "It's a long story. Not one I can get into right now." I glance out the window as we fly down the freeway. "I'm getting on a plane shortly. I'll be home soon and then I will explain everything." My voice starts to shake with unbridled anger. The story of my turning was never one I wanted to relive—and certainly not one I wanted to share with the guys. But I'm left with no choice. They need to know—Calla's life depends on it.

"Lex will meet you at the airport. Whatever this is, Gabriel, we're going to figure it out."

I end the call without another word, glaring at my phone screen for several moments that feel like their own eternities.

Then, with a shaky hand, I dial a number I regrettably know by heart and lift the phone to my ear, my pulse pounding in my throat. I can't say how I know for certain—perhaps it's the familiar weight on my chest and tingling in my veins, or maybe it's intuition. Because Marcel was right. If Dante took her, we'd know it by now, mostly due to his need to brag. No one else would have the guts to make a move against us like this. It... it has to be her.

Each ring feels longer than the last. My heart beats in my throat, and my stomach plummets when the call is answered.

"I was wondering how long it was going to take you to put it together."

My entire body goes rigid at the soft, melodic sound of her voice. I haven't heard it in years, and still, I respond to it automatically. Memories flash in front of my eyes; nights of drinking until we were drunk—on alcohol and blood. Fucking in different clubs around the world, surrounded by vampires and humans alike, but all I saw was red. And her. Always her.

It was a lifetime ago.

"What have you done with her?" I ground out.

Selene chuckles, and the sound presses into my chest, making it harder to breathe. "That's the first thing you want to say to me? After so long?" She tuts her tongue. "I have to say, I'm disappointed."

"I don't care," I snap. "Where is Calla?"

"Your little human is perfectly safe. In fact, she is free to leave whenever she wishes, though considering everything you lot have been keeping from her, she may not want to see any of you ever again."

"What did you tell her?" I growl, barely restrained anger making my voice shake. The driver glances at me from the rearview mirror before quickly returning his attention to the road and switching lanes to pass a transport truck.

Selene sighs as if I'm a child who stepped out of line, and it makes my jaw clench. "Relax, my love," she purrs. "She knows nothing, which I imagine is exactly why she's so upset with you and your boys."

"You don't know anything." I grip the edge of the seat until my knuckles are leached of color. My insides are on fire, and all I want to do is scream. Instead, I pull the phone away from my ear for a moment and suck in a slow, steadying breath. In a low voice, I say, "Tell me where you are, Selene."

"Hmm, now that is tempting."

I close my eyes against the tension building behind them and let out a sigh. She's taunting me, and I shouldn't have expected anything less. Even still, the way it still gets under my skin in seconds is infuriating. "What game are you playing?"

She laughs, and it's a soft, lyrical sound that I used to adore. Now it claws through me like nails on a chalkboard.

"Selene," I growl. I'm losing it; my heart rate has kicked up and my knee is bouncing quickly. The situation is slipping out of my control— that's if I had any to begin with, which when dealing with my sire is unlikely.

"It was lovely speaking with you, Gabriel. I can't tell you how much I've missed the sound of your voice, even when you're cross with me. I do hope to see you soon. We have so much to catch up on, you and I."

Before I can get another word in, the line disconnects.

The phone slips out of my fingers and bounces against the seat next to me. I snatch it up and shove it in my jacket pocket as the driver pulls through the gates leading to the airstrip.

***

After what felt like the longest flight of my existence, I'm back at home in Washington, sitting stiffly on the couch next to Kade. Lex and Atlas are in the chairs across from us.

"Now that we know who took Calla," Kade says, "we just need to find out where they are."

"Selene's got a witch blocking their location," I say, pinching the bridge of my nose as I lean against the back of the couch. "The only shot we have of tracking them is using the bond I have with her."

"You don't think she's blocking that as well?" Lex questions.

I shrug, flicking my eyes over to him. "Won't know until I try it." Tapping into that bond is the very last thing I want to do—I haven't done it in decades—but if it means getting Calla back, I'm going to shove aside all my shit and do it.

"You want us here, brother?" Kade asks, his eyes on me. There's tension in his forehead; he's worried about me, though he doesn't know the history I have with my sire, he—along with the others—can likely sense the unease coursing through me.

I exhale a heavy breath. "Yeah. I know I owe you all an explanation—"

"Stop," Atlas cuts in, shaking his head. "You owe us nothing. Understand?"

"We're here for you," Lex chimes in. "That doesn't come with strings. You tell us what you want and when you want. Your terms, Gabe."

Nodding, I swallow hard. "Let's get this over with," I finally say.

"Try to relax," Atlas tells me, giving me a knowing look. Because the thought of any of us relaxing right now is pretty fucking laughable. Not with Calla out there with a psychotic vampire who is as unpredictable as she is powerful. She and Atlas are fairly close in years, both having been born to vampire bloodlines three centuries ago. He understands the magnitude of being a vampire's sire—another thing they have in common, and something I've never experienced aside from *being* sired.

I close my eyes, taking several breaths to steady my heart rate and even out my breathing. I focus on each core group of muscles in my body, one by one, forcing them to unclench. It takes a good ten minutes before I'm able to connect with the level of calm I'm typically able to achieve in a minute or so.

The room is silent, save for the beating of our hearts and soft breathing. No one speaks, they don't try to interfere, they're just here for me.

I tip my head back against the cushion and exhale slowly, pushing my senses outward. My fangs extend to their full length, my gums throbbing almost painfully. I try to visualize the image of my sire—the memory of her long, ivory hair and brilliant silver eyes. Her alabaster skin and dark lips. Just as her form starts to materialize in my head, every muscle in my body locks, and I grunt at the wicked sensation of hitting a solid wall of nothingness and being blasted backward. My eyes fly open, and I bark out a curse, my nerve endings tingling with electricity.

Kade grabs my arm. "What happened?" His eyes are narrowed, but concern fills his face.

"I..." My voice fades as I turn my gaze to Atlas. "I don't know. I thought it was working. Then it was like I ran into a wall out of nowhere and something shoved me back." I shake my head, trying to clear the thick, heavy fog there. "Could she be blocking me herself?"

Atlas frowns. "I haven't heard of that. The sire bond is an open connection, from the moment it snaps into place until one vampire perishes."

I rub at my temples, willing the deep ache to subside. "Then I have no idea what the hell just happened. I feel like she pushed me out." Shoving my hand through my hair, I get up, cursing again under my breath. Guilt weighs heavy on my chest, and the only way to make it fade is to get Calla back.

"We're going to figure this out," Kade says, looking up at me.

"How?" I practically growl. "You don't know her, Kade. She could be tormenting Calla every second that we don't find her. Messing with her head, *biting her*, telling her everything we've kept hidden to ensure her safety." I scoff, more to myself than at him. "And look where that got us," I grumble. "We have no idea what's happening to her, and this is my fault. Selene is trying to get to me by hurting Calla."

"Gabe, don't," Kade says in a firm voice, getting off the couch in a blur of movement and moving to stand in front of me.

"It's true," I snap. "I'm not strong enough to find out where she is."

Kade steps forward until we're nose-to-nose, and grabs my arms to keep me from moving away. "Yeah, and I was the one here when she left. How do you think I'm feeling about the situation?" His tone is sharp and there's a fire in his eyes that I know is reflected in mine.

I grip his arms, digging my fingers into his leather jacket. "She's in danger because of me," I say through my teeth, breathing hard. My heart is slamming against my ribcage with every painful beat.

Kade lets go of my arms and pulls free of my grip before cupping the side of my neck. "That's enough." His voice carries an authoritative tone I'm not used to hearing from him. He leans in, pressing his forehead to mine. It's cool against my fevered skin, and I shut my eyes, my pulse ticking unevenly.

"Kade—"

"Blaming yourself isn't going to bring her back, so quit it. We're going to find her." He tightens his grip on me, pulling me closer until our chests are pressed together. "Calla is going to come home, and we're going to kill the bitch that took her." He lowers his voice. "And who did this to you."

My chest tightens, and I pull away from him, walking around the couch. I head for the stairs leading to the second level. Lex calls my name, and I hear him move to follow me, but Atlas says, "Give him a minute."

I move with inhuman speed, not stopping until I'm in my bedroom, a closed door separating me from the rest of the world. I fall back against it, my hands clenched into fists at my sides and a muscle in my jaw ticking angrily.

I was our only chance, and I failed. If I'm to believe what Selene said on the phone, until Calla decides she wants to leave, we have no way of finding her.

SIX

CALLA

My footprints have to be imprinted in the floor by this point. I've been pacing back and forth across the room for what feels like hours. I really shouldn't be using my energy where I don't need to, but I've never been this restless. My skin itches and my mind is spinning.

I take a hesitant sniff of my underarm and recoil at the less than pleasant smell. Frankly, I stink. The thought of showering is both enticing and exhausting, but when I try to run my fingers through my hair to pull it back and they get tangled immediately, my mind is made up. I'll shower and then come up with a way out of here.

Closing myself in the en suite bathroom, I flip the lock over, as if that will do anything, and push the thin black straps off my shoulders. I shimmy a little until the slip dress reaches my hips, then falls to the shiny white marble floor in a pile of silk, and I kick it away with a scowl. I pad across the smooth floor and open the massive glass shower door, then frown when I can't find the dial to turn the damn thing on.

"What the hell?" I step back, letting out an annoyed breath when I find a touchscreen built into the wall. "You've got to be kidding me..." I cross my arms over my bare chest, staring at the screen for a few seconds as I pull my bottom lip between my teeth. I tap the screen a bunch of times until I finally figure out how to turn the hot water on. It cascades down from a wide-surfaced waterfall shower head, and I can't help but sigh when I step under the steaming spray.

I close my eyes and tip my head back, letting the hot water refresh me and ease the pounding in my head. I grab bottles and a loofah, scrubbing every inch of my skin until it tingles. The room smells of vanilla and roses, and the idea of staying in here forever is wildly enticing. Here, I can forget about everything. I can pretend for a short while that I wasn't kidnapped—*again*—and that I'm going to have to make Selene believe I've agreed to help her get Gabriel back if I want to make it out of this place.

My thoughts drift to the guys and what they're doing. In spite of being confused and angry as ever at the vault of secrets that seems to get more and more packed, there's a tugging in my chest. I don't want to, but I... I miss them. Lex's dry humor, Gabriel's softness, and Kade's flirting. Hell, I miss Atlas too, even with his constantly stoic and broody demeanor.

My fingers glide across my skin, brushing over the mounds of my breasts before heading lower. I keep my eyes shut, imagining I'm not in the shower alone. That instead, Atlas is here with me and it's *his* fingers teasing my skin as they get closer to the throbbing heat between my thighs. I pull in an uneven breath, leaning against the cool shower tile as I slide my hand down my stomach until my fingers reach my clit. I press my lips together at the bolt of electricity that shoots through me and trace the bundle of nerves at my center in slow, light circles, widening my stance slightly as water continues to shower down on me from above. Steam fills the room, making everything hazy and warm, and my breath becomes heavier. I dip a finger between my folds, sighing softly before quickly adding a second, imagining Atlas holding me back against the shower tile as he torments me with his fingers. I pick up the pace, circling my clit harder and faster with my thumb. Atlas wouldn't be gentle—he warned me as much—and that only spurs me on, my heart rate kicking up and pounding in my chest as pressure builds lower. I bite my lip to keep from moaning, thrusting my fingers harder, curling them at the deepest spot inside me until my knees start to shake. I lower myself onto the marble shower bench, spreading my legs as wide as they'll go, and resume thrusting. I climb higher and higher, all the while, picturing Atlas's dark gaze boring into mine as his fingers move inside me, hard and unforgiving, until an orgasm crashes into me, and I suck in a breath, pressing my free hand against my mouth to stifle the sound.

My cheeks and chest feel hot, almost feverish as I pull my fingers out, cleaning them before I turn off the water and stand on shaky legs to step out of the shower.

I wrap a towel around myself and walk over to the vanity, staring at my flushed appearance in the foggy mirror. *I can't believe I just did that.* But of all the crazy I've gone through in the last... however long I've been here, giving myself the release I desperately needed is probably the least crazy. I had a few minutes of peace and pleasure where I didn't have to think about the shitstorm I have an awful, gut-wrenching feeling I'm about to endure.

I dry my hair with another towel and walk back into the bedroom. In the closet next to the bathroom, I find a pair of black jogging pants and a heavy knit beige sweater—actively ignoring how creepy it is she has a closet stocked with clothing in my size—to tug on over my wet hair, which I manage to comb through after using about half the bottle of conditioner in the shower.

Taking a deep breath, I exhale slowly and open the bedroom door, stepping into the hallway. I peer around both ways, though the room I was in is pretty much at the end of the hall. I start walking the other way, the dark wood floor cold against my bare feet. The walls on either side of me are light gray and clear of any art, with ceilings that are high, lit with pot lights every couple of feet. There's a faint scent of bread in the air and the closer I get to the end of the hall, I start to hear soft music as well. I pause in the doorway, faintly recognizing the space from before Selene saved me from Dante... and then attacked me. My pulse jumps as my eyes flit to the spot on the floor Dante fell to in front of me, but there is no trace of what happened there.

"Oh, hello."

I jump at the timid female voice and whirl around to find an older woman with pale blue eyes staring at me.

She's human.

"I hope you haven't been waiting long," she says, glancing down to the black tray she's carrying. On top is a steaming dish of what looks to be some kind of stew along with a thick chunk of sourdough bread and a glass of water.

"I, uh... No." I shake my head for extra measure, wanting to reassure her that she's done nothing wrong. The thought of her being employed by Selene makes my skin crawl. She looks far too kind to be in this posi-tion, to be working for a vampire thirsty for power. Perhaps she doesn't know the truth about her employer. More likely, the poor human is glamoured.

The woman ushers me to the dining table and sets a spot for me, hurrying away before I have a second to thank her. It's not her fault I'm stuck here, so why shouldn't I be gracious toward someone showing me kindness? The way I see it, us humans have to stick together in this crazy supernatural world.

I take a seat and stare at the food for a few minutes. I'm aggressively *not* hungry, my stomach a swirling mess of nerves. But Selene was right about at least one thing—I need to eat something. I take a small sip of water before picking up the spoon and gingerly scooping some of the stew out of the dish. I lift it to my mouth and force myself to chew, swallowing slowly. I have no doubt whoever made it has cooking experience and uses only high-end ingredients—I wouldn't expect anything else from the vampire who lives here—but each bite I take tastes like dust and sits heavy in my stomach. It takes me a while, but I finish the entire dish, reminding myself with every swallow that I need to regain my strength.

I'm using the last bit of bread to soak up the remnants of the stew at the bottom of my dish when the soft *click, click, click* of heels echoes down the hallway. I glance up just in time to find Selene floating into the room, her fingers wrapped around a cup of tea. She walks over to the table and sits across from me, the subtle scent of peppermint wafting over from her steaming mug.

I finish off the bread, washing it down with the rest of my water, feeling more than a little awkward with Selene watching me silently.

Finally, she says, "I hope that was to your liking." Her tone is kind, almost as if we're friends. It's a laughable notion, one that also makes me drop my hands into my lap so she can't see me clench them into fists.

I offer a single nod in response, not bothering to look at her. Instead, I let my eyes wander across the intricate gold design of the table linen and listen to the soft jazz music still playing from behind a closed door nearby. In the kitchen, I'd guess, where the human Selene is most likely forcing to play housekeeper is probably doing dishes after serving my food.

Selene offers a small laugh. "Oh, come on, Calla. Your silence is absolutely deafening. Please say something. I suppose you might have more questions for me?" she offers. "Ask away. I'm an open book."

I lift my gaze to her face. "How much do you know about the deal my family made with Gabriel and the others?"

She purses her lips, regarding me with an amused look. "I'd venture a guess that I know far more than you do."

"Yeah, well, no one has really explained it to me in detail," I tell her. "Every time I ask, I get vague, non-answers."

She takes a sip of her tea, setting the mug down without making a sound against the table. "That must be incredibly frustrating."

I have the fleeting thought that I may not have the opportunity to ask anyone again, so I swallow past the sudden dryness in my throat and say, "Will you tell me what you know?"

She leans back a little, arching a brow at me. "Hmm. Will you agree to take the deal I put on the table earlier?"

My stomach drops. "I…" I look away, unable to hold her gaze as I force out the words. "I'm thinking about it."

There's a stretch of silence before she says, "Very well. I will share what I know of your bond with the vampires. Consider this your one free pass. I don't make a habit of giving without getting something in return."

I hold back an eye roll, knowing that will likely only result in her changing her mind about sharing information. Instead, I force out one low word. "Noted."

Selene presses her lips together as if she's making sure her lip color is still even. "How much do you know about the oath?"

I frown. "Stupidly little considering I'm the person it affects the most."

Her lips twitch. "Fair enough. Allow me to enlighten you." She moves her hair over her shoulder, fixing her gaze on me. "Your ancestor, whoever it was—"

"My great-great-grandfather," I cut in.

She blinks at me, then continues as if I didn't speak. "He was trying to make a name for himself, to provide for his family. The man was convinced to make an investment in a company on Wall Street. Of course, he wasn't in a place financially to do this, but after being convinced it was so low risk and his return would essentially set his family up for life, he was prepared to use every dollar he had."

My heart is in my throat, and I haven't taken a proper breath since she started talking. Since I learned of the blood oath, I've been equal parts dreading and desperate to find out what really happened. Now it seems I'm about to, and I'm gripped with panic.

"What he didn't know was that the investment he was going to make would only benefit a few people—it was what's now known as a Ponzi scheme.

"Before the money went through, he was tipped off that it was a scam and the company he was investing in was tied to a lot of shady men."

"Dante?" I ask, chewing the inside of my cheek.

She shakes her head. "Dante worked for them. When your great-great-grandfather backed out of the deal, Dante was sent after him to shut him up permanently. They couldn't risk being exposed as a sham. The night Dante went after him, one of your guys—the tattooed one, I think—stumbled upon them. As far as I know, it was by accident. A complete coincidence."

"Wait. Lex is the one who saved him?"

She inclines her head slightly. "Dante has always been an arrogant prick. A popular opinion clearly, because Lex decided to interrupt and mess with him. Lucky for your ancestor, Lex wouldn't let Dante kill him."

"But why?"

She shrugs. "You'd have to ask him."

"Wh-what happened after that?"

"Dante took off, and the man thanked Lex profusely. When he offered Lex anything in return for saving his life—"

I suck in a sharp breath. "You have got to be kidding me."

"You know Lex better than I do," she offers with a light shrug. "He asked if the man had a daughter."

My jaw clenches, and I grab the glass in front of me, only to find it empty. I set it down a little too hard.

"He was confused and told Lex he had a son."

"Let me guess, then Lex said he wanted the firstborn daughter?"

"That part of the story you know."

My eyes burn, and I blink quickly to keep the tears at bay. I wasn't expecting to get so emotional hearing how everything went down. "So what? He just agreed to it?"

Selene purses her lips. "Not at first. He was confused and angry and utterly refused. Until Lex shared his little secret." She flashes her fangs. "When he told him the men he screwed over by going back on his investment were powerful and would continue sending people like Dante after him if he wasn't under the protection of people stronger than them, he didn't have much of a choice. Terrified for his family's safety, he reluctantly agreed and went with Lex to meet the others. And the rest is history."

I swallow hard, pushing my plate away. "Right." Shaking my head, I exhale a slow breath, trying to make my head stop spinning. "And what about Atlas's involvement with the Ellis family? Do you know about that?"

A small smile plays at her crimson lips. "What do *you* know?"

I narrow my eyes at her. "Literally nothing. That's why I'm asking."

"I'm not sure what Atlas is up to with them. Perhaps it's a matter of self-preservation."

My brows pinch together, and I can already sense the beginning of a headache forming in my temples. "I don't understand."

"Being a vampire and keeping the company of vampire hunters is generally not a smart idea, but I'm assuming there's more to it. Atlas isn't so arrogant he would risk his existence without good reason."

What. The. Fuck.

"Vampire hunters," I breathe, nausea coiling in my stomach. I grip the edge of the table, my knuckles turning white under the pressure.

"Ah. This is the first you're hearing of them," she guesses, and I don't bother responding. My reaction is obvious enough. "If I can offer you one bit of advice, Calla—assume everything you believe to be a myth is real. Because it most likely is."

I sit in silence, unable to form a coherent thought, much less an intelligent response.

"You could escape all of this," she says. "If you do as I ask, I can bring back your normal, vampire-free life. Consider what that would mean for you, Calla. You would never have to experience being taken advantage of by the supernatural again. Never glamoured or fed on by a vampire..." She sets her tea down and stands, walking around the table.

I track her movement, my pulse kicking up the closer she gets to me. Before I can attempt to move away, Selene shoots forward at a speed too quick to see and grabs a fistful of my hair in her grip. I cry out as white-hot pain sears across my scalp, and Selene yanks my head back, exposing my throat as she bares her fangs. I don't have a moment to yelp, to beg her not to bite me before she sinks her fangs into my throat.

A scream tears from my lips before she presses a finger against them and the sound stops. My head spins in confusion and the rapid blood loss, and I faintly wonder if I'm being glamoured into silence.

Pain ripples through me like sandpaper in my veins, and I squeeze my eyes shut, screaming internally. I can't move, can't try to shove her back or pull away. Wetness tracks down my cheeks, and a whimper slips through my lips when her grip tightens for a moment before she pulls away from my neck.

When Selene steps back, licking my blood from her lips, I fall against the chair, my shoulders slumping with exhaustion. My eyelids flutter, fighting to stay open as darkness threatens to claim me. My vision ebbs in and out, and there's a dull ringing in my ears.

Selene speaks, but her voice sounds far away and muffled. "Hmm, perhaps now I understand why those boys keep you around." She flicks her tongue along her bottom lip, smirking at me. "You *are* delicious."

Nausea rolls through me as I grip the table in front of me until my knuckles turn white, pulling myself upright as best I can.

She says nothing more before turning and walking away.

I glare at her retreating form and grab the linen that came with my food, pressing it against the puncture marks Selene didn't bother to heal. It takes me at least three attempts to stand. My knees keep giving out, dropping me back into the chair. Tears burn my eyes, and I grit my teeth, hauling myself upright once more. This time, I'm able to stand. I use the table to walk, hesitating when I reach the end. There's still a good ten feet to the hallway without any support. I take a deep breath, putting one foot in front of the other until I make it there and fall against the wall. I manage to use it to make my way back to the room I woke in, closing the door behind me before shuffling to the bathroom where I collapse against the vanity. I stare angrily at the sickly pale reflection looking back at me. She is all too human. Weak.

I drop the bloodstained linen into the sink and back away from the vanity until I hit the closed bathroom door. My knees buckle, and I slide to the floor, pulling my legs to my chest. I bite my lip in an attempt to stop it from trembling, but my chin still quivers as my vision blurs with hot tears. I can't hold them back, not now that I'm alone. They fall down my cheeks, the lump in my throat quickly growing thicker, and the pit in my stomach heavier than ever.

For a moment, I miss how things were. Anything is better than this, including living in a mansion with four vampires who did anything and everything to keep me in the dark. Now, knowing... well, likely not everything, but a lot more than before, I have even more questions that are making my head spin. I shove a hand through my hair to push it away from my face and wince when my fingers brush the bite mark on the side of my neck. Having experienced both ways of being fed on—the pleasurable and the painful—I would take being bitten by one of the guys over another vampire any day.

I sigh and tip my head back against the door. My best friend's family are vampire hunters. Super inconvenient when I live in a house full of them.

As far as I know, Brighton has no idea what her family does. She doesn't know about vampires—Kade made sure of that when I told her about them. Either she honestly had no idea before I blabbed, or she was a damn good actor that day at the waterfront.

Chewing my bottom lip, I tear at the skin there, choosing to focus on the discomfort of that instead of the weight in my chest. I may have gotten answers to some of my questions, but those only prompted more questions. I still have no idea what the guys were planning before Dante swiped me off the street the other night, or how I would've been involved in it. I suppose that's a problem to address once I've made it out of the clutches of the psychotic vampire in the other room. But as it stands, I don't have a fucking chance against her.

When I was a new vampire, following my sire around like the lost puppy I was, we spent a short period of time in Washington, feeding our way through the city, from the seedy bars and nightclubs in the downtown core to a small bed and breakfast we spent one of our first nights together after I'd turned.

Of all the things I can remember from my time with Selene, I wish I could forget that night. We'd spent it drinking at a tiny, hole-in-the-wall pub not far from the B&B. It was long past midnight by the time we stumbled in for the night, of course waking every visitor in the place, as well as the owner. Instead of apologizing, which I immediately sought to do, Selene grabbed the guest closest to her and ripped into her throat.

The rest of that night is a blurry memory filled with terrified screams and blood. So much blood. I lost myself in it. The moment the crimson spilled onto the soft white carpet at my feet, my world narrowed on one thing—feeding.

Between the two of us, we tore through every human in the place. When we left the following morning, there were bodies littered all over the floor and staircase. Blood soaked into the carpet and hardwood, splatters going up the crinkled wallpaper in every room.

We had massacred two dozen humans for no other reason than entertainment.

My stomach roils at the memory; I've never told the guys the story of how I turned. They've gathered over our years together that it was less than voluntary, and they know who my sire is, but that's about it. I don't want them to know what I did or the monster I was. My reluctance to share has nothing to do with them—I trust them all with my life—and has everything to do with my own shame.

I give my head a firm shake to try and clear it. *I need to focus.*

Selene likely still has property in the vicinity, but even with my connections to the local government and law enforcement, I'm unable to track them down. By now, to protect herself from her growing list of enemies, any property she owns in the city is no doubt in someone else's name. I didn't consider myself one of her enemies—not until she came after Calla.

The four of us sit around the dining room table, drinking mugs of microwaved blood. It's taking the chill out of my bones, but that's about it. I still feel weaker than I ever have before. I scowl at the slight tremor in my wrist as I lower the mug to the table.

"We're going to find her," Lex says, and I flick a glance across the table at him. His usually bright white hair is faded and dull. It isn't styled—it's not even combed. It looks as if he got out of the shower, ran a towel over it, and called it good enough. He's wearing a wrinkled black hoodie, with darkness in his eyes that is mirrored on the others' faces as well. I'm sure my appearance is similarly dark and disheveled.

Atlas nods at Lex in agreement, wiping the blood from his lip with the edge of his thumb. He turns his silver gaze to me. "And when we do, you don't need to worry. I will handle Selene."

The knots in my stomach give an uncomfortable, almost painful tug. As badly as I want to shred her porcelain skin to ribbons of flesh and muscle, sink my teeth into her throat and drain every last drop of blood from her body before ripping out her heart and burning it to ash, I *physically* can't. The born vampire that turns a human is protected against them should they ever turn on their sire. I can't bring harm to Selene. And while I can't be the one to bring an end to her miserable, murderous eternity, I will sure as hell be there to watch it come to fruition.

With her many years and powerful bloodline, Atlas is likely one of the only vampires we know that is strong enough to take her on, and he won't be doing it alone. Lex and Kade will back him up. Regardless of the fact he only turned Lex and not Kade or me, the four of us are bonded in a way unlike any blood oath or sire bond—by *choice.*

I nod, frowning at the pull of exhaustion in my muscles. I'm sure they're feeling it too. The blood we've consumed tonight wasn't fresh, and we're all suffering for it. "I don't want to make this about Selene. That's exactly what she wants. Let's just focus on finding our girl."

Atlas claps me on the shoulder from where he's sitting diagonally across from me at the head of the table. "We're going to get her back." His voice is deep and smooth, commanding. He says the words as if there's no other option, and something like hope flickers in my chest.

Kade props his chin on his hand, closing his eyes. "While we're all here, we should probably talk about our friends with the pointy murder devices."

I let out a heavy sigh. "Yeah, all right. When I talked to Marcel last, there hadn't been any new developments from his end to report. I'm assuming that is still the case, otherwise we would have heard from him."

"I spoke to my team in Vancouver about an hour ago. One of our guys intercepted some intel from Ellis Industries regarding a new site."

"Fuck," Lex grumbles, "they found more white ash?"

Atlas nods, his expression grim. "From what I can tell through company communications, they don't plan to start development until the summer."

"Let's burn it down before then," Kade suggests. "Problem solved."

"One of the lesser problems, unfortunately," Atlas says. "The number of hunters is steadily increasing across the map. Our only saving grace at this point is that they have to be more careful with how they're getting rid of vampires. In the age of social media, it's becoming rapidly more difficult to keep the existence of hunters—and vampires—secret from the general population. There's always someone around with a camera."

"Nothing stays secret forever," Lex says in a low voice, his eyes trained on where he's drumming his fingers against the top of the table.

I scratch the stubble at my chin; I still need to shave. "It's going to take a lot for Calla to forgive us... to trust us after keeping Brighton's family's involvement in our world from her." I'd never been particularly fond of keeping her in the dark, but it was necessary. We had no idea what she would do with the information—and she would've had no idea how dangerous that information was in the wrong hands.

I suppose it's too late now. She knows part of the truth at least. And whatever Selene tells her for her own personal gain. I force my jaw to unclench and glance around the table. "Perhaps it's time we show her a little trust?" I offer. "As much as we've asked of her anyway."

Kade tilts his head, looking at me with uncertainty in his tired gaze for a brief moment before nodding. "When we get her back, and we *will* get her back, I think it's time we tell her everything. No more secrets. She's a part of this now."

"She's a part of us," Lex adds.

Another look around the table, and it's clear we're all in agreement. Atlas's jaw is set tight and there's a familiar darkness in his eyes, but he nods, even if he isn't happy about it.

No more secrets.

EIGHT

CALLA

The sound of tense conversation reaches me before I'm fully awake. Muffled, angry voices pull me out of bed, and I wince at the throbbing pain in my neck. I brush the sleep-tangled hair away and trace my fingers over the raised skin, biting my lip as I tiptoe toward the closed door. My movements are slow and hesitant as I wrap my fingers around the cool doorknob and turn it, tensing as I wait for the metal to creak and alert Selene to my presence. Letting out a breath when it doesn't make a sound, I open the door a crack and turn my head so my ear is positioned to hear what's being said from somewhere down the hall, likely the living room.

A gruff curse makes me jump, and my stomach clenches in the same moment my heart sinks as I recognize the male voice. It's Scott Ellis—Brighton's dad.

"You better watch yourself." Selene's voice slices through the silence, sharp and filled with venom. Hatred.

Scott offers a harsh laugh, as if he finds her threatening response to whatever he said to be pathetic. "We'll be in touch."

My brows knit in confusion, and a moment later, the front door slams shut, echoing through the place.

I close the door and lean against it, trying to come up with a reasonable explanation for Scott meeting with Selene. What would a vampire hunter be doing at the home of a born vampire *alone* and without trying to, you know, hunt them? It doesn't make sense.

With a sigh, I push away from the door and walk across the bedroom, slipping into the bathroom to freshen up before changing into a pair of black jeans and a maroon sweatshirt from the closet.

I comb my hair and finally leave the room, walking down the hallway with an uneven pulse and swirling nerves in my stomach.

Rounding the corner into the dining room and living room area, I find Selene lounging on the couch in front of a blazing fire, sipping what smells like coffee from a massive white mug. The half-full french press on the table in front of the couch beckons me closer, but the vampire guarding it keeps me back.

"Good morning," she says without giving any indication that she heard me approach. She keeps her back to me, cradling the mug in her hands, the matte red polish on her nails a sickening reminder of her brutal attack last night.

"Is it?" I blurt before I can stop myself and cringe, quickly recovering by adding, "I mean, that really depends on whether or not you're going to share that coffee."

She chuckles, finally turning her face to look at where I'm lingering near the hallway. "I suppose that's fair considering the drink I took from you last night."

My jaw clenches, and I bite my tongue to keep from saying something that will only get me in trouble. Instead, I force a smile and approach the seating area around the fireplace, picking the gray wing-back chair, keeping as far away from Selene as I possibly can.

The moment my ass touches the chair, the human woman from yesterday hurries into the room with an empty mug, smiling warmly at me as she pours the coffee, setting the mug on the table in front of me.

"Breakfast will be ready shortly," she announces, turning her attention to Selene, and bows her head.

"Thank you," Selene says in a dismissive tone without looking at her housekeeper, and the woman retreats just as quickly as she came in.

I stare at the vampire over my steaming mug, my eyes narrowed as the warmth of the mug in my hand radiates through my fingers.

Selene scowls. "You can lose the judgy eyes, Calla. I compensate her very well for the work she does for me."

"Do you feed on her?" The words leave my mouth before I can stop them. My voice is barely above a whisper, but I have no doubt the vampire heard me.

"No." Her sharp silver eyes slam into me, and she drags her tongue over her dark red lips tauntingly. "I don't need to." Her words hold an unspoken threat that makes my chest tighten.

When she rises from the couch and walks to the dining room table, taking a seat at the head of it, I hesitate before following her. It doesn't take long for the human woman whose name I still don't know to bring out a steaming plate of seasoned potatoes with an omelet folded beside it and a colorful bowl of various berries. My stomach growls, but the savory smell has nausea rippling through me. I need to eat, to keep up what little strength I have, but the thought of picking up a fork and putting food in my mouth makes me want to bend over the side of my chair and vomit on the marble floor. I settle for pushing the food around my plate, forcing myself to swallow a berry every so often. It's not enough, but it's something. And considering my appetite is nowhere to be found since Selene tore into my throat yesterday, maybe I should give myself some credit.

Selene remains silent, sipping from a crystal glass of thick, dark red liquid.

Yeah, that sure as hell isn't helping my nausea.

"Have you given my offer any thought?"

Something in me cracks, and I drop the fork onto the plate in front of me, lifting my gaze to meet hers. "Do you know why they took me?" When she arches a brow at me, I shake my head. "Never mind, that was stupid to ask. Of course you do. That's why you thought getting me to turn on them would be easy, right?"

She purses her dark red lips. "Don't tell me you've made the mistake of caring for them?" Her tone is light, but there's a hint of slightly mocking disappointment there. Are we besties? Hell to the no. But that doesn't mean I want to see Gabriel stuck with Selene. I don't know the story of how he became a vampire aside from it being her who turned him, but if I had to bet—after my short time in Selene's company—the circumstances were less than ideal. As much as I want out of the arrangement that ties me to the guys *for as long as I shall live* or whatever, there has to be a better way. A way that doesn't damn Gabriel to an eternity with her.

"I didn't mean to," I admit, and I have no idea why.

She rolls her eyes. "You're overthinking this entire thing. Help me, and we can both get what we want. I know what you must think of me, but I do care about Gabriel. I turned him all those years ago to be with him forever. I never wanted to be separated from him... and those bastards—" She stops herself when the tone of her voice sharpens, then sighs softly. "They kept us apart for decades, and I want him back. I want my family back, Calla. Surely, you can understand that. Let's work together—this can be mutually beneficial. I want my old life back as much as you want yours."

I swallow the lump in my throat, my jaw clenched tight as I force back tears. Being offered something that would give me everything I want but that I can't accept hurts like nothing I've experienced before. I clear my throat, then say, "How could you break the blood oath anyway? I mean, theoretically?"

Amusement flickers in her gaze, giving me a brief moment to notice the shimmering dark blue shadow around her eyes, lined with a sharp cat-eye flick and long, dark lashes. "I've made many powerful friends over the centuries. Some of which have the power to sever the ties your blood has to the vampires who claim you."

I shake my head at her. "The power to sever a blood oath?" My stomach drops and unease prickles up my spine. "Like... magic?" The word is foreign on my tongue and sounds utterly ridiculous. So much so, I almost laugh.

Her lips twitch. "Don't look so surprised, Calla. Surely witches aren't too far of a stretch of the imagination once you've spent so much time with vampires."

I blink, trying—and failing—to wrap my head around her words. "I just... I hadn't considered that."

She offers a tight smile. "I can see that."

"Okay, so let's say I agree to your terms. You'll let me leave?"

Selene tilts her head to the side. "That's right."

"And you expect Gabriel to what? Just willingly leave his life behind and come join you?"

A chill races through me when the vampire smiles at me.

"He will," she says in a confident tone, "because if he doesn't, you'll be the one paying the price."

"You'll kill me," I say without missing a beat.

She purses her lips and runs her fingers through her hair idly. "Do you want to be a vampire, Calla?"

My brows knit in confusion, and I stare at her. "N-no." That avenue is not something I've ever let myself consider. My answer is more automatic than necessarily truthful, but I cling to it with everything I have, because the alternative... Becoming a vampire is just too damn terrifying to consider. Thinking about tomorrow is too overwhelming at this point. Toss eternity into the mix? No fucking way my mental state will survive that.

"Hmm." Her lips curl into a wicked smirk, as if my answer was exactly what she was expecting—and hoping for. "Then you will have Gabriel return to me. Otherwise, I'll turn you myself."

Panic clamps down on my chest, stealing my breath as my eyes widen. "You can't," I stammer. "I know how vampires are made, and I haven't—" My voice cuts off, and I clamp my mouth shut. She fed me her blood to heal Dante's bite marks and has been glamouring me all week. She could have easily forced me to drink it at any time, and I wouldn't remember. Bile rises in my throat, and I swallow hard. "Wh-what did you do?"

Selene rolls her eyes, managing to make even that look graceful. "No need for theatrics, Calla. Try to understand. I couldn't take any chances. I needed a contingency plan in the event you wouldn't take my deal." She shrugs, as if this whole thing isn't potentially life-changing for me. "So, you're going to go back to your little vampire hostel and tell Gabriel he needs to come back to me. So long as he does as he's told, you have nothing to worry about. My blood will work its way out of your system, same with the venom from my bite, and you'll be fine." Her voice lowers and hardens. "If he doesn't, there won't be a vampire on this earth who will be able to stop me from tracking you down and siring you to me. So really, it's either you or him." The corner of her mouth kicks up. "And no offense, but I'd much prefer him."

I press my lips together to keep them from trembling. "You are fucking insane," I seethe. "This is all some messed up game to you. This is my life. You're screwing with someone's life!"

"A game?" she breathes, a muscle feathering along her jaw as she traps my gaze with hers. Selene shakes her head. "I've told you why this needs to be done, and still..." Her fangs flash, extending to their full length, and I instinctively lean back from the table, my heart beating a little faster. In the time it takes me to blink, she moves, appearing beside my chair and hauling me up by the shoulder. The jerky, quick movement sends the chair to the floor, and I immediately fight to pull away from her. The moment she sinks her fangs into the delicate skin between my neck and shoulder, I scream. I can't help it. As much as I want to be strong and refuse to show weakness in her presence, the agony-filled sound rips through me before I can clamp my jaw shut. Ice fills my veins, but the spot Selene drinks from burns hotter than anything I've ever felt. I use every ounce of strength I have left and struggle against her, pulling hard, which only makes the feeding hurt far worse. Instead, I try pushing her away, but that gets me nowhere as dizziness crashes into me in waves, bringing with it a wicked nausea deep in my belly.

Selene growls at my struggle, shoving me back against the table. The blunt edge digs into my side, but I barely feel it. I put my arms back to catch myself, and my heart races when my fingers brush the knife next to my plate. I pick it up and swing blindly, praying it's enough to get her to stop drinking from me. If she takes much more, I'm going to collapse—and I might not get back up. I pull my hand back as she snarls viciously, then drops the blood-covered silver to the floor. The sound rings through my ears sharply, and I wince, the edges of my vision starting to blur and darken as I sway on my feet.

"You little bitch," she snaps, and her voice sounds as if we're underwater. Muffled and far away. As the wound quickly seals itself, she bares her fangs that are dripping with my blood; my attack did nothing but piss her off.

I open my mouth to say... what? I have no idea. But it doesn't matter. Before I can get a word in, Selene grabs me by the throat and slams my head into the table. Glass shatters and food goes flying. The room spins violently fast around me and every inch of my body hurts. Probably not as much as it should, which isn't a good thing. I'm starting to lose it, to go numb. I pull myself up, gripping the table to remain standing, and the second I catch my breath, Selene comes at me, backhanding me so hard across the face, my mouth fills with blood. I choke on it, spitting what I can onto the floor as I keel over, groaning. Sinking to the floor, my cheek presses against the cold marble. All I can smell is my own blood. The bitter, copper scent makes my stomach clench as my head pounds. Warmth trickles down the side of my face, and I don't have to reach up and touch it to know it's blood.

As my eyes start to close on their own, the pain ebbs away. The chill in my bones thaws, replaced by a soft, pleasant warmth.

I think this might be what dying feels like.

We all sense her at once.

Calla's presence returns just as quickly as it faded just over a week ago.

The four of us converge in the living room within seconds, but before we can get out the door, my phone chimes. With three sets of silver eyes on me, I pull it out and open the text.

"It's Selene," I say in a gravelly voice. "She says not to bother going after Calla. She's... she's heading to us anyway."

What the hell?

I shake my head, anger and confusion coursing through me at record-breaking speeds. A quick glance at the others tells me they're experiencing the same.

"She's just giving her back?" Kade says, crossing his thick arms over his chest. His eyes are narrowed and filled with doubt and suspicion. I don't blame him. He doesn't know Selene—none of them do. They don't know what she'll do to get what she wants—whatever the hell that is this time.

"That doesn't make any fucking sense," Lex adds, his brows furrowed as he looks to me. "What game is she playing, Gabriel?"

I wish I had a better answer than the one I give. "Your guess is as good as mine. None of this makes sense."

Atlas remains silent, but the dark look on his face says it all. He's ready to go to war.

We take turns pacing the room while the others sit around, waiting. It's driving us all nuts, feeling her getting closer. The connection isn't as strong as it once was, which could be from her being away from us for so long. Magic is unpredictable that way.

Half an hour after the text from Selene, a town car with tinted windows pulls into the driveway. We're outside before the vehicle has a chance to shift into park, and Kade is a blur of movement, tearing down the stone steps and opening the back seat. The smell of her blood hits me, and every muscle in my body tenses. My gums throb as a growl rumbles in my chest before I move to stand beside Kade, sucking in a shallow breath at the sight of Calla, half-conscious and covered in her own blood in the back seat.

Lex curses in a sharp tone and moves toward the driver's door, but Atlas grabs his arm, pulling him back.

"He's human. Likely hired help." There's a warning in his voice. Translation: *don't kill the driver*.

Lex tears his arm away from his sire's grip and stomps off toward the house as Kade scoops Calla's limp, entirely too pale body into his arms and carries her inside. Atlas and I follow close behind. I steal a glance at him, wondering if he's struggling to not breathe in the scent of her blood as much as I am. The other two seem to be channeling it into rage. The thought of wanting to taste her blood again—right now of all moments—makes me sick to my core. I wholeheartedly despise the part of me I have to fight to keep control over. The part that wants to feed on the human Kade is laying on the couch with a gentleness I'm not sure I've ever seen from the vampire before.

She's barely alive.

My eyes scan the room, pausing on each of my brothers. There's a fire in Lex's eyes, but something else as well. He's scared—for Calla. Kade is sitting on the coffee table in front of the couch, stroking Calla's matted dark brown hair, brushing the messy waves away from her face. Under her eyes are dark, only made more prominent by her colorless complexion. Dried blood sticks to her chin, almost as if *she* was feeding, and my chest constricts at the thought. The front of her sweater is stained crimson, caused by blood running down her neck from the deep puncture marks there.

Atlas stands behind the couch, his arms gripping the back of it so tight his knuckles have gone white. His eyes are locked on her face, his jaw clenched tight.

"She's waking up," Kade says in a rough voice.

I move forward immediately, standing on one side of Kade, while Lex shifts to the other side.

Her eyelids flutter and her body tenses. When her brows pinch together and her chin starts trembling, I feel as if someone has stuck a hot poker through my chest.

She's in pain.

"Calla," Kade murmurs, cupping her cheek. His thumb brushes over her skin, as if he's trying to coax her awake. "Open your eyes for us. Please." That last word is a faint whisper, tinged with something awfully close to desperation.

I finally let out a breath when she opens her eyes. They're slits at first as she winces at the light above us. Lex quickly moves to shut it off. It's still daylight outside, which likely isn't helping.

"We should move her to the other room and draw the curtains. The sunlight—"

"I don't think we should move her," I cut in, unable to tear my eyes away from her frail body. "Not until she's healed."

Kade leans back slightly as Calla blinks her eyes open a bit more, then he bites into his wrist, moving to feed her—to heal her.

She stiffens, making a feeble attempt to move away from him before gasping for breath and collapsing against the cushions. "N-no," she stammers weakly, her voice raspy, *broken*.

The sound rips right through me, and guilt digs its claws deeper. This... Calla being in this pain is *my* fault. Selene intervening in her life, bringing this upon her... None of it would've happened if it weren't for me and my ties to the vampire who did this to her.

Kade's eyes narrow. "No? What do you mean, no?" He looks to me, then to Atlas, as if searching for direction. His expression softens as he looks back at her, and I know where this is heading. He's going to glamour her.

"Kade," she warns—not that it holds much strength. But he pauses, hanging onto her every word. "Please, no." She shakes her head, making it very clear she doesn't want his blood.

"Why not?" Lex asks, crouching in front of the couch to be closer to her. He slides his fingers through hers slowly, curling them around the back of her hand, his eyes searching her face.

Calla presses her lips together, flicking a glance toward where Atlas stands over her. Her brows pinch again and she lets out a shaky breath. "Selene bit me. More than once. Her venom is in my veins." She closes her eyes again, as if she can't bear to hold them open any longer. "And so is her blood."

"You drank her blood?" Atlas asks, speaking for the first time.

Her lips turn down. "No. I-I mean, yes." Tension fills her features, and she keeps her eyes shut. "I... I don't remember it. I didn't... even know it happened until Selene told me that she..." Her voice trails off and her eyes open, finding mine in an instant and knocking the air out of my chest.

I fight the urge to reach for her, to pull her against me and feel her heartbeat against my chest. To make sure she's really alive. "What did she tell you, angel?" I ask in a gentle tone.

She blinks quickly. "Gabriel, I..." She sniffles, struggling to hold my gaze. "I'm so sorry." Her chin quivers, but she continues, "If I die now, with her blood and venom in my system..."

Kade shakes his head. "Hey." He turns her face to meet his gaze. "That isn't going to happen. You're here, you're safe now."

"Safe." She chokes on the word.

"You need vampire blood to heal," Atlas says in a firm voice.

"What I *need* is for you to listen to me. For once." Her eyes flick between Kade's. "No more vampire blood. Just the thought of it makes me so nauseous my head won't stop spinning."

"Okay," Kade says.

I frown at the back of his head. That's it? We're just going to let her stay in this pain while her injuries heal at a human pace? My pulse kicks up, along with the throbbing in my gums as my fangs threaten to cut through. When a deep growl rattles through me, Atlas moves around the couch and grabs me by the arm, dragging me out of the room. He doesn't stop until we're in the formal sitting room, far enough away that Calla won't hear when I shove him away and snap, "What the hell was that?"

"You needed a minute," is all he says, standing between me and the hallway back to the other room.

"I need for her not to die," I correct him sharply.

He blinks at me. "She's not going to die, Gabriel. Take a breath and calm down. You getting worked up and pissed right the fuck off isn't going to help her. She will heal. Yes, far slower than if she drank our blood, but that's her choice. We're giving her that now, remember?" There's an edge to his voice that makes me think he's not finding it all that easy keeping it together right now either. He's certainly doing a better job at it than me.

"She'll suffer for what she did to Calla," I vow in a dark tone.

Atlas steps close again and claps me on the shoulder. "Yes," he agrees, "and it will be my pleasure to carry that out." He holds my gaze for a moment, then nods. "But for now, we need to take care of the human in the other room." He's right.

I inhale through my nose, pulling in a deep breath to try to center myself, then exhale slowly through my mouth. I nod at him before the two of us walk back to the other room to find Lex cleaning the blood off Calla's face and neck. Kade moved onto the couch in the few minutes we were gone and has Calla in his lap, her back against his chest and their legs stretched out in front of them while he strokes her hair.

Lex sets the bloodstained cloth down and helps her take a small drink of water before he moves out of the way, murmuring about making her something to eat as he heads into the kitchen across the room.

I approach at a calm pace, taking the spot Kade had been in on the coffee table before he moved to the couch with her. Calla's eyes follow me, and I lean forward, catching her chin gently, tilting her face up just enough that our gazes are level. "I need you to tell us what happened, angel."

She blinks at me, slowly registering my words. Her chin trembles as she opens her mouth to respond, then stops. Her jaw clenches against my fingers, and part of me fully expects her to yell, to scream at us for the secrets and lies.

Instead, she bursts into tears.

TEN

The tears come without warning. I've been trying so damn hard to keep them back, because I was terrified that once they started, I wouldn't be able to get them under control. And here we are. My shoulders shake with silent sobs, and I bury my face in Kade's chest, not wanting them to see me like this. The warmth of him, the steady beat of his heart against my cheek is grounding. And as much as I want to scream at them for everything they kept from me, the strength I'd need to do that isn't something I have right now. There's so much more I need to know—that *they* need to tell me, but for once, I'm glad they aren't just yet. I don't think I have it in me right now.

I use the back of my sweater sleeve to dry my cheeks. The tears slow, and I sniffle, staring out at the water in the pool as it glitters in the afternoon sunlight. I feel better, at least a little. The pressure in my chest from holding back the tears has eased, though it's been replaced by a pounding in my head—from the crying. I'm not sure where the tears came from, perhaps feeling relatively safe after not having a clue what was going on at Selene's triggered my body to release what I've been keeping locked up tight. Because, despite the lingering confusion and anger I hold with regards to the secret-keeping—especially about Brighton's family—I *do* feel safe here. With them. But it's moments like these, where that security makes me feel weak instead of strong, and I hate it.

Atlas disappears for a minute before returning, stopping in the kitchen and filling a glass of water before approaching the couch. He holds out the water glass in one hand and opens his other palm to reveal two white pills. "You should take these with food," he says pointedly but doesn't attempt to glamour me to eat something. Huh. Maybe I've finally made some progress then. Or he can tell by looking at me that the chances of vomit ending up all over the floor if he does force me to eat are too high to risk having to deal with.

I take the pills from his hand, then the glass. My hand shakes a little as I bring it to my lips and take a drink before tossing the pills back, followed by another mouthful of water to wash them down. I don't meet his gaze, nor do I thank him. Part of me wants to refuse the painkillers, but without them, the pounding in my temples is only going to get worse.

The five of us sit in silence for a while. I doze in and out of sleep, while Kade continues running his fingers over my hair. I'm clinging to the warmth of his chest against my back more than I care to admit—and I never will out loud.

When I open my eyes next, the sun is setting outside and Kade and I are alone. I rub my eyes and struggle to sit up, finally managing it with help.

"Easy, Calla," Kade murmurs.

"Wh-where is everyone?" I turn to look at him, my eyes tracing the hard lines of his face as I itch to reach forward and run my fingers along his jaw. Softness fills his silver gaze, along with a flicker of concern as he watches me, his dark hair falling across his forehead.

"Atlas is in his office and the others went out to pick up food for dinner and a first aid kit." His fingers brush along my neck, making me shiver as he reaches the marks Selene left on me.

"Not used to needing that, I suppose," I say, lowering my gaze, wanting to close my eyes against his gentle touch.

He laughs softly. "Yeah, not so much." He cups my cheek, tilting my face back up. "How are you feeling? No bullshit."

I blink my eyes open. "Better, I think." The splitting headache is gone, and I don't feel as if my chest is going to explode from the pressure building inside me. My muscles still ache, but I imagine that will last for some time, same with the cuts and bruises I sustained at Selene's hand. But I'd much rather deal with that than risk drinking vampire blood right now.

Kade nods. "Good. Are you hungry?"

I press my lips together. The thought of food doesn't immediately make me nauseous, so that's a step in the right direction. "I can try to eat something."

"Glad to hear it." His fingers slip away from my cheek, and he taps the tip of my nose. "Gabriel mentioned making risotto. Think you'd be up for that?"

I nod, then shift away so I'm not pressed right against him. Sitting up, I slowly drop my legs over the edge of the couch, planting my stocking feet on the floor. I brace my hands on either side of myself and take a deep breath.

"Where do you think you're going?" Kade asks in a gentle tone before I can attempt to stand.

I sigh. "I need to get out of these clothes. Should probably shower too." I feel gross, and there's definitely blood dried into my hair.

In a blur of movement, Kade is in front of me, leaning down and sliding his arm around my waist, guiding me up until I'm standing. My balance is slightly off, so I'm glad he's there to lean against, but I feel ridiculous needing his help just to get off the couch.

"There you go," he says softly in my ear.

"You going to help me in the shower too?" I try to joke. "Wash my hair and everything?"

He doesn't miss a beat. "You say that like I won't." Kade lowers his face, pressing his lips against my hair. "Or are you thinking about the last time I took you in the shower?"

My face flushes, and I close my eyes. "Evidently, *you* are."

He chuckles, then kisses my cheek. "Always. I'm never not thinking about the next time I'll get to have you." His grip on my waist tightens. "But I don't think you're ready for that yet."

No. I suppose I'm not.

Kade helps me to my room and into the bathroom, where he pulls my pants down until I can step out of them as I hold onto his shoulders. I lift my arms over my head, wincing at the ache in them, and he quickly pulls my sweater off, dropping it on the floor. He lifts me onto the vanity without any effort, leaving me sitting there for a few seconds while he turns on the shower and pulls out fresh towels, setting them next to me. His hands find my thighs, warming my bare skin while steam fills the room around us, but his eyes don't wander. He holds my gaze, those bright silver eyes flicking between mine.

"What?" I ask in a low voice, my cheeks filling with heat.

The corners of his mouth curve up. "I'm glad you're back."

I blink in surprise. I'm not sure what I was expecting him to say, but apparently not that. "I..." I can't say it back. Because as much as I'm glad not to be locked up with Selene, I still have a lot to work through with the guys before I get to a place where I'm glad to be here.

"It's okay." He reaches up and tucks my hair behind my ear. "We have a lot to discuss—when you're ready."

My brows pinch closer. "We do?" I ask, hoping he'll offer more than that.

Kade nods, then lifts me off the counter, keeping his hands on my waist even after my feet are planted on the floor. "When you were gone, the four of us agreed it's time. No more secrets."

I drop my gaze so he doesn't see my eyes widen. "Oh." I'm finally going to get some answers, to understand what's truly going on here. It's what I want, and yet, there's a newly forming pit in my stomach telling me that I might not be ready for it.

"Do you want me to help you into the shower?" he asks.

I meet his gaze again. "You're asking this time?"

He smirks. "Yeah. Don't get used to it. I'm being nice because you're all sad and hurt."

I laugh—actually laugh. It's the first time in... I can't even remember how many days. The sound of my own laugh is foreign to my ears. "You're such a gentleman," I remark dryly.

He tweaks my chin. "We both know that's not true." He glances toward the shower before looking back at me. "You're good then?"

"You'll hear if I fall on my ass."

Kade leans in and presses his lips against my cheek. "Take your time and holler if you need me."

I nod silently and watch him leave the room, pulling the sliding door shut. With a deep breath, I step away from the support of the vanity and slowly make my way into the shower, where I proceed to spend the next hour washing every bit of me until I finally feel as if I might have cleaned the time I spent with Gabriel's sire off my skin.

Showered and dressed in my own clothing, I feel significantly better. The hot water eased the aches and pains in my muscles, and the fog in my head seems to have mostly cleared. I think I'm even a little hungry.

I walk out of the closet and freeze when I step into the bedroom and find Atlas standing in the corner, looking out the window with his back to me. My eyes immediately go to the door to the hallway, finding it shut. "What are you doing?" I finally ask.

Atlas turns to face me, and even from across the room, his dark silver gaze does things to me I don't want to think about. Because I am still very much pissed at him, and despite thinking of him while I was trapped at Selene's, I find myself fighting the urge to scream at him.

"Waiting for you," he says in a tone that suggests his answer is quite obvious.

My eyes narrow. "And you felt the need to do that in here?"

He crosses the room at an unhurried pace, closing the distance between us as he says, "Considering I own this house, I can do whatever I like, *wherever* I like."

I fold my arms over my chest, refusing to back away even when he stops so close I can feel his breath against my forehead. I stare at his chest, the sharp, black V-neck shirt he's wearing. "What do you want, Atlas?"

"Right at this very moment?" He snags my chin before I can turn away and forces my gaze up to his. "I'd like to wring your neck for taking off, for running away instead of facing what you found."

My brows shoot up as anger flares to life in my chest. I smack his hand away and step back, glowering at him. "Excuse me?"

A muscle ticks in his jaw, sharp and shadowed with stubble. "What you did was idiotic and immature and very well could have gotten you killed."

My voice trembles as I snap, "Fuck you." If this asshole thinks I'm going to stand here and let him blame *me* for the shit that's gone down, there's no way in hell that's happening.

His lips curl into a scowl. "Glad to see you haven't lost your fire."

"Get out."

"No, I don't think I will," he says in an annoyingly calm voice.

I let my hands fall to my side. "Fine. Stay as long as you'd like, *I'll* go." I move to shove past him, but he catches my wrist and pulls me toward him. When I stumble, falling forward into his chest, he takes that opportunity to back me up against the wall. He drops my wrist, caging me in between his arms and pressing his hands flat against the wall on either side of me. His expression is dark, vicious. I'm prepared for him to rip me apart, quite honestly, and my heart is hammering against my ribcage waiting for the storm to come.

"You," he starts in a low, deep voice, leaning down so his lips are at my ear, "have no idea what I would have done if something had happened to you."

The air is stolen from my lungs in a swift *whoosh*, and I suck in a breath, my heart in my throat. "Atlas," I say in warning, sinking my teeth into my bottom lip. The emotional rollercoaster that is this exchange isn't one I'd like to continue riding.

"I want to lock you up and never let you leave this house." He leans back to look into my eyes. "And I could."

I shake my head. "If this is your way of apologizing for keeping me in the dark, which pretty much led to me being kidnapped and used as a human juice box by not one but two psychotic vampires, you're doing a shit job."

"I'm not apologizing," he says flatly.

My jaw clenches at his tone. "Then what *are* you doing?"

Atlas cocks his head to the side, watching me. "Whatever I want."

I slam my palms against his chest, trying to push him away, but he doesn't budge. Not a fucking inch. "Get away from me."

"Want to try that again with a more convincing tone?" he taunts.

Instead of fighting him, I lean back against the wall, exhaling harshly. "Not really. Want to stop being an asshole?"

He leans in for a moment. "Not really."

I roll my eyes, wishing I could make him feel as out of control as I do. "I thought of you," I blurt, "while I was there. About how angry I was for everything you kept from me, but... also how much I wanted you there."

His eyes dance across my face. "Oh?"

I swallow hard, forcing myself to look at him head-on as I say, "When I was in the shower, fucking myself to feel something, *anything* that could help me escape my reality, I closed my eyes..." My voice trails off as I close my eyes now, then continue, "and when I pushed my fingers inside, I pictured it was you there, thrusting into me while you held me against the wall."

Atlas growls deep in his throat. "What are you doing?"

My eyes fly open, and I arch a brow at him. "Whatever I want," I say, adopting his words.

"Hmm." He drops one hand off the wall, wrapping it around my hip. "And what is it you want, Calla?"

Leaning into his touch instead of trying to push him away, I lick my lips. "What I want?" I echo. "How about the truth? Kade said—"

"I don't care what he said," he cuts me off.

I scowl. "Of course not, because you—"

Atlas seals his lips over mine before I can finish my sentence. For a second, I'm lost in the taste of his lips, the way they move against mine, firm yet unhurried.

I shove him back, and my palm cracks against his cheek.

He blinks at me, surprise filling his eyes as he lifts his fingers to his cheek, which is tinged pink where I slapped him.

My heart is pounding in my chest as we stare at each other in silence. And then I'm reaching for him, grabbing the front of his shirt in my fist and tugging him back to me. I lean up on my tiptoes and smash my lips against his, putting everything into the kiss. Every bit of anger and hurt at him for all of the secrets and lies, the fear I felt when Dante ambushed me on the street outside Brighton's apartment and being kept by Selene, and lastly, the bitter relief I feel being back here.

He grips my hips, hauling me flush against him and pressing me back into the wall at the same time. When he nips my bottom lip, I gasp into his mouth, and he growls in response.

I lean back, resting my head against the wall as I catch my breath. "I hate you," I say, my voice trembling.

Atlas smiles slowly, and my breath catches. It's the first time I've seen him smile. He has a small dimple in his left cheek when he does. He lowers his mouth, brushing his lips on mine. He doesn't kiss me, though. Instead, he whispers, "By all means, hate me for as long as you can, Calla. I'm still going to make you come."

I want to refuse him, to deny that I want what he's offering —*threatening*. But I can't. Even if I say the words, he'll see right through me. Atlas has intimidated and intrigued me from the moment we met, and as much as I wish I could say I don't want him, that I'm not drawn to the out of control way he makes me feel, I'd be lying to both of us if I did.

"Go ahead," he adds, lowering his voice, "tell me you don't want it."

My eyes narrow. "You're an asshole." It's a weak retort, but it's all I can come up with.

He chuckles, turning his head slightly toward the door. "Yes, well, as much as you'd like this asshole to have his way with you, it sounds like Gabriel and Lex are back, so we'll have to pause our little tiff for now." Without so much as a glance at me, he turns and walks out of the room, leaving the door open so I can watch him retreat down the hall.

I fall back against the wall with a heavy sigh, pressing my hand against the pounding heartbeat in my chest.

What the hell just happened?

ELEVEN

Lex and I are putting the last of the groceries away when Atlas comes into the kitchen looking rather... bothered. When I arch a brow at him, he simply shakes his head, shoving his hand through his hair, flexing the muscles in his forearm before dropping onto the couch in the living room. A minute later, the TV clicks on and the soft sound of the local news station fills the silence.

Calla walks in a minute later, her cheeks tinged slightly pink and her jaw set tight.

I want to ask what happened while we were gone, but whatever it was is between her and Atlas.

Her eyes move from me to where Atlas is focused on the screen in the other room. She lets out a little huff before turning her attention back to me. "I, um, need to talk to you."

The sound of her pulse increases, and I nod, shutting the fridge door. "Of course, angel," I say in a soft tone. "Maybe after some food? Are you feeling well enough to eat?"

She presses her lips together. "I'm okay. I... I don't think this should wait any longer."

Lex is across the kitchen, pouring the contents of a blood bag into a glass. "This sounds like something we should discuss together," he chimes in, tossing the empty blood bag in the trash under the sink and coming to stand next to me.

"Probably," she says, stealing another glance toward Atlas. "Where's Kade?"

The moment his name leaves her lips, he appears behind her, close enough she must feel his body there.

"Wherever you want me," he says in her ear.

She yelps, whirling around to face him, and drives her fist into his stomach. "Damn you." Her voice is a little breathless as she scolds him.

Kade grins at her. "Aww, come on. You know you missed me sneaking up on you." He dives down and plants a kiss against her cheek before she can shove him away, but a smile tugs at my lips watching her try.

Atlas takes that opportunity to get off the couch, shut off the TV, and join the rest of us in the kitchen. Lex immediately offers him the glass of blood in his hand, to which Atlas just shakes his head. Lex shrugs and takes a long drink. My gums throb watching the dark crimson liquid slosh around the glass.

I swallow past the fire in my throat and turn my attention back to Calla, who has moved away from Kade and is leaning against one of the islands.

She pulls her bottom lip between her teeth, hesitating.

My chest tightens, wanting to go to her, to wrap my arms around her waist and hold her close. The desire to reassure her that everything is okay is strong. It's a pull I'm struggling to ignore, because I get the feeling based on her response to Kade, that she needs some space. So, as badly as I want to crush her against my chest and make her feel secure, I keep my distance. Because there's also a part of me that longs for her blood, to feel her writhing against me, if the throbbing in my gums and the hardness between my legs are any indications.

Calla opens her mouth to speak, her eyes wider than normal as they bounce between all of us. When nothing comes out, she snaps her lips together, then clears her throat, trying again. "I have a lot to tell you. I know you're going to be pissed, but please let me finish before you say anything or have some supernatural meltdown."

Lex downs the rest of his blood in a matter of a couple gulps, setting the stained glass on the counter behind us. "What does that mean?"

She looks at him and sighs. "Just... I need you to listen, okay?"

I manage to catch her gaze and offer a reassuring nod. "Of course. We're listening."

She inhales deeply, then starts talking quickly. "The night I left here after finding those pages in Atlas's office, I went to Brighton's. Before I made it inside, Dante grabbed me off the sidewalk and knocked me out. I woke up in some fancy penthouse—I'm still not sure where it was—and he was there. I thought he took me as revenge against you guys for the Wall Street deal, but I quickly found out he wasn't the one behind it. Not really. He, uh..." Her voice breaks off, and she blinks a few times, trying to fight back tears. Swallowing hard, she continues, "He bit me. It was the worst pain I've ever felt. I mean, up to that point."

"He's a dead man," Lex growls, his fangs on full display.

Calla laughs, but the sound is void of any humor. "He *is* dead. So you can put your fangs away, Lex."

"Dante is dead?" Kade asks, crossing his arms over his chest.

She nods. "I thought he was going to kill me. And then, he just stopped." Her jaw clenches. "He dropped dead, after she, um—after Selene ripped out his heart." She shakes her head. "I thought she was saving me from him," she says quietly, and her low voice makes me think she's beating herself up more than we know.

"What happened after that?" I ask, my stomach already churning at the mention of my sire.

Calla's brows pinch together as if she's struggling to remember. Her gaze drops to the floor, and she says, "I don't really know. She came at me, then everything went dark. When I woke up next, it was a week later, though I guess I'd been awake before then and don't remember it. She fed on me twice between the time I woke up and when she put me in a car to come back here." A shudder ripples through her as she seems to relive the memory of Selene biting her, and my hands curl into fists at my sides.

Kade growls low in his throat, and Atlas shoots him a warning glare that says, *keep it together*.

"I don't know what the hell is going on with Brighton's family," she says in a more level voice, lifting her gaze to look at Atlas, "but Scott was there. He met with Selene one morning. I don't know what they were talking about, but he left abruptly and it didn't seem good."

Atlas's eyes narrow. "You didn't hear *anything* they said?"

"Not really. I caught the end of their conversation. She sounded pissed, and he told her they'd be in touch."

"Well, fuck," Lex mutters. "Add that to our list of problems."

Calla frowns at him. "I wish that was it." Her eyes flick to me for a split second before they move away, her pulse jumping.

"What else is there?" I ask, that wretched pit in my stomach growing bigger by the second.

"As you could probably guess, she didn't send me back to you out of the goodness of her heart."

Because she doesn't have one.

"She wants something in return," Kade guesses.

Calla nods, her heart hammering in her chest as sweat dots her brow. "She..." Her eyes land on me again, glassy with unshed tears. "She wants you, Gabriel."

My stomach sinks. I'm not surprised—Selene has never been subtle or coy about what she wants—but the thought of returning to her, to even seeing her face, makes me sick. I can count on one hand the number of times in the last century I've vomited, but the bile rising in my throat threatens to increase that tally.

"At first, she wanted me to choose to convince you, but I refused her. As angry and confused as I was—as I *am*—I could never do that to you." She sucks in a breath. "She took matters into her own hands and decided to make you choose—you or me."

"What the fuck does that mean?" Kade demands.

She doesn't take her eyes off me as she says, "If Gabriel doesn't go back to her... she... she's going to turn me into a vampire."

"No fucking way," Lex snarls, his eyes dark. "She's not getting anywhere near you ever again. We're going to rip her limb from limb and set them on fire until she is nothing but ash."

Memories of my life before I met the guys flash before my eyes. The dark period I spent with Selene, the hunger and the bloodshed that followed everywhere we went. The thought of returning to that life grips me with a fear so strong my lungs constrict, making it hard to breathe. But if this is what it takes to keep Calla safe—

"I'll go." The words leave my lips before I realize I've spoken. The pit in my stomach seems to grow blades, slicing through my abdomen and filling my veins with poison that makes me bite back a string of expletives. I know this isn't ideal—for anyone—but I also know what Selene is capable of. I've seen it firsthand, and this is the least of it. So there isn't a choice here, not really. I have to do what she wants.

Kade moves forward, stepping in between me and Calla. "Absolutely fucking not. There is no way in hell we're letting you go back to that psychotic bitch."

Atlas steps up, standing next to Kade. "He's right. We will deal with Selene and we are more than capable of protecting Calla."

Calla scowls from behind Kade. "I want to be able to protect myself, thank you very much."

Atlas glances over his shoulder at her. "Fine. Once you're fully healed and have your strength back, we'll start training again. But don't think I'll go easy on you."

"When have you ever?" she shoots back, and there's a fire in her eyes that despite the fire blazing through me makes my chest fill with pride. Our girl is strong—oftentimes stronger than I think we give her credit for. It's one of many things I admire about her... and the thought of walking away from that and into the arms of the monster who created me has my thoughts moving toward a white ash stake to the heart.

Before I can speak, Calla says, "I'll agree to waiting to train on one condition."

Atlas offers a dry laugh. "There you go again thinking you have any choice in the matter."

Her usually soft, warm brown eyes darken as they narrow on him. "You're not the only person who could train me." Her gaze moves to Kade—specifically the bulging muscles in his arms.

Kade smirks when he realizes she's looking at him. "Oh no. Don't drag me into this."

She rolls her eyes, huffing out a frustrated breath. "I'm not asking for much here, guys."

"What *are* you asking for?" Lex asks.

"Answers. Honesty. *Transparency*."

I glance between the guys, shrugging. We'd been planning to bring her into the fold anyway. This doesn't seem like a stretch. She deserves to know about the world she's living in.

"I want to know everything," she adds in a firm voice, looking at each of us.

Kade tuts his tongue. "Always so stubborn."

She shoots him an annoyed look, which does nothing to diminish the smirk on his lips as he watches her.

Kade glances in Atlas's direction, waiting until he nods to start talking. "Your BFF Brighton's family are vampire hunters."

Calla frowns. "I know that part."

"You also know that before we came for you, we spent some time—"

"Stalking me," she cuts in. "I do recall that part being mentioned, yes."

I frown at the bitterness in her tone and the tension in her body. Seeing her upset doesn't sit well with me. But we all agreed she deserves to know everything, and she's asked for transparency. She's entitled to any response she feels like.

"We gathered information on the people you spent time with," Kade continues. "Brighton included. We knew her relation to the hunters and very quickly deduced that she was not involved with the organization. From what Atlas could gather, Brighton's mother refused to allow her daughter to be a part of it. She didn't want that life for her."

"I met with Brighton a month before we came to your apartment," Atlas says. "I confirmed she had no prior knowledge of hunters or vampires or anything supernatural."

"So her reaction that day when I told her about you guys was genuine," Calla muses, her brows pinched together.

Kade goes on to reiterate the information we've already discussed about the hunters. That they're growing in numbers and that white ash may not be as rare as it used to be.

"What are we going to do about that?" she asks.

Lex chuckles. "You're going to focus on building your strength during training with Atlas and finishing the semester. You've always been adamant about school. Let us worry about this and you worry about that, okay?"

She blinks at him, and for a moment, I'm not sure if she's surprised by his suggestion or pissed that we're attempting to sideline her from the hunter action. Either would make sense at this point.

"Fine," she finally says, "but once school is done for the term—"

"We'll revisit this conversation," Kade says, adopting Atlas's firm tone.

Her eyes narrow on him and a muscle ticks along her jaw. She opens her mouth as if she's about to start arguing again.

"Okay," I say before the two of them can get into it in the middle of the kitchen. "I need to speak with Marcel—update him on the situation. Lex, can you start dinner? I shouldn't be long."

He nods, grabbing his empty glass off the counter and sticking it in the dishwasher before walking to the fridge.

I take that opportunity to slip out of the room, walking into the formal living room at the side of the house and perching on the stiff armrest of the couch. It's no wonder we never use this space—the furniture is most definitely for show and not comfort.

Marcel answers my call on the first ring.

"What's up, Gabe?"

"We've got her back," I tell him. "She was pretty banged up, but she's going to be okay. She already wants to start training with Atlas. We'll keep her safe, but she doesn't like feeling vulnerable, like she can't protect herself."

"Makes sense," he says.

"Yeah." I understand where she's coming from. I'd feel the same if I was in her position, I'm sure of it. "It was Dante that took her, but Selene was behind it."

"Son of a bitch," he says, sighing. "How'd you find her?"

"We didn't," I say reluctantly. "Selene sent her back to us." I fill him in on everything Calla told us, from Dante being dead to Brighton's dad meeting with Selene. "Things could get very messy. I want advanced security measures put in place around here."

"Of course. I'll arrange it immediately." The sound of laptop keys clicking fills the line for a few seconds. "Everything will be set up within twenty-four hours."

"Thank you, Marcel."

"Anytime, my friend. I'm glad your girl is safe."

Something in my chest tightens, and I press my lips together for a moment. "Me too."

"I've got a few calls to make, but I'll send you a confirmation email later once the security is set up. Let's plan to catch up in a few days, but if you need anything prior to then, you know where to find me."

After hanging up with Marcel, I rejoin the others. Lex is reading the instructions for mushroom risotto on his phone, while Atlas, Kade, and Calla are sitting in the living room.

The grim expression on Calla's face is quickly explained when I hear Atlas explaining his involvement in Ellis Industries.

"You're a shareholder in a company whose mission statement might as well be *kill all the vampires*?" She shakes her head. "What the hell?"

"It's important to keep our eyes on all of the moving parts when it comes to the hunters," Kade tells her. "Atlas being inside the company is the best way to do that."

"So long as you don't get caught," she says, directing it toward Atlas. There's worry in her gaze that he seemingly ignores, though I know he sees it as clearly as I do. She shakes her head. "I thought it was an environmental company."

"It is," Kade says, "sort of. They are deeply involved with the protection of certain lands."

"Land where white ash trees are plentiful," I say, walking into the living room and sitting next to Calla on the couch.

She frowns, her eyes flitting between us as she puts it together. "They protect the land where white ash trees grow so they can use them against vampires."

"That's right," Kade says.

Calla runs a hand over her face, and I quickly notice the way her fingers are shaking. "This..." Her voice trails off. "This is insane." Her gaze focuses on Atlas. "You can't—What if they find out who they're in business with?"

He shrugs. "Keeps things interesting."

The muscles in her jaw tense. "I'm serious," she snaps at him.

Atlas sighs as if this whole conversation is an inconvenience to him, and I shoot him a look. "Nothing is going to happen, Calla. They aren't going to find out."

She crosses her arms over her chest. "Really? Because Selene knows about you *and* she knows Brighton's dad. There is absolutely no way that's a coincidence."

"Selene is also a vampire," he counters. "She wants to throw us under the bus, she's getting run over as well."

"That's what you're counting on?"

There's a slightly, barely noticeable shift in Atlas's posture. His patience is wearing thin. I understand Calla's concern—it's nothing I haven't been worried about before, but it's really not the most present issue.

I reach over and wrap my hand around her knee, giving it a reassuring and gentle squeeze. "Everything is going to be all right, angel."

She glances down to where I'm holding onto her and purses her lips before meeting my gaze. "That's not... I just—"

"Trust us." I lower my voice. "Please?"

Calla catches her bottom lip between her teeth, and the urge to lean in and tug it free so I can seal my mouth over hers pulls at me, but I shove it down—for now.

Closing her eyes, she whispers, "I'm trying."

I glance over at Atlas and Kade, who both nod at me.

She's trying. That's really all we can ask for at this point.

My best friend's family is full of vampire hunters.

I lean forward, my elbows digging into my knees, and rake my fingers through my hair. My throat is thick with tears—again—and my head is so light, I'm glad I'm sitting down, otherwise there's a good chance I'd fall on my ass.

I've finally gotten the answers I've been asking for since day one, but I'm finding it all harder to swallow than I was expecting. At least they're being truthful and letting me in on what's going on. Honesty is what I need to help build my trust with the guys, and they are making a significant effort to give me that. It's not lost on me.

"What happens now?" I ask, sitting upright. "I've missed school—people, including Brighton, are going to wonder where I am."

"I dealt with Brighton," Kade says.

Cringing outwardly, I hesitate before asking, "What does that mean exactly? What did you do?"

He rolls his eyes. "Relax. After you seemingly went AWOL, she freaked out and called us. When Gabriel and I went over there to talk to her, I glamoured her to delete and forget about your texts. I also told her you were sick and would be out of commission for a while."

I let out a breath. I guess it could be worse. Except... "How am I supposed to act around her now?"

"Normal?" Lex offers from the kitchen. He's stirring something in a pot on the stove but shoots me a wink over his shoulder.

I stare at him. "That's helpful. Thank you." A pit grows in my stomach. "I know what you said about her mom not wanting this life for Brighton, but do you think they could be planning to use her in the future?"

"It's a possibility, of course, but they tend to start hunters much younger than she is so they can train for years before being used in the field."

I shake my head, still struggling to grasp this revelation. "Vampire hunters," I say in a low voice. "Don't you think their existence is something you should have told me about, I don't know, when I moved in?"

"We're telling you now," Kade chimes in, glancing at something on the phone in his hand.

I huff out a sigh. Maybe I should be more accepting of their newfound willingness to share things with me instead of dwelling on all of the time they kept me in the dark. "Okay," I say, leaning against the back of the couch and crossing one leg over the other. "What's the plan?" I need more to go on; it seems with every answer I'm given, it sparks a dozen more questions.

"We're still gathering information," Atlas says. "It's important not to move too quickly in order to stay undetected within the ranks of the organization."

"Right," I say, dragging the word out, clearly not sure what the hell he means.

"Atlas has a responsibility to help ensure the protection of our kind. The York family is very important in the vampire world. They go back centuries and are one of the most powerful and respected clans to exist."

"That explains a lot," I mutter under my breath.

"Watch it," Atlas says sternly.

"As you can see," Kade says, "our boy here doesn't love the attention being on him."

My lips twitch. I can't help it. I understand the situation is serious, but the small break in tension is appreciated. Despite that, my head still feels as if it's going to explode from all of this new information. And with the looming threat from Selene, the weight on my chest seems to be getting heavier by the second.

Blowing out a slow breath, I get up from the couch and walk toward the kitchen, where the warm, savory aroma of mushrooms and spices infiltrates my senses. I need a break from all the dark and heavy conversation. I steal a look at Gabriel, who is watching me from the living room. "You still owe me a cooking lesson."

He smiles, and the way his eyes soften makes my face heat. "I haven't forgotten," he promises.

"Good, because I'm going to hold you to it." I slide in next to Lex and lean over the stove, peering into the steaming pot of risotto. "Smells amazing."

He snakes an arm around my waist and tugs me against his side, dipping his face to kiss my cheek. "Yes, you do."

I roll my eyes, trying to ignore the way his touch sends my pulse racing. "Is it almost ready?" I hadn't been hungry before, but I can't deny the pang of emptiness in my stomach now.

"Should be." Lex moves away from me, humming under his breath as he walks to the fridge.

I turn around to start setting the table, and my breath catches in my throat when I come face-to-face with Kade. "What... are you doing?" I ask, willing my heart to settle.

He tilts his head to the side, his eyes wandering over my face slowly, as if he's committing it to memory. The corner of his mouth curves into a grin that makes my pulse jump, and when he moves so fast my eyes can't keep track of him, I let out a startled gasp as he throws me over his shoulder.

"Kade!" I punch his back, though nowhere near as hard as the last time he pulled this stunt.

Lex chuckles from where he stands at the stove, shaking his head at us as if we're children that are misbehaving.

"What the hell are you doing?" I groan again, gripping the back of his shirt as the blood rushes to my head.

Kade walks toward the hallway, taking the steps upstairs two at a time, making me bounce against his hard body each time. "I thought we could play a little game before dinner." His grip tightens, making parts of me come to life far quicker than I'd like to admit—or ever will. He strides down the hall and kicks his bedroom door open with ease. Before I know what's happening, he dumps me onto his bed. My head hits the pile of pillows at the top, and I shake the hair out of my face, shooting a glare at him.

"I don't think I want to play your game."

He smirks at me from the end of the bed. "No? Your body tells me something else entirely."

I force out a laugh. "I don't think you're as observant as you think you are, Kade."

He licks his lips. "Hmm, say it again."

I arch a brow. "Say—"

"My name. I like the way it sounds when you say it. Almost as much as I enjoy hearing you moan it."

Heat flares across my cheeks, and I dig my heels into the mattress to push myself up, but Kade is there in a flash, pinning me down with his knees on either side of my hips.

My heart slams against my ribcage, both in surprise and excitement, and I lift my arms in a halfhearted attempt to push him off.

"Come on," he purrs. "You can do better than that." He grabs my wrists, lifting them above my head and holding them there in one hand. "You want to fight me off?"

Oh, hell no, but the thought of trying has me all kinds of tingly.

I swallow past the dryness in my throat and buck my hips, gritting my teeth when the only thing that accomplishes is making the heat between my legs intensify. "Get. Off."

Kade leans closer, and the warmth of his body radiates against my skin, the crisp scent of his cologne clouding my head. "Try again," he taunts, his lips grazing the shell of my ear.

"Fuck you," I say through my teeth, shoving with all the strength I can muster. He doesn't move a goddamn inch. Bastard.

He presses his lips against the pulse at my throat. "Don't rush me." His tone is laced with a deadly combination of arousal and arrogance. I should hate it, but instead, it has my core throbbing.

Two can play at this game.

Pressing my lips together, I lift my hips, grinding against him until his grip on my wrists tightens to the point it almost hurts, and he growls low in my ear.

"You're asking for me to flip you over and fuck you hard and deep."

His words steal my breath for a moment before I can force out, "Actually, I'm pretty sure the only thing I asked for was that you get the fuck off of me." I hadn't *asked*, but whatever. I tug on my wrists and attempt to buck him off with my hips.

Kade chuckles in response. "The sight of you struggling under me when I can smell just how much you want my cock has me rock fucking hard."

Holy hell.

I shake my head, not trusting myself to speak.

He smirks, shifting his knee to press it between my legs, danger-ously close to the throbbing there. "Use your words, Calla."

My head feels fuzzy, and before I can open my mouth and pray something useful will come out, the bedroom door slams shut, and I jump.

Kade doesn't move, save for the bit of hair that falls into his face, and the smirk on his lips remains in place.

"What's going on in here?" Gabriel's voice makes the pounding in my chest increase.

"Not much," Kade answers without moving his gaze away from me.

"Kade is being a total caveman," I shoot over his shoulder, trying to steal a look at Gabriel, but Kade blocks my view completely.

"I can see that." There's a tinge of amusement in his soft voice, and I'm not sure what to make of that.

"Are you going to help?" I ask, tugging on my wrists again.

"You or him?"

The breath halts in my lungs.

Kade finally rolls off me, revealing Gabriel slowly approaching the bed, his eyes blazing with liquid silver.

I scramble up the bed until my back is pressed into the headboard, and my gaze swings between the two vampires devouring me with their eyes. Inhaling sharply, I press my lips together. "Two vampires against one human? Doesn't exactly seem fair."

"We never said we were, angel," Gabriel murmurs, shooting forward in a blur of movement and wrapping his hands around my ankles. He pulls me to the end of the bed until my tailbone reaches the edge, as Kade sits on my right side.

"You still want to pretend you don't want this?" Kade murmurs, watching me with a curious glint in his eyes.

Tension builds in my chest as heat flares across my cheeks. I want to turn my face away, but his gaze holds me in place while Gabriel's hands inch upward at an agonizingly slow pace. I finally lower my gaze, pulling my bottom lip between my teeth.

"You enjoy fighting us," Gabriel muses, sharing a look with Kade that sends my heart racing yet again.

"I..." My voice trails off before I can vehemently deny that. It's true. The taunting and the fighting—it's exciting. As much as I don't want to like it, my body craves it.

Gabriel's lips curl into the most seductive grin I've ever seen, and I'm suddenly frustrated I'm wearing pants, because his fingers are so damn close to the heat gathering between my legs, throbbing and begging to be touched.

"I don't know what you're talking about," I say, moving to sit up, to leave, but Kade grips my shoulders and pushes me back down.

"No?" he checks. "I think you're lying. To us—and to yourself."

I shake my head, knowing full well I absolutely am.

"You know," he murmurs, leaning down until his nose grazes mine, "I could always make you tell the truth." He exhales deeply, stirring the hair at my temple and making my skin tingle.

"Kade." There's a warning in Gabriel's voice, making me consider for a moment that maybe he's taking my side. Instead, he slides his hands up my thighs, curling his fingers into the waistband of my pants, and slowly peels them down to my knees. "I don't think glamour is necessary. She is soaked."

Oh my god. I want to hide my face or have the bed swallow me up, because he's right. I can feel the wetness between my legs, and it's for them.

I go to close my legs, but Gabriel catches them, his fingers pressing into my bare thighs.

"Keep them open," he orders, and his firm tone catches me so off guard, I do as he says, my eyes widening.

Kade lets go of me as he leans back, tugging his shirt off over his head and tossing it behind him. "Your turn."

I narrow my eyes at him. "This isn't strip poker."

"Well, of course not. Lex would be pissed if we played without him." He grins at me. "You can take it off yourself, or I can do it for you. Your choice."

"Choice," I echo breathlessly. "Don't get much of that around here."

Kade rolls his eyes, but they're still alight with amusement. "Especially when you take too long." He grabs the bottom of my sweater and pulls it up, forcing my arms over my head. It ends up on the floor with his shirt, and I'm left with my bare chest on display for both of them.

"I'm torn," Kade says, turning his attention to Gabriel, "between punishing her for misbehaving or ravishing those fucking gorgeous tits."

Gabriel drags his tongue over his bottom lip, then tugs my pants the rest of the way off before answering Kade. "Work fast enough, and you don't have to choose just one." He drops a light kiss to each of my thighs, getting close to the heat between them before pulling back and smiling at me with a dangerous glint in his eyes. "Something tells me she'll thoroughly enjoy both."

Kade hums softly, evidently in agreement. "As much as I'd love to punish you right now, I'm going to explode if I don't taste you soon." He presses his palm flat against my stomach, and instead of sliding toward the heat at my core, he trails his fingers up to my collarbone, applying a bit of pressure. Gabriel watches him, and they seem to share some unspoken words because, in the space of a breath, his fingers delve between my thighs. Kade drops his mouth to my breast, circling the nipple with his tongue as Gabriel traces his finger along my folds, so light it tickles.

I press my lips together to keep from making a sound, refusing to let them hear the pleasure they're giving me.

Kade sucks hard, and I gasp before I can stop myself, clamping my jaw shut and turning my face away. I press my cheek into the mattress, my pulse pounding as he continues sucking, swirling his tongue in circles, then reaches for my other breast, squeezing my nipple between two fingers. Heat floods through me, coloring my cheeks and chest a deep shade of pink as Gabriel teases me, dipping a single digit between my folds before pulling it back and skimming it back and forth across my slit.

"Gabriel," I practically growl, not allowing myself to look at him.

His finger stops moving, and he holds it in place barely inside me. "Yes, angel?"

I squeeze my eyes shut at his tone. He's torturing me on purpose. "N-nothing," I say through my teeth, and Kade chuckles against my skin, making me shiver.

Kade lifts his head, flicking his tongue over my nipple once before snagging my chin and turning my gaze back to him. "Liar."

I lift my brows defiantly and stay silent.

"Tell him," he says in a low voice.

"No—" My voice cuts off as Kade's glamour washes over me. I narrow my eyes, but I can't break his gaze.

"Go on," he encourages.

"I want your fingers deep inside me," I say, "your tongue after that, and then your cock."

"Good girl," Kade praises, releasing me and dropping his lips to my breast, giving it the same attention as the other.

Before I can snap at him, Gabriel inserts a finger so slow I'm going to snarl at him any second now. He slides in deeper, then turns it and presses his thumb against my clit.

I suck in a breath, gasping, "Yes."

So much for not letting them hear my pleasure.

Kade sucks hard, dragging his tongue back and forth across my nipple, and when I feel the sharp tips of his fangs brush my skin, I tense. He stops immediately and leans back in the same moment Gabriel pulls his finger out.

"Calla," Kade says in a gentle voice.

I shake my head, hating the worry I see in his eyes. "I... Sorry. I'm fine."

His brows tug together. "You—"

"I'm fine," I insist, reaching for him. I grab the back of his neck and drag his mouth to mine until our lips crash together. I'm not sure what it was about feeling his fangs against my skin that made me freeze, but the last thing I want to do is spend time exploring that. I would much rather continue what we were doing.

After a few seconds, Kade relaxes into the kiss and tangles his fingers in my hair, pushing his tongue into my mouth. I moan against his lips when Gabriel delves back inside me with two fingers this time. I lift my hips, urging him deeper, and am rewarded when he lowers his mouth to my clit, circling it with his tongue while thrusting his fingers in and out, quicker and deeper each time. He curls them at the deepest part of me, hitting a new spot, and my hips jerk off the bed. I break away from Kade's mouth, groaning as Gabriel continues winding me up. My orgasm builds quickly, and it doesn't take long before I'm racing toward the edge of release.

Kade peppers kisses along my jaw, down my throat, and across my collarbone, pressing against my side. I can feel the length of his erection against my hip, and I boldly reach for him. He sucks in a breath when I start palming him through the front of his pants. I fumble with the zipper, trying to get it open with one hand, while my other stays wrapped around his neck, and grumble incoherently when I can't make it work. He chuckles against my skin and pops the button, tugging the zipper down and pulling himself free. I wrap my fingers around his length and pump slowly, breathing heavily as Gabriel picks up the pace of his thrusts and sucks my clit into his mouth, swirling his tongue around it.

Kade steals my lips again, kissing me hard as I increase the pressure

I have on his cock, and he growls into my mouth. My speed picks up as the tension builds between my legs.

"Fuck," he breathes against my lips.

"I... I'm—" My voice breaks.

"Keep going," Kade orders, and I'm not sure if he's talking to me or Gabriel.

When Gabriel adds a third finger and starts pulsing his lips around my clit, I dive right over the edge, my pussy clamping around his fingers as I cry out my release. The sound is swallowed by Kade's lips against mine, and I ride the wave of my orgasm while continuing to pump my hand up and down Kade's cock. His grip on me tightens a moment later and he growls against my lips, his release spurting over my hand, coating it in warmth.

Kade snags his shirt off the floor and cleans us up while Gabriel drags his tongue along my slit, tasting me. He presses his lips against my skin just below my navel and peers up at me. "Exquisite," he murmurs, making my cheeks flush as I try to catch my breath.

"Agreed," Kade says, kissing me chastely before sliding off the bed and walking toward his en suite bathroom. I can't help but watch as he goes. That man was chiseled by gods, I swear.

Gabriel crawls over me in Kade's absence, tilting my chin up to seal his lips over mine. His mouth tastes a little like melon, and a rush of heat floods through me when I realize I'm tasting myself on his lips. My fingers glide over his shoulder, and I grip the back of his hair, kissing him deeper, hoping he can feel how glad I am to be with him again. I fucking missed him—missed all of them. And I'm going to do whatever it takes to make sure Selene doesn't come between us.

THIRTEEN

Over the next twenty-four hours, a brand new, high-end security system is installed on the property. The existing one we had when the house was built was good enough until Calla came along. With recent developments, something more high tech is necessary. This system includes sensors on every door and window on all three levels of the house as well as cameras that cover every square inch of the property. Marcel also met with and hired a team of security guards to remotely monitor the feed constantly.

Between that and the four of us, there's not a chance in hell Selene will be able to touch Calla again. We haven't heard from her since Calla returned to us yesterday, but I have to assume there's a ticking clock on her threat against Calla's mortality. We'll kill Selene before she ever has a chance to get her fangs near Calla again. My stomach is in knots over it still. After being with Calla last night, I can't stop thinking about how we almost lost her. I would go back to Selene in a heartbeat if I knew it would keep Calla safe, but the others refuse to allow it to happen. They are confident she is safe here with us, but they don't know Selene like I do... The woman is deceitful and manipulative. She gets her way every time, no matter who gets hurt in the process. I've seen it too many times to count. I gave her what she wanted at the expense of others more times than I'd like to admit during my time with her decades ago.

I drag a hand down my face, cradling a mug of microwaved blood in my other hand. I've been sitting in the dark at the dining room table for over an hour now. It's long past midnight, and everyone else is sleeping, but every time I close my eyes, nightmares from my past flash before me, and I jolt upright, wide awake.

"You can't sleep either?" a soft voice says, and I look up to find Calla padding across the floor in her bare feet. She's wearing one of Kade's old T-shirts, and it falls just above her knees, hugging her curves in a way that has me shifting where I sit. With her hair tied up in a messy bun and the soft scent of her rose body wash clinging to her skin, I want to bury my face in her neck and hold her until the nightmares are chased away.

I shake my head, taking a drink of blood. "Are you all right, angel?"

She sighs, dropping into the chair across from me, and offers a faint smile. "Define *all right*."

My lips drop into a frown. "You know you're safe here, don't you?"

Calla bites her lip, glancing down at her lap. "Yeah. I just... How long until Selene's blood and venom are out of my system? Like, for sure?"

I tap my fingers against the side of my mug. I can see the concern on her face, in the way her eyes flick between mine and gleam with uncertainty. I want to take that away, reassure her everything will be fine, but the truth is, Selene is capable of far greater evil than I hope she —or the others—will ever know. "A few days."

She nods absently, finally looking at me. "Will you tell me about her?"

My forehead creases when I lift my brows at her in surprise. "About Selene?" I check, unease swirling deep in my stomach.

"Yeah. I mean, how did you meet? She turned you into a vampire, so I have to assume she was important to you. You're clearly important to her, so much so, she wanted to ensure you would live forever." She grips the back of her neck as she shifts in her chair. I don't like how uncomfortable she is.

"Selene cares about very few things, Calla," I tell her in a soft voice. "Back then, I... I thought what we had was love. I was very wrong. She manipulated me, glamoured me most of the time we were together, which of course I didn't realize until much later."

Her face is several shades paler than when she sat down. "After you turned?"

Nodding, I admit, "I didn't want to be a vampire. When I discovered what Selene was, I wanted to run. I was terrified. But I also cared about her a great deal, so I stayed. She was different then—at least, she made me believe that she was. Kind and gentle; she would never hurt anyone and would survive off donated blood, much like we do now."

Calla frowns. "When did that change?"

I inhale slowly. Searching through memories of that time isn't easy for me, but I want to tell her everything I know. Answer any questions she has, because after keeping her in the dark for so long, it's the least she deserves. "It wasn't all at once. There were small things here and there. And then one night, she wanted me to taste her blood. We had been..."

"Fucking," Calla offers.

I exhale a humorless laugh. "Yes. She had bitten me—it wasn't the first time, but the first time while we were intimate. With my blood still on her lips, she used her fingernail and sliced into her throat, beckoning me to drink from her." I close my eyes for a moment, shuddering at the memory, at how clear it still is all these years later.

"Gabriel," Calla murmurs, and a moment later, her hands wrap around mine. "You don't have to tell me. I can't imagine what you went through at her hands. If thinking about it brings you pain, I... I don't want that."

I open my eyes, dropping my gaze to our hands. The way her thumb is brushing over my skin eases the tension in my chest somewhat, and I manage a small smile. "It's okay, angel. You should know what we're up against."

She nods and continues holding my hands.

"I didn't want to drink her blood. The very thought of it made me nauseous. I tried to refuse her, I *did* refuse her. But she glamoured me; made me think I *wanted* it." I shake my head. "She may as well have turned me that night."

Calla's brows knit. "When did she turn you?"

"Not for months after that. I think she enjoyed being able to feed on me, but she also got satisfaction from me drinking her blood as a human, even though she glamoured me into it every time." I take a deep breath. "When she did turn me, I was angry and scared and confused. My body went through so many changes at once and everything was overwhelming. I didn't know what to do. I relied on her for a time. She was all I knew, so I didn't have much of a choice. I... I did a lot of terrible things I'll never be able to take back. A lot of people died because of me. One day, it was as if I just woke up. I remembered everything she did to me as a human—the pain she caused me and seemingly everyone around us. So, I left. Packed a bag in the middle of the night and never looked back. I had a lot of growing pains and relearning to do when it came to being a vampire apart from Selene, but luckily, Lex and Atlas found me not long after. Everything since then has been okay."

Her jaw clenches and her fingers grip mine with a surprising amount of strength. "Selene deserves to rot in hell for what she did to you." Her voice shakes with anger—anger that's reflected in the darkness of her eyes. There's also exhaustion there in the form of shadows under her lashes.

"Her day will come," I assure her. "Atlas, Kade, and Lex will make sure of it."

"What about you?"

"She's my sire, so I can't directly bring her any harm."

She shakes her head. "That's not fair."

I shrug. "No, but I know what needs to happen will. I've made peace with everything else."

Calla stares at me for a moment. "I've never met anyone like you, Gabriel."

More of the tension in my muscles releases, and the smile I give her feels more genuine and less forced this time. "I could say the same for you."

Her cheeks flush. "I really missed you."

I meet her gaze and pull a hand away from her grip to brush my fingers across her cheek. "That week you were gone was the longest of my existence, angel."

Tears gather in her beautiful eyes, making them glassy. "I'll try not to get kidnapped again," she says dryly with a weak laugh.

I chuckle in response, running my thumb along her jaw. "I hope despite what happened with Selene that you'll believe me when I say that we won't let anyone hurt you ever again."

She drops my gaze, licking her lips and sniffling. "I appreciate the sentiment, but you can't make that promise." She quickly wipes under her eyes before looking at me again. "And I don't expect you to. Atlas warned me that your world is dangerous for humans. I get it. And I'm going to do everything in my power to ensure my own safety."

My eyes lock on hers, and the fierceness in her gaze makes my cock harden. Despite everything she's been through in the last five and a half weeks since the night we broke into her apartment, she hasn't lost her fire. Pride fills my chest, and I stand, moving around the table with a speed too quick for her eyes to follow.

She sucks in a breath, swiveling to face me with flushed cheeks. "What?" she breathes.

I cup her chin, tilting her head back so she's looking into my eyes as my lips pull up into a smile. "I didn't get enough of you last night."

Calla's eyes widen slightly, and she bites down on her lip, making me long to do the same. To claim her mouth and her body as mine.

Without warning, I grip her hips and lift her onto the table, pushing the chair out of the way with my foot before my mouth descends upon hers. She immediately softens against me, leaning in and draping her arms over my shoulders. I tighten my grip on her hips, then slide my hands up her thighs, gathering the material of Kade's shirt as I go.

"Gabriel," she murmurs against my lips, and my cock twitches in my pants.

I bite back a groan; I want to take my time with her.

Pulling back just enough to see her face, I say, "What is it, angel?"

She pulls back and grips my forearms. "Should we really do this? Here, I mean?"

I press my lower half into her, stealing her breath, and the little sound she makes drives the beast inside me wild. "I'm not waiting another minute to have you. Let the entire house hear us." I claim her mouth once more, pushing the hardness between my legs against the heat between hers until she wraps her bare legs around me, digging her heels in to pull me closer. My tongue darts out and flicks along her lower lip until she opens to me, and I deepen the kiss, grazing her tongue with mine. Her hands slide into my hair as her hips desperately try grinding against me, and when she makes a frustrated sound against my lips, I can't help but chuckle. Leaning back, I murmur, "Tell me what you want."

Her fingers grip the back of my hair. "I *need* you."

A shiver trickles down my spine, filling me with heat as I look over her pink-tinged face. I draw one hand up to cup her cheek while the other rests on her bare thigh, and kiss the tip of her nose. "You have me. Always."

A hint of a smile touches her lips, making my heart beat faster. The things this woman does to me... I'll never get tired of them. "Let me rephrase," she says, "I need you *inside me*."

I grin at her, brushing my thumb along her jaw. "Sounds like someone needs to learn patience."

Her eyes narrow and her lips form a pout. "Don't be mean."

As I slide my hand slowly up her thigh, her gaze softens and she opens her legs for me. The only thing keeping me from her sweet, aching core is a lacy black thong that I'd like nothing more than to rip from her gorgeous body. I kiss her again, softly, taking my time exploring her lips as my fingers brush along the material at the apex of her thighs that is already damp. I can smell her arousal, which only feeds my need to claim her. And when she moans into my mouth, pushing against my fingers, my control wavers, and I tug her panties down her thighs. She manages to wiggle them the rest of the way off, and they fall to the floor. I waste no time dipping my fingers inside her. One, then two, then three. Thrusting slowly to start as she breathes harder against my lips. My thumb rubs circles over her clit, making her legs shake, and I pull back to bury my face in her neck, kissing and sucking her skin as she lets out little gasps and moans.

When she reaches for my pants, I don't stop her. I need this as badly as she does. I pull back just long enough to tug my shirt over my head and drop my pants, kicking them away before stepping between her legs again. I wrap my fingers around my throbbing length, desperate to plunge inside of her, but I want to make sure she's ready for me. I run the blunt head of my cock along her slit, nudging it against her clit a few times and making her moan before I drag it back down.

"Gabriel," she breathes, her cheeks pink with warmth.

"I'm getting you ready for me, angel," I tell her, pushing just inside her tight little tunnel before pulling out and rubbing along her slit again.

"You're driving me crazy." She tips her head back, biting her lip as I continue moving against her, and my eyes go to her pebbled nipples through the material of Kade's shirt. I lick my lips, suddenly battling the urge to taste them. Her eyes land on me and she giggles softly before tugging the shirt over her head, tossing it behind me. "Better?" she asks, and there's a challenge in her tone.

"Much," I answer, pushing a little deeper into her pussy this time as I strum her clit with my fingers.

"Mmm..." she moans, closing her eyes and bracing her arms behind her as she pushes her hips forward to the edge of the table.

I pull back once more, adding pressure to her clit, and she gasps sharply.

"Please, Gabriel."

I lean in, capturing her lips in a fierce kiss. "You don't have to beg, angel. I'll give you everything you need." With that, I push all the way into her at a languid pace, giving her a chance to adjust to my size. Her pussy squeezes me like a fist, making my pulse tick faster as I force myself to hold still a moment. "Are you okay?"

She keeps her eyes shut and nods, but her jaw is clenched.

I rub her clit, trying to get her to relax a bit. "Talk to me."

"I'm... good."

I kiss her cheek, then press my forehead against hers. "Relax for me."

"Trying," she says in a shallow voice, and when I move to pull out, she grabs the back of my hip, holding me inside her. "Don't move."

"Okay," I murmur, brushing my lips against hers, and she immediately kisses me back. A few pounding heartbeats later, she slowly starts moving her hips, her breath hitching against my mouth, but she doesn't stop. She pulls back and kisses along my jaw, wrapping her legs around me and urging me on. I take the hint and resume thrusting, picking up speed as she clenches around me, making my head spin with pleasure.

"Lie back," I tell her, and she complies without question. When her back is flat against the table, I slide my hand up her stomach and between her breasts, taking a moment to circle and tweak each nipple as I continue thrusting into her.

"Fuck," she hisses as her legs dangle off the edge of the table, and I grin, moving deeper inside her.

"I've got you." I lean over her, finding a new angle that hits a particularly sensitive spot based on the soft whimper that escapes Calla's lips. My balls tighten when she clenches around my cock again, and her breathing quickens as she meets my gaze. Her lovely brown irises are filled with heat and lust, and the sight of her writhing beneath me almost does me in.

"Gabriel," she breathes, "I'm going to—*ahhh*." She presses her lips together, trying to keep her moans quiet, but I shake my head, pressing my thumb against her clit.

"I want to hear you."

Her cheeks flush a deep pink and another moan parts her lips. This time, she doesn't try to stifle it. "Keep... going. You need to finish."

I don't stop. "Calla—"

She meets my thrusts, tugging me back to her mouth. "Come inside me," she says against my lips, and her words send me over the edge.

I growl deep in my chest, spurting my release into her pussy as I thrust hard enough to feel resistance deep inside her tight channel.

Calla cries out, coming with me a second time, digging her heels into my behind to hold me inside her. "That was amazing," she says, laughing as she rests her head against the table to catch her breath.

Once the aftershocks of our shared orgasm subside, I pull out, my cock twitching at the sight of my release rolling down the inside of her thigh. "It was," I agree, sliding my arm around her waist and helping her off the table. She sways on her feet, but I hold her up easily.

"I think you broke me," she teases, leaning into me.

I kiss the side of her head. "Come on. Let's get you cleaned up and into bed."

She lowers her gaze, those dark lashes of hers fanning her high cheekbones. "I... I like it when you take care of me."

I smile at her. "I'm glad, because I plan to do just that for as long as we're bound."

Once we've showered, I carry Calla to my bed, where she falls asleep a few minutes after her head rests against my chest. I wrap my arms around her, holding her to me as I exhale a heavy breath, finally letting myself relax as I close my eyes and wait for sleep to take me.

FOURTEEN

CALLA

I blink my eyes open, yawning and stretching my bare legs on top of Gabriel's plush black duvet cover. My lips curl into a smile when his arm tightens around my waist, pulling me against him. When I feel his hard length pressing against my thigh, I turn my face into the pillow, muffling the laugh that escapes my lips. Rolling onto my side, I shimmy back, pushing my ass against his erection with a mischievous grin.

Gabriel groans under his breath. "Calla," he murmurs into my hair.

I press my lips together. "Hmm?"

"You're teasing me," he says.

"She's good at that."

My head turns to find Kade leaning in the doorway, his wickedly muscular arms crossed over his broad chest. He's clean-shaven today and dressed casually in navy joggers and a black V-neck. Before I have a chance to respond to that, he struts into the room and flops down onto the bed, effectively sandwiching me between him and Gabriel. He yanks the pillow from under my head, stuffing it under his as I grumble at him, trying to shove him off the bed with zero success. Gabriel chuckles on my other side, and I roll my eyes. "Don't encourage this behavior," I say.

Kade smirks at me. "Wakey, wakey. Time to get out of bed, sleepy-heads. It's almost noon."

Narrowing my eyes at him, I snuggle back into Gabriel's arms. "That's seriously what you barged in here to tell us?"

He reaches for me and taps the tip of my nose. "Nope. Thought you should know that I talked to your professors, and—"

"You what?" I cut him off, my voice pitching higher with unease. The idea of Kade waltzing around campus, *talking* to people I respect about *me*... I grind my molars, waiting for his response.

"They've all agreed to accommodate you finishing the term online."

My stomach sinks, and I suddenly feel claustrophobic between two vampires. "I don't want to take online classes."

Gabriel's thumb brushes back and forth over my hip. I think he's trying to keep me calm, but all I want to do right now is shove Kade onto the floor and yell.

What an infuriating, overbearing—

"It's safer," he explains, ignoring my glare.

"This is ridiculous," I mutter, shifting out of Gabriel's arms. I scoot toward the end of the bed to put space between me and them, then turn to look at Kade. "What will Brighton think? How am I supposed to convince her everything is all sunshine and roses when in reality I'm living with four vampires and her family hunts them for a living?"

Gabriel frowns and reaches for me, but I slide off the end of his bed and stand, crossing my arms. I'm still wearing Kade's shirt, which isn't lost on him, considering the lust-filled look he sends my way.

"You're overthinking this," Kade says with a sigh. "We can make her think whatever we need to—whatever is going to keep you safe."

I blink at him, torn between the fluttering sensation in my stomach and the flare of anger. It's very confusing. "No," I finally say. "I don't want you messing with her head anymore."

He doesn't miss a beat. "Ask me if I care."

Heat rises in my cheeks, and I drop my arms to my sides, closing my hands into fists without thinking about it. "Can you stop being a complete asshole for two seconds, Kade? She is my best friend, and while you don't give a shit about her, I do."

Kade sits up, leaning against the headboard, and pins me with a dark stare. "Forgive the fuck out of me, Calla, if I don't feel the need to accommodate the legacy of our enemy. Especially at the expense of your safety."

"She doesn't even know about the hunters," I shout, my pulse kicking up—along with my blood pressure. "You can't hold what her family does against her. She has absolutely nothing to do with it!"

"This isn't up for discussion, angel," Gabriel says in a gentle voice. "Letting you go to school would be reckless with Selene still playing her games. We can revisit this once she's been dealt with."

My gaze whips in his direction, and I regard him incredulously. Of the four vampires, I really did believe that Gabriel would take my side. I shake my head. "And when will that be?" All of the warmth and pleasantness from waking up in Gabriel's arms has left my body, leaving me standing before them cold and agitated.

Kade and Gabriel exchange a glance, then Kade shrugs, which makes Gabriel frown. He's been doing that a lot lately, but I can't really blame him, considering he's got a psycho ex-lover slash supernatural sire trying to control him.

It's been a day since I returned from Selene's, which means her blood and venom are still in my system. She could still come after me and make good on her threat to turn me into a vampire. My stomach roils at the thought, and I exhale a heavy breath, snagging the guys' attention once more.

Gabriel presses his lips together for a moment before speaking. "Perhaps we can discuss the possibility of you attending classes, so long as Kade accompanies you."

My brows pinch together. "To every class?" As much as I would love to get back to class—to some semblance of normalcy—I can't help but recall the single lecture he went to with me. Of course, I have no idea what the professor taught that day, but I do remember how Kade played my body like a damn instrument. Thinking about him being there for every class... "I don't think that's a good idea."

"We can also hire more private security that will monitor you while you're outside of the house."

"You mean compound," I mutter under my breath. That's more and more what it feels like these days. I sigh. "Look, I appreciate you wanting to keep me safe, but—"

"My plan was far less complex," Kade interrupts, rolling his eyes. He turns his gaze to me. "The semester is pretty much over anyway."

"Kade," Gabriel says, "we're not only trying to keep her alive but happy as well." He looks at me. "Your wellbeing is important."

Kade groans and slides off the bed before I can respond to Gabriel. "You guys..." He shakes his head, walking to the door. "Pains in my ass."

I flip him the bird as he leaves the room even though he can't see it, earning a small chuckle from Gabriel. I sigh, resting my knee on the end of the bed. "This is such a mess." I understand their response to the situation, and appreciate how important my safety is to them, but being locked up, even in a house as nice as this one, is going to make me go stir-crazy. All I've wanted since I got here was normalcy. A sliver of my old life. And with this... I'm being pushed further away from it every day.

He offers me a sympathetic smile. "I know, angel. It'll be over soon, you have my word."

I manage a small smile in return. "Thank you," I tell him, "for caring about what *I* want."

Gabriel nods. "Despite how it may seem, Kade does as well. He's just worried. Having control over the situation makes him feel better."

If anyone understands that, it's me. So as frustrated as I am at Kade, I can appreciate that his overbearing behavior is coming from a good place.

***

After breakfast, I stop by my room and change into a matching black sports bra and legging set and tie my hair up before meeting Atlas in the gym over the garage.

He's hitting the punching bag in the corner of the room when I walk in, not stopping as I approach, though I know he heard me enter.

I steal a water bottle from the mini fridge and crack it open, taking a sip as I sit on one of the mats in front of the wall of mirrors and start stretching. I'm not sure what he'll have me doing today, but warming up is probably a good idea.

I'm bent over, my hands wrapped around my feet to stretch my legs when he finally walks over and acknowledges my presence.

"Morning," he grumbles, grabbing a water bottle and downing half of it before tossing it onto the floor where his hoodie and phone are sitting.

I let go of my feet and straighten, meeting his gaze. "Morning," I echo.

He jerks a hand through his hair and crouches in front of me, looking me over before he says, "How are you feeling?"

I blink at him, surprised at the question. "I... I'm fine. Better."

Atlas nods. "Good. Get up. Ten minutes on the bike at whatever speed and tension you can handle, then we'll meet back here." He doesn't wait for me to respond before straightening and grabbing his phone off the floor. I go from having his complete attention to not existing in the space of a few seconds.

I watch him the entire time I'm riding the bike. He is typing on his phone, lines of tension etched in his forehead. I want to ask what's going on, if it has something to do with Selene or the hunters, but there's also a part of me that doesn't want to know. Not yet. I need to focus on my training, on getting stronger and more skilled—so I can protect myself against the things I'm wary to ask about.

My heart is pounding when I climb off the bike and walk back over to Atlas. He puts his phone down as I approach and turns to face me.

"Everything okay?" I ask before I can stop myself.

Atlas hesitates. "No." He steps closer, his gaze darkening. "There's a vampire who threatened someone who belongs to me." He tilts his head to the side slightly, those liquid silver eyes flicking between mine. "I don't take kindly to that."

I swallow hard, my breath hitching when he glides his fingers along my arms before resting his hands on my shoulders. "And I don't take kindly to being repeatedly used as a pawn," I finally say, my pulse jack-hammering when his thumbs brush over my collarbones. "So teach me how to fight back." I meet his gaze. "Please."

A muscle feathers along his jaw, and he nods, removing his hands from me. "Turn around."

I do as he says, exhaling a slow breath. When he steps in close behind me, I press my lips together, fighting the urge to close my eyes and lean into the warmth of his chest against my back.

Shit, I need to focus.

"Now what?" I force out.

"What does your gut tell you?"

"Uhh, right now, it's telling me to run." The urge to put distance between us is about as strong as the one to whirl around and kiss him, but I'm not about to reveal that.

"That's fair," he says in a low voice, resting his hands on my hips. "Your body recognizes danger. It has detected a predator and your fight or flight instinct has kicked in."

"So I should fight, right?" I say, a little breathless with the way his hands are warming my skin. "That's the whole point of this."

"When it comes to vampires, it's best not to run. But you already knew that. So if you can fight them, do it."

"And if I can't?"

He leans in, his breath stirring the hair tucked behind my ear. "Then you're most likely dead."

"Great," I breathe.

His grip on my hips tightens. "This training is more for your peace of mind than anything else, Calla. You won't have to use what I'm teaching you when we're around."

"There will come a day where that won't be an option, so it's important for me to learn, because if Selene tries to—"

Atlas spins me around to face him. "You don't have to worry about her," he assures me. "She won't get close enough to hurt you, let alone sire you."

The blood drains from my face at the thought, and I try to step away from him, but his grip holds. "Atlas…"

"You're scared of becoming a vampire," he comments, and the gentle tone of his voice is something so foreign to me, I finally look at him. There's no glamour behind his words, but I still find myself nodding. No sense in hiding it.

I don't want to be a vampire.

Atlas exhales through his nose, flicking his tongue over his bottom lip and nodding. "Okay."

"Okay?" I echo, my brows pinching together.

"It's not a discussion we need to have right now, Calla. Let's focus on your training."

"Yes, please," I say in a tight voice, trying to ignore the voice of panic in the back of my head. The one telling me to put distance between me and Atlas, to turn and run the hell out of here—not that I'd get far. The idea of eternity is far too big to think about without raising my blood pressure. I'd much rather focus on learning how to protect myself from being forced into vampirism.

"Good." He steps away from me, walking over to one of the cabinets built into the wall, and pulls something out. He walks back to me and holds his hand out, revealing a black leather-bound blade.

After a moment of hesitation, I take it from him with a frown, turning the sturdy handle over in my hand. "You're giving me a dagger?"

"It would appear that way." I want to roll my eyes at the mocking tone of his voice. Then he says, "The blade is infused with white ash."

My eyes widen. He's just handed me a rare, very lethal-to-vampires weapon. "Don't you think that's a little risky?" I ask him, tightening my grip on the hilt of the dagger, testing the weight of it in my hand. It feels good.

His lips twitch. "If I thought for a second you'd try to use this on me or the others, this would be a much different discussion, Calla."

I arch a brow at him. "What makes you think I won't? I've stabbed you before," I point out.

He wraps his fingers around my wrist, but instead of applying pressure to make me release the dagger like I thought he might, he says, "Are you planning to stab me?"

"No." The word leaves my mouth before I can clamp my mouth shut, the urge to answer honestly too strong to ignore let alone fight.

"What about the others?"

"No."

He drops my wrist, and the glamour falls away. "Until that changes, I'm going to teach you to protect yourself against vampires to the best of your ability."

I scowl and mutter, "I know what you can teach me next."

His eyes glimmer with a hint of amusement. "There is no way to resist glamour."

"Could be fun to try, though," Lex says, strutting into the room with a grin. He walks over to us and throws his arm around my shoulders, eyeing the dagger in my hand. "Oooh, pointy."

I roll my eyes and return it to the sheath. "What are you up to?" I ask suspiciously, shrugging him off me.

Lex pouts. "I'm bored, so I thought I'd come see what the two of you were up to."

"I'm learning how to kick your ass," I say, unable to help the grin spreading across my lips. It feels good to be taking control again—at least where I can.

He glances toward Atlas, who shrugs, crossing his arms over his chest. "Interesting."

"Are you done?" Atlas asks. "You're interrupting. So if you're not going to help, get out."

Lex keeps his eyes on me, pressing his lips together against a smile. "Okay, okay." I think he's going to leave, but instead he says, "I'll help. Where do you want me?"

I arch a brow at him, then turn my quizzical expression to my trainer. "Seriously? I can't beat you yet, and you think adding a second vampire is going to help?"

He shrugs. "A *different* vampire. Fight him for a few minutes so I can watch your technique from an outside perspective."

"I... All right, fine." I go to toss the dagger onto the floor, but Atlas moves too fast for me to track, catching it and shaking his head.

"You're never to take this off. Understand?" I nod, and he kneels before me, wrapping the guard around my thigh. My breath catches as his fingers brush my thigh, and I flush at how close he is to the increasing heat between my legs. I want to close my eyes and let the floor swallow me whole, because he can definitely sense how much this is turning me on.

Once the dagger is secured, he stands and meets my gaze, offering a dark smirk before turning his attention to Lex.

Fuck me.

Lex claps his hands together, and I take a step away from Atlas, sighing as I turn to face my new opponent.

"Keep your stance balanced," Atlas instructs from the sidelines, his arms crossed over his chest and his gaze focused on us. There's a dark determination in his eyes, but something else as well. Something that has heat swirling in my stomach at the intensity of it.

I manage to pull myself out of it and turn my attention fully to Lex as he circles me slowly, his eyes gleaming.

I'm glad one of us is enjoying this...

"What's your move?" Lex taunts, bouncing from one foot to the other.

I jump back when he jabs forward with his arm, his hand outstretched and reaching for me. "My move? To attack the guy who enjoys pain?" I offer a blunt laugh and dodge his second attempt at grabbing me. "You'll probably get a hard-on if I stab you."

He nods enthusiastically. "And then you'll be the one getting stabbed," he shoots back with a wink.

I blink at him. "Oh, Lex. It's a damn good thing you're freakishly attractive, because you sure as hell aren't funny."

Lex moves in a blur, and I don't have a chance to whirl around before he has an arm around my waist, hauling my back against his chest.

I scowl. "How am I supposed to beat someone I can't fucking see move?"

He leans in and nips my neck playfully, and I shove him away with another scowl. Of course, he lets me do it, otherwise his arm would still be locked around my waist.

Atlas rubs his jaw, glancing between us. "You need to anticipate the movement before it happens. You won't be able to move at the same speed as a vampire, so you need to learn to move first."

"Are you kidding me?"

His impassive expression doesn't change, but he leans against the wall, crossing one ankle over the other. "It's not easy, I recognize that, but it's what you need to learn at this... stage of your life."

I prop my hands on my hips, vaguely noticing Lex wander over to the barbells. "What the hell does *this stage* of my life mean, Atlas?"

"He's saying, if you were a vampire, it would be a hell of a lot easier," Lex calls out from the other side of the room.

Atlas shoots Lex a glare. "That is *not* what I'm saying." He turns his attention back to me with a sigh. "It'll take some time, but it is possible to learn. I wouldn't waste my time here if I didn't think you had a shot at getting this."

Now *that* I believe.

I nod. "Let's try again."

Lex appears in front of me, and I jump back, widening my stance to keep my balance steady, and duck when he swings his arm toward me. I kick out, catching his legs, and a grin spreads across my lips when he lands hard on his back.

"Keep moving," Atlas bellows in a low voice from a few feet away.

I fight the urge to look at him, to see what expression is painted on that chiseled face when his voice is that... strained. But I can't waste those precious seconds when I finally have the upper hand.

I slam my knee into Lex's stomach, pressing my full weight into him, then drive my elbow into his throat. He coughs violently, his face going red as he tries to pull air into his lungs. When I reach for the dagger at my thigh to show them both what I would do if this were any other vampire outside of the ones I live with, Lex manages to wrap his legs around mine and flip us over. My back hits the mat, and I don't have a chance to even attempt to roll away and escape before Lex traps my wrists over my head, his legs sandwiching one of mine, putting his knee dangerously close to the apex of my thighs.

"Fuck," I growl, my heart pounding against my ribcage as I glare up at him.

"You did well," Atlas offers, walking toward us at a leisurely pace, his eyes locked on me.

I spare him a glance, blowing the hair out of my face. "Look at me," I mutter, pissed that Lex got the upper hand so quickly.

Atlas's lips twitch, his eyes darkening with desire. "Trust me, I am."

A low rumble sounds in Lex's throat, and my eyes snap toward him, quickly finding the bulge in his pants. A flush fills my cheeks and chest, my skin tingling where Lex's fingers are wrapped around my wrists.

"What's next, coach?" Lex asks Atlas without looking away from me.

My eyes widen. He doesn't... He couldn't possibly mean—

"She clearly enjoys being held down," Atlas muses, walking around the mats as he keeps his eyes on us.

I scowl but I really can't say much, considering I've stopped fighting him. It's safe to say our training is done for the moment.

He drags his tongue over his bottom lip, a glint in his eyes that makes my pulse jump under his scrutiny. "I think she'd enjoy it even more if you slid one of your hands into her pants," Atlas says, his jaw set tight, as if that's what *he* wants to do instead of directing Lex to do it.

Lex's lips curl into a grin as he hovers over me, his usual scent of citrus and spice filling my senses as he switches his grip on my wrists into one hand, following Atlas's direction. Slowly, he drags his fingers across my collarbone before sliding them over my sports bra, down my bare stomach, and pauses at the waistband of my leggings. I'm pressing my lips together, trying to hide how my breathing has picked up, though it's probably more than obvious based on my heartbeat and the quick rise and fall of my chest.

"How wet do you think she is already?" Lex muses.

I narrow my eyes at him, my cheeks flaming as I fight the urge to look away or close my eyes instead. "Says the guy with a hard-on."

Atlas exhales on a short laugh. "Why don't you tell him, Calla?"

It's my turn to laugh. "Fuck off. I never agreed to take your direction when it came to *this*."

Lex glances over to Atlas, then back to me, cocking a brow. "I suppose we'll just have to find out." He presses his palm flat against my stomach and slides his fingers into my leggings. I'm wearing panties, so there's still a thin silk barrier between his fingers and the throbbing heat at my core, but his light, teasing touch makes my breath hitch.

"Hmm," Lex purrs, "you're soaked."

My muscles tighten, and I attempt to press my thighs together, but he stops me.

"Wrong way. I want you spread wide for me." He pulls his fingers out of my panties before tugging them down with my leggings until they're at my knees.

I suck in a shallow breath when the cool air from the gym reaches my entrance. I steal a glance toward Atlas, whose eyes are blazing with lust, though his jaw is clenched as if he's in pain. "What," I say to him, suddenly feeling bold, "you don't want to join? Too afraid you'll break me?" I taunt him with his own words.

Before he can answer, Lex crawls over me again and puts his lips to my ear, murmuring, "Atlas likes to watch."

I shiver at his words, then gasp softly when his fingers brush my sex, tracing along my folds at an agonizingly slow pace. He circles my clit a few times before going back to teasing my folds.

"Ask him," Lex says, looking into my eyes.

"What?" I breathe, hyper-focused on the teasing fingers inching closer to my entrance. My brows pinch together in confusion while my heart pounds against my chest.

He smirks darkly. "Ask him to let me make you come."

"I..." My voice trails off. I try to tug my wrists free, but his grip is impossible to break. I grit my teeth against the spike of pleasure when Lex presses his thumb against my clit and my focus narrows on Atlas as he walks closer and crouches at my side. Before I can turn my face away, he snags my chin, forcing my gaze to his, and stays there. Doesn't say a word, just waits.

Fucking bastards. Both of them.

I could refuse them. Neither vampire is glamouring me, which almost makes it worse. They're making *me* do this on my own. And as much as I'd like to ignore the heat gathering between my thighs and the tension coiling low in my belly, begging for release, I can't.

I hate that I don't hate this.

In fact, it's making me hot. I can feel my muscles tightening, trembling beneath Lex as I stare into Atlas's eyes.

"Let him," I say through my teeth.

Atlas tilts his head to the side slightly. "Sorry, what was that? I didn't quite catch it."

Bull-fucking-shit he didn't. The guy has supernatural hearing.

I narrow my eyes. "Let. Him. Make. Me. Come." I enunciate every word, my voice clear and demanding.

There's a challenge in his eyes that sends liquid heat straight to my core, then he says, "Ask nicely."

My nostrils flare. "Fuck you."

He tuts his tongue. "That's not very nice, Calla."

Lex pinches my folds together, and I gasp at the unfamiliar yet pleasant sensations rippling through me.

"Let's try that again," Atlas offers.

I stare at him for what feels like an eternity before I finally drag in a breath and succumb to his demand. "Let him make me come." My voice lowers to something just above a whisper. "Please."

I'm rewarded with one of his rare smiles as he releases my chin. "Now how hard was that?"

My gaze flicks down to his groin before returning to his eyes. "About as hard as you are."

Lex chuckles, moving his fingers over my folds, spreading them with his thumb and forefinger before dipping inside with a single, blunt digit, curling it in just the right spot to make me suck in a breath. "Right there?" he checks.

I nod before my head falls back against the mat, and I spread my legs as wide as I can with my leggings around my knees.

Lex takes his time warming me up with one finger before adding a second. They glide in and out with ease, and I moan, biting my lip to try and contain the sound. I'm not sure why, though this room does echo a bit, and I don't need the entire house immediately aware of what we're up to in here. Especially considering we're supposed to be training me to fight vampires... not fuck them.

When Lex adds a third finger, I press my lips together at the delicious sensation of being stretched for him, which only makes me wetter, letting him pump in and out easier. I start to close my eyes, but Atlas's commanding voice stops me.

"Eyes on me," he says. "I want to see your face when he makes you come on his fingers."

The tension builds at an overwhelming speed as I force my gaze back to Atlas and bite my bottom lip. My hips jerk, trying to push Lex's fingers deeper as I grind on them.

"Are you going to clench around his fingers?" Atlas asks, his voice thick with arousal.

"Y-yes," I breathe, my clit throbbing almost painfully. "Don't stop, Lex."

"No fucking chance." He picks up the pace, curling his fingers and rubbing hard against the most sensitive spot in my pussy.

"Make her come," Atlas says to Lex without taking his eyes off me.

"With pleasure." His thumb brushes my clit, circling it hard and fast as he pumps his fingers in and out at record speed.

"Holy shit," I breathe, almost choking on the air I pull into my lungs. My pussy clenches around Lex's fingers, and I cry out my release, my eyes locked on Atlas as my orgasm overtakes me. My legs shake, my heels digging into the mat as my heart attempts to launch itself out of my chest.

Lex continues his thrusts as I ride the wave of my climax, my hips jerking off the mat. I settle a few blissful moments later, the aftershocks rippling through me as Lex slides his fingers out and pulls my leggings back up.

Atlas shifts back as Lex gets up, hauling me up with him. I immediately sway on my feet, but he's there to steady me. After a few seconds, I'm good to stand on my own, and I take a step away to show him that. He chuckles, watching me with amusement in his eyes. My gaze swings back and forth between Lex and Atlas, my mouth too dry to say anything, because damn, that was fucking hot.

After our little, uh, *break*, we spend the rest of the afternoon training. I get knocked on my ass several times, but overall, I feel pretty good. I managed to stand my ground for a lot of the session, even for a minute when both vampires closed in on me.

Even when my mind wandered for the briefest of moments to the idea of the three of us doing something a lot more fun than training, especially with Lex's words playing on a loop in my head.

Atlas likes to watch.

After a quick shower, I stand in front of the massive bathroom mirror and run a comb through my hair. There's a soft knock at the door to the bedroom, so I tie the plush white robe around myself and walk over to open it, revealing a smiling Gabriel. The sight of him instantly makes me feel better. Until I'm quickly reminded how easy it could be to lose him.

I clear my throat before saying, "What's up?"

He holds up a white rectangular iPhone box. "Thought you could use a new one."

Taking it from him, I offer a smile. "Thank you. And I'm sorry for losing the other one."

"We found it, but the screen was shattered beyond repair." He shrugs. "It's no big deal, angel, so don't worry about it."

Ha. Right. We've got enough to worry about as it stands.

I reach for him, leaning on my tiptoes and pressing my lips against his cheek. "Thanks again. I'm going to get changed and come out in a minute."

Gabriel nods, stepping back. "Take your time."

Once he's gone and I've closed the door, I pull out the phone to find it already set up. I open a new message, biting my thumbnail as I stare at the screen, considering what to say.

Hey Bri, sorry for the silence on my end. Everything is fine, but I miss you.

I hit send, and a minute later, my phone is vibrating with an incoming call from Brighton.

"Brighton, hey."

"Hey, babe! Are you feeling better?"

I press my lips together. "Definitely. How are you? Have I missed anything good?"

She laughs. "Nah, things have been pretty boring, as usual. Nothing new. Let's meet for brunch on Monday, though. I miss our weekly date."

"Uh, yeah. That sounds good." So long as I can figure out how to convince the guys to let me go.

"Amazing. Listen, I have to run, but text me!"

Before I can respond, the call ends, leaving me with a knot in my stomach. Nothing seemed *off* per se, but with recent discoveries, I can't help second-guessing everything I think I know about my best friend.

I scour the cupboards and fridge, trying to put something together that is going to be relatively edible. I'm still waiting for Gabriel to give me a cooking lesson, but I'm too hungry for that right now. I settle on some chicken skewers I found in the freezer and start cutting up some potatoes to mash.

Lex walks in as I'm preheating the oven. "Does Gabriel know you're using his kitchen?" he asks in a teasing voice, leaning against the counter beside me. "Need any help?"

"Sure," I tell him, "I was going to make a chopped salad if you want to do that." Salads have always been one of my go-to meals. They're hard to mess up and easy to customize with a variety of ingredients to keep them from being repetitive and boring.

"You got it." He pushes away from the counter and walks to the fridge, while I resume chopping up the potatoes.

I suck in a sharp breath when the knife slips, slicing into the side of my hand. "Shit." I press my lips together and turn toward the sink to rinse the cut out, but Lex moves in front of me, blocking my path as blood drips onto the floor between us. "Lex—"

He grins at me, taking my hand gently in his. "Don't waste it." Lifting my hand to his mouth, he drags his tongue along the cut before closing his lips around it.

I wince against the pain ebbing around the wound and yelp when Lex pulls back abruptly, covering his mouth and squinting as if he's trying to convince himself to swallow something he doesn't like the taste of. Instead, he starts coughing, and I frown at him. "Uh, I'll try not to take that as an insult."

When his face reddens and he starts to choke, my pulse races. Before I have a chance to call for someone, Kade, Gabriel, and Atlas all rush into the kitchen. Kade moves to Lex's side, guiding him over to the sink, where he heaves crimson into it.

"What the hell?" I breathe.

Gabriel disappears for what can't be more than a few seconds, returning with a blood bag, which he opens and tosses to Lex. He downs it quickly, tossing the empty bag onto the counter, and coughs a bit more before straightening.

Atlas watches the whole thing with dark, narrowed eyes.

"Are you okay?" I ask Lex in a small voice, unable to ignore the pit in my stomach.

He clears his throat. "Never better."

"What was that?" I demand, looking around at the guys.

Atlas and Gabriel share a look before Atlas says, "Selene must have used a witch to spell your blood to produce an adverse reaction to any vampire who drinks it."

"Likely the same witch who created the barrier spell around Selene's home that kept us from finding you."

I press my hand against my forehead, fighting an oncoming dizzy spell, and lean against the counter. The thought of being manipulated by yet another supernatural is making my skin crawl. "What does that mean? Is it going to go away?"

Gabriel sighs. "Magic like this is tricky," he explains. "It won't go away on its own. The witch who performed the spell needs to reverse it."

"Or die," Lex chimes in. "Dead witch means no spell."

"Right," I say, shaking my head as I straighten, my head a little less fuzzy than a minute ago. "Or the four of you could just keep your fangs to yourself," I offer dryly.

Kade snorts. "As if you actually want that." His eyes snare mine, and the dark heat there warms my core. "Deny it all you want, we know just how much you enjoy being bitten."

I want to look away, to hide the heat flaring in my cheeks, but I don't. Instead, I say, "Whatever. We need to focus on the bigger issue here. Selene didn't get what she wanted. We have to prepare for retaliation."

"I'll take care of it," Atlas says in a grim voice.

My eyes snap to him as my chest tightens, and I walk around the counter to get closer, jabbing him in the chest. "I don't care how powerful you think you are, that woman is insane. You can't just—"

Atlas cracks a smile, stopping my tirade mid-sentence. "You're worried about me."

"I..." I clamp my mouth shut, unable to dispute his claim. Because damn it, I do care. About him—about all of them. "I think we need to explore the idea that killing Selene may not be the best course of action." Glancing toward Gabriel, I quickly add, "She absolutely deserves to die. If you ask me, she deserves far fucking worse, but she's connected to the hunters—at least one of them. We should explore that, get some answers, and then deliver her the fate she deserves."

FIFTEEN

GABRIEL

Listening to Calla at this moment, I've never been more certain of one terrifying thing. I don't wish to live in a world where she doesn't live and breathe.

She is resilient and brave, and in the face of such atrocities as she's experienced since we came into her life, she remains one of the kindest —albeit sharp-tongued—humans I've met.

Calla is absolutely magnificent. Truth be told, her fiery attitude and defiance only intrigue me more, and the thought of one day losing her, whether it be to old age or something else, twists me up inside.

After the incident with Lex in the kitchen, I help her finish making dinner, and the five of us sit around the table in the dining room, mostly picking at our food. No one seems to have an appetite now.

"Maybe I should spend some time with Brighton," Calla speaks up, keeping her gaze on the almost completely untouched plate in front of her. She's pushing the mashed potatoes around with her fork without eating any; she's as concerned as the rest of us, making me wish we could've kept her in the dark a little longer. If nothing else but to keep her from worrying herself sick, which is where I fear she's headed.

Kade looks at her with an arched brow, but before he can open his mouth and say something almost guaranteed to upset her, she drops her fork onto her plate.

"Hear me out," she says in a firm voice, snaring the attention of us all. "We need more information about the hunters. I can get it.

Brighton and I are going to have our regular brunch on Monday, but I could get together with her sooner. Maybe suggest a sleepover at her place so I can search for—"

"No," Atlas cuts in.

"Yeah, not happening," Lex agrees.

I offer her a gentle smile, sympathizing with her desire to help. A quick glance around the table tells me the rest of the guys are feeling something too, because as quickly as they shot down her suggestion, they're all staring at her as if she's the answer to all of our prayers. In some ways, she is. And her protectiveness over us is refreshing. It's definitely new, and it makes me want to steal her away and lock her up in my bedroom. I'd like nothing more than to keep her next to me in my bed and never let her leave. It's a shame we don't have that luxury right now.

"Fine," she grits out. "What's *your* plan?"

"There wasn't a plan, per se, for a long time," Kade tells her. "While the hunters want us dead—and have for decades—we just want to exist in peace."

"For the most part," Lex chimes in with a wink at Calla.

She rolls her eyes at him.

I swallow a sigh. "There are some vampires who are a danger to humankind. It is in their nature—*our* nature—to stalk and prey on the weaker species to survive. Many take pleasure in the hunt. It is because of them that we are all in danger of being hunted."

"That still doesn't answer my question," she says, flicking her gaze between the four of us.

Atlas clears his throat. "It's not a simple answer. Have we considered taking the approach of wiping out the hunters as they wish to do to us? Of course. But the thing is, they also help us, in a sense, by hunting the rogue vampires who are out of control and risk exposing our kind to the general population."

Calla frowns, seeming to run through his words a few times before she says, "So there has to be some middle ground. That's what you're thinking?"

"Not with psycho vamps like Selene running around," Kade grumbles before catching the hardness in my gaze. "Sorry, bro."

I shrug; he's not wrong. Selene is exactly the type of vampire the world would benefit from having hunted.

"What if there's a possibility of working with the hunters?" Calla asks, focusing on Atlas more than the rest of us. It's just as well—my head really isn't in the best place to be having this conversation. Not when I can't get Selene's voice out of it. Calla is expecting retaliation, and she's smart to. Selene is up to something—she always is—and we need to prepare for whatever it is.

"Yeah, that's not going to happen," Lex says. "Too many years of history there."

She crosses her arms over her chest, leaning back against the couch. "I refuse to believe that."

Lex shrugs. "That's your choice. It'd probably be different if you saw them in action."

Calla visibly shudders, and there's a dark pang of guilt in my chest, though I wasn't the cause.

"We need to stay the course," Atlas says. "We'll continue observing the hunters' patterns and what Ellis Industries is up to so we know which groups of vampires we need to alert to keep them safe. While Selene appears to be linked somehow to the hunters courtesy of Scott Ellis, they really are two separate issues."

Calla leans back, straightening in her chair, but remains silent. The tension in her expression is a clear tell of how displeased she is, and I'm a little surprised she doesn't push back more. She's never been one to back away from an argument—even with Atlas, who typically scares the crap out of most people—but she says nothing.

When my phone chimes on the table in front of me, my stomach clenches with unease, as if my body knows who it is before I even pick it up. I stare at the screen, gripping the phone so tight in my hand, it's a wonder it doesn't crack. The message staring back at me is from an unfamiliar number, but the area code is local. It wouldn't matter; the message is very clear.

I've been alive long enough to learn great patience, Gabriel. However, that only extends for so long. Your time is running out. Come to me, or your precious human consort will pay for your mistake. I'm sure you've figured out by now that her blood is tainted. Keep me waiting, and I'll have it altered to be poisonous to her as well.

I read the message three times before shooting off a reply. I shouldn't play into her game, but the anger in my chest pushes me to react before I can stop myself.

You're lying. Always lying.

Her response is quick.

Perhaps I am, but we both know you'll follow my instructions regardless, just in case there's a tiny possibility that what I'm saying is the truth.

A growl tears from me, and while Calla frowns at me with wide eyes, I stiffen when another message comes through.

You have twenty-four hours, my love. I look forward to seeing you soon.

I drop my phone onto the table next to my plate, making the water in my glass ripple. A few seconds later, a final message comes through. An address to a highly sought-after apartment building on S Street.

"Gabriel?" Calla's voice sounds muffled, as if she's calling out for me from the bottom of a well.

I blink at the screen before tearing my eyes away and forcing myself to meet her soft brown gaze. Her eyes are slightly wider than normal and filled with concern. "Everything is going to be fine," I tell her, needing that look of fear to disappear from her face. I never want to be the reason she looks like that.

Her lips turn down and her brows inch closer. "What did she say?"

I exhale a heavy breath, reading the text aloud.

Kade curses, while Lex slams his fist against the table, making the silverware clatter.

"Lex," Atlas warns in a low voice, then turns his gaze to me. "How do you want to handle this? Say the word, and I'll finish it tonight."

Calla opens her mouth as if she's going to protest that, and she'd be right to. We just said that killing Selene before we know what's going on with the hunters is likely not our best option.

The pit in my stomach grows, and I grit my teeth. I've done many selfish things in my life, but I can't bring myself to allow Calla to stand in the line of danger when there's something I can do to ensure her safety.

I clear my throat, forcing bile down, and everyone turns their gazes on me. Taking a deep breath, I say, "I'm going to end this."

Calla shakes her head. "Gabriel—"

"Enough," I cut her off in a sharp tone, standing and ignoring the look of shock on her face. The thought of hurting her makes me want to put my fist through a wall, so I clench my jaw and walk away from the table.

Kade calls after me, but I don't turn back.

My mind is made up. I won't let Selene touch Calla again—even if that means I'm forced to face the nightmares of my past to make sure of it.

SIXTEEN

CALLA

I'm getting to my feet before he disappears down the hallway, practically growling at Kade when he catches my wrist.

"Give him a minute," Kade says.

"Let fucking go of me," I say in a such a calm voice, it sends a chill through me.

His silver eyes narrow, and he holds on for a stretch of silence that seems to last forever. My gaze doesn't waver. I tug on my wrist, clenching my jaw to keep from snarling in his face.

"This is fucking ridiculous," Kade growls, turning to Atlas. "Let's just kill the bitch now. Let her think Gabriel is coming, and then ambush her ass."

"She'll be expecting that," Lex says, his voice laced with agitation; he doesn't want Gabriel to go either. None of us do. "But we need to find out what she knows about the hunters," he says in a level tone. "Whatever that meeting with Scott Ellis was about, we need to know." His eyes shift toward Atlas. "You know we do."

Atlas's expression darkens, and he shakes his head but doesn't disagree. "Kade." His voice is firm. And when Kade releases me, I don't stick around to question the surprising turn of events. If Atlas is on my side, hell must be freezing over. That, or he's as worried about Gabriel as I am.

I hurry out of the room, jogging upstairs, not stopping until I'm standing outside Gabriel's bedroom. The door is closed over, but not shut completely, so I knock once and push it open, letting myself in. When my eyes land on where Gabriel is folding a pair of navy dress pants into a black duffel bag, I slam the door shut. He keeps his back to me, but I watch his shoulders rise and fall as he sighs. Fear and anger go to war inside my chest, making my throat feel as if it's closing in as I struggle to find the right words to express the emotions threatening to break me.

Finally, he turns to face me, his expression gentle yet sad. "Calla—"

"No," I snap, walking closer. I keep a few strides between us. "You're not going, Gabriel." I'm fully aware I'm not physically capable of stopping him, but I still need to say it. He needs to hear the determination in my voice.

He glances at the floor, sliding his hands into his pockets. "There's nothing I can say that will make you feel better about this situation. I'm sorry." He lifts his gaze, meeting mine as he closes the short distance between us in unhurried steps. When he stops right in front of me, my breath halts, and he runs his hands up my arms, along my shoulders, then cups my face, his thumbs brushing over my heated cheeks.

"Kissing me right now isn't going to make this better," I tell him, swallowing past the lump in my throat and willing my heart to return to a normal pace instead of the erratic pounding currently filling my chest.

A faint smile touches his lips, and he tilts his head, his eyes searching mine. "You're right. But I'd like to anyway."

My eyes burn, threatening tears, so I lean into him on my tiptoes, wrapping my arms around his middle and skimming my nose along his. I don't want him to see the tears in my eyes.

Gabriel sighs softly and tips my head back, sealing his lips over mine. I close my eyes, melting into him, losing myself in the warmth and firmness of his mouth against mine. I grip the back of his shirt, clinging to him as if it's the last time we'll touch, because it very well could be. That thought sends me into a tailspin, and I put all of my anger and fear and lust into the kiss, pushing my tongue into his mouth and grazing his as his fingers slide into my hair and tangle there.

I allow myself to get lost in him for far too long before I pull away, pressing my hands firmly against his chest to push back. Shaking my head, I open my eyes and meet his gaze. "No. You're not going to distract me from this, Gabriel."

He frowns, pulling one hand out of my hair and lacing his fingers through mine before I can move away. "Calla—"

"What do you think is going to happen if you go to her?" I demand, fear clawing into my chest like razor-sharp talons. Knowing what she did to him, all the manipulation, going so far as to make him immortal so she could control him forever... It makes me want to scream. That, and use the white ash dagger Atlas gave me to end this whole thing. I'm not naive enough to think I would be successful in a fight against her, though I did manage to stab her... The idea of driving that dagger into her chest sparks something vicious in me that I don't particularly like. I'm torn between wanting to stand back while the guys take her on and learn how to fight her myself.

Gabriel tucks a stray bit of hair behind my ear with his free hand. "I don't know, but I do know what will happen if I don't, and I can't let that come to pass."

"I..." I bite the inside of my cheek, staring hard at where his fingers are wrapped around mine. "I don't want to lose you." My voice cracks, and I squeeze my eyes shut. This wretched feeling of helplessness is threatening to overtake me, and I fucking hate it.

He gives my hand a gentle squeeze. "You won't, angel. I swear it."

I shake my head again, not trusting myself to speak. I need to keep it together right now. If I let myself start to cry, I'm not sure I'll be able to stop.

With a heavy sigh, I pull away from Gabriel and drop onto the end of his bed, glaring at the duffle bag as he resumes packing it.

"You should be catching up on schoolwork," he says in a soft tone, and yeah, I guess he's right. Finals are in less than a month. I have assignments to finish and exams to study for, but I can't help but feel as though all of that is pretty minuscule compared to what's going on here. Gabriel knows how much school means to me, and I can appreciate he's trying to be supportive and leave on a light note, but I'm so torn between sadness and anger at our situation that I continue to sit there silently. School doesn't seem so important right at this moment.

Before long, he zips the duffle bag shut, tossing it onto the floor and sitting next to me. "I know you're scared," he murmurs, running his hand up my thigh, warming my skin. "This isn't easy for me either, but unfortunately, it's our only option right now. There are too many variables in play, and we need to have a better idea of what's going on with the hunters before we rid ourselves of that monster. And we need Selene to think she's getting what she wants so she doesn't come after you again." He angles himself toward me, cupping my cheek with his other hand, and guides my gaze to his. "And to protect you, I will do whatever it takes."

I pull in a slow breath, willing my chin to stop trembling. "You shouldn't have to do *this*."

He smiles. "You don't need to worry about me. I'm not the same man I was when Selene sired me. She'll think I'm there solely because she threatened you, but I'll also be figuring up what she's up to with the hunters." His thumb glides across my cheek, and he lowers his voice. "Selene and I may share a sire bond, but it pales in comparison to the connection I have with you. And the blood oath has nothing to do with it."

Leaning into him, I press my forehead to his, closing my eyes as I listen to the sound of our breathing for a minute. My breath hitches when Gabriel presses closer, gripping my hips and lifting me onto his lap. His lips trail along my jaw, peppering kisses along my skin as I drape my arms over his shoulders. My pulse jumps when the hardness between his legs presses into the heat between mine, making me throb. I turn my face so his mouth collides with mine at the same moment I grind slowly against him. He makes a sound that I think is a delicious mix between a growl and a groan, and lifts his hips, teasing me as his lips devour mine. Gabriel kisses me as if he's trying to commit the feel of our bodies moving together to memory. To be fair, he probably is.

When I moan into his mouth, something in him sparks to life, and he flips me onto my back, guiding me up the bed before crawling over me. I open my eyes just in time to watch him drag his gaze over me as if I'm a sought-after piece of art. There is something deeper than lust and arousal in his liquid silver gaze, and while it scares the shit out of me, I find myself reaching for him, needing him closer.

"Kiss me," I demand in a breathy voice, grabbing the back of his neck and bringing his lips to mine. They meld together, moving slowly as we explore each other. Reaching for the front of his pants, I fumble with the buttons, not able to see what I'm doing. Gabriel chuckles against my lips and pulls away. His knees press into the mattress on either side of me as he rises and undoes his pants. I reach for him again, but he catches my hands and kisses the back of each.

"I'm going to take my time with you tonight," he says in a deep voice.

My cheeks heat, and I stare at him as he tugs his shirt over his head, tossing it off the side of the bed before he lowers himself back to my lips, kissing me reverently. He slides a hand under my shirt, lifting it as he goes to reveal my bare chest. I didn't put on a bra after my post-training shower, and based on the way Gabriel's lips curl into a grin against mine, that was a good call.

I gasp into his mouth when he cups my breast, using his finger and thumb to pinch and roll the nipple into a stiff peak. Heat pools in my belly as he continues to work my nipple, kissing me deeper and switching breasts a few moments later, delivering the same ministrations. My head swims with pleasure and lust and... I want *more*. I lift my hips to press the bulge in his pants against my core and nip his bottom lip, hoping he'll get the idea.

Gabriel slips his hand away from my breast and moves it down my stomach, making my skin tingle and heat the closer he gets to my navel. His lips leave mine, trailing a path of soft, sweet kisses along my jaw. He kisses my temple, my forehead, each of my cheeks, and finally, the tip of my nose, all while his fingers inch closer to the throbbing between my legs. It's almost painful by the time he slides under the elastic waistband of my sweatpants.

"I'm curious," he murmurs, skimming his fingers along my pubic bone, making me shiver. "Are you generally opposed to panties?"

A laugh slips through my lips.

"Because we bought you the nicest, most expensive ones. A whole drawer full of them," he continues.

"Hmm," I say, my chest flushed with warmth as he peers down at me. "And they are very nice. But sometimes bare is better." I flick my tongue along my bottom lip, dropping my gaze to his slightly swollen lips. "Wouldn't you agree?"

Gabriel's mouth curls into a grin. "Most definitely." He makes quick work of dragging my sweatpants down my thighs, sliding back to the end of the bed as he tugs them off all the way, letting them drop to the floor. He runs his hands up my legs, from my ankles to my thighs, and I chew my bottom lip as he slowly spreads them open for him, his silver gaze never leaving mine. The softness in his eyes shifts to something darker—hunger.

My heart beats faster in response, and I grip the sheets on either side of me as he crawls closer, licking his lips and dropping his gaze to my center. My entire body heats and tingles where his fingers brush, featherlight and teasing.

He takes his time, kissing the inside of each of my thighs before skimming his fingers back toward my breasts, this time lifting my shirt higher. I pull it the rest of the way off, my nipples still stiff from Gabriel's previous attention to them. He cups them in his hands, massaging gently as my eyes flutter shut and my back arches. I push into him, moaning at his skilled touch. My heart rate kicks up when his breath tickles my entrance, and my eyes fly open as his tongue flicks along my slit. Barely there, but enough to make my clit pulse with desire. My hips jerk, and he moves his hands from my breasts, gripping my hips and holding them against the mattress as his tongue laps at my folds.

I press my lips together, my chest rising and falling faster when he shifts one hand lower, circling his thumb around my clit while his tongue dips inside me, torturously slow.

"Oh," I breathe, sucking in a shallow breath as he plunges his tongue into my pussy. His fingers press into my hips, and I bite my lip, finding myself hoping he leaves a mark on my skin. I try to lift my hips again, but he holds me down, and the pressure of his fingers biting into my skin paired with the pressure and tension of him working his tongue in and out of me has me panting in record time.

He replaces his tongue with two fingers, thrusting into me a few times before adding a third, making me moan at the sensation of being stretched by him.

"I adore that sound," he murmurs, crawling over me once more and sealing his lips over mine as he continues fucking me with his fingers. "I adore you." The words are a whisper against my lips and they make my chest tighten.

I pull him closer, reaching between us to pull his erection free, moving my hand up and down the thick shaft. "I want you inside me," I say, rubbing the blunt head of his cock with my thumb.

He groans, closing his eyes for a moment before opening them and meeting my gaze. "I wanted to take this slow. Enjoy every bit of you."

"But I'm impatient," I say with a little grin.

His eyes glimmer, and he mirrors my grin, slipping his fingers out of my pussy. "As you wish, angel."

I guide his cock to my entrance, licking the dryness from my lips as he drags it along my slit, coating himself in my juices before pressing the head against my clit. I press my lips together to keep from moaning too loudly, and Gabriel moves to hover over me, positioning himself without haste. I run my hands up his chest and lace my fingers at the back of his neck, pulling his lips to mine to kiss him deeply.

Between one moment and the next, Gabriel pushes inside slowly, stretching me to accommodate him, his breathing almost as ragged as my own. He rests his forehead against mine. "Is this okay?"

My heart pounds against my ribcage as my fingers grip the back of his hair, and I lean back just enough to meet his gaze. "I want all of you."

"You have all of me, angel." He thrusts harder, hitting a new spot deep inside me that sets off sparks of pleasure.

"Yes," I breathe, my entire body radiating heat. "Right there."

His hips slam into mine, over and over, until we're both racing toward climax. My breasts bounce with each thrust and sweat dots my brow. My muscles tense, and in the space of a heartbeat, my pussy clenches deliciously around him. I cry out, my release slamming into me like an unforgiving wave as I continue lifting my hips to meet his thrusts.

They become quicker, his hips jerking as he pumps into me. Moments later, he grunts, squeezing his eyes shut as he releases inside me. His thrusts slow, and he collapses on top of me, his cock still filling me up. With a content sigh, he pulls out and presses a gentle kiss to my lips. He wraps his arms around me, holding me against his side and pulling the covers over our legs. I listen to the steady beat of his heart and fight the urge to close my eyes and cling to this moment.

"I... I can't say goodbye to you," I finally tell him.

Gabriel tucks my hair behind my ear, leaning down to brush his lips against mine. "You don't have to." He kisses me again. "This isn't permanent. Once we figure out how Selene is tied to the hunters, we can eliminate her. Doing that before we know wouldn't be smart, but I promise you, as soon as we know it won't tip anyone off, Selene will very quickly no longer be a problem."

I frown at him. "If I'd overheard more when she was talking to Scott—"

"Stop," he interrupts with a gentle voice. "You have absolutely no blame in this, angel. I can't stand the thought of you believing that."

Exhaling a shaky breath, I meet his soft gaze. "She wants you back because she's desperate for power and worried about her enemies, one of which being the hunters she's somehow in cahoots with. Nothing makes sense, but something about this has her scared. She's acting out of selfishness and fear, so please—I understand you know her better than anyone—but be careful. Fear makes people go to extremes."

He pushes his fingers into my hair, leaning in to kiss my forehead. "I will," he vows. "You can't get rid of me that easily."

I'm not sure how long we stay there, our limbs tangled with each other's, but eventually we have to move.

I slip out from the sheets first, grabbing my clothes off the floor and tugging them back on. Gabriel watches my every move, his cheeks tinged pink and his eyes filled with something that makes my chest tighten. He gets up and finds his clothes as well, kissing me slowly before we walk hand-in-hand to the door.

He squeezes my hand. "Calla—"

"I'm not going to watch you go," I cut him off, unable to meet his gaze. If I'm there, the rest of the guys will have to hold me back to stop me from stopping *him*.

"Okay." His voice is calm, gentle.

The grip around my heart tightens, and I reach for him, lifting onto my tiptoes and smashing my lips against his, hard and fast, before I pull back and open the door. Stepping into the hallway, I pause as if I'm going to say something else—I feel as if I should, but nothing comes.

I swallow hard past the lump in my throat and let the door to Gabriel's room click shut behind me. Tears blur my vision as I hurry down the hallway to the stairs. I manage to hold them back until I'm behind the door to my bedroom, but the moment I fall back against it, I crack, pressing a fist to my mouth to muffle the sound of my sobs.

CHAPTER

SEVENTEEN

GABRIEL

The ride to the address Selene sent feels like the longest half hour of my many years. My pulse is erratic and my stomach is filled with nerves. I managed to keep it together as the guys walked me to the front door, but now that I'm alone—save for the town car driver behind the wheel—fear has dug its claws in me deep. Nausea fills my gut, and several times, I have to clench my jaw and debate telling the driver to pull over so I can vomit outside his car. I manage to swallow down the bile in my throat and try to focus on the quiet jazz music filtering through the car or the humans rushing to get home from work to their families. Thinking ahead, I called out sick to work before I left the house, not knowing how long this arrangement is going to last. I figure my flu excuse is good for at least a week.

Despite the unseasonably warm weather, the driver seems to have the heat on nearly full blast, making the churning in my stomach worse. I grit my teeth, finally flicking the window switch to crack it open enough to get some air. The driver either doesn't notice or doesn't care. He keeps his eyes on the road, humming along to the music.

As I watch the GPS screen built into the dashboard, the minutes until we reach the destination tick down. The closer we get, the faster my heart beats. Despite my deep hatred for Selene, part of me will always have a sickening loyalty to her. I never wanted to see my sire again, but my blood sings as we round the corner onto S Street, connected to her on a level I'll never be able to rid myself of as long as she is alive. Until we find out what her tie is to the hunters and what they're up to, the plan to take her out has been put on pause.

My stomach drops as the car slows to a stop at the curb outside Selene's building. The driver shifts into park and glances at me through the rearview mirror.

"Have a good night," the man says in a polite tone.

I unbuckle my belt and reach beside me to grab my duffle bag, unable to voice a response. Without a word, I go through the motions of opening the door and forcing myself out of the car. Stepping onto the sidewalk, I close the door and walk to the front of the building, where a well-dressed doorman in a dark gray suit and hat, who appears to be in his fifties, nods at me before opening the tall glass door.

I walk inside with my duffle bag over my shoulder, my shoes echoing softly against the shiny white marble floor as I head through the empty lobby toward a bank of elevators in front of me. Everything is white—the floors, the walls, the reception desk. In the air lingers the scent of overpriced cologne and perfume as well as the faint smell of roses, coming from the tall vases around the lobby. The scent makes my chest tighten; I can't help but think of Calla's rose-scented body wash as I walk through the space. Chandeliers hang from the high ceilings, and yet, I still feel as if the room is closing in on me. I press the elevator button, fisting my hands at my sides when I catch the way they're shaking.

Stepping into the elevator, I suck in a slow breath and press the button to the penthouse, because of course Selene lives in the penthouse. Her tastes haven't changed. My eyes stay locked on the climbing numbers above the door, and when the elevator slows to a stop at the top floor, a soft *ding* sounds, and the door slides open, revealing a foyer styled similarly to the lobby downstairs.

A large set of white double doors with a gold P1 placard above them stands between me and my sire.

I close my eyes, taking a deep breath through my nose and exhaling it through my mouth. I force my muscles to unclench and step forward, lifting my hand to knock.

The sound of footsteps coming toward me gets louder, and a moment later, one of the doors opens to reveal an older-looking human woman with kind blue eyes and shoulder-length, graying brown hair. Her lips immediately turn upward into a genuine smile when she sees me, wrinkles becoming more prominent around her eyes and mouth, and she opens the door wider.

So, Selene still employs humans. Not shocking, considering they're easier to control and to dispose of when she's through with them. In the time I spent with her, I can recall at least three different human housekeepers. I'm not certain what happened to them, but I can guess easily enough.

"Mr. Simmons, please come in." She steps aside, gesturing for me to walk into the suite.

I clear my throat and force out, "Thank you." Putting one foot in front of the other, I enter Selene's penthouse, resenting the increase in my pulse as my eyes flit around the light and open space, immediately searching for her. She's here—I can feel it in the tingling along my spine and the pressure in my chest. It easily overpowers the connection I have to Calla at this proximity, and I clench my jaw at that, wanting to snarl.

"May I take your bag? I've set up our main guest suite for your stay." Her voice is soft and pleasant. Perhaps she doesn't know I've been coerced into being here. Though, this woman is loyal to Selene, so maybe she does and just doesn't care.

I hand it over silently, and she beams at me.

"You are a very handsome young man," she comments, taking my bag.

Choking on a harsh laugh, I point out, "You're far younger than I am."

Her eyes sparkle when she smiles. "Yes, of course." She switches my bag from one hand to the other. "Please make yourself comfortable. Miss Selene is finishing a call in the study and will be out to greet you shortly."

I follow the housekeeper through the entranceway to an open living and dining space, decorated in soft tones of gray and white. I walk toward the fireplace, the light and warmth beckoning me.

"Can I get you something to drink while you wait?"

I look back at the human over my shoulder. "Scotch if you have it would be good. Thank you."

She nods. "And would you like anything else? Perhaps a drink with some sustenance?"

Is she offering me blood?

"We keep several types in the house. Miss Selene's tastes shift every now and then," she explains, as if the need to have blood available to serve her employer is completely normal. I can't help but think this woman has been glamoured, likely for years.

My lip curls back, and I shake my head. "Just the scotch, please."

With another nod, she hurries out of the room, leaving me to the crackling flames. I brace my hands against the thick white wood mantle and stare into the fire, trying to convince myself that I'm going to get through this and get back to my brothers and our girl.

My entire body stiffens when she walks into the room. I straighten and turn around slowly to face her. My gaze starts at her bare feet, skimming over her black painted toes. She's wearing a floor-length black dress with a deep V neckline. I force my gaze to her face, and my lungs hollow out when our eyes meet, that damned connection sparking between us.

Her crimson lips curl into a slow grin. "Gabriel," she purrs, "I'm so pleased you decided to join me. I asked Beth to give us some time alone."

I assume Beth is her housekeeper. *So much for my scotch.*

I focus on the borderline painful throbbing in my gums, my fangs threatening to extend as an array of mixed, confusing emotions whirl inside me. "I'm here," I say in a flat voice. "Now I want proof that whatever magic your witch used on Calla has been removed."

Selene sighs as if she's frustrated that I ruined what she thought would be a happy reunion. "I've been in contact with her," she says. "Tessa should be there as we speak."

My eyes narrow. "You expect me to take your word for it?"

She arches a sharply lined brow at me. "God forbid." She lifts her hand, picking thoughtlessly at her black manicure as she says, "Text your boys. Check that I am telling you the truth."

I pull my phone out of my pocket and type out a quick message to Atlas.

There should be a witch there to remove the magic from Calla. Can you confirm?

The text bubbles appear a few seconds later, and I stare at the screen until his message comes through.

Yes. The magic has been lifted. Calla is safe. Are you?

Some of the tension in my chest eases, and I exhale a heavy breath. Before I can respond, Selene appears in front of me and plucks the phone from my hand. She turns it off and tosses it onto the couch behind her, stepping even closer.

I hold my breath, clenching my jaw as she leans in and presses her hands against my chest. "What are you doing?" I say in a tight voice, my hands itching to shove her away.

Selene licks her lips, making the red painted on them shine. "It's been a long time, Gabriel."

Not long enough. I want to tell her to stop saying my name. Each time she does, the sound is like nails on a chalkboard to my ears.

She slides her fingers up to my shoulders and laces them together behind my neck. Her perfectly airbrushed face is so close I can count the lashes fanning her bright silver eyes. I used to be so enraptured by this woman, but now, the sight of her makes me sick. The monster in me may crave our connection created by my death, but I loathe her.

"A long time," I echo, keeping my arms at my sides. "What's your angle here, Selene? What are you hoping to accomplish by forcing me to be here?"

She laughs softly, her eyes alight with amusement. "Forcing you? Please. You could just as easily have refused to come." She lowers her voice. "Your little human consort would have paid the price for that choice, but make no mistake, my love. You had a choice."

"So did you when you chose to take my life from me."

She rolls her eyes. "All these years later, and you're still so dramatic about that. I gave you a gift. You should be thanking me."

Anger crackles through me, hotter than the burning fire behind me, and I grab her hips and turn us around slamming her into the wall next to the fireplace. Growling in her face, I snap, "You want me to thank you?"

Heat flares in her gaze, and the sound of her racing pulse echoes in my ears.

"Perhaps what I did was selfish," she finally says, her voice slightly strained. "I couldn't lose you, so I did what I had to do to ensure I didn't."

My jaw clenches and my fingers dig into her hips. "And yet, you still did."

She nods before cocking her head to the side. "I don't blame you for running," she murmurs, her blond hair slipping into her face. "I was born this way, but I understand how overwhelming becoming a vampire can be. Perhaps if you'd stayed—"

"Perhaps if you had listened when I told you I didn't want this," I cut in, my voice sharp, "we—"

"What's done is done, Gabriel. I'd say you've done exceptionally well for yourself. If you can't thank me for turning you, you can at least admit that."

My eyes narrow, and I pull my hands off her hips. "Why am I here?" I demand.

She purses her lips. "You know, Calla asked me the very same question," she says, sliding her fingers into the hair at the back of my neck.

I swallow my disgust. "So tell me," I implore her, "what are you up to?"

"Hmm, I'm keeping very busy with many things."

My control snaps, and I rip her hands away from me, shoving them down. "Things like Scott Ellis?" I shouldn't have revealed that Calla overheard her conversation with Brighton's father, but the words left my lips before I could stop them.

Selene laughs. "Oh, that sneaky little bitch."

My hand is wrapped around her throat before I know what's happening. "Watch your mouth," I growl in her face.

Her lips twist into an arrogant smirk. "You can't hurt me, and we both know it. So we can continue playing—truly, I'm rather enjoying this hands-on side of you—or we can discuss the hunters."

I pull my hand back as if her skin burned my fingers and shoot her a glare. "Why was one of the most important hunters in the state here with you?"

She presses her fingers to her lips, considering my question. "We have a... mutually beneficial relationship—we have for quite some time."

Tension builds behind my eyes and my jaw aches from clenching so hard. "What kind of relationship, Selene?"

"Hmm," she hums, slipping past me and walking toward a hallway near the massive dining table.

I follow, my footsteps loud compared to her silent ones. "Selene," I snap.

She whirls around, her dress swaying around her, reminding me of the elegance in her I admired so long ago. "I think we could use a drink, don't you?"

"No. Tell me what you're talking about. Now."

She opens her mouth to speak, and I notice her fangs have extended. Despite myself, my pulse races at the sight of them. It's the same response Calla has had to mine.

"Very well," she says with a sigh. "I have a little arrangement with our hunter friends here in Washington and back in New York. In exchange for immunity from them, I hand over other vampires."

My stomach plummets, and I automatically step back, blinking at her in confusion. "You *what*?" I shake my head. She's turning in her own to our enemy—to protect herself. I don't question the need to... put down the vampires who pose a threat of exposing us to the humans, but I highly doubt Selene is making that distinction. No, she'd sacrifice anyone to save her own ass.

Panic lances through me, sharp and painful. We've managed to evade the hunters for over a hundred years, and Selene has been turning other vampires over for potentially just as long.

The amusement in her eyes makes my stomach roil, but I refuse to look away. "I knew you were selfish," I say in a low voice, "but this is on another level. You were born a vampire—you have a birthright duty to protect your people, and—"

"Save it," she interrupts. "Your speech is about five decades too late, my love."

I stare at my sire in disbelief. "If I hadn't come, were you going to turn us over to them?"

Her eyes roam over my face before she licks her lips. "I suggest you go ahead and forget about that boys' club and pet of yours." She offers a victorious smile. "They won't be around to worry about for much longer."

Ice fills my veins, and my fangs split through my gums as I snarl at her. I advance without warning, slamming into her and taking us both to the floor. She manages to flip us mid-fall, and my back hits the hard marble, Selene landing on top of me.

"This isn't a fight you'll ever win," she says, bracing herself, her hands pressed into the floor on either side of my head while she straddles me. "Where's my *make love not war* Gabriel?" she taunts, and I see red.

Throwing her off me, I shoot to my feet and stalk toward her, but she moves behind me before I reach her. I whip around and growl in frustration, because she's right. I won't win this fight; I can't cause her any real harm. Which means I am effectively screwed—and yet, though I'm not arrogant enough to believe I have the strength or ability to overpower the sire connection that controls me, I don't stop. All of the pent-up anger and frustration I've been living with, trapped in a cage of my own making, rushes to the surface, and my control snaps.

Selene appears in front of me and doesn't hesitate before grabbing my hair and tugging my head to the side, exposing my throat. Her fangs sink into my neck before I can move away, and a strangled sound escapes my lips.

Strength flows out of me, and my legs give out. Somehow we end up sprawled across the couch, my gaze falling on the dancing flames as it blurs. The pull of our connection fills me with a contentedness that makes my heart pound, and Selene's lips against my skin transport me back in time to the many nights I buried myself between her legs as she drank from me.

I want to push her away, fight her off, make her stop taking from me just like she always did. Instead, I close my eyes, my limbs unable to move as her venom—and her decades-old power over me subdues my ability to resist her.

Finally, she lifts herself off me, pulling away from my neck and licking my blood from her lips. "I gave them up," she purrs, running her finger along the puncture marks she left in my neck. She licks the blood off her finger and gazes down at me, her lips curled into a cruel smile. "The hunters know where your house is. And they know Atlas, Lex, and Kade are vampires."

Fear cripples me as I stare at her, my heart in my throat and my vision dimming around the edges. "What the hell have you done?"

EIGHTEEN

I allow myself five minutes to cry and then I slip into the bathroom, splash some cold water on my face, and pull myself back together. With a deep, centering breath, I walk back into my bedroom and suck in a short breath when I find Kade sitting on the end of my bed.

"You need to come downstairs." His voice is strained, and he keeps his back to me as I walk closer.

I run my hand over my hair in an attempt to flatten the mess I made raking my fingers through it repeatedly while I was crying. "What's going on, Kade?"

He stands and turns to face me. "We have a guest."

I frown, shaking my head. "What are you talking about?" I don't want to see anyone outside of the vampires I live with right now.

Kade reaches out and laces his fingers through mine, guiding me toward the door. "It's the witch who blocked your location from us and fucked with your blood."

I freeze and dig my heels into the floor. "She's *here*?"

He nods, standing in front of me. "You're safe, Calla. She's here to remove the magic from your blood." His jaw hardens. "Seems Selene is making good on her deal with Gabriel."

"I... um, okay."

His eyes search mine. "You trust us, don't you?"

I open my mouth to respond, but I don't really know what to say. I can't say yes. As much as I'd like to, the word won't form on my lips. But I don't necessarily distrust them anymore. I just... It's complicated.

"Okay, let me rephrase that. Do you trust that we won't let anything happen to you here?"

Pressing my lips together, I meet his gaze and nod.

"Good." He squeezes my hand, and we walk down the hall toward the kitchen and living space.

My pulse is a jackhammer beneath my heated skin, and the moment we step into the room, my eyes go to the unfamiliar face sitting on the couch next to Lex. Atlas stands near the front door, watching like a hawk. His eyes meet mine for a moment before moving to Kade. It's just as well, my gaze flits back to the black-haired witch, and when she turns to look at me and stands, my eyes go wide.

I'm not sure what I was expecting, but someone who looks to be close to me in age wasn't it. She has bright emerald-colored eyes that match the jumpsuit she's wearing, and dark, precise brows. Her pale lips tip up into a faint smile, and she walks toward Kade and me.

"That's close enough," Kade barks when she's a few feet away.

She spares him a quick glance, rolling her eyes. "Bite me."

I step slightly in front of Kade before he can respond. "Um, hi," I say to her. "I'm—"

"I know who you are, Calla," she says with another smile.

"Oh. Right."

"My name is Tessa. And I need to apologize. I don't typically get involved in vampire business. I'd warn you about what terrible company they are to keep, but I fear I'm a bit late with the warning."

I press my lips together. "Uh, yeah. Little bit."

"Right. Anyway, the only reason I agreed to help Selene is because I owed her. I certainly don't make a habit of getting into debt with anyone—especially the immortal type—but I didn't exactly have a choice. Selene saved my life years ago, so when she called in the favor, I couldn't exactly say no."

"Yeah, I don't buy it," Kade says with an edge to his voice and pulls me away from her so I'm standing next to him.

The moment I catch sight of his fangs and the darkness in his eyes, I move in front of him and press my hands against his chest, attempting to push him back. "Don't." I put as much force behind that one word as I can and hold his gaze.

For some reason, the moment I witnessed Selene killing Dante plays over in my head on a loop, and the thought of Kade doing the same to Tessa makes me go rigid with panic. If he kills her, he's no better than Selene, and I can't watch that play out.

Tessa sighs. "You can put the fangs away. I'm not stupid enough to come to a house full of vampires with a nefarious agenda. I'm here to remove the spell I cast on Calla's blood, and that's it."

I believe her. If she was here to hurt me, I highly doubt she would announce her arrival. Plus, I can't help but see a bit of myself in her. Perhaps if the circumstances were different, we could even be friends. I admire her fearlessness, especially being surrounded by vampires—including Atlas York.

Kade drops his gaze to meet mine, and I offer him a nod, hoping that's enough to get him to back down. His chest rises and falls deeply, and his fangs retract, his nostrils flaring when he returns his gaze to Tessa.

I hesitate before pulling my hands away from his chest, and turn to face the witch, noticing the way Atlas and Lex—who is now standing as well—are watching us, ready to move and take her out at any given second. It's reassuring for me, but I can't imagine how it's making Tessa feel. "What do we need to do?"

Tessa slides her hands into the pockets of her black blazer and shrugs. "It's a simple spell reversal. Should only take a few minutes." She steps forward, then pauses. "Your boys aren't going to go all vamp on me when I touch you, are they?" She steals a glance over her shoulder, and her posture stiffens slightly.

"No," I say pointedly, looking between the three of them. My chest tightens momentarily at the painfully obvious absence of Gabriel. I remind myself it's only temporary and try to refocus on the current issue at hand. Blood, spells, magic. Right.

"All right," she says, though I don't miss the tinge of doubt in her voice.

We walk over to the dining table and Tessa and I sit across from each other. Lex and Kade take the seats on either side of me, and Atlas stands near the head of the table, though slightly closer to Tessa.

I'm sure that's not intimidating or anything...

She slides her hands across the table and flips up so her palms are facing up, nodding to them. "When you're ready," she says, "place your hands in mine."

I don't hesitate. Maybe I should, but the thought of getting rid of whatever magic is coursing through me is too enticing to delay.

Tessa's hands are soft and cool as she curls her fingers around mine and closes her eyes. After what feels like an eternity, she starts whispering under her breath—words I can't make out—and her skin heats against mine.

I bite my lip at the sensation, staring at our hands. It doesn't hurt, but as the connection holds, tingles travel through my fingers, up my arm, and eventually start overtaking my body. I grimace at the discomfort that follows, and my pulse races, unsure of what the hell is happening to me.

The guys are tense on either side of me, and Atlas's eyes are narrowed on the witch.

A minute later, the tingling fades, and Tessa opens her eyes, releasing her grip on my hand. Her gaze sweeps across all of us, and she says, "It's done."

My brows tug closer. "That's it?"

She presses her lips together against a smile. "Yep. That's it."

"How do we know it worked?" Kade challenges.

I sigh, getting up and grabbing a knife from the butcher block on the counter. I prick the pad of my finger and hold it in front of me as blood beads there.

No one moves.

I turn to Lex, lifting my hand toward him.

"Yeah, no. I'm good."

"Seriously?"

Tessa laughs. "I'm guessing you tasted her blood while the magic was active?"

Lex scowls in response.

I turn to Kade next, who just shakes his head.

"For fuck's sake," Atlas mutters, walking around the table and grabbing my wrist. He lifts my hand to his mouth and closes his lips around my finger.

My cheeks heat when his tongue glides along my skin, and I quickly pull back. When he doesn't immediately start choking like Lex had, the others seem to relax a little.

I look at Tessa. "Okay. Well, um, thanks?" I cringe at the awkward tone in my voice, but I'm not sure what else to say.

"You don't need to thank me, Calla. You never should have had to deal with this to begin with, so again, I'm really sorry."

"What made you decide to come and reverse the magic?" Lex asks, his eyes filled with suspicion. "Doing it in the first place paid your debt to Selene, didn't it?"

Tessa nods at him. "I didn't feel right about doing it, so having the opportunity to undo it wasn't something I'd pass up."

"Uh huh..." Kade mutters from my other side, clearly doubting her motives.

Tessa arches a brow, flicking her gaze between Lex and Kade. "Wow, you guys must be so much fun at parties."

I choke on a laugh. Damn. I like this girl.

The four of us walk Tessa to the door, and after she's gone, I retreat to my room. Gabriel brought up my studies before he left, and as much as I would rather be in the other room with the guys, formulating a plan to get him back, if I want to pass this semester, I at least need to make an effort to study. Plus, a short break from the supernatural is probably something I need right about now, otherwise my head is most definitely going to explode.

I sit cross-legged in the middle of my bed with textbooks open all around me, scribbling notes here and highlighting passages there.

I'm so engrossed in my sociology textbook that I don't hear the knock at my door or the sound of it opening. When I look up and find Lex leaning in the doorway, I jump a little.

"Sorry," he says with a little smirk, "didn't mean to startle you."

I snap the cap on my highlighter and toss it into the textbook before closing it. "What's up?"

He walks over and sits on the edge of my bed. "Considering it's well after midnight, and you're in here studying, I came to ask you that very question."

I purse my lips. "I lost track of time," I tell him with a sigh. "Finals are, like, next week and I needed something else to focus on for a little while."

Lex nods. "I get that." He reaches over and collects the books, stacking them on the table next to the bed. "You should get some sleep. Aren't you tired?"

"Honestly? No. I mean, I'm physically exhausted, but the thought of sleeping... How can I when I know where Gabriel is and *who* he's with?"

"Gabriel is strong," he assures me. "Whatever happens, he's going to be okay."

I glance down at my lap, unprepared for the sting of tears in my eyes. "You sound so sure."

Lex chuckles, wrapping his hand around my knee. "I've known him for over a century. I am certain."

I nod, still feeling at such a loss. "What are we supposed to do now?"

He exhales a heavy breath. "Now we figure out what the hell the hunters are doing conspiring with a vampire. Once we find out, we can send Selene to the depths of hell and call it a day."

I look up, raising my brows at him. "What?"

He shoots me a wink. "I'm kidding about the hell part. But once we find out what Selene was doing with your friend's father, we can eliminate her, and Gabriel can come home."

"Are you finally going to let me help then?"

"You are, Calla."

My eyes narrow. "That's not... You know what I mean. I can do more, and all of you know it, you just won't let me."

"Why don't we talk about that tomorrow? Today has already been a long one, and I think we could all use a quick timeout before the next period."

"Fine," I finally say. "And a sports analogy?" I shake my head at him. "Know your audience, Lex."

His lips curl into a grin, and he leans in, sliding his hand from my knee up my thigh. "Oh, I know plenty about my audience." His mouth traces the shell of my ear, sending shivers through me, and I lean toward him. He smells faintly of pine and soap and his white hair is still a bit damp from a shower. I trace the lines of vines across his arm while his lips find the delicate skin between my neck and shoulder.

"I want to taste you," he murmurs against my skin.

My pulse jumps, and I tilt my head to the side, offering him my neck. We know my blood is safe now, and the thought of Lex biting me has my belly pooling with heat.

"Mmm..." His tongue flicks out, and he snakes an arm around my waist. "Not what I meant, but fuck, you offering yourself to me like that went right to my cock."

Pressing my lips together, my gaze drops to his groin and my cheeks flush at the obvious erection there.

He leans back and pulls off his shirt before closing the distance between us and dropping his mouth to mine, claiming it. Claiming *me*.

Our lips move together, and I close my eyes, letting him take the lead. Lex guides me onto my back, and I stretch my legs out as my head hits the pillows at the headboard. We lay next to each other on our sides, and he deepens the kiss, grabbing my hips and hauling me flush against him. My breasts press against his bare chest, my nipples pebbling at the friction between him and my shirt.

Anticipation sparks to life inside me, and I can't tug my shirt off fast enough. I break the kiss to do it, but quickly return to his mouth, moaning against his lips when his hands palm my breasts. He uses that opportunity to push his tongue into my mouth, grazing mine sensually as my heart hammers against my chest. Heat gathers between my legs, and before long, I grab his hand and guide it down my stomach to the waistband of my pants.

He chuckles softly, pulling his lips away from me for a moment. "Something you want?"

"Thought I was being pretty clear," I shoot back, the tension coiling in me growing more intense by the second. I hadn't realized how tightly wound I was until he started touching me. And now that he has... "I need you inside me."

He steals my lips again, briefly, then meets my gaze, his own ablaze with lust. "I know exactly what you need, and I intend to give it to you."

Lex moves at a preternatural speed, curling his fingers around the waistband of my pants and pulling them off in a single, quick motion. They end up somewhere on the floor at the end of the bed, but I really couldn't care less. Especially when Lex is looking at me as if he's a death row prisoner, and I'm his last meal.

My gaze locks on his as he crawls up the bed, wrapping his arms around my thighs and spreading them without a moment of hesitation. He holds me wide open and presses a kiss just below my navel, dragging his lips down until his breath tickles the most intimate part of me. His tongue darts out, flicking against my clit a few times before he glides it along my folds. My chest flushes, and I reach above me to grab hold of the headboard, my thighs tensing on either side of his head.

The sight of him between my legs spikes my pulse, and I suck in a sharp breath when he presses his tongue flat against my slit, dipping into me as he drags it back up to my clit, circling it until I'm panting.

He draws my clit into his mouth, sucking it between his lips and eliciting a throaty moan from me.

"You know, some of us are trying to sleep." Kade's voice slices through the haze of lust, and my breath hitches as I turn my head to find him leaning against the closed door.

Lex chuckles, and I press my lips together, the vibrations against my sex making me squirm.

"Well, Atlas went to meet with one of our contacts in Arlington to talk about some hunter activity, so it's just me, but still."

I roll my eyes. "Can we help you, Kade? We're kinda in the middle of something."

He drags his tongue over his bottom lip, looking from where Lex is between my legs to my face. "I can see that." He pushes away from the door, walking toward the bed. "Don't let me stop you."

With that, Lex resumes lapping at my folds, alternating between rolling my clit between his fingers and sucking it into his mouth to swirl his tongue around it. Kade kicks off his shoes and socks and loses his shirt before sliding onto the bed next to me. He snags my chin, turning my face to his and slanting his mouth over mine.

I let go of the headboard and grab onto his shoulders, pulling him closer as my hips attempt to jerk off the bed. Lex has a tight grip, so they don't move much, and I writhe against him as he plunges his tongue into my pussy. My grip tightens on Kade's shoulders, and I moan into his mouth, breaking the searing kiss to suck in a breath of air. Lex thrusts his tongue in deeper, flicking it against my pussy walls as his thumb pulses against my clit. My entire body flushes as I race toward orgasm, and Kade reaches over and tweaks my nipples, sending me over the edge.

Lex glides his tongue out of me, licking up the length of my slit and devouring every bit of moisture there, making my cheeks fill with heat to the point of feeling slightly feverish. He crawls up the bed and lays on my other side, sandwiching me between him and Kade.

I reach for the bulge in Lex's pants, unbuttoning them to pull his cock free. He makes quick work of losing the remainder of his clothes, and without turning to look, I hear Kade doing the same behind me until all three of us are completely naked.

They guide me onto my side, and Lex grips his thick cock in his fist, pumping it up and down as I watch, biting my lip. From behind me, Kade kisses my shoulder, his fangs scraping against my skin and making my pulse race as I shiver in anticipation.

"Not yet," Lex tells him, shifting closer and teasing my entrance with his cock.

"I want it," I murmur, my cheeks hot.

Lex smirks. "Oh, I know you do. And you'll get it. You just need to be patient."

I want to scowl at him and protest that, but before I can, he pushes into me with one deep thrust, and I suddenly have lost the ability to form words.

Kade sucks gently on the skin between my neck and shoulder, swirling his tongue there as his hand slides over my hip and finds my clit, circling it while Lex increases the speed of his thrusts, gliding in and out of me easily.

"We're going to fill you up," Lex taunts, making me shiver. I'm practically delirious with arousal, so all I can do is nod. But when I feel the blunt head of Kade behind me, I tense, clenching around Lex's cock.

"There is no fucking way you're putting that there," I breathe. Even as I say the words, part of me wants to try it.

Kade chuckles, rubbing his cock between my ass cheeks, fueling my curiosity.

Lex smirks. "You can take it," he assures me, slowing his thrusts, but still going just as deep. "You just need to relax."

My brows pinch together as I purse my lips. "I... I don't know."

He nods. "Take a deep breath for me."

As I do, Kade reaches over and opens the drawer in the table next to the bed, producing a bottle of lube.

Heat rises in my cheeks and my gaze swings back to Lex. "How long has that been there?" I hadn't thought to look in the drawer, but there's also a rose gold clit stimulator and a matte black dildo.

Lex's smirk turns into more of an amused grin, and he pumps into me again, holding still deep inside. "It was your welcome package. Clearly I should have left it on the bed instead of in the drawer."

I roll my eyes, biting my lip when he hits a new spot with his next thrust. My pulse jumps at the sound of Kade squirting lube onto his hand. He works it over his cock, then teases my clit with his thumb and forefinger. I inhale through my nose, then exhale through my mouth as he pushes an inch into my ass.

The pressure is the most intense thing I've felt in my life, and I grab onto Lex's shoulder to steady myself, squeezing my eyes shut as I will my muscles not to lock up.

"Keep breathing," he murmurs.

I drag in another shallow breath, letting it out slowly.

Kade pushes in further, rubbing his other hand up and down my back soothingly. "Good girl," he murmurs from behind me, his voice thick with arousal.

Lex slows the speed of his thrusts into my pussy, and my walls clench around him, making him and Kade both groan as Kade pushes deeper into my ass.

"Fuck," I grit out, tensing before I can stop myself.

"Easy," Kade says, gripping my hip to keep me in place, holding his cock still in my ass.

"Look at me," Lex says in a soft tone, and when I open my eyes and meet his silver gaze, my world narrows on him and the tension in my muscles ebbs away, allowing Kade to push in the rest of the way. "That a girl. You're doing so good taking him."

"Holy fuck," I breathe.

Kade starts to pull out, and I grab behind me, holding him there. He chuckles, pushing back in, increasing the burning pressure. "You're driving me crazy," he says against my hair.

"You're literally fucking my ass. Give me a damn minute," I growl breathlessly.

He kisses my neck. "Take your time."

I blow out a breath and seal my lips over Lex's as he continues his gentle thrusts. I grip his shoulder tightly as Kade starts moving again. He starts slow, pulling out an inch and pushing back in, until my muscles loosen up. Eventually, the burning fades, replaced by a pleasant fullness as his thrusts pick up speed.

Before long, everything tightens, and I'm launched over the edge, coming hard on Lex's cock. The muscles in my feet spasm, making my toes curl into the sheets as I cry out my release, my pussy clenching around his thickness.

Lex manages to flip all of us so Kade's back is pressed into the mattress with me laying on top of him, his cock buried deep in my ass, while Lex braces himself on top.

He pounds into me, pushing me deeper onto Kade's cock as he lies beneath me, lifting his hips in time with Lex's thrusts. I bite my lip so hard, I taste blood, and both vampires growl as I moan loudly, making no attempt to hold back.

Lex's movements inside me become short and quick. He grunts, thrusting one final time, then throws his head back, his deep groan filling the room as he fills me. He falls onto the bed next to me and sighs contentedly, a sheen of sweat dotting his brow.

Before I have a chance to catch my breath, Kade plunges his cock deeper into my ass as he reaches around to strum my clit with expert precision. I moan deeply while his mouth trails along my shoulder, and Lex reaches over to move my hair out of his way. As Kade gets closer to my neck, my heart beats against my ribcage, practically shouting at him to bite me.

Seconds later, his fangs sink into my neck, causing another orgasm to whip through me, and I announce my release with an uneven moan.

He pulls away from my neck, leaving the wound open as he continues pumping in and out of me, and Lex's fangs quickly replace his. The sensation of blood flowing out of me paired with the dizzying pleasure makes me feel as if I'm going to float away.

Kade curses darkly, picking up speed once more. A few more thrusts, and he grunts loudly, spilling into me. After a moment, he pulls out slowly, making me shiver as he shifts from under me, tucking against my other side while Lex drags his tongue over the puncture marks, healing them.

The room is filled with the smell of sex and our combined shallow breathing. Lex wraps his arm around my waist, pulling my back against his front, and I in turn pull Kade close, resting my head on his chest while he runs his hand over my hair, kissing my forehead. My eyes flutter shut of their own volition and my breaths slowly even out.

I don't remember falling asleep, but when I open my eyes, daylight streams in through the wall of windows across the room. Lex is still asleep on one side of me, and Kade is on the other. I ache in the most delicious way, my lips curling into a smile as I close my eyes to steal a few more minutes of rest.

Before I can doze off, the chime of both Kade's and Lex's phones wake them, disturbing me as well. We all sit up as they reach for their phones.

"Security system," Lex grumbles, his voice thick with sleep, and slides out of the bed. I can't help but admire his bare ass as he walks to the end of the bed and retrieves his pants.

Kade has the same idea and gets dressed as well, tossing Lex his shirt. With a sigh, I get up too, walking around to my closet and grabbing a navy knit sweater and plain black leggings. I quickly pull them on before opening my underwear drawer and wrapping my fingers around the dagger Atlas gave me. His deep voice echoes in my head.

You're never to take this off.

And I don't. Well, except when I go to bed—though I bet Lex would have found a creative way to use it last night.

I shake my head at the thought and secure it to my thigh before walking back to the bedroom.

The three of us head down the hall to meet Atlas in the kitchen, where he grabs a tablet off the counter and taps the screen several times before looking up. He glances between us, and then the three of them start toward the front door. Atlas must've seen something on the security feed outside.

I rush to catch up to them, shoving my feet into the shoes I left near the door before stepping onto the small concrete porch, leaving the door open behind me in case the need for a quick retreat arises.

There's a woman standing in the middle of the lawn, her black hair blowing in the gentle morning breeze. She looks eerily familiar, though I can't place her, which makes it even more confusing that she's here. As is the silver of her eyes—she's a vampire.

I walk down the few concrete steps and join the guys facing off with the woman. "I—" My voice gets caught in my throat when I look at Kade. His face has gone white as a ghost, and the others are tense where they stand on either side of him.

"Calla, go—" Lex starts.

"Who is that?" I ask, cutting him off.

"She... she's my sister," Kade forces out, his voice strained.

My brows knit when the vampire steps forward, offering a fanged smirk as her eyes sweep across the vampires in front of her before focusing on Kade. "Long time no see, baby bro."

Before Kade or the others can respond, a sharp growl of pain fills the air.

My eyes go wide as she steps away from Kade, leaving the blunt end of a dagger sticking out of his chest before disappearing into the trees at the side of the property, Lex snarling and moving in a blur to go after her.

Kade's silver gaze meets mine, and for the briefest of moments, I see fear in his eyes. He blinks at me, then crumples to the ground as Atlas moves to catch him, and a scream tears its way up my throat.

ENTANGLED IN SCARLET

CHAPTER
ONE

KADE

Being stabbed hurts like a motherfucker.

Fire licks across my skin, radiating from where the dagger sticks out of my chest.

She missed my heart. Barely.

The sky above me is bright, and I squint at the sun, closing my eyes as the sound of Calla screaming rips through the air.

Everything happens in slow motion after that.

Atlas's sharp voice pushes past the fog gathering in my head. "Open your eyes, Kade."

I force them open, only for the world to spin. We're moving—toward the house, I think. My eyes close again; I can't keep them open.

My fangs cut into my bottom lip, and my stomach churns at the taste of my own blood, my head clouding with thoughts of death—the end of my immortal existence—and at the hand of my own sister.

Meredith.

Her name punches me in the gut, knocking the air out of my lungs.

She's alive. But how? Who made her a vampire, and why? Why didn't she come to me after it happened? What in the actual fuck was her reason for stabbing me at our reunion? So many questions and so much pain, I can't breathe.

I'm vaguely aware of Atlas setting me on the couch in the living room as he says something to Calla. It's too muffled for me to make out, but a moment later, he grips my shoulder, and white-hot pain explodes in my chest, filling my entire body as he pulls out the dagger, slamming it down on the coffee table.

I gasp loudly, my eyes flying open as I growl at him before I can stop myself.

"You're welcome," he mutters, his jaw set tight.

"Is he going to be okay?" Calla's voice is small and filled with fear. Atlas glances past me; Calla must be standing behind the couch, but everything still hurts too much for me to turn and look.

"The dagger missed his heart. He'll live but he needs blood."

The room is silent for a moment, replaced quickly by the sound of her footsteps moving away from the couch. When the next sound that reaches me is of her pulling a knife from the block in the kitchen, I force myself into a sitting position, gripping the back of the couch until my knuckles turn white. I peer down at my chest and grumble incoherently. This was one of my favorite shirts.

Calla walks back to the couch, swallowing hard as her pulse kicks up.

I eye the knife in her hand. "What are you doing?"

"Atlas said you need blood." Her voice is shaky but her grip is steady.

"There are bags of blood in the fridge in—"

"Fresh blood will heal you faster," Atlas chimes in.

"It's okay," Calla assures, perching on the couch next to me.

Atlas plucks the knife out of her hand, setting it next to the dagger, and Lex walks through the front door before Calla can say anything.

He looks downright pissed. "I fucking lost her." He focuses his gaze on me. "I'm sorry, brother."

I shrug, still in knots thinking about the target he was chasing. I haven't seen my sister in over a century, and after months of searching for someone who clearly didn't want to be found, the authorities gave up hope that she was alive. Weeks after that, our parents did too.

I need to know what happened. I need to find her and figure out what the hell went down the night she disappeared and the decades that followed. Our parents are long dead, and I've made my own family with Lex, Gabriel, and Atlas, but she's still my sister. Even if she wants nothing to do with me, I need some semblance of closure.

"You good?" Lex checks, glancing between me and the others.

"I'll live," I tell him before turning my attention to Calla. She immediately offers me her wrist, and I don't hesitate. I don't have the control to ease into it or be gentle. My fangs sink into her skin and the taste of her blood explodes on my tongue.

She winces, pressing her lips together, but doesn't pull away. Once my venom has a chance to reach her system, she relaxes, leaning against the back of the couch as a sigh escapes her lips and her eyes flutter shut. The sight sends blood straight to my cock, making it twitch in my pants. Despite almost dying at the hand of my supposed-to-be-dead sister, Calla still makes me fucking hard. It's kind of messed up, but I really don't have the strength to give a fuck right now.

"Kade," Atlas says in warning, and I notice the sound of Calla's heartbeat slowing.

I force myself to pull away and drag my tongue over the puncture marks to seal them.

She blinks her eyes open, smiling softly. "Better?"

I nod, leaning in to kiss her cheek. "Thank you."

Lex walks behind the couch, leaning against the back of it, and lets out a heavy sigh. "What in the actual fuck just happened?"

Despite the warmth of Calla's blood flowing through me, a shiver races down my spine, making my muscles tense. "That was Meredith." The sound of her name leaving my lips after all this time has nausea rippling through me, and I clench my jaw for a moment before I'm able to continue.

"I thought your sister was dead," Lex says, raking his fingers through his already messy white hair.

I blow out a breath, which does nothing to ease the pressure in my chest. "Yeah. So did I." Part of me wants to get off this couch and go after her. Lex couldn't find her after she fled, but maybe I can track her blood. We share the same DNA, so there's a chance I can find her. Though that begs the question of why I never felt her presence before. Excellent. Another fucking question that left unanswered is going to make my head explode soon.

Atlas gets up, walking to the kitchen and pouring a glass of orange juice, before coming back and sitting on the armrest. He tilts Calla's face up with a finger under her chin. "You need to drink this."

She blinks her eyes open and, surprisingly, takes the glass without protest and drinks until it's empty before handing it back to him.

"Good girl," Atlas says.

"Fuck off," she shoots back.

My lips twitch. *That's our girl.*

"What do we do now?" Calla asks, her brows pinching together with worry.

"Add this to our ever-growing list of problems," Lex offers, shrugging.

Without warning, the entire back wall of windows shatter. There isn't a moment to process what just happened before half a dozen men and women dressed in all-black uniforms flood into our home with vicious, hateful expressions and daggers raised to fight—to kill.

Goddamn vampire hunters. Now? *Really?*

They rush forward, but Atlas and Lex are faster.

"Get her out of here," Atlas barks over his shoulder, his fangs bared as he takes on a hunter. The man, who is at least a foot taller than Atlas snarls at him, swinging his fist toward the vampire's face. Atlas laughs harshly, catching the hunter's fist in his hand, and throws him backward, taking out two other hunters.

I'm already off the couch, hauling Calla up and shielding her with my body as we move toward the garage.

Lex smirks from where he's facing off with two female hunters, who apparently thought if they worked together they could take him out. Not likely.

"We can't leave them," Calla cries, her voice pitched high with fear. She tries to dig her heels into the floor to stop us, but I lift her easily and keep moving until we reach the door to the garage. "Kade!"

"They're right behind us. Chill the fuck out." I meet her brown, wide-eyed gaze and smirk. "Please."

She stops fighting me, but her heart is still beating rampantly in her chest.

"Everything is going to be fine," I tell her, pushing the garage door open, then pulling it shut behind us. I have no fucking clue if that's true, but the terror on her face is making me feel sick. I want to do whatever is necessary to make it go away.

The sounds of feet scuffling and bodies hitting the floor inside the house continues as we walk to the Escalade. My gums throb uncomfortably at the scent of human blood hanging in the air. I get Calla into the backseat and slam the door shut, climbing behind the wheel. Atlas's souped-up vehicle isn't my ride of choice, but it's the most practical at the moment. I glance at the bright red Maserati beside us and frown. There's a good chance I won't be able to come back for my baby, and that fucking sucks.

I turn the key in the ignition and start the car just as the door to the house opens and the guys jog toward us, their clothes spattered in blood. Atlas takes the passenger seat, while Lex climbs in the back with Calla.

"Drive," Atlas growls, staring forward.

I pull out of the spot without a word and hit the door opener before peeling out of the garage. Heaviness hangs in the car as we leave the house in the rearview; we all must know we're not coming back here, to the home we built.

We're barely past the Washington city limits when Lex gets on the phone to Marcel. He fills him in on the situation, though Marcel had already gotten a call from our security team notifying him of a breach in the system, they had no idea there had been an attack. The hunters must've overrode the tech; our team didn't even have a chance to move in before they attacked.

"I'll have a team go in and clean things up," Marcel tells Lex. "Keep moving. I'll text you the address to a safe house a few hours from you."

They end the call, and Lex sighs. "You got all that?" he checks with Atlas and me, and we both nod.

"Yeah, no. I don't have super hearing," Calla says. "Someone want to tell me what's going on?"

"We can't go back to the house now that the hunters know about it —about us."

Which begs the question of *how* they found out we're vampires. It doesn't make sense. We've lived for decades—for over a century— undetected by them. What the fuck happened?

"Right," Calla says with a frown I catch in the rearview mirror. "And what about that girl? Meredith?"

My grip on the steering wheel tightens, and I press the gas a little harder. "I had no idea she was alive... or that she had been turned. She, uh, disappeared from a party a long time ago, when we were both still human." I merge onto the interstate and speed up to get into the fast lane before continuing. "We searched for months, but once a certain period of time had passed, she was presumed dead." I swallow hard, surprised at the emotion clogging my throat after so long. "My family, we had a memorial service and buried an empty casket."

Calla sucks in a breath. "I'm so sorry." A moment later, she asks, "Why would she come after you after all this time? Or at all, for that matter?"

I keep my eyes on the road. "Before everything happened, we were very close. Her... her disappearance devastated me. I can honestly say I have no idea why she would try to kill me."

Atlas clears his throat. "Perhaps we should consider the possibility that her attack was a distraction for the hunters' ambush."

My stomach clenches at his words, at his assumption that Meredith could possibly be working with the hunters. I thought I knew her better than anyone else in the world, but I have to look at the facts here. I haven't seen or spoken to her in more than a human lifespan. I have to face the idea that I have no idea who she is now or what she's capable of.

"Well, fuck." Lex's voice is low, deepened with anger. "We now know of at least two vampires who are associated with the hunters."

"Wait. You think Selene had something to do with this too?" Calla asks.

"It really doesn't matter right now," Atlas says, glancing down when his phone chimes. Mine and Lex's do as well. "It's Marcel." Atlas plugs the address he sent us into the GPS built into the dash.

I glance at the map on the screen and sigh. We still have a little over three hours of driving to reach the safe house and decide on our next move.

"You want me to drive?" Atlas checks.

I shake my head automatically. "I'm good."

"Liar," Lex mutters from the back seat. "Pull over and let Atlas drive."

"I said—"

"Kade," Calla cuts in with a soft voice. "Please."

I meet her eyes in the mirror for a moment before letting out a low breath. "Fine." I flip the signal on and pull off to the shoulder, putting the car in park. Unbuckling my seat belt, I get out of the vehicle, pulling in a deep breath. The early afternoon air is warm for the middle of April, but it does nothing to combat the chill in my bones. I can't get Meredith's face out of my head. Or the burn of the dagger she plunged into my chest.

"Kade." Atlas's voice pulls me back, and I blink at him. He claps me on the shoulder. "Do you need a minute before we keep moving?"

I shake my head. "Let's just go." Walking around the front of the Escalade, I climb into the passenger seat and buckle up, staring out the windshield as Atlas gets behind the wheel and pulls back onto the interstate.

CHAPTER

TWO

CALLA

After dozing off a couple of hours into the drive, I come to, blinking my eyes open when I can no longer feel the car moving but instead feel the warmth of Lex's hand against my cheek. The sky outside the tinted windows is still light, and I glance at the clock on the dash—it's a little after five.

"We're here," he murmurs in a tired, soft voice. The darkness under his eyes makes me feel bad for sleeping.

I nod, reaching for my seat belt. Before I can open the door, Kade is out of the passenger seat and opening it for me, offering his hand. Accepting it, I let him help me out of the car, the gravel driveway crunching under my Doc Martens. I sway a little, still not fully awake, and he catches me easily, sliding an arm around my waist.

A quick glance around lets me know we're not in any type of large city. Aside from the small, single-level, white farmhouse up the driveway, there are only pine trees for as far as I can see, their muted green color matching the shutters on either side of the windows in the front of the house. The air is warm and fresh, the late afternoon sun beating down on us.

"Where are we?" I ask as we walk toward the place I imagine we'll be staying until we figure out what the hell happened back in Washington.

The wood steps up to the paint-chipped porch creak under us, and I cringe, trying to step lightly. The only modern thing about this place so far is the lock built into the faded blue door. It's a numbered touchpad that Atlas quickly keys the code into, opening the door.

"Somewhere safe," Lex answers from behind me and Kade. "It's temporary."

The door opens into a small foyer that smells of lemon and something a bit stronger, like some kind of cleaner. I was expecting the air to be heavy with dust and the stench of mothballs, so this is a pleasant surprise. Maybe Marcel had it cleaned while we were on our way here. The floor beneath our feet is a worn hardwood with a dull gray runner stretched along the length of the hallway before us. On the left side of the hall is a set of open double doors that lead into a living room, and on the right are a pair of closed wooden doors that I can guess are bedrooms.

I follow Lex and Atlas into the living room, which also leads to a small kitchen and dining area. This part of the house is surprisingly open-concept for how old I imagine it to be.

Lex drops onto the brown leather couch and lets out a deep sigh but says nothing.

I glance from him to Atlas, specifically to both of their bloodstained clothes. "I don't suppose this place comes stocked with food and clothes," I offer wryly.

Kade slides past me. "Food, probably. Not sure about clothes. I'll go take a look in the bedrooms." He disappears back into the hall, and the sound of hinges creaking fills the silence as he opens the door to one of the bedrooms.

I walk into the dated kitchen, rummaging through various cupboards until I manage to find tea and mugs. There's a kettle already on the stove, so I fill it with water and ignite the burner. It's an old gas stove, so it takes a few tries to light, and while it starts to heat up, I drop tea bags into the mugs.

Atlas starts a fire in the fireplace across from the couch before sitting in a chair that looks about as comfortable as a rock and starts talking to Lex in a voice too quiet for me to hear.

I lean against the counter, closing my eyes as I listen to the kettle heating up. My thoughts drift to Gabriel, making my stomach sink. I can't help but feel as if we left him. Yes, we fled Washington because of the hunters, and Lex said this is only temporary, but we still left him. And with his psychotic ex and sire no less.

When Kade walks into the kitchen, I push away from the counter and approach him. "Any luck?"

He nods. "There isn't much, but it's enough to get out of the clothes we're in and wash them."

"Good." I press my lips together at the distant look in his usually bright silver eyes. "Kade..." My voice is soft, laced with concern. "Are you okay?" I lift my hand to his face, brushing my fingers against his cheek. I want to comfort him, take care of him. Because if I'm doing that, I won't have time to pay attention to the panic filling my veins, wrapping around my ribs, and squeezing my heart. When he exhales a shuddering breath, I realize his fangs are protruding from his gums.

"You need a drink." I move to step back and check the fridge for blood, but he wraps his fingers around my wrist, holding me in place.

"Slow down. It's all right, Calla."

"No. No, it's not. You—"

Kade kisses me. I try to pull back, to ask him what the hell he's doing, but he snakes his arm around my waist, hauling me against him and pinning me between him and the counter. His lips steal my breath, and eventually I can do nothing but succumb to the kiss. Closing my eyes, I relax against him and kiss him back. He's trying to distract me—probably himself too—and for a few moments, I'm going to let him.

When he pulls back, cupping my cheek and brushing his thumb over my skin, I meet his gaze and sigh. "I'm sorry about your sister," I tell him in a voice just barely above a whisper.

He kisses me once more, soft and quick. "Thanks."

The whistle of the kettle breaks us apart, and I walk to the stove and switch off the burner, pouring the water into each mug, before Kade and I carry them into the living room.

The four of us sit without speaking for a few minutes, sipping on tea and watching the flames dance in the fireplace, their soft crackling the only sound in the room.

I think I make it five minutes before I can't take the silence anymore. I set my mug on the oak coffee table and sit back in the black wingback chair. "What are we going to do now that your cover with the hunters is blown?"

Atlas looks to me. "Scott has been calling and texting me since we left Washington."

My chest feels tight at the mention of Brighton's father's name. "What did he say? Does he know I'm with you?"

"I'm not sure if he does," Atlas answers. "Likely not, as none of the hunters were people I recognized from the company, which leaves little chance they'd know who you are."

Lex sits up and takes a drink. "If Meredith is working with the hunters, there's a chance she went back to them after her attack and told them there was a human with us, but that wouldn't mean that they'd figure out who."

"I haven't listened to Scott's voicemails—he left half a fucking dozen—but all his texts say is to call him back. A few empty threats here and there, but nothing seriously concerning at this point."

My eyes widen at his words. *Nothing seriously concerning?* I want to ask what would be considered seriously concerning to him, but I pick up my tea to sip instead. There are a lot of moving pieces, between Gabriel and Selene to Meredith and the hunters—they're all linked, and our best bet is to figure out what the hunters are planning now that they know Atlas, Kade, and Lex are vampires.

I wet my lips before saying, "So odds are the hunters have no idea who I am or my, um, association with you guys. That means there's a chance I can still—"

"Don't bother finishing that sentence," Atlas cuts in, snaring my gaze over the rim of his mug as he takes a drink of his tea. "You already know the answer."

I scowl. "In case you haven't noticed, you three are on the run. You're the vampires. The hunters have no reason to come after me."

"I'm sure they'll find one the minute they put it together that you're with us." Lex's jaw is set tight. If he grips that mug any tighter, it's going to shatter in his hands.

I reach over and pry it from his grip, setting it on the table in front of him. "We're not there yet," I point out. "Now's the time to use me while they're still in the dark. I can get in touch with Brighton and try to figure—"

"Enough."

My eyes snap back to Atlas and narrow. "Fine," I say through my teeth, "then what's your plan that's so clearly better than mine?"

A muscle feathers along his jaw as he holds my gaze, setting his mug down without a sound. "I need to speak with my contacts in New York. I actually put rational thought into my actions and consider the consequences before doing something."

I exhale a harsh breath, anger igniting in my chest as my pulse kicks up. "Oh, get off your high horse, Atlas." Defiance flares to life in me, and I continue, "You just don't want me to help, because god forbid someone else is the answer instead of you."

Kade sighs, exchanging a glance with Lex. "Here we go."

Atlas offers a bitter, humorless laugh. "You don't know a fucking thing."

I arch a brow, crossing my arms over my chest. "Please, enlighten me then."

"There are certain ways things need to be done," he says in a forced level tone. "Until you've lived for a century and understand that, I'm not going to waste my breath with this conversation."

That raises my hackles, and I snap, "You are so fucking arrogant."

"Okay, okay," Kade says, holding his hands up as if he's physically trying to contain the tension that hangs thick in the air. "Arguing about this isn't getting us any closer to a solution. Let's stop now before the two of you either start brawling or fucking in the middle of this sad excuse for a living room."

A mix of darkness and hunger fills Atlas's expression, making it harder to hold his gaze as my body betrays how I feel about Kade's latter concern. Heat swirls low in my belly at the thought of Atlas—*no*. I'm not going there.

I clear my throat, grabbing my empty mug off the coffee table and turning toward the kitchen. "I'll find something for dinner," I mutter, walking out of the room while I still have the will to fight the urge to take a swing at Atlas's infuriatingly attractive face. Fucking stupid supernatural beauty.

An hour later, we are sitting around a round dining table that is most definitely not big enough for four people. Lex and Kade are on either side of me and Atlas sits directly across from me. I managed to cook a beef teriyaki dish without burning the place down, so I'm calling it a win.

Lex and Kade devour their dishes, while I pick at mine, and Atlas leaves his untouched. Asshole. It may not be Gabriel's fancy cooking, but it's at least edible.

My expression must be more telling than I thought, because Atlas's lips twitch as he reaches for the glass of water in front of him.

"What?" I say through my teeth, gripping my fork so hard the metal bites into my fingers.

Atlas shakes his head and pushes his full dish away. "It's nothing personal. It actually smells quite good."

"But not good enough for you." I let go of my fork, letting it clammer against the dish before falling onto the table. "Because nothing is."

His eyes narrow ever so slightly. "Because," he says pointedly, "I need blood."

Oh. *Oh.*

Shit. The others survive off blood and food because they're turned vampires. Atlas can eat human food, but he gets no sustenance from it.

I shake my head, frowning. "I... There wasn't any in the fridge."

"I'm aware," he says. "It's fine."

I finish the water in my glass and am reaching for my knife before I even realize what I'm doing.

Lex catches my wrist. "Calla—"

"He needs blood," I say, holding my hand palm up. "You all do," I add, noticing Lex's fangs are showing.

"Do you know what you're doing?" Kade asks.

I spare him a short glance and nod. "I'm offering myself," I say, "to all of you." The words make me shiver, and my skin tingles where Lex's fingers are still wrapped around my wrist.

"Are you sure?" Lex asks.

"Are you going to kill me?" I ask the three vampires all looking at me as if I'm equal parts crazy and the answer to their prayers.

"Of course not," Kade says.

I nod again. "Then I'm sure. But maybe we shouldn't do this at the kitchen table?"

"Why not?" Atlas chimes in with a straight face. "You ate your dinner here."

I gape at him. I'm about to snap again, to revoke my offer to him specifically, when the unthinkable happens.

Atlas laughs.

What the fuck?

"Ease up, Calla. I'm only kidding."

I blink at him, utterly speechless. "I... Since when?"

The corner of his mouth tugs up, and he shrugs. "Perhaps you bring that out in me."

Heat fills my cheeks, and I want nothing more than to look away. Instead, I stand, setting the knife down. Lex follows my movement, keeping his gentle grip on my wrist, and we walk back into the living room, where I take a seat on the couch. Lex sits next to me on the right, and Kade drops onto the cushion on my left. Atlas walks into the room and stands behind the couch, leaning down and moving the hair away from my neck.

My heart pounds in my chest, threatening to break free of my ribcage, but I don't move. I take a deep breath and close my eyes as Kade and Lex each take one of my wrists while Atlas tilts my head back against the cushions. I press my lips together, whimpering softly when fangs sink into both of my wrists. Atlas's fingers dance along my skin, tracing over my collarbone as his lips graze the shell of my ear, and he whispers, "Breathe, Calla."

I let out a shaky breath, turning my cheek to expose my throat to him.

I don't expect him to hesitate. I don't expect his lips to brush my neck, to kiss my skin. His hand slides against my cheek, cradling my head, and then his fangs finally sink into my neck. My whimper from before is replaced by a breathy moan. The sensation of blood being pulled from me in three different directions leaves me feeling light and warm, and has my core throbbing almost in time with my racing pulse.

The vampires on either side of me slide their hands up my thighs, getting dangerously close to the heat between them, and I bite my lip against the pleasure flooding through me. Can I blame it on the venom coursing through my veins? Because I'm definitely going to.

Kade and Lex pull back, sealing the wounds on my wrists as Atlas continues drinking. A moment later, he finishes, dragging his tongue along my neck slowly as his thumb glides back and forth over my skin. His hand against my cheek keeps my head from lolling to the side, and I fight to pry my eyes open despite wanting to keep them shut. To live in this haze of pleasure and warmth and forget about all the problems we're facing outside of this safe house.

"Calla." Kade pats my knee. "Wakey, wakey. You need to eat something."

"No," I groan, trying to wave him off, "I need to sleep."

"Open your eyes." Atlas's command latches onto me, and my eyes open in an instant. "Good. Now, Kade is going to go get your dinner and bring it in here, and you're going to eat it."

"Hmm... I want grilled cheese."

Lex laughs. "I mean, it's the least we can do. We did just have *her* for dinner." He glances at Atlas. "Give the girl what she wants."

Atlas's fingers slip away from my cheek, and he and Kade walk back to the kitchen while Lex pulls me into his lap, curling his arm around my waist. His fingers trail under my shirt, skimming the skin below my belly button, and my breath hitches. He chuckles softly but doesn't move his fingers any lower, so I relax against him.

After I've devoured two grilled cheese sandwiches, I'm feeling steady enough on my feet to put some distance between myself and any furniture—or vampires—to hold me up. I excuse myself and go in search of the washroom, which I find at the end of the hall. It's nothing special, nothing like what I'd gotten used to at the guy's place. In fact, it's reminiscent of the bathroom in my apartment, and I find myself smiling at the memory. It's strange how long ago that part of my life feels now, when really, it was only just over a month ago. So much has happened these past weeks, it's hard to think of what my life was like before this. Before *them*.

After a lukewarm shower—because this place evidently doesn't have a very strong water heater—I dress in a T-shirt I found in one of the bedroom dressers and pop my head back into the living room to say goodnight.

They don't try to stop me or join me, and while part of me is a little disappointed by that, I'm mostly grateful for the space.

The bedroom I pick has light yellow walls and a four-poster dark wood bed with white sheets. Pulling back the heavy comforter, the faint smell of fabric softener tickles my nose, and I crawl under the sheets, the mattress creaking under me. There's a small table beside the bed with a lamp that's probably older than I am, casting the small room in a soft golden glow.

With a deep breath, I roll over and flick the light out before settling onto my back. I stare at the ceiling, my eyes fluttering shut to the sound of muffled conversation from the living room. Their presence brings me comfort enough to snuggle into this strange bed and pretend I'm somewhere else.

In minutes, sleep drags me under, and I go willingly.

When my eyes open, ice fills my veins, and I shoot upright, gasping for air that isn't there. My eyes whip around the elegant space, and my stomach sinks. *I can't be back here.* The room comes more into focus, and I shake my head. "No..." I scramble off the bed and rush toward the window, my head spinning when all I can see outside is darkness. I whirl around, walking past the blazing fireplace and toward the door, but just like last time, before I can reach for the handle, the door opens. I jump back, gritting my teeth as I wait for Selene to glide in and taunt me once again.

Except, it isn't Selene.

I suck in a breath, hot tears pricking my eyes. "Gabriel?"

He steps into the room, closing the door behind him, and smiles at me. "Hello, angel."

I have no idea what's happening right now, but I throw my arms around his neck, clinging to him with every ounce of strength I have. Granted, that isn't much right now.

Gabriel circles his arms around my waist, holding me against him, and buries his face in the crook of my neck. "I don't know how much time we have," he murmurs.

I close my eyes, inhaling deeply, melting into him. "What do you mean? Isn't this a dream?"

"Calla." His voice isn't unkind, but it has lost its dreamlike warmth.

I pull back enough to look at his face, to run my fingers through his thick copper hair, to gaze into his soft, silver eyes. "What is it?" My brows knit in confusion. "Is... is this *real*?"

He nods. "It's a dream in the sense that you're asleep wherever you are, but I am very much awake."

I shake my head. "I don't understand."

Gabriel offers a small laugh. "I don't either. Not fully. But we don't have time to question it when we don't know if or when it'll end."

I pull in a sharp breath. "The hunters. Gabriel—"

"I know, angel." He frowns. "Selene made a deal with Scott. She traded the names of at least a dozen powerful vampires in the city in exchange for her own protection."

My mouth drops open. "Selene told the hunters where we live. They ambushed the house, and we had to run."

His jaw clenches as the color drains from his face. "Is—"

"Everyone is fine," I rush to tell him. "But, um... Kade. His sister is alive. She's a vampire, and I think she's working with the hunters like Selene is."

His eyes widen. "That's not good. How is he?"

Sighing, I say, "He's putting on a strong face, but I don't think he's okay." I can't imagine how he could be.

Gabriel nods. "Right. Of course he isn't."

I chew my bottom lip, my eyes flicking between his. "How are *you*?"

He smiles sadly.

"Oh, Gabriel." I reach for him again, sliding my hands up his chest. "I wish you were here."

He cups my cheek. "I wish for that too."

I turn my face and press my lips against his palm. "The whole reason you went to Selene was because of her threat against me. The solution to that was to kill her, which we were holding off on doing because we wanted to know more about her relationship with the hunters. Since she outed the guys to the hunters, I don't see why her relationship to them matters much now."

"I didn't know about that until you told me," he says gently.

I scowl. "Of course she kept it from you. Is she still playing the angle that she missed you and wants to be with you?"

He tilts his head, regarding me thoughtfully. "It doesn't matter, angel. I didn't miss her, nor do I want to be with her. Now that I know what she's done, you're absolutely right. There's no sense in keeping her alive."

"Good, so—"

He leans in, pressing his forehead against mine. "But there's nothing you or I can do about that right now. I'm here with her, unable to strike her down myself, and you are somewhere I imagine is far enough away to keep you safe. So how about we just enjoy each other's company while we have it and until we can be together for real?"

The pressure in my chest expands, sending a burst of warmth between my legs, making me throb with desire.

"Are you asking me for dream sex?" I ask, not even attempting to hide my amusement.

Gabriel grins at me. "I very much am, yes."

My nose grazes his, and I brush my lips along his bottom one, kissing him slowly, teasingly. He drops his hands to my hips and spins us around, pinning me against the door before his lips claim mine, taking control of the kiss in a single breath. His tongue glides along my lips, and I part them, letting him in and moaning into his mouth when he presses his lower half against me, igniting a delicious friction between my thighs. He knows where to apply pressure to send a bolt of electricity straight to my clit, and I gasp against his lips.

I break away to moan his name, my nipples stiffening against the T-shirt I fell asleep in. It's currently riding up my thighs, held in place by Gabriel's fingers digging into my hips.

"I want nothing more than to take my time tasting every bit of your exquisite body, but I fear our time will run out too quickly."

I don't think I can handle slow tonight. "Please," I breathe, "I need you inside me."

He picks me up easily, and I hang onto his shoulders as he turns us around and walks to the bed, laying me down before tugging his shirt off, dropping it onto the floor. He does the same with his pants and boxers, leaving him naked where he stands at the end of the bed.

I'm propped up on my elbows, watching his every move. I grab the hem of my shirt, pulling it over my head and tossing it to the side, letting Gabriel see me as I'm seeing him—completely bare.

He crawls over me, pressing his lips just above my belly button, his tongue swirling against my skin and kicking my pulse up. He drags his lips up my stomach, peppering soft kisses along the way, making goosebumps rise on my skin as I press my lips together. My core throbs, and almost as if he senses my need, he presses his knee there, and I let out a breathy moan, pushing my fingers through his hair. His lips close around my nipple, and heat shoots right to my clit, making it overly sensitive. My back arches, pushing my breast into his mouth, where his tongue swirls around my nipple, alternating between sucking and licking. Then he moves to the other side, and repeats his ministrations, leaving me panting beneath him.

"Gabriel," I say, gripping his hair between my fingers with one hand and reaching for his cock with the other. I can feel the wetness already gathering between my legs, and he hasn't even touched me there yet. But I need him to. Now.

I wrap my fingers around his thick length, guiding him to my entrance. I drag the blunt head of his cock along my folds, licking the dryness from my lips before kissing him deeply. I whimper against his mouth when he takes hold of his cock and presses it against my clit before dipping inside of me slowly. I lift my hips, pushing him in deeper, and he groans against my lips. We find a delicious rhythm in no time, and Gabriel alternates between kissing my lips and sucking on the sensitive skin below my ear as he rolls his hips and thrusts into me, slow and deep, then hard and fast until I'm seeing fucking stars.

"Gabriel," I pant, digging my heels into his ass to push him even deeper.

"I know," he says against my skin as his thrusts become more frantic. "Come for me, angel."

His words trigger my release, and my pussy clenches around him, milking his cock as he continues to thrust into me, the sound of his grunts mixing with my moans as he climaxes next, filling me with his release.

Once the aftershocks of my orgasm fade, Gabriel kisses the corner of my mouth and pulls out of me, dropping onto the bed beside me and pulling me against him. I close my eyes, my cheek pressed against his chest as his heart returns to a steady beat.

"Can we stay here?" I murmur with a yawn.

He brushes my hair away from my face, tucking it behind my ear before dropping a kiss to my forehead. "I wish we could. But unfortunately, you need to wake up."

My bubble of warmth and happiness pops, and I frown up at him. "But we haven't been here that long."

He offers me a soft smile. "It's morning."

I blink at him, confusion filling me. "That much time has passed?" Disbelief fills my tone.

He nods. "I'm sorry. I'll see you soon, angel, and we'll figure everything out. I promise."

I want to say more, to hold him longer, but before I can open my mouth to speak, his face starts to fade. Everything around me goes dark, stealing the scene from me slowly and then all at once.

THREE

I'm up before the others, having slept on the couch instead of trying to squeeze into the second bedroom with Atlas and Lex. I considered slipping into Calla's room, but something told me she needed space from us. A bed to herself for the night was the least we could give her.

I didn't sleep much anyway. Not with the flashes of Meredith's face twisted in bitter anger and the sight of her razor-sharp fangs bared at me playing on a vicious loop every time I closed my eyes.

After an all too short workout outside, I take a quick, scorching shower and pull the only clothing I have out of the dryer.

The shitty coffee maker in the kitchen is my next stop after getting dressed. It's a far cry from the machine we had installed in our kitchen, but desperate times and whatnot.

I lean against the counter, glancing around the small, outdated room in the dim morning light just barely starting to filter through the window over the sink. I pull out my phone to check for any communications from Marcel while the machine gurgles softly behind me, filling the space with a warm, rich aroma that calls to me almost as strongly as the scent of blood. Almost.

With a cup of coffee in hand, I walk back to my makeshift couch bed, my steps silent across the peel and stick linoleum in the kitchen to the hardwood in the living room. There's a bit of a chill in the air, and instead of fighting with the thermostat, I strike a match across the brick fireplace and start a fire inside. The flames fill the room with a soft glow and warmth as I lounge on the couch, sipping my coffee. It's almost peaceful—you know, if I could ignore the reason we're here.

Lex rises next, his white hair an absolute mess, which he clearly couldn't give two shits about. He doesn't acknowledge my presence until he has a cup of coffee in his hand. He sits in one of the chairs across from me, glancing into the flames.

"You sleep?" he asks in a deep, tired voice.

"Not much. You?"

He grumbles his agreement.

Atlas's voice reaches me, though he's still in the other room. Sounds like he's on the phone with one of Marcel's guys, arranging for a blood delivery. Good man. As much as I'd prefer Calla's blood over the bagged stuff, we can't all feed from her over and over.

He joins us after ending the call, foregoing the coffee, and drops into the chair next to Lex.

I set my empty mug on the coffee table and sigh. Before I can say anything, Calla's bedroom door creaks open. She makes a stop in the bathroom before padding out to the living room, glancing between each of us, and plops onto the opposite end of the couch.

"Morning," she murmurs, sleep still clinging to her soft voice.

I want to pull her to me, lay her across my lap, and coax her back to sleep. Like the rest of us, she looks exhausted.

She bites her lip, glancing at her lap as her pulse ticks faster.

"What is it?" Lex asks before I can.

"I... had a dream last night. Or, I think it was a dream. I don't know." She looks up again and pushes her fingers through her dark brown hair, pulling it up and tying it into a knot on the top of her head.

"You don't know?" Atlas questions, arching a brow at her.

"I think it was real somehow. I saw Gabriel. I mean, he was with me."

My brows inch up my forehead, and I look from her to the guys to see similar reactions on their faces. We're all confused as fuck. Dreamwalking isn't a vampiric ability that I'm aware of. I steal a glance at Atlas; if any of us would know about it, he would. But he appears as lost as I am by this revelation.

"It could be part of the bond," Lex offers. "We can't say we know everything about the oath, especially when there was a witch involved, right? Maybe Gabriel was able to use his connection to you to reach you while unconscious."

"I was asleep," she says, "but Gabriel was awake."

"Interesting," Lex muses, sipping his coffee. "Perhaps the rest of us should test it out. See if we can all appear in your dream at the same time."

"I've never heard of this," Atlas comments mildly. "It doesn't seem too far outside the realm of possibility, though."

"I wonder if that witch Tessa, the one Selene sent to heal me, could tell us about it," Calla muses aloud. "Do you think we could track her down? I mean, after we get Gabriel back, deal with the hunters, save the world, and all that."

"Funny," I mutter, shaking my head. I understand her curiosity—hell, I'd like to know more about this dreamwalking Gabriel was able to do—but I'd rather not bring a witch into the mix.

"It's something to consider," she says, "and Tessa seemed pretty cool."

"For a witch," Lex grumbles under his breath, and my lips almost curl into a grin.

"What exactly happened in this dream? What did Gabriel say to you?" I ask, my chest feeling oddly tight. Every minute Gabriel is away from us, the pit of worry in my gut grows heavier. There's a sharp pain there too, an ugly flare of jealousy that Calla got to see him, even if only in a dream. We need to get him back for real and take out the psycho blond who has her claws in him.

None of us miss the tinge of pink in Calla's cheeks as she presses her lips together.

"He, uh…" She clears her throat, shaking her head as if to clear it and focus, then starts again. "Selene sold us out. Whatever deal she made with Scott to cover her own ass, she used us to fulfill her end and told the hunters you three are vampires and where to find you."

I grip the armrest of the couch so tight, my fingers tear into the leather. My fangs threaten to slice through my gums as I bite back a growl. Lex looks about five seconds away from exploding with anger, and Atlas is scarily still, his jaw sharp enough to cut glass.

"We're getting him back," I snarl, feeling Calla shift closer to me. She wraps her arm around mine, leaning into me. Glancing down, I blink at her in surprise. I'm not used to someone moving closer when I'm pissed off.

"We will," Lex assures me with a stiff nod.

"No more waiting. We know what Selene is up to with the hunters now—selling us out." Bitterness laces my tone, and the urge to get my fingers around her neck and squeeze until her eyes bulge out of her face is overwhelming.

"I've been thinking about it," Calla says. "I think she figured with us out of the way, Gabriel would be more inclined to stay with her. He'd have no one else."

"That bitch is dead," Lex growls.

"We need to be careful," Atlas chimes in, his posture unnaturally straight. "Considering we're essentially fugitives, and there are hunters all over the place, it could get tricky to return to Washington."

"Fuck that," Lex snaps, his eyes wild—more so than normal—and blazing with anger.

"Lex," Atlas warns, shooting him a dark look. "Take a breath. We'll get him back and deal with Selene, but we need to be smart about how we proceed."

Calla sighs, getting off the couch and walking into the kitchen. A minute later, she returns, cradling a steaming cup of coffee. "Not to sound selfish or anything, but I still have school. The term is almost over, but unless you see us resolving this whole hunter issue over the summer break, I'll need to figure out what I'm doing come the fall. I understand this isn't any of your main concerns, but school is quite literally the only normal thing I have left in my life, so yeah, I'm worried about it."

I stare at her, my gums throbbing as I clench my jaw. I want to be sympathetic and understanding of her concerns, but I can't find the will to give a shit about her going to school. We have much bigger problems to face at the moment—including my sister who I believed to be dead for over a century.

Standing, I walk around the couch and leave the room before I say something that'll only upset her. I find myself in the bedroom the guys slept in, leaning against the wall and looking out the window to the side of the property where the sun is rising.

I hear Lex come in and close the door before he speaks, but I don't turn around.

"Kade—"

"Don't," I cut him off.

He sighs, walking closer. "Talk to me, brother."

With a groan, I turn to face him, leaning against the windowsill. "I didn't want to be a dick, so I removed myself from the situation where I was very close to becoming one."

His lips twitch.

"Don't fucking grin at that."

He doesn't try to hide it. "Come on, Kade. You should be celebrating. I think this is real growth for you."

I glare at him. "Prick."

Lex comes closer, stopping once he's close enough to grab ahold of my shoulders. "I know this is stressful for you. Different from how it's affecting the rest of us. I can only imagine what's going through your head right now, but you're not alone." His fingers dig into my shoulders, massaging them until the tension is forced out.

I hold his gaze and nod.

His hands glide off my shoulders, moving down my bare arms, and when his fingers go to work on my belt, my lips curl into a faint grin. "What are you doing?"

He gets the buckle undone and pops the button on my pants. "I'm going to help work out some of that stress." He shoots me a wink, and I roll my eyes but make no move to stop him. Because as pissed as I am, my cock is already hard, twitching and aching to be touched.

Lex pulls my zipper down slowly, the sound echoing through the room as my heart rate kicks up. He wastes no time sliding his fingers into my boxers and pulling my cock out. He bends slightly, tugging my pants down to just above my knees, then straightens, looking me in the eyes.

I suck in a sharp breath through my teeth and grip the windowsill on either side of me as he wraps his fingers around my thick length and starts moving his hand up and down. I close my eyes, and my head falls back against the window with a thud. It could shatter the glass for all I care, so long as Lex keeps his hand on my dick.

A groan rips through me when he applies pressure, twisting his grip as he pumps and using his free hand to massage my balls. He pauses at the blunt tip of my cock for a moment, rubbing his thumb through the moisture gathering there until I growl at him to keep moving, and he returns to the torturous rhythm of pumping.

My chest rises and falls fast as Lex increases both his pressure and pace, and I grab his shoulder to steady myself. "Don't fucking stop," I bark out, and he chuckles deeply. The sound goes straight to my cock, and everything tightens. I let out a deep grunt, and my release spurts out over his hand.

After we've cleaned up, I pull my pants up and buckle my belt.

"You good?" Lex checks as we head toward the bedroom door.

"Better." I nod at him. "Thanks."

He offers another wink. "Anytime. And I fully expect you to return the favor next time." It's not like we haven't done this before, though it has been a while. Over the years, we've all been together in one way or another. Sometimes one-on-one, other times all together. When you know someone for over a century and build such a unique and strong bond, societal norms really don't matter. How you feel about another person—or *people*, in our case—is far more important.

I laugh, opening the door and stepping into the hallway. "Of course you do."

Back in the living room, we find Atlas and Calla bickering about needing to get back to Washington unnoticed, to get Gabriel out of Selene's clutches before any more damage can be done.

Calla leans against the back of the couch, crossing her arms over her chest. "We know where they are, granted Selene didn't move after throwing you guys under the bus with the hunters, but I don't see why she'd do that. And in my dream, we were in the same penthouse, which could also mean they're still there."

"We'll get him back," Lex assures her, perching on the armrest next to her. "Then we'll figure out what to do about the hunters."

Atlas says nothing, just rubs his hand along his jaw as he glances out the front window.

"The way I see it," Calla says, "we have two choices. Try to work with the hunters by showing them you're not a danger to the humans... or take them out." She glances between us, settling her determined gaze on Atlas. "Are you prepared to declare war?"

His jaw clenches. "That's not my call."

Her brows pinch together as she blinks at him. "Isn't it?"

"Atlas is one of a group of born vampires. His parents basically run the vampire world. He'll need to consult with them."

She catches her bottom lip between her teeth and nods. "And where are they?"

"The big apple," Lex chimes in with a faint grin despite the serious topic of conversation.

Her eyes widen and the beat of her heart shifts, becoming more uneven, as if the thought of the city she grew up leaves her uneasy. "Great," she finally says, "let's get going."

"We're not going to New York," Atlas says.

"Then what are we going to do?" Her voice is strained, and my eyes follow her hand as she seemingly reaches for the dagger at her thigh without conscious thought.

"Take a breath," Lex suggests, his gaze tracking her movement as well. "This shit isn't something we're going to figure out in a matter of an hour."

"He's right," Atlas confirms, looking rather pleased by her instinctive reach for the weapon he gave her.

She scowls, frowning when her phone chimes beside her. The three of us watch her pick it up and read the notification.

"What is it?" Lex asks.

Calla glances up, and her deep brown eyes flit between us as she realizes we're all staring at her. "Relax, guys. It's just Brighton." She taps away on the screen for a few seconds, then sets her phone face down on the coffee table. "Our usual brunch spot is closed on Monday for some private event, so we have to go somewhere else."

"You're not going anywhere near her," Atlas says in a dangerously calm voice.

She's quick to turn a glare on him. "Not going would be worse," she points out. "I've barely spoken to her since being taken by Selene, and she probably already thinks things are weird considering I'm still not back to school." She crosses her arms. "I have to go. I need to see her, and she needs to see that I'm fine, otherwise she's going to start asking questions we don't want."

I purse my lips, looking to Atlas, though he's still staring at her. She's not wrong. The last thing we need is for Brighton to express concern over her BFF to that stab-happy father of hers and mention the sexy group of guys Calla was hanging with at the St. Patrick's Day party last month.

"I have an idea," I offer. "Let's say we let her go. We can pick the location and have our team surround it. Keep eyes on her at all times."

She arches a brow at me. "Because that's not creepy or anything."

"You want to go or not?" I warn. "I'm trying to help you here."

"This is ridiculous," she complains. "Brighton, for one, isn't a hunter. She doesn't even know about them." She shakes her head. "We've had this conversation before and it hasn't changed."

I nod slowly. "If you want to see her, you'll agree to the terms I've laid out."

Lex grumbles in agreement, and Atlas lets a heavy silence hang in the air for several moments before he agrees as well.

She rolls her eyes. "Fine. If that's what it takes."

I could easily make a list of things I'd rather do than spend Monday morning stuck in a car with Atlas, but perhaps I should be grateful he decided to drive me back to Washington to have brunch with Brighton. That being said, I hadn't considered that would mean being locked in the car with him for over three hours. I'd hoped Kade or Lex—or both, honestly—would join us, but they were still asleep when we left the safe house.

Atlas has his phone connected to the sound system, and I'm surprised at how much I don't hate his taste in music. I was expecting hardcore rock or angsty screamo. So when Halsey's *Young God* comes on, I turn my shocked expression to him.

"Why are you staring at me?" he asks after a moment without taking his eyes off the road.

"Uh, no reason. I just... didn't peg you for a Halsey fan," I comment mildly.

"What *did* you peg me for, Calla?" There's a hint of curiosity in his deep voice that has my lips twitching.

"Hmm, you really don't want me to answer that."

He offers a short laugh. "Why? Because I'll be tempted to pull over and show you just how wrong you are about me?"

Boldness grips me, and I say, "Hate to break it to you, but that's not the threat you think it is."

He grips the steering wheel tighter, his jaw working. "And why is that? Because it's exactly what you want?"

Absolutely fucking right it is. We've been playing this deadly game of cat and mouse for over a month now. Something needs to happen before one of us explodes.

I chew my lower lip, pressing my thighs together as heat gathers between them. Swallowing past the sudden dryness in my throat, I say, "Doesn't matter, because you won't do it."

"No?" he challenges.

"You're not going to fuck me in the back seat of your car." The doubt is clear in my voice despite how it shakes. Because as sure as I am that he won't do it, there's a depraved part of me that longs for him to do just that. To show me who he truly is—no holding back. The fear, the not knowing what he's fully capable of, it's dangerously exciting.

Atlas shoots me a dark look that steals my breath. "Who said anything about the back seat?" He shakes his head, returning his gaze to the road as his lips curl into a smirk. "I'd fuck you up here with your back against the steering wheel and let everyone driving by see how easily I can make you scream for me."

My heart slams against my chest, and I tear my eyes away from him, the car suddenly suffocating. I feel Atlas everywhere. As hard as I try to shove him out of my head, it's useless.

"Nothing to say now, huh?" he taunts, gripping the wheel so hard his knuckles are white.

"Pull over," I say, nearly breathless. I need a minute without the movement of this car; I need air.

"You really—"

"Atlas, so help me, *pull over.*"

In the space of a heartbeat, he jerks the wheel to the side, guiding the car off the interstate. Gravel crunches under the tires and kicks up dust, and I have my seat belt off, reaching for the door before Atlas even puts the car in park.

The second the lock clicks open, I all but throw myself outside, slamming the door shut before walking toward the thick line of pine trees that run along the freeway. I make it into the damp forest, the sounds of the cars speeding down the interstate fading into the background as I slowly find my center again.

I hug my arms around myself, attempting to suck in deep breaths of fresh, spring air, but when Atlas appears in front of me, I choke on the air in my throat and come to an abrupt stop.

"What the fuck is the matter with you?" His eyes are narrowed and filled with irritation. "Get back in the car."

"With *me*?" I force out in a sharp tone, taking a healthy step back. "Says the guy who was just talking about fucking me for any passerby to watch."

His hands curl into fists at his sides as his blazing silver gaze dances across my face. He takes a step closer. Then another. One more step, and we're so close the tops of his shoes are almost touching my Docs. Atlas cocks his head to the side, and I hold my breath as he studies me. "That's not why you're angry," he finally says.

I arch a brow at him. "Wh—"

"You're upset because you *want* it."

My mouth drops open, and I grasp for the words to refute his accusation, but nothing forms. Fucking hell. I hate him. More than that, I hate that he's right. The thought of people watching him claim me... My chest flushes, and I desperately want to look away so he can't see the heat in my cheeks.

He chuckles deeply, and before I know what's happening, my fist is swinging toward his face, toward the smug smirk plastered across his lips.

It doesn't connect. *Of course* it doesn't. Instead, Atlas catches my fist in his hand and grips it tightly, pushing me back until I collide with the thick trunk of a tree, its bark rough against my thin windbreaker.

I pull my fist back, and he lets it go. In the time it takes me to blink, he cages me against the tree, his hands braced on either side of my head. My eyes widen at his dark expression, at the sharpness of his jaw. But instead of ducking under his arm and attempting to put distance between us, I press my hands to his hard chest.

"What are you doing?" he growls.

I hold his gaze, the pressure in my chest building. "What are *you* doing?"

He exhales harshly, leaning down so his lips are level with my ear, which presses him so close, my hands are effectively trapped between his chest and mine. "I haven't quite decided yet." His words trigger a shiver to shoot down my spine, and I turn my face away.

In hindsight, that probably wasn't the best move, considering it bares my neck to him.

Atlas wraps his fingers around my throat and presses his thumb against my jaw, forcing my gaze back to him. "I have you all alone out here." He lowers his voice. "There is no one to stop me from doing whatever I want to you." He flicks his tongue over his bottom lip, and I catch sight of his fangs. He chuckles darkly when I suck in a breath. "And you'd let me, wouldn't you?" The fire in his eyes sends heat straight to my core, making my entire body flush under his scrutiny, though he isn't glamouring me.

"You're trying to scare me," I force out in a level tone, shaking my head. "I'm not going anywhere."

The corner of his mouth curls up slowly. "I wouldn't let you if you tried."

My heart is beating so hard I can feel it in my throat. "So do it then," I taunt despite my racing pulse.

He drops his hands to my hips, where his fingers dig into my skin, and though there's a layer of clothing between his skin and mine, heat courses through me. "What, you're not going to fight me anymore?"

I pause, the heat between my legs throbbing with need. "Not today."

A faint growl rumbles in his chest, and he dips his head, sealing his lips over mine in a fiery kiss that swallows my entire world so there's nothing left but him.

My fingers end up in his stupidly soft hair as his trail under my jacket and shirt, teasing upward toward my bra. Our lips battle for control, neither willing to succumb to the other. When his fang slices my lip, spilling my blood into his mouth, his body tenses against mine, the hardness between his legs pressing where I crave him most.

I can't stop the moan that escapes my lips, muffled by his mouth on mine. He leans back, his fangs fully extended and my blood staining his lips. Perhaps the sight should frighten or disturb me. Instead, it only makes me ache for him.

"Calla," he warns, seeing something in my gaze.

I press my lips together, then offer him a faint smile. "How long are you going to make me wait, Atlas?"

He licks my blood from his lips. "Forgive me," he says in a dry tone, "for showing some restraint so as not to fuck you against a tree. How rude of me."

I roll my eyes. "Don't pretend to be a gentleman," I retort. "You were ready to take me in the front seat of your car on the side of the interstate five minutes ago." I palm the bulge in his pants. "Hmm. It certainly feels like you're ready now."

Atlas hisses, grabbing my wrist, but doesn't pull it away. Instead, he captures my lips again, kissing me until my head spins, and loosens his grip on my wrist. I take that as an invitation to keep palming him through his pants, and am quickly rewarded with a deep groan from him. One of his hands slides back up my shirt while the other presses flat against my stomach, then glides under the waistband of my leggings. The moment his fingers brush my folds, electricity crackles through me, and I gasp against his lips.

"Fucking hell," he says against my lips, his voice ragged. "You're practically dripping for me already."

Before I can beg for his fingers, he plunges two inside me, dragging his lips away from my mouth and along my jaw. My hips jerk forward, but he shoves me back against the tree.

"I control this," he says, circling my clit with his thumb as his fingers continue moving, massaging the walls of my pussy.

I pull my bottom lip between my teeth to keep from snapping at him. I won't risk him stopping the movement of his fingers. Fuck, if he needs to be in control, so be it. I'll gladly give it up so long as he doesn't stop.

He undoes my bra, and I've never been so grateful for front clasp bras as when he starts palming my breast, rolling the nipple between his fingers until my breath hitches.

"Yes," I moan.

He picks up the pace of his thrusting fingers and switches to my other breast. My head falls against the tree, my back arching as I push my breast into his skilled hand. When he adds pressure to the thumb against my clit and starts curling his fingers inside me, I suck in a shallow breath, my heart rate kicking up and my knees starting to shake.

"Calla."

My name on his lips makes my pussy clench around his fingers, shooting another wave of pleasure through me.

His voice is low, thick with arousal when he says, "Are you going to come?"

A grin tugs at my lips as tension continues to build between my legs. "You'll feel pretty inadequate if I don't, now won't you?"

"Go ahead," he taunts, "try not to."

There's a challenge in his gaze that I'm tempted to accept, but when his fingers brush a particularly sensitive spot deep inside me, everything tightens seconds before an orgasm rips through me, stealing the breath from my lungs with a deep, loud moan and making my knees buckle.

Atlas catches me around the waist, holding me up, and chuckles. "Valiant effort," he remarks dryly.

I grip the front of his T-shirt, leaning into him as I catch my breath. "Couldn't have you moping the rest of the way to Washington."

He leans in, brushing his lips across mine in a whisper of a kiss. "Stop talking." He presses closer, curling his fingers into the waistband of my leggings, and tugs them down to my knees. "I'm nowhere near done with you, and we're running out of time if you actually wish to make it to Washington."

My stomach clenches with a warm mixture of nerves and excitement, and I reach for him, fumbling with his pants until I get the front open. Before I can slide my fingers past the band of his Calvin Klein boxers, he catches my wrists, and I look up at him, instantly caught in his liquid silver gaze.

"I won't be gentle," he warns.

"I don't care," I breathe.

His nostrils flare, and he shakes his head. "I'm not sure if you're the worst thing for me..." His voice drops. "Or the only thing I need."

"Atlas," I whisper, and he closes his eyes, freeing my wrists. I lift my hands to his face, my fingers grazing his cheeks and the dark stubble along his jaw. I lean up on my tip toes, ignoring the way the bark catches on my windbreaker as I press my lips against his.

He kisses me back, slow and soft at first, but it quickly turns to something far more frantic. We can't get enough of each other. And when I feel the blunt head of his cock teasing my entrance, my pulse races, and I tug him harder against me. He grips my hip with one hand and his cock with the other. Dragging the tip along the length of my slit, he drives me crazy, his lips moving against mine, tasting me—claiming me. When his tongue darts out, flicking along my lips, I part them, letting him in, and gasp into his mouth as he presses his cock against my clit. My hips jerk against him, and he deepens the kiss, grazing his tongue along mine.

Without warning, he fills my pussy with his cock, stretching me and knocking the air out of my lungs. His previous ministrations left me wet enough for him to glide in with one smooth, deep thrust of his hips.

My hands drop to his shoulders, and I hang on, digging my fingers in as I try to adjust to his size. He holds still inside of me, breaking the kiss, and I suck in a breath, my chest rising and falling quickly.

"Relax," he says gruffly, "you're gripping my cock like a vise."

I exhale on a short, breathy laugh. "A little warning next time would be nice."

He leans in, pressing his lips against my cheek. "I did warn you," he murmurs.

I won't be gentle.

Well, fuck me.

I turn my face and capture his lips again, circling my hips as much as I can trapped between Atlas and the tree. The sound he makes against my lips is a delicious mix between a growl and a groan, and it shoots heat to my core.

His lips move to my neck, kissing and sucking there as he pulls out slowly before slamming back into me. He reaches between us to tease my clit with his fingers as he continues his vicious rhythm of hard and deep thrusts.

My head falls back against the tree, and I close my eyes, biting my lip as pleasure floods through me in waves, pushing me closer to the edge.

"Open your eyes," he orders, and I obey without a second of hesitation. "If only you always listened so attentively." He smirks, then adds, "Keep them on me. I want to see your face when you come on my cock."

My cheeks fill with heat, but I hold his gaze as he continues his wicked pace, slowing for a few thrusts before slamming into me so fast my head spins. His fingers circle my clit hard and fast until I'm panting, practically writhing against him.

"Atlas," I breathe, the walls of my pussy clenching around him as the pressure builds to an almost unbearable level.

"You want to come?" he says in my ear, making the hair on the back of my neck stand straight, and slows his pace again, pulling me back from the edge.

I grit my teeth and nod quickly.

He rolls his hips, hitting a new spot, and nips my earlobe. "Say it. Tell me how much you need it."

"Asshole," I grumble.

He holds is cock still inside me and moves his fingers away from my clit, leaning back to look into my eyes and smirk at me. "Try again."

I lick the dryness from my lips and hold his glimmering gaze. "I need you," I force the words out, "to make me come."

He wraps his fingers around my throat, holding me against the tree, and drives his cock into me at an unrelenting pace. With skilled, perfectly timed thrusts, he launches me over the edge, making my body ignite with such a powerful orgasm, my world narrows. Everything clenches, and I cry out my release, gasping his name. I cling to him to stay upright as his thrusts become faster and harder until he grunts deeply, spilling his own release into me.

Atlas claims my mouth as I ride the aftershocks of my orgasm. He pulls back, giving me a moment to catch my breath, and glides out of me. Tucking himself into his pants, he does them up before tugging my leggings back up.

"Will you get back in the car now?"

I consider it for a moment, tilting my head to the side. "Maybe."

His eyes narrow ever so slightly. "You truly enjoy testing me, don't you?"

I shrug. "Maybe."

He shakes his head and places his hand against the small of my back, guiding me the way we came.

Once we're back in the car, I cross my legs, pressing my lips together at the delicious ache between my thighs. "Hmm, you know, I thought about moaning Kade's name just to mess with you, but even I can admit to being too scared of your response to go through with it."

Atlas pulls back onto the interstate, and a muscle feathers along his jaw before his lips twitch. "Wise choice."

***

It's mid-afternoon when we reach Washington. I texted Brighton from the car that I'd be a little late, and when we pull up outside the Tryst café, my stomach is more filled with nerves than I was expecting.

"Calla." Atlas's uncharacteristically soft voice snares my attention, and I turn toward him. "You don't have to do this. Say the word, and I'll handle it."

I smile. "I can't do much about our current... situation, but I can do this." I pull in an uneven breath. "I just need a minute."

"Take as many as you need."

"Can you glamour me not to be so freaking nervous?" I ask with a laugh to show him I'm only kidding; the thought of being glamoured still freaks me out.

"I could," he says, "but I don't think I need to."

His confidence in me is weirdly empowering. So much so, I square my shoulders, take a deep breath, and reach for the door handle.

"We'll have eyes on you at all times. Anything feels off, you get up and walk to the door. Our team will keep you safe."

I glance at him over my shoulder. "And where will you be?"

A dangerous glint fills his eyes. "I'm going to get Gabriel."

I turn back to face him completely, my pulse jackhammering. "What? No. I want to go with you."

He laughs, but it holds little humor. "Too bad. You already have plans."

"Atlas." I glare at him.

"Go on." He nods toward the café. "Out of my car."

I shake my head, knowing full well there's no sense arguing with him. I climb out of the Escalade and slam the door, just in case my death glare wasn't enough to show him that I'm pissed.

He pulls away from the curb, leaving me staring after him until the vehicle disappears around the corner.

With a heavy sigh, I turn and walk into the café, and am immediately enveloped in the smell of coffee beans and fresh baked pastries. If my stomach wasn't coiled with anxiety, it would be downright heavenly.

I swallow hard and keep walking, finding Brighton sitting at a round, two-person table in the middle of the room. Her eyes light up when she sees me coming toward her, and I smile, lifting my hand in a wave. She gets up and throws her arms around me when I reach the table.

"Why do I feel like I haven't seen you in a fucking year?" she asks, finally letting me go and dropping back into her chair.

I set my bag next to hers under the table and sit across from her. "I know, right? Sorry, things kinda sucked for a while. It's good to see you, though."

Her hazel eyes flick across my face as her brows knit. "You're really better?" she asks. "I was so worried about you."

I nod, reaching for her hands and giving them a quick squeeze. "I'm totally fine. I'm sorry I scared you."

She blows out a dramatic sigh. "Okay. You're forgiven. Because I love you and I desperately need to vent."

I laugh, arching a brow at her. "Yeah? Please feel free to go off. I'm all ears, Bri."

She shakes her head. "Food first, then I'll rant."

We grab lattes and croissants before returning to our table. I steal a quick glance around the café, wondering which of the other patrons are really the security team that's here to look out for me. It could be anyone—everyone looks the same in terms of casual street clothes and business attire.

Turning my attention back to Brighton, I wrap my fingers around the mug in front of me, lifting it to my mouth to take a sip of my vanilla latte. It's a bit sweet for my taste, but that's really not my main concern at the moment.

"What's going on?" I prompt her.

She shoves a chunk of pastry in her mouth. "Ugh. My dad. He made me move back in, claiming it was useless to pay for my apartment when he and my mom live in the city. Apparently he wants to spend more time as a family, which is complete bullshit."

I frown. "Why do you say that?"

"I've been back for almost a week and have seen him once. In passing. He's having all these closed door meetings and missing dinner every night. I tried talking to my mom about it, but she just brushes it off."

"He's having meetings at your house?" I ask over the rim of my mug, and she nods, tearing another piece off her croissant. "Is that abnormal? I mean, do you know what they're about?"

She stops chewing and stares at me for a few seconds. Long enough to make my stomach drop. Shit. I probably said too much.

Brighton finally shakes her head. "I haven't heard anything. Nothing that made sense anyway. I just... I'm worried about him. What if he's involved in something dangerous?"

I want nothing more than to comfort my best friend. Especially considering what I know about the things Scott Ellis is involved in. But I need to be very careful what I say.

"Listen," I tell her, "the term is almost over. Why don't we go away for the summer?" I figure I'll need to move around with the guys anyway, so why not have Brighton tag along? If it gets her away from the hunters, I want to make it happen—whatever it takes.

Her eyes widen. "Are you serious? Because I am so fucking down for that."

I nod. "Definitely. We can figure out the details later, but let's do it."

"Holy shit, yes," she shouts, earning a few looks from the people around us that she doesn't even notice. "When are you coming back to school?"

I bite into my croissant, chewing and swallowing before I answer her. "I fell pretty behind when I was sick, so I'm going to finish the term online. My professors have been accommodating, which has been great, but I do miss going to class."

She snorts. "Of course you do."

"I might actually see about transferring to remote courses for the fall term," I say.

Brighton shakes her head. "No. Absolutely not. I need you here, Cal." She looks seconds away from pouting, and I regret saying anything.

"It's not a for sure thing, I've just been thinking about it. I'd like to travel and see more of the world," I explain. "You can't tell me you've never thought about it."

She narrows her eyes at me, but eventually sighs. "Yeah, fine." A smile curls her lips. "Getting away for a while will be so nice," she comments.

"Definitely." I reach across the table and squeeze her hand. "And I get it. Parents can be... tough to deal with. Why do you think I moved away from mine?" I lean back and tear off a piece from my croissant, popping it into my mouth.

"Yeah, I guess. At least your dad isn't some shady businessman."

"Neither is yours, Bri," I lie through my teeth, the buttery pastry suddenly feeling heavy in my stomach. "Just because he has private meetings doesn't mean..." My voice trails off when her gaze abruptly drops away from mine. "Brighton," I say with an edge to my voice, my pulse kicking up. "What haven't you told me?"

She presses her lips together, and when she tilts her head back up, her eyes are glassy with unshed tears. "I... I lied to you before. I did overhear some things." The color leeches from her face and her chin quivers. "It didn't make any sense, but I... um, hacked into his email and found conversations with people that—" Her voice cuts off, and she whips her head around as if she's worried she'll be overheard.

And she will. By the vampire security team the guys sent me here with.

Fuck, fuck, fuck.

They'll report back and tell them what Brighton's telling me.

I reach back across the table, nearly knocking over my mug, and grasp her wrists, squeezing until she looks at me.

Her hazel eyes widen, and a single tear leaks down her cheek. "Calla—"

I shake my head, hoping she gets the message not to say anything else. "It's okay. I know you're not feeling well. Finals are stressing me out too."

Brighton frowns, her brows knitting, but finally nods. "Yeah, sorry." She sniffles.

"Hey, no worries." I hold her gaze. "Everything's going to be fine."

Her expression shifts to one filled with confusion, and I want nothing more than to explain everything to her. She knows more than we can discuss freely here, but I'm sure she—much like I do—has far more questions than answers at this point.

I stand, pushing my chair back. "I'll be right back, just going to slip into the washroom."

She nods in response, and I walk quickly through the café, the sounds of conversation, soft music, and the hiss of a milk steamer filling the space until I close the washroom door behind me, muffling all of it.

Leaning against the door, I flip the lock over and pull out my phone. My finger hovers over Atlas's name, and I bite my lip. Instead of texting him, I open my conversation with Brighton and type a quick message.

Keep your eyes on your phone. Do not look up. We can't talk out in the open here.

Her response comes a few seconds later.

What the fuck, Cal?!

I'm sorry, but I need to know what you heard during your dad's meeting.

The little text bubble pops up, then disappears, then returns. I hold my breath until her message finally comes through, and then my entire body fills with dread.

I know about the vampires.

FIVE

KADE

Lex drags my ass out of bed sometime after noon. The bastard. I was quite content to spend the whole fucking day here. While it's not the most comfortable bed—certainly nowhere near the mattress I was forced to leave behind at our place—I'm more exhausted than I'd care to admit. Despite drinking from Calla and sleeping all night, my muscles ache with tension and the thought of working out makes me want to ignore Lex in the doorway, roll over, and go back to sleep.

Atlas slept on the couch last night because he and Calla were heading to Washington this morning, so I stole the other half of the bed Lex crashed in.

"We have company," he mutters, pushing away from the door-frame, and snags my T-shirt off the floor, tossing it at me.

I catch it out of the air and sit up, raking my fingers through my hair before tugging my shirt on over my head and getting up to follow him into the hallway. "What the fuck are you talking about? No one is supposed to know we're here." My tone is sharp and my pulse ticks faster.

Whoever is here isn't human, otherwise I'd be able to smell their blood. I *do* smell blood, but it isn't fresh and there are about six different sources. We must've gotten blood bags while I was passed out.

"Relax. Come see for yourself."

Stepping into the kitchen, my eyes immediately land on Fallon where she leans against the counter, nursing a cup of tea. She's wearing a skin-tight black leather bodysuit with high-waisted jean shorts and mesh leggings. She looks downright stunning with dark makeup and her bright red corkscrew curls.

Fucking hell. Talk about a blast from the past.

"Kade," she says in greeting, though it's clear by her tone and the smile missing from her crimson-colored lips just how thrilled she is to see me. Evidently, my memories from the night we spent together decades ago are more fond than hers. Perhaps it's the morning after she recalls, when I left her in that hotel room to get back to the guys.

"Fallon," I reply, grinning at her as I cross my arms over my chest. "Long time no see, gorgeous."

She rolls her eyes and takes a sip of her tea. "Charming as ever, I see."

I shrug. "What can I say? Some of us are just born that way." I flick a glance to Lex before looking back at her. "What are you doing here?"

"I've been in contact with Marcel. He told me where you lot were hiding out, so I offered to stop by with some blood and see if there's anything I can do to help."

My eyes narrow on her. "Why would you do that?"

"Because I'm not an asshole?" she offers dryly, then adds in a serious tone, "Because I care about Gabriel." She sets the empty mug in the sink. "I know he's still with that psycho sire of his, but—"

"Not for long," Lex cuts in. "Atlas went to get him."

My gaze swings toward him. "He what?" We didn't talk about that last night. Lex and I were supposed to go with him.

Lex turns to me. "He decided it was best he go alone. He didn't want to risk all of us returning to Washington now that we have targets on our backs."

"And you just let him go?" I snap, my chest tightening. I want Gabriel back as much as he and Atlas do, but the thought of them both being in danger and us being stuck here makes me want to put my fist through a wall.

He blinks at me. "You expected me to stop him? To go against him?"

I growl in response, shaking my head at the ridiculousness of the whole fucking situation. "Fine. So what? We're just supposed to wait here until they come back? What about Calla?"

Lex shrugs. "She's meeting with Brighton, so I guess we'll have to face the outcome of that when she returns, presumably with Atlas and Gabriel."

"You are infuriatingly calm about this," I grumble.

"I recognize there's nothing I can do right now. I'm pissed, but getting all tense like you are now isn't going to change anything or help the situation."

I stare at him, then mutter under my breath, "Whatever."

Sliding around Fallon, I open the fridge and find it stocked with blood bags. I pull out a B-positive and pour it into a glass before popping it into the microwave to heat it up. Once the timer beeps, I take my breakfast and walk into the living room, dropping onto the couch and kicking my bare feet up on the coffee table.

Lex and Fallon join me a couple minutes later, chatting about some broadway show Lex saw the last time he was in New York, while I down the blood in my glass. I feel a bit stronger once I've finished it, but a blanket of lethargy still seems to cling to me.

My thoughts shift to my sister as I tune out of Lex and Fallon's conversation. As hard as I try to recall the last time I saw her before she disappeared—or we *thought* she disappeared—it's blurry. It was before I turned and it fucked me up so badly that thinking about it sends me to a dark place I really don't want to visit. Despite that, I need to know what happened to her and why the hell she's aligned herself with the very people who threaten her existence.

I shake my head, forcing myself to tune back into the conversation happening next to me.

"Have you heard anything from Jase?" Lex asks Fallon.

I arch a brow at her. "Who the hell is Jase?"

She flicks an annoyed glance my way and says, "He's my partner."

I can't help the smirk that forms on my lips. "Oh, really? And how did you two lovebirds meet?" She's so easy to get a rise out of, I can't help myself. Especially if it distracts me from thinking about... other things.

Fallon scowls, shaking her head. "For a century-old vampire, you're a fucking child, Kade." She turns her attention back to Lex, and I don't bother adding that I'm older than a century, because she's clearly done talking to me. "I spoke to him on my way here," she says. "He was heading to Washington to back Atlas up if needed." Her jaw sharpens when she clenches it, gripping the arms of the antique chair she's sitting in. "I wanted to go, to rip that blond bitch limb from limb, but

Jase thought it was best he go instead." She rolls her eyes. "Something about keeping a level head or whatever."

Knowing there's another vampire going after Gabriel with Atlas makes me feel a bit better even though I've never met the guy. He's friends with Gabriel, which means he's one of the good ones—someone we can trust.

Fallon pulls her phone out, reading the screen, and her lips curl into a smile. "They've got him."

My stomach clenches, and I sit forward, staring at her. "What else did he say? What happened? Did they slaughter Selene?"

She shakes her head without looking up from her phone. "All he said is that they have Gabriel."

My eyes shift to Lex, who is reaching for his phone. "Atlas says they're on their way to pick up Calla and head back, but nothing about Selene."

Fuck. That means she's still alive.

"So now we have to sit around for at least three hours waiting for them. Great."

"You need a hobby," Fallon mutters, typing something on her phone.

I shoot her a dark glance even though she's not looking at me. "Oh, I have hobbies. I'm surprised you don't remember. Or maybe you do."

Her fingers freeze and she lifts her gaze to meet mine. "If I recall, you weren't much to remember."

Lex snorts.

I narrow my eyes at her, but before I can come up with a sharp retort, Lex curses, gripping his phone tight enough he's going to shatter the glass screen if he doesn't ease up.

I move over to him in a blur and pry it from his hands. My jaw clenches as I take in the alert from our security team, then I lift my gaze, shifting it from Lex to Fallon. "We have a problem."

CHAPTER

SIX

CALLA

The ugly beige bathroom walls close in on me. Black spots dance across my vision and there's a dim ringing in my ears.

I'm having a panic attack. Right now. Awesome.

Sweat dots my brow and my fingers shake as I struggle to type a response.

When did you find out?

I have no idea what else to say. This whole situation just got a million times more complicated.

A week ago. How do YOU know about them?!

It's a long story.

One that has to do with Gabriel? I know he's a vampire. His name came up in the meeting my father was having. The vampire hunter meeting. Because apparently that's the family business my mom was so adamant I stay out of.

I blink back tears as fear digs its claws deeper into my chest. I want to take Brighton away from all of this. She deserves this life about as much as I do. It isn't fair for either of us.

Yes. There's a lot we need to talk about, but I can't stay in here and text you for the next half hour or my fanged babysitters are going to know something's up.

Calla, are you in trouble?

I almost laugh at her message, because yeah. I'm in so much fucking trouble. And I'm about to make it a hell of a lot worse.

I'm coming out, I type back. *We need to get out of here and somewhere we can talk without being overheard.*

My car is parked out front. When you come out, I'll get up, and we'll leave.

There's a chance one of the vampires watching us will step in and try to stop me from leaving with Brighton, but I'm going to have to take that chance.

With a deep breath, I slide my phone into my back pocket and leave the bathroom. My pulse ticks faster the closer I get to the table, but I force myself to reach for my bag and smile at Brighton.

"Sorry to do this," I tell her, "but I have to get going. It was really great to see you, though. We have to get together again soon. Maybe after finals?"

She stands, shouldering her bag. "Definitely. I think I'm going to stick around and study for a bit, but I'll walk you out."

We walk out the front door, and Brighton pulls her keys out unlocking the car. She meets my gaze, and I nod at her. Without a word, we get into the car and she starts the engine, pulling away from the curb a moment later.

"Where am I supposed to go?" she asks, her voice shaking. She was able to keep it together in the café, but her hands are gripping the steering wheel so tight her knuckles are white. She's freaking out—rightfully so.

"Take a breath," I tell her in what I hope is a calming voice, because I'm sort of freaking out too, but one of us needs to keep a level head. The last thing I need is for Brighton to lose her shit and crash the car. "Head toward the interstate."

She offers a tense nod. "Are you going to tell me what the hell is going on?"

"I told you about the vampires once," I say, watching the confusion pass over her face. "You don't remember because Kade glamoured you to forget."

Her gaze whips toward me and her voice cracks when she says, "What? What does that mean?"

I cringe inwardly as she turns her eyes back to the road. "Do you maybe want me to drive? What I'm about to tell you is pretty over-whelming."

"No," she says quickly, "just keep talking. I want to know everything."

I pull in a slow breath, inhaling through my nose, then exhaling through my mouth. And then I tell Brighton about the blood oath, the night the guys came for me, getting kidnapped by Selene, and everything in between.

Her eyes are filled with tears, and she blinks hard to clear her vision, making the tears roll down her cheeks. "Holy shit, Cal. I... I don't even know what to say. I'm so fucking sorry."

I blink at her. "*You're* sorry? What could you possibly have to apologize for? I'm the one who kept all of this from you."

Brighton sniffles. "Not by choice. I'm sorry I couldn't be there for you through all of that." She pulls one of her hands off the wheel and reaches for me, grabbing my hand and squeezing it. "But I'm here now." Taking her hand back, she wipes the wetness from her cheeks.

"I know, but you probably shouldn't be."

She nods. "Because my family are vampire hunters." Shooting me a wide-eyed look, she adds, "which is not as cool as one would think."

"Right," I say, jumping when my phone starts vibrating from where I dropped it in the cup holder. My heart leaps into my throat when I see Atlas's name on the screen.

"Do you need to get that?" Brighton asks warily.

I bite my lip. Atlas could be calling about Gabriel. Or, the more likely situation, he's calling to reprimand me for leaving the café with Brighton. I'm sure someone from the security team has alerted the guys to my departure by now.

In a split-second decision I'll probably regret later, I shut my phone off and offer her a tense smile. "There is nothing I would rather do less right now."

"Got it. So don't. But you need to tell me where I'm driving."

Before I can overthink it, I type the safe house location into the GPS attached to the dash. "Where's your phone?" I ask her, and she hands it to me. I promptly turn it off and put it next to mine in the cup holder. I can't take any chances that Brighton's dad could be tracking her phone.

My best bet now is to get back to the safe house with Brighton and convince Kade and Lex to take my side to help protect Bri from her family. It's a long shot, but I'm too anxious to think of something better at the moment. One thing at a time.

"Where exactly are we going?" she asks, glancing between the GPS and the road.

"Somewhere safe." I drum my fingers on my thighs in an attempt to distract myself and calm my nerves.

"Will there be vampires there?"

My fingers still against my leggings. "Kade and Lex. Atlas drove me to Washington and he's getting Gabriel back from his sire, though if I had to bet, he's managed that and knows I gave our security team the slip, which likely means he and Gabriel are headed this way as well." They may not be able to track my phone now, but I can't exactly turn off their connection to my blood.

"Right. So your plan is to take me—the daughter of a vampire hunter—to a house full of vampires?"

I look in her direction, pursing my lips. "They aren't going to hurt you. You are one of the most important people in my life. If anything, they'll help keep you safe."

"Safe," she says in a small voice, "from what?"

I frown. "Do your parents know that you know about the vampires and the hunters?"

She shakes her head, keeping her eyes on the road, and a fraction of the tension in my chest eases.

"What do you think would happen if they did?"

"Honestly, I have no idea. When mom was so adamant about me finding my own path or whatever to keep me out of the family business, I just thought she wanted me to follow my dreams. To give me a choice of what *I* wanted." She adjusts her grip on the wheel. "I keep thinking about what would've happened if I'd grown up knowing about vampires. If my mom hadn't kept me away from the hunters."

Nausea ripples through me. "You'd probably *be* a vampire hunter," I say in a gentle tone.

"Yeah. Instead, we're here." She laughs, but it doesn't hold any humor.

"I know you're probably scared and confused as hell right now, but for what it's worth, I'm glad your mom kept you out of it. Otherwise, we would've never met."

She smiles. "Considering the company you're keeping these days, that might not be true."

My eyes widen, but when she bursts into laughter—*genuine* laughter—I join in. "Very funny," I mutter.

Brighton sighs heavily, tipping her head back against the headrest. "This is so messed up, Cal."

"I know, but we're going to figure it out," I tell her, determination clear in my tone.

"Are you trying to convince me or yourself of that?"

My stomach sinks, and I offer a dry laugh. "Both I guess."

My nerves are at an all-time high when we pull into the driveway of the safe house.

"You're sure about this?" Brighton asks, her voice pitchy.

The front door opens and Kade marches outside, his expression grim. Well, shit.

"Too late now," I mutter, unbuckling my seat belt and reaching for the door. "Give me a sec."

Kade rips the door open from the outside before I can and hauls me out of the car. "Are you insane?" he growls in my face.

"Not the welcome I was hoping for."

He pulls me away from the car and toward the house. "What exactly were you hoping for by bringing her here and compromising our location?" His eyes flick to the car before returning to me.

I open my mouth, but whatever response I was going to use dies on my lips. "She needs our help, Kade. Besides, this place was supposed to be temporary, right?"

His eyes narrow sharply. "Not the point. Bringing her here was stupid."

"She's not a hunter."

"Not yet," he snaps. "She lives with them, though. And once her father finds out where she is—"

"She's not going to tell him," I shoot back.

"You think she'll have to? You think he doesn't have her phone tracked?"

I cross my arms over my chest. "Actually, no. I don't think he has her phone tracked. As far as he knows, Brighton knows nothing about the vampires, which was true until she overheard him in a meeting. He doesn't know she knows," I say in a tense voice. "Plus, I turned our phones off."

He exhales slowly, looking past me to the car again. "Get inside. Now."

"Fine," I snap back. "Have you talked to Atlas? Did he get Gabriel?"

"You'd know he did if you answered your fucking phone."

"Are you done yelling at me?" I ask in a level voice.

"Oh, *I* am. Just wait until Atlas gets here."

I roll my eyes, but my pulse jumps at his words. Dealing with Atlas's wrath is going to be a special kind of hell. "What's his ETA?"

Kade purses his lips. "You've got forty-five minutes tops."

"Great," I mutter dryly, glancing toward the house. "Where's Lex?"

"He's inside with Fallon debating the most painful place to get tattooed."

I frown at the unfamiliar name. "Fallon?"

"Friend of Gabe's," he explains, walking backward toward the house. "You better not try to take off."

"Relax, Kade. We drove here, remember? I'm not going anywhere."

He stares at me a moment longer before turning and walking up the porch steps.

I flip him off before returning to the car to grab my bag. "Ready?" I ask Brighton.

She unbuckles her seat belt slowly. "That was intense."

I shrug. "It's all good. Come on."

We walk toward the house, and I can see the fear on Brighton's face. I wrap my arm around her shoulders as we climb the stairs onto the porch. "You're safe here. I promise."

She nods, and we step inside. I close the door behind us and I drop my bag onto the bench against the wall of the foyer. I head down the hall toward the living room, Brighton following me hesitantly.

Lex gets up from the couch the second we step into the room. "You're in big trouble," he mutters, but instead of yelling at me as Kade did, he pulls me into his arms and kisses the top of my head.

I step back in surprise and nod at him. "So I've been told. Lex, this is—"

"Brighton Ellis," he answers for me. "We met at that house party last month."

Oh, yeah. I completely forgot about that.

"Hi again," she says in a nervous tone.

He grins at her, flashing his fangs, and Brighton gasps and steps back.

I elbow him in the ribs. "Don't start."

His fangs retract, and he shoots me a wink before returning to his place on the couch.

We walk into the living room, and my eyes land on a gorgeous redhead sitting with one black mesh stocking-clad leg over the other. Her silver eyes meet mine and her red lips curve into a small smile.

"Hey," I say, "it's Fallon, right?"

She nods. "It's nice to finally meet you, Calla. Gabriel speaks very highly of you."

Heat rushes to my cheeks, and I smile. "Thanks. It's nice to meet you too."

"I bet you'll be glad to have Gabe home. I was just texting my partner, Jase, who was with Atlas when they, uh, picked him up." Her eyes flit between Brighton and me. "Anyway, they should be here any minute."

My heart lurches. *Any minute?* I turn my gaze to Kade. *Forty-five minutes, my ass*, my glare in his direction says.

He smirks, offering a shrug in response.

As much as I'm looking forward to seeing Gabriel, I would quite literally rather do anything else instead of dealing with Atlas.

"Marcel just sent through the details for our new place," Lex says to Kade, showing him his phone.

Kade shrugs. "Not the same, but I guess it'll do for now."

Lex nods in agreement. "It's not forever."

"Do I get to see?"

"Nope," Lex says, popping the 'p'.

I scowl, shaking my head.

"Childish, aren't they?" Fallon offers with a faint grin.

"It's unbelievable," I agree.

Her eyes flash with excitement. "They're here."

My stomach drops, and I shift closer to Brighton as she tenses.

"Calla—"

"It's fine," I assure her, though I really don't know what's about to go down.

As expected, Atlas is the first one through the doorway into the living room. Completely unexpected, though, is Brighton pulling me away from him when he storms into the room.

"Leave her alone," she says to him, her voice cracking but her grip on my arm strong.

He easily pries her fingers off me in a second. "Sit down and shut the fuck up." His voice is smooth, scarily calm.

She does as she's told, her expression passive and her eyes glazed over.

My jaw clenches, but before I can yell at him for glamouring Brighton, he grabs my wrist and drags me down the hall, shoving me into the bedroom and slamming the door shut behind us.

"You ever do something that blatantly idiotic again, and I'll make sure you can't sit for a fucking week."

Is... is he threatening to spank me? I press my lips together, trying to stifle the burst of laughter trying to escape. Because that is the last thing this conversation needs. Atlas is pissed enough as it is. I'm well aware, but I don't know how else to respond to the thought of his palm cracking against my ass cheek.

He growls low in his throat, his eyes filled with the same fire expanding in my belly. "I can smell exactly how you feel about that." His voice is thick with arousal, which only makes my body heat more, a flush creeping across my chest.

"Go ahead," he taunts. "Test me. See where that will get you."

I narrow my eyes despite the pounding in my chest and swallow past the dryness in my throat. "Bent over your knee?"

My quip is rewarded with a dazzling smile, one that steals the breath from my lungs in a vicious *whoosh* and fills me with a swirling mix of fear and excitement.

He stalks forward, a predator hunting his prey, and I instinctively reach for the door handle. He steals my wrist before I can grasp it and lifts both wrists over my head, pinning them to the back of the door with one hand. His other hand grips my hip, holding me against the door.

"I thought about exactly what I was going to do to you the entire drive here," he says, his lips next to my ear.

My mouth goes dry. "Oh?" I force out. "And what did you decide?"

His responding chuckle stirs the hair at my temple, and I gasp when his hand moves from my hip, sliding under the waistband of my leggings, brushing my folds, and dips two fingers into me without warning.

"Interesting form of punishment," I say in a breathy voice, tipping my head back against the door as he pumps his fingers in and out at a languid pace, teasing my clit with this thumb.

His lips find my neck, and I turn my face to the side, baring it to him completely. An invitation in more ways than one. His fangs scrape along my skin, sending a shiver down my spine, and his swift bite steals my breath. He drinks deeply, his fingers curling inside me, driving me wild with a pleasurable mix of sensations.

I press my lips together in an attempt to muffle my moan, but it's still audible enough I blush, knowing everyone but Brighton will hear exactly what's happening in here. But right now, I can't find the will to care.

Once Atlas retracts his fangs and drags his tongue along the puncture marks to heal them, I turn my face toward his, capturing his lips with mine in a sensual kiss that I feel all the way to my toes.

He kisses me back hard, picking up the pace of his fingers in my pussy until I'm moaning without inhibition against his lips.

I'm racing toward climax, my head back against the door and my hips grinding against him.

And then he breaks the fiery kiss and pulls his fingers out of my heat mid-thrust.

"What the fuck?" I growl breathlessly, my chest heaving as I tug on my wrists, wanting to reach for him. "Keep going."

"No," he says simply.

"No?" I echo incredulously, shaking my head. "What, you want to watch me finish myself?" I tug on my wrists again. "Fine. Let go of me, and I will."

He grips my chin, holding me in place as I struggle against him. "You will not touch yourself until I allow it." The power of his glamour pours through me like ice in my veins, but it does nothing to ease the throbbing heat between my thighs.

He lets me go, stepping back and watching me with dark eyes.

I glare at him. "You're an asshole." Ripping the door open, I storm out of the bedroom, blinking past the burn of tears, willing them to recede as I walk back to the living room to see Gabriel.

Calla launches herself at Gabriel the minute she walks back into the living room. He catches her as though he was expecting it and wraps his arms around her waist, holding her to him as if his immortal life depends on it.

Lex watches them for a brief moment, a soft smile on his lips, then turns his attention to his phone. I'm hoping he's communicating with Marcel to confirm when we can move to our next residence, because I'd like nothing more than to get the hell out of this shack. I understand we won't be able to return to the home we built for some time—if ever—but there has to be something nicer than this place where we can stay while we figure this shit out.

I turn my gaze back to Calla and Gabriel and scratch the back of my neck. I guess we're going to ignore what just went down between Calla and Atlas in the other room. Cool.

When she pulls back, her hands clasp his face and they share a moment of just staring at each other before Lex clears his throat.

"Not to ruin what is a very touching reunion, but we've got about a million and one problems to deal with right now."

Calla shoots him a dirty look before focusing on Gabriel again as if Lex didn't say anything. "Are you okay?" she asks him, her gaze roaming over him to check for herself.

His hands drop to her waist, and he nods, pressing a kiss to her forehead. "I'm okay, angel."

After another moment of her staring at him without a word, she finally nods, accepting his answer. "What happened to Selene?" The bitterness in her voice when she says the woman's name is something we all share. Same with the urge to rip the vampire apart and burn her to ash for how she tormented Calla and for everything she's done to Gabriel since turning him.

"Jase and I forced our way past her pathetic security team at the building, broke into her penthouse, where Gabriel was..." Atlas frowns, glancing toward him, and he nods, his expression grim. Atlas clears his throat. "Where Gabriel was being fed on by Selene. They were both so caught up in it, they didn't hear us coming until we were already inside. She shoved Gabriel aside and took off. Jase tried to stop her, while I tended to Gabe, but she got away." Atlas's voice is rough. "No matter, it'll make her death that much more enjoyable when we catch up to her."

My stomach is knotted, my chest filled with a sharp pressure I can only identify as rage. I want that psycho vampire dead as much as the others.

"We're all together again. That's the important thing for now," Gabriel says in a calm tone. "Selene will meet her end, I have no doubt about that."

I don't understand how he's being so chill about this, though he's always been the most level-headed of our group. He's probably just relieved to be back with us.

Atlas is silent and his jaw is locked tight.

"What now?" Lex chimes in. "Are we going searching for the bitch?"

I lean forward, resting my elbows on my knees. "Fallon was in contact with another vampire Selene sired and believes she fled Washington for Chicago, so her and Jase are headed that way to see if there's any merit to that intel before we make any further moves against her. There's no point in doing anything until we know for sure."

Calla glances around the room in surprise, clearly not having realized that Fallon was gone.

"She said to tell you goodbye," Brighton mentions from her spot on the couch.

Calla turns to her friend and nods. "Sorry, uh... about before."

"Everything okay?" she asks quietly, as if she thinks speaking softly will ensure that we—the room full of vampires—won't overhear.

Atlas snickers, and her eyes shift between Brighton and him before she nods again. "Fine." There's an edge to her voice that Brighton frowns at, but she doesn't push the subject.

The human might be smarter than I initially gave her credit for.

I slip out of the room as Calla walks to sit next to Brighton on the couch. Might as well give everyone a few minutes to get reacquainted before we dive into all the doomsday planning. I retreat to the bedroom I slept in last night to steal a moment of quiet, but before I can close the door, Gabriel appears in the doorway.

"Can I come in for a minute?" he asks.

I walk away from the door, leaving it open, and drop onto the end of the bed. I rake my fingers through my hair, then scrub them down my face as Gabriel closes the door and walks closer.

"How are you doing?" he asks. "I've been worried about you since I heard about Meredith's unexpected return."

"Ah, that's right. Gabriel Simmons, dreamwalker extraordinaire." I exhale on a laugh. "We should probably figure that out, huh?"

He offers me a wry smile. "I'll add it to the list." His expression turns serious. "Now answer my question."

With a sigh, I tell him, "I'm probably doing about as well as you are, Gabe. You were locked up with your psycho sire for days. I have a feeling I don't want to know the shit she put you through."

He waves me off and sits next to me. "Nothing I wasn't expecting and haven't been through before."

My jaw clenches. "Whatever it was, that was the last time it'll happen," I vow.

Gabriel nods. "Atlas is pretty upset that she got away. Between that and the stunt Calla pulled..." His voice trails off, and he shakes his head.

"Never a dull moment around here," I offer with a faint grin.

He chuckles. "That is most definitely true." Angling himself toward me, he meets my gaze and asks, "Have you found out anything else about your sister?"

The grin dies on my lips. "Nothing. I don't know how to go about getting in touch with her. Maybe if I knew who her sire is I could, but I didn't even know she turned."

"Right, of course."

"Did Selene mention anything about her?" I ask.

He shakes his head. "I only found out about the hunter attack on the house when I reached Calla in her dream."

"Right. Do you have any idea how you made that happen?"

He offers a light shrug. "All I did was focus on her, on the pull of our bond. It took a while because of how close I was to Selene. Our sire connection was overpowering. But there was a brief moment where I could feel Calla strongly, so I latched onto that, closed my eyes, and willed her to appear before me. I'm not going to sit here and pretend to know how it worked, but it did." He reaches over and rests his hand on my thigh in a comforting manner. "We can explore that later. I know the situation with Meredith is concerning. I can't imagine how you're feeling."

I glance down at his hand on my thigh and exhale a heavy breath, shocked at how much tension eases out of my shoulders at his touch. "I'm at a loss, Gabe," I admit, and I despise how weak my voice sounds. "She clearly hates me, considering she stabbed me in the chest with a white ash dagger, nearly hitting my heart." I swallow the lump in my throat, willing myself to get a fucking grip on my emotions. "All those years ago when she disappeared, I let our parents give up and bury an empty casket."

His fingers wrap around my knee and he squeezes until I lift my gaze to his. "None of that was your fault," he says in a firm voice. "None of it. You were a kid. She was gone for so long, there was no other viable option or anything else you or anyone else could have done at that point. Your family deserved closure."

My jaw clenches when my eyes start to burn. "Closure…" I echo the word, and it tastes like poison on my tongue. "She wasn't dead," I say through my teeth, sniffing sharply as my nose starts to run.

"But she did die," he says in a gentle tone, and he's right.

I nod, dread coiling around my chest like a snake, putting pressure on my lungs and making it hard to breathe. "And now she wants to kill me."

"You don't know that for sure," he points out. "She had a chance to but she didn't. That could mean something."

"Yeah, that she wants me to suffer before the hunters—or *her*—next attack." Even as I say the words, I don't exactly believe them. Despite her attack a few days ago, I can't see Meredith that way. She was never cruel or vicious. She was warm and kind. The type of person that would do anything for the people she cared about. Becoming a vampire, it wouldn't have destroyed that part of her. Even as I sit here with my head spinning, I cling to that. I have to believe it, because the alternative is too fucking devastating to consider. Because if my sister truly hates me… I don't know how I'll live with that.

Gabriel frowns. "Or," he says pointedly, "she's angry but still wants an opportunity to know her brother. Don't you think it's worth finding out?"

I sigh and mutter, "Your optimism can be so fucking annoying sometimes."

He smiles, bumping my shoulder with his. "I missed you too, Kade."

I'm not a vampire, but even I can sense the anxiety rolling off Brighton in waves. Her knee bounces erratically as she chews her bottom lip, staring at the unlit fireplace.

I want to comfort her, to reassure her that everything is going to be fine. She's an adult; she doesn't have to return to Washington—or her family of vampire hunters—if she doesn't want to. As much as I want to keep her with us, that likely won't fly. Brighton trusts the guys as much as they trust her, and keeping her with us would be a hell of a liability, especially if Scott decides to track her down.

With a sigh, I reach over and wrap my hand around her knee, stilling it. "Are you hungry?" I ask softly.

It takes her a second to pull her gaze away from the fireplace and look at me. Her eyes are glassy with unshed tears, and she shakes her head.

"I sure am," Lex chimes in from where he's sitting across from us.

"You know where the fridge is," I tell him without turning my attention away from Brighton.

"Yeah, but I prefer the fresh stuff," he says, and I catch him rising from his seat out of my peripheral.

Brighton stiffens next to me, and I squeeze her knee reassuringly before shooting Lex a glare. "Don't even think about it."

He pouts. "You're no fun." He saunters out of the room, and Brighton finally relaxes a little once he's gone. Fair enough. I understand her unease. Lex is... rather intimidating if you don't know him. Hell, even if you do. His wild eyes and chaotic demeanor still make me nervous a lot of the time. He won't hurt me, that I'm sure of, but besides that, I have no idea what he'll do sometimes.

My eyes flick to Atlas, who has been sitting silently since Kade and Gabriel left the room. His eyes are closed as if he's sleeping, but I have no doubt that he's awake and listening to everything happening around him.

"When are we leaving here?" I ask.

His chest rises and falls with a deep breath, but he doesn't open his eyes. "Once I've decided what to do with your friend."

Brighton sucks in a short breath but doesn't dare say anything.

I offer her a look that I hope says *it's okay*. "I think she should come with us."

His lips twitch, and he opens his eyes, his gaze slicing through me, heating my body with thoughts of what happened between us less than an hour ago. "Is that right?" He rubs his jaw, scratching the stubble there. "Because what could possibly go wrong if we take the daughter of one of the top vampire hunters in the country? Let me think about that for a second." His gaze darkens. "She's not coming."

Lex returns to the living room with a blood bag in his hand. He pulls the plastic topper off and brings it to his lips, shooting a wink at Brighton. He's clearly trying to freak her out, and based on the color draining from her face and her hands shaking in her lap, it's working.

"Seriously?" I snap at him.

He shrugs and continues drinking.

"Ignore him," I tell Brighton.

"Mean," he grumbles, dropping into the chair on the other side of the fireplace and kicking his booted feet on the coffee table. "Can't we just glamour the squirmy one and get on with our lives?"

"No," I say in a harsh voice. "I'm not going to let you mess with her head again."

"I... I won't tell anyone anything," Brighton says in a small voice. "I don't want to be part of anything my family is involved in, I swear. I wish I hadn't found out about it to begin with."

"That would certainly make our lives easier," Kade says as he and Gabriel walk back into the living room. It's not a large room, so having four vampires and two humans really takes the claustrophobic feel to the next level.

I angle my body toward Brighton, while Gabriel grips the back of the couch behind me. As opposed to Lex, Gabriel's presence is calming, reassuring. "Do you want to forget?" I ask her in a soft voice, knowing the guys would be more than willing to oblige wiping her memories.

"Y-yes," she answers in a voice barely above a whisper without meeting my gaze. She lets out a heavy sigh before looking at me. "But I don't want you to go through this by yourself. So, I'm not going to forget. I'm going to be here for my best friend." She reaches for my hands, squeezing them in hers.

"That's touching and all," Lex says, his lips red with blood, "but not your choice. It would be stupid of us to let you go knowing what you do."

"Why?" I push. "The hunters already know you're vampires."

"They may know we're vampires but they don't know about you being with us," Atlas says, "and I'd like to keep it that way."

"We could always send her back to spy on her daddy for us," Kade offers with a bored expression.

I shoot him an incredulous look and shake my head for added measure. "No. Absolutely not."

"We're not going to do that," Gabriel says in a level voice, and a bit of the panic in my chest eases.

"Well, whatever," Kade grumbles. "I don't think we should let her leave without wiping her memories."

"Enough," Atlas calls out, snaring the attention of everyone in the room. "We are not discussing this anymore. Brighton will go back to Washington and live as she did before today's events." His gaze focuses on her, and I can tell by the swirling of his silver irises he's about to glamour her. "You will drive straight home and tell no one what happened today. You will not share this location. You and Calla never left Washington. You sat at the café and commiserated over the big, bad vampires, and then you went home. You will not, under any circumstances, say a word about what you know to anyone outside of this room. Do you understand?"

"I understand," she says automatically.

"Good." He turns his gaze on me, and I narrow my eyes at him. He better not fucking glamour me right now. "Say goodbye to your friend," he says, though his words aren't weighted in glamour.

Brighton and I get up from the couch, walking toward the front door. Once we're outside in the driveway, I wrap my arms around her. I'd like nothing more than to have her stay, to keep her away from the man she calls Dad. But I've lost this fight. It makes me want to scream or cry—or both, honestly. I wish I'd fought harder, but the worst part is, we would've ended up here regardless. The guys will never trust Brighton, same as she'll never trust them. I have nothing to do with it on either side.

"Let me know when you get home, okay?" I say, pulling back. "Oh, and don't turn your phone on until you're back in the city."

She offers me a watery smile and nods. "I'm scared to leave you here." Her eyes shift past me toward the house.

I sigh, understanding her concern. If the roles were reversed, I'd be going crazy with worry. "They won't hurt me," I promise her. "I know things are messed up right now, but they... they're not so bad." I laugh softly, almost to myself. It's wild that just over a month ago, I hated them—I genuinely wanted to *kill* them. And now... I don't know. Things have definitely changed. I'm not exactly sure how I feel about that, and now doesn't quite seem like the time to figure it out. Perhaps when we're not running from vampire hunters while simultaneously hunting a vampire ourselves.

Brighton gets behind the wheel and starts the car, rolling down her window.

"Be careful," I tell her, hugging my arms around myself.

She nods. "You too, babe. We'll talk soon." She slides her sunglasses on and rolls the window up before backing her car down the gravel drive.

I stand there long after her car has disappeared from view.

"You should come back inside."

Gabriel's gentle voice startles me, and I turn around to face him. "This is such a fucking mess, Gabriel." I clench my jaw against the tears burning my eyes.

He tilts his head, regarding me thoughtfully before closing the distance between us in a few smooth strides. "I know, angel." He reaches for me, running his hands up and down my arms, then tucks me against his side, guiding me back toward the house.

Back inside, I grab Gabriel's hand and pull him down the hallway into the bedroom I've been occupying before I can think too much about what I'm doing.

The corner of his mouth kicks up and his bright silver eyes glimmer with amusement. "What are you doing?"

"I'm going to show you how much I missed you, and you are going to distract me from the shit storm that has become our lives." Atlas glamoured me so I can't touch myself to get off. He said nothing, however, about one of the others making me come. I tug my shirt off, tossing it to the side and kicking off my shoes before adding, "Any objections?"

He steps closer, trailing his fingers up my arms and along my collarbones until his hands are cupping my neck, holding me in place. "Absolutely none." He captures my lips in a slow, sensual kiss that leaves me tingling everywhere, heat gathering low in my belly. Pulling me against him, he tips my head back, deepening the kiss as his tongue sweeps across my bottom lip, seeking entrance.

I open to him, grazing my tongue along his and gripping the front of his shirt in my fists. He drops his hands to my hips and lifts me off the floor without breaking the kiss. I wrap my legs around him, gasping into his mouth when I feel his hardness against me. His lips curve against mine as he carries me to the bed, laying me down and hovering over me. His lips part from mine, and he drags his mouth down my throat and chest, between my breasts, making my breath hitch as he quickly moves lower, flicking his tongue against the skin above my navel.

My body is still wound tightly from Atlas's attention and denial earlier, so it takes very little time for heat to gather between my thighs, especially with the way Gabriel is looking up at me through his lashes, as if I'm truly an angel like he calls me.

I press my lips together, watching him pull my leggings down all the way to my ankles, letting them drop onto the floor at the end of the bed before he drops his mouth to the inside of my thigh. I squirm as his lips get closer to my center, and he shoots me a faint grin that says *keep still*.

I nod, shifting up the bed a little so my head rests against the pillows.

The first pass of his tongue along my slit vaults my hips off the mattress as I suck in a sharp breath.

"Easy," he murmurs, gliding his hands up my thighs, spreading them open before trapping my hips so I can't move them again.

I catch my bottom lip between my teeth, keeping my eyes on him as he lowers his mouth back to my core, flicking his tongue against my clit once, twice, three times before he sucks the bundle of nerves into his mouth, swirling his tongue around. I moan deeply, my eyes fluttering shut as his hands slide up my stomach, cupping my breasts through my bra.

I unclasp it, letting my breasts spill out, and his fingers quickly find my nipples, teasing them into hard peaks. I reach down and run my fingers through his copper hair, holding him against my pussy as he devours me.

"Fuck," I moan, my head spinning with ecstasy.

Gabriel takes his time tasting me. Switching from circling my clit with his tongue to licking my folds, dipping inside my tight channel before returning his attention to the bud at my center.

My chest rises and falls quickly as he continues his ministrations, massaging my breasts as I grip the sheets with one hand and his hair with the other.

He groans against my sex, sending vibrations through me, and my pussy walls clench around his tongue, stealing my breath as I come, moaning his name. Gabriel laps up my release, sucking my overly sensitive clit before crawling up my body and sealing his lips over mine.

I taste myself on his mouth, which makes my core tighten with arousal. That paired with the way he's pressing his erection between my legs has me reaching for his shirt, tugging it off and tossing it toward the end of the bed. I waste no time going for his pants, undoing the button and zipper.

"Slow down," he murmurs against my lips.

"I need you," I breathe, sliding my hand into his pants and wrapping my fingers around his thick length. "I think you need me too."

He groans into my mouth. "Always."

In the time it takes me to blink, Gabriel stands and removes his pants before bracing himself over me again.

Okay, so I don't hate vampire speed all the time.

"Hmm, this looks like fun."

I gasp in surprise, leaning up on my elbows to find Lex and Kade in the doorway. "Jesus," I mutter.

"Hardly," Kade remarks dryly.

"Need a hand, brother?" Lex asks, looking at Gabriel and flicking his tongue over his bottom lip.

Gabriel looks down at me, his expression soft. "What do *you* want, angel?"

My eyes widen slightly, and I bite my lip, considering all the things these three could do to bring me pleasure. "I... I'd like them to join us," I say in a quiet voice, my cheeks flushing hotly.

His lips curl into a smile, and he leans down to press a gentle kiss to my lips. "You don't need to be embarrassed."

"Don't worry," Kade says, approaching on my right while Lex comes around to the other side. "Soon the only thing you'll feel is pleasure."

Lex and Kade slide into the bed on either side of me. Kade curls his finger around my chin, turning my face to him and claiming my mouth. My eyes flutter closed as Lex lowers his mouth to my breast, licking and sucking gently while massaging the other with his hand, rolling the nipple between his fingers and making me moan against Kade's lips.

"Her pussy is all yours, Gabe," Lex says with a smirk against my skin that fills me with heat.

Kade reaches between my legs, strumming my clit as Gabriel positions the head of his cock at my entrance. He pushes in slowly, stretching me around his thick length, and my thighs clench around him.

"Relax, angel," he says in a lust-filled voice.

Kade works my clit, pushing his tongue into my mouth as Gabriel's cock slides in further. My pussy grips him tightly, and Kade moves his mouth to my neck, kissing and sucking the sensitive skin below my ear, distracting me from the pressure between my legs as Gabriel pushes the rest of the way into me.

I take a minute to catch my breath, overwhelmed by the combination of sensations happening all over my body.

"Feeling left out?" Lex asks after pulling his lips off my breast.

I blink my eyes open and frown in confusion before I look to the doorway where Atlas is leaning, his arms crossed over his chest and his eyes lit with arousal. I drop my gaze and suck in a breath at the obvious bulge in his pants.

"It's a bit crowded in this tiny ass bed, but I'm sure we can make it work," Kade says.

Atlas walks into the room, but instead of coming toward the bed, he lowers himself into the chair by the window.

Lex chuckles. "Problem solved. Enjoy the show."

Atlas keeps his eyes on me as he reaches for the button on his pants. Slowly, he unbuttons them, dragging the zipper down and pulling his cock free.

Holy shit.

Gabriel moves inside me, stealing my attention, and I press my lips together, moaning softly. He pulls halfway out before pushing back in slowly, steadily. He does it a few more times as my eyes drift back to

Atlas, to where he's pumping his hand up and down his erection. Gabriel's pace is driving me mad, but I'm so caught up in watching Atlas, I can't make my lips move to tell him to go faster.

"Calla," Kade murmurs, nipping my earlobe.

Cue the full body shiver. "Mmm."

He drags his tongue along my neck. "I'm going to bite you."

My pussy clenches around Gabriel's cock, my heart racing with anticipation.

His chuckle stirs the hair at my temple. It's the only warning I get before his fangs sink into my skin, and I cry out in a mix of pleasure and pain.

Gabriel increases the speed of his thrusts, while Kade drinks deeply and continues circling my clit with his fingers. I reach for Lex, finding the front of his pants while keeping my gaze locked on Atlas. My fingers slide past the waistband and wrap around his hot, throbbing erection.

He hisses through his teeth, guiding my hand up and down his shaft at the pace and pressure he wants. "Fuck, that feels so good."

My muscles clench and heat floods through me, drowning my body in pure pleasure. I succumb to the building pressure between my thighs, my pussy clenching around Gabriel's cock as I come hard, crying out, my heart pounding against my chest so fast I'm almost concerned I'll pass out from too much stimulation.

Kade licks my neck, sealing the puncture marks as Gabriel slows his pace.

"No," I breathe, "keep going. You need to come."

"Calla," he groans, his eyes closed and his face filled with pleasure as he drives into me over and over. His muscles tense a few thrusts later as an orgasm rips through him.

Kade kisses me again, blocking my view of Atlas, but his deep grunts fill the room, mixing with Lex's as my hand continues to pump his erection. He tenses, shooting his release onto my hand a moment later.

Gabriel pulls out of me and disappears for a few seconds, coming back with a warm washcloth and cleans between my legs, making me tingle and shiver, my skin still very much sensitive.

Kade kisses my shoulder while Lex cleans our hands and tucks himself back into his pants. I turn my gaze to find Atlas doing the same.

The room is filled with our combined breathing, the smell of sex heavy in the air.

I yawn, curling onto my side and facing Kade, ready for a week-long nap. Gabriel slides in behind him while Lex presses against my back, resting his hand on my hip and his chin on my shoulder.

The sound of Atlas's ringtone makes me lift my head to see him pulling his phone out of his back pocket.

He sighs as if whoever is calling is the last person he wants to talk to, then gets up without a word, giving me one last look filled with something I can't begin to decipher before he's gone.

CHAPTER

NINE

KADE

Calla and Gabriel get dressed before the four of us find Atlas in the living room, tossing his phone onto the coffee table none too gently. The air in the small room is thick with tension, and his expression is grim, making me wish I'd listened in on the conversation from the bedroom.

I drop onto the couch with Lex while Calla perches on the armrest of the chair Gabriel sits in. If I was him, I'd pull her onto my lap in a second. He has far more self-control than I do.

"What was that about?" Calla asks, watching Atlas with a concerned expression. Her cheeks are still flushed, and the sight sends blood straight to my cock. *Fuck.* I need to focus. I tear my gaze away from Calla, focusing on Atlas.

He thrusts his fingers through his dark hair, leaning back against the chair as he rests his ankle on the opposite knee. "I'm being summoned," he says, shaking his head with a single, humorless laugh.

My lips turn down into a frown. This isn't the first time Atlas has been summoned in the time I've known him. And it's never for anything good.

Calla's brows lift; of course she has no idea what's going on.

"So I guess we *are* going to New York," Lex says, picking at a hangnail on his thumb and shifting where he sits. He's connected to Atlas on a more physical level, which means he's likely experiencing some of the discomfort rippling through Atlas right now. I feel for him.

"Wait, what?" Calla cuts in, her eyes wide as she looks from Lex back to Atlas.

He lets out a heavy sigh. "My parents have requested an audience."

She shakes her head, crossing her arms. "They can't call you? What century are they living in?"

Lex snorts, and I press my lips together against a smile. I can count the number of times I've been in the company of Atlas's parents in the last few decades. They are stiff, old-school vampires, but they are powerful and scary as hell. The last thing we need is to get on their bad side. When they call, Atlas goes.

He blinks at her, clearly unamused. "It doesn't work that way." He looks past her to Gabriel, then to me and Lex, and continues, "I'm not the only one being summoned. They've called a summit. All born vampires from the main bloodlines are required to attend, otherwise they must send a proxy."

"Why now?" I ask. "What's happening that they need to bring everyone together?"

"There have been a string of vampire deaths across North America. Far more than we normally see, even with the increased number of hunters. It's starting to garner attention. Many of the older born vampires want to wipe out the hunters to protect their own. They don't care that some of those vampires they want to protect are the same ones who needlessly kill humans for food and for sport."

"I'm going with you," Lex says, his gaze locked on his sire. His pulse is uneven and sweat dots his brow. The poor bastard is nervous. I want to reach over and clap my hand on his shoulder, to offer him comfort, but it'll make him uncomfortable. Lex despises feeling weak just as much as I do.

"No," Atlas says, holding his gaze, "you're not. You need to stay with your brothers and Calla."

"Uh, here's an idea," Calla chimes in, "how about we all go? I don't exactly have a desire to visit my home city, but it seems like the best option. I think we should stay together." She swallows, glancing at her lap for a moment before lifting her gaze to look at Atlas. "You shouldn't have to go alone."

His eyes flick across her face for a moment, his lips set in a tight line. "This isn't up for debate or discussion, Calla. I am going to New York to attend the summit, and the rest of you will stay put and prepare to move to the next safe house."

"I agree with Calla," Lex says in a low voice, and the room falls silent.

Calla is wide-eyed, staring at Lex; she's surprised to have someone taking her side in the conversation. Hell, I'm as surprised as she is, mostly that Lex would say anything to go against Atlas. I don't think that's happened in, well, ever.

Atlas inhales slowly. "Lex, do not—"

"There's no reason we shouldn't go with you," Lex says, cutting him off, and I can see it in his face that he's worried about being away from his sire.

"I can think of several," Atlas barks back.

"You should have backup," Calla says. "You guys protect me with security teams and whatnot. While it's annoying, it's also comforting."

"He isn't in danger," Gabriel assures her. "While these *events* aren't pleasant, they aren't dangerous for someone like Atlas to attend."

She mulls that over. "Then what's the big deal if we come along?" Calla chimes in, facing Atlas. "Haven't you ever heard of moral support? This is the perfect example of a time when it would be helpful."

"What would be helpful is if you'd—"

"Atlas," Gabriel cuts in gently.

His jaw works, and he shoves a hand through his hair, exhaling a harsh breath. "I'll be gone very briefly. There's no sense in dragging you lot there when all you'll be doing is sitting in a hotel room. There are hunters everywhere. New York is one of the highest populated, so it's not as if you three can galavant through Times Square."

"Well, damn. There goes my plan," Calla remarks dryly, rolling her eyes.

Atlas shoots her a dark look. "I'm going alone. End of discussion."

Lex drops his gaze, frowning, but doesn't argue further.

"When do you leave?" I finally ask, knowing there's no sense continuing to try and convince him to let us go with him. That door is shut and locked.

"First thing in the morning, so if you all don't mind, I'm going to pack a bag," he says, getting up and walking out of the room.

Calla frowns, looking at Gabriel, who offers her a reassuring smile.

"Come on," he says, standing and guiding her up as well. "Let's see what we can find to make for dinner."

The two of them head into the kitchen, leaving Lex and I alone.

"Well, fuck," he mutters.

"Agreed," I say and I can't help but fear this is the beginning of a lot worse to come.

CHAPTER

TEN

CALLA

Marcel must've had clothing delivered while I was in Washington, because when I stop in front of the room the guy's have been sleeping in, Atlas is standing at the end of the bed, folding a pair of black dress pants into a duffle bag. His back is to me, but even from across the room I can't help noticing the tension in his shoulders. I mean, Atlas is tense on a good day, but this is different.

"Are you going to continue staring at me from the hallway?" he asks without otherwise acknowledging my presence.

I purse my lips, considering it for a moment before I step into the room and close the door. Kicking off my shoes, I walk over and crawl onto the bed, sitting cross-legged in front of him, the duffel bag between us. I pull at a loose thread on the worn duvet as he shoves a small stack of T-shirts into the bag.

"Something you want to say to me?"

My fingers freeze. I lick the dryness from my lips. "Do your parents know what happened in Washington? The hunter attack on the house, I mean."

"Of course."

"But they don't understand why you might want to stay close to your friends, whether it be here or us joining you in New York?"

"It doesn't matter." His voice is clipped but level.

"Doesn't it?" I'm not sure why I'm pushing it. Maybe part of me hates the power the born vampires seem to have even just over their own kind. That, or maybe I don't want Atlas to leave.

He grips the duffle bag in his fist and practically rips the zipper shut before meeting my gaze. "No, Calla, it doesn't. I have responsibilities. I don't get to choose not to attend because I'd rather stay with my brothers and my—"

"Your *what*?" I cut in, my voice sharper than I was expecting. "What am I to you, Atlas?" I clamp my mouth shut when his blazing silver gaze slams into me. I have no idea where that came from and I certainly don't think I'm prepared to hear the answer, whatever it may be. "Forget it," I rush to say and move to get off the bed, but before my feet can reach the ground, Atlas is there, pinning me flat on my back against the mattress with his fingers locked around my wrists. My heart lurches in my chest as I watch his jaw work, and he glares down at me, his dark hair falling into his face. I have the urge to reach up and brush it back, but he has effectively immobilized me.

"Let me go." My racing pulse and the heat gathering between my legs are really out here trying to make a liar out of me.

"No."

My eyes narrow, and I mutter, "Fine. Then kiss me, you asshole."

The corner of his mouth curls into a wicked smirk. "Earn it."

I blink at him. "What the hell?"

"You heard me." He cocks his head to the side. "Fight me off, and perhaps then I'll give you what you clearly desire." His gaze lowers to where my shirt has ridden up, exposing my stomach.

Warmth floods my chest and cheeks. "Fuck you."

"Precisely." Amusement shines in his eyes as his grip on my wrists tightens. "I'll admit, I've missed our training sessions. It's only been a few days, but I found myself looking forward to them."

I roll my eyes but don't say anything. Because I can't disagree with him. I looked forward to them as well—too damn much. "You're saying this is some impromptu training session?"

"Oh, no." He leans down, pressing his body to mine, his lips at my ear when he says, "This is very real." When he leans back, his eyes are darker and his fangs flash in the light overhead.

I resent the shiver that zips through me. I cover it up with a scowl, thrusting my hips as hard as I can manage in an effort to buck him off. Instead, he lifts my arms above my head, laying me across the mattress so we're parallel with the headboard. His knee presses dangerously close to the throbbing at my core. I inhale and exhale short breaths, glaring up at him where he hovers over me, his gaze trained on my mouth.

"You're making this too easy," he says with a tsk.

My eyes fall to the dagger strapped around my thigh before flicking back to his face. I tug on my wrists until my skin burns under his grip. "Care to provide any advice?" I say through my teeth, my tone laced with bitterness.

"No."

"Do you just like saying that?" I shoot back, stilling beneath him.

His lips twitch. "I told you this wasn't a training session. If I was any other vampire, you'd be drained by now."

"If you wanted my blood, Atlas, all you had to do was ask." The words are out of my mouth before I can stop them.

"Actually, *Calla*, I don't." His mouth is against my neck in the time it takes me to blink, and I suck in a breath as his fangs scrape my skin. "I could do anything to you." He lowers his voice. "And the best part?" His knee inches higher, making my pulse jackhammer as his breath tickles my skin. "You'll let me because you want it."

"No," I breathe. I *lie*. I won't say it—I refuse to give him the satisfaction despite the moisture soaking through my panties, which he can no doubt smell. Fucking vampire senses.

"No," he echoes with a soft chuckle, his lips tracing the shell of my ear. "So if I were to bury my fingers between your thighs right now, I wouldn't find you absolutely fucking soaked for me?"

Holy hell.

I close my eyes, turning my face away. I'm not sure how long I can keep this up, denying what my body craves, even if there's a part of me that hates it.

"Ah, ah, ah. None of that. Look at me." His voice settles over me like a weighted blanket, and I comply without hesitation, his glamour clinging to me and controlling me effortlessly.

When he pulls back, our eyes meet, and I say, "Is this what you want?" I lick my lips. "Me, powerless beneath you, succumbing to your will?"

Atlas's jaw clenches into something sharp enough to cut glass and his eyes search my face as if it holds the answers to his prayers. "You —" He clears his throat. "You have no fucking idea."

I nod, forcing myself to hold his gaze. "Show me."

His mouth is on mine before I can think about what I've asked for. He devours me, his lips moving against mine, coaxing them to part for him, his grip on my wrists loosening ever so slightly. But it's enough.

I bring my leg up, slamming my knee into his stomach as hard as I can as I rip my wrists from his grasp. I roll away, right off the damn bed, landing hard on my hip. I wince as I force myself to my feet, reaching for my dagger before I'm even fully upright.

My eyes snap to the bed where I expect Atlas to be, but it's empty. I whip around, holding the dagger in front of me, and find him standing what has to be less than an inch from the tip of my blade. I start to step back, but he grabs my arm, holding me there.

I open my mouth to ask him what the hell he's doing, but he shakes his head, making the words die on my lips.

"You had me. Don't back down now."

You had me.

His words fill my chest with a somewhat unfamiliar warmth—pride. I got the upper hand. I tricked him and got away. But he's right, whatever upper hand I gained, I just lost it. Great.

I blow out a heavy breath. There's no chance I'm going to pull anything over on him now. "I'm calling it."

Atlas tilts his head to the side slightly. "Why?"

"This would be the part where I'd stab you if—"

"If what?" he cuts in, a challenging glint in his eyes. "If you didn't secretly care about hurting me?"

My eyes narrow and my grip on the hilt of the dagger tightens. I could remind him of the time, mere weeks ago, when I *did* stab him. Instead, I say, "Hardly. You don't even like me. Why would I give a shit about you?"

He laughs, shaking his head again.

"What?" I snap, lowering my arm with the dagger, and secure it back in its holder. We both know I'm not going to use it.

His eyes dance across my face. "You really believe that, don't you?"

I arch a brow, thrown by the softness in his voice. "When people show me who they are, I tend to believe them." And he's shown me more than once.

Atlas nods, his expression turning into something I mistake as thoughtful. Because then he says, "Is that why you let me fuck you against that tree?"

My cheeks fill with heat and my chest tightens, anger flaring to life in me. "I let you *fuck* me because I knew I needed to get you out of my system."

He smirks faintly. "I see. And did you?"

"Completely," I lie through my teeth without missing a beat.

"Right," he murmurs, stealing the distance between us with a single stride. "That's not nearly as convincing when I can hear the blood rushing through your body and your heart beating like a hummingbird in your chest. Not to mention the smell of your arousal."

I shrug, feigning indifference as I work really freaking hard to ignore the pull of desire urging me to grab the front of his shirt and kiss him until I can't think straight.

"Go ahead," he says, "tell me I'm wrong, that you didn't enjoy what I did to you this morning, and I'll forget the whole thing."

I swallow hard, but it doesn't help. "I don't know," I say, apparently deciding to add fuel to this fire, "It wasn't all that memorable."

My stomach swirls with nerves and heat as his lips slowly curl into a smile.

"Shame," he says, reaching for me before I can even consider moving away. He cups the side of my neck to hold me in place, his fingers warm against my skin. "Perhaps you need a reminder." He leans in, dipping his face until our foreheads are touching, and closes his eyes. I hold my breath, preparing for him to kiss me or bite me. Truth be told, I'm not sure which I crave more at the moment.

"Atlas," I whisper, my stomach pooling with warmth. I can't deny how much my body craves him for much longer.

His thumb brushes the pulse at my neck, and his throat bobs when he swallows. "You have one chance to walk out of here, otherwise you're mine for the night. I will not let you go."

I drag in a shallow breath, dropping my facade of indifference. "I'm here," I say in a low voice, gripping the front of his shirt. "I'm not leaving."

His chest rumbles with a low growl, his grip on my neck tightening a moment before he slants his mouth over mine, claiming me completely with a single fucking kiss.

I return the kiss with a fierce intensity, as if I need to prove something to him. Easing my grip on his shirt, I slide my hands up his chest and drape my arms over his shoulders, pushing my fingers into his hair as he tips my head back, deepening the kiss.

My world narrows on the sensations he's wringing from me. I am utterly consumed by this wicked vampire, and there's not a thing I can do about it—nothing I *want* to do. Nothing but this.

Without warning, his hands drop to my hips, and he lifts me

without breaking the kiss. My muscles tense at the sudden movement, and the next thing I feel is the mattress at my back. His lips leave mine, giving me a chance to catch my breath as my eyes fly open to find him leaning over me, his hands pressing into the mattress on either side of me. His legs cage mine in where they dangle off the end of the bed, and when he straightens, moving his hands to the waistband of my leggings and peeling them down to expose my center, my heart races. He steps back, pulling each of my legs out to remove my leggings before kneeling before me.

The sight of Atlas York kneeling between my legs is something that will remain branded in my memory. Because holy shit, it is *hot*.

His hands glide up my legs slowly, his lips trailing after them, peppering kisses and making my skin tingle. He spreads my thighs, holding them open, and the moment his lips brush my folds, I tremble with need.

My chest is splotchy and warm, rising and falling quickly as I keep my eyes on the top of his head.

Atlas drags his tongue along my slit, circling my clit before sucking it into his mouth. He moans, sending vibrations directly to the bundle of nerves in his mouth, and I suck in a sharp breath, gripping the sheets and biting my lip.

He pulls back, resting his chin on my mound. "You still want to pretend you don't remember what I feel like inside you?"

I shoot him a glare. "Shut the fuck up and put your mouth back on me."

He graces me with a faint grin. "You're in no position to make demands." In a second, he has my hips trapped against the mattress. "You'll take what I give you and say thank you."

I open my mouth to shoot a retort back, but before the words have a chance to leave my mouth, Atlas plunges two fingers into my pussy, stealing the words from my lips. "Fuck," I moan, turning my gaze to the ceiling so he can't see the pleasure in my eyes. I expect him to drop his mouth back to my clit, so when his lips press against the inside of my thigh, I peer down at him—right before his fangs sink into the delicate skin there.

I cry out, a mixture of pleasure and pain spiking through me as Atlas drinks deeply. My clit throbs in response, and he pulses his fingers inside me, curling them at just the right spot. I reach under my shirt, hiking it up as my hands slide under my bra, and roll my nipples between my fingers. My breaths come in little gasps, my cheeks hot as I race toward release. Pressure builds low in my belly, and the sensation of Atlas taking my blood while pushing his fingers deep inside me sends me over the edge. The walls of my pussy clench around his fingers, soaking them with my release as he continues pumping them in and out while I ride the orgasm to completion, basking in the delicious aftershocks of my climax.

I shiver when he pulls his fingers—and fangs—out of me. He seals the puncture marks with a quick drag of his tongue along my skin and crawls over me, the bulge in his pants stealing my attention immediately.

"You," I say rather breathlessly, "are wearing entirely too much clothing."

His eyes glimmer with a dangerous mix of lust and hunger as he tilts his head to the side. "Is that right?"

My eyes flick to his erection, and I press my lips together against a smile. "Well, yeah. If you want to do something about that."

He captures my chin and licks his lips. "What I *want* is to fuck that smart mouth of yours."

I stare at him, my eyes widening at his words. I want to look away, to hide the flush of my cheeks. I press my lips together as he watches me.

"Nothing to say now?" he taunts, tugging his shirt off in one fluid motion, dropping it on the floor.

"I've got plenty," I say, reaching for the button on his pants, "but I was raised to know that talking with a mouthful is rude." Of course, my mouth isn't full of anything yet, but I don't know what else to say. Because I'm pretty fucking far out of my element with Atlas.

He laughs, the deep sound filling the room as he pulls back and stands, unzipping his pants and tugging them along with his boxers to his ankles. His cock, now free of its confinement, springs to attention, and I can't pull my eyes away. I still can't believe that thing fits inside me. It makes me shiver at the memory of how it felt, my pussy clenching around it. *I want it again.*

"Come here," Altas beckons me, his voice thick with arousal, and offers me a hand. When I take it, he pulls me up so I'm sitting at the end of his bed, putting me at eye level with his cock.

Something takes hold of me, and I move without hesitation, reaching for him. I wrap my fingers around the base of his thick length, slowly pumping and alternating pressure.

He hisses out a sharp breath, and my lips curl into a satisfied grin. I quite literally have him in the palm of my hand, and as badly as I want his cock buried inside me, I'm not going to rush this moment. Because right now, *I'm* in control. *He's* going to take what *I* give him.

I lean forward as moisture beads at the tip of his cock and lightly flick my tongue along it to capture the saltiness there as I continue moving my hand up and down his shaft.

"Fuck," he breathes, his hand gripping my shoulder firmly but not to a painful degree.

Slowly, I wrap my lips around him, pushing down and taking him into my mouth, my tongue gliding along the underside of his cock. His grip on my shoulder tightens, and I close my eyes, focusing on keeping my throat relaxed so I can take more of him. He moves his hand from my shoulder to the back of my neck, guiding himself in further until he hits the back of my throat. I will my gag reflex not to kick in, my pulse pounding beneath my skin. Finally, he lets up and I pull back slowly, sucking and licking as I start bobbing up and down, taking as much of him as I can. His hand stays wrapped around the back of my neck, but he isn't applying any pressure; I'm still controlling this.

He exhales a harsh, short breath, and I reach down and take his balls in my hands, massaging them as I increase the pressure of my lips around his shaft.

"Calla," he grounds out, and I'm not sure if my name on his lips is a curse or a prayer. Perhaps it's both. "Slow down, or I'm going to come in your mouth in a minute."

My stomach swirls with warmth, the throbbing between my legs growing more intense knowing how much my ministrations are affecting him. I've never been the biggest fan of performing oral, but the thought of driving Atlas to release with my mouth spurs me on, and I move quicker instead of slowing down.

Atlas's grip on my neck tightens. "Fuck, Calla," he growls.

I moan, my lips vibrating against his cock, sucking harder as I continue working his balls. They tighten in my hands, which is my only warning before he groans deeply, shooting his release against the back of my throat. I force myself to swallow as much as I can, but some spills out the side of my mouth, rolling down my chin. Atlas pulls me off his cock and uses his thumb to clean his release off my face. He cups my cheek, dipping his head to kiss me with enough intensity to make me grab him and pull him on top of me. He moves at an inhuman speed, somehow maneuvering us so he's lying under me and I'm straddling his waist, his cock pressing against my back.

I steady myself on top of him, my palms flat against his chest. He grips my hips, and I push my ass against his cock, looking down at him with a grin. His eyes devour me and a muscle ticks in his jaw.

I arch a brow at him. "What?"

He fingers the hem of my shirt. "Now who's wearing too much clothing?"

Offering a short laugh, I pull my shirt off over my head, tossing it to the side of the bed, leaving me in nothing but my bra.

Atlas's fingers skim up my sides, making me shiver, then he reaches behind me and unclasps my bra, pulling it off and exposing my breasts to his hungry gaze.

At that moment, my body floods with heat under his scrutiny. I'm left completely bared to him, and it's making my heart pound in my chest. I turn my face away, suddenly feeling wickedly self-conscious. Atlas has been around for over a century; I can't be anything special. My thoughts veer into dangerous territory, and I'm thinking about all the women he must've been with before me. Surely some of them were far more experienced than I am, and—

"Calla." Atlas's voice pulls me back, but I still can't bring myself to meet his gaze. His hands are back on my hips, his thumbs rubbing slow circles against my skin. "What's going on in that head of yours?" he asks. "Already regretting this?"

My eyes widen. Of all the things he could say, that was the least of what I was expecting. "No."

"Then look at me."

I catch my bottom lip between my teeth, peering down at him, focusing on the dark stubble covering his chin.

He says my name again, and I finally lift my eyes to his, my heart in my throat.

"You are the most stunning creature I've laid eyes on," he murmurs, reaching up to tuck my hair behind my ear. "There is nothing on this earth that will keep me from you." His gaze darkens as his hand returns to my hip and gives it a squeeze. "Wherever you are, I will find you."

Every word in my vocabulary vanishes. Gone. *Poof*. I have no idea what led Atlas to say those words to me, but something in my chest is clinging to them.

Maybe vampires *can* read minds. That, or my face gave my thoughts of insecurity away more than I'd like to consider.

I lean down until my chest is pressed against his and my fingers are in his hair, then brush my lips over his. "I want you inside me," I murmur against his lips.

He nips my bottom lip, his hands reaching around to cup my ass and grind me against his cock. "So take it."

My heart lurches and feels as if it's lodged in my throat. "What?"

Atlas smirks. "Ride me, Calla."

I blush hotly, chewing the inside of my cheek. "Right."

"Lift your hips," he instructs in a deep voice.

I do as he says, and he shifts under me, positioning the head of his cock so it lines up with my entrance. All I have to do is lower myself onto him. He rubs along my slit, coaxing me to push down, and I hold my breath as I sink onto him one inch at a time.

"Breathe," he says, his eyes glimmering with amusement.

I force a breath in and out, lowering the rest of the way so I'm seated on him. I've never been this full before. He feels so much deeper than when he took me against the tree.

Holy hell, this is fucking amazing.

I lift my hips, moving up his shaft before dropping back down a little faster this time, eliciting a moan from my lips.

Atlas closes his eyes, holding my hips, but letting me lead as I balance myself on top of him, alternating my pace here and there, making him groan beneath me.

"That's it," he encourages, reaching between us to play with my clit as I continue to ride his cock.

I tip my head back, closing my eyes as our heavy breathing fills the room. I moan, not even making an effort to be quiet, and Atlas lifts his hips to thrust into me, stealing my breath.

"Yes," I pant, moving quicker still, and my breasts bounce with each thrust.

"Fuck," Atlas groans. "Look at me. I want to watch you take my cock, riding me until you come."

My eyes fly open, meeting his liquid silver gaze as I drop onto his cock over and over, crying out when my pussy walls tighten. My muscles squeeze his cock as his fingers work my clit until I see fucking stars. He thrusts into me hard and fast, his climax quickly following mine, and he announces his release with a deep grunt before pulling me down onto him and sealing his mouth over mine. His lips dominate me as he continues thrusting his hips, and I ride the aftershocks of my orgasm, kissing him back with fervor.

He wraps his arms around me, rolling us so we're lying on our sides facing each other, and pulls out of me without breaking the kiss. I shiver as his cock brushes my clit and slide my fingers into his hair again, pulling him closer to me.

We break apart to breathe, and I trace the lines of his chest with a single finger as he presses his lips to my forehead. It's the sweetest thing he's ever done, and it makes my chest tighten, reminding me that he's leaving in the morning.

"I don't want you to go," I whisper too low for any human to pick up on it.

But Atlas isn't human.

His soft exhale stirs the hair at my temple. "Everything is going to be fine," he says in a level tone.

"You don't know that." I try to pull away, but he holds me against him.

"Let's not talk about it. There's nothing to be said or done. I'm going to the summit. End of story."

"Fine," I mumble, closing my eyes. It's not an argument I want to get into, nor do I have the energy for, especially considering I won't win. Instead of pushing it, I shift closer, resting my head against his chest, and let myself relax enough to drift off, listening to the steady beat of Atlas's heart.

I guess he has one after all.

ELEVEN

KADE

Atlas is gone before any of us wake the next morning. Lex is still passed out when I pry my eyes open and immediately smell the sweet aroma of cooking coming from the kitchen. There's also a lingering scent of coffee, which is what truly hauls my ass out of the rickety bed. I don't bother putting on a shirt, walking down the creaky floored hallway in nothing but my boxers. I round the corner into the kitchen and lean against the wall, my lips curling into a faint smile as I watch Calla stirring pancake batter in a stainless steel mixing bowl. She drops a handful of chocolate chips into the batter and another handful into her mouth.

She's so fucking sexy, I can't take my eyes off her. I want to sneak up behind her and wrap my arms around her, pressing her against me. More than that, the desire to hoist her onto the counter and bury my head between her thighs sends a rush of heat straight to my cock.

Setting the bowl on the counter, she walks over to the stove and flips the pancakes already cooking in the pan, humming softly under her breath before turning toward the fridge. Her eyes land on me, and she yelps, her hand smacking against her chest in surprise.

"What the hell, Kade?" she grumbles, her heart still racing, and I certainly don't miss the way her eyes linger on my bare chest.

I chuckle softly, pushing away from the wall and walking closer to her. "Good morning to you too."

She rolls her eyes, and I half expect her to flip me off, but she just opens the fridge and proceeds to ignore me. Huh. Guess she wasn't so overtaken by lust at the sight of my abs to not get annoyed with me for sneaking up on her.

"You should be in a better mood after last night," I say, my voice laced with amusement. We all heard what she and Atlas got up to, and it took every ounce of self-control I have not to invite myself. Gabriel insisted that we leave the two of them alone—that they both needed it. Which, fine, whatever. But damn. I've only experienced the mastery that is Atlas York in bed on a handful of occasions. The tinge of jealousy was annoying as fuck.

"I'm fine," she says, slamming the fridge door shut and setting the block of butter on the counter.

I hold my hands up in mock defense. "Easy. I'm only messing with you."

"Yeah, well, for once, could you just not?"

The grin falls from my lips. "Hey." I close the distance between us and turn her around to face me. "What's going on?"

Her jaw clenches, her eyes flicking between mine. "Nothing," she says flatly.

I hold her still when she tries to pull away. "Calla."

"Kade," she levels in a tight voice.

I sigh. "I'm worried about him too, but Atlas can take care of himself."

She blinks, her hard expression softening as her brows knit. I can tell she's clinging to a facade of strength, and while I admire the hell out of that, part of me wants her to know she doesn't have to. That we'll be strong *for* her.

"I know," she says. "I still think we should've gone with him."

I move my hand off her shoulder and brush my knuckles across her cheek. "He'll be back and annoying the hell out of you before you know it."

Calla lets out a heavy sigh. "Yeah, all right." Her eyes flick between mine. "I'm worried about you too, you know."

"I'm fine," I say automatically, ignoring the pressure in my chest. I don't want Calla to worry about me, to see the darkness swirling inside me, or the suffocating anxiety I experience when my thoughts drift to my sister.

"I don't believe you," she whispers.

I force a smile. "Okay. Then I *will* be fine."

Calla sighs, clearly recognizing that she's not going to get much more out of me. "You hungry?" she asks.

I tap the tip of her nose. "Sure. I'll go wake the others."

She nods, turning back to the stove to flip the cooked pancakes onto a plate before pouring more batter into the frying pan. "Gabriel's asleep on the couch."

I stop in the living room, nudging the couch cushion with my foot until Gabriel rouses, squinting at me. "Wakey, wakey," I say in a singsong voice.

He blinks his eyes open and sits up, running his fingers through his copper hair. "He's gone."

I nod. "Not sure when he left, but I'm sure he'll check in when he can."

Gabriel returns my nod and stands, shuffling into the kitchen, no doubt to the coffee machine.

I return to the bedroom and grab my pillow, proceeding to smack Lex in the face with it. "Get up."

"Fuck off," he grumbles, rolling onto his stomach and covering his head with the pillow.

"Calla's making breakfast for everyone. Don't be an asshole. Come eat with us."

His responding laugh is muffled by another pillow. "Calla doesn't cook."

"She bakes, though. I think pancakes are essentially baking. She mixed water and some powdered shit." I shrug, tugging the sheets off him and exposing his bare ass. I snicker. "Get up, put on some pants, and come eat."

He groans, turning back over. "In that order?"

My eyes flick to his impressive erection, and I smirk. "Preferably."

With that, I quickly pull on a pair of black joggers and walk back to the kitchen, where Gabriel is leaning against the counter nursing a cup of coffee while he chats with Calla about a French toast recipe he wants to show her when we have a better functioning kitchen.

Once we're all squeezed around the dining table stuffing our faces with pancakes, Gabriel announces that Atlas made it to New York. If I should feel better about that, I don't. Atlas's parents are some of the most wicked vampires in existence. They have zero regard for human life and care only for the preservation of their kind. I have no fucking clue how Atlas can stand them; they scare the absolute shit out of me.

"What happens now?" Calla asks, taking a sip of orange juice. Her pulse is ticking unevenly and her brows are knit.

"We'll head to the new place once Atlas is finished at the summit. It'll depend on what information he brings back what we do after that."

She nods, then sighs softly before pushing her plate away, half-eaten. "I'm, uh, going to get cleaned up." She doesn't wait for any of us to respond before she stands and carries her dishes into the kitchen. Her footsteps grow softer as she walks down the hall toward the bathroom.

My chair scrapes across the floor as I stand, leaving my plate to follow her. I'm not sure what makes me do it, but I need to check on her.

The bathroom door isn't completely closed, so I knock once and slowly push it open enough to slip inside, then shut it behind me. The bathroom is the only part of the house that seems to be newly renovated. With his and hers sinks and a massive claw-foot tub, it looks as if the previous owners started in this room and never had a chance to finish the rest of the house.

Calla is bent over, turning on the water to fill the tub. She stands, turning to face me, and says, "What are you doing?" Her voice is small, tired.

"I wanted to make sure you're okay," I tell her, leaning against the wall beside the door.

She grabs a bottle of bubble bath from the vanity and squirts some under the water. "I'm as okay as any of us can be at this point, Kade."

"That's a copout answer."

"Fine." She sets the bottle back on the vanity and crosses her arms over her chest. "Are *you* okay? With everything going on, you haven't had a chance to deal with what happened with your sister."

So she's going to try and get me to talk again. Arching a brow at her, I say, "I came to check on you, and you're asking how I am?"

Her arms fall to her sides, and she leans against the vanity, flicking a glance toward the tub to check the water level before looking at me again. "Um, yeah. Are you going to tell me?"

I blow out a heavy breath. "Honestly, I have no idea what to do. Or if there's anything I *should* do, for that matter. I don't know what Meredith's plan is, or why she seems to be working with the hunters. At this point, she's the enemy. And yeah, that really fucking sucks." I shove my hands into the pockets of my joggers to hide the way they're shaking. I'd like to believe I've done well hiding how much my sister's sudden appearance has affected me. But the more I think about it, the more it doesn't make sense. I'm so confused, and the only one who holds the answers that will resolve that confusion is my sister.

Calla frowns. "I'm really sorry, Kade. I wish there was something I could do to make it easier for you." She walks closer, stopping an arms' reach away. "You can talk to me about her, you know. Anytime. I'm a good listener."

I offer her a wry grin. "Thanks. I've also been known to be a good listener."

"I'm pretty much at a loss," she admits. "These days, I have no idea what's happening or *going* to happen. There's a new threat every day, and despite that, I find myself worrying about school of all things, which is ridiculous in comparison to the other shit we're facing, I am fully aware of that. And the more I think about the aforementioned shit, the bigger this pit in my stomach grows, because I am scared—so fucking scared of what's going to happen and the possibility that I might lose one of you..." Her voice trails off and her eyes widen; she's surprised by her own words.

She's worried about losing us.

My chest is oddly tight, and I have the urge to wrap her in my arms and never let go, never let her think that anything or anyone could get in the way or threaten what we have.

Calla sighs and finally says, "But I kinda came in here to get *away* from the talking."

I nod slowly, wanting to assure her that I won't push it. "We don't have to talk." I dip my face so my lips are at her ear. "I'm also very good at *not* talking."

The hitch in her breath is all I need. I pull my hands out of my pockets and grab her around the waist, pulling her against me.

"Kade," she breathes, and the sound of my name on her lips goes right to my cock.

"Tell me what you need," I say, trailing my mouth along her jaw as she presses her palms against my bare chest.

She trails her fingers upward as she leans up on her tiptoes and connects them at the back of my neck, turning her face so my mouth lands on hers. She kisses me slowly at first—until I press my lower half into her, then she moans into my mouth, deepening the kiss as she grips the back of my hair.

I return her kiss, guiding us toward the tub, where the water is at the perfect level. I manage to reach over and turn it off without breaking the kiss. I nip her bottom lip, grazing my tongue along it, and her pulse kicks up.

She leans back and grabs the hem of her shirt, quickly tugging it off, revealing her breasts. Her nipples are pebbled, and I lick my lips, wanting nothing more than to drop my mouth to her skin and devour them.

Calla places a finger under my chin, tilting my head up to return my gaze to her face to find her soft brown eyes filled with desire, with need —and I am more than happy to oblige.

I give her a chaste kiss before curling my fingers into the waistband of her pants, crouching as I tug them down to her ankles. Her hand rests on my shoulder as she steps out of them, kicking them into a pile with her shirt. When I straighten, her cheeks are flushed, and I reach for her, tucking her hair behind her ear. I take her hand, guiding her to the tub, and she steps in, lowering herself under the bubbles as steam fills the room, fogging the mirrors and filling the space with a calming haze of eucalyptus and mint.

Stepping out of my pants and boxers, I get into the tub. Calla slides forward, so I lower myself behind her and pull her back against my chest. I move her hair over one shoulder and press my lips to the other, kissing toward her neck, where I suck gently, swirling my tongue against her warm skin.

Calla sighs, tipping her head back against my shoulder. "Touch me," she says in a voice so low any human would miss it.

My lips curl into a grin against her neck. "I *am* touching you."

She lets out a little impatient noise, her hands gliding along my thighs beneath the water. "You know that's not what I mean."

"Hmm…" I lift my hands to her shoulders, massaging them with slow, deep movements. "I think you're going to need to be more specific, Calla."

She inhales slowly. "You're such an ass," she mutters, but her voice is gentle, soft with relaxation.

I chuckle. "You like it."

Calla reaches back and grabs my hands, pulling them over her shoulders and down her chest to her breasts. "Do I need to tell you what to do with these?" she taunts.

My cock twitches at her tone, and I cup her breasts, my fingers working her nipples into stiff pebbles. "I think I can manage."

She sucks in a breath, turning her head and pressing her lips to my collarbone, then my jaw before her lips find mine, and she moans against them.

"I want to taste you," I murmur, nipping her lower lip as my gums throb, my fangs threatening to break through them.

She breaks the kiss, her heart pounding in her chest. "If you want my blood," she says in a shallow voice, "put your hand between my legs and make me come."

It takes every ounce of my self-control not to drive my cock into her from behind. I settle for trailing my hand down her stomach until my fingers disappear under the bubbles and water to brush the inside of her thigh. My lips find her neck, and I kiss her there, running my finger along her folds. Satisfaction floods through me when her breathing hitches, and she spreads her legs open for me. "That's my girl," I murmur, my lips tracing the shell of her ear, making her squirm. I dip a finger past her folds and apply a bit of pressure to her clit, moving my thumb over it in a circular motion.

"More," she demands, breathing heavily, and I am more than happy to oblige.

I slide my finger inside her pussy, curling it before pulling out, then add a second finger, pushing back in to my knuckles.

She bites her lip, her head bent back against my chest and her eyes closed. "Yes."

"You like that?" I drag my tongue along her neck, and she pushes her ass against my dick. "Message received," I say, my lips dancing across the delicate skin below her ear as my fingers pump in and out of her soaked pussy. Her thighs shake and her heels slam into the bottom of the tub.

"Don't stop," she pants, pushing against my fingers, riding them.

"Are you close?" I whisper lowly in her ear.

She sucks in a shallow breath. "Y-yes. Holy shit."

Heat floods through me, and if my dick wasn't rock solid before, it sure as fuck is now. "I want to feel you clench around my fingers as I sink my fangs into your throat."

"Yes," she nearly whimpers, tilting her head and baring her neck to me. "Please."

Her soft words have my fangs slicing through my gums in an instant, and I press my thumb against her clit, circling it hard and fast as I fuck her with my fingers and sink my fangs into her neck. Her sweet, hot blood explodes on my tongue, and I close my eyes, drinking deeply. My cock twitches with need as her blood warms my stomach, and I increase my thrusts into her.

"*Kade*," she cries out in a high-pitched voice, coming around my fingers, squeezing them as she grinds against me, reveling in the pleasure of her climax.

My fingers continue pumping as her legs shake and her breaths come in shallow pants while she rides the aftershocks of her orgasm, her release coating my fingers and seeping into the tub.

When my need to bury my cock deep inside her overpowers my desire for her blood, I pull back, healing my bite, and maneuver us in a blur of motion, spilling a bit of water on the bathroom tile.

"What are you doing?" she asks with a short laugh, still catching her breath.

I reach under the water and lift her leg to the ledge of the tub. "Hold it there," I tell her, fisting my cock in my hand, pumping my hand along its length a few times before lining it up with her entrance. I tease her with the thick head, making her moan as I drag it along her slit, dipping in inch by inch until my full length is buried in her throbbing heat. "Fuck," I hiss out through my teeth. "You feel so good."

"This angle doesn't," she grumbles.

Fair enough. She's on her side with her leg up and her ass pressed against the back of the tub.

"Allow me to fix that." I grab her around the waist and stand while remaining mostly inside her. I manage to get us out of the tub and plant her sweet ass on the vanity. I roll my hips, pushing all the way into her, and she grabs my shoulder, biting her lip to quiet the sound of her moan, with her eyes closed and her head tipped back against the steam-covered mirror.

I pick up the pace and slide my hand up her stomach, between her breasts and past her collarbone until my fingers wrap around her throat. I don't apply pressure, I just hold her to the mirror, my cock hardening inside her at the rapid beat of her pulse against my fingers. My balls tighten, and I groan, pumping hard and fast as tension builds quickly. I reach between us with my other hand and find her clit, flicking it once, twice, three times, making her gasp each time, then rub two fingers over it in a slow, circular motion.

She bites her lip so hard, the smell of her blood hits my senses, and I slam into her.

"Don't hold back," I order. "I want to hear every sound you make as I ravish you."

Her responding exhale is uneven, and when my cock hits a particularly sensitive spot deep inside her, the lovely sound of her moans fill the warm, hazy room.

"Good girl." I reward her by quickening my thrusts, pulsing my fingers around her clit.

"Fuck, I'm going to—"

"Come," I say in a velvet-smooth voice, thrusting so hard her ass slides back on the vanity. "Come for me, Calla."

"Mmm... *ohmygod*, yessss," she cries out, gripping my shoulders so hard, her fingernails bite into my skin. I barely feel it. She could stake me in the fucking heart right now, and I wouldn't give a damn. Not with her wrapped around my cock.

"That's it," I encourage her, driving into her over and over as my own orgasm builds. Her walls squeeze me perfectly, throbbing and clenching around me, and I groan loudly, spurting my release inside her as I come. "Fuck," I growl, tugging her to me and slamming my lips against hers, holding my cock still in her heat.

Our lips move together as if we've been together for over a century. As if our bodies know each other on a molecular level. Which, in a sense, I suppose they do. Blood oath and all.

The idea makes my chest tighten, and I break the kiss. The thought of that damn oath having any part of what we just did makes me feel oddly sick to my stomach.

"You know," she says, resting her forehead against my chest, catching her breath. "We started off in the tub, but I feel dirtier than ever." She plants soft kisses across my chest, and I can't help but chuckle, forcing myself to shove away any thoughts of what brought us together.

I catch her chin, tilting her face up to meet my gaze as I slowly slide out of her. "If you're waiting for an apology, you're not getting one," I tease.

Calla arches a brow at me, her cheeks flushed a lovely shade of pink. "For that?" She laughs. "Hardly."

Offering a grin, I kiss her forehead and grab a towel from the shelf next to the vanity before lifting her off it and wrapping her up.

She holds the front of the towel and walks toward the bathroom door, glancing back at me over her shoulder. "Good talk." She winks at me, and my grin widens.

I take another towel and tie it around my waist, following her out of the bathroom. She walks down the hall to one bedroom, while I go to the other, tugging on a fresh T-shirt and dark jeans. I'm doing up the buckle on my belt when my phone chimes from the wicker—yes, *wicker* —table beside the bed. I snatch it up, expecting an update from Atlas, and the phone nearly slips from my fingers when my eyes land on the message.

We need to talk, brother.

So she knows I'm alive, that her ambush before the hunter attack didn't kill me.

And she has my phone number.

My stomach plummets, and I sink onto the end of the bed, gripping the phone in my hand, and my fingers glide over the keyboard.

Pass. Last time we hung out, you tried to kill me.

Her response comes moments later.

Your humor hasn't changed, K. And I didn't try to kill you. If I'd wanted you dead, you wouldn't be alive.

I despise the way my fingers shake as they hover over the keys.

You know, that's not very comforting. What do you want to meet for?

Once I hit send, I force my legs to stand and walk to the living room, where Gabriel is reading something on his phone and Lex is lounging on the couch, drinking from a blood bag as if it's a juice box.

Lex catches the look on my face and arches a questioning brow at me.

"We may have a problem."

Gabriel looks up from his phone. "What's going on?"

"Meredith wants me to meet her."

"Yeah, no," Lex says. "Sister or not, the little psycho stabbed you."

"Lex," Gabriel warns.

I frown, though I understand where he's coming from. If someone from his past showed up and skewered him, I wouldn't be too keen on him meeting up with them a second time.

"What does she want?" Gabriel asks.

My gaze drops to my phone as it vibrates with another message from Meredith.

I owe you an explanation.

Lex scowls when I read the text aloud. "No fucking kidding."

Gabriel pinches the bridge of his nose, sighing. "Do you want to go?"

My stomach twists. Part of me feels I need to, to hear what she has to say, but the last thing any of us need right now is another ambush. "I... I think so."

He offers a curt nod. "We should at least wait until Atlas is back. We can go with you and make sure she doesn't try to pull anything a second time."

Lex tosses the empty blood bag on the coffee table. "I want proof it isn't a trap."

I press my lips together and type a response to my sister.

My sister.

Fuck. I still can't wrap my head around her being alive—and like me. I have so many questions, but maybe with this meeting, I'll finally get some answers.

Say I agree to meet you. How can I be sure it's not a trap? I'm sure it comes as no surprise that I don't trust you.

I lean against the armrest of the couch after I send my reply and wait.

That's fair. But you should take into consideration that I didn't tell the hunters about the human consort you have.

I bark out a bitter laugh. She thinks Calla is our consort. Vampires have been known to keep humans around to feed on or complete household tasks, but that has absolutely nothing to do with the reason Calla is with us.

I often pretend the blood oath doesn't have anything to do with it either, but that's beside the point.

"She's making jokes now?" Lex says, his sharp silver eyes narrowed on me, though I know his anger is not directed *at* me.

"You could say that. She thinks Calla is our consort."

Lex's expression softens, and he snorts out a laugh. "Right."

I rub my hand down my face, then reply with, *I don't see what that has to do with anything. And why should I believe anything you say to me now?*

A minute goes by. Then two. Five minutes later, she still hasn't responded.

Finally, after what feels like the longest fifteen minutes of my eternal existence, my phone buzzes with her reply.

I've never lied to you before, have I? Being a vampire doesn't change who you are as a person. I'm no liar, Kade.

With a sigh, I write back and tell her we'll meet on Friday at a location to be determined once I know where we'll be and knowing Atlas will be with us again in case I need backup. That also gives me a few days to prepare myself for whatever I'm walking into with her.

This meeting has the potential to be a complete disaster. Despite that, there's a tiny, annoying-as-fuck spark of hope in my chest. And I can't help but cling to it.

"His car just pulled in."

My stomach does a little flip, but I force myself to stay on the couch instead of running outside and launching myself at him.

Atlas was gone for two days. We didn't hear much out of New York during that time, save for a couple of quick texts from him assuring us he was fine, bored if anything, and that he'd fill us in when he got back.

Gabriel gets up and walks to the front door. I catch sight of Atlas through the window in the living room, throwing his duffle bag over his shoulder and walking toward the house, and my breath gets caught in my throat. The pull in my chest and the pounding of my heart isn't something I was expecting.

Lex and Kade disappeared after breakfast to pack what few things we have, but they both walk into the living room and drop into the chairs on either side of the unlit fireplace.

The front door opens and the sound of hushed voices reaches me. My throat goes dry, and I swallow hard, my eyes snapping to the doorway when Atlas steps into the room. He's dressed in all black—combat boots, jeans, V-neck, and a leather jacket. His hair is a mess from the wind and his under eyes are shadowed with sleepless nights.

I'm off the couch, closing the distance between us before I fully come to terms with what I'm doing. Between one moment and the next, I launch myself at him, wrapping my arms around his neck and burying my face in his chest. He stumbles back half a step. Atlas York *stumbles*. Clearly he's as taken by surprise at my greeting as I am. But then his arms come around me—one snakes around my waist and the other slides into my hair, cradling my head against his chest.

I inhale deeply, closing my eyes as his scent envelops me, settling my racing heart. I suppose there was a part of me that was worried about him and I didn't realize how deep that worry ran until I saw him.

"Aww, I love it when Mom and Dad get along." Kade's voice bursts my bubble of momentary calm, and I move away from Atlas, shooting Kade a glare over my shoulder.

When my eyes flit back to Atlas, my chest tightens. He looks like shit. I mean, he's still easily one of the most attractive men—scratch that, *people*—I've ever seen, but his face is a canvas of darkness. His jaw is set tight; he's on high-alert now, but he's also exhausted.

He drops his chin, glancing down at me. "Don't look at me like that," he says in a low voice. "I'm fine."

I shake my head. "Liar."

His lips twitch. "I'll live, then."

Crossing my arms, I narrow my eyes at him. "You—"

"He just needs to feed," Lex interjects from across the living room. "What, they didn't feed you in New York?"

Atlas leans against the door frame as Gabriel shifts around him, walking to the couch and dropping onto it. "Nothing I wanted."

My brows knit in confusion. "You didn't feed at all while you were there?"

"I don't particularly like the way they choose to feed and I didn't have time to find my own means."

Nervously, I ask, "What does that mean?"

"It doesn't matter," he says with a tone of finality.

I want to push, but if I've learned anything being with these guys it's to pick my battles, so I nod. And then I grab his wrist and pull him down the hall toward the bedroom I've been sleeping in. Once we're inside, I close the door and let go of his wrist, moving the hair away from my neck.

He sighs. "Calla—"

"Take what you need."

"It's not your responsibility to ensure I have blood to drink." He steps closer, lowering his voice. "You are not our feeder."

You're far more than that.

He doesn't say it, but with the way he's looking at me, the storm of desire in his eyes, he doesn't have to.

"I don't care," I say, and my voice comes out quieter than I intended. I swallow, then add, "I want to make you feel better. What's wrong with that?"

His eyes flick between mine, and he lifts his hand to my face, his fingers skimming over my cheek so softly I barely feel it. "I haven't fed in a few days, and after the days I've had... I could hurt you."

I reach for the dagger at my thigh, patting it where it sits securely in its guard. "I can defend myself," I offer, my pulse ticking faster.

Atlas presses his lips into a thin line. "Do you truly believe that once I get my fangs in your neck you could fight me off if I lose control?"

"No," I say firmly. I've been training, yes, but I'm not naive enough to believe I could fight off a vampire once they sink their fangs into me. "I don't think you'll lose control."

"Then you are too trusting."

I shrug. "I never said I trusted you."

"Didn't you?" he questions with a subtle tilt of his head. "You're offering yourself to me knowing full well you won't be able to defend yourself if things go wrong. You're trusting that things won't go wrong. That I have control enough over the monster in me that wants to tear into your carotid artery and devour your blood."

Without missing a beat, I say dryly, "And they say romance is dead."

He exhales a short laugh, shaking his head. "Calla—"

"God, Atlas," I cut him off. "Quit being such a martyr. Do you really think the three other vampires in this house would sit by and let you suck me dry?"

He lets out a heavy sigh before his dark gaze falls on my neck, making my throat go dry. I instinctively step back, then remind myself that I wanted to do this. His silver gaze slams into me a moment before he strikes, moving at a preternatural speed. His arm circles my waist, pulling me flush against his chest as his other hand cradles the side of my head. A low growl rumbles through him, and I close my eyes, tilting my head to the side seconds before his fangs sink into my neck, stealing my breath. There's a brief moment of white-hot, searing pain, but then it's gone, replaced by warmth and pleasure.

Atlas drinks deeply, and I lean into him, giving myself over to the endorphins rushing through me. I gasp softly when his erection presses against the throbbing between my legs. Heat gathers low in my belly, and my breasts tingle with the desire to be touched. I press my lips together to keep from moaning and cling to him, my head starting to spin.

A minute later, he pulls back, dragging his tongue over the puncture marks on my neck. He keeps his arm around me, and I sway into his chest.

"Calla, open your eyes for me."

"Hmm..." I try to pry them open, but they're too heavy. I just want to sleep and for him to keep holding me. My skin tingles everywhere he touches, and I feel as if I'm floating on a cloud of warmth.

He grasps my chin, tilting my head up. "Don't make me feed you my blood."

Right now, that doesn't sound as awful as it usually does. In fact, the thought only makes the heat between my legs intensify.

A rumble of laughter vibrates through his chest. "Yeah, that's what I thought. Come on. You need to eat something."

We start walking toward the living room, and by *we* and *walking*, I mean, Atlas practically carries me there with how much I'm leaning on him just to stay upright.

I've never felt so equally weak and aroused before. It's an odd thing.

Atlas guides me to the couch, and Gabriel is there a second later, setting a plate with a sandwich and glass of orange juice on the coffee table in front of me.

I smile at him as I reach for the glass, my hand shaking a little. "Thanks."

Four sets of silver eyes are honed on me while I inhale the sandwich, washing it down with the juice. With food in my system, I gain back some of my strength and don't feel as if I'm going to pass out at any second, which is nice.

Gabriel sits next to me, while Atlas leans against the mantle between Kade and Lex.

I turn my gaze to Atlas. "Are you going to fill us in on what went down in New York?"

A muscle in his jaw ticks, but he nods. "I don't agree with what they've decided to do, but I was outvoted by a lot," he prefaces before sighing. "Many of the older born vampires want to take out the hunters, starting with the headquarters in Washington using the information I've gathered from being inside Ellis Industries. I have names and addresses of most of the D.C. hunters... and I provided that information during the summit."

"Shit," Lex mutters, rubbing his jaw.

Gabriel and Kade remain silent, and the food in my stomach suddenly feels like concrete.

I clench my jaw against the nausea rippling through me and swallow past the bile rising in my throat. "What does that mean?" I force the words out, willing my stomach to settle.

Atlas's expression remains impassive. "There has been an attack planned. Its goal is to wipe out as many of the hunters as possible in one night. It's happening in three days. We needed time to spread the word to as many vampires as possible and get them on board for the attack. The idea is to attack every place we can simultaneously so there's little chance of a real fight."

Tears prick my eyes and my mouth fills with saliva as my stomach churns more violently. If the vampires attack Scott Ellis, Brighton is in just as much danger as he is. And as conflicted as I am over finding out that Scott basically runs the hunters, he has always been kind to me since Bri and I became friends years ago. The thought of their family home being attacked by vicious, vengeful vampires makes my head spin so fast my vision blurs.

My chest fills with pressure and my hand flies to my mouth. I'm off the couch in a rush. Gabriel reaches for me, but I pull back and run to the bathroom. I drop to the floor and barely manage to get the lid of the toilet up before I empty my stomach into the bowl. Tears roll down my cheeks, and I jump when a hand touches my shoulder. Wiping my mouth with the back of my hand, I turn my head enough to see Atlas crouching behind me. I blink at him in surprise; he's the last one I would've guessed would come after me.

Atlas moves his hand from my shoulder and collects my hair, pulling it away from my face just in time for me to turn back to the toilet and heave until my throat is dry and my head is pounding. He rubs my back until I stop vomiting, then stands and walks over to the vanity, filling a glass with water as I sink onto the floor, leaning against the wall and struggling to breathe. Each breath is a short, shallow gasp; it feels as if someone is standing on my chest, crushing my lungs, and darkness dances along the edge of my vision.

Atlas appears in front of me again, crouching and bringing the glass to my lips. He helps me drink a little, but I immediately start coughing, which doesn't help with the hyperventilating I'm already doing.

He sets the glass on the floor beside me, holding my gaze. "You need to breathe, Calla."

I'm fucking trying, I want to say, but the words... I can't make them form, so I just shake my head, continuing to fight for every breath.

His eyes soften a fraction, and I think I see concern in them. His hands land on my cheeks, soft but firm, and he snares my gaze. The moment his glamour falls over me, the tightness in my chest eases.

"Breathe," he murmurs.

I try to pull in a breath and find I can. It's a bit stunted, but my lungs fill.

"Good. Now let it out slowly."

I close my eyes to focus, letting the air out through my mouth.

His glamour holds despite our eyes no longer being locked; his fingers graze my cheeks, holding the connection. "Again."

We sit on the floor as I regain the ability to breathe on my own. Eventually he releases me and we end up sitting next to each other against the wall.

"I understand your concern about what came of the summit," he says in a level voice. "This isn't something I wanted." He turns his head to look at me. "I give you my word I will make sure Brighton is safe. She will not be harmed."

I bite my bottom lip to keep it from trembling. Brighton doesn't deserve to be anywhere near this. She also doesn't deserve to lose her father, but that—asking Atlas to spare the life of Scott Ellis—isn't going to happen. I'm grateful he at least cares enough about me to ensure Brighton will be okay, but that is going to leave me having to help my best friend through losing one of her parents.

I'm unsettled at how strangely calm Atlas is over this whole situation. It's mass murder. Granted the humans they'll be going after have killed countless vampires, it doesn't change the facts. Not to mention, these are the same people who attacked all of us at the house, so it's a little hard not to be twisted up about everything. I don't know how to feel or what to do.

I tip my head back against the wall, closing my eyes and pressing my fingers against my temples in an attempt to alleviate the pounding there.

"Do you want me to stay here or do you need a minute to yourself?"

I want him here as much as I want to be alone. It doesn't make sense, so I tell him, "A minute, please."

"Of course." He stands, and I open my eyes to watch him walk toward the door. "Kade mentioned something about a meeting with his sister. I'll go speak with him, and you can join us when you're ready." He gives me one last look, his expression filled with something I can't quite decipher. It's as if he wants to say something more. Instead, he turns and leaves the room, the door clicking shut softly behind him.

I stay on the floor, leaning against the wall and sipping from the glass of water. My head still hasn't stopped spinning, and the more I think about everything that's about to happen, the worse it gets.

I thought being kidnapped and held captive by four vampires would be the most messed up thing to ever happen in my lifetime.

How unbelievably wrong I was.

THIRTEEN

We spend one more night at the shitty little safe house before hitting the road Friday morning.

No one is in a particularly good mood, and nothing—not even strong coffee and sugary breakfast pastries—is going to help. Between the outcome of the summit and the tension over this meeting with my sister, we're all on edge. That, and I know Calla is worried sick about her human bestie. In hindsight, it might've been better for her to have stayed with us if Atlas is going to waste energy trying to protect her from the attack.

We ride in silence for over an hour. Atlas and Gabriel are up front, with Lex and me in the middle, and Calla is passed out in the very back. It doesn't surprise me. I'd been up several times through the night and could hear her tossing and turning. She wanted to be alone, and none of us pushed it.

I glance at the GPS, my stomach getting queasy as we move closer to our destination. I want to believe I'm not nervous about this meeting, but if it goes anything like the last one...

Nope. Not going there. This time will be different. Everything is on *my* terms. I'm going to get the answers I need to stop my thoughts from spiraling trying to figure out what the hell happened to my sister after she disappeared.

Meredith agreed to meet at a location of my choosing, so Gabriel found a place between the safe house and where we're headed, which apparently is a small town in Connecticut. It's not permanent, but until the hunters are dealt with, we can't return to our home in Washington.

Calla stirs in the back seat, blinking her eyes open and yawning. My dick twitches in response, and I find I have the urge to reach for her. It's a constant desire, really.

Lex glances up from his phone, having heard her wake, and turns to look at her over his shoulder. "Good morning, sleepyhead." He shoots her a wink, to which she responds by covering her face with her arm. Cute.

I reach to the back seat and run my fingers up her arm, circling them around her wrist and prying it away from her face. She grumbles at me, but eventually gives up, opening her eyes.

"Are we there yet?" she mumbles tiredly.

"Almost, angel," Gabriel calls back from the passenger seat. "Just under an hour now."

Hearing that makes my chest tighten, and I grit my teeth. My gaze drops when Calla entwines her fingers through mine.

"You okay?" she whispers, her gaze soft.

I give her hand a squeeze. "You don't need to worry about me."

"But I am worried about you," she says, and her eyes widen slightly, as if she's surprised by her own words.

"Aww, thanks," I tease her, rubbing my thumb over the back of her hand, hanging on tighter when she tries to pull away.

Calla rolls her eyes. "You're so annoying."

"Yeah, but you like me. Admit it."

"I'd rather choke to death on my tongue," she says with a painfully fake smile, tugging on her hand until I let go.

Lex snorts, having turned his attention back to his phone. A quick glance shows me that he's texting back and forth with Marcel about our next safe house to ensure everything is set up for our arrival this afternoon.

Calla's eyes shift between Lex and me. "Can I go back to sleep now?"

"I suppose you could, or I could come back there and we could do something a lot more fun."

She stares at me, trying to keep a straight face, but I don't miss the leap in her pulse. I could back off, but instead, I keep pushing.

"Remember the night of the house party? Sitting in the back of this car with Lex and me on either side of you?"

Her cheeks flush a lovely shade of pink and her refusal to answer only spurs me on.

"No?" My eyes flick between hers, and I unbuckle my seat belt. "Shall we remind you?"

Calla scrambles upright and shoots me a glare. "I remember perfectly." She swallows hard and tucks her legs onto the seat.

Lex pouts without turning back to her. "So no reminder then?"

"You've been staring at your phone this whole time," she says, "I figured you were looking at porn for your spank bank. I don't think you need me."

He pockets his phone and undoes his seat belt, moving into the back seat before I can and before Calla can make a sound of protest. "You severely underestimate your own allure," he says in a low voice, capturing her chin between his fingers.

Calla wets her lips, and the sound of her racing heart pounds through the vehicle. "My *allure*?" She laughs softly. "Is that your weird way of saying I'm better than porn?"

"No competition," he answers without hesitation.

"Gee, thanks," she remarks dryly, knocking his hand away from her face. "Now will you let me go back to sleep?"

"I could," he muses, licking his lips as he holds her gaze, "or I could make you come so hard you'll be energized for the rest of the day."

Her mouth drops open for a moment before she realizes and snaps it shut. You'd think she'd be used to hearing things like that by now— at least from Lex.

"I'm good." She turns her attention out the window next to her, and I shoot Lex a smirk. He flips me off and grabs Calla's ankles, pulling them out from under her and across his lap. She immediately tries to get away, which of course only encourages Lex to trap her against the seat. He makes quick work of unbuckling her seat belt and using it to secure her wrists above her head.

"What the fuck," she snaps. "Cut it out, Lex." She tugs on her wrists and tries to kick him in the stomach. "Let me go."

He winks at her, leaning down until his face is a breath away from hers. "If I thought for a second that's what you actually wanted, I might consider it."

Her eyes narrow sharply, flicking toward me for a moment as her chest heaves from the exertion of trying to break free of her bindings. "Are you enjoying this?"

My lips curl into a grin, and I try to ignore the discomfort of the bulge in my pants. Watching her struggle is getting me hard as fuck. "Not nearly as much as you're about to be."

She stills against the seat and looks back at Lex but says nothing. She has apparently reserved herself to silence.

"What, are we playing the quiet game now?" I ask.

Lex chuckles. "Not for long." He captures Calla's chin, holding her gaze. "Tell me what you want."

Calla stiffens for a brief moment as Lex's glamour slams into her, then visibly relaxes. "I..." The word hisses through her teeth as she tries to fight his glamour.

"Go on," he murmurs, and a quick glance at his crotch shows me how much this is turning him on as well.

Gabriel and Atlas remain silent up front, choosing instead to turn up the music and ignore the three of us.

Her expression is vacant as she stares into his eyes. "I want... you to..." She swallows hard. "Get the fuck off me and quit acting like a damn caveman."

His shocked expression mirrors mine. He pulls back, letting go of her chin, and shakes his head.

My eyes shift between the two. "Did she just—"

"I think so," Lex says without taking his eyes off her.

"I resisted glamour," Calla says, pressing her lips together to hide a smile. She's proud of herself, and I can't really blame her.

"How?" Lex asks, his brows pinching closer.

Calla tugs on her wrists, shooting him a look. "How the hell should I know?" Her legs are still draped over his lap, but she manages to sit up.

"Are you guys listening to this?" I say, looking toward the front of the car.

Atlas's grip on the wheel tightens, and he exchanges a look with Gabriel. "Perhaps the back seat of a moving vehicle isn't the optimal place to explore this," he offers in a tight voice.

"Try it again," Calla says, and my head whips toward her, though she's still looking at Lex.

"Really?" he asks.

She nods. "I want to see if I can do it again."

The corner of his mouth kicks up as he makes the connection once more. "Tell me the truth," he says in a smooth voice, sliding his hand up her leg. "If I was to slide my hand into your panties right now, how wet would I find you?"

Her jaw clenches and her brows knit in concentration as she actively attempts to fight his glamour. "I'm…" She clears her throat, and her hands curl into fists where they're still bound in the seat belt above her head.

"Tell me," Lex pushes.

A shudder runs through her and she grits her teeth as her cheeks flush, whispering, "I'm soaked."

Lex breaks the connection, his hand wrapped around her thigh. "Good effort." He shoots her a wink.

She rolls her eyes. "Whatever. Can you untie me now?"

"Say please, and I'll consider it." His hand slides higher, and her breath hitches, her gaze dropping to where Lex's fingers inch closer to the apex of her thighs.

"Go to hell," she mutters instead.

He shrugs. "Don't think for a second I won't drag you there with me."

She manages to twist her wrists enough to get one free, but I reach back and catch it before she can take a swing at Lex.

"Ah, ah, ah. Hitting isn't nice," I tell her.

She huffs out a breath, then clamps her mouth shut when Lex cups her through her pants. His thumb presses down, and she bites her lip, staring at the roof of the vehicle.

"Are you going to be a good girl and let me make you come?"

Her eyes snap to his, and she opens her mouth but no words come out. Her pulse is pounding beneath her flushed skin, and I can smell her sweet arousal as clearly as I bet Lex can.

He tilts his head to the side, watching her for a few seconds before he says, "I'm going to take your silence as a resounding yes." He wastes no time sliding his hand into her pants, and I keep my eyes on her face. Her eyes widen slightly, and she bites her lip so hard I'm waiting for her to bleed.

"Let go," I tell her, my thumb brushing over the pounding pulse at her wrist. "Give yourself over to the pleasure."

She sucks in a sharp breath as Lex pushes his fingers inside her. Twisting her wrist in my grasp, she grabs a hold of me, digging her fingers into my arm. "Fuck," she breathes, her chest rising and falling fast as she opens her legs wider.

"Good girl," Lex says in a voice thick with arousal. "Lift your hips for me."

She complies, and he tugs her leggings and panties halfway to her knees. His thumb presses against her clit as he pumps his fingers in and out of her pussy, filling the car with the smell of her. It makes my gums and my dick throb with the desire to fuck and feed from her.

Lex pulls his fingers out and sticks them in his mouth, sucking them clean before lowering his head between her legs. Calla's grip on my arm tightens when Lex drags his tongue along her slit before swirling it around her clit.

Fucking hell, my dick is rock hard at this point.

Calla lets go of my arm, and I slip into the back seat, guiding her onto her back with my legs spread open on either side of her. It's a bit of a tight squeeze, but Lex hauls her closer to him, making it work. I hiss out a sharp breath when she reaches over her head and palms the front of my pants. She's playing with fire if she thinks she can tease me without following through.

I cover her hand with mine, pressing down harder, and groan. I make quick work of popping the button on my pants and unzipping them before pulling my cock out. Her fingers wrap around it immediately, moving at the perfect rhythm. I desperately want to bury myself between her thighs, but the back seat of Atlas's car isn't exactly conducive to that. Besides, Lex is taking care of that quite well at the moment.

Calla moves her thumb over the head of my cock, using the moisture beading there to glide smoothly up and down my shaft as Lex devours her pussy with his tongue. Her speed picks up as Lex's movements quicken, and pressure builds in my balls as she continues to pump. Her gaze is glued to where Lex is positioned between her legs, and she moans softly, her cheeks bright pink.

"Don't stop," I tell her in a gravelly voice, and her grip tightens a little, making a deep growl tear from my throat and my fangs extend. *Fuck.* I'm going to come any second, and Calla looks to be just as close, her breaths coming in short pants as her heart pounds loudly. "Make her come," I order Lex, fighting the urge to sink my fangs into Calla.

She sucks in a sharp breath, her fingers stilling around my shaft for a few seconds as the sounds of her unbridled moans fill the car. Her fingers start moving again, pumping my cock harder and faster as she comes around Lex's tongue. He stays between her legs, lapping up her release as if it's his last meal on this earth, and I grunt, my muscles tensing as my orgasm whips through me and I come. My release coats Calla's hand and thick ropes trail up the length of her arm.

It takes me a minute to catch my breath and tuck myself back into my pants.

Gabriel offers a handkerchief from the front—because of course Gabriel has a handkerchief—and I clean myself off Calla's skin, while Lex tugs her leggings back up, making sure her dagger is secure, and presses a kiss to her cheek.

"Thanks for the road trip snack," he tells her with a wink.

She groans. "You are so annoying."

"You didn't seem to think so a minute ago." He lowers his voice. "Don't worry. You can get me back later tonight."

She chokes on a laugh. "Don't count on it."

He pouts. "You're so mean to me."

"If you three are done," Atlas calls from the driver's seat, "we'll be arriving in about twenty minutes."

My stomach sinks as panic starts to claw at my chest. I enjoyed the distraction for a little while, but the reality of what we're about to do is settling in again.

"Hey." Calla's soft voice catches my attention, and I meet her gaze. Her eyes flick between mine, and she nods. "Everything is going to be okay."

I force a smile, more grateful for her at this moment than she could possibly understand. I just hope to hell she's right.

The address we sent Meredith to meet us at is an old brewery one of Marcel's contacts owns. It was shut down years ago and is pretty much in the middle of nowhere. We have to drive on a gravel road for the last ten minutes of the trip to reach it, which thrills Atlas to no end; he's always been protective of his car.

My leg bounces as we pull up outside the tall factory building, and Atlas kills the engine.

"You ready, brother?" Lex asks, slapping a hand on my shoulder.

"Not in the slightest," I grumble, turning around in my seat. "Let's get this over with."

The five of us get out of the Escalade, and Atlas steps in front of Calla, blocking her path.

"What is your problem?" she says, crossing her arms as she looks up at him.

"You're staying here."

"The hell I am," she shoots back.

"You'd like to test me?" he asks in a mild tone.

She doesn't back down even when he steps closer, towering over her. "Considering you're being ridiculous, yeah."

Gabriel sighs. "Come on. We're wasting time standing out here."

"Agreed," Atlas says without looking away from Calla. "Get back in the car."

"Fuck off." She moves to step around him, but he grabs her arm and drags her backward. "Atlas!" His name comes out as more of a growl as she attempts to dig her heels into the gravel.

"If we're trying *not* to attract attention, perhaps we should move this inside?" Lex offers, looking rather bored of the whole thing, though I don't miss the way his jaw is clenched or the way his eyes dart around, surveying the area.

Atlas curses under his breath and releases her, turning and prowling toward the building. The rest of us follow him, and Calla shoots daggers at the back of his head. He breaks the deadbolt and unchains the heavy metal door, swinging it open with a loud creak, and we file inside.

The interior of the brewery is dark and cold. Several of the window panes have been smashed out and no doubt the electricity hasn't worked for years. Our steps echo off the concrete floors as we walk around stacks of empty kegs. The scent of yeast and sulfur lingers in the air, so faint I'd guess that Calla can't smell it, but it tickles my nose.

Every tiny sound catches my attention, and my gaze whips around the space. I can't remember a time I've been so on edge. Perhaps when I first turned...

The door creaks open again, and we all turn at the same time.

Daylight streams into the darkness, and Meredith's form is a silhouette in the doorway as she steps inside, letting the door close behind her.

My heart rattles in my chest as she walks closer, and Atlas steps forward. We didn't discuss exactly how we'd handle this meeting, and I didn't tell my sister I wasn't coming alone, though she should have expected as much.

Her silver eyes run the line of us, widening slightly as she takes in the fact she is severely outnumbered. Not to mention, Atlas's reputation precedes him in the vampire community. If I didn't know him, didn't care for him as if he'd been the one to turn me, I'd be scared shitless of the guy.

She steps back, pressing her lips together as the color drains from her face. "Kade," she says in a low voice. "I... I thought we were meeting, um, alone."

"Not a chance," Lex says before I can offer an answer.

Meredith frowns, glancing down and making her black, shoulder-length hair fall forward. She reaches up and tucks it behind her ear. "Right. I guess that's fair."

"Considering you stabbed me last time, I'd say so." I have so much I want to say, to ask, but I can't make the words form. I shake my head. "Why are we meeting, Mer?"

Her eyes move from me to the others and back. "Can we talk somewhere a little more—"

"Nope," Lex cuts in. "Whatever you need to say to your brother, say it now, or you can walk right back through that door."

She blinks quickly. It's almost as if... *Is she going to cry?*

I fight the urge to step forward, to comfort her even after all this time. Even after she ambushed us with the hunters. Because she's still my sister.

Meredith clears her throat, walking closer to our group, stopping once she's a mere few feet away. "Kade," she starts in a low voice. "I... I know you deserve an explanation."

I find myself nodding. "What the hell happened to you, Mer?"

"That is sort of a long story." She takes a deep breath, tugging the lapels of her denim jacket tighter around her narrow frame. "The night I disappeared, the party I was at was attacked by a group of vampires. Everyone was killed. I should have died that night, but..." Her voice trails off, and she kicks at the concrete floor with a booted foot. "I caught the eye of the vampire leading the group. He was impressed that I was still breathing after having my throat nearly ripped out. So he saved me, fed me his blood, and took me with them. For months, he used me as his personal feeder, until one day... he fed me his blood and then snapped my neck. I was asleep for days, and when I woke, my throat was on fire. I had this unquenchable thirst and I... I was so scared. I quickly realized that I'd been turned into the very monster that had stolen my life."

I'm clenching my jaw so hard, my gums are throbbing and tension is building in my temples. My hands curl into fists, and I shove them into my jeans.

"It took me almost a decade to get a handle on my bloodlust." Her gaze drops to the floor, and she sighs. "I killed a lot of people figuring it out."

"What about the vampire who turned you?" Gabriel asks.

Meredith shrugs. "What about him? Once I woke and found out what he did to me, I fled. I didn't want to be part of the group of monsters that found entertainment in slaughtering random college students just trying to have a good time on a Friday night."

"Fine," Lex chimes in. "You became a vampire, struggled to adjust, and then joined forces with the very people who wish to eradicate our kind?"

Her eyes hold mine despite Lex's words. "I allied with the hunters to protect myself."

I frown at her. "Protecting yourself from the hunters?" If Selene had done it, maybe we need to consider that other vampires have as well.

She hesitates, then shakes her head. "From my sire. Turns out he didn't take too kindly to me running from him. He tried to track me down a few times, but I'd made friends among the hunters. They took care of him for me."

Anger pulls at me, and a muscle ticks in my jaw. "Did you know when I became a vampire?"

Meredith presses her lips together before nodding. "Of course. I kept tabs on my family. I witnessed the devastation our parents experienced when I went missing, when they never found me." She blinks quickly, her eyes glassy. "I was there the day the three of you buried my empty casket."

"We looked for you," I say, my voice uneven. "Months went by, and the police were no help whatsoever. I didn't want to give up, but they... Our parents needed closure, Mer. *I* needed closure. We were looking for someone we were never going to find." Recalling that time makes my head spin and my stomach churn, especially now knowing what really happened to my sister.

She nods. "But you didn't know that back then. I was still out there."

"So why didn't you return home?" Atlas speaks up.

Her eyes snap to him. "I couldn't. It wasn't safe. Even once I'd gotten a grip on my hunger and the urge to tear into the throats of everyone I passed on the street, my sire was still out there." Meredith turns her gaze back to me. "If I went home to my family, I would be putting them all at risk. He'd come after me and hunt you all just to get back at me for leaving him. And after the hunters killed him, I thought about going home to be with my family, but I... I couldn't do it."

Gabriel exhales softly, and I don't have to turn my gaze toward him to know there's a look of sympathy on his face.

"So you just let us believe you were dead?" I snap before I can stop myself.

Her gaze hardens. "After everyone gave up on finding me, yes I did, brother. And I was angry, so fucking livid. I could forgive Mom and Dad. They were weak and broken before I disappeared. But you..." Her chin quivers. "You just let them give up on me. *You* gave up on me."

I swallow the lump of emotion in my throat and force out, "Is that why you stabbed me?"

She exhales a humorless laugh. "Perhaps. That blond vampire, Selene, told the hunters about you lot. I knew I had to see you before they wiped you out, so I volunteered to lead the ambush. I was meant to kill you to distract the others so that when the hunters attacked, they'd be successful in killing you all."

A growl rumbles through Lex's chest, and he starts to move forward until Atlas grabs him, pulling him back without a word.

Meredith clasps her hands together, sniffling. "I couldn't do it. I knew the moment I saw you, I wouldn't be able to go through with it."

"But you still stabbed me."

She nods. "I was still angry."

A laugh escapes my lips. "And now?"

"I've had time to process everything with a clearer head and I..." She looks away, lowering her voice. "I want to know my little brother."

My chest fills with pressure and my throat feels as if it's closing in. My heartbeat kicks up and my eyes search hers, looking for any hint of dishonesty. There's nothing in her gaze but fear and longing. I believe she's telling the truth, and I want to know her too.

"What about the hunters?" Lex demands. "You think you can just walk away from them?"

She spares him a glance. "I've gotten pretty good at running." She looks back at me and steps closer. "What do you think? Can we forgive one another and be part of each other's lives? Eternity is a long time to live without family."

"He *has* a family," Calla snaps, speaking up for the first time.

Meredith's eyes go to her, and she offers a faint smile. "You're human."

Calla crosses her arms over her chest, standing taller. "Do you have a point or do you just like stating the obvious?"

Lex snorts and Gabriel rests a hand on Calla's shoulder.

Meredith blinks in surprise. "She's a bit mouthy, isn't she?"

"A bit," Lex echoes with a laugh, and Calla shoots him a glare.

Meredith focuses on me again. "What do you say, baby bro? Will you give us a chance to get to know each other again?"

I blow out a breath, nerves swirling in my stomach like a wicked hurricane. I haven't felt so entirely out of my element in decades. "Yeah," I finally say after several beats of heavy silence. "I'd like that."

Between one moment and then next, Meredith closes the remaining distance between us and wraps her arms around me. I stiffen in response, and it takes a few long moments before I relax enough to hug her back. There's a new kind of pressure in my chest, and I think it might be hope.

Then the brewery doors fly open, breaking off their hinges, and hunters flood the room.

Betrayal whips through me as everything moves in slow motion. Lex grabs Calla, shoving her toward Gabriel before storming forward with Atlas, fangs bared. Gabriel catches Calla easily and moves her behind him, putting himself between her and the mob of angry humans.

The sound of daggers being unsheathed rings in my ears as I look toward my sister. My stomach plummets when I catch the look of shock and horror on her face. She wasn't expecting us to be ambushed, which means... she didn't betray me this time.

No time to think about that now. I reach for her, wrapping my fingers around her wrist and pulling her toward me within seconds of her ending up with a dagger in her chest.

Three hunters close in on us, and Meredith growls at the curvy blond one. "What are you doing?" she hisses despite it being painfully obvious. They're here to wipe us out and they used my sister to track us down.

Blondie doesn't answer her. Instead, she swipes the air in front of her with her dagger, making us move backward.

Several more hunters spill into the room, bringing the total to at least a dozen. My eyes shift between them, then move to where Atlas is tearing into the throat of a middle-aged hunter. His blood sprays across the concrete floor, and Atlas tosses his lifeless body aside, moving onto the next target.

"Kade." Meredith's voice shakes, and I snap my attention back to the small group of hunters attempting to back us into a corner. *I think the fuck not.*

"Get behind me," I bark at her, my fangs slicing through my gums.

"No way," she snaps back, baring her own fangs at me.

"Fine," I say through my teeth, "then get ready to fight."

Before I can move, she snarls and launches herself forward, grabbing the blond hunter by her hair, yanking her head back and sinking her fangs into the woman's throat. She cries out in pain, and the other two hunters descend. Not quick enough. I move in a blur, grabbing both of them by their throats, then slam their heads together, effectively knocking them out cold.

Meredith drops the hunter to the floor near the others, and she moans, her eyelids fluttering as she struggles to stay conscious.

We immediately jump into the thick of the fight, where Lex is facing off with a hunter whose arms have to be even thicker than mine, which is saying something. He's managed to get a few good hits in; Lex has blood leaking from a gash over his eye and rolling down his chin.

"Kade, behind you!" Calla's voice slices through the sounds of fighting, high-pitched and filled with panic. *What the fuck is she still doing here?*

I whirl around just in time to block the dagger that was headed for my heart. Meredith snarls and kicks the hunter's legs out from under him. She doesn't hesitate—between one second and the next, she snaps his neck, dropping his body carelessly and stepping over it.

I find myself shaking my head, wanting to close my eyes and erase the picture of my sister slaughtering these people despite their intentions for us. Seeing my sister as the same monster that looks back at me in the mirror has my blood running cold and my heart cracking in my chest. I don't want this life for her. But it's too late.

Another swarm of hunters marches inside, and Atlas and Lex tear their way through them, only experiencing minor injuries. Nothing a little blood won't heal in a matter of minutes.

Gabriel hangs back, guarding Calla, while Meredith and I charge forward to back up the others. The smell of human blood is overwhelming. We're all covered in it. The monster that lives inside me revels in this chaos. My lips twist into a dark grin as I grab another hunter, a pretty brunette one. Her eyes widen, but she doesn't have a chance to beg for mercy before I rip through her windpipe and shove her toward another oncoming hunter. He's younger, probably seventeen or eighteen, and his eyes are as wide as saucers when he catches the still body of his fallen comrade.

Two hunters move around him, charging toward me. I slide out of the way, and when I turn to take them on, I freeze. They managed to grab hold of Meredith. My world narrows on them, on the dagger they have poised over her heart.

"Let her go, and I'll end your pathetic life quickly," I say slowly in a low voice, a muscle ticking in my jaw.

The hunter shrugs as if he doesn't care either way and drops his arm with the dagger as the guy on her other side rolls his eyes.

Meredith frowns briefly and takes a step forward. Her entire body goes rigid, and panic floods through me. It's swiftly replaced by white-hot pain and fury when a third hunter attacks from behind, shoving his dagger through her back until it protrudes from her chest. He yanks it out, replacing it with his hand. Meredith shrieks in agony... until the sound is cut off as the hunter pulls back with her blood-covered heart in his hand.

The sounds of battle behind me fade as I watch my sister fall to her knees, her face turning gray as the life leaves her eyes. And then her heart hits the floor with a sickening *thump*.

I see red. I give myself over to the monster wholly, letting it control me as I black out with rage and tear through the rest of the hunters.

At some point, Atlas pulls me back, and I stumble, unable to fight any more. It takes me a few seconds to refocus, and I frown at the figure stepping through the open doorway.

Calla sucks in a sharp breath, her hand wrapped around Gabriel's arm and her pulse pounding like a jackhammer.

"Well, this is quite disappointing," Scott Ellis says, rubbing a hand along his neatly trimmed beard. He's dressed in the same all-black uniform as the rest of the hunters, but he makes no move to join in on the fight.

At least half a dozen more hunters filter in behind him, poised with daggers and ready to fight.

Fucking hell, it never ends.

Atlas steps forward, intentionally blocking Calla from view, and wipes the blood from his mouth. "My sentiments exactly."

Scott frowns, his eyes moving past Atlas and filling with confusion. "Calla?" Anger flares to life in his gaze as he looks at each of us. "What are you doing with her?" he growls.

"Nothing she doesn't enjoy," Lex says with a smirk.

"Lex," Atlas snaps. The *this isn't the time* is unspoken, but it's certainly clear in his tone.

Scott ignores them both, focusing on Calla. "It's going to be okay. I'll get you out of here and away from these monsters."

The hunters flanking him charge forward, and I prepare myself to rip these motherfuckers to shreds. But I don't get the chance. Gabriel appears in front of the rest of us and goes absolutely ballistic.

I've known Gabriel for over a century, and never in that time have I seen him like this. He slaughters the hunters in a matter of seconds. Blood and organs paint the dirty floor, and the hunters' fearless leader runs out the door while the rest of us are enamored by Gabriel's equally graceful and lethal attack.

"Fuck," Lex snaps. "More are coming. We have to get the hell out of here."

Leave. We need to leave.

This place is filled with the bodies of almost two dozen hunters.

And my sister.

I can't tear my eyes away from her. The image is burned into my mind for the rest of my immortal life.

Lex's voice sounds far away when he says, "We need to leave *now*. Before the rest of the bastards show up."

"I'll deal with Scott and grab the car. Meet me around the back of the building," Atlas says in a voice that is dangerously calm, then quickly disappears through the doorway outside.

Calla appears in front of me and reaches for my face. "Kade," her voice is soft, so soft I want to close my eyes and wrap myself in it. To forget every other fucking thing and just exist with her in a world where I didn't just watch my sister get her heart ripped out.

"Let's go, brother," Gabriel says.

Between him, Lex, and Calla, they manage to drag me away from the piles of bodies.

Everything from that moment until we're speeding down the interstate is a blur. I stare out the window from the back seat, barely feeling Calla's fingers slide through mine. She squeezes, and I'm not sure if she's trying to get my attention, but I can't bring myself to look at her.

Losing my sister the first time just about ruined me. I can't fathom how I'll survive it a second time.

FOURTEEN

CALLA

My heart hurts for Kade. For everything he's been through and the sister he lost after coming so close to getting her back. She was ripped away, and there wasn't a thing he could do to stop it.

As I stare at him, the desire to take away his pain—to bring it on myself even—is jarring. It's something I wasn't expecting and am not sure what to do with. It buries itself deep in my chest, digging its claws in until I force myself to look away from Kade.

By the time we reach Monroe, Connecticut, we've driven through the darkest part of the night.

Atlas, as usual, is behind the wheel. Kade is next to him in the passenger seat, staring blankly out the windshield as the headlights illuminate the road in front of us. There are no other vehicles around us, making the atmosphere eerie, especially paired with the layer of misty fog we're traveling through.

Lex is passed out across the seat behind Gabriel and me, snoring softly. Under different circumstances, it would be cute. But here we are running for our lives—again.

And now Brighton's dad knows I'm involved with the vampires, which really isn't something we need. I can't be sure what he'll do. Will he bring it up to Brighton with the expectation that I told her about the vampires? Should I text her? If Scott wasn't monitoring her phone before, I'd bet good money he is now.

I try to close my eyes and get some rest, but it's useless. My stomach is so twisted in knots, and despite the fact I didn't participate in the fight at the brewery, I still somehow ended up covered in blood. We all are, and it's all I can smell. Atlas's poor car is going to need to be deep cleaned at this point.

The sun is just starting to rise when we pass the town sign welcoming us to Monroe.

"It's a quiet place to lay low for a while," Gabriel says in a soft voice.

When I turn toward him, he's already looking at me. "Right. How many vampires are in this town?"

"Four," Atlas says from up front, turning down a residential street where the streetlights are flickering, stuck in that period between night and day.

Four?

Oh.

These guys are the only vampires in town.

"Is that safe?" I watch out my window as we pass by gorgeous houses, both uniform yet slightly unique, with perfectly manicured lawns on both sides of the street. "I mean, a small town filled with only humans... Won't that attract attention we're not looking for?"

"It's okay," Gabriel assures me. "Marcel set us up with a rental property in a neighborhood with mostly young professionals. We shouldn't stick out, and—"

"And hopefully, we won't be here long enough for it to be a problem."

My eyes shift from Gabriel to the back of Atlas's head. "Okay." I don't have much of a choice but to trust them. "What about blood? Does Marcel have a contact at the local blood bank or something?"

Gabriel offers me a faint smile.

"Of course he does," I say under my breath.

Atlas slows as we reach the end of the street, which I'm realizing now is a cul-de-sac, and pulls into a circular driveway, stopping the car outside a stunning colonial home.

Gabriel reaches behind us and shakes Lex awake as the others get out of the front. I climb out of the back with the intention of grabbing Kade's hand, but he's already halfway up the porch steps when my feet hit the paved driveway. I frown as he reaches under a mat on the porch and pulls out a key, opening the front door and disappearing inside.

"He needs some time."

I jump at the sound of Atlas's voice at my ear, then turn my head to look at him. "I want to help. He doesn't deserve to be in this pain."

Atlas's tired eyes flick between mine and he nods in understanding. He reaches for me, placing his hand at the middle of my back, and guides me toward the house.

The floors and doors are dark wood and the walls are a pristine white. It feels classic and elegant and definitely not a place five people in bloodstained clothing should be occupying.

"We need to wash our clothes," I announce around a yawn and tug my shirt off over my head.

"I see a very kinky game of strip poker in our future," Lex says with a grin as his eyes drop to my chest.

I cover myself up and roll my eyes. "It's like seven in the morning. Can you chill?"

The guys strip to their boxers, leaving their shoes on the porch. I do the same and step out of my pants, collecting everything and wandering through the house until I find the laundry room at the back of it. Once our clothes are in the washing machine, I wander back toward the front and find the others in what appears to be a formal living room with stiff furniture and a massive white brick fireplace but no TV.

"Home sweet home," I mutter, dropping onto the floral patterned couch next to Gabriel. It feels all kinds of wrong to be sitting around nearly naked with three sexy as hell men in an unfamiliar house.

"Not for long," Lex says in a low voice. "Once the hunters are wiped out, we can return to our actual home." I find myself missing the mansion. At first, I hated the place. It was my gilded cage. But at some point—and I'm not sure when exactly—it became more than that. Nowhere has truly felt like *home* to me—certainly not the city I grew up in—but it could have. Maybe it still could.

"Let's not get ahead of ourselves," Gabriel says.

I open my mouth to question what's going to happen next when my phone chimes from where I left it in the laundry room. With a sigh, I get up and retrieve it. My pulse jumps when I see Brighton's name on the screen. I snatch up my phone and read her message, holding my breath the whole time.

Do you have any idea why my dad is asking a million questions about you and how we met, when we met, where we met? He's being super freaking weird, Cal.

I lean against the washing machine, chewing my bottom lip as I try to come up with a response that isn't going to make her freak out more.

What did you tell him? I type back.

Not much. The truth, which he already knew. That we met at school in freshman year.

Before I can type out a reply, another message comes through.

Something is going on, I can feel it. He's sending me and my mom on a vacation out of nowhere and he's not coming with us. It doesn't make sense. He doesn't know that I know about the vampires...

I blow out a heavy breath and craft a response that details what went down at the brewery and what the old vampires have planned for the hunters. I don't disclose our location, but I tell her we're hiding out until the attack the vampires have planned. I also add that she can't tell her dad any of this, though it seems as if he already knows about the looming attack.

My head is going to explode.

I exhale a short, humorless laugh at her message. As much as I hate that Brighton is now somewhat involved in this crazy mess, I'm glad to be able to talk to my best friend about it. But it also means I have to live with the fear that she's going to end up hurt because of it—because of me.

Same here. But seriously, you and your mom should go. Things are going to get ugly fast, and you shouldn't be around for it.

If Scott somehow got tipped off that the vampires are planning an attack in a couple of days, we could have a problem. Well, the vampires could. This really isn't my fight, though I'm forced to watch the outcome either way.

We're going, don't worry. Are you sure you're safe?

No. I'll probably never be *safe* as long as I live in a world with vampires.

Yes, I write back.

Good, she replies. A moment later, another message comes through. *I'm going to lose my dad, aren't I?"*

Her words feel like a punch to my gut, and I blink back the tears that prick my eyes. How am I supposed to answer that? She already knows the answer, but I think she needs someone else to tell her. To confirm her fears.

I don't know for sure, but there's a very good chance, yes.

Brighton's reply doesn't come until five minutes later. My chest feels tight until the phone buzzes in my hand, and then my stomach sinks.

I appreciate your honesty. Something's going down here. I'll text you later.

My fingers hover over the screen as if I'm going to type a response, but nothing comes. I guess there's not much else to say at this point.

I walk out of the laundry room, stopping outside of the main floor bathroom, and find a linen closet. I reach up on my tiptoes, grabbing a black fleece blanket and wrapping it around myself before returning to the living room where Atlas is starting a fire in the fireplace.

"Brighton's father knows something," I say as I walk back to the couch. Within seconds, I have three sets of silver eyes staring at me expectantly. "He's sending Brighton and her mom away."

A muscle feathers along Atlas's jaw, and he grabs his phone off the mantle, lifting it to his ear as he walks out of the room.

I frown, turning toward Gabriel. "Do you think Scott knows about the plan for attack?"

He reaches toward me, resting his hand on my knee over the blanket. "It could mean that or any number of other things. Seeing you shocked him and could very well be why he's sending them away. If he thinks you're tied to us, he could be acting proactively to protect his family."

I glance from where his hand rests on my knee to his face. "From me?" I ask, my brows pinching together.

"I don't know, angel, but we're going to figure it out."

"Isn't your bestie not being around when the vamps attack her daddy a good thing?" Lex asks, lounging sideways in the wingback chair next to the fireplace. He stares at the flames, drumming his fingers on his bare thighs.

"That's not the point," I tell him. I may not agree with what Scott is doing, but Brighton doesn't deserve to lose her dad.

He only shrugs in response, and I'm reminded once again that the vampires I'm bound to couldn't care less about Brighton. They're only concerned about the threat posed by her family and the rest of the hunters. I've never felt so stuck in the middle before, concerned both for my best friend and the vampires I've come to care for over the last month and a half of being with them.

I can't just sit in this room that reminds me of a fucking museum and stare at the wall, so I get off the couch, deciding to explore this place we'll be staying in until we can go back to Washington.

The entire place is elegant but old fashioned. With crown molding and oil paintings on the walls. It's kind of creepy, like a dollhouse... until I wander downstairs to the basement. I'm expecting concrete floors and total darkness, so imagine my surprise when I find a theater room with plush black recliners and a giant projector screen built into the wall.

Okay, this totally makes up for the lack of TV in the living room upstairs.

I step into the room and find the remote, turning on the screen and finding it hooked up to some sort of system that has every streaming service imaginable. If I had to guess, we probably have Marcel to thank for this. I haven't met the guy yet, but he seems to work magic to help the guys—and me too, I suppose.

I flip through the different streaming services and find a serial killer documentary that I haven't seen yet. I've been a little too preoccupied to keep up with new true crime releases. Turning it on, I flop into the middle recliner in the front row, snuggling in with my blanket and using the remote to turn the lights down.

The show is about a half hour in when Lex's voice startles me.

"What in the fucking hell? Have I entered an alternate reality?"

I chuckle, pausing the documentary and turning to find him standing in the doorway, stunned as I was upon finding this room. "Right?"

His eyes flick to the screen, and he arches a brow. "What are you watching?"

Pressing my lips together, I hesitate before saying, "Uh, it's a true crime documentary."

Amusement fills his features, and he walks into the room, dropping into the seat next to mine. "I knew you were dark like me," he says, shooting me a wink.

I roll my eyes. "You can only stay if you're not going to talk through the whole thing."

Lex presses his hand to his chest, his expression now serious. "You have my word."

"Yeah, okay," I remark dryly, turning my attention back to the screen.

"You going to share that blanket? My clothes are still in the dryer."

"Do you want to share my chair too?" Sarcasm drips from my tone, and Lex laughs. Without warning, he stands and scoops me up before sitting back in my spot—with me in his lap.

"You're right. This is definitely much better." He's grinning down at me, his breath soft against my forehead.

Heat fills my face as his lower half presses into me, and I shake my head, hoping my hair will hide the blush in my cheeks. "I didn't... Never mind." I turn the show back on and slowly relax in Lex's arms.

Halfway through the show, my eyelids start to feel heavy. They flutter as I yawn, and Lex's arms tighten around me. His lips brush the shell of my ear as he says, "We're watching a show where they're describing how this guy brutally slaughtered a bunch of people, and you're all cozy and trying not to fall asleep."

"Hey," I grumble, "don't judge. Serial killer documentaries relax me."

"Of course they do," he says, and I can hear the grin in his voice without looking at his face.

"Whatever. You're sporting a hard-on, so I'm not sure how you get off mocking me."

"I'd be happy to show you how I get off," he says in a low voice, nipping my earlobe.

My pulse leaps, and I immediately regret my choice of words. "Lex..."

"Hmm?" He nuzzles my neck, dragging his mouth across my skin, licking and kissing as my heart kicks up. The only thing between us is the blanket I'm wrapped in and some flimsy undergarments.

"What are you doing?" I ask, my voice a little breathy.

He slides his hands under the blanket, and the cool air makes me shiver before his fingers touch my bare skin, brushing up and down my sides. "Exactly what you want me to," he answers, gliding one hand up to slide under my bra and cup my breast while the other moves slowly, heading for the heat gathering between my thighs.

I pull in a shallow breath, tilting my head back against Lex's shoulder and closing my eyes. The voices from the documentary fade into the background as I lose myself in Lex's touch, letting everything else fall away. His skilled fingers tweak my nipples and massage my breasts, alternating from one side to the other while his other hand hovers at the thin lace of my panties.

My clit throbs with need, and I quickly grow so impatient that I grab his hand and guide it into my panties, moaning softly when his fingers brush my folds.

"You know exactly what you want, don't you?"

I arch my back, pushing my breast into his hand. "Right now, I want you to stop talking."

He chuckles, pinching my nipple so hard a spike of pain flashes through the pleasure filling me. "Then I'm going to need *you* to talk. Tell me exactly what you want, and if you're a good girl for me, maybe I'll let you come."

Boldness grips me—I have no idea from where—and I say, "I want you to do whatever you want to me. To take complete control even when I try to fight you. *Show* me what I want." I'm tired of having to say what I want. For once, I want to be told. Because fuck, I need to not have to think for a while.

Lust flares in his liquid silver gaze as he settles me in between his legs. There's something else there too. Something that steals the breath from my lungs. *Hunger.*

"You want me to fuck you into submission?" he taunts in a low voice, running his middle finger along my slit. "I am more than happy to oblige."

Everything in me tightens and my entire body flushes with heat. I'm suddenly too warm in the blanket, and my heart is pounding in my chest.

"You like the sound of that, don't you?" He dips his finger inside easily, gliding through the moisture already gathered there.

"Y-yes," I whisper.

His lips find my neck again, grazing faintly over my pulse. "Open for me."

I spread my legs, making the blanket fall open. The cool air tickles my bare skin, and I suck in a breath when Lex pushes deeper into my pussy, adding another finger and working my clit with his thumb. My hips grind against his fingers, trying to get him even deeper, but he snakes an arm around my waist, holding me still. I struggle against him, trying to feed the friction between my legs, but he stills his fingers inside me.

"Settle down," he murmurs, his lips moving up to brush my ear.

I shiver but keep my mouth shut.

Lex resumes pumping in and out of me, keeping his arm trapped around my waist, and I bite the inside of my cheek when his erection presses into my back. He increases the speed of his thrusts, curling his fingers and hitting my most sensitive spot. I grip the arms of the recliner on either side of us, my breathing coming in short pants as he works me to the brink of orgasm. Pressure builds low in my stomach, my muscles tightening and my pussy clenching around his fingers as he pushes me to climax.

"That's it," Lex says in my ear, "give it to me."

I cry out, gripping his thighs as pleasure spikes through me so intense I can't feel my legs. I come hard on his fingers, and he continues pulsing them inside me, rubbing my pussy walls as I ride the delicious aftershocks of my orgasm.

I squirm in his grasp when he pulls his fingers out, and my stomach clenches when he lifts them to his lips and licks them clean.

"You really are my favorite flavor." He drops his hands to my hips and lifts me easily, turning me in his lap so I'm facing him, straddling his legs. "Now," he says, lifting his hips enough to tug his boxers down, freeing his thick cock, "you're going to take all of me inside you and you're not going to come until I allow it. Understand?"

I swallow hard, my throat suddenly dry. "I... Okay."

Lex offers a dark smirk that makes me lower my gaze away from his. "Good answer." His voice is filled with power and control, making it almost embarrassingly easy to follow his every command. It's exactly what I needed, and it's making me so fucking hot, I couldn't deny it if I wanted to.

Licking my lips I lift myself up as Lex positions the head of his cock at my entrance. I grip his shoulders to keep steady and slowly start to lower myself onto his shaft, letting out a soft moan the deeper he fills me. My pussy stretches to accommodate his size, and I squeeze my eyes shut, focusing on my breathing as I sink the rest of the way onto him.

"Mmm, fuck, you feel so good wrapped around my cock. I can feel you throbbing and tightening around me. You're doing so good."

My previous release makes moving up and down his shaft easier, and I blush at the feel of it leaking down my thighs.

"Again," he orders, capturing my chin with his fingers and bringing my mouth to his. His lips devour mine as I lift up and sink back onto him once more, shivering at how deep he reaches at this angle.

We find a steady rhythm as our lips battle for control, and he pushes his tongue past my lips, flicking it across the roof of my mouth. When his grip on my hips tightens and he starts pushing me down harder on his cock, my pulse jackhammers, and I moan into his mouth. My head spins faster with each thrust, and Lex doesn't ease up at any point. Instead, he lifts his hips, thrusting up into me as I bare down on him. The pressure and friction quickly builds to a near unbearable level, and his lips pull away from my mouth, trailing along my jaw before his fangs graze my neck, teasing the pulse there.

"Lex," I breathe, my heart fighting to break free of my rib cage.

"Stay right there," he says in a thick voice, slamming his hips upward, pushing himself so deep it knocks the air out of me with a shallow gasp. "Don't come yet. I want you on the edge until I'm ready to come inside you."

His words ignite an indescribable pleasure that shoots straight to my core. I throw my head back, moaning without reservation as I continue riding his cock, my breasts bouncing in front of his face.

"I'm so close," I pant, whimpering when Lex reaches between us and strums my clit.

Lex groans. "Not yet." He pulls me against his chest and continues thrusting his hips. His lips find my neck and he sinks his fangs in, drinking deeply as I cry out in a mixture of pleasure and pain. The latter lasts mere seconds before my whole body is flooded with the most euphoric sensation, I can't hold back any longer. He pulls back a moment later, kissing me hard, his lips tasting of copper.

"I'm... *fuck*, I'm going to—"

"Come for me." Lex thrusts hard, his cock throbbing inside me. "*Now*."

I cry out my release as my pussy clenches around him, and he grunts loudly, announcing his own climax as he shoots his release into me.

"Holy shit," I breathe, catching my breath with Lex's cock still buried between my thighs. I feel wickedly energized but lethargic at the same time.

Lex smirks at me. "You are amazing. The feel of you wrapped around my cock... I could fuck you for hours."

I shiver at the thought. "Hmm, well as nice as that sounds, this human could use a bit of recovery time. Maybe a nap and some food."

He leans in and kisses my cheek, chuckling softly. "I suppose we can arrange that." He lifts me off his cock and stands, carrying me toward the staircase as the documentary continues in the background.

FIFTEEN

KADE

I open my eyes to darkness outside the window next to the bed I fell into hours ago. Hunger rips through me like fire in my veins, making me shoot upright and swing my legs over the side of the bed. It takes longer than it should for me to remember where we are. To remember what happened that led us here.

I suddenly wish I was still unconscious.

Getting up, I find my clothes clean and folded at the end of the bed. I put them on and make my way back to the main floor of the house. The sound of steady breathing from the bedrooms upstairs tells me everyone else is asleep, and the clock on the stainless steel stove in the kitchen makes me realize why. It's nearly three in the morning.

With a sigh, I open the fridge, grateful to find that Marcel's blood bank contact came through and stocked us up. I snatch a bag of B-positive and let the door close, then search the cupboards for a glass, which I proceed to fill halfway with blood and the rest of the way with whiskey from a bottle I can say with confidence Gabriel left on the counter.

I sit at the head of the old oak table in the attached dining room overlooking the yard. Thick trees line the area, making it feel more private despite being in a residential neighborhood.

Downing half of my drink, my hand shakes as I return the glass to the table. My chest is filled with pressure I haven't experienced in a very long time, and I struggle to ignore the burn of tears in my eyes. I stare hard out the window, into the darkness, begging it to consume me.

I wince when my fangs slice through my gums and cut into my bottom lip. I wipe the blood away and take another drink.

The hunters will pay for what they did. I don't care what Meredith promised them, or even that she stabbed me. I was given the chance to have a life with my sister—my family—and they took it from me.

I'm so lost in anger, I don't hear anyone approach.

"You're going to break that glass if you hold it any tighter," Calla says in a soft, sleep-filled voice.

Even in the dark, wrapped in a bedsheet, she looks angelic. Perhaps I understand a little more why Gabriel is constantly calling her *angel.*

She steps closer, the moonlight from the window next to me illuminating her features, and I quickly turn away, not wanting her to see my face—my fangs or the tears in my eyes. I take another drink, setting the glass down in a steadier motion this time.

"Hey." Calla walks around the table and stops in front of me. "Don't hide from me." She kneels, placing her hands on my knees. "You said that to me once, remember?"

As if I would forget any moment that involved her, especially considering it didn't involve clothing.

I swallow past the thick, suffocating feeling in my throat and finally meet her gaze. "Of course," I murmur.

Her lips curl into a faint smile. "Good." She lowers her gaze a moment, her lashes fanning her cheeks. "Kade, I don't know what to say or do. I... I want to help you."

I slip a finger under her chin, tilting her head up so I can look at her face again. "I appreciate that."

Her eyes search my face. "I can't imagine the pain you're going through. I've never had a sibling, so I don't understand that kind of bond. Do you want to talk about it?"

"No." My voice is hoarse. What I *want* is to rip into the throats of every hunter on this earth. An unrealistic goal, maybe, but the rage simmering inside me is only growing more intense. The bloodlust searing my veins is like nothing I've experienced before, not even when I first turned. I want them all dead. I want to bathe in their blood and listen to the sweet sound of their terrified screams as I end their lives. Every single fucking one of them.

"Okay," she says, her voice filled with understanding. She stands and grabs the chair closest to her, sitting with her knees brushing mine. "What can I do?"

I try to smile, to show her how much it means that she wants to bring me comfort, even after everything *she's* been through. "Distract me. Let's talk about something else." I don't enjoy daydreaming about mass murder when Calla is looking at me with soft eyes. I want to shield her from the monster inside me.

"Um, okay." She chews her bottom lip before flicking her gaze up to meet mine. "Tell me about how you became a vampire."

I stare at her, my eyes widening. "Are you sure you want to know?"

She tucks her legs onto the chair, sitting cross-legged, and nods. "I know Gabriel was turned by Selene and Lex was turned by Atlas, but I don't know your story and I'd like to."

I've never told anyone the story of how I turned, but I find myself wanting to share with Calla. We know everything about her life; the least I can do is tell her about mine. How I came to be what I am now.

She must take my silence as reluctance to share, because she reaches for my hands and says, "You don't have to tell me, Kade."

I lace my fingers through hers and give her hands a gentle squeeze. "I want to. I'm afraid it's not some dramatic or heartbreaking story, though. You might be disappointed."

Calla arches a brow at me. "Why do you say that?"

"Because," I say, "I became a vampire by accident."

Her eyes widen, and she presses her lips together to try and hide a laugh. "I don't understand." She shakes her head. "How does one *accidentally* become a vampire?"

"As a human, I had a group of friends that happened to be vampires. I suppose the company I kept was a bit of a hazard in itself."

She gives me a knowing look. "Right."

I acknowledge the look with a nod and add, "They didn't make a habit of it or anything, but on occasion they'd feed on me. It was fun. Most of the time we were drunk—they enjoyed the blood and I enjoyed the bite." I meet her gaze. "I know you understand that part." I can see the tinge of pink in her cheeks even in the dim light of the dining room.

"So, what?" she says, freeing her hands from mine and leaning against the back of the chair. "One of them turned you?"

"Not exactly." I pull in a deep breath, let it out, then tap into my memory of my last night as a human.

The club is rowdier than normal tonight. The line wound around the block, though our group walked right through the front door as soon as we arrived. Perks of my friends being able to glamour the doorman.

Will and James head for the bar immediately, while I stick with Sophia and Marianne. They're laughing with their arms draped over each other, murmuring too low for me to hear over the music.

Sweat and booze cling to the air, together with the heavy scent of tobacco. It makes my head swim as the girls start dancing around me, laughing and chatting about the new jewelry they picked up at the market earlier. The guys return a few minutes later, and Will sticks a drink in my hand.

We drink and dance for hours, lost in the lights and the music... until Sophia catches the eye of a man at the bar. He saunters over, trying to get her to dance with him. She's polite at the beginning, smiling and waving him away, but the longer he persists, the more agitated she becomes. She can handle herself, there's no doubt in my mind, but the scene playing out before me makes me think of my sister, of whatever happened the night she disappeared.

My eyes dart around, looking for the others, but I don't see them anywhere. I'm stepping in between Sophia and the drunk man before I can stop myself. I shove him back hard, putting distance between him and Sophia, which only pisses him off. His face is red with anger and maybe some embarrassment as we seem to have attracted a bit of a crowd.

"Back off," I snarl at the burly man.

He barks out a laugh and comes at me, his muddy brown eyes bloodshot. "Take your own advice before I snap you in half, mate." His eyes shift back to Sophia. "No need to worry, gorgeous. I'll take you back to mine and show you a real good time."

His words set off a rage in my chest I've never felt before, and I swing my fist toward his face. My punch snaps his head back as pain flares through my knuckles, and I curse under my breath.

"Kade!" Sophia's voice slices through the music and the crowd.

When the man's group of friends rushes over, flanking him, I have the sense to know I might've made a mistake.

Everything happens so fast. The group of guys closes in on me, slamming their fists into my face, chest, and gut, and at some point, I end up on the grimy tile floor, being kicked in the stomach.

I spit blood out, groaning, which is easily drowned out by the yelling, and before long, someone is hauling me to my feet. My one eye is almost swollen shut already, but I faintly recognize the silver-eyed man practically carrying me through the room, the sounds fading in and out around me.

James kicks the door to the men's room open and shouts at the few guys in there to get out. Once we're alone, he locks the door and sets me on the bench next to it, capturing my chin and tilting my head back to look into my eyes.

"You got yourself into quite the battle."

I groan in response, letting my head fall back against the wall. I feel like a complete idiot. Sophia could have easily dealt with that disgusting man all on her own, but I decided she shouldn't have to.

James pats my cheek, and I wince at the pain that shoots through my face. "Come on." He opens his mouth, his fangs flashing in the light, and sinks them into his wrist before bringing it to my mouth. My lips close around the wound without hesitation, and I swallow a mouthful of his blood, then another, and the pain filling my entire body starts to ebb away. Moments later, it's gone completely. He pulls his arm back, and I reach up to touch my face and find there to be no pain there. I can see clearly from both eyes and my wounds are completely healed.

I shake my head. "I'll never get over that."

James grins at me, offering me a hand up. "Let's get out of here, yeah?"

I can't agree fast enough—I'm very much ready to leave this place.

We slip back into the loud room; everyone is dancing and drinking as if nothing happened, and we move along the edge of the room to a side door, which James pushes open to an alleyway next to the building. I see the others waiting for us at the opening and start toward them with James at my side.

We're about halfway to the street when an angry voice shouts from behind us. Before I can turn, a gunshot cuts through the air. It rings in my ears, vibrating through my skull as fire spreads through my chest. I glance down to find my gray button-up turning red. My head spins, and I reach to touch the redness growing on my shirt. I think I hear Marianne shout my name just before my legs give out and I sink to my knees, falling onto my side as it becomes impossible to breathe. My cheek is pressed against the cold, wet pavement, and my vision blurs with tears as blood spills out of my mouth.

The faces of my friends fade in and out above me.

Will pulls me into his lap and holds my head steady. His voice is muffled when he says, "You're okay. You're going to be fine."

Except, I'm not. I'm dying.

"I gave him my blood, Will," James speaks up.

"I know that," he says in a low voice. "So he's going to be all right."

Sophia meets my gaze. "You can let go, Kade," she says in a soft voice. "We'll be here to help you when you wake." She and Marianne take each of my hands and hold onto me as my eyes close, putting an end to my mortal life.

"You died because you were sticking up for your friend." I reach out and pry the empty glass from his hand before he shatters it, setting it on the table and pulling my chair closer. "You didn't deserve what happened to you, but your death was a noble one, if that makes you feel any better."

Shit, that sounded so lame. I want to take it back until he offers me a faint smile.

"It turned out okay," he says, "but it sucked for a while."

I nod in understanding. "Are you still in contact with those vampires?"

Kade shrugs. "For a while. We grew apart when I met Lex and Atlas, but we do touch base every decade or so. Marianne and Sophia ended up getting married. They live in Italy right now, I believe. James prides himself on being an eternal bachelor. He travels a lot, so I'm not sure where he is these days."

"What about the other guy? Will?"

I nod. "Will fell in love with a human about thirty years ago. They got married, and he turned her."

"Where are they now?"

He lowers his gaze, frowning. "Marianne contacted me last year and let me know they'd been killed by hunters."

My eyes widen as my stomach sinks. "Shit, Kade. I'm so sorry to hear that."

He nods. "I've gotten used to losing people. When you live forever, that's just part of the adjustment. Granted, it's a bit harder when you lose people who were also meant to live forever." Shadows cloud his face, and I know he's thinking about Meredith again.

I reach for him once more and slide my fingers through his. Standing, I push my chair in and wait for him to do the same before I guide him out of the dining room, and we walk hand-in-hand to his bedroom.

Kade walks over to the bed and drops onto the end of it with a sigh. He drops his chin to his chest, his palms flat against his thighs. "You don't need to hang out with me," he says in a low voice. "If you want—"

"What I want," I cut him off gently, approaching the bed and stopping in front of him, "is to be here for you." I run my fingers through his hair and smile when he finally looks up at me. "Now, come on. I think you could probably use a bit more sleep." I sure as hell could. "Lift your arms."

He arches a brow at me but eventually does, and I pull his shirt off. I point to his pants. "You want to sleep in those?"

"If you want me naked, all you have to do is ask." The words are definitely something I'm used to Kade saying, but his tone is distant. He's trying to put on a strong face but he's really hurting. There's a deep struggle in his eyes that makes my chest ache.

I try to play along, offering him a brilliantly fake smile. "You caught me. Please, oh please, take your pants off."

He shoots me a tired smile, leaning back on the bed to undo his pants and wiggle out of them. Once he's left in just his boxers, he sits up, and I walk around the bed, pulling back the sheets. He follows my movement and gets up, coming to my side and sliding under the sheets.

I wait for Kade to get settled before I go to the other side and undress, keeping only my shirt and panties on before crawling in beside him. I wrap my arms around his waist, pressing my cheek to his bare chest. I close my eyes against the warmth of his skin, listening to the steady beat of his heart as his breathing evens out.

"Thank you," he murmurs, fading into a place where the harsh reality of his life can't reach him, and I hold him tighter as he falls asleep in my arms.

I wake to the smell of two of my favorite things: coffee and bacon. And then I realize my legs are tangled with Kade's, bringing a rush of warmth to my cheeks and much, much lower. He's still sound asleep, so I'm careful not to move and disturb him. I hold my breath when he shifts slightly, and my eyes widen when his erection presses into my thigh. I close my eyes, trying my best to ignore the rush of heat between my legs—not to mention the throbbing there.

Kade nuzzles his face between my neck and shoulder, making me shiver. I keep my eyes shut and lay my hand over his heart, letting him know I'm here with him. I suck in a breath when his fangs scrape my skin.

"Good morning," I force out in a soft voice.

"Mmm," he breathes against my skin.

I press my lips together, hesitating a moment before tilting my head to give him clear access. "It's okay," I tell him. "Go ahead."

Instead of sinking his fangs into my neck as I'm expecting him to, he kisses the spot just below my ear. "Thank you, but in this state, I'm afraid of how easy it would be to lose control, and I... I don't want to hurt you."

I open my mouth to tell him I trust him but stop myself, nodding. I'm not entirely sure I *do* trust him, especially right now. He's hurt, on edge, and even he's not confident in his ability to control himself. "Blood bag it is. Let's go eat."

We get dressed and head to the kitchen, where we find Gabriel making breakfast. The island is covered with platters of eggs, bacon, hash browns, pancakes, and fresh berries.

My stomach growls, and I don't waste any time finding a plate and loading it up with food. I plop down at the end of the table in the adjoining dining room where Lex is already eating, and Gabriel sets a steaming cup of coffee in front of me. "Thanks," I murmur around a mouthful of scrambled eggs, and he smiles at me.

Kade comes in with a piece of bacon hanging out of his mouth, a plate with more bacon in one hand, and a tall glass of blood in the other. He sits next to Lex, who throws his arm around Kade's shoulders briefly before returning his attention to the food in front of him.

Gabriel joins us a few minutes later, and we eat in silence.

I'm the one to break it several moments later when I ask, "What's going to happen once the vampires start their attack on the hunters? Won't that ignite a full-on war?"

Atlas chooses that moment to waltz into the room, holding his phone and a coffee cup. "It'll depend on how the hunters around the globe respond to the initial attack." He sits at the other end of the table, setting his phone down and taking a drink. "It's essentially a reminder of which species is more resilient and powerful. The hunters have been around nearly as long as we have, and there are blips in history where their presence is more pronounced—like now, for instance—but that will change, as it always does."

I frown at the onslaught of information. "So history is just going to continue repeating itself?"

"It's more complicated than that, angel," Gabriel says in a gentle tone, lifting a forkful of hash browns to his mouth.

"I don't think it is," I argue. "You're reminding the humans where they—*we*—hang on the food chain. There's nothing complicated about that." Disappointing as hell, sure, but not complicated.

I don't know what else to say—there really isn't anything else *to* say. It's out of my hands and even Atlas's, I figure.

Clearing my throat, I stand, pushing my chair back and grabbing my dishes to take to the sink. "I'm going to get some air."

A quick trip to the bathroom, and I'm ready for a run. Physical activity has always helped me to clear my mind, and the sun is shining brightly this morning, which I'm hoping will improve my mood.

I walk out to the hallway, scrolling on my phone to find a good playlist, and stop abruptly at the sensation of someone moving past me at an inhuman speed. I exhale a heavy breath, lifting my gaze to find Atlas blocking the front door with his arms crossed over his chest.

My eyes narrow, and I take another step forward, slipping my phone into the pocket of my leggings.

He shakes his head. "Do not pass GO. Do not collect two hundred dollars."

"He makes jokes now," I comment wryly.

"Oh, I'm very serious. You're not leaving."

"Would you chill? I'm going for a run. You can't keep me locked in here."

His expression darkens, and he lowers his voice. "Want to bet?"

"No," I reply firmly, "I want you to get the fuck out of my way."

"You're not going out there," he says simply, and when I open my mouth to argue, he continues, "It's not safe now that the hunters know you're associated with us."

I blink at him. He's... concerned about me. Or he just wants to hold power over me. Again. "I can't stay cooped up in here, Atlas. I'm going stir crazy. I need to blow off steam." I swallow hard and say the word I absolutely loathe using in conversation with him. "Please?"

He narrows his eyes, glaring at me so long I'm fully expecting him to refuse. But then he says, "Fine. I'll go with you."

That's kind of the opposite of helpful, considering I was going to get my mind *off* the vampires, but I suppose I should take what I can get.

"Great," I deadpan, sticking my headphones in and cranking up the music on my phone as we walk out the front door.

We start at a light jog, and my feet hitting against the sidewalk in time with my slightly accelerated heartbeat makes me feel significantly better than sitting at the dining room table discussing the impending vampire hunter war. And yet, I'm still thinking about it. What it'll mean for me and the guys, Brighton and her family... I change the song on my phone and pick up my pace, trying to drown out my thoughts. That, and ignore the vampire easily keeping pace beside me. As hard as I pretend he's not there, I can't help but feel him all over.

I give my head a shake as we round the corner and pick up speed again. There's a park ahead with what looks to be a walking trail, so I set my sights on it, my feet pounding the pavement and gravel through the park until we hit the dirt path. I slow my pace a little in case we run into other people, but Atlas evidently doesn't share that concern. Between one moment and the next, he grabs me around the waist and hauls me off the trail into the forest, knocking my headphones out in the process.

"Atlas! What the hell?" My heartbeat pounds in my throat and my vision blurs with the inhuman movement until my back hits the hard bark of a tree. I immediately start fighting him, throwing my arms out and shoving as hard as I can. It does virtually nothing besides exert my already low energy.

"Enough," he says, gripping my wrists in one of his hands and lifting them over my head.

I glare at him, my chest heaving between us. "What are you doing? Is this our thing now?"

His lips twitch for a split second. "You'd like that, wouldn't you?" His eyes glimmer. "If I took you against this tree and fucked you so hard you couldn't walk back to the house."

I swallow past the dryness in my throat. "You'd look pretty funny having to carry me back there."

Atlas leans in until his nose grazes mine. "Perhaps a risk I'm willing to take."

"Like giving a shit about human life?" I blurt.

He pulls back, his brows knitting as he lets my wrists go. "What?"

My pulse kicks up, but I don't attempt to move away. I have no idea what I'm doing, but with everything going on, I feel as if I'm spiraling, desperate for something concrete to hold onto. "Do your parents know you care about a human?"

He grasps my shoulders, not holding me against the tree anymore, just holding me. "Why are you asking me that?"

"You have to do what they say, that was made clear to me with what's been planned for the hunters." I drop my gaze, staring at the brush at our feet. "I guess I'm just wondering what'll happen when it comes to what they want you to do with me."

"They're indifferent to our arrangement." His grip on my shoulders loosens. "It's not something they're concerned about, Calla."

I say nothing, but my pulse is still pounding from running—and being this close to Atlas. I guess I hadn't realized just how worried I was about Atlas's parents and what they thought about their son's... whatever I am. I've been so tangled up with worry over Kade and Brighton I didn't really consider what it all meant for *me*—until now, apparently.

His eyes dance across my face, and when I turn away, he drops one hand from my shoulder and snags my chin, forcing my gaze back to his. "You're safe. They aren't..." He sighs, lowering his voice to something so calm and soft, it's almost unrecognizable. "I'm not going to let anyone bring harm to you."

My chest tightens, and I hold his gaze. "Okay," I finally say.

His thumb brushes over my jaw. "We should get back. I don't like being out in the open like this." He steps back, giving me space, then we walk back to the trail before picking up the pace and jogging toward the house.

I walk up the front steps ahead of him and reach for the door. Before my hand can wrap around the handle, Atlas pulls me back and spins me around. I don't have a moment's warning before his lips are on mine. His arm snakes around me, hauling me against him as his mouth devours mine in an all-consuming, world-narrowing kiss.

For a brief time, we're just two people losing ourselves to each other. It's incredible and awful, and I want nothing more than to pretend it'll last forever.

Something in me cracks as fear digs its claws deep into my chest. I never wanted this—I dreaded the day the vampires would come for me —and now, all I can think about is how scared I am to lose them.

I break the kiss, leaning my forehead against his jaw while I catch my breath. "I need to ask you something."

"So ask."

"Would you stay out of the attack if I asked?" Now that I don't have to worry about Brighton's safety, that leaves plenty of room for concern over the guys. I'm not sure if the others are expected to participate, but Atlas definitely is.

He leans back as his eyes roam over my face. "Worried about me?"

"Don't answer a question with a question," I grumble.

"Well, we're not close enough to drive to Washington in time anyway, so I guess I'll sit it out." A flight would give him plenty of time to be there for tonight, but I'm not about to offer that up. I'd be telling him something he already knows, anyway.

"Will that get you in trouble?" I ask in a quiet voice. Everything I've heard about Atlas's parents makes me hope I never have the misfortune of meeting them.

The corner of his mouth quirks. "I think the ability to be grounded becomes a little less effective after you've lived for over a hundred years."

I shoot him a look. "I'm so glad you can find humor in this."

"You'd be smart to as well. Otherwise, this is going to get very dark, very fast."

Too fucking late.

SEVENTEEN

KADE

Nemone of us slept longer than a few hours last night. When Atlas and Calla got back from their outing—and sucking each other's faces on the front porch while Lex and I watched from the living room—we passed the time watching shitty reality television in the insane theater downstairs. Lex ordered enough pizza and wings for an army, and the four of us stuffed our faces. Atlas took his time eating a single slice, I think mostly to have something to do with his hands. We were all antsy and on edge, having decided to stay away from Washington and any of the other hunter attacks that took place simultaneously last night.

Sitting together in the living room, we wait for Atlas's phone to ring, for one of his contacts from New York to brief us on the stats of the attack.

Calla's asleep in one of the bedrooms; Gabriel suggested there was no sense waking her until we had information to offer, and we agreed with him.

My phone chimes from the coffee table, and I lean forward on the couch enough to see Marcel's name on the text alert. I swipe it up and scan the message. It's short and to the point, just like Marcel.

"The Washington house has been cleaned out and rented," I announce to the guys, my shoulders feeling heavier than they did moments ago. That place was home to us. We had it built from designs Atlas created. It's another loss I can't seem to accept.

"How long is the lease?" Lex asks, frowning.

"Marcel didn't say." I shrug. "Probably a year."

Gabriel says nothing. He continues staring out the front window in thought, one leg crossed over the other.

What I wouldn't give to know the thoughts in his head right now.

"It doesn't matter," Atlas says, taking a drink from his mug. If I didn't have heightened senses, I'd think he was drinking coffee, but the thick, coppery scent of blood makes my nostrils flare.

Lex nods, kicking his legs up on the coffee table. "You're right. Whenever we're ready to go back, Marcel will take care of it. Glamour whoever's in there to pack up their shit and get the fuck out."

He's not wrong. Still, the thought of someone else living in *our* home makes my hands ball into fists. We wouldn't be in this mess if it weren't for the hunters.

Gabriel wets his lips, reaching into his pocket when his phone chimes. "It's Fallon. They went to Chicago after leaving us and they spotted Selene last night." He types a message back, then tells us, "I've asked them to keep tabs on her until we can get there. I don't want them taking her on themselves."

"Good. We deserve the pleasure of ending her miserable existence," I say in a sharp tone. I'm itching to shed some blood. Anything to sate the angry demon making a home in my chest.

Atlas is next to pull out his phone and stares hard at the screen. Before he can tell us what's going on, Calla shuffles into the room still in the black T-shirt and sweatpants she fell asleep in, rubbing the sleep from her eyes.

Fucking hell. I immediately want to tug her into my lap and bury my face in her neck. My cock twitches in my pants, and I grit my teeth. Now is *not* the time.

"Any news?" she asks around a yawn, dropping onto the couch next to me and hugging her knees to her chest as her tired gaze moves between us.

"Just now," Atlas says, and we all turn our attention to him. He clears his throat. "My advisors from Chicago and New York report that nearly fifty vampires were killed during the raids last night. Dozens more were injured but are now fully recovered after feeding."

Calla gasps softly at his words and wraps her arms around her legs, her brows pinching together. She's conflicted. Here she sits as a human in a room full of vampires while we talk about other vampires killing humans. The worst ones, the ones who want to kill *us*, but still. I understand what must be going through her head, because when I thought Meredith betrayed me, I still couldn't find it in me to hate her, to not *not* want to know her, given the chance.

"And the hunters?" Gabriel asks. "How many were lost?"

"Lost?" Lex says with a bitter laugh. "Ain't no loss, brother."

Gabriel sighs. "You know what I mean."

"At least three hundred," Atlas says. "We don't have final numbers yet, but it's predicted that number will climb as the day goes on."

"What about Scott?" Calla asks in a small voice, her pulse ticking faster with each passing minute.

"I can't confirm either way at this point," Atlas tells her. "I'm in touch with the team in Washington, so I'll know more soon."

With a short nod, she gets up and walks to the kitchen, where I can hear her getting a mug out of the cupboard and pouring herself some coffee.

"Well, I can't just sit around here all day," I say, getting off the couch. I noticed a pool in the backyard when we arrived, so I head outside into the sun, tugging my shirt off and losing my pants before diving into the water. Swimming laps back and forth across the pool, I focus myself on the movement of my arms, kicking hard, while remaining at a human pace. My muscles won't tire like they would when I was human, but the exertion is still a decent distraction. Until an even better one walks out the back door onto the deck with a steaming mug in her hands and walks toward the pool.

"I didn't even notice this place had a pool," she says, dropping onto one of the lounge chairs and taking a sip of her coffee.

I swim to the edge closest to her, propping my arms on the concrete lip of the pool. "Are you planning to sit there and watch or are you going to come in this time?"

Her cheeks turn pink as she presumably recalls the day at our house in the pool when I feasted between her lovely thighs.

"I..." She glances down at her clothes. "I don't have a suit."

The corner of my mouth kicks up. "Hmm. I'll give you one chance to guess what I'm wearing."

She rolls her eyes. "I'm not jumping in there naked, Kade. Nice try."

"Why not?" I push, gliding away from the edge and back as she watches me.

Calla gestures around. "Uh, what if someone sees?"

"Someone like who? Gabriel?" I add with a faint smirk, rather enjoying this moment being so reminiscent of the last time we were near a pool together.

Her cheeks flush hotter, and she shakes her head. "This place might feel secluded, but it's still fairly suburban."

I let out a heavy sigh. "Fine. Be like that. I suppose I'll just keep swimming laps to try to keep myself occupied."

She sets her mug on the deck next to her chair and pins me with a half-hearted glare. "Are you trying to get me in the pool with pity?"

I shrug. "Is it working?"

Holding my gaze for a stretch of silence, she blows out a breath and stands, tugging her sweatpants down until they fall to her ankles. She steps out of them and kicks them aside, then walks closer to the pool, crossing her arms over her chest.

"Come on," I encourage. "The water is nice and refreshing."

She chews her bottom lip, glancing back toward the house for a second before turning back to me and moving to sit at the edge, dipping her feet then her legs into the pool.

I swim to her, sliding my hands up her bare legs and holding her gaze as I reach her panties. "Are these coming off?"

Her gaze lowers as if she's trying to see what I'm wearing, and I can't help but chuckle. Her eyes find mine once more, and she presses her lips together. My hands go to her waist, soaking her T-shirt as I pull her toward me and into the pool, deciding I'd rather let her make the move to undress then guide her into doing it.

She grabs my shoulders, her breath hitching as I lower her into the water. She slowly relaxes as her feet touch the bottom and the water soaks through her shirt. She leans into me, gliding her fingers through my hair and resting her forehead against mine. "So, what? We're just going to distract each other with sex in the pool of a stranger's house?" Her voice is soft, barely above a whisper, but I catch every word.

Nodding, I slide my hands around to cup her ass and press her against my cock beneath the water. "Any objections?"

Her pulse races, and she lifts her chin, sealing her lips with mine.

Message fucking received.

I kiss her hard, closing my eyes and losing myself to the feel of her against me. She makes a soft noise that goes straight to my dick, and I squeeze her ass, lifting her up so she can wrap her legs around me.

Our lips battle for control, and I tear her panties clean off, tossing them onto the deck, and she yelps against my lips. *So much for waiting for her to undress.* My teeth catch her bottom lip, and I nip it gently, keeping my fangs retracted even as she grinds against me, tempting the monster just below the surface.

"Kade," she moans, leaning back to catch her breath.

I turn us around and pin her against the side of the pool, kissing the tip of her nose. "Tell me," I murmur, "would you like me to fuck you with my fingers, my tongue, or my cock?"

Her eyes are filled with hunger and her lips curve into a smile she doesn't try to hide. "You're making me choose?" She flicks her tongue over her bottom lip. "What if I want all three?"

I press my lips to hers in a chaste kiss, then dip my hand between her thighs, tracing along her slit with two fingers. "I'll give you anything you desire, Calla. Never doubt that for a second." I push inside her at the same moment I capture her mouth again, reveling in her warmth, in the taste of her lips, and when she kisses me back, grinding herself on my fingers, I'm about to lose my fucking mind with the need to bury my cock between her thighs.

She grips the back of my hair, moving her lips with mine as her heart thumps in her chest. I circle her clit with my thumb for good measure, picking up the pace of my fingers and curling them to hit the spot that'll drive her wild. Her pussy clenches around my fingers, and my cock throbs in response, my balls tightening.

"I need more," she murmurs against my lips, and holy hell, it's so sexy I couldn't deny her if I wanted to; she doesn't need glamour to control me.

I pull my fingers out, making her shiver with delight, and tweak her clit before lining my cock up with her entrance. I tease her with the blunt head, and her chest rises and falls quickly as she stares into my eyes, pleading. I push inside her all the way in one smooth thrust, her pussy already wet enough to allow me to glide in easily. I groan, completely sheathed in her heat, and give her a few seconds to catch her breath before I start to pull out slowly.

She grabs my hip, holding me inside her. "You feel so good." Her voice is low and breathy and her cheeks are flushed beautifully; I'd like nothing more than to have this vision of her etched into my mind permanently.

Pressure fills my chest at the thought. I never want to let this stubborn as hell, sharp-tongued, and unbelievably compassionate human go. She is very easily the best thing to happen to me—to any of us, I think. And I very much intend to show her that.

I roll my hips, pushing in deeper, and she presses her lips together,

her eyes fluttering shut as her face fills with the most serene expression. She slides her hand from my hip to my ass, digging her fingers into my skin, and I in turn pick up the pace of my thrusts, pounding into her until we're both breathing heavily. Her pussy clenches around me, and I steal her mouth as she cries out in pleasure, kissing her as she squeezes my cock, soaking it with her release. My muscles tighten and the most delicious pressure fills me just before my climax crests and I come hard, filling her with my release as she moans, riding the aftershocks of her orgasm.

Our lips part, and we catch our breaths, but I make no move to pull out of her heat. I kiss each of her cheeks, then her forehead.

"I've never had sex in a pool before," she murmurs with a soft laugh.

I chuckle, tucking her hair behind her ear and tweaking her chin. "Glad I was your first."

"Mmm. Do you plan to stay buried between my thighs for the rest of the day, or...?" There's a playful glint in her eyes that I can't help but grin at.

"Perhaps," I taunt, dipping my face to kiss her again, slow and deep, until her pulse is racing once more. I lean back, flicking my eyes between hers. "As much as I'd like to, we should probably head back inside and see what's going on."

Her smile fades quickly, and she nods. "Okay, fine. But you know, you fucked me with your fingers and your cock." She lowers her voice, pressing her chest against mine. "But I didn't get your tongue."

My cock twitches inside her, and I smirk. "Oh, I'm well aware. I'm saving my dessert for later."

Her pussy clenches around me again, and she pulls in an unsteady breath.

"Come on," I say, sliding my cock out and guiding her to the other side of the pool closest to the house. I jump out, then turn and offer her my hand. She takes it, and I pull her up, her T-shirt clinging to her and making her nipples stand out. Fuck. I already want her again.

Later, I vow to myself. Something tells me I'm going to need something to look forward to.

EIGHTEEN

CALLA

I leave Kade's side when we return to the house and head upstairs to the bathroom across the hall from where I've been sleeping. Turning on the shower, I peel off my wet T-shirt, dropping it into the sink and catching my flushed complexion in the antique, gold-framed mirror over the marble vanity. My cheeks and chest are tinged pink and my hair's a mess of tangles and saltwater from the pool. Besides that, though, I look... happy. Which feels all kinds of wrong considering everything going on around me, but I suppose I should be grateful that I can experience some goodness even with shit hitting the fan.

After my shower, I tug on a clean pair of black leggings and an over-sized sweater. My stomach grumbles as I'm yanking a brush through my wet hair. Evidently I worked up quite the appetite in the pool.

I'm about to go downstairs to start making something for lunch when my phone starts vibrating from the bedside table. I walk over, and when I see Brighton's name on the screen, I snatch it up and answer it. "Tell me you're okay," I say quickly.

"Your concern for my daughter is meaningless when you choose to spend your time with monsters, Calla."

Scott.

So he wasn't killed during the raids.

"Where is Brighton?" I say with an edge to my voice. There goes my appetite.

"Brighton," he says, "is not who you should be worried about."

My hand curls into a fist at my side as I start pacing the bedroom. "What the hell does that mean?"

"Choices have consequences." His voice is level and calm.

A surge of anger flares through me in response. "You have no idea what you're talking about," I say through my teeth, clenching my jaw. I'm not about to tell him about the blood oath, that my being with the vampires was never a *choice*. I have a feeling it wouldn't really matter to him at this point, anyway. "What do you want, Scott?"

"Personally, I want nothing. My organization, however—"

"If this is a recruitment call, you're wasting your breath," I cut in.

He laughs. "Noted. It's a shame, though. You certainly have a fire that would make you a strong candidate."

"I'm hanging up now," I practically growl into the phone.

"You'd be wise to consider your options, Calla. *You* may be safe for now, but what of the others you care for?"

My stomach drops and ice fills my veins. "What did you just say?"

The line goes dead.

"Fuck," I shout at the empty room. Storming to the door, I rip it open and rush downstairs.

Kade and Gabriel aren't around, but Lex and Atlas are sitting at the dining room table, drinking blood from tall crystal glasses. They both turn to look at me when I burst into the room, out of breath.

"Calla?" Lex says, arching a brow at me.

"He's alive," I force out, swallowing hard. "Scott is alive, and I... I think he threatened me. I don't know—he hung up on me before I could get him to elaborate."

Lex's fangs flash in the light over the table, and he gets to his feet in a flash. "He won't be alive for long."

"Lex," Atlas says in a deep voice, "take a beat." His sharp eyes focus on me as he stands. "Tell me exactly what he said."

I rehash the short conversation, clenching my phone in my hand. "What the fuck am I supposed to do with that?"

"We'll handle it," Atlas tells me, lines of tension creasing between his brows.

My phone goes off again, and my pulse jumps. Atlas pries it out of my hand easily before I can catch a glance at the screen, and when I reach for it, he holds it away from me.

"It's your father," he says.

My heart stops. "Give it to me."

Instead of heeding my demand, Atlas answers the call, lifting my phone to his ear. I try to grab it from him, but he turns away, and Lex catches my wrist, pulling me toward him.

"Mr. Montgomery," Atlas says in a smooth voice, "what can I do for you?"

I look between Lex and Atlas, knowing Lex can hear the call just as clearly as Atlas can, while I'm left in the dark. "What's going on?" I ask.

Lex frowns but says nothing, freeing my wrist from his grip.

Atlas turns, meeting my gaze and nodding. "I understand. Let me speak with her, and we'll sort things out." He ends the call, setting my phone on the table.

"I haven't spoken to my father in over a month." My voice sounds hollow. "What is going on?" I demand. "What the hell happened?"

Gabriel and Kade slip into the room, concern etched on their faces, and I know something is very wrong.

"Your mom was in an accident. Someone blew through a red light and hit her. She's in surgery now. Your father couldn't tell me anything more."

I stare at his face, my throat too thick to force any words out. My chin trembles and my vision blurs with hot tears. Without warning, my legs give out, and Lex moves to catch me around the waist before I collapse onto the floor.

"Calla," Gabriel starts.

"No," I croak, tears rolling down my cheeks. I shake my head, my heart thumping so hard in my chest it pulses in my throat. "This isn't happening."

Gabriel steps in front of me, taking up my whole world. "Listen to me, angel. We're going to get in the car right now. We'll be in New York in an hour."

I get the feeling back in my legs enough to stand on my own and wipe the tears from my cheeks. "He did this," I say in a shallow tone. "Scott told me the people I care about weren't safe. I didn't think... How could this have happened?"

"He must've had someone set up to cause the accident at his direction," Kade comments, his arms crossed over his chest where he leans in the doorway, his expression as murderous as I feel right now.

"We don't know for sure that it's related," Lex offers. "Sure, it looks like it, but it's New York. Dozens of car accidents happen every hour."

I shake my head. Deep in my gut, I know this isn't a coincidence. The hunters did this.

My mom could die because of the hunter's war with the vampires.

The hospital lights are bright, and my nose burns with the harsh scent of antiseptic in the air as I charge toward the information desk inside the triage center. We find out my mom is out of surgery, and I start crying again because she made it through the procedure—*she's alive.*

After what feels like the longest elevator ride of my life, we reach the surgical recovery floor, and I nearly throw myself off the elevator and sprint toward her room, my Docs smacking the shiny white tiles as I weave in between hospital staff.

I skid to a stop outside her room, suddenly frozen, unable to move my feet to step inside.

My dad looks up from the chair he's in across the room, and his bloodshot eyes fill with tears as he gets to his feet and comes toward me.

"Dad?" I whisper, silent tears rolling down my cheeks.

"Come here, sweetheart." He wraps his arms around me, holding me as sobs tear through me, and I cling to him, the pressure in my chest finally exploding.

"Is she going to be okay?" I ask after getting the sobs under control. I glance past him to where the curtain is pulled over so I can only see the lower half of her body, which is covered in blankets.

"She pulled through the surgery, but she hasn't woken up yet. The doctors said it could take some time, so we just need to try and be patient." He runs his hand down my hair, tucking it back. "Did you come alone?"

I shake my head, sniffling. "They're in the hall," I say in a low voice.

His jaw clenches as disgust fills his expression.

"Dad, please. Just forget about that right now."

He pulls me into another hug, then guides me over to the bed.

I suck in a short breath at the sight of my mom hooked up to too many machines to count. There's an oxygen mask over her mouth and nose, IVs connected to both arms, and bandages covering several areas of her arms, face, and chest.

"Calla," my dad says in a soft voice.

I force my eyes away from Mom. "Why did she need surgery?"

He frowns, hesitating as if he doesn't want to tell me. "She had some internal bleeding and a punctured lung, which is what required the surgery. They inserted a chest tube, so she'll be here a while when she wakes, but you know your mom. She's stubborn. I know she'll make it out of this."

We sit around her bed, and I take her hand, holding it between both of mine.

Hours pass. Nurses come and go, checking over the machines and even bringing me a blanket at one point.

I'm not sure where the guys are. Half of me wishes they were by my side, but the other half is glad they're not. I don't have the mental capacity to think about that right now, so I don't even try.

Sometime after dinner, I send my dad home to change and eat a proper meal.

I must have dozed off, because I open my eyes to find a woman in a white coat standing at the end of the bed, looking over my mom's file.

"Sorry to wake you," she says in a gentle voice, offering me a kind smile.

I sit up, wiping my eyes, and shake my head. "It's fine. How is she?"

The doctor's smile slips a little. "Usually by this point, we start to see some improvement, but there's nothing yet."

My mouth goes dry. "What does that mean?"

"She's in a coma." Her tone is soft, but her words shoot ice through my chest.

I stare at the woman, then snatch the file out of her hands as if I'm going to be able to make sense of what's inside. "But she's going to wake up, right?"

"Her body needs time to heal. That could take days or weeks, maybe longer."

"You didn't answer my question," I say, dropping my eyes to the file in my hands. I flip through the pages. They aren't just records of this hospital stay. I come across the one from five years ago when Mom had brutal kidney stones, then the documentation from my birth.

"We'll continue to monitor her," the doctor says as I continue thumbing through Mom's file.

My eyes catch on another hospital stay a few years before I was born. I squint at the words, sure I'm reading them wrong. This must be a mistake. Something from someone else's records that was misfiled.

"What is this?"

The doctor sighs. "I really shouldn't be allowing you to see that. Medical records are—"

"What is this?" I repeat, shoving the file back at her.

She scans the page and frowns. "Oh. Your mom was admitted for a delivery, but unfortunately, it looks like the child didn't survive."

I blink at her, my thoughts spinning and moving too fast to string together anything coherent for almost a minute. "She had a baby before me," I say to myself.

"Yes. I'm sorry, you shouldn't have seen that. I'd think if your mom wanted you to know about the child, she would have shared it with you."

Something clicks, and the words fly out of my mouth before I can think to stop them. "Was the baby alive when it was delivered?"

She frowns, dropping her gaze to the file once more. She flips a couple of pages and nods. "According to the death certificate, she lived a few hours."

She.

Oh my god.

My world narrows. Black dances around the edges of my vision and my heart slams against my chest.

"S-she?" I whisper. "My mom had a baby girl before I was born?"

The doctor nods. I watch her mouth move, but I can't hear anything over the ringing in my ears.

I wasn't the firstborn Montgomery daughter.

Whatever debt my ancestors owed to the vampires—the blood oath was never mine to fulfill.

FATED
IN
RUBY

CHAPTER
ONE

LEX

New York City, a long fucking time ago...

The street is quieter than normal. The quiet that comes from thick, heavy snowfall, muting the sounds of people and cars. The air is so cold my lungs sting with each fogged breath as I hurry down the slick sidewalk toward the parking garage a few blocks away from my office building. My face is frozen, and I curse the white shit covering my path... and my decision not to park closer to the office this morning. Considering my odds of getting a spot on the street in the downtown core were slim, I hadn't bothered wasting my time driving around. I'd overslept and really fucking needed a coffee.

I pick up my pace, jogging down the cement steps into the parking garage, my messenger bag bouncing against my hip.

It takes three tries for my engine to turn over, and I toss my bag onto the passenger seat, cranking the heat before backing out of my spot and heading toward the street.

The road conditions get worse as I make it out of the city toward the bridge, and I—for approximately the millionth time since I started working for my company three years ago—regret not spending the extra money to get a townhouse in the city.

Cranking the heat higher, I drum my fingers against the steering wheel to the soft rock song on the radio. Messing with the tuner, I try to find a *station that will come through clearly, but most are static and cutting out from the weather.*

I take my eyes off the snow-covered road for a second. And a second is all it takes.

A horn blares.

I slam the brakes.

The car doesn't stop. In fact, the packed snow under my tires makes them slide, sending my car across the lane—straight into the traffic traveling in the opposite direction.

I don't have a moment to react or even a second to close my eyes or yell.

Everything happens at once. The truck slams into me, shattering the windshield. The airbags blow, knocking the air out of my lungs, and my head snaps back against the seat so violently the world darkens to nothing.

I don't know how much time passes.

Am I dead?

I don't think I'm dead.

I can't hear or see anything.

The reason I don't think I'm dead? Everything hurts like hell. A pain so intense it might actually be keeping me alive, if that's even possible.

Cold seeps through me, and slowly—so fucking slowly—the sounds of horns blaring and people shouting break through the ringing in my ears. Everything is muffled, and I can't seem to remember how to open my eyes. Wetness drips down my face. I groan. At least, I think I do. Or maybe I'm screaming. Crying out for help from the darkness threatening to steal me away.

I'm scared. Scared I'm going to let it take me without a fight, because anything has to be better than the agony I'm in.

Glass trickles in from somewhere, hitting the dash as the sharp scent of copper mixed with burning rubber assaults my nose.

At some point, I manage to pry my eyes open.

There's a man at my side, standing in the open door.

Oh. The door isn't open—it's gone.

His eyes are too light and his lips are turned down into a frown. He looks angry and confused and sad all at once. When he opens his mouth, I can't hear the words he's saying. Shaking his head, he leans inside the car, pressing himself so close, my body explodes with white-hot pain.

"... shattered nearly... bone... your..."

My skull is pounding, but as the seconds tick by—or maybe it's minutes or hours—the pain fades into numbness, and I can't help but fear that isn't a good thing. I want the pain back. It means I'm still alive.

"...going... be dead... the next... if I... something. I... help"

His hands cup both sides of my neck, holding my head up despite it wanting to fall back against the seat.

I struggle to focus on his face. The harsh lines of his jaw, his defined brows, the dark stubble on his cheeks. The vision of him blurs, ebbing in and out.

My eyes flit to his mouth when he speaks again. I think he asks for my name. But when I open my mouth to respond, nothing comes out.

The man nods. "...figure... later." He flicks his tongue across his lips, and I blink at the sight of his elongated canines.

I've fucking lost it. I'm seeing a man with fangs standing in front of me while I die.

I always joked about going to hell, but perhaps it's really happening, and this guy is going to take me there.

He moves in a blur, sinking those impossibly sharp fangs into my neck.

I don't move, don't make a sound. The pain I would expect to feel having someone tear into my throat doesn't exist in my reality. In fact, after a few seconds, there's a trickle of warmth that seeps into my veins. I close my eyes against it, clinging to that tiny bit of pleasure in this nightmare.

And then he grips my jaw, forcing my mouth open and pouring in something warm and thick.

My eyes pop open to find his wrist pressed against my lips.

His blood. I'm drinking his blood.

I don't have the strength to stop myself from swallowing mouthfuls of the coppery liquid.

After I swallow a few times, he pulls his wrist back, and I catch sight of the puncture marks before they disappear, as if they were never there.

Sirens echo in the distance, getting closer, and I blink at the man who both drank my blood and fed me his, in utter confusion.

"... part isn't... be... pleasant... I'm sorry... make it quick."

I don't have time to grasp his words before he reaches for me once more and ends it all in one fatal motion.

If this is what hell feels like, I should have been more concerned about ending up here. My entire being hurts so deep it's otherwise indescribable. Darkness surrounds me and my veins are filled with liquid fire. My head is pounding with what feels like a splitting migraine and my throat is full of sandpaper.

"Alexander."

Someone is calling my name from far away. The voice is muffled and deep... and vaguely familiar. I've heard it once before.

I try to speak, but nothing comes out.

"You need to drink."

Yes. Water. I need water.

Reaching blindly, still unable to pry my eyes open against the pain paralyzing me, I grunt when my hands hit a solid wall of muscle.

"Open your eyes," the voice demands, and it's as if I needed him to tell me to, because I manage to do what he says.

My eyes are immediately overwhelmed, trying to focus on everything at once. The man sitting in front of me, the luxurious space we're in, the darkness outside the window across the room. I get stuck on the woman sitting off to the side. She can't be much older than twenty. I'm only in my mid-twenties, but still. She looks uncomfortable and out of place here. But she smells absolutely amazing.

What the fuck?

My eyes snap back to the man and widen as my brows scrunch together.

"It's okay," he assures me.

I swallow, wincing at the pain scratching at my throat. "What," I force out, "happened?"

The man frowns briefly. "Long story short, you died. Sorry."

My heart lurches at the same time my stomach drops, and I feel as if I'm going to vomit all over this guy in a second.

"There was an accident. Your car slid into oncoming traffic and you were hit head-on by a truck. I was driving behind it and saw the accident happen."

I'm actually fucking dead?

"So this is hell?"

His lips twitch for a split second. "Depending on how you look at it, I suppose it could be."

I blink at him. "Huh?"

"I'll explain everything, but you need to drink first."

My eyes drift back to the woman. "Who's she?"

"Your dinner," he answers simply. "You'll feel much better once you drink."

My eyes widen again, and I try to move away from him, though the second I do, pain flares through me, stopping any further movement. "You're crazy," I stutter.

"Many would agree," he offers. "I'm Atlas. Also, a vampire, as you will be once you drink and complete the transition."

Suddenly things start to come back. The crash. This man. His fangs.

"You... you killed me!"

He scoffs. "I saved your life, actually. You're welcome."

I drag my hands down my face, my fingers cold and shaking. "I don't want to be a vampire." My voice is empty, tone vacant.

"You'd rather be dead?" He shrugs. "Fine. Don't drink. I really don't need the hassle of siring someone anyway."

I shake my head, which doesn't help the spinning. "I don't... What are you...?" I can't finish a fucking sentence at this point.

The man—Atlas, apparently—sighs heavily. "To become a vampire, you need to die with both vampire venom and blood in your system, which you did. Then you come back to life in a sort of in-between state, which you have. You either drink human blood and become a vampire, or the pain you're feeling will get worse until you ultimately die. Again. For good."

I grit my teeth. "Why?"

"That is a very loaded question, Alexander. One with several possible answers. Are you asking why vampires exist, or why I chose to turn you into one?"

Another wave of fiery pain flares through me, and I grip the sides of my head, squeezing my eyes shut and groaning. "Why did you do this to me?"

Atlas inhales deeply. "I... am not quite sure yet." He stands and approaches the woman, offering her his hand, which she takes immediately, before walking back to me. The woman sits next to me while Atlas remains standing.

"You... you want me to drink her blood?" I force out, wincing at the dryness in my throat.

He grabs the woman's wrist, lifting it to his mouth and biting into it without hesitation. She sucks in a breath, then sighs softly, closing her eyes and falling against the back of the couch. Atlas pulls back after a moment and offers me her wrist, seemingly unconcerned that her blood is dripping onto the hardwood.

"Time to choose," he says in a flat but not unkind voice. "Drink now and live forever, or don't and die."

My eyes hone in on the blood pooling around the puncture marks on her wrist. Somehow I can smell it, and the harsh copper scent is making my gums throb, filling my head with a haze of... hunger.

I'm moving before I can stop myself, cradling the woman's wrist in my hands, lifting it to my mouth. I close my eyes, pressing my lips to her skin and trailing my tongue along Atlas's bite mark. The second I taste her blood, my veins sing with relief. The pain disappears instantly, and I moan at its absence, drinking deeply. The woman's blood flows easily, filling my mouth, and with every swallow, I feel stronger. Within seconds, the throbbing in my gums intensifies to an uncomfortable level. Before I know what's happening, fangs slice through, and I pull away from the woman's wrist only to tug her closer to me and sink my new, lethally sharp teeth into her neck.

She cries out, but the sound is quickly replaced by a lust-filled moan.

I swallow mouthfuls of her hot, thick blood, growling deep in my throat as the sound of her pounding heartbeat fills my ears. The longer I drink, the more it slows. I don't stop—I can't.

I lose track of time, of everything but the taste of life exploding on my tastebuds.

And then Atlas says, "Stop now or she'll die."

I don't care.

"Alexander." His tone sharpens.

I don't care. I don't stop.

Atlas sighs.

The woman's heart slows until I can't hear it anymore. Until it stops beating.

"She's dead," Atlas says mildly.

Finally, I pull back. I blink at the sight of the woman slouched against the couch, blood dripping from her neck and her eyes rolled into the back of her head.

Fucking hell.

I just killed someone.

I'm... a monster.

"What..." I choke on the word, lifting my hand to my mouth, and gasp when my finger touches a razor-sharp canine.

Atlas shrugs, unbothered. "It happens. Don't worry about it. Most vampires kill their first feed."

"I... I didn't mean to." I wipe my mouth with the back of my hand.

"The hunger will control you if you don't learn to understand it. There is much you will need to learn, Alexander. Your life as a human is over. Consider this your rebirth."

I frown at my name. It doesn't feel like me anymore.

Alexander died in that car.

"You're looking at me strangely."

Exhaling slowly, I lift my gaze to his. It's the first time I've noticed his eyes are silver. "I don't think I want to be Alexander."

He nods. "What would you like me to call you then?"

I scratch the back of my neck. I don't think I'm ready to part with my old life as much as I'd like to believe I am. "Lex," I finally say. "I want to be called Lex."

TWO

CALLA

The soft, steady *beep, beep, beep* from the monitor Mom is attached to is driving me crazy. I've been pacing her hospital room for almost an hour, my Docs squeaking against the pale beige tile each time I turn and switch direction. It isn't making me feel better, but I sure as hell can't sit still. My stomach is a mess of nerves and my head is spinning. Every time I try to wrap my head around the news that I'm not the firstborn Montgomery daughter, my pulse jack-hammers and a wave of nausea-filled panic floods through me. And the thought of the guys having overheard the conversation terrifies me. They're keeping their distance, but they can't be far. Which means, if they were listening, they know.

What does this mean for me—for us?

If the oath is void, if it was never mine to fulfill... will they let me go?

Do I *want* them to?

It's all too much to think about right now. There are so many ques-tions, so many what-if scenarios whipping around my thoughts; my head already feels seconds away from exploding. Between the blood oath, the hunters, Brighton, and Mom's *accident*, I have no idea what to do. I want to run. Desperately. Run until there's no such thing as vampires and hunters and blood oaths. More than that, though, I want to kill Scott Ellis for what he made happen; there is no doubt in my mind he's the reason my mom is lying in a hospital bed right now. He deserves to suffer for what he did; my mom has nothing to do with the vampires, and he went after her to get at me. To *punish* me for being associated with the vampires. As much as the idea of taking one of Brighton's parents from her makes me sick to my stomach, the dark desire I have to see him fall overpowers it.

Without thinking, I pull my phone out of my pocket and tap Brighton's number. The line doesn't ring—it goes straight to voicemail, and I hang up without leaving a message. I can't take the chance of Scott intercepting it, which is why I don't text her either.

Instead, I keep pacing.

My dad comes into the room by the time I've bitten my thumbnail painfully short, holding a paper to-go cup in each hand. He's at least changed his clothes since I arrived yesterday—when I sent him home to have a break—but he looks exhausted. Dark circles under his eyes, messy gray-brown hair, and the wrinkles around his eyes are more pronounced than usual. He appears... frumpy. Which is so incredibly not like him, it worries me.

"You'll wear the tile down to the subfloor if you keep that up, kiddo." The corner of his mouth pulls up slightly, but the smile is forced, and we both know it.

I pause, dropping my hand back to my side. "Yeah."

He walks closer, frowning in what seems to be realization. "Caffeine might not be the best thing for you right now."

He's not wrong; my pulse is already erratic and my thoughts haven't stopped racing since—

"Dad," I blurt in an uneven tone. I can't keep this to myself a second longer. My thoughts are tangled like old Christmas lights, and there's no chance of getting them straight on my own.

He sets both cups on the rolling table at the end of Mom's bed. "What is it, Calla?" He shrugs off his navy rain jacket, draping it over the chair closest to him, then gives me his full attention.

"I..." My voice cuts off. Shaking my head, I clear my throat. "I know you and mom had... um, lost... a baby before I was born."

His brows furrow as his face falls, and he inhales deeply before nodding. "We did. How did you—?"

"I read Mom's medical records," I blurt. I don't feel bad for doing it, considering it's likely the only way I would've ever known about the child they had before me.

"I see," he murmurs in a tired voice. "I'm sorry you found out that way. We should have told you."

"Were you going to?" I ask.

He opens his mouth, then seems to consider what he's going to say. A moment later, he frowns. "It was never a discussion your mom and I had."

Nodding, I say, "So no, then." I steal a glance toward the door before looking back at him. "The baby was a girl." My chest is tight, my throat dry as I force out, "What if this means something? For the oath?"

Dad blinks at me before his eyes widen. "I don't..." He looks over his shoulder at Mom, then back at me. "We shouldn't talk about this right now."

He's probably right. There's no telling who is listening, and the most important thing right now is that Mom gets better. But my head is going to explode if we don't.

"I know it's not the best time or place, but please. I've spent every single day since being told about the oath believing that my future would never be my own. That I wouldn't get to choose what I wanted to be, where I wanted to live... anything. And if that somehow isn't the case—if I *do* get a choice—I want to know. Now."

"I understand, Calla, and you absolutely deserve that. You deserve everything you want out of life, and answers to your questions are the least of what you should get." The sadness in his eyes gives me pause.

"But you don't know, do you?" I ask in a low voice, and he shakes his head after a beat of silence. "You... you never thought to look into it?" There's an edge to my voice, a sliver of hurt in my tone that makes him take a step toward me, but I shift backward.

Dad sighs. "After we lost the baby, your mom and I went through a very difficult period. Her more than me, of course, but I struggled with not knowing how to be there for her in the way she needed. I am sorry to say that trying to figure out what our dead child meant for the oath didn't cross my mind." His eyes are glassy and he turns from me for a moment to wipe the unshed tears away. When he faces me again, he says, "I don't want you to think I'm dismissing this, because I'm not. But I thought once before I was going to lose your mother. Now this happens, and I..." His voice cracks, and he sniffles. "I love you more than life, Calla, but I need to focus on your mom right now. Please try to understand?"

I nod stiffly, because I do understand—I almost lost my mom. "Okay. We can talk about this later."

Later isn't going to be anytime soon, so I go back to pacing.

Dad sits at Mom's bedside, reading yesterday's paper and glancing over at me every few minutes. He sets the paper in his lap and sighs. "Why don't you go for a walk?" he suggests. "Clear your head. Maybe get something to eat?"

I stop pacing and purse my lips. I haven't in a while, and despite all of the upset, I am pretty hungry. My eyes flit to Mom, and I frown, not wanting to leave in case she wakes while I'm gone.

"Calla," Dad says in a soft tone. "Go on. Please."

Finally, I nod. "Call me the second anything changes."

He nods.

Staring at him, I say, "Promise me."

He offers a tired look, setting the paper aside and standing. He walks over to me and touches my cheek in a gesture that's meant to be comforting. As conflicted as my feelings are toward the man who raised me, I don't pull away when he drops his hand and wraps his arms around me. In fact, I hug him back, because despite everything, we're the ones here for Mom and we need to stay strong together—for her.

"I promise, kiddo," he says softly. "Now go." He releases me, kissing the top of my head.

I blink back tears as he appears to do the same, stepping away from me and forcing a watery smile. I do my best to mirror it, then turn and leave the room, sniffling and wiping the wetness that escaped my eyes and fell down my cheeks.

The stark white, obscenely bright hallway makes me squint as I walk across the shiny tile, avoiding the eyes of the nurses and other people passing me going in the opposite direction.

I should step outside and get some air. Or find the cafeteria and pray there's something relatively edible there. I'd even settle for microwaved mac and cheese at this point.

Instead, I head toward the visitor lounge, where the vampires I may or may not be bound to are waiting for me.

The moment Calla walks in, the lot of us stand from the particularly uncomfortable plastic waiting room chairs, and her stride falters. She stays near the doorway, her eyes flicking between us. I haven't seen her this hesitant since the night we showed up at her apartment in Washington, and that was nearly two months ago.

"My dad thought I needed a break," she finally says in a quiet voice. "I guess my pacing was stressing him out," she adds with a half-hearted shrug.

Gabriel moves toward her before any of the rest of us can, touching her cheek gently before wrapping his arms around her. He holds her to him while he smooths his hand over her hair. It's a mess of dark brown waves, which is to be expected given the circumstances, but I think all of us—save maybe for Atlas—are fighting the urge to bring her comfort in any way possible. Kade would probably brush her hair if he wasn't standing silently in the corner of the room. His eyes are on Calla, but they're distant—near-vacant. It makes my stomach twist with unease. There's something more going on there, but I'm not entirely sure how to breach the topic with him. He lost his sister at the hands of a hunter and watched it happen. Granted their relationship was complicated, but not having the opportunity to change that is clearly eating him up inside.

"How are things going?" I ask after Gabriel pulls back, letting Calla out of his arms but staying close to her side.

She presses her lips together, tilting her head slightly. "You haven't been listening?" Her quiet tone is laced with mild disbelief.

I shake my head. I'd been focusing on some trashy reality show on the flatscreen across the room, figuring whatever was happening between Calla and her parents wasn't my business. I'm not sure I would've taken that same stance even a month ago, but here we are. This scrappy little human has changed all of us, even if we don't want to admit it.

"I was listening," Atlas says in a level voice, and Calla frowns, nodding.

"What are the rest of us missing?" I ask, glancing at Gabriel, who shrugs. Evidently, he wasn't listening either.

Calla lets out a heavy sigh and walks over to one of the chairs, dropping into it before locking eyes with Atlas. "I wasn't the firstborn Montgomery girl."

My eyes go wide and my head whips toward Atlas.

"What?" Kade speaks for the first time since we arrived. His voice is low, gravelly. It makes Calla turn her gaze toward him.

"Uh, yeah." She folds her hands in her lap. "My mom had a baby girl before me. She only lived for a few hours, but..." She trails off, dropping her gaze to her lap.

"The fuck?" I mutter. "What does that mean?"

Gabriel's brows knit as he looks between Calla and Atlas. "It's entirely possible the claim we have to Calla is invalid. The girl we were owed lived; however, not long enough for us to fulfill the blood oath."

"I don't understand any of this," Calla mumbles, "and honestly, I can't think about what it means right now." Her voice cracks and her throat bobs as she swallows, refusing to meet any of our gazes.

Gabriel wraps his arm around her shoulders, pressing a kiss against the side of her head. "We will figure it out later. Right now, you need to focus on being here for your mom."

She clears her throat and nods, then says to no one in particular, "I want whatever security team you had for me looking out for my parents instead. This... this can't happen again."

"Of course," Gabriel assures her. "Fallon and Jase have several trusted friends in the city, and I will contact them personally and ensure things are taken care of."

"Thank you." She sits up straighter, her back pressed into the chair.

"I want Scott Ellis dead." Her voice doesn't crack this time, but her eyes are glassy with unshed tears.

The room falls silent for a moment before Kade claps his hands together, a dark look plastered on his face. "Now that's a plan I can get behind," he says, coming over to where the rest of us are standing around Calla.

She blinks, making the tears roll down her cheeks as she nods at Kade. "Good." When Gabriel pulls a handkerchief out of his pocket and holds it down to her, she arches a brow at him. "What's that for?"

He regards her thoughtfully and says in a gentle tone, "Angel, you're crying."

Calla takes the handkerchief and quickly dries her cheeks before handing it back to Gabriel. Her gaze passes over each of us until her phone chimes. She pulls it out, and a look of what I can only describe as a mix of hope and relief fills her face.

"What is it?" Kade asks.

"My mom is awake," Calla says in a thick voice, standing and pocketing her phone. "I—"

"Go," I tell her. "We're not going anywhere."

Her eyes meet mine, and something in my chest feels weirdly pulled toward her. She opens her mouth as if she's going to speak, but then shuts it, opting to nod instead. Without another word, she walks out of the waiting room, leaving a heavy silence in her absence.

Kade scowls, taking the seat Calla left. "Every fucking day it's something new. What the hell are we going to do about this?"

"Perhaps it's worth asking Calla what she *wants* to do about it?" Gabriel offers, raking a hand through his mop of copper hair.

I shove my hands into the pockets of my black jeans and move to lean against the wall next to the doorway. "She's not getting out of this on a technicality." My words are harsh, I'm well aware, but the thought of having Calla walk away from us... I don't want to consider it as a possibility. If that makes me a monster, so be it.

Gabriel offers me a look of understanding but says, "If the oath has no bearing on her, she shouldn't have to—"

"Have to what?" I cut in, irritation prickling at the back of my neck at his words. "Be stuck with us? I think we all know just how much she doesn't hate it, despite what she'd often have us believe."

"It's not as if we're torturing the girl," Kade adds in an absent tone. "Far from it, in fact. She can hardly deny that."

"You'd consider holding her against her will in the absence of a valid agreement?" Gabriel questions, keeping his eyes on Kade, though the words are meant for both of us.

"Do you honestly believe it'd be against her will at this point?" I challenge. "Or, just maybe, we're not giving our girl enough credit. You said it yourself and you're right. Perhaps she *wants* to be with us. Otherwise, what's to keep her from running away? She's still here, isn't she?"

"Her mom is laid up in a hospital bed, for one," Kade says. "You really think she'd take off now?"

My lips press into a thin line for a moment, then I grumble, "Probably not, no."

"Enough," Atlas says, crossing his arms over his chest. "As far as our current problems go, this is the least concerning." His dark expression and sharp tone are clear—this isn't up for discussion at the moment.

"Fine," Kade mutters, "then let's talk about how we're going to deal with the son of a bitch who almost killed Calla's mom."

"I think that's a conversation Calla should be present for," I chime in, "considering from the sounds of it, she'd like to be the one to do it."

"Calla isn't killing anyone," Atlas says, though even he appears rather conflicted about it.

"No?" I offer. "Who are we to deny her that pleasure?" Okay, so *pleasure* might not be exactly the right word in this case, but the anger and hatred in Calla's voice when she told us she wanted Scott dead makes me think her taking him out should be left on the table. And I'll be more than happy to help should she need it.

Atlas sighs, as if I'm testing his patience. "If it's truly what she wants, fine. But you know as well as I do it would feel good for about three seconds, then she'd have to live with the weight of killing someone for the rest of her life."

"Taking a life means something different when you're a vampire," Gabriel says. "I fear it would break her, especially with the target being the father of her best friend."

Kade shrugs. "I say we kill them both."

Atlas pinches the bridge of his nose, shaking his head. "Kade."

I stare at Kade, unsure what to say. Deciding to take out Brighton is a bit extreme, even for us. I can't help but think he wouldn't be so determined to shed blood like this if his sister hadn't just been killed. It isn't an excuse for him lashing out—and I'm sure as hell glad he didn't offer that *suggestion* while Calla was still in the room—but I understand it's coming from a place of pain and trauma, whether he'll admit it or not.

"Oh, come on," Kade continues. "As if you haven't already considered it. That girl is as much of a threat as her father is."

"Calla would disagree," Gabriel says.

"I don't give a fuck, Saint Gabriel," Kade snaps. "It isn't her species at risk, ergo it isn't her call."

"Enough, Kade," Atlas shoots at him. "This is not the place to be having this discussion."

Kade looks as if he wants to argue, but eventually backs down, pressing his lips into a tight line and shaking his head.

My gums throb with discomfort, the hunger clawing at me despite the swirling unease in my stomach. I'm not accustomed to arguing with my brothers, and I feel the overwhelming need to ease the tension between us.

"Anyone else fucking starving?" I ask.

That's something we're in undeniable, eternal agreement over.

FOUR

CALLA

My heart pounds in my throat as I all but sprint back to Mom's room. The second I step inside and see her eyes open, mine fill with tears. I rush forward, and surprise flickers across her worn-out expression.

"Calla, what—?"

I have my arms around her, burying my face against her shoulder and the stiff, scratchy material of her hospital gown, before she can finish her sentence.

"Easy, honey," Dad says from where he's sitting in a chair on the other side of the bed.

Squeezing my eyes shut against the tears, I stay there for several seconds longer, then pull back and wipe my cheeks, perching on the edge of the bed. "Sorry. I'm just glad you're okay."

"Me too, sweetheart," she says with a faint smile, reaching for my hands. "You didn't need to come all the way from Washington. I hate to take you away from your studies—I know how important school is to you."

I frown. "Of course I needed to come, Mom." It doesn't matter that I didn't come here from Washington or that we're essentially on the run from hunters or that the blood oath might be void. All that matters is my mom is alive and she's going to be okay.

"Don't get me wrong, I'm happy to see you, but I'm fine. Just a little accident."

I'm not surprised she's trying to downplay what happened to her. Hell, I'd do it too. It makes thinking about it easier. Which is why I make the choice not to tell either of them the truth—that the *accident* was intentional. The guys will make sure they're protected from here on out, so it won't do any good to reveal Brighton's father was behind the crash. I fight the urge to clench my hands into fists; I can't stop thinking about the phone call I had with Scott before he tried to kill my mom. He will pay for what he did, but it's hard to pretend the thought of taking one of Brighton's parents from her won't hurt like hell.

Revenge is a conflicting desire, and I'm not entirely sure what to do with it right now.

The doctor chooses that moment to pop her head in and check on Mom. She lifts her chart from the holder at the end of the bed and reviews Mom's vitals, checking over the machines, which I think are monitoring her blood pressure and heart rate.

"How's it looking?" Dad asks, reaching mindlessly for Mom's hand. She glances down at the touch and smiles.

"I'm pleased with your improvement," the doctor says to Mom. "I'd like you to stay for a few more days to ensure you remain stable and nothing else comes up, but things are looking quite good at this point."

"Is it really necessary for me to stay?" Mom asks, glancing between Dad and the doctor.

"I'm afraid I must insist on it," she replies with a smile.

I, for one, won't argue on Mom's behalf when it comes to this. I'd much rather she stay under the supervision of medical staff until they're sure she's completely fine.

"Don't worry, dear," Dad says to her, "you'll be home before you know it, and I'll be here with you until you're ready to leave."

She sighs, sneaking a glance at me, and I nod in agreement with the others. "All right, fine," she says finally. "Can I at least get a proper meal?"

Dad laughs. "Whatever you want, it's yours."

The doctor slips out of the room, and I can't help but smile watching my parents. Despite the years of resentment I held for my father, for what he kept secret, seeing him with Mom is a reminder that he's a good man. He loves us, regardless of the blood oath he neglected to share with his wife before she became pregnant with his child. And now... well, now it may not even matter.

"Honey," Mom says, pulling my attention back to her. "I do appreciate you being here, but I'm sure you need to get back to Washington and study for finals."

I don't bother telling her that I've been out of school for a while. Unfortunately, it's pretty close to the bottom of my list of problems at the moment. And as much as I don't want to leave my mom here like this, it's not safe to stay in NYC. The hunters will know I'm here and likely assume the guys are with me, which pretty much makes them sitting ducks... er, vampires. Whatever.

Concern for their safety wasn't anything I thought would even be on my radar, but there's an uncomfortable tension in my chest that proves it very much is. I would be wrecked if any of them were hurt— or worse—because they were here to support me.

Do I have any idea what's going to happen? No.

If the blood oath is in fact void and I am, for all intents and purposes, free of Atlas, Lex, Kade, and Gabriel, what will happen? I have no freaking clue, and the thought alone makes my pulse race and my palms sweat. We'll have to face it eventually, but given the choice to stay with the guys or explore the future I never thought I'd have... I'm not sure what I'll do.

"I don't want to leave you," I tell Mom in a low voice, my throat thick with emotion I'm struggling to hold back.

"I'm okay, Calla," she assures me. "I'll get out of here in a few days, and your father will take care of me at home."

I hold her gaze for several seconds, then finally, I sigh in defeat. "Okay." I reach for her hand and give it a gentle squeeze before looking across the bed at my dad. "I'll go back on the condition that you keep me up to speed with everything happening here. I want to be updated at least three times daily and—"

Mom laughs, cutting off my tirade. "Honey, relax. We will make sure you know what's going on, but please don't worry about me. You heard what the doctor said. I'm okay." Her voice is gentle but firm.

I give her a hug, hanging on a little longer than normal, and kiss her cheek. "Call me if you need anything, okay? Please?"

She presses her hand against my cheek, smiling at me. "Sure. Take care of yourself, Calla. I love you."

I blink back the sudden rush of tears and nod. "I love you," I echo.

After another extended hug, Dad walks me to the door, where we share a hug as well.

"Keep me posted," I tell him, sniffling as I glance at Mom over his shoulder. Her eyes are closed again, the machines around her beeping steadily.

"Calla, I—" His voice cracks. "Stay."

My brows shoot up, and I shake my head. "What? Dad—"

"You don't have to go with them," he says in a hard voice. "We'll figure out the blood oath. This could be your way out. You don't have to go back to Washington. We can have you transferred to NYU to finish your degree. You can live at home or we can get you an apartment in the city—whatever you want."

I don't bother telling him that I'm not going back to Washington. That would require a much longer conversation about the hunters that I don't have the mental capacity to have at the moment.

Instead of addressing his offer, I ask, "Are you going to tell Mom that I found out about the baby?"

"Yes. Stay, and when she's better, we can tell her together. I never thought we'd have a chance to save you from those monsters, but this... If the oath was technically fulfilled by your sister the moment she was born, it was never your burden to bear, Calla. I am so sorry you've had to live with it as long as you have and that I never considered this before."

"It's not that simple, Dad. This is a potential loophole to the oath, sure, but..." I trail off, not sure how to explain to my dad how I've come to care about the vampires who took me from my apartment—my life —two months ago.

His face falls, and he reaches for my hands, holding them in his against his chest. "Please, Calla. I know this is scary, but if it means your freedom, we need to at least try."

I press my lips together, willing my chin to stop trembling. "There's more to it than you know. I'm sorry, Dad. I don't know how to explain everything to you right now, but there's far more at stake at the moment. I... I have to go." I swallow the lump in my throat, pulling my hands back before wrapping them around my dad in a quick, tight hug. I kiss his cheek, then turn and walk away without looking back.

CHAPTER

FIVE

LEX

Calla is silent the entire drive from the hospital to the hotel Gabriel reserved a suite at. Understandable, of course, but not something I'm used to. I decide quite quickly that I don't like it. I much prefer her sharp tongue and wit. It was clear when she returned to the waiting room and announced she was ready to leave that she didn't truly want to, but none of us questioned her or mentioned the conversation we all overheard between Calla and her father. Of course he wanted to save her from us, that much wasn't surprising in the least. What did confound me was her response. It was almost as if she wasn't sure she *wanted* to be free of us. I sure as hell don't want to let her go, voided blood oath be damned.

Once we've checked in at the hotel and settled into the penthouse suite, Kade disappears into the bathroom, the shower turning on a moment later. Gabriel and Atlas sit in deep blue armchairs across from each other in the living room, and Calla busies herself making tea in the full kitchen on the far side of the suite, keeping her back to us.

I fight the urge to go to her, knowing she probably needs some space to figure things out. That does nothing to appease the monster in me that wants to devour her. My cock twitches, and I groan inwardly, considering joining Kade in the shower, but he seems even less approachable as of late. Looks like I'll just have to deal with the hard-on I'm sporting until I can deal with it myself. In the meantime, I distract myself by listening to the steady beat of Calla's heart from across the room. I never expected something so mundane to be so calming, but I suppose there are a lot of things about the human in our midst I never could have expected.

When Kade reappears from the bathroom, his hair damp and smelling of aftershave and mouthwash, the five of us sit down together.

Calla folds her legs under her and sips her tea before looking at each of us. "We need to talk about the oath. Whether or not it's void, I think we all know we're bound in ways that have nothing to do with the agreement my ancestor made with you." She sets the steaming mug on the small, marble side table in between her chair and mine. "I'd like to make contact with the witch Selene sent to undo that blood spell. Maybe she knows more about the oath and can provide a definitive answer to its validity."

"I will track her down," Gabriel offers.

Calla nods, then a moment later sighs. "Something I don't understand is your ability to track me. Clearly, we're still connected in some way, which makes me think the oath could be valid."

"Not necessarily," Atlas says. "There's a bond between us, yes, but that may not mean what we've believed it to mean. We are connected to your blood, that much is true. Because you are born into the Montgomery line, we can sense you as I'm sure you could sense us given the proper training and time."

She blinks at him, her pulse ticking faster beneath her skin. "What does that mean?"

"It means we're connected, but it's possible that because you're not technically the firstborn daughter since the blood oath was entered into, *your* life isn't promised to us," Gabriel answers. "We have been connected to every Montgomery born since the agreement was made. The bonds were never incredibly strong—nothing like that of a vampire and their sire, for instance—but they were there. Each time a Montgomery child was born, we would have to check if it was a girl, and when it wasn't, we'd learn to ignore the bond until it faded completely."

She falls silent, dropping her chin slightly as her shoulders slump. "What about the girl born before me?"

I rub my jaw, leaning my elbow on the armrest of my chair. "We felt the bond snap into place when the child was born, but it broke so quickly, we didn't have a chance to check if it had been a girl. Your mom wasn't the first to lose a Montgomery child, but the others were lost much earlier on."

Calla's shoulders move as she sighs, picking at a loose thread on her shirt before she lifts her head to look at me. "You didn't bother to check this one?"

I shake my head. "It happened during a time where things between the vampires and hunters were... much like they are now. We had more immediate concerns."

She nods, but her gaze is nearly vacant, caught somewhere between shock and loss. "Okay," she finally says, flattening her hands on her thighs.

"Okay?" I ask, searching her face.

Calla shrugs. "What do you want me to say? What's done is done, and none of us can change the past. Right now, I think the most important thing for us to do is focus on the future. Things aren't exactly sunshine and rainbows, remember? We need to make a plan." She goes to stand, but Gabriel stops her.

"Slow down, angel. We don't need to do anything right this second."

"We shouldn't waste any time," she tells him, shifting her gaze toward Kade, then Atlas. "You know it as well, if not better, than I do."

"Perhaps," Gabriel continues, "but we also need to take care of each other. You should eat something and get some rest."

"Our problems aren't going anywhere," I add, echoing Gabriel's concern for Calla—and the rest of us. "They will still be problems tomorrow."

She pulls her bottom lip between her teeth, seemingly considering our words. My gaze gets stuck on her mouth, and the desire to reach for her, to taste her lips, nearly overtakes my control.

"Lex," Gabriel says in a firm voice, eyeing me sternly from beside her.

I shrug, my lips curling into a grin. "Sorry?"

Calla rolls her eyes, a tinge of pink filling her cheeks under my stare. "You are not."

My grin widens. "Yeah, I'm not." I stand, offering her my hand. "I think it's time we let ourselves forget about the day, enjoy each other's company, and—"

"Get naked?" Kade offers, flashing a bit of fang.

"Preferably," I answer, shooting Calla a wink.

She eyes my outstretched hand, and her pulse ticks faster as she slowly reaches for it, placing her palm against mine before standing from the chair.

I guide her toward the king-size bed across the room as Kade and Gabriel trail behind us. Pulling back the heavy duvet with one hand, I keep my other wrapped around Calla's. Then, without warning, I scoop her up, surprised when she instantly wraps her legs around my waist. "That a girl," I murmur, dropping my mouth to her collarbone. Her skin is flushed and warm, and it shoots right to my cock, making it throb with the need to take her.

She drags her tongue along my bottom lip before pushing it into my mouth, deepening the kiss as she buries her fingers in my hair.

I barely hear the sound of Atlas growling across the room over the sound of Calla's pounding heartbeat. I fucking love that I can get her going this easily.

Gabriel and Kade move around us, sliding into the bed, while I lay her in between them, breaking the kiss for a brief moment before Gabriel takes my place, capturing her chin and tilting her face toward him. Their lips meet, and I step back to tug my shirt off, dropping it onto the dark stained hardwood as Atlas stalks toward us, his gaze dark and hungry.

I make quick work of losing my pants, catching Kade's gaze as I turn back to the bed. Something in his eyes calls to me, and I'm moving before I even realize what I'm doing. My hands close around the hem of his shirt, and I pull it over his head. I enjoy the view of his thick, toned muscles, dragging my gaze down his chest toward the dark hair leading to the waistband of his jeans. I unbuckle his belt as Atlas moves beside me, catching Calla's attention. Her eyes widen slightly, taking in the situation, and her heart races. Her bare chest is flushed, and Gabriel unclasps her bra, freeing her breasts and quickly dropping his mouth to them, kissing and sucking, filling the room with the sound of Calla's short breaths and moans.

It's a good thing our suite came with a massive bed, because in a matter of minutes, all five of us are piled into it.

Atlas slowly pulls Calla's pants down to her ankles, and she shivers, her skin covered in goosebumps. She holds her breath as he pulls off his shirt and lowers himself between her thighs, burying his face there, and if that sight isn't enough to set me off, nothing is.

I slide my hand into Kade's boxers and free his hard cock, pumping my hand up and down its length as my gaze bounces between him and what Atlas and Gabriel are doing to elicit the most delicious moans from our girl.

"Fuck," he grunts, gripping the sheets on either side of him. His hand finds Calla's, and their fingers intertwine. Kade's head falls back against the pillow and his eyes close as he bites his lip, thrusting his hips up. I alternate speed and the tightness of my grip, moving at a speed no human could match and making his breath come faster. He opens his eyes and lifts the hand that's holding Calla's, offering me her wrist. I don't hesitate—at that moment, I can't. My fangs extend to their full length, and I sink them into Calla's wrist, groaning as her hot, sweet blood explodes over my tastebuds. It fills my gut with warmth and my dick gets even harder. I close my eyes, reveling in the spark of energy zipping through my veins as I continue pumping Kade's cock. I pull away from Calla's wrist when I've had enough, opening my eyes as Kade guides their intertwined hands back to the mattress, leaning over to lick the wound shut. I reach down and cup his balls in my free hand, massaging them in time with my movements along his throbbing shaft. His jaw is clenched so tight it looks sharp enough to cut glass, and his eyes fly up to meet mine. My breath stills at the darkness there, despite the way he's moaning as I work my hand over his cock.

"Kade—"

"Shut up," he growls. "Don't fucking stop."

Atlas peers over Calla's thigh at us, arching a brow for a brief moment before returning to his ministrations, making her cry out as he devours her pussy with his mouth. Gabriel seals his lips over hers, kissing her deeply, muffling the sound, and rolls her nipple between his fingers. Her back arches, her hips vaulting off the bed, and Atlas quickly traps them against the mattress, fucking her pussy with his tongue until she's trembling, coming hard against his mouth while Gabriel devours hers. Atlas licks her clean before standing and moving behind me, capturing my attention. He nods toward Calla, then smoothly takes over pumping Kade's cock as I shift over, quickly removing my pants and boxers, freeing my wicked erection.

Calla's eyes widen, bouncing between my cock and my face, and I can't help but grin as I run my hand along my thick length. I take note of the bulge in Gabriel's pants and nod at him before turning my full attention to Calla and the beautiful blush in her cheeks. I lean down, placing a soft kiss against her lips but pulling back before she can respond. "Tell me," I murmur, my lips tracing the shell of her ear, "would you like Gabriel to fuck that gorgeous ass of yours while I bury my cock in your pussy?" I press another chaste kiss against her lips, then move to her other ear. "Or shall I be granted the pleasure of stretching you there?"

"Fucking hell," she mutters breathlessly.

I tut my tongue, meeting her gaze. "That's not an answer, Calla."

Her eyes are narrowed but filled with arousal. "I don't care, just fuck me."

I run the blunt head of my cock along her folds, adding pressure when I reach her clit and making her suck in a sharp breath. "So demanding," I purr as Gabriel shifts off the bed and removes his pants and boxers, his cock hard and thick. I lick my lips, turning my gaze back to Calla. "I've been thinking about burying myself between your lovely thighs for too long now." I move without warning and at a speed too fast for her to track. In the time it takes her to blink, I've grabbed her and maneuvered myself under her. She yelps in surprise, which very quickly morphs into a moan when I grab her hips, lining my cock up with her entrance, and sink inside her, stretching her tight walls. I groan as she squeezes me, her head thrown back, pushing her breasts out toward my face. The bed shifts as Gabriel moves behind her, and I catch the hot as fuck sight of him running his hand along his shaft as he gets ready, lubing himself up before rubbing Calla's back. She's still managing to hold herself up as I thrust in and out of her pussy, but something tells me once Gabriel pushes into her, she won't be able to for long.

Her eyes widen and her heart races when Gabriel settles behind her. She bites her lip, her gaze locked on mine, and a sliver of panic flickers across her face.

"Relax," I murmur. "Keep your eyes on me and just breathe."

Gabriel's hands slide over her hips, and I keep still inside her pussy. "Angel?" Gabriel checks in a velvet-soft voice.

Her eyes flick between mine. "I'm okay." She takes a deep breath.

I nod in encouragement. "Good girl. Just like that."

Gabriel pushes his cock into her ass slowly, and she tenses.

"Fuck," she hisses, collapsing on top of me, pushing my cock in deeper.

"Shh," Gabriel murmurs, leaning over her to kiss the skin below her ear. He gives her a minute to adjust to him, stroking her back soothingly. "I'm going to go deeper now."

I reach between us and find her clit, circling it with my thumb as I continue holding still inside her, which is one of the fucking hardest things I've done in my many years on this earth when all I want to do is pound her pussy until my release fills the deepest parts of her.

Slowly, her muscles start to unclench and she begins to relax.

"That's it," I murmur. "Take a deep breath for me now."

Just as she does, Gabriel pushes the rest of the way into her, so we're filling her completely.

"Keep breathing, angel," Gabriel says in a thick voice. He's holding back as well.

"I'm... trying." Her cheeks are flushed and her chest rises and falls quickly with each breath.

"You're doing so well," I tell her, circling her clit faster as I lean up to seal my mouth over hers. She kisses me back, moaning against my lips as Gabriel starts to pull back before pushing in deeper. The movement stimulates her pussy, and she clenches around me. I thrust my hips up, tilting my head to deepen the kiss, and the three of us find a steady rhythm in a matter of thrusts, while Atlas continues working his hand over Kade's cock.

Calla pulls her mouth away from mine, crying out as her muscles tense, squeezing both Gabriel and me. Pressure builds low in my stomach, and we're both thrusting into her at an inhuman speed, vaulting us all over the edge. The room fills with the sounds of our combined orgasms—deep moans and near-animalistic grunts.

Gabriel pulls out of Calla's ass, collapsing into the chair against the wall next to the bed to catch his breath, and Calla falls onto the bed next to me as I slide out of her pussy.

Kade grunts deeply on my other side, and I turn to watch as Calla's lips press along my collarbone. A few more firm, quick pumps and he finds his release, groaning loudly despite trying to press his lips shut to muffle the sound. He slides out from under Atlas and gets off the bed before any of us can reach for him. A moment later, the door to the bathroom slams shut, and Calla flinches next to me. I glance down at her, and she's already looking at me.

"He's not—" she starts.

"I know," I say with a sigh.

"What can we do?" she asks in a small, tired voice.

"I think we should give him time and space," Gabriel answers from her other side.

"I'm worried about him."

I slide my hand into hers and give it a squeeze. "Me too, but it'll be all right."

"I... okay," she finally says. A moment later, her stomach rumbles loud enough, we don't need vampire senses to hear it.

Atlas glances over at us from where he's standing at the end of the bed. "Room service it is," he says, walking into the living room and picking up the hotel phone to call down to the kitchen.

I push my hearing out, trying to focus on Kade, but all I can hear is his breathing. It's still a bit fast, but it's evening out. The heavy pit of concern in my stomach grows bigger still. Gabriel's right—he needs time and space. But I can't help but worry if we give him too much, we could lose him.

Half an hour later, we're sitting around the living room in different stages of undress, watching some ridiculous rom-com Calla picked out and stuffing our faces with a variety of deep fried foods.

Despite the war raging on between the vampires and hunters outside this hotel room, it's dangerously easy to sit here—with my arm around Calla's waist and her head resting on my shoulder as she drifts off to sleep—and pretend this moment of peace is real. That it's something we can have long-term.

I'm not naive by any means, but fuck if I don't want it to last.

CHAPTER
SIX
CALLA

For the briefest of moments when I wake the next morning, my thoughts aren't plagued with vampire wars and blood oaths. There are a few short minutes of peace where all I think about is the feel of Atlas's tongue devouring me, or Lex's cock buried deep in my pussy, or Gabriel's in my ass, until nothing else but them exist in my world.

A sigh escapes my lips, and without opening my eyes, I reach out... only to find the massive bed empty.

I yawn, rubbing my eyes as I prop myself up on my elbows. Sunlight fills the room, making it look even fancier, if that's possible. The crisp white sheets and soft gray walls are simple yet elegant. As is the silver and crystal chandelier that hangs over the bed from the vaulted ceiling. The sliding frosted glass door that divides the bedroom from the rest of the suite is closed over almost completely, but the sound of the guys' muffled voices reaches me from the other room.

They're talking quietly, but I can hear the sharp anger in Atlas's voice. Gabriel seems to be the one offering calm responses to whatever is being said, which doesn't surprise me, considering he's always been the calm in the storm when it comes to them—at least in my experience.

I stretch my legs out and push the duvet off before swinging them over the side of the bed. I wrap the bedsheet around me and walk out to the living room to see what's going on, the soft white material trailing behind me like a gown.

The guys stop talking and turn their attention toward me the moment they sense me there, and Gabriel stands, walking toward me as he rakes a hand through his messy copper hair.

"Good morning, angel," he greets in a soft voice, smiling at me. His chest is bare, and my eyes immediately drop to the tight muscles there, inching even lower to the black trousers he's wearing dangerously low on his hips. His voice nudges my attention back upward. "Are you hungry? We can have room service brought up, and there's a French press on the counter that's fresh."

"I'm not hungry," I tell him, swallowing hard and forcing myself to refocus. "What's going on?" When none of them answer my question, I fold my arms over my chest as best as I can while still covering myself with the bedsheet and sigh. "I'm not going to take silence as an answer this time. Tell me what's going on. You guys stopped talking the second I walked into the room."

"I, for one, was distracted by the mere thought of your naked body under that sheet," Lex says with a wicked smirk that sends heat through me despite my irritation at them for being annoyingly unforthcoming. I should be used to it by now, but I thought we'd turned over a new leaf, so why are they hiding something from me now?

"Yeah?" I say, playing into his words. "Tell me what you were talking about, and maybe I'll give you a better look." I'm entirely not serious, but Lex seems to consider it, while Atlas and Kade exchange a brief look, and Gabriel doesn't take his eyes off me.

Atlas clears his throat, snagging my attention. He's the only one of the group fully dressed, wearing dark gray slacks, a black V-neck, and a leather jacket, with his hair combed back. The others are in various stages of undress—Lex's white hair is slicked back and still wet from a shower, but he's wearing jeans and shoes, though no shirt. Kade has clearly not showered. His hair is a mess and he's wearing nothing but a pair of black boxer shorts. The dark circles under his eyes make my chest ache for him, and I have an awful feeling whatever situation I've just walked into is going to make that ache much more painful.

"There was another attack against the hunters about four hours ago," Atlas says. "I didn't know it was happening until it was already underway."

My eyes widen and my grip on the bedsheet tightens. "Another attack so soon? Why?"

"The vampires who orchestrated it didn't want to give the hunters a chance to recover from the initial attack."

My stomach drops in the same moment my heart leaps into my throat. "Was Scott killed?" That should have been my first question, though I'm not sure if I'll be happy about it or resentful that I didn't have the opportunity to strike him down myself. I shudder at the heavy sensation that grips me. I'm thinking about killing another human being. Despite the awful things he's done, I'm terrified of what these violent urges might suggest about me.

Atlas shakes his head. "No, he wasn't. However, Brighton's mother was. Scott had been checking in on her and Brighton when it happened. There was a group of vampires tailing him, and he managed to escape, but unfortunately she did not."

Tears fill my eyes, and I shake my head, backing away regardless of the devastating knowledge that I have nowhere to go. *Because nowhere is safe even under the protection of four vampires.*

"Brighton?" I force out, and my voice cracks.

"She's fine," Kade chimes in without looking at me. His bare feet are propped on the armrest of the couch where he's lounging, staring at the ceiling. "She wasn't with them when the attack happened."

But she easily could have been.

I immediately feel the urge to go to Brighton, to be there for my best friend—to comfort and protect her. Panic consumes me, pressing on my chest so hard I can't breathe. I try to swallow past the dryness in my throat, but it does little to help the feeling of suffocating. My head swims as dizziness floods through me and each breath becomes harder than the last. I can't think straight. Too much is happening.

Gabriel reaches for me, and I reel back, my vision blurry with tears.

Lex stands, as if he too is going to come toward me, his brows drawn together in concern. "Calla—"

"No," I croak. "This isn't... I can't..." My chest heaves as my breaths come in short gasps. *I can't breathe.*

Before I know what's happening, my legs give out. Gabriel catches me around my waist before I hit the floor, holding me against his chest.

The room tilts around me, darkening as the sounds around me start to fade in and out, echoing through me.

"Look at me, angel." Gabriel's voice somehow slices through my hysteria, and the moment our eyes meet, I am grounded. "Breathe," he says in a voice that leaves no room for anything but compliance. The power of his influence settles over me like a warm, weighted blanket, filling me with comfort and steadiness—enough to allow me a moment to catch my breath. At that moment, I can't even contemplate attempting to resist the vampire's glamour—I don't *want* to. He can pull me out of this never-ending fall I'm experiencing, and I'm desperate enough not to fight him.

I inhale deeply, holding his gaze as he nods in encouragement, then let the breath out slowly, finding I'm able to stand again. My legs are still a bit unsteady, but with Gabriel holding me, I'm not worried about ending up on the floor.

"There you go," he murmurs. "Stay with me and keep breathing slowly." His fingers splay across my cheek, warming my skin as my pulse slowly returns to a normal pace.

"She good?" Lex asks from somewhere behind Gabriel.

"She's just fine," he answers without breaking eye contact with me, and I find myself nodding.

"I'm better now," I say in a low voice.

Gabriel nods, then pulls his gaze from mine, severing the glamour, but makes no move to shift away from me.

I turn my face and press my lips to his palm in a soft kiss. "Thank you," I whisper. I wasn't prepared for the moment where I would thank a vampire for glamouring me, but here we are.

Glancing past Gabriel, it appears that Lex and Kade slipped out of the room. Something tells me—and I hope—they might have gone for breakfast for me and blood for them.

Atlas lingers, always in the background, always watching. His silver eyes are focused, but I can see the exhaustion behind his sharp facade.

I slip into the bedroom and put yesterday's clothes back on before returning to the living room, where Atlas and Gabriel are drinking coffee on the couch.

"I have no idea what I'm supposed to do now. I still want to kill Scott for what he did to my mom, but how can I be okay with taking Brighton's only living parent from her?"

Atlas sets his mug on the table and says in a flat voice, "That's not your call. Scott will die either way."

"So what you're saying is you're going to kill him?" I ask.

"Well, Lex seems to think we should leave that pleasure to you. If you're not too emotional to handle it."

My stomach drops at his tone. It's devoid of any true emotion and it rubs me in all the wrong places. "Do you expect me to be...? What, like you? Of course I'm going to be emotional about it. This is my best friend's father, not just some random hunter. Brighton already lost one parent. *I* almost did too. You expect me to be okay with this?"

Atlas's sharp eyes flick between mine, missing the pain I'm sure is filling my own gaze. "I'm not saying you have to do it, Calla. I'm saying if that's what you *want*, the kill is yours."

We stare at each other for a moment. I swallow past the emotion building in my chest, then open my mouth to respond, but nothing comes out.

The worst part? Atlas is right. Scott needs to die—and that's going to break Brighton.

I flee the room without another word. I don't know what to say at this point. My throat is thick with unshed tears, and I turn on the shower as if that will cover the sound of the sob clawing its way up my throat. I pull my phone out of my back pocket and dial Brighton's number. The line doesn't even ring once before I get an automated message that says, "We're sorry. The number you have reached has been disconnected or is no longer in service."

The phone slips from my hand, clattering against the white marble vanity as I stare at my reflection in the mirror. It's one with bright lighting all around it, which really doesn't help the washed-out and splotchy look of my face.

I turn on the cold water and splash my face, pressing my fingers to my temples as wetness trails down my cheeks, dripping onto the front of my shirt. I look into the mirror as if my reflection is going to tell me what to do, how to survive this and get through it unscathed. A voice in the back of my head, low and cruel, tells me I won't. I won't make it through this without loss, whether it be one of the vampires I've come to care for, my family, or my best friend.

In this world, no one makes it out alive—even if they're meant to be immortal.

Walking the streets of New York City makes me reminiscent of the days I lived in Brooklyn and spent much of my time in the city. Of the nights I spent going from bar to bar with friends after long days in the office, meeting women I never knew the names of—nor saw more than once. On occasion, maybe twice.

Walking this path with Kade now, heading toward a blood bank, where Marcel assured us the staff would be accommodating and supply us with blood during our stay in the city, I can't help but worry about the vampire beside me. Even last night, with my hand wrapped around his cock, he was distant, and he seems to be growing more so every day. None of us expect him to be okay, to bounce back to normal after watching his sister who he just reconnected with be killed by hunters, but I refuse to let him suffer in silence. If the roles were reversed, he'd be the same way with any of us.

We pass a couple slow walkers and round the corner to a less busy street lined by red brick row houses, and I punch him in the shoulder, firm but lighthearted. "You can talk to me, you know." I'm not sure how else to breach the subject and get a conversation going. In the decades I've known Kade, I've never seen him like this, which makes me wary on how to approach the matter.

He huffs out a humorless laugh, keeping stride next to me. "About what?"

I shoot him a sideways look, shrugging with my hands in my jacket pockets. "So we're just going to pretend that you're totally fine and not being super weird, even for you?"

It's Kade's turn to shrug. "No idea what you're talking about." It takes him a moment to realize I've stopped walking, and he turns around, arching a brow at me. "What?" he asks.

"You know what," I tell him. "You're not okay. We all know it. We all see it every single day and none of us know what the fuck we're supposed to do to help you."

He glances skyward, his shoulders rising and falling with a sigh. "There's nothing for you to do, Lex. I don't know what you want me to tell you. This is me. Living with what happened. And the moment I get my hands on any one of those hunters, I'm going to shred them to ribbons." His fangs are fully extended by the time he finishes speaking, and I take a quick glance around to make sure we're not being watched.

I blow out a breath. "Yeah, that's all fine and good, but I'm worried about you. We all are."

"No thanks," Kade says plainly, pursing his lips as he shoves his hands into his pockets and rocks back on his heels.

I step toward him. "The fuck? What do you mean, *no thanks*?"

He blinks at me. "I don't want your worry. It's useless to me."

I grab the front of his leather jacket and pull him off the street, hauling him into an alley between two concrete buildings, and slam him against the solid wall. "You need to get your shit together and talk to us, brother. I understand everything with the hunters was bad and you need time to heal from the loss of—"

Kade growls, cutting me off. "What I need, *brother*, is to kill some hunters."

I don't let him go. In fact, I tighten my grip on his jacket, leaning in so close our heavy breaths are mixing. "I understand. Whatever you've got going on in your head, it isn't your burden to face alone. We're here for you. You're my brother, as much as Gabriel and Atlas are. We are a family, however dysfunctional we are sometimes, so don't block us out now. We've been through so much shit together. Don't let this be what comes between us. I want them dead as much as you do. I swear, I will make it happen. These attacks will only continue and we will make sure the hunters fall."

Something in Kade's gaze wavers, and he swallows hard, his jaw clenched tightly. He drops his cheek to my shoulder, letting out a shuddering breath, and we stand there for a moment.

I inhale deeply, closing my eyes at the crisp, clean scent of him, and press my lips together. His lips brush my throat, and my heart races, my pulse zipping with energy. I tip my head to the side slightly, licking my lips, and whisper, "Go ahead." My heart beats faster and my dick hardens.

There's a brief moment of hesitation before Kade sinks his fangs into my neck.

I gasp softly, pulling in a slow breath as my blood flows freely into his mouth, and he groans against me, palming the front of my pants while he feeds. My blood won't give him much sustenance. Maybe a bit from the last human blood I had, which is typically why vampires don't feed off each other, but it does bond us in a way that some would be uncomfortable with.

Kade and I—we've always had a deep level of understanding for each other, being able to give the other what they needed, even knowing what they needed before they knew it. It's something I'm not prepared to lose. I'm going to do whatever it takes to get the Kade I know back, to save him from the demons I know are trying to control him. Because I've felt them too.

I push against him, desperate for the friction he's creating between my legs, and when he shoves his hand past the waistband of my pants and wraps his hand around my throbbing cock, I growl a curse at him.

His fangs retract, and he laps at my neck while moving his hand up and down my length before pulling it out of my pants to give him better access. He grabs my shoulder and turns us around so I'm against the wall now. I lean against it, tipping my head back as Kade pumps his hand faster, alternating speed and pressure enough to drive me fucking wild. My blood stains his lips and my gaze flicks to his eyes, but he's staring at my cock, his pulse pounding just as hard as mine.

"Fuck," I groan through my teeth, warmth spreading through me as if I had been the one to feed. "You're going to make me come." The muscles in my stomach clench and the tip of my cock glistens with moisture, but Kade's movements don't slow. In fact, he works me harder, faster, until my breath hitches and my muscles coil tight. I grunt, spilling my release onto Kade's hand.

"Feel better?" he asks, a hint of a smirk on his lips as he kneels, cleaning his hand in a puddle of rainwater.

I tuck myself back into my pants and arch a brow at him. "I was going to ask you the same thing."

He straightens, offering me a one-shouldered shrug. "Distractions help, I guess, but the anger I've felt since Meredith... it doesn't go away,

Lex. It ebbs and flows, and when it's at its greatest height, I'm worried about what I could do."

I nod in understanding, then ask, "To us?"

"Calla mostly," he admits. "The rest of you can protect yourselves."

"Yes, and we'll protect her too." I shake my head. "Kade, you're not going to hurt Calla."

"No more than we already have, you mean," he comments in a low voice.

The warmth in me is quickly washed away. "We've done some shitty things, yeah, but I think we all can tell how different things have become. We care about the fiery little human, and I can say with some confidence that she cares for us as well."

"What do you think she'll do once we figure out if the oath is valid?"

A heavy pit of unease unfurls in my stomach, and I shake my head again. "I have no fucking clue."

"You want her to stay as much as I do," he says.

"I do," I answer without hesitation.

Do we deserve her? Abso-fucking-lutely not.

But she has become part of us, and it'll be a cold day in hell before any of us let her go without a fight.

That being said, if we find out Calla wasn't meant to be ours, and she decides to leave, we'll have to set her free. But I hope—more than I'd care to admit—she *chooses* to stay.

CHAPTER

EIGHT

CALLA

I sit on the shiny white marble floor of the bathroom, scrolling through old photos of Brighton and me, knowing it's not going to make me feel any better but unable to stop myself from doing it. Will looking at pictures from the spring break we spent in Mexico bring her mom back or stop the vampires and hunters from killing each other? Of course not, but it's sure as hell a decent, albeit short-lived, distraction.

After half an hour, I force myself up from the heated tile and am walking toward the bathroom door when my phone chimes with a text message from an unknown number.

My heart beats faster as I read the message.

Hey, it's Tessa. We met a while ago when I reversed the magic in your blood. Gabriel reached out and said that you wanted to talk. What's up?

I chew my bottom lip, staring at the message, unsure how to reply to that. When I met Tessa back in Washington, she seemed like someone that I could be friends with, so I feel a little bad reaching out to her now when I need something.

I type out several responses before landing on one, short and sweet.

I have questions I'm hoping you can answer.

Her response comes a few seconds later.

I'll do my best. Where and when can we meet?

I'll have to check, I type back, *but the sooner the better.* I need to figure out what the hell is going on with this blood oath, what it means, and

502

also about my newfound ability to resist glamour. And at this point, if I don't get answers soon, I'm going to lose my damn mind.

Let me know when and where, and I'll be there, she says.

One last look in the mirror, and I take a deep breath, running my fingers through my hair to fix the mess it has become, and walk back to the other room.

Atlas and Gabriel are still in the sitting area. Atlas is on his phone and Gabriel is sipping from a cup of coffee.

I pocket my phone and approach them. "How long are we going to stay in New York City? I heard from Tessa, and we're trying to make plans to meet up."

"We'll be here until we get more information from our contacts in Washington on the latest attack," Atlas says.

"I'll take you to see Tessa," Gabriel chimes in. "I know you want answers and from what I know of Tessa, I believe we can trust her, at least with this."

I pull my phone back out and let Tessa know we're still in New York City. She responds a minute later, saying that she needs some time to deal with things on her end but can fly here in a couple of days to meet us. We agree she'll let us know when she arrives and leave it there for now.

I drop onto the couch next to Gabriel and sigh. "I'm worried about Brighton. I tried calling her but her phone was disconnected, which I assume we have Scott to thank for. I want her kept safe. Is there any way someone in Washington can figure out what's going on? And maybe bring her here?"

"No," Atlas cuts in. "We're not going to lead the hunters directly to us."

I don't miss a beat in my response. "Brighton isn't a hunter."

Atlas just shakes his head without looking up from his phone.

"I just want to know that my best friend is alive." I choke on the words, pulling back when Gabriel tries to reach for me.

"I'll get in touch with her," he assures me, "but that's the best I can do right now."

As scared and as angry as I am, I do know that, but I also know I can't just sit here doing nothing.

I get off the couch and find my shoes, lacing them up. Figuring this hotel is fancy enough, they should have a gym, and I need something to keep my mind occupied.

"Where are you going?" Gabriel asks, but before I can answer, Atlas stands, setting his phone on the table. "I'll go with you," he says as if he read my mind and knew I was planning to go searching for the gym.

I didn't exactly want company, but if Atlas is anywhere near as conflicted as I am with what's going on, I understand the need for the distraction, so I don't argue.

We head there together, and I frown when we step inside the bright, open room and I realize there are a few people already working out, one woman jogging on the treadmill and one guy spotting another on the bench press in front of a wall of floor to ceiling windows over-looking Central Park.

Without hesitation, Atlas uses vampire speed to appear before each person, glamouring them to leave the gym. I walk further into the room as they head for the door without acknowledging me. Once they're gone, Atlas locks the set of frosted glass double doors and prowls closer to me. Despite the cold air being blown into the space, a flush spreads across my chest under his predatory gaze.

I arch a brow at him as the room seems to get smaller, then shift back a few steps, bumping into a mini fridge stocked with towels and water bottles. My eyes snap back to Atlas, who continues closing the distance between us at an unhurried pace. "What... are you doing?"

"You wanted a distraction," he answers simply.

"Yeah, well, so did you. That's why we're here."

"Exactly," he says, the corner of his mouth quirking ever so slightly.

"I was going to run on the treadmill or lift weights. I don't know what you're doing," I tell him, propping my hands on my hips.

His eyes fill with hunger, and in a split second, I maneuver around him, putting space between us once more, which makes him smirk.

"Don't back down," he says, a hint of amusement in his voice as he turns to face me again.

"You want to fight?" I say, my brows lifting. "Here? Right now?"

He inclines his head in acknowledgement, and I drop my arms to my sides, shaking them out.

"Okay," I say, drawing out the word, "but I'm out of practice, so no vamp speed and no glamour." I walk over to the padded mats, not having to look over my shoulder to know Atlas has followed. I tug off my T-shirt, leaving me in a sports bra and leggings.

"I remain thoroughly amused you think I need any of that to beat you," he muses, again coming closer, and pulls his shirt over his head, tossing it with mine before nodding at my bra. "Your turn."

I roll my eyes, standing my ground this time. "Fuck off. Let's just do this."

"Come at me," he prompts, a glimmer of amusement lightening his eyes.

I have the stark realization that I could all too easily become addicted to this playful side of Atlas. It doesn't come out often—he won't let it—but I find myself enjoying it way too much each time it does.

I step forward, raising my arms, closing my hands into fists, and jab out with my right arm. He ducks, moving behind me, but I spin away before he can get his arms around me from behind and smack them down before getting in a punch to his chest. He advances again, grabbing my wrist and spinning me around, pulling my back against his chest. I immediately try to pull away, to escape his grasp, but he holds firm without a single ounce of effort. *Fucking vampire strength.*

"What now?" he murmurs, his lips against my ear.

My throat is dry, but I manage to force out, "Ideally, I would reach for my dagger and stab the shit out of you."

"Hmm," he says, "and where is your dagger, Calla?"

I grit my teeth, trying again to break free despite how pointless it is. There is no world where I can overpower Atlas, and he fucking knows it. "Well, I didn't think it would be very wise to wear it around a hotel with a bunch of humans."

He exhales a slow breath. "What did I tell you?"

"Not to take it off," I say in an agitated tone. "But—"

"But nothing." He snakes an arm around my waist, his lips teasing the pulse at my throat, making my breath hitch.

I flush hotly. "Fine." Then I mumble much lower, "Sorry."

"Don't apologize to me. You're the one who's dead." He bites the side of my neck without breaking the skin, as if he's intending to prove his point.

I scowl, attempting to elbow him in the ribs. "Uh, touché. Or, I don't know. Does that count if you're born a vampire? Like, you're born dead or...?"

His low chuckle in my ear makes me shiver, and I fight the urge to close my eyes and grind my ass against the very obvious erection he's pressing into me. "You pose an interesting question that I actually don't have the answer to," he says.

"Well, fuck, alert the media," I remark dryly. "That's a first."

"Cute," he throws back, nipping my earlobe. "Are you going to try to get out of this or are you enjoying it too much?"

I clear my throat. "Feels like you're the one who's enjoying it too much."

He pulls back and spins me around to face him, moving so fast the room blurs for a second. He snags my chin, forcing my gaze to his, and dips his face so his lips nearly touch mine. "You forget I can smell your arousal."

My gaze lowers as heat fills my cheeks. "Good for you."

His lips brush mine. "It's rather distracting, actually."

I lean in before I can stop myself. "Then do something about it."

His lips curve into a wicked smirk. "Perhaps once you've worked for it."

I roll my eyes, but follow him across the room to the bench press and set up the weights.

Atlas spots me while I lift. I manage a few sets before a sheen of sweat covers my chest and forehead, and I grunt with exertion, returning the bar to the rack after my fifth set. I haven't lifted that much in a while, but I feel good, *strong*. Atlas walks around the bench as I sit up, and my breath catches when he crouches at the end of it, his hands going to my hips and spreading my legs open.

"What are you...?" His hand brushes my core through my leggings, cutting my voice off. He reaches up, sliding his fingers into the waistband of my leggings, and pulls them down. I lift my ass, and he pulls them and my panties down to my ankles, leaving me bare to him. He doesn't hesitate. His tongue is between my legs in an instant, and I press my lips together, suppressing a moan.

"You know," I say breathlessly, "I really hope they don't have a security camera in here."

Atlas pauses, looking up at me from between my thighs. "I don't give a fuck."

"Noted," I breathe, and he returns his mouth to my pussy, licking then sucking my clit into his mouth. He has my head spinning in record time, and I grip the sides of the padded bench, my chest heaving with short breaths as I race toward release. His grip on my hips tightens, and he pushes his tongue deep inside me, his fingers finding the bundle of nerves at my core and driving me over the edge.

"Fuck," I moan. "Right there."

Atlas chuckles, sending vibrations straight through my core, and flicks his tongue along my pussy walls at a speed and pressure that renders me completely speechless as pleasure floods my entire body. I cry out, clamping my thighs around his head, sweat rolling down my temples as I ride the electric aftershocks of my orgasm.

Without warning, he pulls me off the bench onto the mats, hovering over me as he cages me in between his arms. "Is this enough of a distraction for you?" he taunts.

"Uh-huh," I answer, still trying to catch my breath. "You?"

"It will be."

He stands and tugs off his pants, tossing them behind him before crawling over me again, lining the head of his cock up with my entrance. My body trembles in anticipation, and I reach for him, but he grabs my hands, trapping them above my head as he slams into me, stealing my breath, and seals his lips over mine, kissing me hard and filling me to the hilt. I moan against his lips as he pulls out and thrusts back into me.

I suck in a breath when I realize his fangs have extended, and the thought of him sinking his fangs into me steals my breath anew.

"Tell me what you want," he says against my lips.

"You know."

"Of course I do," he says smugly. "I want to hear you say the words."

"You are so bossy," I grumble.

"And yet, you're so fucking wet for me because you like it and you *hate* that you like it."

"Fuck you," I growl, and he chuckles against my lips.

"What is it you think we're doing, Calla?" His blazing silver eyes flick between mine. "Now, say the words, or I'm going to stop everything."

He wouldn't. I pull back enough to glare at him.

"You think I'm not serious?"

I swallow my pride, my eyes dropping to his mouth where his fangs are visible. "Bite me." The words leach from my lips as my pulse skyrockets, and his lips curl into a dark smirk. Atlas grips my jaw, tilting my head to the side, and lowers his lips to my neck. He drops featherlight kisses there, continuing his thrusting, then a moment later, his fangs sink into my throat, and I gasp sharply. The spike of pain is quickly replaced by the most euphoric sensation that makes me sigh, and the sensation of blood being pulled from me as he fills me with his cock makes my heart pound and my head spin. A pleasure I've only experienced since meeting the vampires.

Atlas fucks me until nothing exists in my mind but him. My muscles clench around him, and I come hard, crying out as Atlas pulls away from my neck and kisses me again. His thrusts become harder and faster, until he finds his release, grunting against my lips.

We find our clothes and get dressed, and I down half a water bottle as we walk back to the suite where Lex and Kade have seemingly just gotten back.

Lex takes one look at us and grumbles, "I always miss out on the fun."

After what few belongings we have are packed, we check out and leave the hotel, getting into the Escalade to head for the place Marcel rented for us until we decide if we're returning to Monroe, to Washington, or where we're going next.

It's nothing fancy or like what we lived in at home, but it'll do for the time we're here. Our temporary accommodation is a simple, three-story row house with old wood floors and exposed brick walls in several rooms, including the main floor living room. There's even a small weight room on the second floor for Calla and Atlas to go at each other and a kitchen big enough for Gabriel to cook, with updated stainless steel appliances.

He and Atlas left shortly after we arrived to meet with Atlas's parents. After they found out their son was in New York City, Lenora and Simon wanted to know why. Translation: they demanded an audience with him, and Gabriel tagged along as backup. Doesn't hurt that the Yorks have a soft spot for Gabe. The guy knows how to charm anyone—old, important-as-fuck vampires or otherwise.

The plan is to tell them our trip here has to do with Selene. Gabriel's friends, Fallon and Jase, live in the city and are helping us track her down. We don't want them to know the reason we came was actually because Calla's mom was hurt and she needed to see her. They would see the move as stupid and weak, playing into the hands of the hunter who caused the accident for likely the very purpose of getting us here. Our trip has been uneventful on the hunter front so far, but our security team is very good at what they do. It would take significant manpower to get anywhere near us. After the attack at the house and the one Kade lost his sister in, we've reinforced our team tenfold. This isn't the first time the hunters have grown significantly in numbers in a short period of time and decided they were strong enough to over-throw and effectively wipe out the vampires. It seems it doesn't matter how many times history repeats, how many times the hunters lose, every handful of decades, they think they've discovered the answer to getting rid of us. Of course, it never works—it never will. Our species was made to outlast humanity... so the inconvenience of the hunters coming to interfere from time to time is just something we've gotten used to. But this time, perhaps it is different. With Calla now involved, the stakes are higher for us. The hunters—that prick Scott Ellis specifi-cally—have something to leverage, and we have something to lose. And none of us are willing to let that happen.

While Atlas and Gabriel are gone and Kade is in the shower, I flip through the channels on the television until Calla plops down next to me. She tucks her legs under her and leans against the back of the couch, shifting her eyes toward me. "Will you tell me about the night you made the deal with my ancestor?" she asks. "Why did you do it, knowing it would ruin my chance at a future that I chose? I mean, I know you didn't know me then, but did you not think about what this would do to the person the oath was connected to?"

Well, fuck. I suppose I shouldn't be surprised that she's asking. If anything, I should be surprised it took until now. I don't have an answer. Well, not a good answer, one that will appease her. The truth is going to be sorely disappointing. I rake my hands through my hair, then drag them down my face, sighing deeply. "Calla," I say in a soft tone, "I wish I could tell you there was some important reason I needed to make that deal, but honestly, I was bored." I glance at her, and her eyes narrow ever so slightly as she shakes her head.

"You were *bored*," she echoes, disbelief filling her tone, making it sharper.

"Hey, I told you that you weren't going to be happy. That's who I was back then. I wasn't thinking about you. I figured it would be a form of entertainment when the time came. And you know, I wasn't wrong."

She scowls, and I almost wish I could take back what I said. Almost. "I'm so glad I can be a form of entertainment for you, because that's all I could ever hope for in my life. Entertainment for a group of arguably psychotic vampires who seem to hate everyone else but are okay with sharing me."

"Right," I tell her, not really knowing what else to say at that point. She's not wrong. The four of us would kill anyone who laid a finger on our girl, but we're all more than okay with each other bringing her levels of pleasure she's never and could never experience apart from us. I suppose that's what knowing one another for over a century allows for. Honestly, I haven't given it much thought. The four of us with Calla feels natural. Sometimes, it's the only thing that seems to make any sense.

"I don't understand how this bond between us works. You said it was something to do with my blood and being connected to everybody in my family line, but this feels different." Her voice softens a bit. "I mean, doesn't it?"

I nod in agreement, because she's right. It *is* different, but it has nothing to do with the oath or our connection to her blood. It's *her*, and I'm not exactly sure how to say that. "I don't know what you want me to tell you, Calla."

She huffs out a breath, and something tells me she isn't sure either. Not truly. "Tell me why you came when you did. What was it about that night? That moment in my life that you decided, *yeah, now seems like a great time to waltz in and flip everything upside down for this girl who's just trying to get through college.* Can you explain that to me, Lex?"

I pull back, surveying her face—her firm expression and the darkness in her eyes. "I know you're upset, that you've been upset since it happened—even when you didn't hate being with us. But does it really matter now? If the oath is invalid or never should have applied to you and you're free to go, does it really matter?"

"I suppose that'll be something I need to decide once I talk to Tessa. At this point, I can only hope she has some answers that you guys obviously don't."

"That's fair," I offer, kicking my legs up on the coffee table and resting my hands behind my head, my fingers laced together. "I know what I did was shitty, okay? And your reaction, knowing that it hurt you, makes me want to apologize. But then, I think that if I hadn't done it, I... I wouldn't know you. So, I can't sit here and truthfully tell you that I'm sorry, because I'm not."

She stares at me for a moment, then swallows hard. "Well." She pauses. "Thanks for your honesty, I guess."

I sit up straight and angle my body toward her. "Calla." I wait for her to look at me before I say, "You being here has changed everything. You understand that, don't you?"

I don't miss the way her pulse kicks up or the flush in her cheeks as she stares back at me. "You know," she says in a quieter voice than I was expecting, "the time I spent waiting for you to come for me, not knowing when it would be... That was worse than anything I've faced since the night you all showed up at my apartment."

"We should have called first," I say jokingly.

She punches me in the arm, and the strength behind it makes me grin. Our girl is strong—in many ways. "You didn't answer my question," she finally says.

I nod. "You got very close to Brighton, and while we considered the possibility of that coming in handy, we were also wary of it backfiring. We decided it wasn't worth the risk and that we needed to step in before things could potentially get out of hand."

She turns on the couch, resting her back against the armrest and facing me. "What, were you concerned her dad would recruit me to the hunters and *I'd* end up coming after *you*?" She laughs as if she's kidding in her suggestion, but the thought had crossed our minds. "Seriously?" she asks, slightly taken aback.

I shrug, unsure what to make of her response. "It was a possibility we had to consider."

Calla purses her lips in thought. "And yet, Atlas insists on me carrying a weapon that can kill you and is constantly training me to—"

"Protect yourself," I interject. "He knows as well as the rest of us that you won't hurt us. Same as you know we won't hurt you." There might've been a period of time when that wasn't true, but it has certainly passed.

She huffs out a breath, pulling at a loose thread at the hem of her shirt. "Why is this so complicated?"

I itch to reach for her, to pull her into my lap and hold her against me. "Because we live in a world full of nightmares most people could never imagine."

"The nightmares have to end sometime," she murmurs.

With a sigh, I say, "Not when you live forever."

She lets out a little laugh. "You're like the worst vampire salesman ever, Lex."

My lips twitch. "Sorry, didn't realize I was in a pitch session."

She lifts her head to smile at me, her eyes holding mine. "Are... are you glad Atlas turned you? Now, I mean? Looking back on it?"

"I am," I answer sincerely. "Sure, it's had its challenges. There's no shortage of them when you have to learn a new way of living." I tilt my head, searching her face for some hint as to why she's asking.

She chews her bottom lip, nodding. "Right. Of course."

"Why do you ask?" I ask in a gentle tone.

Calla shrugs. "Just curious. You all have such different stories, it's interesting to see how you all came together."

While I don't exactly buy the entirety of her response, I don't push it. Something tells me she's not ready to explore the real reason for her question.

CHAPTER

TEN

CALLA

If waking up on my twenty-fourth birthday, in an unfamiliar house, with four vampires that are, like, ten times my age isn't weird, then maybe I've spent too much time with them.

After my conversation with Lex yesterday and turning another year older today, I can't stop thinking about my future. I hadn't planned to ask him about becoming a vampire, because despite him not regretting his choice, that's still not a life I can see for myself. Immortality is, quite frankly, terrifying to consider. Add vampire hunters into the mix, and it's enough to thrust me into a tailspin of panic, so I shut down that train of thought immediately.

I make no move to get out of bed despite the warm, bright sun shining through the third story window. I lay on the soft covers, staring outside, watching people as they walk past. I'm tempted to go back to sleep; I don't think I've had a restful night in weeks. But the scent of coffee is like a siren's call, pulling me out of the comfort of the bed. I walk down the hallway and both sets of stairs, following the scent to the kitchen on the main floor. The closer I get, the sweeter the smell becomes. I step into the room and find Gabriel pulling dishes down from an upper cupboard.

He smiles the moment I enter the room. "Happy birthday, angel," he says, walking over to me with a cup of coffee in his hand. He leans in, pressing his lips to my cheek in a soft kiss, and when he pulls back, he hands me the coffee.

"Thank you," I tell him with a smile.

His eyes search mine. "Did you sleep okay?"

"Sure," I say noncommittally, and he gives me a knowing look. I shrug, taking a sip of the godly bean juice. I bump my shoulder against his. "The coffee helps."

He watches me a moment longer before letting it go, walking back to the stainless steel stove.

"What are you making?" I ask, leaning against the island in the center of the kitchen. "It smells amazing."

Gabriel keeps his back to me, grabbing a spatula off the counter next to him. "Well, I wasn't sure if you would want waffles or pancakes or French toast, so I—"

"You made all of them, didn't you?"

He turns to face me again and nods. I can't help but grin at the faint pink tinting his cheeks. *Gabriel's blushing.*

"That was very kind of you," I tell him, taking another drink. "And this is amazing. You never disappoint."

"At least where cooking is concerned," he says, then immediately looks as if he regrets saying that.

"Yeah, let's not talk about the other stuff today. Please. Can that be my one birthday wish?"

"You could have anything and that's what you want for your birthday?" Kade says, walking into the room and stealing a piece of French toast off the platter beside the stove. He doesn't bother putting it on a plate, he just folds it in half and shoves it in his mouth, eating the slice in two bites.

I press my lips together, the warmth in my chest traveling slightly lower at the hungry look in Kade's eyes. "Well, I guess that depends," I say, "on what else is being offered."

"Whatever you want," Gabriel says, "it's yours."

I laugh, setting my mug on the island counter next to me. "I don't know if you can offer me that."

"Is that a challenge?" he asks, a glint in his eyes that shoots heat straight to my core, because I am *so* not used to this side of Gabriel, but I definitely like it.

"No," I say, "I just... I want to eat my breakfast and maybe pretend like our world isn't about to explode. Sound good?"

Gabriel nods solemnly, and Kade sighs as if he's disappointed by my request, walking around the kitchen to pour himself a cup of coffee.

By the time Gabriel finishes putting all the food out, Lex and Atlas join us in the small dining room off the kitchen. There's a floor to ceiling window at the head of the mahogany dining table which has light reflecting off the crystals from the modern chandelier hung over it.

Lex pulls me against his side and kisses my cheek. "Happy birthday," he murmurs, his lips tracing the shell of my ear.

"Thanks," I say back, wrapping my arm around him in a sort of half hug.

"So, Atlas," Lex says dramatically, "what did you get our girl for her birthday?"

I roll my eyes at Lex. "Yeah, I'm sure—Never mind. I... I don't need anything. I just want to make sure everybody I care about is safe. Which frankly seems to be too much to ask right now, so I'm good. I don't need anything."

"I was going to offer a morning training session where I might just let you win," Atlas says with a small twist of his lips.

"Yeah, I don't believe that for a second, but I'll take it. You're on."

"You know, I thought you might say that."

"That's great. Now if you don't mind, I need to eat some food. And everything smells so fucking good, I might not actually be able to move after."

"Now that sounds like the type of breakfast I'd be in for," Lex says, shooting me a wink.

"Lex, could you cool it on the sexual innuendos?"

He snorts. "As if. And you like it, don't even lie."

Instead of answering, I take a sip of coffee and shift my attention to filling my plate with a pancake, a waffle, and a slice of French toast before piling it high with syrup, raspberries, and powdered sugar. I take a seat at the table, and the guys sit around me.

"There's got to be something we can do today," Lex says around a mouthful of French toast.

I immediately shake my head. "Really, I don't want to do anything. I've never been one to care too much for birthdays, so it's all good. And we have far more important things to worry about right now than me turning another year older."

"Yeah, what are you now, thirty-seven?"

I shoot Lex a dry look. "I don't think that's really insulting until you *are* thirty-seven. And you're calling *me* old? Really?"

Gabriel chuckles from behind his coffee cup, and I turn my attention to the plate in front of me, then proceed to stuff my face.

My phone rings as I'm finishing my last mouthful, and when I see my mom's caller ID, I get up from the table and answer the call in the kitchen. "Mom, how are you doing?" I ask, finding the need to do something with my hands, so I start putting the leftover food in the fridge.

"Hang on, hang on," she says, laughing softly, and then proceeds to start singing happy birthday.

I'm surprised at the tears in my eyes by the time she finishes the song. I swallow past the lump in my throat. "Thanks, Mom," I say in a thick voice, closing the fridge as I hold the phone to my ear with my shoulder. "Seriously, how are you doing?"

"Much better."

Grabbing the sponge from the little dish beside the sink, I wipe down the island counter. "You promise you're not just saying that to make me feel better on my birthday?"

She laughs. "Calla, I'm serious. I'm okay. You don't need to worry about me. They're taking very good care of me. And so is your father, around the clock."

"Well, good, but you'll let me know if you need anything, right?" I toss the sponge into the sink and lean against the counter.

"Of course, sweetheart. Are you doing anything for your birthday?

"Um..." My voice trails off, and I chew my thumbnail. "Yeah, I think I'm going to rope one of the guys into giving me a cooking lesson. Maybe eat some cake. I hear that's customary for birthdays. But I don't want to keep you. Please make sure you're resting and not pushing yourself too hard and—"

"Calla," she cuts in. "Don't worry about me, okay? I will keep checking in with you. You will know if anything changes. I love you. Now, please go enjoy your birthday."

With a heavy sigh, I finally concede. "I'll talk to you later, okay?"

"Of course. I love you, sweetheart."

"I love you too, Mom."

"Wait, wait, wait!" Dad shouts in the background.

"Hey, Dad," I say, assuming Mom has me on speakerphone.

"Happy birthday, sweetheart," he says.

I smile, though he can't see it through the phone. "Thank you."

"You're getting old. What are you, late thirties now?"

I roll my eyes, knowing Lex is most likely in the other room laughing his ass off after having made that same quip. "Yeah, it feels like that some days," I tell him.

"Well, just know that we love you. Talk to you soon."

"Okay, Dad. I love you too."

"Bye, sweetheart," Mom says, and we end the call.

Later that afternoon, after a training session with Atlas where he does *not* let me win and in fact kicks my ass several times, Gabriel brings me into the kitchen, where he has one of the counters covered with those reusable mesh grocery bags, and they're full of food.

I turn to him, a bright smile on my lips. "You're finally going to give me a cooking lesson," I say. He must've heard me on the phone with my parents. Though I wouldn't put it past him to have already had this planned.

He nods, smiling back at me. "Better late than never."

I scan the bags, my interest piqued. "What are we making?" I ask, walking toward the counter. I peek inside one of the bags and find a loaf of French bread. I'm already excited. "I hope this is to make garlic bread," I tell him.

"Of course," he answers, coming behind me. "I figured we'd start with something fairly easy and something I know you'll enjoy because I've made it before."

"Yeah, I'm pretty sure I've enjoyed every single thing you've made, so that doesn't really narrow it down, Gabriel."

He's still smiling when he says, "What do you think about lasagna?"

"I think I want to eat it. So yeah, let's do it. What do we do first?" I ask.

"Wash your hands and then we'll preheat the oven and start mixing the ingredients and cooking the meat and lasagna noodles."

I pull my hair back with the elastic around my wrist, sweeping it off my neck and into a messy bun on the top of my head before washing my hands, with Gabriel using the sink next to me.

He proceeds to pull out a frying pan before turning to me. "We're going to cook the meat first. I picked up ground beef. We're also going to need to cut up onion and garlic to cook with it." He sets me up with a cutting board and a knife, and I start chopping the onion while he minces the garlic.

"There's a joke in here somewhere," I tell him, glancing over at his cutting board.

He chuckles, softly leaning over to press a kiss against the side of my head. "Garlic is one of my favorite ingredients to cook with."

"That makes me so happy," I tell him. "I could live off garlic bread. You know, if it was sustainable." Once the onion and garlic is chopped, we add it to the frying pan with the ground beef, and I mix it all together over the burner, then lean against the counter while it cooks. "What's next?" I ask him.

"We'll add the tomato paste and sauce as well as crushed tomatoes with some water and seasonings once the meat is cooked."

"That seems simple enough," I tell him, pursing my lips.

"Yes, this recipe is not as complex as it is lengthy. You do have to simmer it for a while. At least an hour, I've found, while stirring it occasionally to prevent it from sticking to the pan and burning."

"Wow. You should have your own cooking show." My tone is teasing, my lips twisting up at the corners.

"You think so?" he asks with a grin, and I nod in response. He cages me in, his arms gripping the counter on either side of me, and presses his forehead against mine. "I know you said you're not one to celebrate birthdays, but I for one am very grateful for your birth."

My cheeks flush, and I close my eyes as his lips brush mine. I lean into him, sealing my lips over his and kissing him deeply. His hands drop to my hips and pull me against him as his tongue slips into my mouth and he kisses me as if I'm the first breath of air he's taken in days.

My world narrows as my head spins and warmth floods my chest— and much lower when I feel the hardness between his legs press against me.

"You know, I had a feeling Gabriel would be a hands-on teacher in the kitchen." Kade's voice reaches me, and Gabriel chuckles against my lips, pulling back and kissing my cheek before stepping away. Kade walks around us to the fridge and pulls out a blood bag, ripping it open and drinking directly from it without even warming it up or putting it in a glass. He slides onto the counter beside where we were working, drinking in silence with his eyes locked on me.

I pull my bottom lip between my teeth to keep from frowning at him. Instead of responding to his behavior, I busy myself pulling out the necessary ingredients to make chocolate cupcakes to go with dinner. I mix the batter while Gabriel continues working on the lasagna, sticking my finger in the bowl and sucking the sweet, chocolatey goodness off before pouring it into a cupcake pan. My eyes whip toward Kade at the sound of his low growl and my cheeks flush as his eyes devour me.

"Do you need to take a walk?" Gabriel asks him.

His lips twist into a smirk. "That's not what I need."

I prop my hands on my hips, staring at him pointedly. "You want to help me make the icing?"

He slides off the counter and comes towards me, tossing the empty blood bag on the counter behind me. "Hmm, that depends," he says in a low voice, dragging his tongue over his bottom lip. "Do I get to lay you across this counter and lick it off you?"

A laugh escapes me before I can stop it, though neither of us miss the jump in my pulse. "It's my birthday. Maybe I should get to eat off you."

His smirk widens. "You will hear no arguments from me on that." He moves at a speed I can't track, grabbing my hips and lifting me onto the counter. His mouth is on mine before I can take a breath, and I make a startled noise against his lips. Without thinking, I wrap my legs around him, pulling him as close as he can get with the counter there, and he kisses me hard. My heart slams against my ribcage when I feel his fangs extend, but he's careful not to let them slice into my lips.

When he pulls back to give me a chance to catch my breath, his eyes flick between mine, and my gaze drops to the bulge in his pants before swinging toward Gabriel, who is watching us with hunger in his eyes.

"You want in on this, Gabe?" Kade says in a smooth voice.

I don't wait for him to answer. I reach out, offering him my hand. He steps closer, taking it and letting me pull him toward Kade and me. Once he's close enough, I slide my fingers into his hair and bring his mouth to mine, kissing him as warmth flares to life in my stomach.

Kade slides his hand up my thigh slowly, teasing me while one of Gabriel's hands finds its way under my shirt, the other braced on the counter. His mouth explores mine, his tongue pushing past my lips and flicking across the roof of my mouth. I push my chest into his touch, and he cups my breast, making me thankful I didn't bother with a bra after my post-training shower. His fingers circle my nipple before pinching it, making me gasp against his lips at the same moment Kade spreads my legs open, pressing his thumb against the heat at my core through my leggings.

"I want to bury my cock here," he says in a husky voice that sends shivers through me, because fuck, I want that too. "Hmm," he hums. "But first, I want a taste of our birthday girl."

Gabriel pulls away from my lips, sliding his hand to my hip, then uses both hands to lift me just enough for Kade to peel my leggings and panties down to my ankles before tugging them off completely.

My bare ass is on the counter we were just preparing food on, and that feels all kinds of wrong—for about five seconds.

My focus narrows on Kade's head between my legs. He trails his lips from my knees up the inside of each of my thighs until I'm practically squirming. Gabriel guides me backward until I'm laying across the island countertop. He pushes his hands under my shirt, dragging it up until my breasts are exposed, then pulls it off over my head. He leans over the counter and kisses me slowly, deeply, his fingers brushing over my collar bones, featherlight, until they reach my chest. I tip my chin up to kiss him back, moaning into his mouth as he cups my breasts, massaging them with skilled fingers as Kade continues to torture me with his teasing kisses against the delicate skin of my inner thigh.

"I've barely touched you, and you're already dripping for me," Kade purrs, and my cheeks flush hotly. He's right; moisture seeps from me, my core throbbing in response to his words.

His tongue flicks out, licking up my slit, and I practically whimper against Gabriel's lips. My back arches off the counter, pushing my breasts into his hands.

Kade sucks my clit into his mouth, swirling his tongue around it, and plunges two fingers into my pussy, making me see stars.

I cry out, breaking my kiss with Gabriel, my chest heaving with short breaths. "Fuck," I breathe, my hips moving against Kade, pushing him deeper inside me.

He thrusts hard and fast, curling his fingers at just the right angle to have me moaning in seconds. Heat shoots straight to my core and I clench around his fingers, riding them as his mouth devours me, licking and sucking at alternating speeds and pressures until my head is spinning. Gabriel continues palming my breasts, rolling my nipples between his fingers. His lips find the sensitive skin of my neck just below my ear, his breath stirring the hair there. "Are you going to come for him, angel?" His words propel me closer to the edge, the muscles in my stomach coiling tight.

"Yes," I pant. "Kiss me."

His lips are on mine in a second, devouring me as thoroughly as

Kade is. My heart pounds in my chest and my head feels light enough to float away. I'm floating on a cloud of blissful pleasure that I would give anything to last forever.

Seconds later, my pussy clenches around Kade's fingers and I'm launched over the edge, overcome with an earth-shattering orgasm that has me moaning against Gabriel's lips and grinding against Kade's face and fingers as I ride it out. He licks me clean before straightening and helping me sit up as Gabriel comes around the counter, leaning next to me.

"One down, twenty-three to go," Kade comments with a smirk, licking his lips.

I stare at him, still trying to catch my breath. "What the hell are you talking about?"

Gabriel shakes his head, chuckling softly. Clearly, he understood what Kade meant.

"Birthday fucks," Kade says.

I choke on a laugh, taking the shirt Gabriel offers me and tugging it on. "Do you want me to live to see my twenty-fifth birthday? Because I'm pretty sure letting you fuck me twenty-four times in one day would kill me."

After eating far too much lasagna and garlic bread at dinner, to the point my jeans are too uncomfortable to stay in, I slip away to the bedroom to change into leggings.

There's a soft knock at the door as I'm tying my hair back.

"Come in," I call out.

A moment later, Lex slips into the room, closing the door behind him. "Are you ready to go?" he asks, his gaze sweeping over my clothes.

I arch a brow at him, shaking my head. "Go where, Lex?"

The corners of his mouth curl into a grin, and I'm immediately suspicious. "Do you trust me?" he asks.

I prop my hands on my hips. "I don't know how to answer that."

He walks over to me at an easy pace, and part of me wants to step back, but I stand firm, though my hands drop to my sides as those silver eyes search mine. "Do you trust me?" he asks again. His tone is devoid of any humor, so I take a moment to consider it. I press my lips together, unable to form a response. Lex grins. "You didn't immediately say no, so I think we're making progress."

I roll my eyes. "Yeah, okay, so what? Where are we going?"

"I think it's time you get a tattoo," he says.

I blink at him. "Just because I didn't say that I don't trust you doesn't mean I'm going to let you tattoo me, Lex."

He reaches for me and tweaks my chin before I can move or slap his hand away. "We'll just see. How about this? I'll let you tattoo me if you let me tattoo you."

I lean against the dresser, staring at him. "You realize I have no experience in repeatedly stabbing somebody with a needle, right?"

He shrugs, as if that's the least of his concerns. "You'll catch on quick."

"Okay," I say, drawing the word out. There's a mix of nerves and excitement in my belly, making me antsy. The weight of his gaze doesn't help either. "Are you serious?" I check.

His only response is a confident grin.

There are several beats of silence before I sigh heavily. "Let's do this."

He offers me his hand, and I find myself reaching for him without even thinking about it. Our fingers lace together, and we walk downstairs to the main floor, where the others are lounging in the living room.

"I can't believe you convinced her," Kade says, sipping his glass of whiskey. I'm not sure if he's drinking more blood or booze these days, but it seems to help. To numb the anger and sadness radiating from him since he lost his sister for the second time. As much as it hurts me to see, if that's how he needs to cope right now, who am I—or any of us —to interfere? Kade doesn't seem like the type who would respond well to an intervention, though I do still think we need to do *something*. The anger and guilt and sadness he's harboring would rip even the strongest person apart.

"Honestly, same," I tell him. "This is crazy, right? Like, I shouldn't do this."

Kade shrugs. "It's not the end of the world, Calla. It's just a tattoo."

"Yeah, just a permanent marking on my body. Not like it's forever." My tone is dripping with sarcasm, but I press my lips together at the last word. *Forever*. Heat gathers my cheeks, and I drop my gaze to the floor. Something about the word holds new weight, and I have a feeling it has to do with the people I'm sharing my life with. Perhaps it's another reminder of my mortality. Knowing that Lex, Kade, Gabriel, and Atlas will live forever, whereas my life is a ticking clock.

"Come on," Lex says, tugging on my arm, and we head outside where the Escalade is parked at the curb. Lex opens the passenger side door for me to climb in, then shuts it and moves around the front of the vehicle using vampiric speed. In the time it takes me to blink, he's behind the wheel, starting the engine.

"Let me guess," I say as he shifts the car into drive and pulls onto the street. "You know another tattoo artist?"

"Not exactly," he says in response, pressing the gas harder.

I turn and look at him, my brows drawing together. "Uh, what does that mean?"

"Well," he says, drumming his fingers against the steering wheel. "Let's just say I found a tattoo studio that we're going to *borrow* tonight."

My eyes widen, and I smack his arm. "Lex! We're going to break in somewhere?"

He grins without looking at me. "You don't need to sound so horrified. I'll leave money."

"Yeah, and what if we get caught?" My voice increases in pitch with each sentence.

"Then I'll deal with it," he says, amusement lacing his tone. "You need to chill."

I shake my head, staring out the windshield. It shouldn't surprise me that Lex planned to have us break into a tattoo studio in the middle of the night. And the more I think about it, the less it does surprise me. What actually does is the lack of reluctance on my part. I trust that Lex will take care of it if something goes down. If the cops show up and try to bust us, he'll glamour them to fuck off. So really, the stakes aren't that high. At least in that respect. I'm absolutely still panicking over the thought of letting him near me with a tattoo gun. And yet, here I am. I don't think he would have forced me into the vehicle back at the house if I'd flat out refused, and I'm not sure if that says more about my progress with him or vice versa.

I exhale slowly, stretching my legs out and say, "All right."

"See?" he says, "This is gonna be great." He cranks up the music, filling the space with The Weeknd's *The Hills*. The bass makes the car vibrate, and I close my eyes, getting lost in the music. Lex rolls down the windows, letting in the crisp late-April evening air, and I breathe deeply, allowing myself to enjoy this moment, however fleeting and temporary it may be.

CHAPTER

ELEVEN

LEX

The tattoo shop is in one of the nicer neighborhoods in the area, and as we get closer, I can feel the nerves radiating off Calla in waves. She has to know I'm not going to let anything bad happen, otherwise she wouldn't have gotten into the car. If she didn't want to be here, she wouldn't be.

I park the car on the street and hop out, walking around the front and opening Calla's door, offering her my hand.

She stares at me, her expression filled with uncertainty and her lip caught between her teeth.

"Come on," I encourage with a charming smile, leaning toward her. "We do have all night, but I have other things planned for you I'd very much like to get to."

Her eyes narrow slightly, though the slight tinge of pink in her cheeks makes me think her head went the same place mine did. Finally, she takes my hand and allows me to help her out of the Escalade.

"We can't exactly walk through the front door," she says. "I'm sure they have a security system."

I shrug. "I'm sure they do, which is why we're gonna go through the entrance at the back and also why I had Marcel's team hack into their system and disable any alarms."

"This is quite the elaborate birthday gift, Lex. Breaking and entering. Wow, so nice of you."

I laugh softly, squeezing her hand as we walk to the back of the tall

525

and narrow, gray brick building through an alley between it and what smells like a butcher shop, and come to a stop at a solid metal door. I purse my lips, looking at the lock. I could probably try picking it but it'd be easier just to break it, so that's exactly what I do.

Within seconds, the door is open, and I usher Calla inside, closing it behind us. I keep the main lights off as we walk down a short hallway, our shoes echoing off the black marble floor. The space smells of citrus-scented cleaning products and antiseptic. There's also a bit of cologne that lingers in the air. I had scoped out the place earlier while Calla was training with Atlas and knew it would work perfectly.

I peek into one of the rooms and find it set up with a padded chair and a tattoo station, so I guide Calla inside, flicking on the light. The floor in here is white, contrasted by black walls with a gold zig-zag pattern. There's a shelf on the wall across from the door that's lined with black binders—samples of the artist's work, no doubt, considering there isn't any on the walls like in most places.

"You're going to show me how to do this, right?" she asks, pulling her hand free from mine and holding it up to look at it. Her fingers are shaking a little, and she presses her lips together. "I'm not sure this is such a good idea. I'm not going to be able to stop shaking the entire time, and your tattoo is going to look like a toddler did it."

I can't help but grin at that. "You're cute."

"Yeah, you're not going to think that when I fuck up the art that is currently on your body."

"Whatever you do is going to be perfect," I tell her, "but if it makes you feel better, I can glamour away your nerves, steady your hand."

She steps back immediately, her posture stiffening and her breath hitching. "You know I don't like it when you guys do that."

I hold my hands up in a gesture that's meant to be calming. I don't want to ruin this evening before the fun has even started. "I know. I'm not saying we have to, I'm saying it's an option. Whatever you want."

After several beats of silence, she huffs out a breath and plops down on the rolling stool. "Okay, I... Fine, I guess. But it better be temporary and very specific to what we're doing. And please make whatever it is you're having me draw on your body very simple and small and—"

"You're overthinking this," I cut in using a light tone, walking over to her. I slide my finger under her chin, tilting her face up so her eyes meet mine. "This is supposed to be fun. Relax. I'm not worried and you don't need to be either. Just have fun and enjoy your birthday."

"I don't think my idea is the same as yours when it comes to fun."

"Hmm, I think we both know that's not entirely true," I point out, smirking.

"Fine," she concedes and rolls toward the tattoo station, looking over all the instruments, and picks up the tattoo gun. "What am I supposed to do with this? Just draw?"

I cough to cover the sound of my laugh and shake my head subtly. "There's a little bit more to it than that."

She sets the gun down and shoots me a dry look before pulling her hair back. "Well, you're going to have to show me."

I nod. "Okay. What do you want on you?"

She seems to consider that for a moment, her eyes trailing the length of my bare arm to the vines and roses there.

"I don't think you're ready for a sleeve just yet," I tease.

"Funny," she deadpans. "I don't know. What do you think I should get?"

I shrug. "It's your body. It needs to be something that represents you or something you love. Or it can be fucking random, it doesn't matter. You can put as much or as little thought into it as you want. People get tattoos for all kinds of reasons, some for no reason at all. What do you think about the outline of an orchid? Maybe somewhere along your wrist or your thigh? I mean, you can put it somewhere you can cover up if you want or somewhere you can see at all times. It's totally up to you."

She tilts her head back and forth, thinking about it, then says, "Yeah, I like that idea. Something minimal and delicate. Maybe on the side of my wrist going up towards my elbow?"

I nod. "We can do that no problem."

"Okay, so what are you entrusting me to put on you?" she asks.

"I figured I'd let you do whatever you want."

She bursts out laughing. "That is very dangerous. I am no artist. I need a very simple design with an easy to follow stencil, and also maybe a shot of something strong to convince me this isn't the worst idea in the world."

"Fair enough," I say, more than a little amused with her. "I'm sure I can find something around here. And that might help steady your hand. Do you want to go first?"

"Uh, I guess?" she says, though it sounds more like a question with the increase of pitch near the end. "How long is it going to take?

"Ten, maybe fifteen minutes tops. The design I'm thinking for you is quite simple, not a ton of detail or shading necessary, so it won't take long at all. It'll take longer to set everything up than it will to actually tattoo you."

"Okay." She drags the word out, nodding as if she's talking herself into it.

I pat the chair and say, "You get settled in here. I'm gonna go find something to drink and be right back." I pause in the doorway, feeling the need to make sure she's on board and comfortable with being here. "You can still change your mind. If you truly don't want to do this, we don't have to." The corner of my mouth tugs up. "Believe me, I have no problem jumping to the second part of our plans for tonight." My cock twitches in my pants just thinking about taking her in that chair.

Calla folds her hands in her lap, looking at me with a bright-eyed expression. "No, I want to. Ever since that night you took me to Scarlett's, I've thought about getting one."

"Okay. Sit tight, birthday girl." I shoot her a wink, and she switches from the stool to the lounge style tattoo chair as I leave the room to search for a bottle of liquor. It's not difficult to track down. In fact, they have essentially an entire bar set up in their kitchen. I snag a bottle of tequila and head back to the studio, where Calla is lounging on the chair, her legs crossed at the ankles, staring up at the ceiling as her fingers tap along her thighs.

I saunter back into the room, the bottle of tequila in my hand, and walk around the lounge chair to drop onto the stool. I crack the bottle open, taking a long swig before handing it to Calla for her to do the same.

She swallows a mouthful, cringing, and sucks in a breath after she swallows. "That tastes like shit," she says.

I chuckle. "Yeah, well, it's an acquired taste. Are you ready?" I ask.

She puffs out her cheeks and offers a nervous laugh. "Yes?"

"Is that a question?"

"No. I mean, yes, I'm ready. Let's do it." She holds the bottle of tequila in her lap while I turn and start preparing the ink and gun after pulling on a pair of black gloves. "Aren't you gonna make a stencil?" she asks. "I mean, I don't have a lot of experience when it comes to tattoos but from what I've seen, they usually do."

I glance at her over my shoulder. "If that will make you more comfortable I can, but it's not a difficult design. I was planning on free-handing it."

She hesitates, pursing her lips. "Don't fuck it up," she says, offering me a hard stare.

I nod, barely containing my amused grin. "I thought you trusted me to do this."

"I do. I just don't want a wonky orchid on my arm."

"All right, I'm going to do a stencil, because you're just going to—"

"No, Lex, it's fine. Just do it."

I shoot her a wink, then turn back and continue preparing the instruments. When the gun is loaded up, I turn back to her and shave the small portion of skin I'm going to be inking. "Ready?" I check.

Her eyes meet mine, and she nods. "On a scale of, like, one to ten, how bad is this going to hurt?"

The corner of my mouth tugs upward. "It'll hurt far less than me sinking my teeth into you. How's that?"

Her cheeks flush and she looks away. "Yep. Okay, cool."

"No need to get uncomfortable, Calla." Especially considering how much we both know she likes to be bitten. I don't bother saying it aloud—I don't need to. My cock hardens just thinking about it.

"I'm not," she insists. "Just start before I freak out for no reason and change my mind."

"Okay," I say, lowering the gun to her skin. I start the design that I had pulled up on my phone, going for a few seconds before stopping. "How's that?" I check.

"Huh," she says, surprise filling her tone. "Yeah, that's not bad actually."

I can't help the smugness in my voice when I say, "I told you."

She rolls her eyes. "Yeah. Okay, just keep going."

The entire design takes about ten minutes. When it's done, I set the gun down and rip off the gloves, tossing them into the wastebasket on the other side of the table. I wipe her skin clean and let her take a look at the design. "You like it?"

"Holy shit. I'm kind of obsessed."

"That's good, considering it's kind of permanent."

She grins, still looking at the tattoo.

I wrap it up and tape the bandage to make sure it heals properly.

"Can I tell you something?"

I don't miss a beat. "Anything."

"I really don't want to tattoo you."

I laugh deeply, sliding my hands up her thighs. "It's okay. I wasn't going to make you do it."

"I'm not saying I couldn't do it," she points out. "I'm just saying I really don't want to fuck it up."

"It's all good," I tell her. "It's your birthday. We can do whatever you want."

She presses her lips together, her eyes flicking between mine. "The entire time you were sticking a needle in my skin, all I could think of was—"

"That time at Scarlett's?" I cut in, tilting my head to the side.

She nods, placing her hands over mine, her thumb tracing back and forth across the top of my hand. "I mean, we're already here. We've already broken probably multiple laws by breaking in, so we might as well—"

Before she can finish her sentence, I tug her forward, slamming my mouth against hers, claiming her lips with my own.

TWELVE

My world narrows on the feel of Lex's mouth on mine. He braces himself on the back of the chair with one hand as he leans over me and slides his other hand into my hair, gripping the back of my neck and holding me in place.

Our lips move together, battling for control in a way that makes my pulse surge and my heart pound against my chest as if it's attempting to break free of my ribcage.

I grip the front of his shirt, wanting him closer, pressed against me everywhere possible. I push my tongue into his mouth and grin against his lips when he groans in response.

After a blissful moment, Lex pulls back a little. "Tell me what you want," he murmurs, his lips brushing the line of my jaw.

I keep my eyes closed, licking my lips. "Whatever you're thinking," I say, slightly breathless, "that's what I want." Lex has never been one to disappoint, and right now, I really don't want to have to think.

He drags his mouth down my throat, kissing softly and making my skin tingle at his touch. "You'll need to be wearing far less clothing for what I'm thinking," he says in a low voice, looking at me with a dark, hungry gaze, though his fangs aren't visible—yet.

I nod, reaching for the waistband of my leggings to tug them down. Lex grabs my wrists and in a nanosecond has them above my head. I gasp softly, not expecting the movement.

"Keep them here," he instructs. "Let me take care of you."

I bite my lip, gripping the headrest of the chair and nodding.

Lex's eyes glimmer with amusement as they trail the length of me, from where my nipples are sticking out against my T-shirt to my Docs. He slides his hands up my thighs, warming the skin beneath my leggings, and I hold my breath as he gets dangerously close to the heat between my legs. His hands reach my hips and he drops them inward, brushing his thumb over my clit, making me gasp. His eyes flick to mine, darkening with desire. "You know," he murmurs in a husky tone, "I was going to reward you for handling your first tattoo so well, but I think I'll make you work for it a little longer."

My eyes narrow. "Mean," I grumble.

He presses his thumb down, and my hips lift at the same moment a moan tears its way from my lips. "Needy little thing," he muses.

"If you don't touch me," I say, holding his gaze, "I'll touch myself. You're more than welcome to watch."

Lex shakes his head, tutting his tongue. "Hmm, no you won't. I told you to keep your hands where they are."

I arch a brow at him. "You also said it was my birthday and we could do whatever I wanted. I didn't think you'd torment me before fucking me."

"Patience," he says in an amused tone, leaning in and brushing his lips across mine in a whisper of a kiss before pulling back again.

I scowl, though the sound is half-hearted. "You may have forever, but I certainly don't."

Lex chuckles and finally curls his fingers into the waistband of my leggings, dragging them slowly down my legs until they fall onto the floor in a pile along with my panties. "I'm dying to bury my cock in that sweet pussy of yours, so this is torment for me too."

"So shut up and put us both out of our misery."

He smirks. "Oh, I will, but first I think I'll make you come with my tongue. I want to taste you just as badly as I want to fuck you."

Heat fills my cheeks and pools low in my stomach. My skin feels ultra heightened, and when Lex presses his mouth just below my belly button, I pull my bottom lip between my teeth, my core throbbing with need.

The first pass of his tongue along my slit has me trembling, closing my eyes and fighting the urge to grip his hair and grind against his face. He holds me open to him, swirling his tongue around my clit until I'm panting, and when he plunges it inside me, I clench around him, unable to stifle my moan. Lex sucks and licks and thrusts his tongue in and out, pulsing his fingers against my clit in perfect timing. In minutes, I'm panting, desperate to feed the need to come. My breasts tingle, and I want nothing more than to reach for them, but I'm concerned Lex will stop fucking me with his tongue if I disobey his instruction to keep my arms above my head.

He hits a particularly sensitive spot deep in my pussy, and I suck in a sharp breath, moaning his name. He picks up speed, devouring me with his mouth as I writhe against him, my fingernails biting into the back of the chair. Pleasure floods through me in waves, and I succumb to it, crying out my release as a powerful orgasm rips through me. Lex licks me clean, making me shiver as I continue to ride the delicious aftershocks. He kisses the inside of each of my thighs before pulling back, grinning at me. He holds out his hands, and I take that as permission to move my arms, taking his hands and letting him help me sit up. I'm still catching my breath when he drops a soft kiss against my temple and murmurs, "I'm going to fuck you now." In what feels like less than a second, Lex unbuttons his pants, pulling his cock free and stroking it a few times.

Before he can make a move, I lean forward and lick the blunt head, making him hiss out a sharp breath.

"Calla—"

"You had yours, now I get mine," I say before swirling my tongue around him, pushing him into my mouth until he hits the back of my throat.

Lex closes his eyes, gripping the counter behind him. "Fuck. You are perfect. So fucking perfect."

His words make my heart beat faster, and I bob up and down his cock, taking as much of him into my mouth as I can, and reach out to massage his balls in my hand. I want to drive him crazy like he does to me. And based on the way he's biting his lip and thrusting his hips forward, I'm heading toward that accomplishment pretty damn quickly.

"If you don't slow down, I'm going to—"

I pick up the pace, using my other hand to pump the base of his cock as I swirl my tongue along the rest of him. He curses, grabbing the back of my hair but continuing to let me control this. A few more thrusts, and his balls tighten in my hand as he grunts and spurts his release onto my tongue. I swallow it down and pull back, wiping the back of my hand across my lips before grinning up at him.

He pulls me off the chair completely, lifting me up, and I wrap my legs around his waist, holding onto his shoulders as he grips my hips.

"I'm nowhere near done with you, but this maybe isn't the best place for the rest of what I have planned."

My eyes widen, a flush creeping across my cheeks. "Oh?"

He leans in, pressing his forehead against mine. "Two words."

I laugh, giving him a chaste kiss. "We are not playing strip poker."

Lex groans, letting me down. "Way to be a party pooper, birthday girl."

After we put our pants back on, we head out to the car. I'm surprisingly giddy over it for having been so nervous at the thought of giving Lex control like that, but I'm thrilled with the outcome. The tattoo is a delicate outline of an orchid and it's easy enough to cover up—not that I can see myself ever wanting to.

There's a warm tingling between my thighs which is more pronounced than the itch of my new tattoo. Having my way with Lex in the tattoo studio made me think of the night at Scarlett's place in Washington where I had sex with him for the first time. His intensity knows no bounds and steals my breath every time. I've come to crave it like an illicit drug, and I ride the high of what we did the entire way to the house.

He helps me out of the Escalade, lacing his fingers through mine, and we walk inside together.

Kade is lounging on the couch in the living room with a half empty wine glass of liquid too dark and thick to be wine, and Atlas is sitting across from him with his nose in a book. He glances up when we enter the room, his eyes landing on the bandage around my wrist and his lips twitching briefly. "Do I want to know what he convinced you to get?"

"What, you don't want to see my *Calla loves Atlas* tattoo? The heart around our names is the best part." My voice is dripping with fake sweetness, but the sarcasm laced through it sort of negates it.

He arches a brow at me, looking as if he's going to respond but instead lowers his gaze back to the book in his hand.

Kade sits up, peering over the back of the couch at us. "Seriously," he says, "what did you get?"

I can't help but smile thinking about the gorgeously simple design. "An orchid."

"An orchid?" he echoes. "What the fuck is an orchid?"

Lex snorts, giving my hand a gentle squeeze. "It's a flower, you dumbass."

"Her favorite," Gabriel says, walking into the room from behind us. He pauses at my side, leaning in and kissing my cheek before going to the chair opposite Atlas.

"And it's stunning." I squeeze his hand this time. "Lex is an artist, in case you guys didn't know." I stifle a yawn, slipping my hand free from his. "Now, if you don't mind, I'm going to get changed. I'm about ready to pass out, but you four feel free to play strip poker without me."

"Where's the fun in that?" Lex asks, frowning at me.

"Not fucking happening," Atlas chimes in.

I laugh softly, walking out of the living room and upstairs to the room I've been staying in.

My phone chimes with a new text as I'm getting changed. I grab it off the nightstand to find a message from an unknown number wishing me a happy birthday. My stomach clenches, and I can't help but hope it's Brighton. Instead of responding to the text, I call the number immediately. The line rings and rings, and just when I think it's going to click over to voicemail, the call is answered. There's dead air for several seconds before I say, "Brighton? Brighton, is that you?"

"Happy birthday, Calla."

My eyes fill with tears, my throat clogged with emotion. I press my fist against my lips to hold in the sound of my tears. "Thank you. I... I don't know what to say. I'm so sorry about what happened to your mom. She didn't deserve that. *You* didn't deserve that. I wish there was something I could do to make it better. I want to be with you, to be there for you. I can't even imagine what you're going through right now. I... I almost lost my mom and I can't—I just... I'm so sorry, Brighton."

"You want to do something?" she asks. There's an edge to her voice that makes me tense. "Because there is something that you can do to help me."

I catch my bottom lip between my teeth, hesitating before I ask, "What is it, Brighton?"

"I know you're in New York City. I know what happened to your mom, and I'm sorry, but if you want to help, you can trick those vampire friends of yours—those *monsters*—and lure them to the hunters. I can text you a location. They'll take care of them for good, and you can have your life back. You never wanted this, did you? I can help you get free of them."

My stomach drops at the coldness of Brighton's tone, and her words make me want to vomit. "I... Brighton, I can't." Those are the only words I can muster. My head is spinning. Just the thought of betraying the guys makes me want to cry. Despite how they came to be in my life, I'm in a place now where I can't imagine it without them. And even if I could—even if I decided to walk away from them—I would never be okay with turning them over to be executed.

The silence on the line is deafening and seems to last forever. Until she says quietly, "Then you're not really sorry, are you?"

My mouth drops open, my chin quivering as my vision blurs with an onslaught of hot tears. "That's not fair."

She sighs, sounding more agitated than I've ever heard her before. "Look, I know you think you care for them, and maybe they've even done some nice things since they kidnapped you weeks ago, but it's not real, Calla. You never had a choice in any of this."

I squeeze my eyes shut, silent tears rolling down my cheeks. "You're wrong," I force out, my voice breaking near the end. "I may not have chosen to be with them in the beginning, but whatever I feel *is* my choice. Brighton—"

The line goes dead, leaving me distraught. Bri is just in shock. She's trying to figure out how to grieve the loss of her mom, and in her own mind, she probably thinks she's trying to protect me. But this isn't really what she wants. She didn't mean it when she asked me to send the guys to their deaths. If she believed I truly cared for them, she wouldn't ask me to do something that would cause me so much pain I can't put it into words. Because, yeah, if something happened to one of the guys, that would fucking hurt.

My hand shakes as I open the text conversation and type out, *I'm so sorry. I love you.* I wait for a few minutes, dropping onto the end of the bed and staring at the screen. But when no response comes after ten minutes, I set my phone beside me and fall back against the mattress, tears leaking out the corners of my eyes as I stare at the ceiling.

At that moment, I make the very conscious—albeit potentially stupid—decision not to tell the guys about what Brighton said. If they were listening, they heard it anyway, but I'm not going to bring it up if they don't.

As much as I don't want them in danger, I'm worried if they know what Brighton asked me to do, they'll decide she needs to be dealt with along with her dad, and that terrifies me.

Calla's bestie wants us dead.

I suppose that's fair, considering her mother was killed by vampires, but that doesn't excuse Brighton asking Calla to help lure us out for the hunters to attempt to pick off.

Will she come out and tell us or will she decide to keep it from us?

The call ended abruptly almost an hour ago, and Calla hasn't come out of the bedroom since. Fifteen more minutes pass before she comes out, and I approach her in the hallway.

"I was wondering if you were going to join us again," I say, grinning softly. "How's the arm?"

"Huh?" She shakes her head, refocusing on me. "Oh, it's fine. Kind of itchy but it doesn't hurt."

I nod. "That's normal." My eyes dance across her face, looking for any hint she might give up the information I'm waiting to hear.

"Yeah," she says absently. "Um, thanks again. Maybe you can show me another time, and I'll try it on you."

I nod slowly. "Is there anything else?"

Her pulse jumps and her eyes narrow a fraction. "What do you mean?" she asks, swallowing hard.

I shrug. "Nothing in particular. I was just curious. You look like there's something on your mind."

"Lots," she says.

"Anything worth noting?" I press.

"Is there something *you* want to talk about, Lex?"

I shake my head. "I don't know, Calla, is there?"

"Okay, why are you being weird?" She crosses her arms over her chest, pinning me with a glare. "And since when do you beat around the bush?"

I step closer, right into her personal space. "I thought I would give you a chance to tell me yourself."

Calla stands her ground, her expression as tense as her posture is rigid. "I don't know what it is you want me to tell you."

"Hmm, I'm pretty sure you do." I snare her gaze, putting glamour behind my words as I say, "Tell me about the phone call with Brighton."

She visibly shudders, gritting her teeth and staring at me hard. A few seconds pass. It turns into a minute, and she doesn't speak but she does look downright pissed, her eyes flashing with anger and her hands balling into fists at her sides.

"That is so fucking annoying," I grumble, preparing to try again.

Gabriel comes up the stairs before I have a chance and says, "What's going on?"

I focus on Calla, lifting a brow at her. "Do you want to tell him, or should I?" I offer.

She looks as if she's about to tear my head off, which if I wasn't so pissed, would be an absolute turn on. She keeps her arms crossed and focuses her attention on Gabriel, speaking to him as if I'm not even here. "Brighton texted me from a new number, so I called her. I think she's in a really bad place since her mom was killed and I think Scott got to her because—"

"She wants to kill us, essentially," I cut in, leaning against the wall in the hallway. "And she wants our girl to help."

Calla blows out an agitated breath. "It's not *you* in particular, it's just... it's vampires. Vampires killed her mom. She doesn't know—"

"You're just coming up with excuses for her because you don't want to admit your bestie is a vampire hunter now."

She glowers at me. "We don't know that she is. Wanting vampires dead and being the one to kill them are two different things."

"What did she say to you, angel?" Gabriel asks in a level, calm tone. Always the fucking voice of reason, Gabe is.

"Well, she... she wanted me to get you guys somewhere the hunters could take you out." She shrugs. "I don't know where. She said she'd send me a location, but that was before I told her I couldn't do what she was asking."

Gabriel frowns and nods. "I see. Was there anything else?"

Calla shakes her head. "I tried to talk to her, but she hung up on me. She knows about what happened to my mom and that we're here. I just—I'm worried about her."

"Oh, that's sweet," I remark in a dry tone. "You're not worried about us?" It's petty, but the thought of anyone threatening my brothers puts me on high alert, and this situation has me agitated as hell.

Calla's brows tug together and her gaze flips between Gabriel and me. "Of course I'm worried about you, but we have each other. Who does Brighton have besides her psychotic father, who, for all we know, is manipulating Brighton to do his dirty work?" Her tone is biting by the time she finishes her sentence. She's come to loathe Scott Ellis as much as the rest of us after he almost killed her mother, and I suppose we should consider the possibility that sick bastard would use his own daughter to get what he wanted—the four of us dead.

"What, you're her only friend?" I say anyway, still pissed Calla was going to keep this information from us.

"I'm her only friend that knows about vampires. I just... This wouldn't have happened if you guys had let her come with us."

"I understand you're upset, angel. We'll talk more about this tomorrow, but for now, try to get some rest." He shifts his attention to me. "I'm going to go talk to Atlas," he says, touching Calla's arm in what I think is meant to be a comforting gesture, before walking away.

Calla attempts to walk away too, but I step in front of her.

She sighs. "Lex—"

"You can't keep secrets from us, Calla."

Her lips part in surprise before she scowls. "That is a two-way street if you want me to hang around." Her eyes widen as if her own words shocked her, and she pushes past me, hurrying away.

We haven't discussed the blood oath connection and what'll happen if we discover it has no bearing on Calla, but that comment—and her reaction to it—makes me think she's thought quite a bit about it.

I fight the urge to go after her. Instead I take a page from Gabriel's playbook, knowing he would suggest I give her some space. She's under an immense amount of stress, and while she seems to be mostly adjusted to having us in her life, we can't expect her to be okay with everything that goes along with that.

I can't help but feel a little bad for upsetting her, but any information about the hunters is incredibly important. Knowing that does nothing to diminish the pit in my stomach, and I make a mental note to speak to Calla later on and apologize for trying to force the information out of her—not that it worked. I think at this point, the rest of us are just as intrigued and curious about how she's able to resist our glamour as she is.

That witchy friend of Gabriel's sire better have some fucking answers.

FOURTEEN

CALLA

The next morning, I wake with my stomach in a ball of nerves. My head is spinning, trying to come up with all the questions I want to ask Tessa about the blood oath and my newfound ability to occasionally resist a vampire's glamour. None of it makes sense, and part of me is worried that even if she's able to answer my questions, I still won't have the clarity I'm so desperately searching for.

I take a shower to try to wake up and calm my nerves, scrubbing my skin with a rose scented body wash and standing under the hot spray of water far longer than necessary to wash my hair. I eventually force myself to get out, dry off, and put on a pair of black high-waisted jeans, tucking in a white tank top. I comb my hair and apply a little bit of makeup to make myself look a bit more alive before heading down-stairs to the kitchen to get a cup of coffee.

Gabriel is standing next to the coffee machine, sipping from his own mug, and smiles when I walk into the kitchen. "Morning, angel," he says softly.

"Morning," I say back and approach as he pours me a cup. "Thanks," I murmur, taking it from him.

"Are you ready for today?" he asks.

"Yes and no," I answer honestly. "I think I'm putting too much hope in getting answers from Tessa, and surely that's not fair to her."

Gabriel nods in understanding. "Tessa has been a part of this world for quite some time. If anybody can help, it's her."

I take a sip of my coffee, nodding. "Thanks again for setting this up."

"Of course," he says. "We'll head out in a few minutes. When you're ready, okay?"

"Sure," I say.

Atlas walks into the room with damp hair and a black V-neck that is at least a size too small for him and clinging to the hard muscles in his stomach. My eyes get stuck on his arms, and I lift my mug to cover the flush of my cheeks

His eyes shift between Gabriel and me, holding mine for a moment. "I've ensured we'll be the only ones in the café, and Marcel has a team that will sit outside and secure the building."

With a sigh, I say, "This is ridiculous." While the security team is quite good at discretion, the thought of constantly being monitored is creepy. You'd think after looking over my shoulder everywhere I went in the years leading up to the guys coming for me I'd be used to feeling as if I was being watched all the time. I thought that would stop since I joined the ones who were watching me. How wrong I was.

"It's for your safety," Gabriel says in a gentle tone. "And for ours as well. We can't be sure what the hunters are planning, and considering Scott knows we're in New York City, we can't be too careful."

"I understand," I say, setting the mug on the counter. "Are you coming with us?" I ask Atlas.

"Yes. We're all going."

"Super," I remark dryly. I'm sure Tessa is going to be thrilled with my posse of testosterone. I'm not fully versed on the history between the vampires and witches, but I do know they aren't BFFs. I'm lucky she agreed to this meeting, otherwise I really have no idea where I'd go searching for answers.

Atlas doesn't crack a smile. Instead, he turns and walks out of the room.

"Geez," I mutter, "who shit in his cornflakes this morning?"

Gabriel offers a faint smile. "He's just concerned for everyone, that's all. He takes a lot of responsibility in keeping the people he cares about safe. Which, believe it or not, Calla, includes you."

I press my lips together, unsure how to respond to that. The thought of Atlas giving a shit about anybody, especially me, is hard to swallow. But the more I think about it, something deep inside me knows it's true—and that same part knows I care just as much for him.

The café is completely empty of patrons when we arrive except for one round table near the back of the room where Tessa sits, watching the door as we walk in, the old-fashioned bell above our heads chiming to announce our entrance. Her bright emerald eyes flash with recognition when they land on me, and she stands, offering a wide, unreserved smile as we approach that somehow eases a good amount of the nerves in my stomach. I realize as I walk across the worn hardwood floor that, despite the circumstances of this visit, I'm happy to see her. A hell of a lot more than the last time when Selene sent her.

"Hello again," she says, tucking her ink black hair behind her ear to reveal a line of dainty silver studs along her earlobe. Today she's rocking a plum-colored blouse tucked into acid-washed jean shorts and shiny black Doc Martens that I'm immediately obsessed with. I'd much rather be meeting up to go shopping with this girl than to discuss supernatural shit, but here we are.

"Hey," I say, jerking my thumb behind me. "Sorry for the entourage."

She presses her mauve-stained lips together against a smile and nods. "It's okay. I understand. Do you want to sit? I assume your guys bought this place out, so we might as well get something to drink and eat. I'm starving."

I laugh softly, surprised at how genuine it sounds. "Yeah, that sounds good."

Tessa and I sit across from each other at the small table while the guys pile into one of the booths along the front window not far away, chatting softly. We both order chai tea lattes and chocolate croissants. Tessa also orders a yogurt parfait and a fruit salad. She munches on the fruit as she says, "So, what can I help you with?"

I take a deep breath, glancing sideways toward the guys before I focus my gaze on her. "I'm not sure how much you know about why we're together. Essentially, my family made a deal with them—Lex specifically—wherein the firstborn daughter from my bloodline would be promised to them for saving the life of my ancestor who got into some shady business a long time ago. Fast forward to when I was born, they thought the oath was being fulfilled with me, but my mom had given birth to a baby girl prior to me. The baby died shortly after she was born, but she did live for a period of time. Basically, we need to know if that child fulfilled the oath, meaning it doesn't—or never really did—apply to me."

Tessa pauses, her fork halfway to her mouth, then sets it down, leaning back in her chair. "That is... Wow, I'm sorry. That's a lot."

"Yeah," I say with a breathy laugh. "I only recently found out about it, so the last time we met, we didn't know about this."

"Right," she says, tapping the side of her mug with a black-painted nail. "I suppose..." She pauses, pursing her lips in thought. "Magic is tricky, but that sounds like a loophole if I ever heard one. That baby girl your mom lost is who would've 'belonged' to your vampire friends over there. You are the second born Montgomery daughter, correct?"

"Yes," I say in a quiet voice, my stomach clenching painfully.

"Well, I think that's your answer, Calla."

I frown, my heart pounding in my chest. Though I'm not sure if it's because Tessa just told me that technically I'm free, or because now I have to decide whether or not I'm going to stay with the guys.

"Not the answer you were hoping for?" she asks, flicking a glance towards the guys.

I shake my head. "I just... I wasn't sure what to expect."

"Care to elaborate?" she offers.

"For the better part of two months, I thought we were connected because of the oath. Because of some mystical connection between our blood, but—"

Something like understanding flashes in her eyes, cutting me off.

"What?" I ask warily.

Tessa smiles at me, her expression thoughtful. "Calla, whatever connection you feel to them has nothing to do with magic."

My stomach drops at the certainty in her tone, because as scary as it is, deep down, I know she's right. "Right, well..." I trail off and clear my throat. "We're sort of dealing with a lot of different things right now and this is just an added level of complication." That reminds me of Tessa's connection to Selene, and I take a sip of my latte before I say, "No offense, but you seem too nice to be friends with someone like Selene. I mean, have you met her?" Not the subtlest shift of topic, but I'm desperate to veer away from the whole feelings conversation, especially with the guys well within earshot.

Tessa pops a blueberry into her mouth, offering a short laugh. "We're less friends and more acquaintances through debt." Her gaze drops to the table for a few seconds before she meets my eyes again. "Selene saved my life a long time ago, which left me indebted to her.

That's the reason I agreed to spell your blood against the vampires. I owed her one and I didn't have a choice."

"She saved your life? Selene? We're talking about the same vampire, right?" Sure, she stopped Dante from draining me like a juice box, but only to torment and hold me captive herself. "Can I ask what happened?"

"Yeah, I mean, it's taken me some time to move past it, but it was back when I discovered what I was. I obviously didn't know what magic was prior to that night. When I was born, my parents put me up for adoption. They suppressed my magic with a cloaking spell in hopes of giving me a normal life. But when I got old enough, the spell failed and my magic went out of control. I didn't know how to handle it—I didn't even know it existed." She pauses. "I accidentally set fire to my adoptive family's home."

I keep my mouth shut so my jaw doesn't drop open, but my eyes still widen. "What happened? I mean, did they...?"

"They survived," she says, nodding. "Barely. The authorities couldn't figure out how the fire started and how I was unharmed, so they decided to send me to a psychiatric hospital. Somehow Selene caught wind of what happened and she knew—or she could guess—it had something to do with magic. She intervened and took me some-where I could learn to control and use my magic. So, yeah, I kind of owed her."

"Wow, that's intense."

"You can say that again. It hasn't been easy. Learning everything and living in this world—the witches, vampires, hunters—but I think it's important you decide what you really want. And even if it's not the easiest option, you have to fight for it. You and I are the same in that we have a timeline, Calla. We are mortal and our time on this earth is limited. If we don't do what is right for us, I think that's the biggest tragedy of all."

I'm surprised at the tears gathering in my eyes and I blink them away quickly, nodding at her. "There's something else," I say. "I have, on occasion, been able to resist the vampires' glamour. I have to really focus, and if I'm vulnerable in any way emotionally or otherwise, like if I'm tired, it doesn't work. Do you know anything about humans resisting glamour?"

She tilts her head to the side, regarding me curiously. "No," she says, her tone laced with surprise. "I mean, *I've* learned to mostly resist it, but there are still some vampires, depending on their age and their pedigree, that are still able to get past my defenses, but I have magic at my disposal. I'm kind of baffled that you're able to."

I rake my fingers through my hair, sighing. "Cool. So I'm a supernatural anomaly. That's great."

She chuckles softly, and I hear one of the guys snicker behind us. My money's on Lex. "I'd like to see it, if that's okay?"

My stomach clenches at the thought of willingly having the vampires try to glamour me, but I reluctantly agree with a single nod.

We all get up and walk to a more open area of the café, pushing some tables out of the way. Gabriel steps up first, and Tessa stands at the sidelines, watching closely as Gabriel meets my gaze and murmurs in a hypnotic tone, "Lift your right leg."

The muscles in my leg tense, and I clench my jaw, unable to break his gaze. I imagine putting all of my weight into my leg to keep my foot planted on the ground, visualizing that it's glued there by cement and there's no chance I have the strength to lift it. A few seconds pass. Then a minute. Finally, Gabriel blinks, severing the glamour, and my muscles relax.

"Interesting," Tessa muses.

Gabriel offers me a smile, and I turn my attention to Tessa. "Yeah, but it doesn't work all the time."

"No," she agrees. "It's definitely mind over matter. I could see you fighting it with the way your body tensed and the crease between your brows. You really had to put some thought behind how you were resisting it."

"Right," I say, "but sometimes I can't get to a place where that's possible."

"I understand what you're saying. I'm not sure there's a workaround for that. I could stand here and tell you not to get emotional and you'd be able to resist glamour whenever you want, but the reality of that is it's not always possible."

"How is it *ever* possible?"

"Hmm, I can't say with complete certainty, but it likely has to do with your emotional connection to each other."

Shifting the weight between my feet, I say, "If that's true, I probably can't resist glamour from a vampire I don't know or have a connection to."

"That's right. Sorry, I know it isn't convenient. The fact you're able to resist *any* glamour is impressive."

"Gee, thanks," I remark dryly.

She offers me a knowing smile. "Do you want to try again?"

I shrug, blowing out a breath. "Sure, why not?"

Tessa glances between the vampires, then points at Kade, who shakes his head. "I'm good. I'll just observe." His voice is detached, his eyes unfocused.

I frown, worry creeping in again, but Tessa doesn't seem to notice as she skips past him and moves to Lex, who shoots me a wink as he walks closer and captures my gaze. "You want to punch Atlas in the face." His glamour washes over me, and I ball my hands into fists at my sides, fighting to put up a mental block against his words.

I shake my head. "You don't need to glamour me for that to be true," I remark dryly, and he bursts into laughter, Gabriel and Tessa chuckling as well.

"That's cute," Atlas says in a dry tone, taking Lex's place in front of me. His glamour slams into me without warning, and I immediately know I'm in trouble. "Take your dagger and stab Lex in the shoulder."

My hand is reaching for the weapon before I can even attempt to stop myself, pulling it from the holder at my thigh. I spin around to face Lex, moving at a speed I didn't even know I was capable of. He's able to stop my arm, gripping my wrist so tight I drop the dagger before I can stab him with it. The pain lancing down my arm severs the glamour, and I blink hard, shaking my head to clear the fog there. Lex frees my wrist, and I bend to pick up the dagger, returning it to the holder before turning back to Atlas and Tessa.

"Two out of three isn't bad," she says. "Plus, Atlas here is stronger than the others based on his bloodline, so you did quite well."

Atlas shoots me a smug grin, and I flip him off.

Tessa and I return to the table for her to grab her things.

"Thanks again for meeting me. I really appreciate it."

"Of course," she says, lowering her voice. "And listen, I know what I told you might not have been what you wanted to hear, but the choice is yours to make. I can't offer you advice. If you knew more of my history, you probably wouldn't want it anyway. But feel free to contact me whenever."

I pull her into a hug, I think surprising both of us, and smile at her when I pull back. "You too. Don't be a stranger. Oh, and nice shoes."

Tessa glances down, her lips curling into a grin. "I have to confess, I bought them after meeting you and seeing yours. They looked so cool, and I've never owned a pair. I rarely wear anything else now."

My smile widens; I can't help it. "I hope you know, we just became best friends."

"Hey, no arguments here. I think we could both do a lot worse," she jokes.

We laugh, walking toward the front door, and Tessa offers a quick wave to the guys on her way past. Pausing in the doorway, she turns back to me and says, "Keep me posted on things, yeah?"

I nod, sliding my hands into the pockets of my pants. "Definitely."

"Take care, Calla. I'm sure we'll chat soon."

"You too," I tell her, then watch her get into the back of a town car. As the car pulls away from the curb and drives away, I frown at the pang of sadness in my chest. I've never had many friends, and connecting with Tessa so easily is making me miss Brighton.

Instead of returning to where Lex, Atlas, and Gabriel are sitting, I find Kade at the counter, munching on what looks like a carrot muffin. "I want to talk to you."

"Lucky me," he says, swallowing, and sets the muffin on the counter. "To what do I owe the pleasure?"

"Kade," I say softly, shaking my head. "I... I'm worried about you. We all are. You've been off for a while." I press my lips together. I can practically feel the darkness in him, and it scares me. Even more, thinking he's going through this alone makes it ten times worse.

"You don't need to worry about me, Calla. I don't want to add to the weight on your shoulders."

I grab his face, holding on even as he tries to pull away. "Kade, I promise you, we will make the hunters pay for the pain they've caused, for the damage they've inflicted. I will learn how to fight and I will kill them myself."

His eyes soften a fraction and his hands go to my hips, pulling me closer. "I've done nothing good to deserve you," he says in a voice barely above a whisper, dropping his forehead to mine.

I close my eyes and press a kiss against his cheek. "It's gonna be okay," I murmur before pulling back. I take his hand, and we walk over to the others, where Gabriel is drinking what looks like a cappuccino and Lex is stuffing his face with a croissant.

Lex wipes his mouth and stands, taking my other hand. "My turn." Kade lets go of my hand, and Lex pulls me aside.

"What is it, Lex?" I'm really not in the mood for another lecture from him, and honestly, after everything today already, I don't want to talk anymore.

He stares at the ground for a few seconds before lifting his gaze to meet mine. "I'm sorry for yesterday. It was wrong of me to try to force information from you, no matter what it was in regards to. I'm sorry for upsetting you."

I blink at him in surprise. The last thing I was expecting was for Lex to apologize for, well, anything. I nod slowly. "Thank you, I appreciate that. And I do forgive you. I understand why you did what you did, but please don't do it again. That being said, I'm sorry I was going to keep information from you that could have turned dangerous. I was scared and I didn't know how all of you would react. I'm *still* scared. Brighton is my best friend, and if anything happens to her, I don't know what I'll do."

Lex nods this time. "We'll figure it out, okay?" He holds his hands out, and I slide mine into his. He wraps his fingers around my hands and squeezes reassuringly. "We still have a lot to talk about, but I know how overwhelmed you are, so why don't we just take a beat, yeah?"

I exhale a heavy breath. "Please."

Lex lets go of my hands, slinging his arm around my shoulders as we walk back to the others. "Oh, and one more thing? Next time Atlas glamours you to stab me, could you try just a little harder to resist?"

I passed out on the couch last night after about six too many glasses of whiskey, evidenced by the ache in my neck when Calla shakes me awake the next morning.

"What is it?" I grumble without opening my eyes. I can already tell the sunlight streaming in through the living room window is going to burn when I do manage to pry them open.

"Lex, get up." The tone of her voice, the seriousness of it and the worry it's filled with, make my eyes fly open.

I cringe as I sit up. "What's going on?" I demand.

"Kade is gone," she says. Dark circles line her eyes, and the tension in her jaw has me standing in an instant.

Dread floods through me, heavy as concrete, settling in my gut, and my fang slices through my gums before I can even try to hold them back. "What do you mean, *gone*?" My voice is as close to desperate as it gets, and I grab her shoulders, needing an answer right fucking now.

Gabriel comes into the room with Atlas behind him. "He wasn't here when we woke up," Gabe says.

Fuck.

Fuck.

One of two things has happened. Either Kade lost his shit and took off, or the hunters have him. The former seems likelier than the latter, considering the rest of us are still here and unharmed. If the hunters came for us, they wouldn't have just taken Kade and left us alive. If anything, they would've taken Calla to get to us. That thought makes me growl, my grip on her shoulders tightening. "We should've kept a closer eye on him. We knew he was struggling—we should have made him talk or get help or… fucking *something*, I don't know." Guilt claws at me, its talons sharp and unforgiving.

Calla grabs my forearms, digging her fingers into my skin until I realize I'm probably holding her too tightly and ease my grip. "We'll go look for him," she says, her forehead creased with worry. "And *when* we find him, we will—"

"I'll go," Atlas cuts in, shrugging on his worn black leather jacket. It's nearly May, though the cold weather in New York seems to be lingering.

Calla steps away from me and grabs her jacket off the back of the couch. "I'm coming with you."

"You're not." His voice is firm, but I see the fire in her eyes.

"Atlas, now is *not* the time—"

"You're not coming with me. Stay here."

She tries to walk to the front door when Atlas turns his back on her, but Gabriel catches her around her waist pulling her back. "Are you fucking kidding me right now?" she demands. "Kade is gone. We should all be out looking for him."

Gabriel remains calm despite the cold glare Calla is shooting at him. "It's not safe. Atlas will find him," he insists in an attempt to placate her.

"If it's not safe for us, it's not safe for them," she counters, pulling away from him, though she doesn't attempt to follow after Atlas.

"Atlas knows what he's doing," I chime in, raking my fingers through my hair, which I'm sure looks extra crazy from sleeping on a couch cushion. "He will be fine. He'll find Kade and bring him back here. Everything will be fine, Calla." I'm talking to her but also to myself, repeating the words over in my head in hopes that I'll manage to trick myself into believing them. I have complete confidence in my sire; Atlas will find Kade wherever he ran off to, but I get Calla's urge to join the search. I feel it too.

She blows out a frustrated breath, the faded Pink Floyd T-shirt she slept in riding up and exposing a sliver of her stomach. "This is ridiculous," she says, shaking her head. "We can't catch a fucking break."

Gabriel's phone chimes, and he pulls it out of his pocket, reading it over before he says, "It's from Fallon. They found Selene and want to know what they should do."

Great. Another problem. What fucking impeccable timing.

"I'm going to give her a call." He glances between me and Calla. "Are you good to handle this?"

I nod in response, and Gabriel slips out of the room, leaving me alone with Calla. I walk over to her, snagging her chin and tilting her head up to look at me. "Breathe," I tell her. "I see you slipping and I understand. Everything keeps getting piled on, and if I had to bet, you probably feel helpless right now." *I sure as hell do.*

She pulls her face away from me, exhaling harshly. "Yeah, just a bit."

"I think we need a distraction. You up for a game of hide and seek?" I ask with a grin. It's more than a little forced, but I hold it anyway.

Calla laughs, giving me an odd look. She thinks I'm kidding.

"I'm completely serious," I say. "You go hide…" I lower my voice, then add, "and if I find you, I get to do whatever I want with you." I smirk at the jump in her pulse and the heat my words bring to her cheeks.

She crosses her arms over her chest as if to hide the perkiness of her nipples, though I can still sense just how excited my idea makes her. The sweet smell of her arousal makes me want to throw her onto the couch and take her right now. Fuck the game.

"Hmm, okay, I'll play. But you do have a slightly unfair advantage, supernatural senses and all, plus being able to use our connection to find me. It won't be a very fun game when it's over in five seconds."

I hold my hands up. "I promise, no vampire abilities. Until I find you, then they're fair game." I'm dying to sink my teeth into her again. Not to mention, I'd give anything to bury my cock between her thighs, because I need the distraction just as much as she does.

She chews her bottom lip, considering it. "Okay, fine. But if you cheat—"

"I'm not going to cheat, Calla. Now, you have ten minutes." I meet her gaze and offer a dazzling, albeit slightly predatory smile. "Time to hide."

Her eyes widen before she takes off out of the room and down the hall. I listen for a few seconds before purposely pulling back my heightened senses, staying true to my word.

I poke my head into the kitchen, where Gabriel is still on the phone with Fallon. He nods at me, letting me know he'll fill me in later, and then I proceed to start searching the rooms on the main floor before heading upstairs.

Either Calla is really fucking good at this game, or I am shit without my vampire senses, because thirty minutes go by, and I still haven't found her.

I'm walking out of the bedroom she's been staying in with only a few more rooms to check when the faint creak of a hinge catches my attention down the hall. I pause, pressing my back against the wall, and wait. She must be in that bedroom waiting for a chance to change hiding places, perhaps to somewhere I've already searched. It's a smart plan in theory, but she's about to be caught. My gums throb at the thought of capturing her, and I lick my lips.

A moment later, Calla darts out of the room, spotting me a second later. She curses and makes a break for the stairs. I catch her easily, snaking my arm around her waist and pulling her against me halfway down the stairs as I chuckle victoriously.

Between one moment and the next, Calla sinks her teeth into my shoulder hard, and I let go of her, cursing in surprise. She catches the banister to keep herself from falling and rushes down the rest of the stairs—only to run right into Gabriel. He steadies her, glancing past her to me, and I offer him a grin. His eyes darken slightly as they shift back to Calla, and in a flash, he has her over his shoulder, carrying her up the stairs toward one of the bedrooms as she curses him out for not playing fair. I follow behind them, my cock hardening and my gums throbbing even more now, to the point of pain. I fight to keep my fangs retracted as I close the bedroom door behind us.

Calla isn't getting away this time. And I'd say, with the way her heart is trying to beat out of her chest, she damn well knows it.

Gabriel sets her down far gentler than I would have, and the moment her back hits the mattress, she scrambles up toward the headboard and tries to get off the bed, losing her sweatpants in the process when Gabriel grabs for her ankles and pulls them clear off. He doesn't make a move to stop her further, and she gets around him, stopping in her tracks when her eyes land on me. Her gaze flicks toward the door before returning to me.

I shrug. "Go for it."

She narrows her eyes at me as her pulse kicks up. "This doesn't feel like hide and seek."

My lips curl into a smirk. "It's not. I won that game." I take a step toward her, and she presses her lips together. "This is my prize. And Gabriel's, because I like to share. I'm a good friend like that."

Calla rolls her eyes. "Technically, Gabriel caught me. *You* lost me."

"You *bit* me," I toss back at her, very much enjoying the ping pong of banter we've got going on.

"Touché," she deadpans.

I offer her a grin and delight in the soft gasp that escapes her lips when my fangs extend.

Gabriel moves silently behind her, sliding his arm around her waist and caging her against his chest. Before she can protest, he presses his lips against her neck, and she leans into him, her head tipping back onto his shoulder as she catches her bottom lip between her teeth. Her gaze holds mine as Gabriel reaches around her with his free hand, sliding his fingers into her black lace panties. Her eyes widen a moment later, and she pulls in a shallow breath before her eyelids start to flutter shut.

I move closer, my erection protesting being trapped beneath the fabric of my pants. I reach forward and rip the little bit of fabric off of her. "Eyes on me," I order, sliding my hand into my pants and freeing my cock. I stroke myself, watching Gabriel thrust his fingers into Calla's pussy as he holds her against him, no doubt grinding against his own erection.

Tension coils tight in my stomach as I increase the speed of my hand, and Gabriel matches his thrusts in time with my pumps. Calla's eyes bounce between my face and my cock, her cheeks flushed and her expression filled with arousal. Gabriel tweaks her clit, and she moans, arching against him.

"Are you going to come on his fingers?" I ask in a husky tone, my breathing increasing as I continue pumping up and down.

She nods, biting her lip.

"Say it."

"Fuck off," she hisses, reaching back to bury her fingers in Gabriel's hair and pressing her lips against his collarbone. She breathes hard against his skin, grinding her hips into him as he adds another finger and uses his thumb to circle her clit.

Calla is panting now. "I can't... I'm going to... My legs are going to give out."

Gabriel's lips trace the shell of her ear. "It's okay, angel. Let go. I've got you."

Her moans get louder, and Gabriel once more increases the speed of his thrusts, pushing her over the edge. She cries out at the same moment her knees buckle, and Gabriel stays true to his word, catching her before she collapses. He carries her back to the bed, setting her on the end of it before tugging off his shirt and sliding in behind her. I waste no time fitting myself between her thighs as she falls back against Gabriel. He moves back so she's nearly laid flat and rubs her shoulders in a slow, circular motion, eliciting a soft moan from her. I lift her shirt, pressing my lips against her stomach, then take my cock in my hand and trace back and forth along her entrance.

Calla shivers, her chest rising and falling fast. "Lex…"

"Don't worry," I say in a soft voice, "I won't make you beg." I slam into her, stealing her breath. I bury myself in her warmth, all the way to the hilt, and groan at her tightness. I will never tire of this feeling, of Calla wrapped around my cock. "Hmm, Gabriel got you nice and wet for me." Her release makes it easy to thrust in and out at a quick pace, and I lose myself in the feeling of her pussy clenching around my cock, milking me as she moans without abandon. The sound is fucking music to my ears.

I pound into her, pressing down on her hips and groaning as pleasure fills me, shooting to my cock and tightening my muscles. I grunt, slamming into her hard and fast, and find my release just a few thrusts later, spilling my release deep inside her.

Calla's climax follows only moments later, her hands gripping the bedsheets on either side of her and her head thrown back against Gabriel's chest.

"Holy shit," she breathes, the muscles in her thighs twitching as I pull out of her.

I chuckle softly, my own breath stilted, and offer her my hands. When she takes them, I pull her into a sitting position, and she glances back at Gabriel—more specifically to the bulge in his pants. She turns and crawls up the bed to him, sealing her lips over his. I'm not sure what I want to see more—Calla riding him or swallowing his cock.

"Angel," he says softly, gripping her hips.

"You haven't come yet," she points out in a soft voice. "And you technically won the game." She kisses him again. "Take your prize."

"Are you sure you're ready for more?"

Ah, Gabriel. Always the gracious lover.

She nods. "I'm ready for *you*."

Gabriel smiles at her as if she's his world. "Hang onto my shoulders, yeah?" He licks his lips, pulling his thick, solid cock out of his pants. "I want you to ride me."

Calla's pulse jumps as she nods again, holding onto Gabriel's shoulders and lifting herself up. I watch from the end of the bed as she lines him up with her entrance and sinks down onto his cock, letting out a low moan as she takes all of him.

"That's it," Gabriel murmurs, holding her hips steady.

She lifts up, then drops back down, making Gabriel groan, tipping his head back against the black wrought iron headboard as he watches her through hooded lashes, his eyes ablaze with lust... and something deeper than that.

Calla picks up speed, nearly bouncing on his cock less than a minute later, her breaths coming hard and fast as she pants, gripping Gabriel's shoulders so tight her fingernails have left indents in his skin.

"Yes," Gabriel says, holding her gaze and thrusting his hips up each time she slams down on him. "Don't stop, angel. You're doing so good."

"Mmm," she hums, circling her hips and moaning loudly. "I'm so close."

"Come for me," he says, pulling her against him, and captures her mouth with his. Their movements become quicker and near-frantic as they chase each other to orgasm.

She breaks the kiss, panting hard. "Gabriel... *ahh*."

"Yes," he groans. "That's it. Come."

The sounds of their combined release fills the room, and I can't tear my eyes away. Watching them is so fucking hot. My cock is twitching, ready to take her again. Gabriel too.

Calla collapses against Gabriel's chest, his cock still buried in her pussy, and she stays there as their breathing returns to normal.

"That's it," I say, smacking the mattress. "When Kade and Atlas get back, we are *finally* playing strip poker."

Gabriel chuckles at the same moment Calla scowls, and I just grin at both of them.

SIXTEEN

By the time Lex, Gabriel, and I pull ourselves out of bed and have lunch, over an hour has passed. I volunteer to clean up and wash the dishes, considering Gabriel cooked and, quite honestly, I could use time to myself with a slightly less sexually charged distraction.

I'm just about done loading the dishwasher when the front door flies open, slamming into the wall. I hurry into the hallway and suck in a sharp breath when I see Kade next to Atlas—covered in blood.

Gabriel and Lex show up behind me in an instant, then very deliberately step around and in front of me. Kade, on the other hand, doesn't look at me. He simply drops his chin and walks upstairs. A moment later, the bathroom door slams shut and the shower turns on.

The rest of us gather in the living room. I linger in the doorway while Atlas, Lex, and Gabriel sit around the coffee table.

"Where did you find him?" Lex asks, his voice deep with concern.

Atlas sighs, pushing his fingers through his hair, and I can't help but notice how absolutely exhausted he looks. It makes my chest ache; we're all wearing thin. Atlas's eyes meet mine briefly before he turns his attention to Lex. "I found him," he says, "with his teeth stuck in a... *professional dancer* at a club about thirty minutes from here."

Gabriel frowns and Lex scoffs. "A professional dancer? He was fangs deep in a stripper?"

Atlas sits back, rubbing his jaw. "By the time I got there, he had killed half a dozen people."

"Fuck," Lex says in a low voice.

Gabriel closes his eyes a moment, shaking his head, and lets out a sigh. "It's good you found him. A spectacle like that was just asking for a hunter ambush."

I push away from the doorway, turning to walk back into the hallway. They don't need me to be part of this conversation, but there's a pressure in my chest that makes me think the vampire upstairs does.

"Where are you going?" Atlas says, and I don't turn back around.

"I'm going to check on him." Despite the ice that shot through my veins hearing what he had done, my need to comfort him outweighs any fear I might have.

"That's not a good idea," Atlas warns.

"He won't hurt me," I say over my shoulder, though it may be more to convince myself than the others. Even if something happens, there are three other vampires who would have my back.

I force my legs to carry me down the hall and up the stairs, pausing outside the bathroom, my hand hovering over the doorknob. I take a deep breath before I slip inside, closing the door behind me. The room is hazy, filled with steam and the all-glass floor to ceiling shower is fogged up, though I can still see Kade's broad form under the rainfall showerhead. His hands are braced on the white marble tile, his head bent forward as the water hits his back. Blood rolls off of him, staining the tile at his feet. He doesn't acknowledge my presence for a few seconds, and when he speaks, he doesn't look at me. "You shouldn't be in here." His voice is practically unrecognizable. It's dark, vicious, as if he hates me. It feels like a punch to the gut. I want to turn and leave—I don't want to see him this way. But I can't. My feet are rooted in place.

"I'm not leaving," I say, surprised at the steadiness of my voice. I walk closer to the shower, and he finally turns to meet my gaze, his silver eyes slamming into me like a freight train. I swallow hard at the menacing expression on his face. His fangs are protruding from his gums, and he makes no attempt to retract them. He's trying to scare me away, but I refuse to give into it, to the fear that wants me to believe that Kade is a monster who doesn't care about anything or anyone, when I know full well that isn't true.

Instead of leaving, I pull off my shirt and drop it on the floor, then step out of my shorts, leaving myself naked before him.

The darkness in his eyes—at least some of it—shifts to something I'm a little more familiar with. Hunger. Lust.

The muscles in his shoulders tense. "Calla," he warns.

I close the rest of the distance between us, opening the shower and stepping inside before I can talk myself out of it.

"What are you doing?" he demands, turning to face me as the water cascades onto my face.

"You are not alone," I say firmly, reaching for him.

He grabs my wrists in a tight grip, pushing me until my back hits the opposite wall. He lifts my arms over my head, pinning them against the wall. "Do you know what I did?" he whispers.

My stomach drops. "I... Yes."

"What makes you think I won't do the same to you?"

I force myself to hold his gaze despite the pounding in my chest and the alarm bells blaring in my head, screaming at me to get away from him. "Do you want to?" I ask in a quiet voice.

He lowers his face until his lips are at my ear. "I want to fuck you so hard I can't think straight. I fear that it's the only way I can escape the horrors playing on repeat in my head."

"You're worried that's going to scare me away?" I ask.

"No, Calla, I'm worried that I'll lose myself. That I'll lose control and tear your throat out to devour your blood."

I nod slowly. "Yeah, I'd rather you didn't do that."

He laughs harshly, the sound void of any humor.

He's hurting so badly, so deeply. There's nothing I can do to fully erase that pain, but maybe I can numb it for a short while. Offer him some bit of reprieve.

I lean forward as much as I can with my wrists trapped against the wall and press my lips to his. Kade stands frozen for a moment before he slowly starts to kiss me back. He takes a step closer, his chest touching mine, and my nipples harden as I feel the hardness between his thighs against my stomach.

"Let me touch you," I say against his lips and tug on my wrists.

He holds them against the wall, water dripping down his face as he pulls back just enough to look into my eyes. "You want to touch me? To stroke my cock until I can't hold back any longer and climax with your name on my lips, covering you with my release? Is that what you want?"

I can't read the tone of his voice—I also can't deny how hot his words are making me. Because yes, that's exactly what I want. "I want to take care of you."

His grip tightens for a moment before he releases me, his hands trailing the length of my arms, then down my stomach. He steps back, and I lower my arms, flexing my fingers a few times to get the blood flowing again. As hot as being pinned against a wall while naked is, it does get uncomfortable after a while.

Instead of wrapping my fingers around his erection, I sink to my knees in front of him. His broad upper body blocks the water from hitting me, and I lean forward, licking the head of his cock. I swirl my tongue over the tip a few times, looking up at him. His eyes are blazing, liquid silver that I immediately get lost in.

"Keep teasing me, and I'll fuck your mouth raw," he warns, his tone low and jagged.

After a few more swipes of my tongue, I close my lips around him and suck, pulling him into my mouth. A rush of excitement zips through me and heat pools low in my stomach when Kade hisses out a sharp breath before groaning.

"Hmm," I hum, making my lips vibrate against his cock. I pull back, flicking my tongue over his head before taking him back into my mouth, hollowing my cheeks as I suck on him.

He grabs the back of my head, and my pulse races, but I give myself over to the idea of bringing him pleasure in hopes of helping him through what I can only imagine is one of the darkest periods of his incredibly long life. I let him guide me up and down his cock, relaxing my jaw as he thrusts his hips forward, filling me to the back of my throat.

"Do you want me to come in your mouth?" he asks in a thick voice. "Because if not—"

I grab his ass, sucking harder in response.

"Fuck," he curses, breathing hard. His grip on my hair loosens a little, but I don't relent. I bob up and down until Kade stiffens, grunting as he climaxes and shoots his release onto my tongue and against the back of my throat.

I swallow what I can as he steps back, his cock gliding over my tongue as he pulls it out of my mouth, then let the water wash away what spilled over my lips.

Kade helps me up and slants his mouth over mine the second I've taken a breath. Our kiss is fiery. It's a battle for control, and I'm not giving in this time. Not even when he grabs my chin, tilting my head back slightly to deepen the kiss.

"Fuck me," I breathe, tugging him closer and pressing my forehead against him. "Lose yourself in me."

"I could hurt you."

"So hurt me," I offer, my voice strong, unwavering.

His eyes widen, filling with horror, and he recoils.

"There," I say quickly. "That look on your face right now is why I know you won't."

"Calla." My name on his lips sounds desperate. I'm not sure if it's a prayer or a curse.

I drape my arms over his shoulders and press my breasts against him, licking my lips. "I'm here," I tell him, kissing each of his cheeks. "It's okay."

His gaze holds mine and his throat bobs when he swallows. "Turn around."

I bite my lip, nodding, then pull my arms back and do as he says. I'm facing the shower wall with my back to Kade, my pulse pounding beneath my skin as I wait for him to make a move.

Kade wraps his hand around the back of my neck and presses me flush against the marble tile. His chest brushes my back, and he traces the shell of my ear with his lips. "Would you try to stop me if I wanted to fuck your ass?" he murmurs, and shivers race down my back.

I close my eyes and turn my face so my cheek is pressed against the wall. "No."

He nips my earlobe, making me jump. "Hmm... Didn't think so." He snakes a hand around me, quickly finding the heat between my legs. Kade rubs my clit in a precise, circular motion before dipping two fingers inside my throbbing pussy. "I think I'll fuck you here, though. You make such lovely noises when I do." He pulls his fingers out and licks them clean before dragging the head of his cock between my ass cheeks. He kicks my legs apart a bit more, and I bite the inside of my cheek, practically vibrating with anticipation.

I brace myself against the wall and pull in a deep breath, but Kade slams into me from behind before I can let it out. "Fucking hell," I gasp.

Kade chuckles darkly, pressing his lips to the side of my neck as he holds still inside me. The walls of my pussy clench and stretch around him, unprepared for the invasion, and my heart pounds against my ribcage. He reaches around to stroke my clit as he pulls back, then slams into me again.

His thrusts are hard and fast. Unrelenting.

I moan, blinking back tears at the intensity of the sensations setting my body ablaze. "Kade," I breathe, my head spinning with lust.

"Fuck," he growls, picking up speed.

Seconds later, he sinks his fangs into my shoulder, and I whimper, my pussy clenching around his cock. He drinks deeply, pounding my pussy and strumming my clit like an instrument. He certainly knows exactly how to play my body to elicit a favorable response.

My chest rises and falls fast, my hardened nipples overly sensitive as they brush the marble tile with each thrust. "Make me come," I pant, tension and pleasure coiling in my stomach. I'm so fucking close.

He pulls back, licking the puncture marks to close them, then flicks my clit hard, shifting the angle of his thrusts to hit a new spot deep inside me, and ignites a world-narrowing orgasm.

I clench around him, coming hard and gasping, reaching behind me to grab onto him, to hold him against me as I come undone. Hell if I know how I managed to stay upright during that.

Kade pulls out of me, making me shiver with the aftershocks of my orgasm, and turns me around to face him, kissing me softly. "You truly are an angel, aren't you?" he murmurs, his eyes flicking between mine.

"A corrupted one at this point," I tease, sliding my finger along his jaw and kissing him once more. I pull a bottle of body wash off the ledge next to us and squirt some onto my hand, lathering it before I start to wash the remnants of blood off him. I take my time washing everything away, then move onto his hair, because I know how important it is to him under normal circumstances.

Once we're done in the shower, I tug on a robe and guide him out of the bathroom after he's dried off. We walk into the connected bedroom, and I manage to get him into bed without protest. The exhaustion in his eyes makes my chest tighten. He hasn't had a decent rest in far too long.

In that moment, I find myself wishing I could glamour him to close his eyes, forget about everything, and have a restful sleep. But I can't. So I do what I can and pull the blankets up around him, sighing softly.

"Thank you," he says.

I smile. "You're welcome." Resting my hand against his cheek, I say, "Now get some sleep, okay? Please?"

Kade nods.

I pull back and turn to walk out of the bedroom. I'm barely two steps away when Kade's saying my name stops me.

"I haven't loved many people…" he continues, his voice trailing off. I can't bring myself to turn back to him, though I can't figure out why. "I thought maybe I forgot what it felt like. But now I know, each time I look at you, that feeling I used to be so familiar with comes back a little more."

My heart is in my throat and the air gets caught in my lungs. *Fucking breathe. Inhale, then exhale. You've been doing it for twenty-four years. You know how.*

"Calla."

"Kade," I force out, turning enough to look at him over my shoulder.

"Look at me, please. I would very much like to see your face when I tell you that I love you."

I suck in a breath, whirling around to face him with wide eyes. "You just—"

"I love you," he repeats, his lips curling up at the corners.

"I…"

Kade props his hands behind his head against the pillow. "You don't need to say anything. Nothing will change what I've said." He licks his lips, his gaze flicking toward the doorway before returning to me. "You should go back downstairs. Sounds like Gabriel's almost done cooking dinner."

I press my lips together but find myself nodding. "I'll make sure they save you some in case you're hungry later."

He smiles, turning onto his side and settling into the bed. "You're good at taking care of people," he mumbles, his eyes sinking shut.

I step forward and lean over, kissing his forehead gently before walking out of the bedroom, closing the door behind me.

My head is spinning as I fall back against the wall in the hallway outside the bedroom. I press my hand against my chest and feel my heart pounding there.

Kade told me he loves me.

Holy fuck. As if this entire situation with the vampires could get any more complicated.

I've never allowed myself to consider love in connection with any romantic partner because I knew the fate of my future was sealed. Even now, when it might not be, I'm not sure how to handle the admission.

I care about Kade as much as I do the others. But love? I… I'm not sure I *can*.

In a mixed daze of post-orgasm bliss and confusion, I head back downstairs and run into Atlas on my way to the kitchen. He blocks my path completely, and I am so not in the headspace to battle with him right now. Before I can speak, he steps closer, and I freeze, waiting to see what he's going to do. He leans in and presses his lips against my cheek. "Thank you," he says in a low voice, "for helping Kade."

I step back and nod. "Of course."

"I underestimated you," he admits, his brows pinched.

I blink at him in surprise, not entirely sure what he's making reference to exactly, but manage to recover quickly. "You'd be smart not to do that anymore," I advise him.

He graces me with one of his rare smiles. "Noted."

"'Anymore'?" Lex asks, poking his head into the hallway from the living room. "Does that mean you're staying despite the oath bullshit?"

I walk around Atlas and into the living room, taking the glass of wine Gabriel offers me. I swallow a mouthful and meet Lex's expectant gaze. "Where else am I going to go? There are both vampires and vampire hunters who want to kill me."

Gabriel nods, but there's sadness in his expression. "If you want to go," he says, "we'd ensure you were safe."

I'm still very conflicted over what I want. A month ago, I desperately wanted my freedom, my shot at a future of my choosing, but now... The thought of living a life without the guys makes my chest hurt.

If this is what love feels like, I'm not sure I want it.

SEVENTEEN

I'm getting fucking sick of being shaken awake. This time, it's Atlas whose face is right in front of me when I open my eyes. His grim expression makes me shift upright and lean against the headboard. Kade grumbles at the movement from beside me. We fell asleep talking about where we'd go if we can't go back to Washington. We talked about France or Italy, or how lovely it would be to sit poolside in Bali or Ibiza. The thought of Calla not being there with us, though, made none of the options all that appealing to either of us.

"What the fuck?" Kade growls, covering his head with a pillow as he turns away from us.

I glance at the clock on the small table next to the bed, then arch a brow at Atlas. "It's four in the morning. What's wrong?"

"Downstairs," he says, already heading for the door. "Now."

He's gone before I can say another word, and I sigh. I rake my fingers through my hair and glance over at Kade, whose bare ass is on display. I give it a firm smack and swing my legs over the side of the bed, standing and walking around to his side.

"Fuck off," he says, the sound muffled.

"Come on, get up." I grab his arm and tug on it. "Something's up. We have to see what's going on."

He scowls, turning over and glowering at me. "It's still fucking dark out. What time is it?"

"I don't know," I lie. "Let's go. And put some pants on. I don't think it's the time to be walking around with your dick out."

Kade glances down and shrugs. "You certainly didn't complain about it last night."

I roll my eyes. "Get the fuck up before Atlas loses his shit."

He exhales a dramatic breath. "Fine, fine."

Five minutes later, the five of us are sitting around the living room. Calla is curled up in a blanket on the couch next to Gabriel while he chats softly with Atlas, who is sitting in the armchair across the room.

Kade shuffles into the room and uses the wall to keep himself upright, whereas I lean in the doorway between the hall and living room, wanting to go back to bed as soon as possible. I'd barely gotten an hour of sleep before Atlas woke us.

"Are you going to tell us what's up?" Calla asks around a yawn. Her eyes are squinty, as if she's fighting to keep them open.

"About twenty minutes ago, I received a call from my parents' head advisor. Marcel and several other members of our team have also been in touch. The hunters are fighting back all over North America."

"Fighting back?" Gabriel asks in a tired voice.

Atlas nods. "They're executing counter-attacks against the vampires targeting them. They must have someone feeding them information about the attacks planned against them, because they've become too prepared for them otherwise."

I push away from the doorframe, crossing my arms over my chest as I stand at the back of the couch, looking at Atlas. "Fuck this. It's time to get our hands dirty and enter the fight. Enough is enough. I'm ready to shed some blood and put an end to this."

Gabriel frowns. "I'm not sure that's the best course of action. Diving into the fight now isn't ideal with the other situations we need to work through." He rubs the stubble along his jaw, glancing at each of us for a moment. "That being said, if it comes down to it, we need to protect our own—ourselves and each other."

"Agreed," Atlas says.

"So we're going to sit on the sidelines and see what happens?" Calla says, her brows furrowed.

"We know what happens," Kade chimes in, his chin nearly touching his chest as he keeps his gaze on the floor. "When you live forever, history tends to repeat itself. Once in a while, the hunters get on some power trip and think they can eliminate the vampires. They ignore the long-standing history between us. Never have they succeeded in their mission to rid the world of us—obviously—and they won't."

"And they never fucking learn," I say, irritation making my tone sharp. Not that anytime the hunters decide they can overpower us in numbers and strength is a particularly convenient time, but now—with everything coming up about the blood oath and trying to hunt Selene—is pretty much the worst possible timing to have to deal with hunters trying to punch outside their weight class.

"Does this mean we still can't go back to Washington?" Calla asks.

"No," Atlas says. "We'll go home today."

Huh. That's news to me.

Her eyes widen. "Wait, really?"

"Why now?" Kade follows up, his head tipped back against the wall now. He appears as exhausted as the rest of us, though some of the darkness in his eyes has faded, which makes me feel slightly better. I'm still worried about him, but I think Calla's strength got through to him last night. And I am beyond grateful for that.

"Lenora and Simon believe we're here because of Gabriel's sire. Knowing them, they are attempting to verify that. If we stay longer, they're sure to figure out we lied about our reason for being here."

"God forbid," Calla mutters tiredly.

"You wouldn't be saying that if you knew them," I comment mildly. Atlas's parents are some of the most powerful and vicious vampires to exist. They have no regard for human life and believe their son should share the same view. If they found out we came here for Calla to see her parents... I don't think any of us want to see what would happen in that instance.

She sighs. "Whatever. If we're going back to Washington, I want to see Brighton."

"We'll discuss how we are going to deal with Miss Ellis once we're home," Atlas says in a voice that leaves no room for further questions, much less argument.

Calla frowns at him but doesn't push it.

"While we're all here," Gabriel says, crossing one leg over the other and resting his ankle atop the opposing knee.

"Does it have to be now, Gabe?" I say, my brows pinching together. "Can we at least make a pot of coffee first?" It's clear we're not going back to bed, so might as well try to bring myself somewhat to life with a shot of caffeine.

"I'll do it," Calla says quickly, pulling herself off the couch and keeping the blanket wrapped around her shoulders. She can't get out of the room fast enough.

I have the itch to reach for her as she passes me, but I force myself to focus on Gabriel.

He scratches his jaw. "Fallon and Jase have been keeping tabs on Selene in Chicago, but the longer they wait to make a move while they continue tracking her, the bigger chance there is that she's going to figure out she's being watched."

"Lex and I can meet up with them in Chicago while you and Kade take Calla back to Washington," Atlas says.

Calla pokes her head back into the room, her eyes narrowed at Atlas. "Absolutely not."

He draws in a slow breath, turning his attention to her. "Want to try that again?"

She crosses her arms. "I said, no, Atlas. I know you're not familiar with the word, having heard it on so few occasions, but I would've thought you'd be used to it from me by now."

The corners of his mouth twitch ever so slightly. The movement is brief, barely enough to catch; Calla likely missed it. "Careful," he warns, his silver gaze sharp and the tips of his fangs visible. If I had to bet, he hasn't fed in a while, and Calla seems to taunt the monster in him—in all of us, really. And as dangerous as it is, the allure is near impossible to ignore.

Calla doesn't flinch. "We need to stay together," she argues. "I don't want you sending them with me for protection or whatever when the two of you are going after that psychopath." She shakes her head and repeats herself in a firmer tone. "*No.*"

The coffee machine gurgles from the kitchen, and Calla retreats once more, presumably to get some coffee.

I turn my attention to my sire. "I'm on board for Chicago. I say let's go and deal with the bitch. We can certainly take her out without these two." I jerk my thumb toward Kade, then Gabriel. "No offense."

"Fucker," Kade mutters under his breath halfheartedly, and Gabriel says nothing. He wouldn't be able to do anything against Selene even if he wanted to.

Calla returns to the living room with a steaming mug of coffee and lowers herself back onto the couch. We're all watching her as she takes a small sip and sets the mug on the coffee table in front of her before settling into the cushions. A moment later, she realizes and scrunches her nose up in an annoyingly cute way I can't ignore. "What?" she mumbles, her cheeks turning pink under our gazes.

"We will all go to Washington," Atlas says to Calla, then turns to Gabriel. "I imagine Fallon and Jase have backup if necessary?"

Gabriel nods.

"Good." Atlas stands. "Give them the order to kill Selene by whatever means necessary."

My chest tightens and disappointment flows through me. "I thought we were going to take her out."

He shrugs. "It's not worth the hassle of us all going to Chicago to deal with her when there are already people we trust there that can handle it."

I frown at him but don't say anything further. I was ready to fight, to punish the vampire who tortured Calla and had her hooks in Gabriel so deep for decades, but Atlas was quick to concede to Calla's wish that we all stay together. She is changing all of us in different ways—even big, bad, powerful Atlas York, and I'm not even sure he realizes it.

<hr />

After we've packed, we head to the airstrip and board the York family private jet, courtesy of Atlas's mother and father. The interior is all black leather and dark wood. It smells mildly of lavender and sage, no doubt cleaned pristinely just before we boarded.

Kade drops onto the couch in the middle of the plane, keeping his sunglasses on and crossing his arms over his chest as he stretches his legs out. In minutes, before the plane has even taken off, he's asleep. As jealous as I am, I'm glad he's getting rest. He needs it the most of all of us right now. That, and an escape from reality, even just for a little while.

Gabriel and Atlas sit across from each other near the front of the plane, drinking what looks and smells like whiskey from crystal glasses and speaking softly about future plans to return to the house we built in the Palisades. It may be a far-off goal, but I'm looking forward to returning to the only place I've ever felt like home, and I think the others share my sentiment.

I guide Calla to the back of the plane, sitting next to her as she starts reading something on her phone. She seems content to pretend I'm not here, but I'm in the mood to mess with her a bit.

"Whatcha reading?" I ask in a light tone, leaning in until my shoulder brushes hers and peering at the screen.

"A book." She turns it away from me without a word as the plane taxis to the runway.

"Oh, come on. Let me see," I drag out the word. "I won't judge." The plane engine powers up, vibrating the cabin, and a moment later, we accelerate down the runway.

Calla huffs out a laugh as we ascend into the air. "Judge all you want, Lex. I really don't care."

"Tell me what you're reading then," I challenge, shooting her a wink. "Oooh, is it a dirty book?"

She rolls her eyes. "You are insufferable."

"Hmm." I lower my voice, speaking softly into her ear. "Will you say that after I make you come in that chair?"

"What?" she squeaks, her pulse jumping.

I smirk at her. "Want to join the mile high club?" The race of her heart and the flush of her cheeks tells me all I need to know. I lean in, dragging my tongue along her neck before pressing a kiss against the pulse point at her throat. Her breath catches, and I slide my hand up her thigh, teasingly slow.

"Lex," she says, her voice strained.

I press my finger against her lips. "Shh." Reaching for the seat belt, I move at a speed too quick for her to track and use the material to secure her wrists to the armrests. She immediately tries tugging on them to free herself, but the woven strap—and my handiwork—is too strong to break.

"What are you doing?" she asks, glancing down at her restraints before looking up at me.

"Making sure you don't move," I tell her, giving a quick pull on the seat belt to make sure it's secure.

Her eyes narrow. "Let me go."

I purse my lips, shaking my head. "Go where? We're over thirty thousand feet in the air."

She holds my gaze, looking rather unimpressed. "You know that's not what I mean."

I get up from my chair and lean over hers, close enough our noses nearly touch. "Why would I let you go when I could do this instead?" I trail two fingers down the center of her chest slowly, heading toward her navel and keeping my eyes locked with hers. She swallows, her breath hitching when I reach the waistband of her dark gray joggers.

Without hesitation, I slide my hand into her panties, brushing the soft, delicate skin of her folds. She catches her bottom lip between her teeth, tipping her head back against the seat, then lets out an uneven breath.

"Calla?" I murmur, my lips tracing the shell of her ear.

"What?" she grumbles through her teeth.

My lips curve into a grin. "Do you want my fingers inside you?"

Instead of answering me, she arches her hips, causing the tips of my fingers to dip between her folds.

I pull my hand out of her panties. "Ah, ah, ah."

She exhales a frustrated sigh. "Stop tormenting me."

"But it's so much fun," I counter in a voice laced with amusement. Playing with her is the highest level of entertainment I've found in a long time. Even better, I know she enjoys it just as much as I do, whether she admits it or not. I tease her over her joggers, sliding my hand between her thighs and tracing the outline of her panties before pressing my thumb against her clit.

Calla sucks in a sharp breath. "Fine. You're so determined to hear me say the words? I want you to fuck me with your fingers, your tongue, your cock—whatever. Just *fuck me*."

"So impatient," I tsk.

She glowers at me. "I know what I want and I'm not afraid to ask for it. Now fuck me or leave me alone to read my book in peace."

"Fine," I say, "but first I want to show you something." I grab my duffle bag off the chair across the aisle.

"Oh, god." She sighs. "Do I even want to know?"

I chuckle. "Let's find out."

She arches a brow at me but stays silent.

Unzipping the bag, I reach in and search for the box Kade and I picked up before we left Monroe. "We picked this up for your birthday and then forgot to give it to you. Apologies, it's not wrapped."

"Um, okay. I thought the tattoo was my birthday present. I don't need—"

I pull out the box and set it in her lap, grinning as her cheeks turn pink when she sees the dark purple vibrating dildo. "I'm sure you'll find a use for it."

"You give me gifts like this, and I might not have a need for you."

"Sure," I remark dryly. "I'm not worried. I don't see sex toys as my enemy. If anything, they're amazing teammates."

"Right, okay. Cool. Not sure how I'm supposed to use this when you've tied my wrists to the seat, but thanks?"

I take the box back, popping it open and sliding out the toy. "Allow me." I toss the box aside and lift the dildo to her mouth. "Open."

Her eyes widen, and she hesitates, but eventually she does as I say. I slide the toy along her tongue, and she closes her lips around it, making my cock twitch in my pants, imagining her doing that to me. I pull it out of her mouth, and it's shiny with her saliva.

"Good girl," I say in a low voice. "Now lift your hips."

She plants her feet on the ground and arches forward enough for me to pull her joggers and panties down to her knees. The moment her ass is planted back in the seat, I have the dildo between her legs, vibrating against her clit.

"Shit," she hisses, her lips parting in a soundless gasp.

I spread her legs as wide as they'll go in the chair and drag the head of the toy along her slit, turning the vibration higher with each pass.

She pulls against the restraints, glaring at me as I tease her over and over. I'm sure I'll pay for it later, but right now it's just too damn good to resist.

I turn down the vibration a bit and push the tip of the dildo inside her pussy. Her muscles tense, and she presses her lips together. I slide it deeper, using my other hand to circle her clit slowly, and when I start to pull it out, she closes her thighs, holding it inside her.

"Don't you dare," she practically growls, her chest rising and falling a little quicker than normal.

I push it in deeper, making her suck in a shallow breath. "Better?" I ask smugly, twisting it and turning up the vibration.

She nods quickly, her hips arching as I pull it back slightly before thrusting it deeper once more, eliciting a sweet moan from her lips.

"So responsive," I murmur. "I should tie you up more often."

"More," she demands, ignoring my taunt.

I pick up the speed of my thrusts, again increasing the intensity of the vibration, and Calla gasps sharply, her eyes closing as her head falls back against the seat, and she tugs on the restraints. My thumb circles her clit hard and fast, and her thighs shake as an orgasm washes over her. She grips the armrests until her knuckles are white and presses her lips together in a feeble attempt to quiet her moans.

I pull the vibrator out of her, switching it off and tossing it onto the chair across the aisle. Before she can open her eyes, I slam my mouth against hers, kissing her deeply and gripping her chin to hold her to me. She responds immediately, kissing me back with fervor and breathing heavily into my mouth. I lean back and undo the restraints.

She immediately grabs the front of my shirt, drawing me back to her mouth, and we kiss once more. Her tongue dances along mine before retreating, and I nip her bottom lip playfully.

As I'm dropping back into my seat, Atlas saunters over with his fangs bared, likely having smelled Calla's arousal. I can tell by the look in his eyes, though, he doesn't want to fuck her at this very moment. He wants her blood.

Without a word, Atlas grabs her wrist and pulls her out of the chair. Her jaw is set tight, her eyes roaming over his face as he guides her toward the other couch opposite to where Kade is asleep. He sits, pulling her onto his lap, and she steadies herself by grabbing his shoulders. She licks her lips, and Atlas's eyes drop to her mouth, darkening. Calla moves her hair over one shoulder, exposing her neck and tilting her head to the side as she leans in, pressing her chest against his. His hands go to her hips, settling her in his lap, and I watch with fascination as they seem to communicate without words before Atlas sinks his fangs into her throat.

Calla makes a short sound of discomfort before her tense expression relaxes, and she sighs softly, leaning fully into Atlas as he closes his eyes and drinks deeply. The pounding of her heart slows as the seconds tick by, and when Atlas pulls away from her neck, he shifts her off his lap and onto the couch. She slumps back against the armrest, a look of serenity overcoming her features.

Atlas gets up as Gabriel comes to sit with her, putting his arm around her shoulders and guiding her to rest against his side.

The smell of her blood in the air makes my fangs slice through my gums, and I lick my lips. As much as I want to drink her blood—as much as the monster that craves her warmth and her life is pushing me to take from her—I hold myself back. We don't need her passing out before we land in Washington.

Instead, I get up and walk to the front of the plane, grabbing a blood bag from the mini fridge at the bar, hoping it'll be enough to sate the monster for now.

EIGHTEEN

CALLA

When we touch down in Washington, there's a black town car waiting at the private airstrip. The four of us pile into the back while Atlas takes the passenger seat, speaking in a low voice to the driver.

In minutes, we're on the road, and I stare out the window at the familiar buildings and signs, wondering if we'll end up at another safe house.

When we pull up outside the hotel Brighton had booked a room for me on the night I tried to escape the guys, I shake my head. The others don't seem to notice, but when we get out of the car, I shoot Atlas a look, knowing he would have been the one to arrange this, to which he offers me a quick smile.

The bastard actually made sure we got the exact suite I'd stayed in, and while the four of them sit in the dining room area, I slip away to the bedroom to check in with my parents. I call my dad's phone in case Mom is resting and I'm surprised when she's the one who picks up. "Oh hey, Mom. How are you doing?"

"Calla, sweetie. I'm doing well, all things considered."

"Yeah?" I check. A tinge of worry still lingering in me. I wish I'd gotten to see her again before we left the city, but once the hunter situation is dealt with, I tell myself, I'll go back to New York and have a proper visit with them. Part of me wants to ask if Dad told her about the oath and about me finding out about the baby, but I can't bring myself to say the words. So I say, "We're back in Washington."

"That's good, honey. So exams must be coming up, right?"

I bite my lip, wondering how I should go about telling her that I didn't finish the semester. "Yeah, I'm actually taking a brief pause on school. Things got very complicated way too quickly for me to keep up with everything." That has nothing to do with school and everything to do with the chaos that my life has become in a matter of a couple months.

"Calla—"

"Mom, I know. I don't want you to worry. School is still my priority. I'm not going to drop out—I will graduate, I promise you."

"I'm just worried about you, that's all."

"I called to check in on *you.*"

"Yeah, well, we did me. I'm good. Now let me worry about my daughter. It's natural for a mother, okay?"

"Things are... fine," I tell her, surprised to find my chin wobbling and my vision blurring. I want to confide in my mom, to hear her advice on what I should do about the guys, about Brighton, about Kade telling me he loved me—about *everything,* and yet instead I say, "I won't keep you. I just wanted to make sure you were still doing good."

"Calla, why do I feel like there's something you want to say but aren't?"

"There are things I want to say that I *can't,*" I tell her, which is mostly true. "But I should be able to tell you soon, I hope."

"I don't even want to ask this, but are those boys taking care of you?"

I press my lips together. "Mom, I don't think you can call them *boys* when they're significantly older than you."

She sighs. "I try not to think about it that way, to be honest."

"Yeah, you and me both. Listen, I should go but I'll check in with you soon, okay?"

"All right, sweetheart. Know that I love you."

"I know. I love you too."

After ending the call with my mom, my finger hovers over Brighton's name, and I fight the urge to call her. I want to reach out to her, to meet up with her now that we're back in the city. I think a face-to-face conversation would do a lot more than speaking over the phone or by text. More than that, I want to hug my best friend.

I chew my thumb, staring at the screen, and then my fingers are moving. I open a new text and ask her to meet, knowing that one if not all of the guys might actually kill me for this. I pace the bedroom until her response comes in a few minutes later. And then I sit on the end of the bed, reading it over three times.

Calla, I'm so sorry for how things went the last time we spoke. It wasn't fair what I asked you to do and I feel like I'm losing my mind.

I sniffle, blinking back tears, because I understand that completely. And I want to go to her but I know the guys will never allow that in a million years. So instead of trying to keep it from them, I walk back out to the living room catching Gabriel's gaze.

"Go for a walk with me? I could use some fresh air."

We head down to the lobby, but before the elevator reaches the ground floor, Gabriel pushes the emergency stop.

"Is there something you want to tell me, angel?" he asks in a gentle tone, his expression open, willing me to confide in him.

"Yes," I answer honestly. "I've been in contact with Brighton—just today. Not that long ago when we were upstairs. I want to meet up with her and make sure she's okay, but I knew if I tried to do that without telling you guys it wouldn't go over very well."

Gabriel presses lips together and nods slowly, leaning against the elevator wall. "Thank you for trusting me enough to bring this to me. And, Calla, I understand your concern for your friend, but we can't help her. Not only will interfering with Scott's daughter bring more unwanted attention on us, Brighton hates vampires for what happened to her mom. And rightfully so. But there will never be enough trust between us to make whatever you're thinking or hoping work."

I bite down on my bottom lip to keep it from trembling as tears burn my eyes. I never thought the day would come where I was torn between my best friend and them. I open my mouth to respond, but Gabriel's phone chimes.

He pulls it out and frowns. "It's Atlas. We need to get back upstairs."

My stomach drops, and I shake my head. "What, why? What's going on?"

He hits another button, making the elevator start moving again. "There's an attack happening on a community of vampires on the university campus." The elevator reaches the lobby, and we take it back up to our floor.

Back in the room, Atlas, Kade, and Lex are scrambling around, getting changed and drinking the blood bags we brought from the plane.

I tie my hair back and down half a bottle of water, trying to calm my nerves.

"I called Marcel. He's sending two of his guys to stay here with you," Lex says.

I bark out a choked laugh. "What the fuck did you just say? I'm going with you."

"You should stay behind, angel," Gabriel says softly.

I ignore him, my eyes falling on Atlas, and I can see the debate happening in his expression. He's considering glamouring me into submission. I hold his gaze, daring him to do it. My narrowed eyes tell him that I will be beyond livid if he goes through with it.

When he steps forward, I force myself to stand my ground. He stops right in front of me, wrapping his hand around my thigh, touching the dagger there. His eyes travel the length of my body as he leans in, his breath tickling my cheek. His jaw is set tight, his eyes dark and serious. "Look at me."

I do despite the fact his words hold no weight of glamour. The intensity of his gaze burns right through me.

"You do not hesitate, you understand me?"

My eyes widen as my pulse jumps. I swallow hard past the dryness in my throat. I'm not exactly sure I can kill humans but I find myself nodding anyway.

Everything happens so quickly. We're in the car, speeding towards campus in the dark. I don't immediately see chaos when we arrive, but the moment we get out of the car, I hear the sounds of battle and my blood runs cold.

Our group rushes toward the fight, Lex and Kade on one side of me, and Gabriel and Atlas on the other. We round the corner of one of the buildings and nearly trip over a female vampire trying to flee, with blood-soaked clothes and wide silver eyes. She appears weak and scared and young—so fucking young it makes my chest ache. Gabriel stops her, making sure she's relatively unharmed before letting her go. She disappears in a blur of movement a moment later.

Once we get close enough, I notice there's a large group of people, some moving in blurs of shapes and others trying to tear them down with guns and daggers.

The guys dive into the fight, whereas I stay near the outside. I'm not so arrogant I think I can dodge a bullet at close range. My eyes fall on a wounded vampire several feet away. There's a dagger sticking out of his chest, but he's still moving. I race over to him, darting around several hunters covered in blood, whether it be their own or that of a vampire, I can't tell in the dark. I fall to the ground at the vampire's side and pull the stake out of his chest.

He coughs up blood, and it spatters across his cheek. His eyes widen when he realizes I'm human. "Why... are you helping me?" he says in a broken voice.

"I'm not with them," I insist. "I'm not a hunter." I toss the dagger far enough away he won't be worried I'm going to stab him with it.

"It scraped my heart. It's going to take me too long to heal. There are too many hunters..." His voice trails off as fear fills his dirt and bloodstained features.

My eyes don't leave his face. If he doesn't heal and get out of here, it's very possible that another hunter will come for him. So I do something potentially stupid and offer him my wrist. "Don't take too much," I warn him. "There are four very scary vampires here who will actually kill you if you hurt me."

There's no hesitation in his movements. He grabs my wrist, and I see a flash of his fangs before he sinks them into my skin. It doesn't hurt as much as I was expecting it to. Maybe it's because I gave myself willingly.

A moment later, I cringe when I hear Atlas shout, "For the love of god, Calla," and I know I'm going to pay for this act of kindness on my part later.

The vampire on the ground pulls away from my wrist, and I cover it with my palm. I help him up, and he offers me a grateful smile before he disappears into the night. I turn and come face-to-face with Atlas.

"Are you fucking kidding me?" he growls, fangs bared.

"We don't have time for this," I mutter. "I helped him. It's fine. Get over it."

His eyes are ablaze with pure fury. "Do you know how many vampires are around right now?"

"Yes, and we're trying to help them, so quit being jealous someone else had my blood and—"

"Enough. Do that again, and I will drag you back to the car myself and make sure you stay there. Don't give me that look. I don't take too kindly to others having what's mine." It goes without saying that Gabriel, Lex, and Kade are the exception.

Heat floods through me, stealing my breath at his possessiveness. I don't know if I want to kiss him or punch him, and we really don't have time for either.

He rips the dagger out of its holder at my thigh and shoves it into my hand. "A lot of good it does you there. Hang on to this. Use it and —" His voice cuts off, and he sighs, muttering a curse under his breath.

I shake my head, searching his face. "What? Why is your face like that?"

A muscle ticks in his jaw. "You're going to be upset with this."

"I mean, add it to the list. What is it, Atlas?"

"Your friend is here."

"What?" I turn and find Brighton fighting alongside the hunters, her father not too far away in a white dress shirt spattered with blood. While it's clear to me the hunters are severely outnumbered, clearly it's not so much to them, because they continue fighting.

Brighton's eyes turn to me and widen. She shakes her head, abandoning the attack she was carrying out. Tears fill her eyes, and I charge forward, ignoring any and all caution as I stomp through the battle, with Atlas at my side. Except, I'm not heading for Brighton. My sights are set on Scott.

"Are you ready to do this now?" Atlas asks. He knows exactly what I need to do.

"I don't know," I admit, his words catching me up as we continue toward them.

"Calla, what are you doing?" Brighton asks, panic filling her eyes, and I barely hear her. I want to be understanding of her being here, I really fucking do, but right now, I can't find the grace to grant her that. And there's not a chance in hell of finding it for her father.

Scott finally sees me, recognition flaring to life in his gaze.

"You fucking monster," I seethe before he can say anything to me. "You put your own daughter in danger to settle some score?"

"That's not what's happening!" Brighton attempts to denounce my claim with tears in her eyes. I have no clue why or *how* she's standing there defending her father. "I'm fighting for my mom, Calla."

I shake my head, flinching at the sound of a pain-filled scream from somewhere behind me, and keep my eyes on my best friend, the desperation in her gaze no doubt reflected in mine. "It was your mom who fought so hard to keep you out of this fight, Bri. She didn't want this life for you, remember?" It was never a secret that she wanted to keep Brighton out of the family business—the secret had been what the business *was*.

Scott grabs Brighton's arm, but I grab the other before he can pull her away from me. "You don't have to go with him. *Please* don't go with him," I implore her, knowing at that moment and despite the dagger clenched in my other hand, I won't be able to kill Scott myself. As desperate as I am to avenge what he did to my mom, I can't do that to Brighton. Seeing her like this now, I'm not sure she would survive it.

From my peripheral, I catch a quick glance at Atlas helping a couple of vampires who are being ganged up on by half a dozen hunters. He moves with a lethal grace, striking them down with his bare hands in a matter of seconds.

Brighton sniffles, snapping my attention back to her as tears roll down her cheeks, and she lowers her voice. "He's my dad, Calla. He's all I have left."

My heart cleaves in two, and I shake my head, letting go of her wrist. "All you have?" I whisper, betrayal whipping through me like ice in my veins, and I struggle to hold her gaze.

Scott clears his throat and pulls Brighton away from me. "It's time to go."

"Don't," I warn her, my eyes wide as I stare at her and my grip tightening on my dagger, as if I could use it to keep her with me. "If you go, you're dead. They *will* kill you—I won't be able to stop them."

"She's dead if she stays," Scott hisses, tightening his grip on the dagger in the hand he doesn't have wrapped around Brighton's arm.

"You started this," I growl at him, my voice sharp and filled with venom. "You're severely outnumbered here, Scott. You brought your daughter into this, and—"

"Brighton," he cuts me off, blatantly ignoring my presence. Brighton gives me one last tear-filled look before she turns and runs toward the parking lot with her father.

I can barely see, my eyes overflowing with tears. I stumble back, nearly tripping over a body. I'm not sure whether it's a vampire or hunter. The numbers are dwindling and there's death on both sides. But there's a sick part of me that's glad Scott got away only because it means Brighton is safe.

I don't try to stop them, because if we kill Scott, they'll kill Brighton too. I try to blink the tears away, but they fall down my cheeks, and I wipe my face with the back of my hand, sniffling as my nose runs. My eyes fall on Kade, who looks near demonic in battle.

Something in him has snapped, I realize with a tightness in my chest that makes it hard to breathe.

He's ripping through hunters too quickly for them to even attempt to fight back. He notices Scott and Brighton getting away and starts toward them.

A strangled cry gets stuck in my throat, and Atlas pulls him back.

I rush toward them as Kade fights Atlas's grip, gnashing his bloody fangs in Atlas's face. "Kade!" I scream, my voice cracking with pain.

His eyes swing toward me, and he blinks, then stops fighting Atlas. "Calla—"

"Please," I force out through my tears, "just... let them go. *Please.*"

His jaw hardens, his gaze lowering for a moment before meeting mine. "Okay," he finally says, stepping away from Atlas and toward me. His nostrils flare, and he frowns. "You're bleeding."

"No, I... Well, yeah. I'm okay, though." He must've been too wrapped up in his lust for hunter blood he didn't realize when Atlas did that I'd fed that vampire.

Atlas keeps his eyes locked on Kade for a moment before they flick to me. A second later, he moves in a blur and reenters the fight. Scott and Brighton might've fled, but other hunters are still determined to spill vampire blood tonight.

Gabriel is the farthest away, helping another vampire to his feet, and Lex howls in delight, tearing into a hunter's throat and spraying blood on the lawn.

I cringe at the vicious sight as Kade moves around me to follow Atlas back into battle.

Between one moment and the next, hands wrap around my shoulders from behind and I'm flying toward the ground. I don't have time to put my hands out and catch my fall. I land hard on my hip, and pain explodes along my side. Before I have a second to recover, I'm flipped over and end up face-to-face with a very pissed off vampire, his fangs snapping way too close for comfort.

"Hunter," he snarls in my face.

"I'm not! Get... off of... me," I hiss, struggling beneath the dark-haired vampire. His mouth is already covered with blood, and I cringe as it drips onto my face. My stomach roils as his fangs get closer to my throat, and panic claws into me as I reach around desperately. I wrap my fingers around the dagger at my thigh, pulling it out of its holder and gripping it tightly. I try again to shove him off, but he growls in my face, slamming me hard against the ground. I cry out, my vision blurring, and he presses his body into me, sinking his fangs into my shoulder.

My muscles tense, and I yelp in pain. Something in me snaps, and I use every ounce of strength I have to thrust my arm up, sinking the dagger into the vampire's chest. I have no idea if I hit his heart, but he reels back and falls to the ground beside me.

Gabriel is there, pulling me off the ground and holding me upright, while Lex pulls the vampire up and tears into his throat so hard his head rolls off his neck and lands in the grass with a sickening *thump*.

I turn away, pressing my face into Gabriel's chest as nausea rolls through me like a vicious wave. Pain radiates through my whole body as blood seeps through my shirt. Consciousness threatens to slip away from me, my vision dimming around the edges, and I fight to cling to it.

"Calla," Gabriel says, supporting the majority of my weight; I'm far too unsteady to stand on my own. "Keep your eyes open. You're okay, angel. Everything is going to be okay."

I don't feel okay.

The sounds of pained and angry shouts grows quieter as Gabriel guides me away from what's left of the fight, while Lex rejoins Kade and Atlas, striking down more hunters with dangerous ease. Sirens blare in the distance; we don't have much time to get out of here before the authorities arrive.

"Did I kill that vampire?" I force out, trying to look back to where his decapitated body landed in the grass.

"Lex did," Gabriel answers in a gentle voice.

My brows pull together and even that hurts. "So I... I didn't hit his heart?"

"No, you didn't."

Relief floods through me. Sure, he still ended up dead, but not by my hand. I'm glad I was able to defend myself, but if anything, this reaffirmed that I'm not ready to kill anyone. I'm not sure I'll ever be ready for that.

Things seem to end quite quickly after that, or maybe I just go numb. I'm not really sure. By the time Gabriel and I make it to the car, the others have joined us.

Atlas immediately crowds my personal space and snags my chin, tipping my head back and looking into my eyes. "You forgot something."

I squint at him through the pain pounding in my head. "What?"

He holds up my dagger, still covered in that vampire's blood. After wiping it off on his shirt, he returns it to the holder at my thigh and leans in until his lips are at my ear. "You did good."

My stomach flutters despite the pain radiating from the rest of me. Atlas is proud of me and that's doing weird things to my heart. I lean back a little to look at him, and my stance falters. He catches me around the waist, holding me against his chest.

"Calla." His voice sounds far away.

Darkness crowds my vision again and my ears start ringing. Shit. How hard did I hit my head?

"Calla?" Atlas's face blurs in front of me. "Fuck. Lex, you drive." He tosses the keys before sweeping my feet off the ground and cradling me against his chest as he gets into the car.

Gabriel is in the seat beside us. "She needs—"

"I know," Atlas cuts him off, looking down at me.

My chest tightens at the worry in his eyes. I'm not entirely sure what he's referring to. I want to suggest a doctor or a hospital maybe, but I have a feeling that's not where we're going.

The movement of the car doesn't help matters, and I squeeze my eyes shut, clenching my jaw so I don't whimper in pain.

"Calla, I know you're in pain, but I need you to look at me."

I manage to pry my eyes open enough to see Atlas's face.

"There you are," he murmurs in a voice so soft it nearly doesn't sound like him. "Listen to me. I'm going to take the pain away, all right?"

"Wha—?" Realization hits me, and I groan. "No."

Something like a tinge of reserved amusement passes over his features. "You can complain all you want and try to stab me later, but this is what's happening."

I narrow my eyes. I want to pull away from him, but there's not a shot in hell I have the strength for that.

Atlas lifts his arm, and I see a flash of his fangs before they're in his wrist. A second later, he pulls it back. "Are you going to make this difficult?"

After glaring at him for a good ten seconds, I shake my head. The thought of drinking his blood makes me all hot and panicky, but the pain and blood loss I'm experiencing outweigh that—barely.

"Good. You can close your eyes if that'll help."

I wet my lips, managing to lift my hands and cradle his wrist in them. He brings it to my mouth, and my pulse kicks up the moment before I close my lips around the blood pooling on his skin. My eyes flutter shut as his blood coats my tongue, warming my stomach as it glides down my throat. Almost immediately, the pain fades. The pounding behind my eyes and the pain in my side is gone. The skin around where the vampire bit my shoulder tingles, healing as Atlas's blood flows through me.

He pulls his wrist away from my mouth, and I think I shock both of us when I lick my lips, because what the hell? Why am I acting like I want *more*?

I drop my gaze, trying to ignore the heat flaring in my cheeks. "I... um, thanks."

He nods and helps me sit up but makes no move to shift me off his lap.

We're back at the hotel shortly thereafter. The guys glamour anybody who sees us on our way back to the suite, considering we look like we just participated in a massacre, which I suppose we did.

The guys take turns showering the blood off of them and they collectively decide to toss their clothes. When it's my turn for the shower, Lex offers to help, but I wave him off, needing a minute to myself.

I stand under the hot spray of water, letting it mix with my tears and the blood rinsing off my skin.

Tonight is a turning point. Brighton has made her choice, and I think... I feel that I've made mine.

We're on opposite sides of a war that neither of us should have to be involved in, and I'm not really sure how to deal with that right now.

After my shower, I wrap myself in the plush hotel robe and walk back out to the main living space. Gabriel's in the kitchen with Kade where they're sipping on glasses of whiskey.

Atlas is on his phone, speaking quickly and with a grim expression on his face, likely reporting back to somebody in New York who will relay whatever message he gives to his super scary, super powerful vampire parents.

Lex is lying on the couch, watching some trashy reality show.

We sure are a sight to be seen.

I perch myself on the armrest of the couch, vaguely paying attention to the TV, but not really able to focus on the drama unfolding. Not when I have so much of it in my real life.

Lex sits up as Gabriel and Kade come into the room and says, "We all need to decompress. I think we should have a game night."

I groan. "My god, Lex. Please don't say—"

"I think we need to do it. I think we really do need to play strip poker."

"What is with your fixation on this game?" Gabriel asks.

"I don't know, man. I just think it would be fun. Plus, I'm really fucking good at poker."

Kade says nothing, which concerns me, especially after seeing him in battle tonight. He catches me looking at him and arches eyebrow at me as if to ask why I'm watching him. I arch one right back, to which he smirks faintly, shaking his head and downing the rest of his drink. "If we're doing this," he says, "I'm going to need another drink."

"I'm going to need several," I mutter.

"Strip poker?" Gabriel is looking at Lex. "Really?"

Lex grins and nods, looking like a kid on Christmas morning who was told he would be going to Disney World.

An hour later, the five of us are in various stages of undress in the living room of our hotel suite. I'm on the couch with Kade, while Lex sits on the floor with his back against the couch, and Gabriel and Atlas are occupying the armchairs opposite us.

"You know," I say to Lex, trying and failing to suppress a wry smile as I run my fingers through the back of his hair, "for the guy who has been so insistent on playing strip poker, you kinda suck at this game. So much for being 'really fucking good at poker,' huh?"

He grumbles something under his breath that I don't quite catch, snatching one of the decorative pillows from the couch to cover his crotch.

"Now don't be a poor sport, Lex," Kade says, taking a drink of his whiskey and blood cocktail before setting the glass on the coffee table. I've gotten fairly skilled at mixing alcohol and blood tonight. I'm also apparently quite good at poker, considering I'm still wearing my T-shirt, bra, and panties. Kade is down to his boxers, as is Gabriel, and Atlas has only lost his jacket, shirt, and shoes. Because *of course* he's also good at poker.

"I have a better game," Kade offers, angling himself toward me.

I arch a brow at him. "Oh? Another one that will leave poor Lex in his birthday suit I hope?"

Kade smirks, running his hand up my bare thigh and making my skin tingle under his touch. "That's the idea. Though you, my sweet and fiery Calla, are still wearing entirely too much clothing." He slides his finger along my hip, under my panties, and tears them clear off me before I have a second to protest, dropping them in Lex's lap.

My cheeks flush hotly, and I narrow my eyes at him. "Your game is to ruin my clothes?"

He catches my chin, leaning in until his lips nearly touch mine, and my senses are overwhelmed by a mixture of citrus and whiskey and Kade. "My game is to see which of us can make you come the hardest."

Holy fuck.

My pulse cranks way up, pounding like a jackhammer beneath my skin, and my throat goes dry.

The corner of his mouth kicks up, and he says, "I thought that might pique your interest." His mouth is on mine before I can respond, his tongue teasing my lips and coaxing them open until they part and he pushes into my mouth. Our tongues dance as I lean into him, my eyes shut and my stomach fluttering like a jar filled with butterflies. When he pulls me onto his lap and his erection presses between my thighs through his boxers, I gasp against his lips. He grips my hips, and they instinctively start moving, seeking to address the growing friction at my core.

Lex shifts behind me, his chest against my back as he leans in to press his lips against my shoulder. He slides his hands under my shirt and bra, cupping my breasts and tweaking my nipples into stiff peaks.

I moan into Kade's mouth, grinding harder against his erection. I slide my fingers into his unbelievably soft hair, gripping the back of it, and reach between us with my free hand, palming the bulge in his boxers. He stiffens and groans against my lips, nipping my bottom one with his teeth.

"Keep moving like that," he says in a low voice, "and I'm going to fuck you so hard the game will be over before it even starts."

I rest my forehead against his, catching my breath. "Still sounds like a win to me."

Lex presses his lips just below my ear, his tongue darting out and teasing the sensitive skin there. "Not before I have a chance to devour you again." He pinches my nipples, and I yelp in surprise more than pain. He pulls his hands out of my shirt, then promptly pulls it up and off over my head. I turn in time to see him toss it toward Gabriel, who shakes his head, grinning faintly as he watches us.

"Fear not. You'll have your turn, brother," Lex tells him.

"I certainly hope so," he says, holding my gaze, and I smile, biting my lip as my face warms.

Kade's grip on my hips tightens, pulling my attention back to him. He slides me off his lap, laying me across the couch with my back against his bare chest, and Lex grabs one of my ankles, pulling it over the edge until my foot touches the floor and I'm spread open for him.

My breath catches in my throat as he licks his lips, his gaze locked between my thighs, filled with a hunger that makes me shiver. He kisses from just below my knee all the way up my thigh, and the moment his lips brush my folds, I sigh, tipping my head back against Kade's shoulder. He kisses my cheek, snaking his arm around my waist, securing me to him as Lex licks the length of my slit.

"Fuck," I breathe, closing my eyes as pleasure floods through me and warmth fills my stomach.

Kade sucks on the crook of my neck, his tongue swirling in circles against my skin and making my nipples tingle as I imagine his tongue giving them the same treatment.

Lex slides his hand up my thigh, lapping at my folds with his tongue as his thumb finds my clit and teases it until I'm squirming against Kade's hold. His tongue plunges into my pussy, and I moan, reaching for something, *anything* to hang onto. Kade's hands find mine, and I lace my fingers through his.

Lex pulls his hand away from my clit and uses both hands to hold me open to him, his tongue bouncing between sucking my clit and plunging deep into my pussy until my head is spinning and I'm gasping for breath, writhing against him.

In minutes, I'm racing toward orgasm, my heart pounding in my chest and the muscles in my thighs tightening as I reach climax and cry out, squeezing Kade's hands until my knuckles are white and moaning loudly.

Lex leans back, grinning at me as he licks his lips and heat fills my cheeks. Kade frees one of his hands from mine and curls his finger around my chin, turning my face so my lips meet his, and he kisses me deeply. When he pulls back, I'm desperate to suck air into my lungs. As my body vibrates with electricity and pleasure, still riding the aftershocks of my orgasm.

When Lex stands and heads toward Atlas, my eyes widen, but Gabriel quickly replaces him in front of me, the bulge in his boxers distracting me from watching what Lex is going to try with Atlas.

I pull my other hand free from Kade's and reach for Gabriel—more specifically the waistband of his boxers to pull his cock free. Excitement fills my stomach and my core continues to throb as he lowers himself onto the couch, but instead of kissing me, his lips meet Kade's as he lines his cock up with my entrance and pushes into me with ease. I slide my hands up his bare chest, holding him and getting lost in the scene of him and Kade exploring each other's lips. His cock pushes in deeper, hitting a particularly sensitive spot, and I press my lips together, moaning once more. He pulls nearly all the way out before thrusting back into me. He finds a steady rhythm, rolling his hips and hitting a spot deep inside me over and over that has me panting in a matter of minutes. He pulls back from Kade's mouth only to seal his lips over mine, and I lose myself in the feel of his lips as he picks up the pace of his thrusts, and Kade reaches between us circling my clit with his fingers.

It doesn't take long for another orgasm to rack my body, leaving me a trembling puddle of pleasure. I don't think I could stand if I had to at this point. Gabriel slams into me a few more times before the muscles in his thighs tighten, and he grunts, shooting his release into me and kissing me hard.

I manage to catch the scene of Lex going down on Atlas past Gabriel's shoulder, and my pussy clenches around Gabriel's cock at the sight of Atlas's head bent back against the chair, his eyes shut, biting his lip with a look of pleasure etched into his usually sharp features. I don't know what it is about the sight of the most powerful vampire I've met in that position, but when Gabriel moves inside me again, I'm overcome with another orgasm, and I grab his face, bringing his mouth back to mine as my hips arch, trying to push him deeper inside me.

Atlas grunts across the room, gripping the arms of the chair until his knuckles turn white, and he shudders.

Lex swallows Atlas's release and rocks back on his knees, smirking at me over his shoulder.

"Perhaps we should move this into the bedroom?" Kade suggests as Gabriel slides out of me, dropping a soft, sweet kiss to my forehead.

Lex moves at vamp speed into the other room, and we all turn to look at him through the open sliding barn-style door into the bedroom.

Gabriel moves off me, helping me sit up, and Kade gets off the couch, following Lex's lead.

Atlas rolls his eyes, tucking his cock back into his boxers and standing, walking toward the kitchen instead of the bedroom. He comes back a minute later with a glass of blood in one hand and a bottle of water in the other. He hands me the water, and I take it, murmuring a quick word of thanks before unscrewing the cap and downing half the bottle. I set it on the coffee table and get up, somewhat surprised my legs are strong enough to hold me upright.

Gabriel slides his arm around my waist anyway, and I don't protest when his other arm curls around the backs of my knees and he sweeps me off my feet, carrying me into the bedroom, with Atlas trailing behind us.

Despite the massive bed, it's still a pretty tight fit for the five of us. I end up sandwiched in the middle, with Kade and Gabriel on one side and Atlas and Lex on the other.

Pressure builds in my chest as each of the guys turn their attention to me. My heart pounds in my chest, and this time, it has less to do with the orgasms that tore through me moments ago and more to do with the weight of the words on my tongue, daring to be spoken.

"Angel?" Gabriel murmurs, his eyes dancing over my face and lit with concern. "What is it?"

I swallow past the lump in my throat, then sigh softly. "I don't care about the blood oath," I finally say. "Despite it being the catalyst of what brought me to you, it won't be the reason I choose to stay." I take a moment to look each of my vampires in the eyes. "I'm not going anywhere, because as much as I *can* see my life and my future without the four of you, I... I don't *want* to. So whatever happens, whatever we're forced to face, it will be together. I'm here and I'm yours, as much as you are mine."

The following morning, the lot of us are sitting around the dining room table at breakfast. Gabriel made some egg frittata thing, and Calla insisted on walking down the street to a local bakery to pick up muffins, which Gabriel was more than happy to take her to do.

After her speech last night, the four of us are coming to terms with her decision to stay with us despite finding out that in terms of the blood oath, she had no obligation to and could be free of us at any time.

I'd never admit it out loud, but what she said made me want to wrap my arms around her and never let her go. She has certainly made our lives interesting these last two months and brought light into the darkness for all of us.

Gabriel's phone starts ringing as we're finishing up breakfast, and he sets his coffee down, answering the call on speaker. "Fallon, what is it?" he asks.

"Gabe, I don't want you to panic, because we're good, but we were involved in a little, uh… situation."

Gabriel frowns briefly. "What kind of a situation, Fal? What happened?"

"We were attacked by hunters," Jase says.

"Son of a bitch," I growl under my breath.

"What the fuck happened?" Kade asks.

"We were ambushed," Fallon says. "I don't know if the number of hunters in Chicago has increased all of a sudden, but it felt like every single one was in on this attack."

"How did you escape it?" Atlas chimes in.

"Yeah, that's the thing," Fallon says with a tone of unease. "Selene saved our lives."

"You're going to have to say that again," I tell her, "because I'm certain we did not just hear you correctly."

"Oh, no," she says, "you did. We would be dead if it wasn't for her. Needless to say, our cover is effectively blown, so I'm not sure what you want us to do now."

"Fucking hell," Kade curses, slamming his fist against the table.

"Did she say anything to you?" Gabriel asks, raking his fingers through his already messy copper hair. There's a haunted look in his eyes, and I'm sure his head is spinning as fast as mine is, trying to decide what the hell we're going to do.

There's a chance Selene didn't tie Fallon and Jase to Gabriel. I don't know that they ever met—I doubt it. But Selene was obsessed with Gabriel. She would know if anyone so much as breathed on him.

"It doesn't fucking matter," I chime in. "Just because she saved a couple of lives, it nowhere near makes up for everything she put Gabriel and Calla through. She's a dead woman."

Kade and Atlas both nod their heads in silent agreement, while Gabriel sits quietly. Calla stares at her lap, her jaw set tight. "I don't really know what to do with this information," she says in a low voice.

Gabriel sighs. "Are you sure you two are okay?" he checks.

"Yeah, man. We're good," Jase says.

"Do you know where Selene is now? Atlas asks.

"No. After she saved us, she took off pretty quickly. If you guys are going to come, now is the time. I doubt she'll stick around much longer, and we can't exactly go looking for her again without raising suspicions if we happen to find her."

"I'll call you back," Gabriel says. "Be safe." He ends the call, gripping his phone in his hand tight enough the glass cracks, and he drops it onto the table, cursing under his breath.

Calla reaches for him, wrapping her hand around his arm, and he lets out a slow breath. "I'm sorry," she says in a gentle voice.

He somehow manages to smile at her.

"You think she knew who they were?" Kade asks. "Could she have saved them with the thought of using it later to get back to you?"

Gabriel rakes his fingers through his hair, shaking his head. "I truly don't know. But why would she take off after saving them if that was the case?"

"Perhaps that's something you can ask her before I tear out her esophagus," I offer. "I think we better get back on the plane." There is no way in hell we're letting that psycho bitch get away again.

Atlas stands. "I'll call Marcel and arrange for the flight and have a car pick us up. Get ready and pack some clothes." He turns his attention to Calla. "I don't suppose there's any point in me asking you to stay behind?"

She regards him curiously. "You would ask?"

They stare at each other for a moment before Atlas sighs. "Never mind."

She nods, a hint of a smile on her lips.

In ten minutes, we each have a duffel bag packed and meet in the living room. We're about to head out when Atlas glances down at his phone, and his expression hardens.

"What is it?" Kade asks.

"New York is calling. We are being summoned—all of us."

"What for?" Gabriel asks.

Atlas shakes his head. "It doesn't say, but if I had to guess, it's probably about the hunter attack last night. Evidently it has garnered some media attention and there's some concern from the Capitol."

"What does that have to do with us?" Calla asks. "I mean, besides us having been there? What is there to say about it now?" Her voice is even, but she won't meet his gaze. Her pulse is also slightly elevated and sweat dots her brow. She's trying to project confidence, but I can see how nervous she is and I don't blame her one bit.

He blinks at her, his expression void of any emotion. "I don't know, but this isn't a suggestion."

"Right," she says, pressing her lips together, and doesn't add anything else.

"I'll call Fallon back and let her know we have to make a pit stop in New York before we head to Chicago," Gabriel says.

I lean against the back of the couch, sighing. I can't help but think this *pitstop* is going to be a lot more than that.

I've only been summoned to New York with Atlas one other time and that was shortly after he sired me. Lenora and Simon made it known they weren't happy Atlas had turned me and also made it very clear that Atlas's position in this world was more important than I would ever understand. It didn't matter Atlas had little desire to participate in the politics of their world—they refused to allow anything else for their son.

So here we are, heading back to the Big Apple to face what is sure to be a complete shit storm.

TWENTY

I can only recall ever being this scared twice in my life. The night the vampires came for me and when I thought my mom was going to die.

There's a black town car waiting for us at the airstrip in New York when we land, with tinted windows and men in suits standing outside. One opens the door to the back seat, and we pile in, Gabriel and Atlas on either side of me, with Kade and Lex in the seats behind us. No one speaks—the car is deafeningly silent as we drive away from the airstrip. The car ride feels simultaneously too long and too short. I keep my hands on my thighs, pressing my fingers into my skin so my knees won't bounce. I don't know who the guys in the front are, but if they're affiliated with Atlas's parents—which I figure they must be—I can't show any sign of weakness, despite the way my heart pounds, causing my pulse to race.

I considered I would eventually be forced to meet the scary, all-powerful York vampires who produced one of the most difficult and intimidating people I've ever met in my life, but I certainly wasn't prepared for it to be today.

Atlas keeps his gaze trained forward, his jaw set in a tight line. His stone cold demeanor sure doesn't make me feel better about the situation.

I pull my bottom lip between my teeth, chewing it absently as I stare out the windshield. When I taste blood, I tense, my eyes widening. *Shit, shit, shit.* I didn't get a good look at the men in front of us so I'm not sure if they're vampires. My anxiety heightens tenfold, and I jump when Gabriel places his hand over mine on my thigh, my gaze whipping toward him.

He leans in, his lips brushing my ear. "They're human," he whispers. "Breathe, angel."

I close my eyes, trying to focus on the warmth of Gabriel's hand on mine, grounding me. Despite my aversion to glamour, part of me wishes I'd asked one of them to use it on me to chill the fuck out. Pulling in a deep breath, I turn my head slightly so my hair acts as a curtain to my face, then let it out slowly.

"That's it," Gabriel murmurs, gliding his thumb back and forth across the top of my hand. "You're okay."

"I'm freaking out," I admit in a hushed tone.

Gabriel sighs softly. "I know, but I need you to trust that we're not going to let anything happen to you. Can you do that for me?"

I hesitate, pressing my lips together. Not that I have much of a choice in the matter, but I appreciate Gabriel's words. And when my chest tightens and my breath hitches, I come to a realization that somehow makes me even more anxious. "I trust you," I say, swallowing hard. "All of you."

Lex and Kade both reach for me from the back seat, each of them touching one of my shoulders, and I turn my gaze toward Atlas to find him already looking at me. His expression softens ever so slightly, and he offers a subtle nod. There's an understanding between us that, at this moment, requires no physical touch.

And oh my god, I am so damn screwed because, despite my best efforts, I've fallen for him—for all of them. The knot in my stomach tells me there's no coming back from this. Whatever happens, these guys—these equally lethal and caring vampires—are my future.

Not much later, we pull off the main road and continue driving, thick forest lining both sides of the vehicle. There isn't another car or building in sight, and we eventually slow to a stop in front of giant wrought iron gates. The driver rolls down the window, speaking too soft for me to hear to a woman stationed there in an all-black uniform.

A moment later, there's a loud clicking sound, and the gate slides open. We drive through, and my breath catches when my gaze falls upon the house we're driving toward. *House* isn't the appropriate word for this place. It's more like a palace compound and looks like something out of a movie. It's ridiculously huge and impeccably landscaped, with a long reflection pool leading up to the front of the building where our car slows to a stop once more.

The two guys up front make no move to get out, and a third man in a suit walks out of the building, heading toward the car, and opens the door at Atlas's side. "Mr. York," he greets in a level, polite tone. "Good to see you, sir."

Atlas nods at the man but says nothing, getting out of the car. At the last moment, he finds my hand and squeezes it once without looking at me, and I think it's meant to reassure me, but the mess of nerves in my stomach don't know how to react.

I slide out of the car behind him as Gabriel gets out the other side, with Lex and Kade following after me.

"I'll have someone collect your bags," the man says, still only addressing Atlas. "Your parents are waiting for you inside."

Atlas nods again and starts toward the building. The four of us follow him, Kade and Lex on either side of me, with Gabriel taking up the rear. They are essentially caging me in between them, which should make me feel safer, but right now, I'm suffocating. If this meeting is about the hunter attack, my presence doesn't make all that much sense, considering I'm not a vampire or a hunter. Which makes me think my being here is due to some creepy fascination the Yorks have with their son's human... whatever I am, and that really doesn't make me feel better about the whole situation.

We walk up wide marble stairs with massive pillars on either side, and I don't think I could feel more wildly out of place anywhere else.

The man who greeted us opens the tall, glass door, holding it as the five of us file inside what I am reluctant to call a foyer because of how ridiculously huge and fancy it is. The marble from outside carries in and the ceilings are at least two stories high. Directly in front of us is a staircase leading to the second floor and an intricate chandelier hanging from the ceiling. On one side of the lavish entrance is a sitting area with a white stone fireplace that sits unlit and a sleek black grand piano. The other side has several sets of doors, all closed, and stunningly detailed canvases hung between them—oil paintings, I think.

"Mr. and Mrs. York are in the formal dining room," the man announces.

Gabriel touches my back gently, guiding me forward, and I follow Atlas down a brightly lit corridor, my Docs echoing softly on the marble floor. I wipe my palms on my thighs and pull in several deep breaths, but it does nothing to help the anxiety in my chest, making my pulse pound beneath my skin.

We stop outside a set of solid black double doors, and the man opens them, stepping aside for us to walk in.

The space is just as fancy as the one we came from. There's a long, dark wood table in the middle of the room with chairs set around it, and at the head of the table is a man nearly the spitting image of Atlas, though he appears maybe twenty years older than the vampire at my side. My heart slams against my ribcage and my feet stop moving. Terror grips my body, and I wish nothing more than for the floor to open up and swallow me whole.

The woman to his right is the most stunning person I have ever laid eyes on. Lenora York has long auburn hair, striking silver eyes, and sharp features like Atlas. She's dressed as if she's attending the Met Ball, and I can't help but glance down at my own clothes. I nearly laugh at how ridiculous I look in comparison. Her eyes travel over us, focusing on me for a split second before landing on Atlas. Her lips curve into a subtle smile, and she stands, smoothing the front of her red wine colored dress. She moves away from the table, gliding toward us with graceful ease. "Atlas, my son, welcome home." She stops in front of him, kissing each of his cheeks.

"Mother," he says in greeting. "I'm afraid we can't stay long. There's a matter we need to attend to in Chicago."

Her brows crease and what could be misconstrued as concern passes over her features. "Chicago?" she asks, sounding mildly disappointed.

"Yes. Gabriel's sire is there, and we would like to deal with her before she can leave the city."

"I was under the impression Selene was residing here in New York, which was the reason for your previous visit."

My heart skips a beat, and I pull in an unsteady breath. Something tells me she wouldn't take too kindly to knowing she was lied to.

"No one likes her, so she moves around a lot," Lex says in a dry tone, and my eyes widen slightly, but I stay silent, my jaw clenched so tightly it's causing my gums to throb in protest.

Lenora purses her lips, clearly unamused. "I see. No matter, we appreciate you coming to us on such short notice. Please allow us to handle the issue in Chicago. I would hate for it to take you away so quickly."

"That won't be necessary," Atlas says, his voice is smooth but firm.

It's hard to believe he's speaking to his own mother. There's no love or fondness in his voice. It's strictly business. "I'm sure we can settle whatever is going on here and be on our way shortly."

She frowns, turning to Gabriel, who she reaches her hand toward. He immediately takes it, stepping forward, and brings it to his lips, brushing them over her knuckles. "Lovely to see you again," she says in a softer tone than I was expecting to hear from her.

Gabriel nods. "A pleasure, as always. I apologize that our business elsewhere must interfere with this visit."

She pulls her hand back smoothly and smiles at Gabriel. "Nonsense. I understand your sire has caused many issues for you and I will be happy to have her handled."

I watch Gabriel's face, though he gives no hint as to what he's thinking.

"I, of course, appreciate your generosity," he says, "however, I must insist we deal with this particular issue ourselves. Selene has caused a great deal of anguish, and though I cannot personally deliver the action against her that she deserves, I need to be there when it happens."

Just when I expect her to refuse him, Lenora nods. "I understand. We will have the plane ready to take you there after our visit. Please, come sit. We were just about to eat." She moves down the line toward Lex, leaning in to kiss his cheek, then does the same to Kade, pausing in front of him. "I understand you lost your sister during a recent hunter attack."

Kade's eyes widen, as if he wasn't expecting her to bring it up. "I... Yes," he finally says.

She nods. "And you killed the hunter responsible?"

A muscle feathers along his jaw as his gaze darkens. "I did."

"Good." With that, she returns to the table where her husband is standing at the head. No sympathetic words or comforting gestures. Just *good*. She doesn't even acknowledge my presence, which, not to sound self-absorbed, but I figured was kind of a big deal. I'm not about to complain about it—I'd be more than happy to go unnoticed this entire visit, though I have a feeling that's not going to happen.

We walk over to the table, and Atlas takes the spot to his father's left, shaking his hand before the rest of the guys do the same, which leaves me standing there feeling absolutely ridiculous. I'm not sure how I'm supposed to address these people. These vampires, they're royalty in their own world, but from the things I've heard about them, I'll dislike them as much as I'm terrified of them.

"And you must be Miss Montgomery," Simon says in a deep voice. His gaze slams into me, and my entire body fills with discomfort. I want to step away—run away, actually. But I force myself to stay where I am and nod.

"Calla," I say, thankful my voice doesn't crack.

He offers me his hand, and I hesitate before placing my palm against his, and he covers it with his other hand. "Charmed to meet you."

I force a smile and murmur, "Thank you," because what the fuck else am I supposed to say? It's not exactly nice to meet him too, and I'm not about to lie to someone who can kill me with a subtle flick of his wrist.

The corner of his mouth quirks slightly as I've seen Atlas's do on occasion, and he releases my hand. I let it fall back to my side, fighting the urge to curl it into a fist. My eyes shift toward Lenora who is watching me with a look of distaste. *Perfect. She already doesn't like me.*

I inhale slowly through my nose and say, "That is a beautiful dress, Mrs. York." The moment the words leave my mouth, I want to kick myself. It sounded stupid to my own ears, so I can't imagine what the rest of the room is thinking. *Why am I complimenting this woman?*

Her eyes trail the length of what I'm wearing and a smile settles on her lips. "Thank you, Calla. Perhaps I can find you something more appropriate to wear after our meal."

I bite the inside of my cheek to keep myself from saying what I really want to say and nod. "That's very kind of you."

"It is my pleasure, dear," she says in a voice drenched in haughty, fake politeness.

"Shall we eat?" Simon suggests, and we all sit around the table.

I pick the spot next to Atlas, while Lex sits on my other side and Gabriel takes the seat next to Atlas's mother as Kade drops down next to him. A moment later, a group of waiters file out of a door across the room, each carrying a different tray or bottle around the table. Wine glasses are filled with champagne and a second glass is filled with what I immediately recognize as blood. The waiter approaches my chair to pour, and Atlas moves before I can, covering my glass. Without a word, the waiter moves on and fills Atlas's glass. He pulls his hand back, and I let out the breath I was holding.

Next, the waiters bring out plates filled with lamb, seasoned potatoes, and a variety of steamed vegetables. Despite my nerves, my stomach growls at the decadent smell of everything, and we eat in silence for a while before Atlas speaks up.

"I understand the situation in Washington last night was not ideal."

Lenora stops him with a quick wave of her wrist. "We are dealing with that, son. It is nothing to worry about."

Atlas takes a drink of champagne, shifting his gaze between his parents. "I see." His voice is hard. "Then why are we here?"

Simon takes a drink from his glass of blood, setting it on the table and shifting his gaze from Atlas to me. I freeze with a forkful of potato halfway to my mouth. I set it down on the plate quickly and press my lips together. "You are here," he says, "because your mother and I thought it was important to discuss Miss Montgomery's place in your lives."

Gabriel clears his throat. "With all due respect, sir, I don't understand why Calla's place in our lives is relevant to anyone but us."

Lenora sighs, as if she's disappointed in him for speaking. "Gabriel, consider how it reflects on us to our people—those who look to us to set an example—when they catch wind of the four of you keeping a human pet."

My blood runs cold as my gaze snaps toward her, and I tighten my hands into fists under the table, my entire body tensing. I bite my tongue hard, stopping before I can taste blood, figuring this is not the best place for that to happen, considering I'm sitting around a table full of vampires.

"Sorry," Lex cuts in, "you're concerned about optics?"

She doesn't even spare him a glance when she says, "Essentially." Finally, she turns her attention to me, and I fight to hold her gaze, because what I really want to do is lunge across the table and slap her across the face. *I am no one's fucking pet.* "I understand the agreement that was made which outlined the plan for your future, Calla, has been nullified based on new information being brought to light."

"So what?" Kade cuts in. "Yes, the blood oath is void with regards to Calla. She is free to do as she wishes and she wishes to stay with us. What does that matter?"

She lifts her chin, turning her face toward Kade. "It matters greatly, and you should know this by now. You have been well-acquainted with Atlas for many decades. At this point, you should understand the importance of his role in our society. This arrangement you have created with Miss Montgomery is not something that can continue as it stands." When her eyes shift back to me, I open my mouth, but she continues speaking before I have a chance to say anything. "You thought your future was tied to these creatures based on an agreement that was made prior to your birth. It is quite unfortunate you had to live any part of your life believing you had no control over your own future. I have sympathy for you in that regard, Calla. But, my dear, the oath is void. You are free to leave. That is the choice you should make."

I swallow hard, blinking against the sudden burn in my eyes. Anger heats the blood in my veins, and I straighten in my seat. "I have made my choice already."

"Hmm," she says, glancing toward her husband. "You see, that is a problem for us. The way you are now will not stand."

I lick the dryness from my lips, shaking my head. "I don't understand."

Lenora takes a sip of her champagne, sparing Atlas a brief glance before returning her attention to me. "It is quite simple. We are giving you two options. You can choose to be glamoured and forget about the vampires you have met along with everything that has happened since they took you."

"The fuck—" Kade snaps.

My eyes narrow, and I shake my head, cutting him off. "Yeah, no. That is *not* an option. Now that I actually have a choice in how my future will play out, I'm sure as hell not going to let anyone try to push me toward something I don't want."

"I understand," she says in a level tone. "Perhaps you will feel more motivated to choose the other option."

"The one where we get the fuck up right now and leave?" Lex says, his expression grim and his fangs fully extended.

"Sounds good to me," Kade adds, dropping his fork onto his plate so carelessly I'm shocked the porcelain doesn't shatter.

"Enough," Simon snaps, silencing the room.

My heart pounds so hard in my chest I can feel it in my throat. I grip the arms of the chair, and everything in me is screaming to run, to get as far away from these vampires as possible.

"There is no need for theatrics," Lenora says with a sigh.

"We are not going to force Calla to do something she doesn't want to," Gabriel says in a firm tone. His jaw is set tight as he looks at her.

She tilts her head ever so slightly, as if to question his stance. "Unfortunately, that is not your call."

I swallow the bile in my throat. "What are you saying?" I force out. "What is my other *option*?"

My stomach drops when her gaze flits to me, as if part of me knows what she's going to say before the words leave her bloodstained lips.

"Mother, no," Atlas cuts in with a sharp, venom-filled voice, making me jump.

Lenora tuts her tongue, barely sparing him a glance before she focuses on me once more. "Calla, you will either forget everything... or you will become a vampire."

Unraveled by Desire

Forget everything or become a vampire.

My gaze drops to the glittering plate of half-eaten food in front of me. The decedent smells wafting under my nose from the lamb and potatoes turn my stomach. Nausea ripples through me as my hand slips off the table, dropping to my thigh, where I instinctively reach for the dagger strapped a few inches above my knee. I curl my fingers around the hard white ash as my pulse races.

My lips part in surprise when Atlas covers my hand with his before I can pull the dagger out of its holder.

Ice fills my veins and the air in my lungs gets stuck there. Betrayal whips through me, tendrils of dread weighing my shoulders down as I turn toward him with a glare. How can he sit there and take his parents' side when they want me to—

"No." Atlas tightens his grip on my hand and shakes his head so subtly I almost miss it. I have no idea if he's speaking to me or his mother. Maybe both of us.

What the fuck is happening right now?

I turn my head at the sound of a deep growl from across the table to find a look of pure rage etched into Kade's darkened features. Lex is nearly vibrating with anger beside me, and Gabriel is sitting deadly still, his jaw set in a tight line.

Taking a deep breath, I lick the dryness from my lips and pull my hand away from Atlas's rigid touch. "I am not going to become a vampire." I'm shocked my voice doesn't waver or crack. Screw that. I'm fucking proud it doesn't.

Simon sets his fork down next to his plate and offers me a barely-there smile. "Then you should be happy to get your life back."

Kade scowls. "Even if Calla was agreeable to being glamoured to forget vampires, that option isn't viable. The hunters will come after her for having been associated with us. Without her memories, she'll be in greater danger from them."

Lenora arches a brow at him. "The girl's safety as a human isn't our concern."

Well, fuck you too.

I clench my jaw to keep from snapping at her, knowing full well she can backhand me across the room and break my bones effortlessly.

She lifts her cloth napkin to her lips, dabbing at literally nothing before setting it back in her lap. She oozes pretentiousness, and I can't help but wonder how the hell Atlas has put up with her for so long.

"Lenora—" Gabriel starts, and she holds up her hand, silencing him.

"This matter is not up for debate or discussion, boys." Her sharp silver gaze slides to me. "You have one month to decide what you'll do. If in one month you're neither a vampire nor living blissfully unaware of vampires, I will kill you myself. Understood?"

"Understood?" I echo incredulously. "Fuck you." The words are out of my mouth before I've even realized what I said. My eyes pop wide, and I push the chair back as I stand.

I think one of the guys calls my name, but my ears are ringing so loud as I retreat the way we came in, I can't be sure who it was.

I nearly trample one of the house staff in my haste to get out of that room and mutter a quick apology. The slight, middle-aged woman steadies me and offers a polite smile, which immediately makes me feel worse for nearly taking her out. And when I spot the partially healed bite marks along her arms and on both sides of her neck, I recoil, unable to stop a frown from forming on my lips as the bottom one quivers.

"Can I help you find something, dear?" she asks, unfazed by my reaction to her.

"Bathroom," I force out between shallow breaths, because there's a good chance I'm going to hurl or collapse, and I'd rather have some semblance of privacy to do either.

The woman nods and points to a door across the grand entryway.

I'm heading toward it before she can say anything else. I grip the handle and burst inside, slamming the door shut behind me and flipping the lock out of habit more than anything else. Because in a house full of vampires, that tiny piece of metal is virtually useless.

Stumbling toward the white marble vanity, I grip either side of the sink and stare at my pale, wide-eyed expression as I try to stop hyperventilating. I can't seem to pull in a steady enough breath to fill my lungs, and the longer I try, the harder it becomes.

I have about three seconds of warning to drop to my knees and grab the toilet before the contents of my stomach come back up and into the bowl. I heave until my throat is raw and tears burn my eyes. There's a dull pounding in my temples a few minutes later when I lean back and flush the vomit away.

After forcing myself to stand, I turn on the faucet and rinse out my mouth, wiping away the tears that slipped down my cheeks. My complexion is flushed and uneven, my eyes still glassy. I don't feel in control of my body as I rake my fingers through my hair and try to catch my breath. I clench and unclench my hands at my sides, closing my eyes to help me focus better.

Breathe in.

Hold it.

Breathe out.

My breathing is almost back to a relatively normal pace when a knock sounds at the door.

CHAPTER

TWO

ATLAS

I can't recall ever feeling so... *fuck*, I don't know. Angry? Helpless? Disappointed in my own forsaken family? Take your pick.

She doesn't deserve this. After everything she's been through—everything *we* put her through... If Simon and Lenora are the reason we lose Calla, I will never forgive myself. I've lost a lot because of the vampires who raised me—the most notable being my humanity many times over the decades—but I'll be damned if they ruin what we've only just started with Calla.

The strangled, desperate sound Calla makes from behind the bathroom door when I knock shoots a dagger of pain straight through my chest, and I grimace at the foreign sensation.

As the seconds tick by, my muscles tighten, and I knock again. Still nothing. I reach for the handle to find the door locked and press my lips into a thin line. Calla's heart pounds loud and fast, and the soft sound of her sniffling makes me want to rip the door off its hinges. I'm at quite a loss on what to do with that.

"Calla." My voice comes out low and even. It likely won't bring her comfort as much as Gabriel's would, but I was out of my chair and following Calla before I fully realized what I was doing, besides pissing off my parents further.

There's movement on the other side of the door, and a moment later, the lock flips over.

I open the door, stepping inside and closing it behind me, and find

610

Calla sliding down the wall until she settles on the floor. Bringing her knees up to her chest, she wraps her arms around her legs and looks up at me through damp lashes.

With a sigh, I approach slowly and slide down next to her, stretching my legs out in front of me.

We sit in silence for a few minutes, and I listen to the uneven sound of Calla's breathing. I want to take away her pain, her fear, her anger… but I also know I'm the cause of at least some of it. And maybe at one point I didn't care, but it'd be a lie if I said that was still the case. I can't be sure exactly when the shift happened, but I find myself caring for the human next to me, which is something that hasn't occurred in a very long time. Perhaps seeing her like this, so scared and vulnerable, is bringing it out in me, but my instinct tells me to protect her at all costs—to show her I will.

"I don't want to be a vampire," she finally says, her voice barely above a whisper.

I keep my gaze trained forward. "I know."

She sniffles. "But I… I can't… I don't want to forget you." There's a slight uptick in her pulse as she tries to take a deep breath. "I've tried, even before this, to think about the future. It was going to come up at some point, but I'm not ready for it yet."

The last thing I want right now is to let this infuriating little human go, but I can't help the annoying voice in the back of my head telling me that we never should have had her to begin with. That she deserves so much better than us.

"This could be your chance," I say quietly. "Your way out. The hunters are still a concern, but we would make sure you were protected even if you didn't know who we were." Even as I speak the words, I hate each and every one of them with a burning passion.

Her breath catches. Out of the corner of my eye, I catch her shaking her head before dropping her forehead to her knees.

"I want to go home," she finally whispers, her voice low and thick with more tears. Then she laughs—it's a humorless, sad noise that gnaws at my chest. "I don't even know where that is anymore."

It sure as hell isn't here, and I'm not going to make her stay here a minute longer.

I get up and extend my hand to her. With a shaky breath, she slides her hand into mine and allows me to help her stand. She chews her bottom lip, blinking at me, which makes fresh tears roll down her cheeks. My eyes flick between hers as I step closer and brush them away.

Calla stands before me like a deer in headlights, clearly not having expected the gesture, and I nearly smile. To be fair, it was slightly uncharacteristic.

"Oh, come on," I say, trying for a light tone. "Don't look *so* surprised. I can be nice."

The corners of her mouth curl just a little, but the movement doesn't reach her eyes. They are still filled with fear and pain, and I'd do fucking anything to take that away if I could—which starts with getting out of here, so I turn to guide her out of the bathroom.

"Atlas."

The crack in her voice as she says my name stops me dead in my tracks. The absolute power this woman has over me and she doesn't even know it...

I stand in front of her and cup her cheeks in my hands, tilting her head back enough for our eyes to meet. "I know." I put as much sincerity into those words as I can, needing Calla to understand that I'm with her.

Her watery eyes flick between mine, her brows pinching together into an expression so desperate I find myself vibrating with anger at myself for allowing her to fall into a position like this. We fucking *put* her here, and I take full responsibility for it. Remove me and my twisted family of power-hungry vampires, and Calla wouldn't be at risk of losing her memories or her mortality.

Her tone is firmer when she says, "I don't want to go back out there."

Frankly, neither do I.

The idea of facing Simon and Lenora York once more makes my skin crawl and my gums throb as my fangs threaten to descend. My dynamic with them has never been that of a normal parent-child relationship. It's always been more pawn-puppet with their role in our society. The vampires have always looked to them as leaders for as long as I can remember, and at this point, I'm not sure why. They're as feared as they are respected, which is why I know there's no way out of this mess aside from the options they've presented to Calla. There are too many vampires who will do whatever they ask without question. It would take them disappearing for this problem to go away, and while some have tried to take down the esteemed York dynasty, none have succeeded. Even if I... even if *we* could, in theory, I'm not sure that's something I could bring myself to do, regardless of what I feel for this human who has effectively tilted the axis of my world as much as we have hers.

Exhaling a heavy sigh, I say, "Well, unfortunately, we can't stay in here." The guys are waiting in the foyer just outside the bathroom, and the tension is palpable even through the door. I pull my hands away from Calla's face and slide an arm around her waist. "Listen to me," I say, my mouth at her ear. "We're going to get out of here, and no one is going to touch you."

Her body leans into me; I'm not sure she even realizes it. "You're touching me," she mumbles back.

I almost smile. I don't often, but somehow she forces it out of me on occasion. "I'm not no one," I shoot back in a low voice. If she tries to deny it at this moment, I can honestly say I'm not sure what I'll do. Perhaps nothing here, but the very second I get her alone—

"No," she near-whispers, "I guess you're not."

Something in my chest gives an uncomfortable tug as I reach for the handle and open the door, revealing the other vampires who've fallen madly for the same human I have.

I reach for Atlas without thinking, needing the contact of his skin against mine more at that moment than I ever have before. I wrap my fingers around his forearm as he opens the door, and a flicker of relief sparks to life in my chest at the sight of Gabriel, Kade, and Lex.

They won't let anything bad happen to me.

It's hard to believe I once thought *they* were a bad thing that happened to me.

"Time to go, angel," Gabriel says in a gentle voice as Atlas and I step out of the bathroom.

"Yes, please," I agree, loosening my grip on Atlas's arm when I realize my nails are digging into his skin, creating little crescent indents. "Sorry," I murmur.

He drops his gaze to where my fingers are brushing over his skin. "Mark me any way you like, Calla." When his sharp silver eyes slide to mine, I press my lips together and dip my chin, overwhelmed at the intensity of his expression.

"Let's get the fuck out of here. Car's waiting outside," Lex says, moving to stand on my other side while Gabriel and Kade walk behind us. We quickly depart the way we came in, this time the house staff are nowhere to be seen. It's just as well—If I didn't have to see anyone associated with Atlas's parents again, that would be fine by me. Save for their son, of course.

Atlas sits up front with the driver, who introduces himself as Theo

—part of Marcel's team, which makes me feel slightly better than riding in a vehicle driven by the York's staff. At least I know Marcel is loyal to the guys and doesn't want to, you know, kill me one way or another. It's the little things.

"How are you doing?" Gabriel asks from the seat next to me.

I roll my head against the back of the seat to look at him, then shrug. "Kind of like I'm in a nightmare that I can't wake myself from."

Kade drops his hand onto my shoulder from the seat behind me and gives it a squeeze. "We've got you. You know that, right?"

"I... don't think it's that simple anymore," I reply.

A frown turns Gabriel's lips down, and he sighs. "Unfortunately, I believe you're right about that."

I nod slowly as Kade continues massaging my shoulder. "So what now?"

"What do you want to do?" Lex chimes in.

Biting the inside of my cheek, I glance forward to Atlas before saying, "I know we need to get to Chicago, but I'd like to visit my parents first." With all this talk and stress about my future, I need to see them. Because if I have to make this huge decision, I'm not doing it without talking to my mom first. As strained as our relationship has been in the past, this is bigger than any lingering feelings I may have to do with the blood oath. Besides, I'm not prepared to live—for however long that may be—harboring anger or resentment toward them, because in the end, the only person it'll hurt is me. And holding onto those feelings when my life with the guys—current situation aside— has turned into something I never could have expected and now can't think about giving up doesn't make sense.

"I'll take you to see them," Gabriel offers, sliding his hand into mine where it sits on my lap.

I turn my attention back to him and manage a small smile, curling my fingers around his. While I'd like to see my parents alone—without my entourage of vampires—that's hardly going to fly at this point. "Okay," I finally say, "thank you."

Atlas tells Theo the address, then turns in his seat to face us. "We'll drop you off and touch base with Fallon to get an update on the situation in Chicago."

"Aww, I wanted to see Calla's childhood bedroom," Lex grumbles from the back seat.

Atlas's gaze flicks to me, and I roll my eyes. The corners of his mouth twitch, and he shakes his head at Lex.

I tune out for a while, pulling my phone from my jacket pocket. I haven't used it much lately, and my stomach drops when I turn it on and find a slew of missed calls and messages from Brighton. Listening to the voicemails isn't an option with the guys around, but I scroll through the messages.

Hey, can we talk?

Calla, I'm worried about you.

I have no idea what's going on. If you're ignoring me, I understand, but please let me know you're okay.

Please answer me. I need my best friend.

I made a huge mistake. Please call me.

The knots in my stomach get tighter with each message, and I shove my phone back into my pocket. I can't deal with this right now.

A few minutes later, I recognize the neighborhood we're driving through as the one I grew up in. My stomach swirls with nerves knowing what I need to talk to my parents about and concerned with how they're going to react. I imagine it's something they've considered, knowing their daughter was promised to a group of vampires, but that doesn't make the conversation any easier to walk into.

The car pulls up outside my parents' place, and Atlas gets out, opening my door. I take the hand he holds out to me, and gasp in surprise when he pulls me in close, dropping his lips to my cheek. "We'll figure this out."

I wrap my arms around him tightly—tighter than I have before—and breathe in his scent. It makes my chest tighten when my thoughts immediately drift to the possibility that I may one day soon not remember it—remember *him*.

Once we pull apart, I duck my head back into the car for a second and say, "Don't get into too much trouble without me."

"Right back at you," Lex remarks with a wink.

Gabriel comes around the car and nods at Atlas before he gets back into the passenger seat, then the two of us walk toward the door.

Mom is flying outside and down the porch steps before we're even halfway up the walkway. She throws her arms around me, squeezing me so tight I can barely pull in a breath, but I don't care. I hug her back just as hard. It's safe to say her almost dying helped close the chasm that was between us for years.

"Hey, Mom," I say, laughing softly as I step back.

She hangs onto my arms, looking me over as if she didn't see me not that long ago in the hospital. "I had no idea you were here!"

"Uh, yeah. It was an unexpected trip."

Her eyes fill with concern. "Calla, what's going on?"

"Perhaps we should go inside?" Gabriel offers in a smooth voice, stepping up beside me and offering my mom a polite smile.

Her gaze shifts to him and narrows. "*You* are not welcome in my home."

"Mom," I say, pulling her attention back to me. "Please be nice."

She opens her mouth as if she's going to argue but then closes it and nods, wrapping her arm around my shoulders and hugging me against her side as we walk inside, with Gabriel trailing behind us.

Dad comes into the hallway from the living room, and his eyes light up when he sees me. "I wondered what your mother was rushing out the door for. She's been ordering Amazon packages almost daily, so I just figured it was a delivery."

Mom smacks his arm, and he chuckles.

"We're not here long, but I wanted to visit."

Dad's eyes slide to Gabriel and his lips turn down. "I see."

"Hello, Mr. Montgomery."

Dad crosses his arms over his chest, looking less than thrilled at Gabriel's presence. "Which one are you?"

Gabriel smiles as if the question wasn't meant to offend him, which I'm sure it was. "Gabriel Simmons, sir. It's nice to see you again."

I press my lips together. *Sir.* Gabriel's at least five times my dad's age and, oh my god, how have I not thought about that before?

"Mmm hmm. And is there a reason you needed to escort my daughter to her own home?"

I take a deep breath, but before I can respond, Gabriel chimes in, calm as ever.

"I assure you, it's for her safety as much as it is for yours and your wife's."

He scoffs. "Bullshit."

Closing my eyes, I say, "Dad, please. Can we at least pretend to get along for a few minutes? Today has been really shitty, and I just need a break from the chaos. Please."

His stoic demeanor cracks, and he frowns at me. "What's going on?"

I nod toward the living room, and we all walk from the hallway and sit around the coffee table in the middle of the room. Gabriel sits in the armchair we inherited from Dad's mom's apartment when she passed away years ago. It's incredibly ugly, but Dad refused to get rid of it because it was her favorite. My mom sits next to me on the love seat, while my dad remains standing, leaning in the doorway between the living room and dining room.

"You have a lovely home," Gabriel says, leaning back and resting his ankle on top of the opposite knee.

Mom hesitates, looking toward me before turning her attention to him. "Thank you."

"Where are the others?" Dad asks, his arms still crossed.

"They are arranging our travel to Chicago," Gabriel offers, and just when I think he's going to stop there, he continues, "The vampire who turned me is residing there, and we've been tracking her so we can move in and kill her."

My eyes widen, hardly not expecting Gabriel to put all of that out there. I suppose he's not concerned with sharing information with my parents at this point, but still. *I'd* rather they didn't know everything going on in the non-human part of my world. Which, regrettably, is becoming more and more by the day—especially after the visit with Atlas's parents.

"Since when do vampires kill other vampires?" Mom asks, her brows scrunched together as if she's trying to make it make sense.

"Since they abuse their power and hurt people who matter to me."

I shoot him a look that says *enough*. They don't need to know about the time I spent with Selene. Of all the things that have happened since the guys came for me, *that* I wouldn't mind being wiped from my memories.

"I see," Mom says, shifting her focus to me. "Do you need anything while you're here? How long can you stay?"

I offer her a smile. "I'm okay. Really."

"Coffee?" she offers. "I could make coffee."

"Sure," I answer. "I can help while Gabriel and Dad chat."

Okay, so throwing Gabriel to the wolves—well, *wolf*—wasn't the nicest thing I've ever done, but I need a minute to talk to my mom, and Gabriel seemed all too open to sharing things with my parents; I'm sure they'll find something to talk about.

We get up, and I offer Gabriel a faint smile, hopefully conveying that I'll make it up to him.

In the kitchen, Mom scoops coffee grounds from the tin into the machine while I pull down mugs from the cupboard above the dishwasher, setting them on the counter before leaning against it. "I have to ask you something," I force out, unable to look at her face as the words leave my mouth.

She closes the lid and turns the machine on before giving her full attention to me. "What is it, sweetheart?"

"If I, um… I mean, I'm not sure yet, but…" I sigh, trying and struggling to find the right words. "There's a lot you don't know and a lot I hope you never have to know, but this—"

"Calla." She moves in front of me and takes my hands in hers. "Take a breath."

I finally look at her and immediately wish I hadn't. The concern on her face makes my chest seize with pressure. "I'm not even sure where to start," I whisper. "I have so much going on in my head, I can't keep up with everything. I certainly don't expect you to."

She offers me a small smile. "Well, I can't try until you tell me what's going on."

I take a deep breath and say, "The blood oath that tied me to the vampires is void, and now I have to choose to have them glamour away my memories and go back to my life before they came for me, or become one of them."

My mom recoils, her grip on my hands tightening as her bottom lip starts to tremble. Her brows crease and her eyes water as she shakes her head adamantly. "How is that possible?"

I swallow the lump in my throat, unable to hold back my emotions at seeing my mom upset. "The oath would have applied to the baby girl you and Dad had before me and lost, so it never was mine to fulfill."

Recognition flickers in her eyes and a pained expression fills her tired features. "Oh, Calla. Honey, I am so sorry. We should have—"

"Mom, it's okay. This isn't… None of this is your fault." My voice is firm; she has to know I don't blame her for anything that's happened.

"I should be happy about this. You can get your life back, move on from this nightmare, and…" Her voice trails off, and she frowns at me. "But you're not sure that's what you want, is it?"

I press my lips together, trying desperately to hold back the tears threatening to spill down my cheeks if I blink. "I…" I look away.

"You care for them," she offers in a low voice.

"I didn't want to. I tried to fight it at first, but the longer I spent with them, the more I realized they weren't as bad as I thought they'd be. And I couldn't force myself to hate them when I thought I'd be bound to them for the rest of my life. I couldn't live like that."

Mom releases a shaky sigh and swallows hard as the coffee

machine gargles behind her. "I'm really trying to understand, honey, I am. I can't imagine what you've been through these last two months, and while I'm glad they seem to have been taking care of you, I'm not sure I can get past the reason they're in your life. I'm still working through that with your father if I'm being completely honest."

"I get that," I tell her. "And just because I've somewhat made my peace with it doesn't mean you automatically have to. It affected you differently, and you have every right to work through it however you need to."

Her brows lift, and she shakes her head, offering me a watery smile. "When did you get to be so wise and graceful?" She smooths a hand along my hair and settles her gaze on me before she says, "What do *you* want, Calla?"

I hold her gaze, the pit in my stomach growing as dread weighs my shoulders down. "I don't want to be a vampire, Mom." I blink back the tears burning my eyes. "I'm terrified of losing control of myself—of losing myself in general, actually. I don't even fully know who I am yet, and now I'm faced with this choice that doesn't really feel like a *choice* and it's going to change the path of my life. Again." I force myself to stop rambling before I go blue in the face. Because, like I told Atlas, today isn't the first time I've thought about becoming a vampire. It's hard not to when I spend every day surrounded by them. There's probably a small part of me that wants it—at least certain aspects of it— and that scares me even more.

"Have you considered the other option?" she asks.

"Of course. But the thought of forgetting them... it hurts."

"It wouldn't hurt forever," she says gently, "and you'd get your life back."

I frown, and my voice lowers. "This is my life now." The words are heavy on my tongue, and I realize the weight of them is the truth.

Her eyes shift away from me as if she can't bring herself to look at me as she says, "Then it sounds to me like you've made your choice."

"My *choice* is them, *not* becoming a vampire."

Mom shakes her head. "And why exactly are those your only options?"

"That," I say in a tight voice, "is a somewhat complicated story."

"Try me," she insists, and I sigh.

"One of the vampires, Atlas, his family is kind of important in the vampire world. I guess his parents are like royalty or something. A lot of people look to them for leadership, and apparently, their son having a 'human pet' is a bad look."

"A human—You have got to be kidding me." Her voice is filled with anger, which is also reflected in her eyes, and I can't say I blame her because I'm pissed about it myself. There is absolutely nothing I like about Atlas's parents, what they stand for, or the power they hold over their son. Nothing about this situation is fair, and even worse, there's nothing I can do about it. So here I am, again, powerless to what's going to happen to me.

"I told you, it's complicated."

She scoffs. "There's nothing complicated about that, Calla. Atlas's parents are threatened by you. That much is clear."

I nearly laugh at that. "I don't know, Mom. These people are terrifying. They don't care about human life, like, at all." I almost tell her what Lenora said about me essentially not being their problem if I lose my memories and the hunters come after me. My parents already know enough about the supernatural world—there's no reason for them to be burdened with the knowledge of the hunters as well.

Mom wraps her arms around me, and I lean my cheek on her shoulder, closing my eyes and allowing the familiar warmth of her and the aroma of the coffee brewing behind us to bring me a brief moment of peace. Because I really fucking need it.

"Will you stay here tonight?" she asks softly.

I pull back and smile at her. "If I stay, Gabriel has to as well."

She presses her lips together, then nods. "I figured as much. I'd just like to have my daughter under my roof for one night." She lifts her hand to my cheek and holds it there. "I miss you."

I cover her hand with mine. "I miss you, too."

With coffees in hand, we return to the living room, where Dad and Gabriel seem to be engaged in a surprisingly friendly conversation. Gabriel can turn on the charm when he needs to, though I am surprised he managed to win my dad over.

I drop down on the couch next to Gabriel and offer him a mug. "Looks like we're sleeping over. Hope that won't cause any problems," I murmur.

He takes the coffee, his eyes dancing over my face. "I've already let the others know."

I arch a brow at him, panic creeping through me and making my chest tighten. "You were listening?"

"I caught the tail end, that's all. I was checking to make sure you were okay."

I take a sip of my coffee before setting the mug on the table in front of the couch. "Okay."

"What were you guys chatting about?" Mom asks, sitting across from us in the chair Gabriel had been occupying before we'd slipped away.

Gabriel and Dad share a brief look before Gabriel turns his attention to me and smiles. Dad does the same to Mom. Evidently neither is going to share, and I'm sure as hell going to press Gabriel about it when we're alone.

The ceiling of this hotel room is filthy. It's safe to say it hasn't been cleaned since the building opened a few years ago. Granted, no human would notice; however, it's all I can focus on as sleep evades me.

Lex and Kade are asleep in the bedroom across the suite from me. As much as the support of the guys helps on most occasions, I find myself needing more tonight.

Unfortunately, she decided to stay at her parents' house.

I considered having Gabriel bring her back here but ultimately decided that wasn't a fight I wanted to get into. Calla has been through a lot, even just in the last twenty-four hours, and as much as I want her at my side, she more than deserves time with her family.

Closing my eyes, I force my muscles to unclench and try to ignore the weight sitting on my chest like a pile of rocks.

I've never been this unsure, this conflicted. I've always done what Simon and Lenora expected of me, even if it was the last thing I *wanted* to do. But this... forcing Calla down one of two paths—neither she wants—I'm not sure I can do.

Sleep eventually drags me under, and when I open my eyes, I'm no longer in the hotel suite with the dirty ceiling. I'm surrounded by dark windows and black silk sheets—the Washington house I designed for us.

I sit up slowly, my eyes flitting around the room at inhuman speed, taking in the familiar space. Something tugs in my chest when my eyes land on where Calla is leaning in the doorway.

Fuck me. This isn't real.

Her cheeks are flushed and her beautiful, soft brown eyes are filled with desire. I can hear the pounding of her heart from across the room, and my cock hardens at the sight of her in that black lace slip.

"What is this?" I force out, my eyes hyper-focused on her.

She pushes away from the doorframe, padding across the dark wood floor toward the bed. "Remember the time Gabriel was able to reach me while I was asleep?"

I arch a brow at her, leaning against the headboard. "You're telling me we're dreamwalking?"

It's one of our lesser utilized abilities and only works when the vampire is extremely focused. I've done it on a handful of occasions—closed my eyes, pushed my thoughts outward to the person I was trying to reach, and connected with them. It helps when they're open-minded and willing, though born vampires have the ability to dreamwalk even if the other person isn't willing—it just takes a bit more concentration and it helps if the vampire has fed recently, putting them at their strongest.

And on nights such as tonight when some of us are apart physically, it is certainly a handy ability to have.

She nods. "Gabriel was able to connect with me easily from the same room, and I..." She trails off, her cheeks becoming pinker. "I missed you, so I asked him to try reaching you."

The corner of my mouth twitches as I watch her move closer. "What was that last part? I want to make sure I heard you correctly."

She offers me a dry look. "Getting so old you should have that vamp hearing checked?"

"Cute," I deadpan. "You didn't miss Kade and Lex?" As soon as the question leaves my lips, they waltz through the doorway. "Hmm." I glance at both of them, then chuckle as Gabriel saunters in behind them. "Well, this is new."

Kade shoots up behind Calla and scoops her into his arms before depositing her onto the end of my bed. She yelps in response, her heart racing, and she manages to kick him in the stomach as she sits up on the mattress.

"This way, we're all together," Gabriel comments, standing next to Lex.

My eyes shift from him to where Calla is sliding up the bed toward me. Part of me wants to flip her over and take her from behind while she screams into a pillow, but that's not what she needs right now, so I forcefully lock up the monster inside me and grip Calla's chin between my fingers. Her eyes flick between mine, searching for what I can't tell, but she wraps her fingers around my wrist and leans in, pressing her lips against mine. Her kiss is soft and warm and *her*. I'll never tire of this human, which doesn't bode well for me in our current situation.

I tip her head back and deepen the kiss, sliding my fingers along her jaw to cradle her neck. The moan that leaves her lips goes straight to my cock, and my gums throb with the urge to sink my teeth into her throat.

The bed shifts as Lex and Kade slide in on either side and Gabriel sits at the end. Calla pulls back, her eyes bouncing between each of us as her cheeks flush a deep pink.

"Angel?" Gabriel says in a gentle voice.

"I'm okay," she tells him, "I'm just... glad we're all together."

"For as long as you want," Kade says, and his devotion to her is plain as day on his face. I think we all recognize the danger in that, but it's not something any of us can deny let alone fight at this point.

She turns toward him, sliding her hand up his chest and into his hair as she leans in and seals her lips over his. He growls deep in his throat and grips her hips, lifting her into his lap as he kisses her. The moment she pulls back for air, Kade pulls the slip over her head, leaving her completely naked. The monster in me roars, and I clench my jaw, forcing my fangs not to extend.

"Fuck. You are perfect," Kade murmurs to her, tucking her hair behind her ear before he tugs his T-shirt off, tossing it to the side.

Lex catches my attention on my other side as he does the same, then glances at my bare chest, smirking briefly. My lower half is covered only by a sheet because sometimes sleeping with clothes on is a nuisance.

Calla shifts on Kade's lap, grinding against the bulge in his joggers, making him groan. He shares a lust-filled look with me, and I move at inhuman speed, hauling Calla off his lap and holding her between my legs, her back against my chest. Kade and Lex grip each of her thighs, spreading them slowly as Gabriel moves up the bed, sliding his hands up her legs as he gets closer to her center. Her breathing hitches, her heart hammering in her chest as Gabriel drags his tongue over his bottom lip.

I drop my mouth to Calla's shoulder, kissing her bare skin as Lex and Kade turn their attention to her chest. Her soft, breathy moans fill the room as they swirl their tongues around her nipples before sucking them into their mouths. She sucks in a sharp breath when Gabriel leans in and licks the length of her slit before circling her clit with his tongue.

My fangs slice through my gums, and I can't stop the primal growl that passes my lips. I pull back in time to keep them from sinking into Calla's shoulder, and she turns her face to look at me. She pulls her bottom lip between her teeth for a moment, watching me curiously before she releases her lip, and the corner of her mouth curls up.

"What?" I mutter in a low, gravelly voice.

"Since when do you show restraint?"

I offer a short laugh. "You have no idea, Calla."

She purses her lips. "Okay, well, don't. Not tonight."

Arching a brow, I say, "What are you asking?" I know exactly what she wants, but she's going to say it out loud.

Her eyes narrow slightly, and she bites her lip again, her eyes flicking to where Gabriel is licking between her legs.

"Eyes on me," I demand in a voice that leaves no room for debate.

She looks at me again. "Don't tell me what to do."

"I'll tell you what to do, and you'll do it," I taunt, wrapping my fingers around her throat. Not tight enough to affect her breathing, but firm enough she knows I'm in control here. "Now, tell me what you want."

"I—*fuck*," she moans as Gabriel slides a finger inside her and sucks her clit into his mouth. Lex and Kade are trailing their lips along her collarbone, alternating between kissing her skin and teasing her nipples.

I press my lips just below her ear. "Hmm? What was that?"

"Bite me," she breathes, her head rolling to the side against my chest, baring her neck to me.

My cock twitches, and I'm sure she can feel its length against her back. I hone in on the bulging vein in her neck, my gums throbbing painfully until I sink my fangs into it. Calla's blood pours into my mouth, exploding on my tongue, and I groan, swallowing deeply as I snake my arm around her waist, holding her tightly against me.

She moans deeply, gripping the sheets on either side of her. Her hips jerk, but Gabriel chuckles and moves to hold them down as he devours her.

I pull back and close the puncture marks with my tongue, kissing

Calla's shoulder softly as I breathe in her scent. Her blood warms my stomach and dulls the ache in my chest, and when she tips her chin up and kisses my jaw gently, it knocks the air out of my lungs. Something so small and simple makes me want to burn down the world to keep her safe and do whatever it takes to make her happy. The feeling is foreign to me, but I already know learning to live without it would make us all miserable.

Calla's breathing shallows, and Gabriel adds another finger, picking up the pace of his thrusts. He licks toward her navel, nipping and sucking her skin, while Lex and Kade continue their ministrations, attending to Calla's breasts.

I push her hair away from her face, lowering my mouth to hers, swallowing the sound of her moan when Gabriel hits a particularly sensitive spot inside her. Our lips meld together and battle for control. I flick my tongue along her bottom lip, seeking entrance, and she immediately parts for me. I slide my tongue into her mouth, grazing it against hers, and her fingers find their way into my hair, tugging hard as she kisses me with fervor. Her pulse kicks up, her chest rising and falling fast. A few seconds later, she breaks the kiss, crying out with her release, her head bent back against my shoulder.

Lex and Kade pull away, grinning at each other, and I catch sight of Gabriel lapping up Calla's release, making her shiver. Peering down at her face, I can't help the small curve of my lips at her serene, satisfied expression.

Kade yawns, and Calla laughs at him. "Sorry, are we boring you?"

"Fuck no," he says. "This is exactly how I want to spend all of my time, quite honestly."

Lex snorts. "I believe it."

"Perhaps we should all get some actual rest and reconvene tomorrow?" Gabriel suggests.

Calla frowns. "But you guys didn't... I mean..."

I slide my finger along her jaw, curling it around her chin and tilting it so she's looking at me. "Tonight was for you."

She presses her lips together, then opens her mouth.

"Don't argue with me," I cut her off. "You won't win this one."

Her eyes narrow slightly, and there are several beats of silence before she says, "Fine."

I grant her a faint smile. "Good girl."

She bats my hand away, scowling half-heartedly.

Lex leans in and kisses her cheek. "Good night, beautiful."

Before she can respond, Kade swoops in and covers her mouth with his. "See you soon," he murmurs to her, getting off the bed and following Lex out of the room. Gabriel joins them a moment later, leaving Calla and I as she gets off the bed, pulling her slip back on, her eyes locked on me.

"What are you thinking?"

She chuckles. "I was going to ask you the same thing."

I cock my head to the side, watching as she sits on the edge of the bed, tucking her hair behind her ear. "There is a lot I'm not sure I can properly articulate tonight, Calla," I tell her.

"Oh, heavy," she comments, reaching for my hand and sliding her fingers through mine. Her thumb brushes over my knuckles, and I find myself so taken with that small act that, despite the weight on my shoulders, it brings me a sense of comfort I'm wholly unfamiliar with.

"You should go," I tell her.

She blinks at me, her eyes searching my face. She hesitates before saying, "Um, okay. Are you all right?"

I shake my head. "What do you mean?"

Surprise flickers across her face. "With everything that's happened, I—"

"You're asking about *me*?"

Her brows tug closer together as she holds my gaze. "Why are you surprised by that?"

I drop my gaze, unable to look at her a moment longer with this new kind of pressure in my chest. "Not surprised, just undeserving."

Her grip on my hand tightens. "Okay, no. You don't get to do that." Her voice is sharper than I expected, and my eyes flit back to her face. "You're an asshole. You don't get to make me feel bad because you're feeling bad."

"I'm sorry." Those words leave my lips on very few occasions, but I genuinely mean them in this instance.

"Good." She pulls her hand back and stands. "I'll see you tomorrow."

I fight the urge to reach for her and pull her back into my bed. I don't care that it isn't real. I want her here with me. Instead, I nod. "Sleep well."

Calla walks out of the room, and the scene starts to fade around me. I close my eyes and let the darkness take me with it.

We check out of the hotel first thing and head for Calla's parent's house. After last night, it's safe to say we're all antsy to reunite.

Kade lets Gabriel know we're on our way, and by the time we pull up at the curb outside, they're waiting on the porch, along with Calla's mother and father. Calla hugs each of them, hanging on tightly as if she isn't going to see them again. They dote on their daughter, and it's hard to ignore how loving they are toward her—and how reluctant they are to let her leave.

I stand near the car while Kade and Lex walk toward the house. This display isn't something I need to involve myself in, and quite honestly, I'd like nothing more than to wrap this up and get on the road. The scene of loving parents and their child isn't something I've ever experienced with my own, which is yet another stark reminder of just how twisted our society—and my family's place in it—is.

After another round of hugs, Calla and the others walk toward the car. I open the passenger side door for Calla, and she climbs in without a word, refusing to meet my gaze. I catch the unshed tears in her eyes as I close the door, while the others slide into the back.

Getting behind the wheel, I start the car and pull away from the curb without looking to see if Calla's parents are still standing on the porch. Something tells me they'll stay there until our vehicle is out of sight.

"Where are we going?" Calla asks, staring out the windshield.

"Marcel's," I answer, switching lanes to pass a group of motorcyclists not going fast enough for my current level of patience.

"Here in New York? I thought we were going to Chicago?"

"We are," Kade answers from the seat behind me. "But first, we need to touch base with Marcel, and he owns a vampire-exclusive boxing club in the city."

"Why?" she asks, pulling her phone out of the duffle bag at her feet. "What's going on now?"

"Nothing new," he says. "Hunter attacks are increasing in numbers quicker than normal, and it's garnering more attention."

"They've doubled in a matter of days," Lex adds.

Calla doesn't respond to that. Her head is bent as she reads from her phone, tapping her finger against the side of it.

"Something you want to share?" I ask, keeping my eyes on the road.

She sighs. "Not really. I'm fairly certain I know what you'll all say."

"Humor us," Kade says.

"Brighton keeps texting me. She said it was a mistake taking her father's side and she doesn't want to be a hunter. She's scared and is asking for help."

Lex barks out a laugh. "Right."

Calla frowns. "I'm not sure what to believe."

"Believe that her father is a manipulative piece of shit who is probably using his daughter in an attempt to set a trap for us," Kade says in a somewhat aggressive tone.

"We don't know that," she says back, her free hand clenching into a fist against her thigh. Her pulse is ticking faster, no doubt Kade's words shooting her blood pressure higher. It's a possibility we need to consider, and I'm not about to put the guys or Calla in a position to be ambushed by Scott Ellis.

"We don't know that Scott didn't text you from Brighton's phone," Lex points out.

"So what? I'm supposed to leave my best friend on read *in case* it's not her texting me, even though she's asking for my help?"

"For now," I say, "yes."

The anger and frustration rolls off of her in waves, and she's silent for several beats. "Fine," she finally mutters, keeping her head down.

I hold out my hand, waiting for her to give me her phone.

"What the hell do you want?"

"Hand it over," I say without looking in her direction. There's no way she's keeping it now that 'Brighton' has made contact with her.

She scowls. "As fucking if."

Irritation prickles across my skin, making the back of my neck tingle. "You want me to pull over and take it from you, Calla?"

"No. What I want is for you to chill out, Atlas," she snaps, emphasizing my name. "If you can't trust me not to put all of us in danger, then I think we need to reevaluate what it is we're doing here."

I put my hand back on the wheel, gripping it until my knuckles are leached of color, and push harder on the gas. Now is not the time to get into an argument; I trust Calla, but there's not a chance in hell I trust that friend of hers. She is loyal to her own blood.

As loyal as you are to yours? an infuriating voice croons in the back of my mind.

I let out a harsh breath, clenching my jaw so tight my teeth hurt. A curse flies from my lips as I almost miss the turn, slamming on the breaks and whipping the wheel around to take it at the last second.

Calla gasps sharply, grabbing the handle above her door, while Lex whistles under his breath from the seat behind her.

"You good?" Kade asks, and I shoot him a dark glare through the rearview mirror.

A few minutes later, we pull into the lot of Marcel's boxing club. Calla gets out the second I shift into park, slamming her door and stalking toward the building as if she's been here before. Lex and Kade follow after her and Gabriel lets out a sigh. Before he can say anything, I grumble, "I don't want to hear it, Gabe."

"Okay," he says in a level tone, getting out of the vehicle and walking toward the entrance with the others.

The inside of Marcel's club is industrial in appearance, with concrete floors, black brick walls, and an exposed ceiling with large metal pipes. Fluorescent bar lighting hangs from several of them, but the lack of windows doesn't offer any natural light. One wall is lined with punching bags attached by chains to a thick metal beam above our heads, and the middle of the space is occupied by a large boxing ring. A few people are using the bags and others are lifting weights in front of a wall-sized mirror at the far end of the room.

Gabriel is already chatting with Marcel, while Kade and Lex start sparring in the ring, because of course they are.

My gaze falls on Calla, who is wandering around the room taking the space in. She trails her fingers along a few of the punching bags as she passes them, and ends up leaning against the ropes of the boxing ring, watching the guys throw punches at each other. They move at inhuman speed, and while I can see them clearly, they're likely blurs of movement to her, and yet, she watches in awe.

As she watches them, I watch her. I can't help it. The woman infuriates me as much as she intrigues me, and there are very few people—none human, save for her—who can do that.

Lex manages to get the upper hand and knocks Kade on his ass with a loud crash against the floor of the ring.

Calla grins at them, shaking her head as she watches with amusement as Lex helps Kade up, smacking him on the back.

"Thanks, fucker," Kade grumbles, punching Lex's shoulder.

Lex shoots him a wink. "Anytime."

Calla ducks under the rope and jumps on Lex's back, wrapping her legs around his waist and her arms around his neck. "My turn."

Lex laughs, grabbing under her knees to steady her. "Yeah?"

Kade jumps the ropes and grabs a can of beer from the mini-fridge against the ring, cracking it open as he leans against the padded corner.

I walk closer to the ring, listening vaguely as Gabriel talks to Marcel about the attacks. He's sending us a report of the most recent stats, which we'll discuss before heading for Chicago.

Jumping into the ring, I catch Calla's gaze, and she slides off Lex's back.

"Oh shit," he says with a laugh. "I'm out of here." A second later, Calla and I are the only ones in the ring, and she's glowering at me.

"Go ahead," I offer in a level voice, steadying my stance.

She crosses her arms over her chest, arching a brow at me. "What exactly are you giving me permission to do?"

"You're pissed at me, so let's get it out of your system."

"Right, and you think inviting me to fight you is going to make me feel better?"

I cock my head to the side, holding her gaze. "We won't know until we try, now will we?"

She drops her arms to her sides, blowing out an agitated breath. "I don't think so. We both know how it's going to end, which isn't going to improve the situation."

With a brief twist of my lips, I move too fast for her eyes to register, stopping close enough I can feel her breath against my skin.

Calla sucks in a breath and moves to take a step away from me, but I catch her wrist, holding her in place. "Atlas—"

"We're doing this," I cut her off. "Now, focus and fight me."

Her features harden when she realizes I'm not messing around. She pulls her wrist out of my grip and widens her stance.

I advance again, shifting around to attack from behind. I grab the back of her neck, and she throws her elbow back, catching me in the ribs hard. Of course, it's more annoying than painful, but it still puts more distance between us, which allows her to whirl around and slam her fist into my jaw. I lift my hand to rub it, and the second time she attempts to hit me, I catch her fist in my hand, closing my fingers around it tightly, and spin her around, hauling her back against my chest. She immediately tries to pull away, but I'm not about to let her go. The sound of her heart pounding in her chest calls to the beast in me like a siren. I drop my mouth to her shoulder and bite down without my fangs, to send a message. *You lose.*

"Fuck you," she snaps, the anger clear in her voice as it shakes.

"You only get a reward if you win," I taunt lowly, my lips teasing the shell of her ear.

She scowls, trying to pull away again. This time, she reaches for her dagger. Between one moment and the next, she stabs backward blindly, and the damn thing sinks into my thigh.

I growl loudly and let go of her, stumbling back as pain shoots through my veins. My eyes fall to where the dagger is sticking out of my leg, and I blink at it before lifting my gaze to where Calla is staring at me, wide-eyed with flushed cheeks and a racing pulse.

Slowly, I reach for the dagger and pull it out, gritting my teeth against the fiery pain licking up my thigh. My blood drips onto the floor of the ring. I grab a towel hanging over one of the ropes and wipe the dagger clean, walking back to her and sliding it into the holder against her thigh. "Not bad," I say mildly.

The anger remains in her voice when she says, "I'll aim higher next time."

I laugh, caught off guard by her dig. "Yeah?" I step in closer, forcing her back until she collides with one of the padded corner posts. Her eyes narrow, flicking between mine as I cage her in between my arms.

"You want to get stabbed again?" she warns.

"Perhaps we should get going?" Gabriel asks from somewhere nearby. I'm so focused on Calla, I didn't catch his approach.

I keep my eyes on her. "Not sure. Calla?"

She lifts her chin in what I can only imagine she intends as an act of defiance.

My brows lift. "Are you done?"

She blinks at me. "Me? Am *I* done? *You* started this!"

I dip my face closer, my nose nearly touching hers. "I mean, are you done being pissed at me?" I ask in a low voice.

She opens her mouth to respond, but nothing comes out, so she snaps it shut, clenching her jaw. "That depends on you," she finally says.

I exhale through my nose, stirring the hair swept across her forehead. "What would you like me to do? Shall I kidnap your friend from her father?"

Tension creases her forehead as she stares at me. "That's not... I just want to make sure she's okay."

"And I need to make sure you stay alive. In their eyes, you may as well have fangs."

Calla frowns. "Brighton—"

"Is a hunter now," I cut in. "You can stand there and try to deny it all you want, but that is the truth. You've seen it with your own eyes, whether you want to accept it or not."

She blinks quickly, swallowing visibly. "She doesn't want to be, which is exactly why we need to help her." Calla shakes her head. "We're talking in circles, Atlas."

"I'm aware," I remark dryly.

She lowers her gaze for a moment before meeting my eyes. "Please." Her voice is quiet, small. Concern is clear as day on her face, but I can't put the others—my *family*—in danger for a human we don't trust.

I inhale slowly, dropping my hands off the post on either side of her. "Is she in immediate danger?"

"What?"

"Do you believe her father will harm her?"

Her eyes widen slightly. "No, he wouldn't."

"Fine." I step away. "We need to get to Chicago, but we'll address Brighton's situation once Selene is dealt with."

Calla bites the inside of her cheek, then nods. "Fine."

"I don't suppose you'd agree to stay with Marcel while we—"

"Nope," she interjects in a firm voice, her eyes daring me to challenge her.

My lips twitch briefly. "Of course not."

I could easily make her stay behind, but we've come to a place where that no longer feels like the right move. As much as I want to protect her from our world, she's a part of it now. She's not helpless—far from it—and we'll have her back regardless. Calla is family, and more importantly, she *chose* us.

FIVE

CALLA

Fighting with Atlas leaves me feeling all kinds of conflicted. My skin is warm, and I'm vibrating with unbridled energy.

My stomach is also growling non-stop.

We left my parent's place before breakfast this morning, and I hadn't been hungry then, anyway. Turns out, fighting a vampire is quite the workout.

Atlas glances over at me from the driver's seat and then turns on the signal to get off the interstate. A few minutes later, we're in a drive-thru lane ordering food.

My phone chimes while we're waiting in line, and I grab it from the cup holder.

Hey! How's it going? I've been thinking about you. Hope you're well!

I smile at the screen, and Kade tugs on the back of my hair from the seat behind me. "Quit it," I grumble, batting his hand away.

"What are you smiling about?" Lex asks.

"You guys are so nosy," I say. "It's Tessa."

Lex shakes his head. "Who?"

"The witchy girl," Kade tells him.

"Oh. Right. Since when are you two besties?"

Since you won't let me talk to my actual best friend, I want to say. Instead, I shrug. "We've kept in touch a bit since the whole blood spell thing."

We move up slightly in line, and I scan the menu. Everything sounds good, but I'm pretty close to starving at this point, so that is likely a contributing factor.

"Huh. What does she want?"

I roll my eyes. "She's just checking in. You know, being nice? People do that sometimes."

Lex whistles. "Someone is hangry."

At the window, Atlas orders coffee for everyone and breakfast sandwiches for the rest of us.

"You're not hungry?" I ask automatically.

"That very much depends on if you're offering to feed me," he answers in a serious tone, without looking at me. He's sliding his credit card out of his wallet as we inch toward the window.

"If that's on the menu, I want to change my order," Kade says close to my ear, and I shift away, pressing closer to the passenger side door.

"Nope," I shoot back. "You'll have to pick up some blood bags and behave like civilized vampires. Sorry."

Lex snorts. "You're no fun."

I elect not to answer, instead focusing on my phone as I reopen my conversation with Tessa.

Things have gotten even more complicated since we last spoke, I text back.

Seriously? Do tell. I thought things were already pretty intense.

I press my lips together; she's not wrong. I type a long paragraph, telling her everything that happened with Atlas's parents and the ultimatum they gave me. Given she's one of few humans I still talk to, I'm curious to get her take on the situation.

Holy shit. Calla, that's insane. I've never met Atlas's parents, but with their reputation, it doesn't really surprise me. I'm so sorry you're dealing with this. Do you know what you're going to do?

Chewing my bottom lip, I pull my legs onto the chair, folding them to sit cross-legged. Atlas pays at the first window, and we proceed to the second, where he's handed a tray of drinks and a brown paper bag that smells heavenly.

I eat half my breakfast sandwich before pulling my phone out again.

No. I thought I did, but I keep going back and forth while also trying to come up with an alternative. Some sort of loophole that is going to allow me to continue living as a human in a world of vampires. Seems pretty unlikely, but stranger things have happened.

I jump when my phone starts ringing, then swipe across the screen to answer the call.

"Sorry, I'm not a huge texter, and this conversation felt important," Tessa says.

"No, it's okay, but I'm not alone."

Tessa sighs dramatically. "Well, your vamp boys are just going to have to deal with you talking to someone besides them."

I can't help but laugh, knowing the odds of them listening are pretty high. "Right."

"What are you doing now?" she asks.

"Heading for Chicago," I tell her. "We're still in New York at the moment."

"Your parents are there, right?"

"Yeah, but we were visiting Atlas's."

"Visiting seems like too mild a word for what that was," Tessa comments, empathy clear in her tone.

I sip my coffee, ignoring the way the breakfast sandwich is settling weirdly in my stomach. "No kidding."

"Why don't I meet you in Chicago and we can have a girls' weekend? Get your mind off things?"

I pull my lip between my teeth, surprised at the burn of tears in my eyes. I would love to have even a few hours of normalcy, to think about something other than the fate of my future—and it being in someone else's hands.

"That sounds really great," I say, swallowing the lump in my throat.

"Should you confirm with your supernatural security team?" she checks with a short laugh.

Fuck that. I'm *not* asking for permission. "I'll text you the address of where we're staying when we arrive."

"Okay, great. Booking a flight to O'Hare as we speak."

"Thanks, Tessa. I really appreciate this."

"Hey, me too. Truth be told, this trip is as much for me as it is for you. I could use the time away from here."

I frown, though she can't see it through the phone. "You've heard all my grievances. What's happening on your end?"

"Uh, too much to get into right now. I'll fill you in when I see you."

"Deal. Safe travels."

"You guys, too. See you soon."

Once I get off the phone with Tessa, I stick my coffee in the cup holder and curl up in the seat.

"We're not going to talk about that?" Lex says.

"What's there to talk about?" I grumble, my eyes already starting to close.

"Calla's making friends in the supernatural world," Kade says, his voice laced with amusement. "We should be proud."

"And we trust this witch?" Lex asks doubtfully. "She was working with Selene at one point, remember?"

Gabriel chimes in before I can turn around. "She did that to fulfill a debt. She chose to come back of her own volition to remove the spell, which she didn't have to do," he points out. "And I looked into her. There's a mentor at the academy she's at that I've known for years. He vouched for her, and I trust his judgment."

My brows lift at that, though I guess I shouldn't be surprised at least one of them did some digging on Tessa. The whole professor and academy thing has my interest piqued, and I make a mental note to ask her about it. I didn't peg Tessa as the private school type, and something tells me there's a story there.

"Good enough for me," Kade says.

"Hmm, fine," Lex mutters. "I guess Calla can have her girls' weekend with the witch. But if you're doing something fun, I'm going with you."

I roll my eyes, choosing not to respond to that. "We're not driving the whole way to Chicago, are we?" I direct the question to Atlas, and he shakes his head.

"We could've flown out of the city, but after yesterday, I'm far less inclined to use family resources. I have connections of my own at a private airstrip about an hour from here."

I nod, resting my head against the back of the seat. "Wake me up when we get there," I say around a yawn, closing my eyes.

I drift in and out, listening vaguely to the casual conversation happening between the guys. Lex is still determined to return to the Washington house sooner rather than later, and it's clear the others want the same. I fall back to sleep listening to Kade complain about how they'll need someone to go in and deep clean the place before we can go back.

The next time I open my eyes, I'm in someone's arms. I squint against the light and determine it's Gabriel carrying me from the car toward the charter plane.

"I could have walked," I mumble.

He grins down at me. "You looked so peaceful asleep. I didn't want to disturb you."

"Yeah, so peaceful when you're not running your mouth and getting into trouble with Atlas," Lex chimes in, walking on Gabriel's right with a duffle bag over each shoulder.

I shoot him a look, then turn my face back to Gabriel. "You can put me down now."

"If you insist," he says lightly and sets me down, keeping his arm around my waist until I'm steady and step away from him.

The five of us climb the stairs onto the plane, and I plop down in one of the chairs near the middle of the cabin. I never flew private before I met the guys—it certainly is a perk. No long security lines or lost luggage and unlimited drinks. I'm not sure I can go back to stale airplane pretzels after this.

Atlas talks to the pilot while the rest of us settle into our seats, Gabriel taking the seat next to me.

I glance over at him to find him already looking at me. "How are you doing?" I ask in a soft voice. "I know the reason for this trip must make you feel, well, I'm not exactly sure. Are you nervous or sad or happy you'll finally be rid of her?"

He places his hand on my armrest, palm up, and I slide my fingers through his. "I'm going through a range of emotions. Losing my sire will hurt physically because of our blood connection, but mentally and emotionally, it will be a great relief. She's had her claws in me for so long. I can't properly express how much I am looking forward to being free of that."

I squeeze his hand. "Have you ever thought about what your life as a vampire would be like if you were sired to someone else?"

Gabriel considers that. "Not really. The influence Selene had on me was relatively short-lived for someone immortal. Of course, I wish she'd never held any power over me, but dwelling on it now does nothing to erase the past. All I can do now is move forward and build a future for myself with the people I care about." His thumb traces back and forth across my skin as he speaks in a gentle tone. "Are you thinking about what *your* life would be like as a vampire?"

My eyes widen, his question taking me off guard. "I... I guess I am. I don't know." I stare at my lap, a new pressure building in my chest as the weight of my words settles there. "I feel like my head hasn't stopped spinning for two days."

Lex drops into the chair across the aisle and spins it to face us. "Would it help to make a pros and cons list of both your options?"

"Or say *fuck it* to both and let's come up with a plan that allows Calla to remain as she is," Kade offers mildly, walking over with a crystal champagne flute filled with blood.

I laugh, but the sound is far from humorous. "Right. You want to go up against the Yorks?"

He shrugs, downing half the glass. "You know, Calla, being a vampire isn't the worst thing in the world. It does have its perks."

"True," Lex agrees. "The speed and strength are quite convenient in many instances."

Kade nods along, then adds, "You can experience and explore anywhere you want—you literally have all the time in the world."

Gabriel gives my hand a squeeze, turning my attention to him. "The heightened senses are my favorite part. They are overwhelming to begin with, but once you get used to them... you'll see the world in a completely different way. It's quite beautiful."

Atlas walks over, glancing between us, but adds nothing to the conversation before picking a seat on the opposite side of the aisle and pulling out his phone.

We take off a few minutes later and fall into a comfortable silence. I play over the guys' answers in my head, considering what my life could be if I choose eternity. The idea of leveling the playing field with the guys is definitely a pro, but having to drink blood to survive? The thought makes my stomach churn.

"You're thinking about the blood, aren't you?"

My eyes swing to Kade. "Um, yeah."

"When I was human, I was the most squeamish person you could imagine. I mean, pass-out-looking-at-a-needle squeamish. The sight of blood made me sick to my stomach... until I turned. It's like a switch is flipped and your body recognizes it's required to live."

"And you don't need to bite people to get blood," Gabriel says, still moving his thumb back and forth along my hand. "The first time, you'd need to feed from the vein to complete the transition, but after that, you can drink blood bags if that's what you want."

"I see you as a B-positive vamp," Lex says with a grin.

I wrinkle my nose at that.

"All vampires have their preference," Gabriel continues, "but blood is blood."

I nod along, considering I don't have any room or experience to argue his words, and Gabriel shoots me a reassuring smile. It's a lot to consider, but hearing from Gabriel, Lex, and Kade about their own transition experiences is enlightening.

"Aren't you even a little bit curious?" Kade inquires.

I want to say no, but there's a part of me that is curious despite the fear surrounding that option and denying it won't do me any good, so I shrug. "I guess. Considering it seems to be the only alternative to forgetting nearly everything from the past two months."

"It's not something you have to think about right now. One thing at a time." He gives my hand one more squeeze before standing. He walks to the front of the plane and pulls a drink out of the mini-fridge, then grabs a second and walks over to sit with Atlas.

Before I can close my eyes and even attempt to fall asleep, Lex drops into the seat Gabriel vacated and twirls a strand of my hair around his finger.

"What do you want?" I grumble, tiredness clinging to me like a weighted blanket.

He pouts. "I'm bored."

"You're bored?" I echo. "Why exactly is that my problem? I'm not the only one on this plane."

"Yeah, but you're my favorite to play with." He leans in until his lips graze my ear. "And I'm pretty sure you enjoy it too."

I turn my face to look at him and catch Kade watching us with an expression that catches my breath. His eyes are devouring me as if I'm completely naked, and heat rushes to my cheeks in response.

Before I can register what's happening, Lex pulls me into his lap so I'm straddling him, and Kade moves at an untrackable speed, taking my seat.

"Fuck," I mutter, grabbing Lex's shoulders to steady myself so I don't fall against his chest. "A brief warning next time wouldn't kill you."

"It'd ruin the fun, though," Kade says, moving the hair away from my neck and brushing his lips against the delicate skin there.

Lex grips my hips, pressing down, and I gasp as his erection teases the heat between my legs. He chuckles in response, leaning in until his nose grazes my cheek. "You like that?" he murmurs, tightening his grip.

"Hmm." I bite my lip, closing my eyes as Kade continues kissing and sucking my neck. He alternates between using his teeth and tongue against my skin, shooting heat straight to my core as I grind against Lex, grinning when his breath catches.

"Are you going to come like this?" he purrs. "Grinding yourself against my cock?"

I open my eyes and lick my lips, rolling my hips as his fingers dig into my skin. I probably could bring myself to orgasm this way, but it would be a hell of a lot more enjoyable without clothing in the way. "You'd like that, wouldn't you?"

The corner of his mouth kicks up, his eyes flicking between mine. "I'd much rather make you come with my cock inside that sweet pussy of yours, but I'll take what I can get."

Take whatever you want. The words are on the tip of my tongue, but when I open my mouth to speak, Kade sinks his fangs into my shoulder, and I cry out as a sharp mix of pleasure and pain washes over me like a vicious wave. My grip on Lex's shoulders tightens, and my core throbs, desperate for the friction as I grind harder against his erection.

"I need more," I breathe, looking into his eyes.

One of his hands slides from my hip down to my thigh, inching closer to where I want him. He drags his thumb over my center, and I catch my bottom lip between my teeth to keep from moaning. As much as I like the pants I'm wearing, I'd like nothing more at this moment than for Lex to rip them off.

"Better?" he teases in a light voice, his lips brushing my cheek.

I press my breasts into his chest as I attempt to get closer. "More."

"So needy," Kade murmurs after retracting his fangs, lapping at the marks he left on my shoulder.

I reach over and find the hardness between his legs, smirking. "Touché."

His hand covers mine, moving it along his erection as he pulls in a shallow breath, groaning and tipping his head back against the leather seat.

I let him control the motions as I become hyper-focused on how close Lex's fingers are to my clit. He's touching everywhere but the sensitive bundle of nerves there, and it's driving me crazy. I press my lips together when he slides his fingers past the waistband of my pants into my panties, brushing along my folds. My breathing picks up, anticipation filling my chest with a near unbearable pressure, and I turn my face toward him again, resting my forehead against his.

Lex dips a single finger inside me and sucks in a breath. "You're already so wet."

"Hmm," I hum, moving against his finger to push him deeper.

"Ah, ah, ah." He pulls his finger out and continues teasing my folds.

I groan, leaning back enough to glare at him. "What the hell?"

"Only good girls get to come," he says with a smirk.

My eyes narrow, and I try to shift off his lap, but he tightens his grip, holding me there. "Lex—"

He plunges two fingers inside me without warning, and I gasp, unable to hold back the moan that he pulls from me, curling his fingers and grazing them along my inner walls. His thumb finds my clit and circles it hard and fast, and his other hand moves from my hip to the side of my neck. He uses his thumb under my chin to tilt my head back and slants his mouth over mine, swallowing my sounds of pleasure as his fingers work inside me, thrusting and teasing at alternating speeds until my head is spinning and my chest is rising and falling fast against his.

Kade groans next to us, watching as he continues moving my hand over the bulge in his pants. "Don't come until Lex tells you to," he says in a voice thick with arousal.

I break the kiss, moaning as Lex curls his fingers deep in my pussy. The pressure between my legs builds quickly, and seconds later, I'm racing toward orgasm—until Lex pulls his fingers out completely, the waistband of my pants snapping against my skin. My eyes pop wide, my chest heaving. "What the fuck?" I growl breathlessly, ripping my hand away from Kade's erection. If I'm not getting off, he sure as hell isn't either.

"What did Kade say?" Lex taunts, his eyes hooded.

I place my palms against his chest, pushing away from him. "I wasn't—"

"You little liar," Kade says in a voice filled with amusement.

I flip him off, keeping my eyes on Lex. "Are you going to make me ask for it?" I ask, arching a brow and rolling my hips into him.

He hisses out a breath. "This is my game," he says in a low voice. "You don't have control here."

I kiss his jaw, nipping at the skin; I don't try to be gentle. "No?"

Lex turns his face, so his lips brush mine. "Hmm... no." In a flash of movement, he lifts me off his lap, stands, and sets me in the chair before walking toward the front of the plane to the mini-fridge. I'm left completely unsatisfied, staring after him, my core throbbing with need and wondering what the female version of blue balls is called.

"He'll pay for that," I mutter under my breath, and Kade only chuckles in response.

I cradle a margarita in my hand, licking the bit of salt from the rim off my finger. Typically tequila isn't my hard liquor of choice, but when Lex insisted we eat at a Mexican restaurant, it seemed fitting to order one. One very quickly turned into a giant pitcher when the rest of the table decided to indulge as well.

Lex is complaining there isn't enough liquor in the batch when Tessa walks in, a duffel bag slung over one shoulder. She's wearing a cropped black tank top and olive-green leggings with running shoes—definite comfy travel attire, but she also makes it look effortlessly stylish. Her black hair is pin-straight and nearly reaches her waist.

I get up from in between Gabriel and Atlas and meet her halfway across the room, hugging her tightly. "How was your flight?" I ask after we break apart. She isn't wearing any makeup, though she's the type of person who naturally looks good without it.

"Good! It's great to see you in person again," she says as we return to the table.

Gabriel offers her a warm smile, while the others watch her with mild interest.

Kade stands and offers her his spot across from me, and she sets her bag under the table, thanking him and sitting down. I return to my spot, while Kade grabs a chair from the table next to us and flips it around, straddling it before diving into the bowl of chips in the middle of the table.

"What brings you to Chicago?" Tessa asks as I reach for the pitcher of margaritas and pour her one.

I steal a glance at Gabriel before returning my gaze to her and say, "Selene is here."

She nods, recognition in her emerald gaze. "I see. And what about your trip to New York?" Her eyes are focused on my face, her head tilted to the side slightly as she waits for me to respond.

I press my lips together, trying to think of a concise and accurate way to describe the shit show that went down at Atlas's parents. "Well," I say, "you got the CliffsNotes version."

She offers a short chuckle. "Yeah, but something tells me it's slightly more complicated than that."

I finish pouring her drink and set the pitcher back on the table. "It always is."

"Do you know what you're going to do?" she asks.

"Nope," I answer a little too loudly, popping the 'p'. Maybe I'm drinking this margarita a little too fast. The warmth in my cheeks and stomach can attest to that, along with the haze of pleasantness starting to settle over me.

Tessa nods, seemingly in understanding, and glances around the room. "Do you know where the restroom is in this place? I could use a second to freshen up after my flight."

"Sure," I say, standing. "Follow me."

We walk to a hallway near the back of the restaurant and find the line for the restrooms. "This place has been packed since we got here," I tell her, cringing at the size of the line.

She smiles. "No worries. I'm not in any rush, I just wanted to talk to you without your fang club."

"Right." I drag out the word as the line moves a little. "I honestly have no clue what I'm doing. I try to think about my life one way, and it sucks. I try to think about it the other way, and it hurts so bad I can't even imagine agreeing to it. I know this whole thing started so messed up and it's been messed up for weeks... I just don't know anymore." I sigh, leaning against the wall. The guy ahead of us slips out of the line and walks the other direction, putting us closer to the front.

"Are you leaning one way or another?" she asks as the bathroom door opens and a couple practically fall out of the doorway, clutching onto each other and laughing as if they'd just heard the funniest thing in the world.

Tessa and I exchange a slightly amused glance, and I shrug in response to her question. "I keep going back and forth."

The single bathroom across the hall opens up, and Tessa grabs my wrist, pulling me inside and closing the door. She turns on the sink and starts washing her hands. "Have you talked to them about it?"

I lean against the wall beside the door, surprised to find the washroom clean and pleasant-smelling, like citrus. "I mean, sort of? They gave me a pros and cons list of becoming a vampire. And I don't know if it's just the blood thing that bothers me or the fact that I would have to be taking from someone or something else just to survive. I'm not a vegetarian or anything, but this just feels different. And don't even get me started on the thought of living forever, because that is just too much for my brain to wrap around. I can't even think about the next five years, let alone the next five hundred without spinning into a complete panic."

"I get that," she says sincerely, grabbing a paper towel from the dispenser and drying her hands, tossing the crumpled bit into the trash next to the sink. She leaves the water running, and her eyes meet mine in the mirror over the sink. "I have the ability to slow my own aging and to essentially prolong my life, but I'm still mortal if I don't actively do those things. I'll grow old and die like everyone else."

"Right," I say, "and I don't even know how it works. Atlas's parents appear older than him. Obviously they are, but he's significantly older than he looks. They all are. Will I look like this forever? Will I look a little bit older but stop aging at some point? I don't…"

She turns to face me and puts her hand on my shoulder in an attempt, I think, to calm my rambling. "A lot of vampires use magic to alter their appearance. That's probably what Atlas's parents have done. They don't want to appear so young their people don't think they can look to them for leadership or guidance. But they don't want to look their age either."

"So you're telling me the guys have chosen to look as they do? Like they could look different?"

She grins softly. "As far as I can tell, they have not altered their appearances in any way. They look as they did when they were turned. Atlas on the other hand, as a born vampire, stopped aging when he reached maturity."

"Really? He looks older than, you know, mid-twenties."

"Yeah, well, guys mature slower than we do, sooooo," she jokes. "But in all seriousness, as a born vampire, he was able to decide when he would stop aging and there would have been a spell cast. But it's not something that he has to continuously keep up. It's a one-and-done sort of deal and then if he were to decide that he wanted to appear differently, that would be a different story. He would need to go to another witch and have them perform magic on him. Likely more than once to keep it up."

I rake my fingers through my hair. "This is all so complicated, and I don't know why I haven't thought about it before. Maybe it's because I'm thinking about it for myself. But either way, I feel like my head is going to explode."

A small smile plays on her lips. "And the margaritas help with that?"

I wrinkle my nose. "They don't *not* help," I say, raking my fingers through my hair before I continue. "There was something else that I wanted to talk to you about."

She leans against the vanity. "Oh?"

"We're going up against Selene, and there's not much I can do to help but I have been training with the guys. I trained a lot before they came into my life too, so I'm not completely useless. But there is something that I need to ask for your help with."

Her eyes search my face, calculating. "What is it?"

"I need you to spell my blood like you did before, making it poisonous to vampires. I don't know what's going to go down and I just want to make sure that I have a defense mechanism in place should anything happen. But can you make it temporary? Like to only last a few days? Is that a thing? Or will I have to bother you again to undo it?"

She offers me a wry smile. "Yeah, I can do that for sure. And I can make it temporary. Though I can't give you an exact timeline on when it will be at its strongest and when it will fade. Magic is fickle like that. It doesn't always do exactly what you want. But that spell is fairly straightforward, and I am confident it will do what you need.

"That's great. Seriously, thank you."

"Of course. I know we haven't known each other that long but I do consider you a friend, Calla, and I'd like to stay in touch no matter what happens. I hope you know that I'm here for you."

I clench my jaw as my eyes start to sting. I don't want to cry in front of her but I also want her to know how much that means to me. "Thank you," I say, hoping the sincerity in my voice rings clear. "I feel the same. If there's anything I can ever do for you, I hope you'll ask. And also tell me about what's going on with you."

She laughs softly. "That is a very long story, and while I do want to share it with you, maybe we can wait until after you've made your big, life-altering decision. I think you have enough on your mind right now and I really don't want to add to it."

I shake my head. "No, no, no. Come on. It can't be that bad, and honestly, I would rather think about somebody else's problems for a second."

"We're going to do the spell first, then I'm going to have at least three margaritas, and then I *might* be in a position to tell you about my crazy life."

"Well, all right then. Sounds like a plan to me."

"Give me your hand," she says in a smooth voice. I offer it to her, and she flips it over so my palm is facing upward. She uses her thumbnail and slices into my palm. I suck in a breath as blood pools in my hand, and she starts speaking in a low voice I can't pick up. After a minute or so, the blood in my hand starts to sizzle and bubble, my skin warming under her touch. It doesn't hurt, but the tingling becomes uncomfortable after a few moments before stopping altogether. The heat is replaced by cold, as if I'm holding an ice cube in my hand, and I try to pull away on instinct, but Tessa holds firm. She continues speaking under her breath for another minute before she closes my palm and turns it over, letting go.

When I open my hand to look at it, the blood is gone and there's a faint silver line in the center of my palm. "That's it?" I check, turning my hand back and forth to inspect it. I don't feel any different, but I don't doubt Tessa's ability, considering she's put the spell on me before and I had no idea... until Lex bit me and thought he was going to die— uh, again.

She nods, mild amusement on her face. "Yep."

"How come you didn't have to cut me open when you spelled my blood last time for Selene?" I ask.

"I did it this way, using your blood, so I could have more control over the spell. Last time, I only needed to be close to you to perform it."

I arch a brow at her, cringing slightly. "Are you saying it was like a *watch me while I sleep* situation when you did it before? Were you, like, standing outside my window?"

She gives me a look. "Do you really want me to answer that?"

"Yeah, no, probably not. Okay," I say, wiping my hands on my pants despite there being no blood left over. "Margarita time."

CHAPTER

SIX

ATLAS

After last night's tirades at the Mexican restaurant Lex picked for dinner and drinks, I'm not the least bit surprised to be the first one awake.

I slip out of the California king the five of us slept in, glancing back over my shoulder to find the others all still sleeping soundly. Calla is pressed in between Kade and Gabriel, her head against Gabe's chest as she breathes evenly. It's the first time I've seen her relatively relaxed since before the dinner with my parents and knowing that feels like a hot poker through my chest.

Lex sighs in his sleep, shifting closer to Kade and curling against his back.

I watch them a moment longer before walking out of the bedroom into the main sitting area in the suite. Instead of dropping into one of the stiff wingback chairs, I step outside onto the terrace.

There are hints of light in the sky, but the air is still crisp with night. It's my favorite time of day; the darkness just before dawn. The world is quiet and I can let myself think about things other than the burdens I carry.

I lean against the railing, looking out over the city. Chicago has never been anything special to me. Once we complete the task we're here for, I'll be just as pleased to leave.

The sound of the glass door opening behind me causes me to turn my head. The smell of coffee and blood reach me simultaneously, and I turn fully around to face Calla.

"Did I wake you?" I ask, glancing down as she holds out the mug filled with coffee as if she's planning to keep the blood for herself. I arch a single brow at her.

"Kidding," she says with a tired smile and pulls the coffee closer to her chest, handing me the blood.

My lips twitch as I take it from her. "Thank you."

She nods, taking a sip of the coffee as she cradles it in her hands. "I just got up. The bed was crowded, and yet, I knew you weren't there the moment I opened my eyes." Her cheeks go pink a second after she realizes what she's said.

I step in closer and take the mug from her, setting them both on the small marble table between the bistro chairs next to us.

Her eyes narrow slightly, watching me like a hawk. "Taking coffee away from me is about as dangerous as taking blood away from you, F-Y-I."

"You know, I think I'll be okay." I can't help the smugness in my tone. The back and forth we get into is far too entertaining to deny.

She reaches for the coffee, but I catch her wrist and pull her toward me before turning us around. I walk her backward until she hits the balcony wall.

The sky is painted with streaks of morning behind her—between Calla and the sunrise, it's the most stunning thing I've ever laid eyes on.

"Atlas, what are you doing?" she asks in a soft voice, sliding her hands up my chest and gripping the cotton of my T-shirt between her fingers.

I pause, my gaze flitting over her face before meeting hers. "You are so beautiful." The words leave my mouth as I lift my hand to her face, brushing the hair back and tucking it behind her ear.

Her pulse jumps and her lips part. "I... Are you okay?"

"Why? Because I gave you a compliment?"

"Um, yeah, pretty much." She pulls her bottom lip between her teeth, lowering her gaze.

I slide my finger under her chin, tilting her head back up, and use my thumb to free her lip. "What are you thinking about?"

Her brows tug closer. "Everything." She shakes her head and turns around to face the lightening sky.

I step up beside her, watching her face as she looks out over the city. "Calla—"

"What do you think I'd be like as a vampire?" she blurts.

I blink, leaning against the balcony wall. "A pain in my ass, probably."

She scowls, shooting me a glare. "Gee, thanks, asshole." She turns away to stomp back inside, but I move quicker than her, blocking the door. "Move," she snaps, blinking quickly.

"No." I step closer.

Calla lifts her hand, but I catch her fist before it can connect with my face, gripping it tightly. "Let go of me." Her voice wobbles, and I immediately drop her hand.

"I'm sorry."

She looks away, sniffling. "Since when?" she mutters dryly.

"That's a more complicated question than you know, Calla." I sigh, snagging her chin once again and making her look at me. Her watery eyes are like a punch to my gut, and I frown. "You are one of the strongest people I have ever had the privilege to know." I slide my fingers along her jaw and cup her cheek, brushing away a tear. "You handle anything that comes your way with grace and courage, and no matter what happens, we've got you."

Her jaw clenches against my hand as she tries to reign in her emotions and hold back more tears. "I... I'm scared. More scared than I've ever been in my life. And I've lived with looking over my shoulder everywhere I went for years before you guys showed up."

Nodding, I murmur, "I know. Believe me when I say I would do anything to take that fear away."

Her eyes flick between mine. "I don't want to die—that whole part freaks the hell out of me—but I'm more scared of who I'll be... what I'll want to do once I've tasted human blood. I've seen what it can do to people and I... I'm terrified of what I'll become."

Her vulnerability cracks something inside of me wide open, and I pull her against me. Wrapping my arm around her waist and burying my other hand in her hair, I hold her to me. Her heart beats like the wings of a hummingbird and her breathing is uneven as she struggles to keep it together. "Listen to me," I say in a soft voice close to her ear. "Becoming a vampire won't change who you are, Calla. It will only heighten everything about you."

She pulls back enough to look into my eyes, and the vulnerability in her gaze fills me with the urge to hold her tighter. "Would you...?" Her voice cracks, and she clears her throat, starting her sentence over. "Would you be the one to do it? I mean, would I have a choice?"

I stare at her for a moment without responding. Quite honestly—and surprisingly—this is the first I've thought about that particular part of Calla potentially becoming a vampire. Which one of us would turn her. In a matter of seconds, I come to the conclusion that *I* want to be the one to sire Calla. I wet my lips, regarding her curiously. "Who would you have do it?" I ask.

She blinks at me, silent for a moment before she shrugs. "I'm not sure that it really matters, does it?"

It's my turn to shrug. "There are certain benefits to being turned by a born vampire," I offer.

"Benefits?" she echoes, arching a brow at me.

"Added layers of protection considering my lineage, stronger abilities because it's my blood, that sort of thing."

"Oh," she says quietly, "good to know, I guess."

"If becoming a vampire is what you decide," I say, looking into her eyes, "I want to be the one to turn you."

Her lips part in a silent gasp as her eyes widen slightly. "I, um... okay. If that's what I decide. But I..." She trails off, shaking her head.

"No, tell me," I push. "You what?"

She exhales a heavy breath. "I'm just surprised, I guess. I thought... Well, I didn't think you even liked me."

An unexpected chuckle escapes my lips, and I reach forward, tucking her hair behind her ear. "You drive me absolutely insane on a regular basis, that is very true." When her eyes narrow and her lips part, I quickly continue, "Before you go running your mouth at me like you so enjoy doing, hear me when I say that I will do everything in my power to make sure you are safe and happy. Even when you piss me off."

Calla seems to consider that for a moment before saying, "It sounds to me that you don't want me to undergo a vampire lobotomy then?" She tries to make it sound like a joke, but her voice doesn't lend any humor.

I pull in a deep breath, letting it out slowly. "Calla, isn't it obvious at this point? We're terrified to lose you, myself included. You're struggling to picture your life without us—I promise we're all doing the same."

She drops her chin, sighing quietly. "I hate this."

"I understand." I pull her against my chest again, smoothing my hand over her hair. "You're not alone in this or anything else. If you have a worry or grievance or fear, those burdens aren't yours to carry alone."

Her pulse jumps, and she buries her face in my chest, clinging to me. She doesn't offer a response, but I wasn't expecting one. So long as she knows we're beside her no matter what, that's what is important. She's part of us now, and we take care of our own.

Calla and I walk back inside a few minutes later as the others get out of bed and head to the kitchen, filling glasses with coffee and blood to start the day.

It's going to be a fucking long one.

"They were supposed to meet us an hour ago," Kade grumbles, tapping aggressively on his phone. "Something's up."

We're sitting in the parking lot of an old factory that has long been abandoned. When Gabriel spoke briefly with Fallon last night, they agreed to meet here.

"Maybe they got held up," Calla offers, though her tone suggests she doesn't believe that. Her expression is strained, her eyes filled with concern, and the tension in her muscles is visible by how stiffly she's sitting in between Lex and Gabriel.

"Or maybe it's a fucking ambush," Kade says tightly.

The sound of tires screeching fills my ears, and I cringe at the sharpness of it. The others exchange glances, Kade looking at me from the passenger seat.

"Incoming," Lex mutters, and we get out of the vehicle, keeping Calla between us as a black SUV with tinted windows speeds toward us. The driver slams the brakes, making the tires squeal against the pavement, and I squint slightly, trying to make out the shapes through the windshield, but it's too fucking dark.

The back doors open, and two vampires I don't recognize jump out, walking around to stand at the front of the vehicle with their arms crossed over their chests. They make no move to engage with us, but we're all on high alert as Fallon gets out of the passenger seat with a grave expression.

Gabriel and I move at the same time, stepping in front of Calla, and shifting her behind us. Then Gabriel steps toward Fallon, concern filling his face. "What's going on, Fal?"

"What the fuck is this?" Kade says, his fangs bared.

Fallon shakes her head. "I'm so sorry," she says in a broken voice, and my eyes snap toward the car where Jase stumbles out of the back-seat. He's clearly had the crap beaten out of him, blood streaking his hair and covering his clothes. He has several bite marks on his arms and throat, and he walks with a subtle limp.

Calla gasps from behind us, and my jaw clenches. Before anybody can ask what the hell happened to Jase, two more SUVs tear into the lot and at least a dozen vampires spill out of them.

"Fucking called it," Kade mutters under his breath.

"Very helpful," I snap at him, scanning the group of vampires oppo-site us. They're young, all turned—I'm assuming by Selene.

The devil herself, the vampire we're here to hunt slides out of the backseat of the first SUV.

Kade growls deep in his throat, and Lex grabs his arm before he can shoot forward and attack. We need to be smart about this; she has the numbers, though we don't yet know how skilled they are when it comes to fighting—and fighting other vampires at that.

Selene walks around to the front of the SUV, her heels clicking on the pavement. "Well," she says, scanning the lot of us with a sharp gaze before flipping her long, near-white hair over her bare shoulder. "This is quite the welcome committee. I hope you don't mind, I brought my own." She licks her deep red lips, the corners of her mouth curling into a grin as her eyes land on Gabriel. "Hello, love."

"Don't you speak to him," Calla snarls with venom in her voice, squeezing through the space between Gabriel and me. Her heart is racing in her chest and her jaw is set tight. The hatred in her expression is cold, dark. I've never seen her like this, not even the night we broke into her apartment in Washington.

Selene barely glances at Calla, annoyance flickering across her face. "I see you still have a pet. Honestly, Gabriel, it's rather tacky at this point."

"Enough," I cut in sharply, my gums throbbing from the pressure of my fangs threatening to extend.

She turns her attention to me, her eyes glimmering with amuse-ment and lust; it turns my stomach. I want to rip this monster's throat out with my teeth for what she's done. "Atlas, how wonderful to see you again."

I ignore her words and nod toward Jase. "What happened here?"

Selene casts a sideways glance at him before returning her gaze to me. "I don't appreciate being watched and tailed. Especially after I so graciously saved these pathetic excuses for vampires from a group of hunters." She picks a fleck of lint off her emerald knee-length dress that fits her like a second skin. The deep V-neck leaves nothing to the imagination as her breasts nearly spill out of it. Between the heels and the dress, it's clear she wasn't anticipating a fight. At least not one she'd participate in.

I shake my head, exhaling a long breath. "Fallon, get him cleaned up and fed," I tell Gabriel's friend without looking away from Selene.

Fallon hesitates. "Are—"

"*Go.*" I toss her the keys to our vehicle.

She catches them and, moving at an inhuman speed, she slides her arm around Jase's waist and guides his arm over her shoulders to help him walk to the car. They peel out of the parking lot moments later.

Selene's entourage of vampires exchange subtle glances before moving to flank their sire. Their fangs are bared, their silver eyes gleaming with bloodlust as they stare at Calla. They were likely turned in the last few months based on their evident struggle to keep their fangs to themselves.

"You should teach them control," I comment in a mild tone, inclining my head slightly toward the salivating vampires.

She presses her lips together, seemingly displeased, but says nothing in response to my observation. Instead, she focuses again on Gabriel. "Care to explain why you're keeping tabs on me? I'd much prefer you came to me yourself instead of sending your annoying little friends."

"I'm here now," Gabriel says in a level voice, moving closer to her.

A couple of Selene's vampires snarl, moving at heightened speed, and they each grab one of Gabriel's arms. A bad move on their part, considering Gabriel can't hurt Selene despite wanting to tear her to pieces. Evidently, she hasn't taught them that bit of being sired to her. Perhaps she didn't find it important and instead taught them blind obedience.

Calla steps forward when Gabriel tries—with intentionally minimal effort—to break free of their grasp, and I shift sideways, blocking her path. My lips twitch when she punches me in the back and huffs angrily. I can't communicate with her that Gabriel purposely isn't fighting them off as a way to keep them occupied.

Lex advances toward Selene, his fangs fully extended and a growl tearing from his throat. Four of her vampires dive into action, their sights set on Lex, to prevent him from getting close to Selene. He whistles, chuckling as he goes head-to-head with a broad-chested male vampire. "You guys are so whipped, it's sad. I'm sad for you." He's taunting them, getting in their heads and distracting them so he can take them out with the least effort possible, because that's Lex. *Work smarter not harder*, he loves to remind us.

Gabriel continues his half-hearted struggle with the vampires on either side of him, while Kade and I exchange a glance. I nod subtly toward Calla, motioning for him to stay close to her so I can tear through the other vampires. I want this fight over quickly. It's been a long time coming, and we're all ready for the end to come.

The next ten minutes pass in a blur of tearing flesh and spraying blood. These turned vampires are nowhere near a match for my years or bloodline. I attack ruthlessly, pulling out hearts and ripping out throats with my teeth. The monster in me revels at the blood dripping from my fangs, staining the front of my shirt. My heart beats wildly in my chest, excitement making my pulse tick faster. I don't often allow myself to be this way, but when I do... Well, the blood-soaked pavement covered with vampire corpses speaks for itself. A few of them fled before I could get my teeth in them, which is as unfortunate as it is pathetic.

I turn in time to see Lex creeping toward where Selene is trying to speak to Gabriel, desperation creeping into her tone as she realizes things aren't going the way she expected them to.

Lex's arm arches through the air, his fist flying toward her face, but she manages to duck at the last second and kick his legs out from under him. He curses loudly, breaking his fall gracefully before shooting back up and kicking her hard in the stomach. She clocks him in the face, which gets Kade worked up enough to go after the remaining vampires Selene brought, who are still holding onto Gabriel.

I move back toward Calla, who is staring at me with a mix of shock and something that is definitely not fear. She's more like us already than she wants to admit, but this certainly isn't the time to bring that up.

Gabriel shoves one of the two remaining vampires toward Kade, who sinks his fangs into his throat, tearing through his flesh, while Gabriel shoves his hand through the other's chest. The vampire freezes, going stiff, his silver eyes widening and filling with tears as his mouth forms a perfect 'O'. Seconds later, Gabriel pulls his hand out, the vampire's bright red heart clutched in his fist. Gabriel drops it, snapping the vampire's neck a moment before he crumples to the ground.

Kade pulls back, blood covering his lips and chin, and grins manically at Gabriel. The vampire in his grasp growls weakly, and Kade pulls a dagger out of the waistband of his pants, driving it into the vampire's heart through his back. Kade tosses the still body next to the other dead vampire and joins Lex in the fight against Selene, who, glancing around at all of her fallen vampires, isn't looking so confident anymore. She may be powerful, but there's no way she'll make it against all of us.

Calla grabs my arm and leans up to speak in my ear. "I want this one."

Fuck. My cock twitches at the tone of her voice, the viciousness that fills her words.

"Are you sure?" I ask, keeping my eyes on Kade and Lex as they take turns dodging attacks from our target while getting some non-lethal hits of their own on her. There's a gash across her left cheek and another near her ear, staining her hair and dripping down her neck and chest, disappearing between her breasts.

Gabriel backtracks to where Calla and I are standing. "Angel, this isn't—"

"My fight?" She shakes her head and continues in a firm voice, "I disagree."

He moves to her other side so she's standing between us. "Of course it is," he assures her, "I just don't want you to think this is going to prove anything to us. Or that you need to."

She turns her dark gaze on him, releasing my arm. "This isn't about you all. It certainly has nothing to do with what you think of me. I want this for *me*, Gabriel."

He nods, turning his attention to the others. "Lex, Kade," he shouts, and Calla doesn't waste any time charging toward the fight. Gabriel and I follow on her heels.

Kade slams his fist into the side of Selene's head, and she stumbles to the side—probably regretting her choice of footwear right about now.

She snarls, catching her balance, and whirls around, but Lex is right there, taking a swipe at her and digging his nails deep across her chest.

Calla halts, her eyes widening as Selene growls in pain. Kade attempts to wrap his arms around Selene from behind, but she slams her head back, smacking into his face, and he falls backward a few steps, reaching for his nose as blood gushes from it.

"Fucking hell," he hollers.

Lex moves in again, fury in his gaze and blood running down his face from a cut just above his right brow. When Lex shoots forward to attack, Selene shoves him away and moves at preternatural speed, grabbing Calla by the throat and pulling her close. "Hmm, you know, it's been too long since I tasted something as sweet as you were, pet, and I could use the boost."

Before any of us can get to her, Selene sinks her fangs into Calla's neck. She cries out, the sound strangled and filled with pain.

Gabriel and I both move for them, but a second later, Selene stiffens, pulling away and recoiling from Calla... who is *grinning*?

Holy hell. She planned for this.

The vampire chokes and spits blood onto the pavement as she claws at her throat as if it's on fire.

Everything moves in slow motion as Calla's blood soaks the front of her shirt. She reaches for the dagger at her thigh, pulling it out and lifting her arm as she stalks toward the vampire who bit her. "What's it going to take for you vampires to stop underestimating me?" With a steady, unforgiving swing, Calla buries the dagger in Selene's chest.

The vampire's eyes pop wide, filled with disbelief. She sinks to her knees, and Calla pushes the dagger in deeper and gives it a rough twist, her heart jackhammering in her chest.

Selene's bloodstained lips open and close as if she's trying to force words out, but all that comes are gargled noises and short gasps for breath.

Calla backs away, her hands shaking at her sides as Selene reaches for the dagger sticking out of her chest, unable to grasp it as her wide eyes roll into the back of her head. She collapses to the side and twitches for a few moments that seem to last a small eternity before she finally stops moving.

CHAPTER

SEVEN

CALLA

Selene's blood is spattered across my face, hot and wet against my lips.

It's not the first time I've consumed her blood, but it's sure as the white ash dagger sticking out of her unmoving chest going to be the last.

I stumble back until I hit a solid wall of muscle. Hands grasp my shoulders, turning me around until I'm eye level with Gabriel's chest.

"Look at me, angel." His voice sounds far away despite him being directly in front of me. My entire body feels tingly and uncomfortably warm to the point where sweat dots my brow and upper lip. I press a hand against my stomach, cringing at the way it clenches and churns, taking in the bloody bodies scattered across the pavement—including the one I killed. I swallow the bile burning my throat, gritting my teeth against the waves of nausea.

"I think she's in shock," Kade says walking into my line of sight and standing next to Gabriel. "She's white as a sheet and her pupils are blown."

"That was the hottest fucking thing I've seen in a long time," Lex adds from behind me.

Gabriel sighs, stepping away to give me some space. "Not now, Lex."

I lick my lips, cringing as I taste the copper bitterness of Selene's blood. I try to wipe it off with the back of my hand. "I... I'm okay." I turn to look back at the body, but Lex is blocking my view.

He shoots me a wink. "You were badass."

I blink at him as my shoulders start to feel heavy. "Um, thanks."

"All right," Atlas says, snagging my attention as he plucks keys from the pocket of a dark-haired dead vampire, and walks over to us. He tosses the keys to Lex and a lighter to Kade. "Let's get this dealt with and be on our way." He invades my personal space without hesitation and grips my chin, looking into my eyes. "Okay?" he says in a quieter voice.

I manage a subtle nod in his grasp.

"Good girl."

I turn away from him as my cheeks heat because I should definitely *not* be turned on right now, but the warm tingling between my legs apparently didn't get the memo.

I just killed someone.

Granted, that someone was a monster who absolutely deserved it. That doesn't change the fact I now have blood on my hands —literally.

I walk over to Selene's body, crouching before it, and exhale a shaky breath before reaching for my dagger and pulling it out of her chest. Using the bottom of her dress, I wipe the white ash as clean as it'll come and return it to the holder strapped to my thigh, standing and walking away from my first kill.

Something tells me if I choose to remain in the world of the super-natural, it won't be my last.

Back at the hotel, we take the elevator to our room without a word to each other. The silence is deafening, but I also can't bring myself to speak. What would I say, anyway? *Great job, team?*

Once we're inside our suite with the door closed, I finally ask, "Has anyone heard from Fallon?"

Gabriel pulls his phone from his back pocket and nods. "Jase is okay. Fallon got him fed and he's healing normally. She said to call once things are settled so they can bring our car back."

"That's good," I say, pulling off my dirty shoes and dropping them near the door. "I'm glad he's okay." When I straighten, the room spins around me, and I reach out for anything to steady myself.

Gabriel is there in an instant, sliding his arm around my waist. "Easy there. Come on. Let's get you cleaned up."

I lean into him as we walk past the kitchen, where Lex and Kade are drinking tall glasses of blood. Atlas took a call out on the terrace the moment we got in, and I already know I don't want to hear what it's about.

In the bathroom, Gabriel leaves me leaning against the marble vanity for a brief moment while he slides the double doors closed and turns on the shower. When he returns to me, he says, "Arms up."

I comply without protest, and he pulls my shirt off over my head, dropping it into the sink behind me. Next is my bra, then my leggings and panties. I lower my gaze, huffing out a sigh. "This is so annoying. I shouldn't need help taking a fucking shower. I just..." I choke on the lump in my throat, blinking hard at the tears forming in my eyes.

I'd *wanted* to kill Selene. God knows she deserved it. It should have felt *good* to punish her for what she did to me, to Gabriel. But killing another person—vampire or not—seems to be taking a toll on me I certainly wasn't expecting.

"It's okay," Gabriel assures, holding his hands out to me. I take them, letting him lead me toward the shower. He pauses at the large glass door, and in the time it takes me to blink, he undresses.

I'm not sure I'll ever be entirely used to all the vampire quirks.

We step under the hot spray of water, and I sigh, closing my eyes as it cascades over my stiff shoulders and back, loosening my muscles almost instantly.

Gabriel stands behind me, pouring rose-scented body wash into his hand and starts massaging it into my skin, his touch careful and tender.

"Hmm. That feels good," I murmur, tipping my head back against his chest.

"I'm glad," he says softly.

I pry my eyes open and turn to face him after several blissful moments. "I should have said this already," I say, tilting my face to meet his soft silver gaze. "I, uh, I'm sorry."

He frowns faintly. "I don't understand."

"About Selene. You wanted her gone as much as the rest of us—probably more—but I'm sure losing her isn't easy, so I just... I want to make sure you're okay." Some of the pressure in my chest lessens when Gabriel smiles at me.

"Oh, angel," he murmurs, cupping my cheeks in his hands. "You don't know how much that means to me. I assure you, I'm all right. Yes, there is a physical loss I can feel, but mostly, it's relief. Like there's been a significant weight lifted from my chest. An absence of pressure. I am thankful you had the strength and courage to do what I could not." He leans in, closing the remaining distance between us, and slants his mouth over mine, kissing me deeply. Warmth floods through me, and I press as close as I can get as our mouths move together. Gabriel parts my lips with his tongue, flicking it along the roof of my mouth and making me gasp as the hardness between his thighs teases my entrance. His hands move from my face to my hips, gripping them firmly and guiding me backward until the backs of my knees touch the shower bench. His lips leave mine, trailing along my jaw to my neck, and he inhales deeply. "I'd like nothing more than to taste you right now," he breathes against my skin.

I shiver, tilting my head to the side and baring my neck to him. "Go ahead," I whisper, anticipation making my breath short.

He chuckles softly and kisses my neck before leaning back to look into my eyes. "I'm not going to bite you, angel."

"Oh." *Oh.*

My eyes widen as Gabriel lifts his hands to my shoulders and guides me down until I'm sitting on the bench. He lowers to his knees in front of me, halting my breath in my lungs as his hands rest on my thighs before slowly spreading them open.

Taking his sweet time, Gabriel trails kisses along the inside of my thigh. Just when I think he's going to put his mouth where I desperately want it, he moves to the other thigh and peppers kisses there. The closer he gets to my core, the deeper it throbs. I open my mouth to complain, but before I can get a word out, his tongue delves between my folds, licking the length of my slit.

"Ahh," I moan, my head falling back against the shower wall.

Gabriel's lips close around my clit, and he sucks it into his mouth, swirling his tongue until my breathing goes shallow, and I wrap my legs around him in an attempt to pull him closer. I grip his hair in my fingers, breathing heavily as he thrusts his tongue inside my throbbing core, flicking it along the sensitive walls of my pussy.

"Right there," I tell him, closing my eyes and giving myself over to the intense pleasure he's bringing me. With his tongue inside me, all thoughts of Selene and the decision I have to make are obliterated. The only thing I can think about is how good Gabriel is making me feel.

He uses his fingers to spread me wider, then teases my clit with his thumb. Heat floods through me, pooling low in my belly before my muscles tense, my pussy clenching around Gabriel's tongue. I cry out as an orgasm tears through me, and Gabriel holds me open to him, lapping up my release as I shiver with pleasure. My thighs shake, and Gabriel chuckles against my skin, making me jolt at the sensation.

"So sensitive," he murmurs after leaning back, trailing a finger along my folds.

I press my lips together, blinking my eyes open to look at him between my thighs. "Hmm."

He braces his hands on my knees, straightening, which effectively puts his cock level with my face.

Licking my lips, I lean forward enough to flick my tongue along the tip of his impressive erection. He tastes salty, and I take more of him into my mouth as he hisses out a sharp breath.

"Calla..." He slides his fingers into my hair but doesn't apply any pressure; I'm in control here.

I take his length as deep as I can until he hits the back of my throat. I hold his fiery, lust-filled gaze as I drag my tongue along the underside of his cock as I pull back, then suck him back into my mouth. I find a steady rhythm, bobbing up and down his shaft as he cradles the back of my head in his hand, groaning as I increase my speed and pressure. He leans forward, pressing his other hand against the shower wall behind me, his body blocking most of the water from hitting me. I close my eyes and relax my throat, taking him even deeper as I reach around and massage his balls.

"*Calla*," he grounds out through clenched teeth, breathing heavily. "If you keep going, I'm going to come in your mouth."

If his words were meant to be a deterrent, it doesn't work. I pick up my pace once more, my pussy tingling as evidence of my arousal leaks out, rolling down my thigh.

Gabriel's muscles tense as I continue swallowing his cock, and seconds later, he grunts loudly, his grip on the back of my head tightening as he shoots his release down my throat. I swallow as much as I can, the warm saltiness of him coating my lips and tongue as he pulls his cock out of my mouth and helps me stand.

I move under the spray of water, rinsing the rest of him off my chin and chest before he steals my lips again, kissing me feverishly. "I want you," I say against his lips, pressing my chest into his.

Gabriel nips my bottom lip and murmurs, "Wrap your arms around my neck." When I do, he turns us around to the back of the shower and presses me against the cool tile without breaking the kiss. He nudges my legs apart with his knee, and then I feel him at my entrance, teasing my clit with the blunt head of his cock. My heart races, and I bury my fingers in his hair roughly, urging him to sink into me. I moan into his mouth as he pushes inside my throbbing heat, clenching around his length as he fills me to the hilt. He moves his mouth to my shoulder, kissing and sucking my skin gently as he gives me a minute to adjust. "You feel so good."

I pull in an uneven breath. "Yeah, well, there's a very good chance you're going to have to keep me from falling when my legs give out."

Gabriel chuckles softly. "I've got you, angel. Always."

And then he rolls his hips, moving deeper inside me, and I'm pretty sure I see literal stars.

He pulls almost all the way out before thrusting back into me, alternating speed with each thrust until I'm panting.

"Please," I breathe, my brows drawing together as I hold his gaze.

"You are so beautiful," he says in a voice thick with arousal... and something deeper.

That does me in completely.

Pleasure shoots through me like lightning, and I come hard, clenching around his cock and milking it as he continues thrusting, following me over the edge not long after.

I collapse against him, and true to his word, Gabriel catches me around the waist, keeping me upright. He kisses me gently and grabs the loofah from the little hook above the tap. After squirting soap on it, he proceeds to trail it over my shoulders, washing my arms, chest, and back. After he's finished, and my skin is tingling with warmth, I take the loofah and do the same for him before reaching to turn the water off.

When we step out of the shower, Gabriel wraps a soft, fluffy towel around me, pressing a kiss against my forehead. The room is filled with steam and warmth. The smell of the soap and us clings to the air, and I close my eyes to live in this moment for a little while longer.

"Thank you," I say in a voice close to a whisper.

"Thank *you*," he echoes, tying a towel around his waist.

Once we're dressed, we return to the living room, where the others are sitting around the coffee table. There's a hockey game playing on the TV on the wall, but no one seems to be paying much attention to it.

I drop onto the couch next to Kade and yawn, leaning against the armrest and letting my eyes close.

"Hey," Kade says, touching my arm. "You need to eat something before you go to sleep."

I pry my eyes open and sit up, shaking my head at him. "Not hungry." Honestly, even if I wasn't so tired, the thought of eating makes my stomach churn.

Surprisingly, they don't push it, though the look on Atlas's face makes me think he's considering it.

I close my eyes again... until Kade touches my arm—again. "What?" I grumble.

"Come on," he says, and the couch shifts slightly when he stands. "I'm taking you to bed."

Parts of me like the sound of that despite the exhaustion clinging to my muscles, and before I can respond or even attempt to open my eyes again, Kade picks me up bridal-style and walks to the bedroom, laying me down on the bed and pulling the heavy duvet over me.

I grab his arm before he can move away. "Stay with me."

"I'm not going anywhere," he assures, sliding into the bed next to me.

I curl into his chest, resting my cheek over his heart, and drift off to the steady sound of Kade's breathing.

The following morning, Calla and I take the elevator down to the parking garage and head out to have breakfast with Tessa before she returns to Oregon. I don't trust the witch completely, but Calla has taken to her, and quite frankly, if it keeps her away from Brighton Ellis, I much prefer it. At least the witches aren't trying to wipe us out—at the moment. Having confirmation from Gabriel that the girl checks out also makes me feel better about Calla associating with her. I've only heard good things about the academy she's from, so I don't have any reason to keep Calla from spending time with her.

"Do you remember the last time I took you to meet a friend and you decided to do something stupid? Let's not have that happen again."

Calla scowls at me. "I seem to recall something else about that time." She folds her legs under her, staring out the windshield when I look over at her. "Something to do with a tree... Hell, I'm pretty sure I still have marks on my back."

My cock twitches, and I grip the wheel tighter, remembering vividly how good Calla felt as I took her against that tree. "Careful," I warn in a low voice.

"Or what? You'll pull over and do it again?" she taunts.

I turn my gaze to her, arching a brow as I pin her with a heavy stare I know will warm her insides. "Want to make it to breakfast?"

She presses her lips together, her pulse thumping beneath her skin.

A faint growl echoes in my throat, and I turn my eyes back to the road. "Don't look at me like that."

"Like what, Atlas?"

My nostrils flare. I can fucking smell her arousal, and it has effectively roused the monster in me. "Like you're considering missing breakfast so I can make you come."

"Hmm, what an interesting story you've created for yourself." Her voice is soft and mockingly sweet.

"You're playing a dangerous game," I tell her, flicking a glance to the GPS built into the dash. We're only ten minutes away from the diner, and I could do so much to her in that time.

"I'm not playing a game." She stretches her legs out, and the moment she squeezes her thighs together, I nearly lose control and pull the damn car over. Instead, I offer a low chuckle, pulling one hand off the steering wheel and gripping her thigh over her skirt. She sucks in a breath, her heart racing in her chest.

"No?" I check, sliding my fingers from the top of her thigh to the inside, reveling in the warmth there. It wouldn't take much for me to push her skirt up and slide my hand into her panties, but if she wants to play this game, I'm going to show her what she's up against.

"Nuh-uh," she says in a breathy voice, staring pointedly out the passenger window as her hands grip the seat on either side of her.

I graze my finger along the center of her panties. "Try again."

"Atlas, we can't do this here," she says, desperation creeping into her tone, though she does nothing to try to stop me.

"You sure?" I press my thumb against her clit, and the sound she makes goes straight to my cock.

"My god," she breathes.

I smirk. "Am I now?"

Her gaze whips toward me, her complexion flushed and uneven. "You are—"

"Shall we contact your witch friend and move this breakfast to lunch?" I challenge, tracing my finger back and forth over her panties.

Her eyes narrow at me, and despite the anticipation written all over her gorgeous face, she says, "No."

I pause the movement of my finger, exhaling a sigh. "How disappointing." I pull my hand away, putting it back on the wheel, and turn onto the street as instructed by the GPS.

"Fuck me," she grumbles under her breath, so low any human

wouldn't have heard it. Her cheeks turn pink when I chuckle as if she had momentarily forgotten about my heightened hearing.

When we pull into the parking lot, Calla unbuckles and pulls out her phone, typing out a message—presumably to let Tessa know we're here—as she asks, "I don't suppose you'll wait in the car?"

I don't bother voicing a response as I get out and walk around the vehicle to her door, opening it and waiting for her.

She blinks at me, then sighs in defeat. "Of course not."

We walk inside, the bell above the glass door chiming to announce our arrival. The buzz of voices is rather distracting as I scan the room. Nearly everyone here is human, save for myself and two vampires near the back of the room. Their eyes turn to me the second we walk in before they drop their chins in a subtle nod. I have no idea who they are, but many vampires know who I am.

Tessa—who appears to be the only witch in here—stands from a booth along the window, waving at us.

Calla's face lights up and a smile curls her lips. The sight gives me pause, and I can't stop looking at her. The warmth in her smile and the softness in her expression... it threatens to steal my breath away.

She walks toward Tessa without waiting to see if I follow—it's pretty clear she couldn't care less—and wraps the witch in a tight embrace.

Tessa arches a brow at me over Calla's shoulder. "You brought the grumpy one," she says to Calla while keeping her eyes on me.

Calla laughs as the two pull apart. "He has his moments."

My lips twitch, though I'm sure the *moments* she's referring to aren't the ones I'm thinking about.

Calla's breath catches when she notices me watching her, and she presses her lips together. Hmm. Perhaps we *were* thinking the same thing.

The girls slide into either side of the booth, and I take a seat next to Calla, perusing the menu pointlessly while they chat about what they're going to eat.

When the waitress—Carol, according to the name tag on her plaid button-up—stops by our table, she brings a fresh pot of coffee and fills the mugs already in front of us.

"Thank you," Tessa says with a bright smile, pouring at least three sugar packets into hers.

"Of course, hon," Carol says. "You all need another minute with the menu?"

Calla and Tessa exchange a grin before the witch orders the largest stack of pancakes this place offers with a side of bacon and sausage and a fruit salad.

Calla turns to me. "What do you want?"

You. The word is on the tip of my tongue, and the jump in her pulse makes me think she can see it in my eyes. My lips twitch, and I turn my gaze to the waitress. "I'm all set, thank you, Carol."

Her cheeks go pink and her heart races at my attention, though she's likely old enough to be my grandmother—if I was the age I appear to be. Carol quickly gathers the menus and makes a beeline for the double doors presumably leading to the kitchen.

"Uh oh, Calla," Tessa says in an amused tone. "You might have competition."

She snorts, hiding her grin with her mug as her eyes shift from Tessa to me. "I think I'm good, considering that poor woman's heart was going to give out if Atlas looked at her any longer."

I take a drink of the coffee, surprised to find it doesn't taste like complete sludge. These hole-in-the-wall diners are always hit or miss, but Carol can make a decent pot.

Tessa taps her fingers against the side of her mug, peering around the room before she says quietly, "The spell on your blood will wear off in a matter of days, but if you want it removed now—"

"Remove it," I tell the witch. It's purely selfish, but I'm craving Calla's blood like never before; it's been too long since I tasted her.

Tessa's dark emerald gaze hardens as she turns it on me. "I wasn't asking *you.*"

"You can remove it," Calla says without looking at me. "Its intention was fulfilled, as you know, and honestly, I'd rather not have unnecessary magic just hanging out inside me."

She nods, pulling her black hair back haphazardly using an elastic from around her wrist. "If you're sure."

Calla extends her arm, sliding her hand across the table, offering it to Tessa. I watch closely as Tessa takes her hand and slices into Calla's skin with her nail, my jaw clenching as bright red pools in her palm. The witch closes her eyes, reciting some Latin incantation that makes the blood in Calla's palm bubble briefly before it sinks into her skin, the cut healing itself. The whole thing takes about five minutes, and while they are focused on it, I'm watching the room to make sure no one is being nosy. If Carol comes back, I can handle her easily enough—probably wouldn't even need to glamour the lady.

Calla pulls her arm back, inspecting her palm by poking at it with her finger. "All good?"

I return my attention to the table, my focus narrowing on Tessa. She hasn't been practicing that long from what I understand, but the girl is powerful and certainly someone we'll need to keep our eyes on. I'm not sure what her backstory is, but from what I've seen, she's confident in her abilities.

Tessa nods, sipping on her coffee that's more sugar than anything. "All good."

Calla smiles at her. "I really appreciate it. You saved my ass, so thank you."

"Selene bit you?" she asks, though she doesn't sound surprised.

"Of course she did," Calla says, "and then I daggered her psychotic ass."

I don't miss the way her knee bounces under the table as she recounts taking down the vampire. As confident as her words sound, taking a life—even that of a monster like Selene—took a toll on her.

By the time the mountain of food arrives, the girls are chatting about Tessa's life in Oregon and planning a trip for Calla to visit during the summer. I want to shoot it down immediately, but the light in Calla's eyes while they talk about it makes me bite my tongue as I remind myself that she deserves a life outside the four of us, even when that is a difficult pill to swallow.

The girls are reluctant to say goodbye once the bill comes to our table, and Tessa throws her arms around Calla when we get to the parking lot, making her promise to keep her updated on everything happening until they see each other again. At the last moment, she faces me with an expression sharp enough to cut glass and says, "You take care of her."

I hold her gaze, nodding once. Hmm... perhaps she's not the worst person for Calla to have in her life. "Safe travels home."

Once we're in the car on our way back to the hotel, Calla tilts the seat back slightly and shuts her eyes, sighing softly.

"Thanks for breakfast," she murmurs. "It was nice to see Tessa again."

I slow to a stop at a red light, glancing over, and can't help but smile at her soft features. In all my time on this oftentimes dreadful earth, I've never cared so much for a human. And while that is a very dangerous thing, I know there is absolutely nothing that could make me stop. I let myself look at her a while longer as I wait for the light to change. "You're welcome."

"I know you don't like her, though I'm not sure why. Maybe it's a vampire thing, but—"

"She's not all bad," I cut in, keeping my gaze trained forward. Truth be told, the way she acted so protective over Calla, it did make me like her more, though I choose to keep that to myself.

"You guys did your background check and Gabriel said she's trustworthy, so can you try to be chill about me having someone in my life that isn't you? The whole territorial thing is annoying as fuck."

I chuckle softly, adjusting my grip on the wheel for no reason other than to not reach for Calla. I'd like nothing more than to pull this car over and show her just how territorial I am. Instead, I say, "Duly noted."

"Good," she shoots back, "because you guys aren't coming with me to Oregon this summer. It's a girls only trip, so you'll just have to learn to live without me for a while." Her pulse jumps at the same moment my chest tightens. Those words hold new meaning, which is clearly not lost on either of us.

"Let's get through this month before you start talking about the summer." I steal a brief glance at her. "Okay?"

She presses her lips together, staying silent as she nods.

A few blocks later, a call comes through the Bluetooth in the car. Kade's name shows up on the screen, and I answer it immediately. "Where the fuck are you?" Kade asks. "We ran into a bit of a situation."

Calla looks over at me, but I keep my eyes on the road. "What happened?" I demand.

"Happening," Kade corrects. "Hunters. Too fucking many of them. You need to get here. Now. I just sent you our location. It's a feeder spot about twenty minutes from the hotel. Fuck! Got to go! Hurry up!"

The call ends, and I slam my foot down on the gas, taking a sharp right turn. Calla grabs the handle above her door, her breathing speeding up, though she stays silent. I open Kade's message and tap his location, projecting it onto the GPS screen. Fuck, we're still ten minutes away. I press the gas even harder, speeding down the street and tapping my thumb against the wheel to remind myself not to grip it hard enough to rip the leather.

I don't know what we're showing up to, how many hunters are there, or if anybody's injured, but knowing my family is in danger has me seeing red. I turn the car down the alley beside the building and I can already hear the fighting going on inside. Several of the windows are smashed, glass littering the sidewalk, though pedestrians don't seem too concerned. They cross the street to avoid the broken glass without paying much attention to what's going on inside. I throw the car into park and turn to Calla.

"Don't," she says before I can tell her to stay in the car.

I grit my teeth, rolling my eyes. "Don't die," I growl at her and get out of the car, hearing her follow.

Calla runs next to me, and our shoes crunch over broken glass when we round the corner from the alley and walk through what used to be the front door of the feeding facility.

I grab Calla's wrist, pulling her back against my chest just as a hunter flies through the air in front of us, smacking against the wall with a grunt, then falls to the tile floor, his eyes rolled into the back of his head.

"Oh my god," she whispers in horror.

"Welcome to the party!" Lex shouts from across the room, holding a middle-aged hunter by the throat, her eyes wide and filled with a twisted mix of hatred and fear. He grins and moves at inhuman speed, sinking his fangs into her neck. She screams in pain, her face going white as a sheet before she passes out, going limp against Lex. He scowls, pulling back and dropping her body to the floor just as another hunter comes at him, a dagger in each hand. The two struggle, and the hunter manages to drag his dagger across Lex's chest. He hisses in pain, snarling with his fangs bared and still stained red with the other hunter's blood.

The white tile floor is littered with bodies, both human—hunters and feeders alike—and vampires. The smell of blood is strong in the air, and there's enough of it to make even my gums throb.

A vampire speeds toward us—Calla specifically—and I step in front of her. "Mine," I growl with a sharp glare, fully expecting a snide remark or a punch in the shoulder from Calla, but she remains silent. Smart girl.

The vampire backs off immediately, grabbing a hunter off another vampire seconds before she would've ended up with a dagger in her heart.

With a quick scan, I take inventory. There are at least a dozen vampires including my guys, but I count thirty hunters still fighting.

Kade moves through the crowd and snaps the neck of a hunter trying to sneak up on Gabriel.

Make that twenty-nine hunters.

All of the feeders are either dead, passed out from fear, or fled before Calla and I arrived.

"Keep your back to the wall," I bark at her over my shoulder. "Don't let anyone get behind you—hunter or vampire. Trust no one but us."

Her jaw is set tight as she nods, retrieving the dagger from her thigh.

I don't want to leave her side, but this fight will be a lot easier if I actually participate. I've trained our girl well; Calla will defend herself as needed.

Holding her gaze a moment longer, I flash her a grin. Her eyes widen in surprise, and I take off across the room, gutting three hunters of their entrails in my wake. Hot blood sprays over my face and clothes. I taste it on my lips, and it has the monster in me roaring.

Three hunters have managed to corner Lex while Kade is fighting back-to-back with Gabriel. I'm about to intervene when at least four hunters close in on me, grabbing at my arms. I snarl viciously, throwing them off, but not fast enough.

Lex screams, and my head whips toward the sound to see his silver eyes widen and filled with shock and agony. I look down and find a dagger sticking out of his chest.

"No," Kade hollers, grabbing the hunter closest to him, and tears through the flesh of her throat, spitting it at the hunter trying to take on Gabriel. He retches, and in the seconds he's distracted, Gabriel snaps his neck.

The two of them rush toward Lex, taking out several hunters on their way. My vision is blocked by three more hunters, and I very quickly lose what little patience I'd been grasping. I smash two heads together, reveling in the *crack* their skulls make on impact. They drop to the floor as another vampire joins me in the fight against the others.

We take half a dozen of them out within minutes. It would've been faster, but I couldn't stop looking over to where Kade, Gabriel, and Calla are standing around Lex.

I whirl around as a hunter tries to sneak past, and she freezes, her eyes going wide. She can't be older than twenty. Her clothes are free of blood and the dagger in her shaky hand is clean—she likely hasn't fought a vampire here.

My lips pull back, and I bare my fangs at her. When her eyes shimmer with tears and her chin starts quivering, I shake my head. "Go," I growl in a menacing voice.

Shock fills her features for a second before she turns and runs, dropping her dagger in her haste to get away.

With the other vampires in the room fighting their way through the rest of the hunters, I manage to make my way over to Lex and the others.

"Talk to me," I say, shoving my bloodstained hair out of my face.

Lex is sitting upright on the floor, his back against the wall. "Yeah, I'm not feeling so hot," he says weakly, his eyes half-closed.

I look around the room, searching for a feeder that's still alive, but there aren't any.

"Get him up," I tell Kade and Gabriel. "We'll get him back to the hotel and—" My nostrils flare and my fangs extend at the smell of Calla's blood. I turn my sharp gaze in her direction to see she has sliced her wrist open with her dagger. Her blood spills onto the floor, and she kneels in front of Lex, lifting her wrist to his lips.

"Drink," she says in a firm voice.

His eyes fly open, narrowing on her as she presses her wrist against his mouth.

Kade and Gabriel stand by on either side of him in case he snaps and tries to attack Calla in this state. I don't think he will, but better safe than sorry, especially right now.

Lex opens his mouth, his lips closing around the wound. Color floods back into his face seconds later as he swallows mouthfuls of Calla's blood. She whimpers softly when he wraps his fingers around her wrist and sinks his fangs in, drinking deeper.

I crouch behind her, smoothing a hand over her hair. "Just breathe," I say softly in her ear.

"I'm fine," she insists, but I can hear the pain in her voice. Lex is too injured to attempt to make this feed pleasant for her, so despite her being willing, it'll still hurt.

"Easy, Lex," Gabriel says, watching closely with a slight frown.

Kade's eyes are locked on Lex's face. "Okay, that's enough."

He doesn't stop.

Calla's pulse spikes with panic, and both Gabriel and Kade tense, watching him closely, as if they're ready to move in an instant to pull Lex away from her.

I give him five more seconds. "Lex." My voice is low, firm. It reaches him on a level that makes him stop immediately. I don't use our sire connection often—in fact, I can count the number of times on one hand—but this moment warrants it. As much as he cares for Calla, he isn't in control—he wasn't going to stop.

His eyes open, and he pulls back, Calla's blood dripping from his fangs, down his chin. "I... sorry," he murmurs to her, wiping his mouth with the back of his hand and retracting his fangs. Shame ripples off him in dark waves, his pupils dilated and his brows tugged close together.

She shakes her head, blinking slowly. "You don't need to be. I'm okay." She stands, then immediately sways on her feet.

I straighten in a flash and catch her around the waist, guiding her to lean into me as Kade and Gabriel haul Lex off the ground.

The few vampires lingering watch us curiously. I glare at the one male who looks a little too long at Calla, probably wondering what she's doing with us. *None of your fucking business.*

Kade disappears for a minute, reappearing with a cooler filled with blood bags, which is presumably the reason they were here in the first place.

"I want to go home," Calla mumbles, her eyes no longer fully open.

"Ah, shit," Lex says, looking over at her and frowning. "I took too much."

"She'll be fine," Kade assures him, though his tone is tense. I can tell he doesn't want to be angry with Lex, but he put Calla in danger. He lost control of his bloodlust because of his injuries, and if we hadn't been here to stop him, things would've been a lot worse. "She's probably loving how nice Atlas is being to her right now."

I roll my eyes but don't bother responding. The five of us walk out of the facility, each covered in too many types of blood to count.

Calla's words play over in my head as we get in the car.

I want to go home.

So do I, my stubborn little human. So do I.

Back at the hotel, Lex flops onto the couch and turns on the television, flipping through the channels. He still looks a little worse for wear, but certainly better after drinking from Calla. He's quieter than normal, still feeling ashamed for losing control with Calla, and there's no sense in trying to reassure him she's fine. He can see it for himself.

Kade tosses him a blood bag, tearing into one himself and forgoing a glass. The two of them drink straight from the bag, tossing the empty plastic onto the coffee table once they've sucked them dry.

Lex grabs the television remote again and changes the channel from whatever cartoon garbage he'd found less than five minutes ago to a local news station.

My stomach drops when I catch the heading at the bottom of the screen.

ALLEGED SUPERNATURAL ATTACK IN VANCOUVER.

"What the fuck?" Lex snaps, sitting up in a flash, his eyes popping wide.

Kade and Gabriel move to stand on either side of me, and Calla walks around the couch and sits next to Lex, staring wide-eyed at the headline, her mouth open slightly in a silent gasp.

"...cell phone footage submitted to us anonymously. We must warn viewers that what you're about to see is very graphic." The image of the news anchor switches to a shaky video of a dark-haired female vampire attacking a man outside what looks to be a nightclub. She pushes him against the brick wall, throws her head back with her fangs fully extended, then sinks them into the man's throat.

"Fucking hell," Kade growls, gripping the back of the couch.

"Did we just get outed on national television?" Lex asks, his voice tight and his jaw sharp.

"It would appear that way," Gabriel says in a dangerously calm voice.

I stare at the television, waiting for my phone to ring.

"What happens now?" Calla asks in a small voice, glancing at each of us. Her gaze stops on me last and holds; she expects me to have an answer.

Raking my fingers through my hair, I let out a heavy sigh. "I don't have a fucking clue," I admit, the words tasting bitter on my tongue.

"This has never happened before?" she asks.

"Not like this," I tell her. "Living in the age of social media where everyone has a camera in their pocket... it's changed things for us." I turn my gaze to the guys. "Get on the phone and connect with as many of your contacts as possible. We need a game plan to handle things moving forward."

We don't give ourselves a moment to react further than we already have. Every second we don't move on this, the worse it's going to get.

Lex stands, pulling his phone out of his pocket, while Kade slips out to the terrace, his phone already against his ear.

"Do you think the hunters have something to do with this?" Calla asks, her brows pinched together.

I shake my head. "We can't know for sure either way, but it doesn't matter all that much. It's out there."

"Right," she mumbles. "Do you think the hunters will go public now? They could use this as an opportunity to recruit new members by preaching public safety and all that."

"Calla—" I start in a sharp tone before catching myself. I soften my tone and continue, "I understand this is overwhelming for you, but I can't stand here and answer your slew of questions right now."

She drops her gaze, and I immediately feel like the biggest asshole on the planet. I clench my jaw to stop myself from apologizing. I can't worry about her feelings at this very moment. I need to get a handle on the situation.

Kade pokes his head back inside, still on the phone. "Word is spreading quickly."

I pinch the bridge of my nose. "Where?"

"Down south," he answers, and I get a flash of his fangs. His pulse is erratic, though his expression is stoic—he's trying to keep up a calm and collected facade, but the only one he's likely able to fool is Calla. Even she might be able to see through it at this point.

"In the Midwest too," Lex adds, holding the phone against his ear with his shoulder as he pours a second blood bag into a glass this time. He's been a stress eater since I've known him, and it's safe to say the exposure of our kind is stress-inducing.

Son of a bitch.

"There's too much widespread exposure to cover up," Gabriel comments in a level voice, though his expression is strained with concern as he scrolls on his phone. He's always been more of a suffer in silence type, but it's safe to say he's as stressed as the rest of us.

I nod stiffly, letting out a heavy sigh when my phone starts buzzing in my pocket.

That took longer than I was expecting.

"What?" I bark into the phone.

"Atlas, this is Terrance Walker. I work for your parents."

"Sorry for your luck, Terrance," I mutter. "What do you want?"

There's a brief space of silence before the man says, "As you're aware, we have members within the government across the globe. However, there are more human than vampire government officials, most of which weren't previously aware of our existence."

I grip the phone tighter, already irritated with this man's voice. "What's your point, Walker?"

"This is a major problem—"

"You don't say," I snap, cutting him off, and Calla frowns at me from the couch. I turn away from her, pacing the length of the hotel suite.

Terrence clears his throat. "Mr. York, this... *situation* will cause mass panic if we do not get it under control very quickly."

"How do you expect us to do that?" I growl, nearly crushing the phone against my ear.

"Your father is about to go into a meeting with Da Silva."

"The Chief of Staff?" I mutter. "Why?"

"Because he has the President's ear, that's why."

"Fine. What do they want me to do?" I ask, because there must be something. There always is.

"I've arranged a meeting for you with the senators in Washington."

"To do what exactly?" I ground out.

"Now more than ever, it's important for certain people to know where they are on the food chain."

I close my eyes, the urge to throw my phone across the room prickling along the back of my neck. "I'd like to speak with my father," I finally say.

He sighs as if I'm wearing on his patience. *Touché, Terrence.* "I told you, he's—"

"Have him call me." I pull the phone away from my ear and end the call, my temples throbbing with pressure. Walking back to the couch, I drop down next to Calla and toss my phone carelessly onto the coffee table.

"I want to help but I don't know how," Calla says in a low voice.

I pause, turning to her and offering a tight smile. "You can't."

She bites the inside of her cheek for a moment before asking, "What are you going to do?"

"Apparently meet with some senators and force their loyalty. Make sure things happen how we need them to." I can't help the bitterness in my voice. Close to half of the current senators are vampires, several of which are born vampires. It's the rest—the humans—we need to deal with.

"That could solve our hunter problem," Gabriel offers with a sigh.

"And cause several more." Raking my fingers through my hair, I grimace. I need a fucking shower. "If the vampires completely take over the government, that's going to create a severe power imbalance."

Gabriel frowns. "Seems there will be one either way—whether it be vampires against hunters or vampires against unknowing and innocent humans."

"There's never a shortage of problems," I grumble.

He laughs softly. "You thrive in chaos, my friend. Lean into it."

I arch a brow at him.

"You don't want to become your parents. I get that. But this is your opportunity to take a stand, be a leader in something you believe in."

I push my tongue against the roof of my mouth, grinding my molars. I'm not sure how to respond or what to do with that. Gabriel isn't wrong. I look at Simon and Lenora York and see everything I don't ever wish to be. They'd like nothing more than for me to be a carbon copy of them—a ruthless vampire, well-respected—or feared, depending on how you look at it—by our species.

"Your expression makes me think things are about to get a hell of a lot more complicated."

I exhale a breathy laugh. "If I take a stand, Gabriel, it won't be next to my parents... it'll be against them."

A heart beats steadily against my cheek. I blink my eyes open slowly, a grin curling my lips as I realize I'm tangled up with Kade and Lex. I snuggle into Kade's warm chest, peering down to find Lex's arm snug around my waist, his cheek pressed against my back.

I close my eyes, breathing in deeply and feeling safe. Comforted. *Loved.*

And because I evidently can't just let things lie, I force myself to picture a life without them.

I'd likely go back to Washington and finish getting my degree, then visit my parents in NYC for a while... maybe look for a job there.

But what about the hunters? I'd still have a target on my back, and while the guys said I would be protected if I chose to leave them, there's no way I'd agree to take resources from them to protect themselves.

And if I went back to my life before the vampires, would I have to forget Tessa? The thought of giving up that friendship makes me frown, opening my eyes again.

There are too many questions I don't want answers to.

Thinking about Tessa, I can't help but consider my friendship with Brighton—yet another complication to my decision. If I decide to become a vampire, that is pretty much damning any relationship I could have with her.

Either way, I lose things that are important to me.

Kade shifts next to me, inhaling slowly and kissing the side of my head, lingering as if he can sense the turmoil inside me. He slides his finger under my chin, tilting my face up, and brushes his lips against mine. Warmth fills my chest as I kiss him back, closing my eyes, desperate to lose myself in something good.

"Morning," he murmurs against my lips.

"Hmm," I mumble back, dragging my tongue over his bottom lip.

He groans, kissing me for a moment longer before pulling back and splaying his fingers along my cheek. "You are beautiful, you know that?"

I lean into his touch. "With bed head and morning breath?" I tease.

"Bed head sounds like something I can get behind," Lex says in my ear, his grip around my waist tightening and his erection pressing into my back.

I roll my eyes, though he can't see it, my cheeks flushing. "You are insufferable."

He nuzzles my neck, biting me playfully, sans fangs. "And you fucking love it."

Kade grins at me as I keep my back to Lex.

Lex yawns loudly and stretches out, unwinding his arm from my waist. "I need a coffee," he announces, sliding out of bed and walking toward the double doors that lead into the common area—completely naked.

Kade chuckles softly, kissing the tip of my nose. "Never a dull moment."

"You're not wrong," I agree, admiring the view of Lex's backside.

He pulls the doors over, shooting us a wink before disappearing.

"Where are the others?" I ask.

He listens for a moment. "Atlas is on the terrace talking to his father and he does not sound happy."

I frown. "Atlas or Simon?"

"Both," he answers with a grimace.

Sighing, I say, "He deserves better than them."

Kade nods, his brows scrunched together. "I know."

Several beats of comfortable silence pass between us before I ask, "Where's Gabriel?"

"Not here." He slides his hand down to my hip, pulling me closer. "I wouldn't be surprised if he went to visit Fallon and Jase."

I reach for him, sliding my fingers into his hair, pushing the soft, dark brown curls away from his forehead. "Makes sense. They're good friends," I muse. "I'm glad he has them."

Kade leans in, grazing his nose along mine. "Hmm, and I'm glad I have you."

Our next kiss is slow, deep, and leaves me tingling with warmth in all the right places.

I rest my forehead against his, breathing deeply. "I know we have a lot to deal with, but I—"

"Calla," he murmurs, kissing me once more. "I want you right now too."

I chew my bottom lip, trying not to smile, then pull back and arch a brow at him. "How'd you know that's where I was going with that?"

The corner of his mouth kicks up. "Just a lucky guess." He lowers his voice, his eyes darkening with lust as they hold mine. "That, and I can hear your pulse quickening."

I swallow. "That could mean anything."

He cocks his head to the side, staring at me hungrily. "And how wet you are? Could that mean anything?"

I scowl, though the annoyance is half-hearted. "Maybe," I grumble.

He chuckles, tucking my hair behind my ear. "I'd very much like to fuck you now if you don't mind."

I lick my lips, a soft laugh escaping. "I'm sure I can be persuaded."

"Challenge accepted." His lips are on mine again, his hands sliding down to my ass, gripping it and pulling me flush against him.

I gasp into his mouth when his erection finds the building need between my thighs, and I lean back for just enough time to tug my T-shirt off, tossing it behind me.

"Fuck," he near-growls, his gaze dropping to my bare chest where my nipples have hardened into stiff peaks. "You are absolutely perfect."

My lips part, and I reach for him, needing him closer. "Take me," I breathe, my pulse jackhammering. "Please. I need you."

"I should take my time with you but I don't think I can right now." His voice is thick with arousal, his fingers digging into my hips before sliding into the boxer shorts I stole from Gabriel's bag last night. Kade presses his thumb against my clit before entering me with two fingers. I'm already so wet, he glides in easily as I reach for him, sealing my mouth over his and kissing him hard, putting all the emotion flooding through me into it. He makes a sound at the back of his throat and curls his fingers deep inside me, hitting a spot so sensitive, I nearly come right then. In response, I reach between us and palm the front of his sweatpants, my heart pounding hard in my chest as I stroke his erection.

He pulls his mouth away from mine, groaning. "If you keep doing that," he says in a low voice, "I'm not going to last long."

I can't help the grin that curls my lips. "We're not taking our time right now, remember?" I offer.

He holds his fingers still inside me but continues circling my clit idly with his thumb, making my breasts tingle as pleasure fills me.

"Glad we're in agreement on that," he says gruffly, picking up the pace of his thrusts again. He fingers me so hard and fast, I clench around him in minutes, panting as I come hard. I slide my fingers past the waistband of his pants and grip his solid length, pumping up and down a few times before freeing his cock. I lick my lips, staring at it as my core throbs, and he slides his fingers out of me, making me shiver.

"Roll over," he says in a surprisingly firm voice that leaves no room for questioning or hesitation.

I roll onto my stomach, resting on my elbows as my cheek hits the pillow. Kade wraps his hand around my hair, holding it tightly, and slaps my ass. I gasp and then giggle. It didn't hurt, but I wasn't expecting it.

"Tuck your knees under you."

I follow his direction and immediately feel him behind me. His free hand slides along my back and rests on my hip. Seconds later, the blunt head of his cock teases my entrance, and I suck in a breath, my pulse racing. Kade slams into me, stealing my breath, and I turn my face to whimper into the pillow as his cock thrusts into me, unrelenting.

He finds a steady rhythm, rolling his hips, slamming into me, and I grip the sheets on either side of me, hanging on for dear life as he owns my body completely.

My moans are muffled by the pillow, and Kade tugs my head back, growling softly. "I want to hear you scream."

Holy fuck.

He increases his speed, sliding his hand around my hip to play with my clit. My breathing comes in short, shallow gasps as he moves faster than I can keep up with. My pussy clenches around his cock, and I see stars as an orgasm rips through me, my nerve endings nearly exploding. I collapse against the bed, and Kade pulls me up, continuing his thrusts until he grunts, spilling his release inside me before collapsing next to me on the bed.

We catch our breaths before Kade pulls me into his arms,

smoothing his hand along my hair and kissing my temple. "That was something," he says with a soft chuckle.

"Yeah," I breathe, "you could say that."

"Are you okay?" he checks, searching my face with attentive silver eyes.

"I'm... That was amazing."

"Glad you think so too."

My heart is still beating faster than normal, but I'm able to catch my breath as I run my fingers over the tight muscles of Kade's stomach. He kisses the side of my head again and murmurs, "I love you, Calla."

I close my eyes, inhaling slowly. "I love you, too." The words leave my lips as if they're the most natural I've ever spoken. I hadn't expected to say it at that moment but I know it's true. I do love Kade—and not just Kade. I love them all.

I open my eyes to find him frozen, those silver eyes locked on my face and widening slightly. His mouth curls into a slow grin as he snags my chin, tipping my head back. "Say it again," he murmurs.

I lower my lashes, unable to hide my smile, then meet his gaze once more. "I. Love. You."

He shakes his head, leaning in until his lips brush mine in a whisper of a kiss. "You have no idea how fucking amazing it is to hear you say those words."

I lean the rest of the way in, sealing his lips with mine and kissing him deeply, showing him I mean every word with all of my heart.

Once we get cleaned up and dressed, we join the others in the common area of the hotel suite. They are sitting around the dark oak dining table, sipping blood. Lex is double-fisting a mug of coffee and a glass of blood, and I just shake my head at him, walking past toward the kitchenette as he shoots me a wink. I grab a cup of coffee, wrapping my fingers around the mug, the heat radiating through my fingers as I take a seat at the head of the table. The others are chatting about plans for the hunters and what our next steps are, while I sit in silence, sipping my coffee.

"You're awfully quiet," Lex observes.

"She's probably still recovering," Kade says with a grin in my direction.

My lips twitch briefly but my pulse ticks unevenly in my throat.

"What's going on, angel?" Gabriel says, reaching for me and resting his hand on my forearm.

I glance down at it, holding my gaze there as I lick the dryness from my lips and clear my throat. "I don't need a month."

"What do you mean?" Kade asks.

I bite the inside of my cheek as my pulse ticks faster, and lift my gaze, looking at each of them. "The ultimatum Simon and Lenora gave..." I shake my head, still having a difficult time with the reality of it. "I don't need a month to decide what I want." My eyes land on Atlas, and a muscle ticks along his jaw as he holds my gaze.

"Calla—"

"I've decided." I swallow past the lump in my throat, refusing to let emotion clog my voice. "I'll become a vampire." I sit back, moving away from Gabriel's touch. "I... I'm terrified, but more so of losing you all than learning to live as one of you. This wasn't an easy decision, but my feelings for all of you won out over my fears of this choice I'm making. Especially after seeing Lex hurt by those hunters... I need to be able to protect the four of you like you protect me. I can't constantly be side-lined because I'm a breakable human."

"That's not how we see you," Kade says in a firm voice, his eyes locked on me. Lex nods in agreement.

Atlas shakes his head. "You don't have to do this, Calla," he assures me. "We will find a way to elude my parents so you can remain human and keep your memories."

I blink at him in surprise. I'm not sure why it's the first I'm hearing this from him. Perhaps he wasn't expecting me to make this decision, or at least make it so quickly. "I can't... I don't want you going against your parents."

"But I would. I *will*—for you."

I drop my gaze for a moment before returning it to him and smiling. "You don't know how much those words mean to me, and I know you mean them, but I've made my choice. And it's not all bad. There are *some* things I'm actually curious about when it comes to being a vampire, and I know you'll all be there to show me the ropes and teach me the ins and outs." I had hoped saying the words aloud would make me feel better about them, but the fear is still rooted deep in my chest.

"I think we should discuss this further," Gabriel says in a gentle tone.

Offering him a soft smile, I shake my head. "I appreciate that you want me to be happy, and of course I hope to get to a place where I am as a vampire. That being said, there's nothing you can say now that will make me change my mind. Please respect that."

Gabriel tilts his head to the side slightly, searching my face for a moment before he nods. The others remain shockingly silent when my gaze slides to each of them, prepared for more than one objection. The lack of protest is mildly shocking and it almost makes me smile. It shows the progress we've made—we've finally reached a point where they treat me as an equal. And it makes me fall for them even more.

"Thank you." I slip away to take a shower and collect my thoughts—and there are many. I'm not sure when I woke up this morning if my decision had been made completely, but the longer I think about it, the more I know I've made the right choice. I've decided not to live without Kade, Lex, Gabriel, and Atlas—which means I've also decided to live forever.

I wasn't exaggerating when I told them I'm terrified. There are so many questions. *Everything* is basically a giant question mark, and I'm not sure what's going to happen. But the same could be said had I picked the other option. At least this way I know the guys will have my back. They'll teach me what I need to learn to survive and enjoy life as a vampire.

After my shower, I sit on the end of the bed with my phone in my hands. I've started calling my parents' number several times but I always disconnect before the line actually rings. *Maybe I should wait until after the transition to call them.* No. No, I can't do that. Despite everything we've been through since I found out about the oath, they deserve to know what's happening with their daughter. I'm worried that if I don't tell them before it happens and have to face them as a vampire to break the news, I'll regret it forever. And forever will have an entirely different meaning to me then.

My knee bounces uncontrollably as I bite the inside of my cheek. I go over in my head what feels like a million times what I'm going to say to them. Another ten minutes pass before I'm finally somewhat satisfied with the script I've come up with.

I take a deep breath, psyching myself up, and finally complete the call. With each ring, my anxiety rises higher. And when my mom answers, my stomach plummets and I forget everything I was going to say.

"Calla, honey, how are you doing?"

"Hi... Hi, Mom."

"What's the matter? What happened?"

I take a deep breath.

"Calla, talk to me." Panic creeps into her voice. "Are you okay?"

"I'm sorry," I say quickly. "I'm okay. I just—I have something to tell you and Dad." I sigh when my chin starts trembling. "I should tell you this in person but I don't think I can, and you deserve to know—"

"Calla, you can tell me anything. I'm going to love you no matter what. Whatever you're about to say does not change that. And I know I speak for your father as well. So take a deep breath and say what you need to say."

I swallow hard, squeezing my eyes shut for a few seconds before I say, "What we were talking about the other day. The ultimatum I was given by Atlas's parents. I've decided what I'm going to do."

"Okay." The mix of emotion in her voice—in that one word— makes me regret this phone call. I wish I'd had one of the guys handle this part, though it wouldn't have been fair at all, it would've been easier.

I swallow past the lump in my throat and force out, "I'm going to become a vampire." The words taste like poison on my tongue, and I immediately grit my teeth against them.

She sucks in a sharp breath, and it's a punch to my gut. "Oh, Calla..."

Tears fill my eyes in a matter of seconds. "I tried, Mom. I really did. The more I thought about it... I just knew I couldn't live with the other option."

"Are..." She sniffles. "Are you absolutely sure?"

"I'm sure. As scared as I am, I feel in my gut this is the right thing."

"It doesn't seem that way to me," she says in a gentle voice. "You sound so upset, Calla."

"Yeah, well, I don't exactly *want* to be a vampire, but the other option is not a better alternative, so this is what I've decided. I can learn to live with one but not the other."

There's a stretch of silence, and just as I'm about to ask if she's still there, her voice comes through quietly. "Okay, sweetheart."

My chest tightens at the emotion in her voice. This can't be what she wants for me. "It must be difficult to hear, Mom. I'm sorry."

She sighs. "I'm so, so sorry. I feel like this is my—"

"No," I cut in. "This is *not* your fault. You didn't even know until it was already..." My voice trails off. That's not entirely true. She knew about the oath after her first daughter died. Perhaps that would have stopped some people from trying again, but knowing her, she needed to be a mother. She deserved that. And as complicated as my relation- ship with my father has been, I don't even blame him anymore. Blame isn't going to change my reality. Nothing is at this point. This is what is happening. The more I sit with it, the more I'm coming to accept it even as I struggle with what's to come.

"Can... can you tell Dad?" I ask, feeling awful putting it on her, but I'm not sure I can repeat this a second time.

"You should talk to him," she says. "He might be able to give you a different perspective. Maybe change your mind."

I close my eyes against the burn in them. "Mom, I can't. Please..." If they start trying to convince me to change my mind, I'm not going to be able to hold it together.

"I've already lost you once," she says in a thick voice, and I can hear her struggling to keep it together.

"Mom, you're not losing me. I promise. Whatever happens, you will never lose me." The pit in my stomach grows heavier because I shouldn't make that promise, not when I don't know I'll be able to keep it.

"I never wanted this for you, sweetheart. I've been so scared every single day since you left for school and I..." Her voice cracks and she stops talking.

"I know," I tell her. "You had as much control over this as I did, so believe me, I understand. And I don't blame you—for any of it."

She sniffles again. "You've become such a strong young woman. I can't tell you how proud I am of you, Calla."

A tear rolls down my cheek, and I don't bother wiping it away. "Listen, I'm going to come to you guys," I say, "once it's safe. A lot is going on, and I'm not sure where I'm going to be. I mean, what state I'm going to be in once it happens."

"I understand, honey. Just know that I'm here for you. I meant that. I love you and I'll support you however I can. You make sure those boys take care of you."

I smile faintly. "That is one thing you never have to doubt. I should go, I love you both and I'll talk to you soon."

"We love you, too, Calla. Forever."

The line clicks off, and I quickly wipe the tears from my cheeks, sniffling and clearing my throat as I stand, leaving my phone on the end of the bed as I walk out of the bedroom.

Lex is grinning as if he's done something bad, and I narrow my eyes at him. "What's going on?"

Kade glances sideways at him and rolls his eyes, chuckling softly.

Atlas remains silent, but Gabriel offers me a warm smile. "We're going to celebrate today."

I arch a brow. "Celebrate what, exactly?"

"You," Atlas says, snaring my gaze. "We're celebrating you, Calla."

Heat rushes to my cheeks, and I blink quickly. "My last day as a human?" I offer.

"You've made your decision," Gabriel says, "but that doesn't mean it needs to happen today or tomorrow or even next week. We can wait until you're ready."

"Or at least until our deadline, right?" I ask somewhat sarcastically.

He frowns slightly, then nods.

"I don't want to wait. I think it'll just make it harder. This is my decision, and I need to start living my life this way."

Lex slaps his knees and stands. "Well, all right then. Let's celebrate your last day as a human."

"Okay," I say, dragging out the word. "How exactly are we going to do that?"

TEN

ATLAS

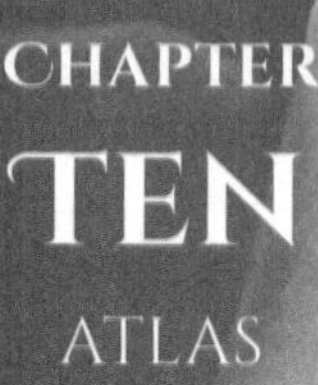

If I hadn't already killed Lex once, I'd be damn near tempted to do it now.

Apparently, his grand idea of celebrating Calla's last day as a human is to attend every fucking tourist attraction in New York City.

Because certainly roaming around a city filled with people who have likely either seen the news about vampires or are keen to hunt us for sport—or both—is a smart move.

I should be pissed. Hell, I shouldn't have allowed it, but Calla... She looked so happy. I haven't seen her laugh and smile that much in, well, ever. At least not in the time she's been with us.

She deserved absolutely everything she wanted today—and I wanted her to have it.

Luckily, we didn't run into any issues—no hunters or television crews. I'll have to get my ass to Washington sooner than later to help clean up the situation—not for my parents but the other vampires in my life that I genuinely care for. Their lives are in danger too, and I won't stand for it.

"For someone who grew up here, you've seen very little of your own city," Lex comments mildly as we make the short walk back to the hotel from the subway—another human experience we had to have instead of taking our own vehicle. Granted, driving in the city is a major headache, so I didn't mind the underground excursion.

Calla shrugs, adjusting her *I* ♥ *NY* ball cap Kade bought her at one of the many gift shops we stopped in today. "I never thought to be a tourist in my own city." She jumps onto Kade's back, wrapping her arms around his neck, and he laughs, grabbing the backs of her knees, holding her steady as we keep walking.

"Where else do you want to go?" Lex asks.

Calla purses her lips in thought. "Italy, for sure. Hmm... Scotland and Ireland. Oh, I want to visit Tessa in Oregon at some point this summer. I've also never been to New Orleans, so that's on my list as well." She slides off Kade's back as we round the corner toward the hotel. "But honestly, right now? I want to go back to Washington."

I slow my stride and walk next to her. "We'll leave soon."

She nods silently, pressing her lips together as if she wants to say more, but I don't push her.

We walk through the lobby of the hotel, and Calla leans against Gabriel's side as the elevator ascends to our floor. When we get back to the room, Lex and Kade drop the gift shop bags onto the coffee table and collapse on the couch. Gabriel follows Calla to the kitchenette and speaks softly to her while she fills the kettle with water and turns it on.

"What happens now?" Calla asks, looking my way as she drops a tea bag into a mug.

"We'll start when you're ready," Gabriel assures her, his hand resting on the small of her back.

She turns her attention to him. "I... Okay."

The five of us sit around the collection of shopping bags. Calla pulls her hat off, tossing it on top of the pile, and sips her tea.

"Do you have any questions?" Kade asks, watching her so closely I'm not sure anything could break his focus.

Calla leans back against the couch, tapping her finger along the rim of her mug as she stares into it. "How long will it take to, um, you know."

Kade's eyes flick to me, and I nod. "Once you have vampire venom in your veins, you'll need to drink vampire blood."

"And then I have to die," she says in a low voice and lifts her head to look at me, "right?"

"That's right."

She nods slowly, her pulse kicking up. "Will it hurt?" She cringes the moment the words leave her lips, her brows knitting.

"I promise you it won't," I tell her.

"Unless you're already dying painfully when it happens," Lex chimes in, shooting Calla a wink. "Do not recommend."

Her lips twitch briefly, but the smile doesn't reach her eyes. "I don't want to know how you'll do it, but what happens after that?"

"When you wake, you'll need to feed on human blood," Gabriel answers her. "We'll take care of that."

"I'm not going to try to kill everyone, am I?"

Kade laughs, and I shoot him a look.

Calla's eyes widen, and she stands, setting her mug on the edge of the coffee table before walking around the couch. "I don't want to hurt anyone." Her gaze flits around the room, never stopping anywhere for long. "Please, I... Don't let me."

I move in front of her, blocking her from pacing. She stops abruptly and steps back, pressing her lips together as her pulse races. She's panicking, and I don't blame her—but I can make it easier on her.

"Calla," I say in a smooth voice, closing the distance between us again.

The fear in her eyes slams into me like a train as her chest rises and falls quickly. She swallows. "Atlas, I—"

"I know," I tell her. "It's okay."

"I'm scared." The words leave her lips in a whisper.

"Let me help you," I offer softly, opening my arms to her. When she steps in, I draw her against my chest, resting my chin on top of her head. Her heart pounds in her chest and her breaths come in quick, shallow pants. I run one hand up and down her back, the other cradling her neck. She buries her face in my chest, gripping my shirt in her fists, her hands shaking.

The others sit silently watching us, their expressions serious and focused, as I'm sure mine appears as well.

"Take a deep breath for me," I murmur, focusing glamour into my instruction as I continue stroking her back.

Her chest rises slowly, then falls when she exhales shakily.

"Good girl. Again. Feel your breath start to even out and your nerves start to calm. Everything is going to be fine. You're okay. We've got you." Once her breathing evens out, I pull back just enough to meet her gaze. "Okay?"

Her eyes flick between mine, and she hesitates before nodding. "You... glamoured me." She blinks a few times as if it's just hitting her now.

I offer a faint smile, tipping her chin up with my finger to look into her eyes. "You can yell at me later."

"I won't," she says in a low voice, "not for that."

I chuckle. "I'm sure you'll find something."

"I'm sure you'll do something that warrants it," she throws back.

"There's our girl," Lex chimes in from across the room.

I keep my eyes on Calla, nodding.

"Let's just get this over with, please," she says, wrapping her fingers around my wrist and pulling my hand away from her face. She pulls her hair over one shoulder, baring her neck to me.

"So you'd like me to do it?"

She freezes, her brows inching closer together. "I... Aren't you?"

I drag my tongue over my bottom lip, my gums already throbbing with the urge to let my fangs extend and sink into her skin. "If there are no objections." I look at the others, and they all nod in response. All the reasons I gave Calla for why I should be the one to turn her are things they already know. I didn't expect any of them to be against it but figured it was best to ask one last time. My attention returns to Calla. "Is this what you want?"

She blows out a breath, swallowing hard before she nods. "Yes, I want you to do it."

I grip her chin once more, forcing her to hold my gaze as my fangs break through my gums. "This is your last chance to change your mind, Calla."

She shakes her head in my grasp despite the race of her pulse, her eyes stuck on my fangs. "I've made my choice, Atlas."

"All right," I finally say, dropping my hand to my side before I turn her around, pulling her back against my chest. I move her hair away from her neck, my fingers grazing her warm, soft skin. The monster in me beats against its cage, growling to be set free, to claim her with my venom and blood, but I keep it at bay.

Calla shivers against me, drawing in a slow breath, as the others stand and walk closer to us. I may be the one turning her, but she belongs to all of us—just as we all belong to her.

Kade laces his fingers through hers as I press my lips to her neck, brushing my lips across her skin softly before sinking my fangs into her. Her breath catches, and she whimpers as I close my eyes, drinking deeply. Her blood coats my tongue, exploding on my tastebuds. *Fuck.* I'll never get enough of her.

I know the moment my venom reaches her bloodstream, because she moans softly, leaning into me fully. I hold her, my heart beating faster as I swallow mouthfuls of her blood.

A few moments later, it's time for her to drink from me. I hold my wrist out, and Lex sinks his fangs in, opening my veins for her. I bring my wrist to her lips.

"Drink, angel," Gabriel says in a calming voice.

Her lips close around Lex's bite, her tongue sweeping across my skin as my blood pours into her mouth. She makes a faint noise of protest, but I hold my wrist firm against her lips. She wraps her fingers around my arm, and just when I think she's going to attempt to pull it away, she grips it harder and drinks deeply.

I seal the marks on her neck and peer down at her, watching her feed from me. I smooth my hand along her hair, reveling in the sensation of having blood pulled from my veins by her. It's a sight I wish to burn into my memory.

The moment she stops drinking to catch her breath, the wound seals itself, and she breathes a little sigh of something I'd like to mistake as annoyance. I enjoy Calla drinking from me.

Her pulse beats steadily as I hold her, pressing a soft kiss to the side of her head. "Okay?" I murmur.

"Yes," she says in a voice so filled with strength, I know I'll burn the entire fucking world to the ground to make sure she's okay.

And then I snap Calla's neck.

"She's been out a while," Kade says, peering at her still form on the couch. Concern is etched into his features. We're all on edge, he's just not trying to hide it.

"Give her time," Gabriel says from the chair he pushed next to the couch and has been sitting in for over an hour.

My gaze is locked on her face, watching and waiting for a muscle twitch. I haven't turned a vampire since Lex; I know I did it right, but my pulse is still pounding as if I could've done something wrong.

I can't—we *can't lose her.*

Lex drops his arm around Kade's shoulders. "Come on. Let's go find someone for our girl to eat when she wakes."

He stares at Calla several seconds longer before Lex physically drags him away.

"We'll be back," he tosses over his shoulder as they leave the hotel suite.

I rake my fingers through my hair, walking around the couch to sit in the other chair, and let out a heavy sigh.

"Talk to me," Gabriel says, keeping his eyes on Calla, though I know his words are meant for me.

"She didn't want this, Gabe," I say in a low voice, shaking my head.

"Maybe not at the start," he agrees, "but she wouldn't have gone through with it had that still been the case. She's too damn stubborn to back down from a fight—even one as potentially fatal as going up against your parents."

I exhale a laugh, though there's nothing funny about that. Gabriel is right. Calla is far too strong-willed to give up even in the face of fear. She chose this—she chose *us*. And I will do everything in my power to ensure not a day goes by where she regrets her decision.

Oh, hell. I fucking love her.

It's not something I've experienced for a very long time outside the three other vampires I've spent decades with, but this... annoyingly breathless feeling in my chest is unmistakable.

Gabriel turns to look at me and chuckles softly. Evidently, I'm not doing a very good job at masking my emotions.

I groan, letting my head fall against the back of the chair.

"We all do, Atlas, and I suspect it's very much reciprocated."

I nod, because I'm not sure what else there is to say.

"Are you going to tell Simon and Lenora she's in transition?"

My hackles raise just thinking about it. They'll want to see it for themselves, and Calla is going to be in no position to deal with them as soon as she wakes.

I opt for sending a brief message to their secretary, letting them know what's going on and that we'll be in touch. Not ten minutes later, I receive a curt response, surprisingly right from my father.

Your mother and I look forward to welcoming Miss Montgomery to the family personally in due course.

I'm not sure if I was looking for validation, and if even a small part of me was, I should know better. I'll never do anything good enough in their eyes, and I'm finally reaching a point where I'm beyond trying.

I grip the phone tighter in my hand. If I have anything to say about it, Calla will never have to endure their presence again.

After seeing Calla with her parents, it's painfully clear what I've missed with my own. The only relationship I have with Simon and Lenora feels businesslike. Transactional. I can't recall a time I felt differently, when Lenora and Simon cared for me as their child as opposed to a powerful vampire that makes them look good or bad depending on my actions.

That's not family.

And despite my relationship with my parents, I *do* have a family—Gabriel, Kade, Lex, and Calla.

Thump... thump... thump.

I'm off the chair and leaning over the couch in less than a second. "Calla," I say softly, brushing my knuckles along her cheek.

Thump thump... thump thump... thump thump.

The door to the suite opens, and Kade and Lex walk through with a girl who can't be much older than Calla. Her expression is blank, and she's entirely too calm for the situation she's been brought into; they've glamoured her.

Thump thump... thump thump... thump thump.

My gaze drops back to Calla as the others join us around the couch. I shove the bags off the coffee table and pull it closer, perching on the edge as I take Calla's hand in both of mine.

A muscle feathers along her jaw and her brows scrunch closer as her nostrils flare. She inhales sharply, and her newly silver eyes fly wide open.

CHAPTER

ELEVEN

CALLA

My throat is on fire.

It's a white-hot pain I've never felt before. My gums throb and my temples ache with an oncoming migraine; my body knows what it needs to douse the flames.

White noise fills my ears. Slowly—so fucking slowly—sounds start to trickle in. Too many beating hearts to count. Televisions in rooms nowhere near me. Unfamiliar voices. Bottles clinking together in the lobby bar.

Someone is sitting next to me. I open my mouth, at least I think I do, but fire licks up my throat, and I can't speak.

"Calla." Atlas's voice is strong and clear, dissolving the fog trapping me in this dreadful in-between state. His knuckles brush along my cheek, and my eyes shoot open.

Too much comes into focus at once, and I squint at the overwhelming amount of light.

"Give it a minute." Gabriel's voice is smooth, calming. "Blink a bit and allow your eyes to adjust." I follow his instruction and find that it helps.

"How do you feel?" Kade asks, standing next to Lex at the back of the couch.

I peer up at him and reach for my throat, wrapping my fingers around it as if I can squeeze the burning sensation out.

697

"That's normal," Lex says. "It will lessen once you feed, but it never fully goes away. You'll learn to ignore it most of the time."

Finally my gaze shifts to Atlas—my sire. He's sitting at the end of the couch, watching me closely. "I..." My voice cracks, and I try to swallow. "I have to feed now?"

He nods, shifting closer. "You don't need to be afraid."

"I'm not," I say automatically. It's a fucking lie and a blatant one at that. I'm terrified.

You made this choice, I remind myself. *You can handle this.*

I start to get up, and the guys all move with me, staying close but giving me room to breathe.

When my eyes land on the pretty brunette sitting across the room, the throbbing in my gums becomes overwhelming. Pain radiates through my temples into the back of my head.

"She was drinking a strawberry daiquiri when we found her, so she might even taste a little fruity," Kade says with a smirk.

I lick my lips, my heart pounding in my chest. "Who is she?" I ask without taking my eyes off her.

"It doesn't matter," Lex says mildly.

I walk toward her, the guys following a few strides behind me. The girl watches me approach, and where I expect to see fear in her eyes, I'm surprised when she smiles at me.

"She's glamoured," I say to no one in particular.

"Yes," Gabriel answers. "It's easier this way."

The girl—who has to be close to me in age—stands when I get a few feet from her. She pulls her long, wavy hair over one shoulder and turns her head to the side, baring her neck to me.

My heart beats in my throat as I step in close enough to feel the heat radiating from her. Her pulse is steady, even. I wrap my hands around her shoulders, needing something to hold onto. My eyes land on her neck, to the vein protruding ever so slightly with each beat of her heart.

"Is someone going to tell me how to do this?" Desperation creeps into my tone as I grip the girl's shoulders tighter.

"You're doing just fine," Atlas says.

"Just lean in and bite," Lex says.

I fight the urge to growl at him, because that *really* isn't helpful advice. I have no fucking clue what I'm doing. I close my eyes and inhale slowly. The girl's scent fills my nose, and I gasp softly. *She smells good.* I lean in, and my pulse skyrockets when a sharp flash of pain fills my mouth. It's gone as quick as it came, but left in its wake are new, razor-sharp teeth. *Fangs.*

"I'm sorry," I whisper to the girl. No sooner are the words out of my mouth does the fire in my throat burn hotter than ever. A snarl passes my lips and a new sensation fills me. In the space of a heartbeat, I grip the girl's chin and sink my fangs into her neck.

My entire body explodes with sensations completely new to me. This is unlike any time I've ever tasted the guys' blood. This... this is euphoric. This is *everything*. The hot, coppery liquid coats my tongue, filling my mouth as I drink deeply, swallowing mouthful after mouthful, feeling more incredible with each one. The girl leans into me but remains silent. Warmth floods through me, and the fire in my throat finally fades almost completely. The ache in my temples is gone, and I feel stronger than I ever have.

"Calla." Gabriel's voice interrupts my haze of pleasure. "Listen to her heartbeat. You need to stop or you risk hurting her."

His words register, but part of me doesn't care. The part that is starved and needs *more*.

I sink my teeth in deeper, and the girl makes a soft noise, leaning more against me as I continue drinking.

"You can choose to let her live," Gabriel says.

"Oh, chill out, Gabe," Lex chimes in. "Take what you need, Calla."

I swallow more as a bit rolls down my chin. I pick up on the sound of the girl's heartbeat. It's slowing way down, and I'm holding her upright at this point. I should stop. *I don't want to stop.*

No. I don't want to kill her.

I growl deep in my throat, struggling with the powerful pull to keep feeding, to drain her. I force my head back, pulling my fangs out of her neck, and shove her toward Gabriel before backing away, breathing heavily, pressing my fist against my mouth.

Gabriel disappears into the bedroom with the limp human in his arms, and I shake my head, her blood dripping from my lips and down my chin.

"I... Is she?"

Kade glances over his shoulder, then turns back to me. "She's alive."

Relief floods through me, and I blink back tears. I don't know what I would have done if I'd killed her.

"Take a deep breath," Atlas says, walking closer.

"I almost—"

"But you didn't," he interjects. "And quite frankly, most vampires do kill their first feed, so you're already ahead."

"Yeah, way to make the rest of us look bad," Lex says with a grin. "Day one, and you're a more skilled vampire than I am."

I nod slowly, my heart still racing as I lift my hand to my mouth and wipe the blood from my lips. "I, um… need a minute." Without waiting for a response, I hurry out of the common area, slipping into the bathroom and sliding the fogged glass door over. I cringe when I leave streaks of blood and quickly turn the sink on, scrubbing my hands. The water turns pink, and I keep scrubbing, using several pumps of soap in an attempt to cover the metallic scent that seems to be burned into my nostrils.

Don't look, don't look, don't look.

Chanting the words over and over only works for about five seconds before my gaze flicks up to my reflection in the massive mirror over the vanity.

I pull in a shuddering breath, my eyes—my *silver* eyes—widening. I blink a few times as if that'll make them return to the brown I'm used to. Nope. They are definitely silver now. And holy shit, feeling my fangs break through my gums and *seeing* them are two wholly different things. It doesn't help that my lips and chin are still covered in that girl's blood.

The bathroom door slides open, and somehow I know without looking that it's Gabriel who came to check on me. I can't pull my gaze away from the mirror, from the fangs poking down from my gums.

"You'll get used to them."

"Will I?" I prod gingerly at them, pulling my hand back and frowning at the bead of blood on the pad of my finger. Oops.

Gabriel walks closer, standing at my back, and smiles softly at me in the mirror. "I've never been more confident in you, angel."

I try to smile, but the action is painfully forced. Instead of trying to fake it, I grab a washcloth from under the vanity and soak it with hot water, cleaning the blood from my face.

"How are you doing?"

I set the cloth down and turn around to face him. "I'm alive. Well, sort of, I guess, right?"

He offers me a thoughtful look. "You're as alive as the rest of us."

I nod. "Everything is heightened. I… I can *hear* the electricity racing through the wires into the lightbulbs in here."

Gabriel smiles. "You'll adjust to that, and once you do, you'll be able to focus on what you want and ignore the things you don't."

My brows lift. "How?"

"Staying fed helps," he offers. "Besides that, it's just something you'll get better at with time. In fact, you'll likely come to enjoy the heightened senses."

A spark of excitement flares in my chest, making my breasts tingle, and my eyes widen. I was not expecting *that* response.

He runs his hand up and down my back soothingly. "Do you regret it?" he asks in a low voice.

His question makes me pause. It's not one I'm sure I can answer after being a vampire for approximately ten seconds, but there's a sliver of hope in my chest, a bit of pleasant warmth that tells me I've made the right decision.

"No," I finally say, "I don't regret it."

Gabriel's heart beats a little faster and *holy shit*, I can hear his heartbeat. He chuckles softly. "Pretty cool, isn't it?"

"Yeah, actually," I admit, frowning a little when my tongue inadvertently grazes one of my fangs. "Why won't they go away?"

Gabriel slides his finger under my chin, tipping my head back slightly. "Open." I follow his direction, and he peers into my mouth before letting me go. "You're probably still hungry," he finally says.

I wrinkle my nose. "I don't want more blood."

He chuckles. "You may not want to drink it, but it's what your body craves and needs to survive now."

Exhaling a sigh, I mumble, "Can I have some people food?"

"You can have whatever you wish, Calla," he tells me, resting his hand against the small of my back and guiding me out of the bathroom.

We walk into the common area, and I slide into one of the chairs at the dining table, drumming my fingers against the wood top. "Where's the girl?" I ask no one in particular.

Lex takes the chair across from me and says, "Gabriel healed her all up and glamoured her to forget tonight. She's currently asleep back in her suite and will wake tomorrow believing that she had a little too much to drink tonight and that's it."

Ah, glamour. Something else I'm going to have to figure out. Nope. Can't think about that right now. One thing at a time. I survived the transition and didn't kill my first feed—maybe I should be celebrating right now.

I lean back in my chair, glancing over to the couch where Kade and Atlas are sitting, watching me. "I can hear, like, everything."

"We're surrounded by people," Kade says. "Once we're home, it won't be this overwhelming."

I press my lips together, nodding. Thank god, because this noise is irritating as hell. Something tells me I could tune into individual conversations if I focused, but right now, it's a bunch of muffled noises, as if I'm stuck in the middle of a crowd.

"Do you have any questions?" Atlas says, resting his arm along the back of the couch.

"Can we order room service?"

Kade laughs deeply. "You mean—"

"Food," I cut him off. "Preferably something with grease. Fries, onion rings, mozzarella sticks."

"I could fuck with some onion rings," Lex says, getting up and walking toward the bedroom. "I'll call down to the kitchen."

"Get me a burger," Kade hollers to him.

"Oh, me too," I say, then look at Gabriel and Atlas. "What about you guys?"

Atlas shakes his head while Gabriel purses his lips, then goes after Lex.

An hour later, our suite is filled with greasy goodness, and the five of us sit around the dining table filled with food. My stomach grumbles at the savory scents wafting through the air, and I fill my plate with a little bit of everything and my burger.

I shove a handful of fries into my mouth and chew for a few seconds before stopping. They taste... weird. I swallow what's in my mouth and try biting into an onion ring. Same thing. I drop it into my plate and go for a mozzarella stick, because those never let me down. Even dipping it in marinara sauce doesn't help.

I sit back and shake my head, shocked when my fangs slide back into my gums. "Why does everything taste weird?"

"Give it some time," Kade offers. "Things will taste different now, especially while your taste buds adjust. You'll notice it less and less with each meal."

"So my taste is different? Will it go back to normal?"

Gabriel nods. "Yes, it's different, and for the most part, you'll enjoy human food less than blood, but it won't always taste as strange as it does right now."

"Okay," I grumble, picking up my burger. It looks juicy and delicious, but if it's just going to disappoint me, I don't even want to bother biting into it.

"Hang on," Lex says, getting up and walking to the kitchenette. He opens the fridge and comes back with a blood bag and a glass, tearing the bag open and pouring the blood into the glass. He slides it across the table to me and winks. "This will satisfy you far more than any of the food on the table."

My fangs pop out again, and I can't help the shiver that zips through me. They have a mind of their own it seems. I reach for the glass and take a drink. I quickly down half the contents, and what I do next shocks everyone.

Kade recovers first and grins at me. "Did you just—"

"It's like ketchup," I interject in a defensive tone, picking up a blood-covered fry and tossing it into my mouth. It actually tastes better this way, and I'm not sure how I should feel about that, but it doesn't matter. If this allows me to eat normal food and enjoy it, I'm going to keep dipping things in blood.

"Ketchup," Kade echoes, shaking his head with an amused expression.

I flip him off and grab another fry. As weird as this is—and it is really fucking weird—part of it feels... normal.

After dinner, we wander over to the couch. I tip my head back against the cushion, sighing heavily. I've never been so simultaneously wide awake and exhausted, horny and anxious before. I can see and hear things I couldn't before, and the sensory overload is making my skin tingle.

Kade squeezes my thigh, and I turn my head to look at him. "How are you doing?" he asks, brushing his thumb back and forth.

I shrug, not sure how to put into words what I'm experiencing. He's gone through it, he understands what's going on inside me, so I don't have to tell him.

"You'll need some time to adjust," he says. "The emotions and sensations that are overpowering now will become more manageable each day, and you'll find yourself starting to feel more, well, you again."

"I am very much looking forward to that."

"I get that," he says. "What else are you looking forward to? Aren't you a little excited to play with your new abilities?"

I press my lips together, mulling over his words. As much as I've been stuck in fear mode, worried about hurting innocent people because I can't control my newfound lust for blood, I haven't really given myself an opportunity to be excited about the prospects this life offers me. "Yeah, I guess I am." The super speed and strength *are* rather appealing, especially when I'm training with Atlas.

Kade grins. "Don't worry. I see that look in your eyes. We're not going to let you hurt anyone, so you can stop freaking out over that, okay? We've got you."

I do find some relief in his words. I trust them. Nodding, I close my eyes, listening to the sounds of the guys' hearts. Is it freaky that I can hear them so clearly? A little, but it's also rather comforting.

"Come on," Kade says, patting my leg.

I groan. "Where?" I am most definitely not in the headspace to go out in public.

Lex chuckles from across the room, and I glance over to find him scrolling on his phone. Atlas and Gabriel slipped out to the terrace, and I'm too scared to try and hear what they could be talking about.

Kade stands from the couch and offers me his hand. I sigh before taking it, letting him pull me up. "What are we doing?" I ask as we walk toward the bedroom.

He squeezes my hand. "I'm going to make you feel better."

Warmth fills my cheeks and chest—and much lower. I press my lips together, my pulse ticking faster as my breasts tingle, thinking about having sex with Kade at vamp speed.

He chuckles. "Not that." We walk through the bedroom to the en suite, and Kade lets go of my hand, going over to the massive clawfoot tub and turning the faucet on. As water fills the tub, steam fogs the room and the mirror above the vanity. I slowly start undressing as Kade adds Epsom salts, bubble bath, and lavender essential oil to the tub.

He turns back to me when I'm down to my bra and panties. In the blink of an eye, he moves in front of me. "I understand if you'd like some time to yourself."

My eyes widen, and I shake my head. "Please don't leave me." The words are out of my mouth before I've had a chance to register them.

Kade cups my cheeks in his hands. "Hey," he murmurs, "you're okay. I'm not going anywhere."

"Sorry, I just—"

"You never need to apologize to me, okay?" His eyes search mine. "I've got you." He leans in and kisses me softly, pulling away before I have a chance to reciprocate.

Once the tub is full and nearly overflowing with bubbles, Kade turns the water off. I walk over, and Kade slides his fingers up my arms, then under the straps of my bra, pulling them off my shoulders before reaching around and unclasping the back. I push my panties down, shimmying my hips until they slip off onto the floor, and I kick them aside with my bra. I reach for the button on Kade's pants as he tugs his shirt off, and then we're both naked.

Kade steps into the tub first, holding his hand out to me. I take it, following him in and under the water, and he draws me back against his chest. My body fills with warmth, in part because of the water temperature, but mostly because of Kade's cock pressed against me, making my core tighten with desire.

"This is nice," I say with a soft sigh, closing my eyes and resting my head against his chest. The water is loosening the tightness in my muscles and the lavender oil is easing the tension in my temples.

Kade dips his head and kisses my shoulder. "You did beautifully today."

I bite the inside of my cheek. "I'm just glad I didn't kill that girl."

"We wouldn't have judged you if you had," he comments.

"I know but I would have judged myself. I don't want this change to mean *I've* changed. I need to still be me."

"And you are," he assures me, his lips trailing from my shoulder to my neck as he draws my hair away from it. "Your will is much too strong to be wiped away by vampirism."

My chest tightens, and I'm taken aback by the sting of tears in my eyes. "I... um, thank you for saying that."

His arm circles my waist, and he holds me against him. "Of course. It's only the truth." He kisses my neck. "And you need to know that we're all here for you every step of the way. You're part of us —forevermore."

TWELVE

ATLAS

"I don't understand why we're doing this right now," Calla grumbles around a yawn, crossing her arms over her chest. To her credit, she at least showed up in proper clothing—a matching emerald sports bra and leggings—and her hair is swept off her neck in a messy bun atop her head. She looks stunning despite the look of annoyance on her face. Hell, even her scowl is nice to look at. Perhaps that's because I enjoy testing her so much; she responds beautifully—it's thoroughly entertaining.

"Because we'll be leaving shortly, and I need to make sure you're prepared for what comes next," I tell her, walking closer.

The hotel fitness room is empty at this time of morning—no glamour required, though that would have been an interesting test for our girl. One thing at a time.

Her arms drop to her sides, and she frowns. "We have to deal with the hunters." Her pulse jumps. "And I have to face my best friend who is likely going to hate me now."

The sadness in her eyes makes me want to comfort her, but that's not something I can do when it comes to this. Odds are, she's right. Brighton lost her mom, putting her in a very vulnerable state, which made it all too easy for her prick of a father to turn her into what he always wanted her to be—a vampire hunter. Which doesn't bode well for the brand-new vampire in front of me.

"Calla, I—"

"Never mind." She shakes her head, and it's just as well. I don't know what I was going to say at that moment anyway. "Let's just do whatever it is to reassure you I won't be killed the second we run into a hunter."

I nod, moving to stand an arm's reach away. "You have a solid foundation, which is good. Now you have heightened speed and strength. It'll work to your benefit once you learn to use it." My gaze lowers to her thigh; she's not wearing the dagger I gave her.

She follows my gaze. "It felt weird to keep wearing it, considering..." Calla shrugs. "Plus it'd be pretty embarrassing during a fight with a hunter to get stabbed with my own dagger, so I figured I'd eliminate the opportunity."

My lips twitch, though the thought of Calla getting hurt, especially at the hands of a hunter, makes me want to lock her up to *eliminate the opportunity*, as she put it.

"You're looking at me like you want to strangle and fuck me at the same time, and I'm really not sure what to do with that right now."

I close the remaining distance between us, snagging her chin and looking into her eyes. "Right now, I want you to focus on why we're here."

Her eyes narrow slightly and defiance flickers in their silver depths. "Liar."

I cock my head, watching her. "Try that again?"

"Have you already forgotten that I can hear your heartbeat just as you can hear mine?" Her lashes lower as she glances down. "And I don't need vampire sight to see how hard you are."

I can't help but chuckle at that, because she's not wrong. Interesting. We've leveled the playing field—this could be fun.

She steps back out of my grasp. "Let's get this over with. I'm starving and I don't even want to think about what that means now."

"After last night, I figured you'd be ready to swap milk for blood in your Cheerios."

She glares at me. "Oh, he makes jokes now. Super."

Instead of responding, I advance without warning with the intention of slamming her onto the mats beneath us. Considering she can nearly match my strength now, I don't have to hold back in training her.

She darts away at the last second, and I whip around to find her across the room, bent over with her hands on her knees. "Holy shit, my head is spinning," she says breathlessly.

"You're much faster now," I offer mildly.

She straightens and shoots me a look. "You don't say."

I shrug. "You'll get used to it. In comparison to the other things you've already tackled, it'll be easy."

Her brows lift. "I'm going to hold you to that."

"Be my guest." I move again, this time going past her to attack from behind, but she whirls around, throwing her fist out. It connects with my chest, knocking me back a step, and despite the surprising flare of discomfort it brings, I can't help but be proud.

Calla grins triumphantly, and I use that split-second distraction to grab her shoulders and throw her down onto the mats, hovering above her. Her grin quickly turns into a scowl. "Fuck," she mutters.

"Good effort," I say, leaning down, "but don't let yourself get distracted next time."

She rolls her eyes and manages to flip us over so she's above me. I make no effort to move because this position really doesn't bother me. "Are you satisfied that I'll be able to defend myself against a hunter?" she asks, tilting her head to the side as she stares down at me.

"What would satisfy me, Calla, is if you never had to be in that situation."

She opens her mouth to respond, then pauses. "Well, that's not the reality we live in, because I'm not going to sit back and watch the rest of you fight. Definitely not now. This is my battle as much as it's any of yours."

Because of me. The words attempt to claw their way free, but I lock my jaw, refusing to speak them. There's a good chance the possibility of Calla becoming a vampire would have come up at some point regardless of my parents, but it happening so soon, that's on me. It's not the reason I wanted to be the one to do it—at least not completely —but it means I feel a strong responsibility for her.

"You're being too quiet," Calla says, shifting on either side of my legs, her knees pressing into my thighs.

My eyes narrow on her mouth. "And you're talking too much." I lean up and steal her lips, grabbing her hips and grinding her against my cock.

"Atlas," she gasps into my mouth, her heart racing, and I kiss her harder, digging my fingers into her hips through her leggings. She pulls her lips from mine. "I... can feel you."

I chuckle. "That's the idea."

She pulls back enough to look at me, shaking her head and pressing her hands flat against my chest. "Not *that*. I mean, you. Your desire for me, your fear of what's coming, your ridiculous need to take on everything alone because you don't want to burden the people you care about."

My muscles tense, and I stare at her in disbelief. I've heard of this happening before with the sire connections, but have never experienced it firsthand. But the more I let it sink in, I realize that I'm feeling everything from her as well. I've always been in tune with Calla, but this is on a deeper level. It's exactly as she said. I can sense her desires and fears and needs.

"I'm going to need you to say something," she says, panic slipping into her tone.

"We're connected."

"Yeah, no shit, but—Wait." Her eyes widen. "You mean because you turned me? Is this some freaky sire thing?"

I offer a tight, unamused smile. "It would seem that way."

She drops onto the mat next to me, groaning at the ceiling. "You've got to be kidding me," she grumbles.

I don't bother getting up. "This isn't exactly ideal for me either," I shoot back, unease prickling along my spine. Having Calla in tune with my emotions is not something I considered when deciding to turn her, which is my bad. It's also very fucking inconvenient. Just because things have evolved with us doesn't mean I want her to be able to sense what's going on inside me at all times. And I can tell by the pissed off expression on her face the feeling is mutual.

She sits up and crosses her legs, facing me. "Can we, like, turn it off?"

I turn my head to look at her. "That would be a no."

"Fuck me," she mutters.

"I know you'd like me to, but we have other things we need to do."

"Shut up," she barks, getting up off the floor, and paces for a few moments. "Maybe Tessa can do a spell to block it or something."

I clench my jaw at that because as much as I don't enjoy every aspect of this connection, the thought of using magic to alter it feels inherently wrong. "We're not doing that."

She scowls. "Then what do you suggest we do?"

I rake my fingers through my hair, standing from the mats. "I don't know at this very moment. Perhaps we can work together and learn to block each other out when necessary."

"So all the time?" she shoots back dryly.

I chuckle humorlessly. "And you were worried you'd lose yourself when becoming a vampire. I can say with the utmost confidence that you're still the same pain in my ass you've always been."

Calla flips me off with both hands. "I'm going back to the room." She heads for the door, but I move faster, crossing the room in a second to block her exit. "Atlas," she warns.

"Hang on a minute," I say.

She lets out an exasperated sigh. "What is it?"

"I don't want you to eat anyone you may encounter between here and the room. Should I go with you?" I'd rather run on the treadmill for a while, but this is more important.

Calla scowls. "No. I think I can make it on my own."

I search her eyes as she holds my gaze. "You won't bite anyone on your way back upstairs. Do you understand?"

"Yes, I understand." Her voice is level and honest.

I nod and step aside to let her leave. "I'll be up soon."

"Okay." She opens the door, then freezes and turns back to me, letting the door close. "Hang the fuck on. Did you just glamour me?" Before I can answer, she continues, "You totally did."

She's damn right I did. I'm not taking any chances. With everything going on in the news and the increased number of hunters, we can't be too careful.

"Just when I thought the playing field was even," she grumbles under her breath.

I hold back an amused grin. "If it makes you feel better, the others won't be able to anymore."

"Just you. Let me guess, perks of siring me? Or is it because you're extra special and was born a vampire?"

"Probably a bit of both," I tell her. "Now off you go." I open the door for her, waiting for her to leave.

She shoots me one more wildly unimpressed glare before she turns and walks out of the fitness center toward the bank of elevators down the hall.

Once she's on the elevator, I let go of the door and walk toward the row of cardio machines as it closes. Instead of getting in a short workout as I'd planned, I frown when my phone starts buzzing in my pocket. I pull it out and sigh as tendrils of dread wind through my chest.

I sit on one of the workout benches and answer the call with, "What is it?"

"Hello to you too, son." Simon's deep voice comes through the line, and I grit my teeth.

"I'm busy, so unless you—"

"Watch your tone with me," he growls. "Get back to Washington now. It is time to put the hunters in their place again. You need to eliminate the senators associated with them during the meeting Terence has scheduled for you tomorrow. We need to send a very strong message, and it needs to be done before the news coverage grows more widespread."

I don't bother telling him it's too late for that. "I'm not going to do that," I say in a tight voice. Every muscle in my body is tense, and I suddenly wish I hadn't sent Calla away. As much as I don't want her involved in this, I'm craving her presence deeper than ever at this moment.

"I am not asking, Atlas. This is your duty as a part of our—"

"Family?" I cut him off with a harsh laugh.

"Your mother and I have built an image among the vampires that is well-respected. We will not have you ruin it because of some ludicrous vision you may have."

"Has it ever occurred to you, *father*, that you have absolutely no idea who I am or what I want?"

There is a stretch of heavy silence before Simon takes a deep breath. "You are an incredible disappointment. You are far too weak to be any son of mine. Forget about the meeting, Atlas. I will have this handled without your involvement." He hangs up, not allowing me another word. It's just as well, considering I have nothing left to say.

The ding of the elevator catches my attention, and I move across the room in a blur, opening the door to find Calla standing at the elevators. I stalk down the hallway toward her, and she briefly looks as if she's considering making a break for it but thinks otherwise at the last second.

"What are you doing?" I demand.

"I... I got on the elevator, but then I felt this intense, dark pressure in my chest. I can't explain it better than that, but it made it hard to breathe, so I got off to come back to you and heard you on the phone."

I arch a brow at her. "So you decided to stand outside the door and eavesdrop on my conversation?" I should have sensed she was there, or even heard her, but I was so wrapped up in the conversation—if that's what you can call it—with Simon that I didn't realize I wasn't alone.

Calla presses her lips together for a moment, holding my gaze. "I'm sorry." She steps in and lifts her hand to my cheek. "The things Simon said to you..." Her voice is low as her eyes flick between mine, and she brushes her thumb along my skin. "They aren't true."

My heart rate increases and the pressure in my chest lessens slightly. I rest my hands against her hips and lean closer, inhaling slowly and finding a brief moment of peace in her floral scent. It's warm and soft and wholly *her*.

"You are anything but weak, Atlas, and I'm sorry he has made you feel that way." Her lips brush mine in a whisper of a kiss as her heart beats fast in her chest. "You deserve so much better than them."

I close my eyes and pull her against me as she wraps her arms around my neck and kisses me fully. I allow myself to get lost in her, kissing her deeply and sweeping my tongue along her lips until they part for me, then push inside her mouth, grazing her tongue with mine.

Pulling back before things get too heated in the middle of the hallway, I rest my forehead against hers. "Thank you," I murmur, opening my eyes to look into hers. What I see in their depths makes my chest fill with a different kind of pressure. One filled with warmth that makes my skin tingle and my pulse jump.

Her eyes widen and her cheeks flush hotly. "Damn it," she says under her breath.

I tilt her chin up with my finger. "Don't worry, I won't make you say it out loud."

"I..." She clamps her mouth shut, and I wait patiently before she finally says, "Okay. I won't make you say it, either."

Those three words don't need to be spoken aloud, though. We both know it, both can *feel* it between us.

We get on the elevator to go back to the room, and I stand near one wall while she stands near the opposite one. "Do you want to see your parents before we leave the city?" I ask. Now that I'm not rushing back to a meeting with the senators, we could stay longer, though I know all of us are anxious to get back to Washington.

Calla tips her head back against the wall and sighs. "I do, but I don't think I'm ready for that." She looks over at me. "I don't want to scare them and I'm nervous about hurting them. I don't think I will. I mean, I know you guys would step in before anything could happen, but that in itself freaks me out too much."

I nod as we get close to our floor. "That's understandable. We can come back whenever you're ready. Or they can come to Washington. Whatever you want."

"Thanks, Atlas."

It's safe to say I shock us both when I smile at her. It's genuine and full, nothing like the faint grins and brief lip twitches I've shared with her in the past.

Something so small shouldn't feel like a turning point, and yet...

We leave to drive back to Washington after we've all showered and had breakfast. The toasted ham and cheese sandwich I ordered tasted slightly better than dinner last night, but I did drink an entire blood bag beforehand. As much as I don't want to admit it helped, it's pretty hard to deny. If it's going to allow me to eat food normally, I guess I shouldn't bristle at it. Drinking blood is part of my life now, and the faster I can get to a place where that feels normal, the easier meals—and life in general, I suspect—will be for me.

We stop for gas somewhere in Maryland, and I convince Gabriel to come with me to the café across the road while the others fill up the vehicle. And by *convince*, I mean, I asked him, and he was happy to, because it's Gabriel.

As we walk into the building, Gabriel grabs my wrist and says, "Keep your sunglasses on."

"What—" My eyes land on the TV attached to the wall across the room. It's broadcasting the news—a segment on how to identify a vampire—and at least half a dozen patrons along with the young blond woman behind the counter are watching it. "Oh my god," I breathe.

Gabriel's hand is at the small of my back. "If we try to leave now, it'll bring attention to us. Walk up to the counter and order your drink."

"I... Okay." Despite the uneven ticking of my pulse, I force my legs to carry me forward.

"Hi there," the barista—Deb, according to her handwritten name badge—says in an overly friendly voice. "What can I get for you?"

"Um." Panic seizes my throat as the audio from the TV overtakes my thoughts.

Gabriel steps up next to me with a charming smile. "Sorry, Deb. We're not used to such a vast menu. I'll take an iced Americano, and she'll have an iced coffee, please."

Deb smiles brightly, her cheeks tinging pink as her olive-green eyes linger on him. "Of course! No problem at all. I'll get that started for you right away." Deb taps on the screen in front of her, and Gabriel pulls out his card to pay.

My eyes narrow behind my sunglasses, and my throat rumbles with a low growl. There's a throbbing in my gums that makes me want to open my mouth, but I lock my jaw.

"Calla," Gabriel says so low only I can hear him. "Control."

I pull in a breath, but instead of it centering me, the girl's scent wafts over to me, and my fangs poke through my gums.

Fuck, fuck, fuck.

I turn away from the counter. "I'll meet you outside." Forcing myself to walk at a normal pace, I cross the room, counting my steps to keep my thoughts on something besides lunging across that counter and tearing into Deb's throat just for smiling at Gabriel.

Back at the car, Lex arches a brow at me. "You ditch Gabe?"

I shake my head. "I left so I wouldn't attack the blond behind the counter."

Kade laughs deeply. "Oh, we're going to need more than that. What happened?"

I thrust my fingers through my hair, then tie it in a loose bun at the back of my head with the scrunchie from around my wrist. "I'm not even a jealous person, but she was all smiley with him, and it rubbed me the wrong way. I could actually picture myself jumping the counter and tearing into her throat."

"Oooh, our girl is territorial," Kade says with a grin, pushing his sunglasses onto his head, which immediately reminds me of the broadcast inside the café.

I grab them off his head and cover his eyes again. "You need to keep these on," I say as Atlas walks out of the gas station and rejoins us. "We all do. Probably a good idea to wear colored contacts when we're in public too."

"Those fucking hunters can't keep anything to themselves, can they?" Lex grumbles, adjusting his shades.

Gabriel walks back to the vehicle and hands me my iced coffee. "One cream, two sugar."

"Thanks," I say, taking it from him. I drink hot coffee black, but iced? I need some creamy sweetness. "And sorry about, um, you know."

He offers me a smile. "No apology necessary. You handled yourself quite well, angel. I'm proud of you."

My cheeks heat, and I take a sip of the iced coffee as I walk with him around to our side of the car. "Why? Because I didn't bite her head off?" We climb in and buckle up while Atlas and Lex get into the driver and passenger seats up front and Kade slides into the seat behind Gabriel.

"Exactly," he answers. "A lot of vampires so young wouldn't have been able to fight that urge. You did very well."

"Oh." I set my drink in the cup holder beside me, feeling a bit better about the whole situation. And hearing Gabriel say he's proud of me makes me want to throw myself at him, which isn't entirely new but it's certainly heightened right now.

We get back on the road, and I doze off for the last half hour of the drive, only waking when Kade touches my shoulder to let me know we've arrived back in Washington.

The house we're parked in front of looks like something out of a magazine, which I suppose shouldn't surprise me at this point. The guys have impeccable taste, and if we can't go back to the house they built together, this will have to do for now.

"Can I assume Marcel is to thank for this place?" I ask no one in particular as we get out of the vehicle, duffle bags in tow.

"Of course," Kade says, "but mark my words, we will be back in *our* home soon."

"And what of the people who live there now?"

"Hmm, if you're good, maybe we'll let you devour them."

I smack him hard in the shoulder. "I'm serious, Kade."

He rubs his shoulder. "Did it sound like I was kidding?"

My eyes narrow, but before I can respond, Gabriel steps up next to me and says, "We'll ensure they have a place to go and cover all moving expenses."

Kade groans. "Ugh, Gabriel. Always the knight in shining Armani."

He shakes his head, pulling his sunglasses off and tucking them into his V-neck. "Don't you ever get tired of being such a saint?"

"It's called being a decent person, Kade." The *you should try it sometime* is implied by my tone, and he rolls his eyes.

He takes my bag off my shoulder and slides it onto his, walking ahead of us. "Look at me, being a decent person."

"Would you like a prize?" I call after him sarcastically.

"If it's you offering, you're fucking right I do." He stops at the massive front door and pulls his phone out, looking at it before punching a code into the keypad. The lock turns over, and Kade opens the door, gesturing for me to walk ahead.

Lex whips past me through the front door. "I call dibs on the en suite bedroom."

"Hey!" I call after him. "I just died and came back to life. I think I should get the primary bedroom."

Kade chuckles as the rest of us walk into the high-ceiling foyer. "Already playing the newbie vamp card?"

"Damn right I am." I don't wait to start exploring. Where the guys' place was bright and open, this place is more closed off, with dark wood accents in each room. It's a two-level house with the kitchen, dining, and living rooms on the main floor along with two bedrooms that are connected by a bathroom with doors on either side.

I wander upstairs and find four more sizable bedrooms, including the primary with the en suite, which Lex surprisingly did leave free for me. There's also an additional bathroom on this floor as well as a room set up as an office with massive windows and built-in dark wood bookshelves.

Backtracking to the living room downstairs, I rejoin the others, dropping onto the couch with a sigh. "It's a nice place," I say, then add, "How long are we going to be here?"

"It's hard to say," Gabriel answers.

I nod. I wasn't confident in getting a definitive answer because everything is so up in the air, but I had to ask just in case.

"How are you feeling?" Lex asks, perching on the armrest of the chair Kade's sitting in.

"Okay, I think. I feel... more awake, if that makes sense? Maybe it's because I can see and hear things stronger now, I don't know."

He nods. "That's likely part of it. Some people adjust to becoming a vampire easier than others, and I'm happy you seem to be adjusting quite well. I think I can speak for all of us when I say how impressive you've been right from that first feed."

"Thanks." I smile at Lex before my gaze flicks toward Atlas, but he's looking down at his phone. "I want to check on Brighton," I announce, shifting the topic of discussion away from me. Despite everything that went down the other night and her leaving the hunter fight with Scott, I'm worried about her. "I'd like to help get her away from the hunters and her dad. This isn't the life she wanted, and her mom would be devastated if she could see her daughter now."

"Not our concern," Kade says, and I shoot him an icy glare. I knew garnering any sympathy for her from them would be a challenge, but the complete lack of empathy in his tone makes my fangs push against my gums.

"What Kade means is that we—which includes you—are in a very difficult position. Brighton's connection to the hunters is stronger because of her father's position within them, making any involvement by us too dangerous, especially with you being newly turned."

"You think Scott's watching Brighton's every move? Maybe she—"

"I guarantee you he is," Atlas says, pinning me with a stare. "He's dedicated to the cause in such a way it means more to him than his family. He will not hesitate to use his daughter to get to us."

"Maybe *we* should be using her to get to *him*," Lex chimes in, raking his fingers through his hair. He hasn't colored it in so long that his light brown roots are showing.

I gape at him. "Lex, we are *not* kidnapping Brighton."

He shrugs. "You were the one who wanted us to get her away from them."

"Yeah, for her sake. Not to use her as some pawn in this war against the hunters."

"I think we should wait and see what happens with the senators," Kade says, glancing toward Atlas.

"I'm not waiting for them to make a move against the hunters. This is still our fight."

Kade leans back in his chair. "Okay. What do you want to do then?"

Atlas drums his fingers against the armrest of his chair. "I want a fucking break," he finally says, not really looking at any of us. "It's been a long few days."

"That's an understatement," Lex says, and I can't disagree.

I don't want to drop the Brighton situation, but I can see I'm not getting anywhere with them at this very moment, so I put a pin in it, prepared to take matters into my own hands if necessary very soon.

Gabriel touches my thigh, and I turn my attention to him. "How are the cravings? Do you want anything to drink?"

I press my lips together. The fire in my throat from before is a dull ache at this point. Faint enough to ignore, especially with everything else going on. And I'm pretty sure my stomach is in too many knots to even attempt putting something down there—blood or otherwise. "I'm good right now, thanks."

"Marcel is going to have blood delivered tomorrow," Kade says, but I'm barely listening. Gabriel's hand on my thigh, as simple a gesture as it is, has my complete attention. His touch is fire, making my skin tingle even through the fabric of my leggings, and I desperately want him to slide his hand higher and dip between my legs. To relieve the ache building at my core, because holy shit, it's never been this intense before. His thumb brushes back and forth, and my breath hitches, heat pooling low in my belly as my entire focus is swallowed up by his touch. Every part of me is oversensitive; I either need him to move his fingers closer to my center or take his hand off me so I can get into a very cold shower.

"Calla?"

"Huh?" I lick the dryness from my lips, tearing my gaze away from Gabriel's hand. I'm not even sure who said my name. My cheeks flood with heat as I glance around at each of the guys.

Lex smirks at me. "Something you need?"

There's no sense in trying to hide it—the entire room can hear my shallow breathing and my uneven pulse. They can smell the arousal soaking through my panties. At one point, that would have mortified me, but now? I'd rather they know what I want, so long as they give it to me.

"Perhaps we should finish this conversation tomorrow," Gabriel suggests, and I'm inclined to agree, considering I have no idea what they were talking about, anyway.

"Works for me," Kade says with a hungry gaze trained on me. He stands from his chair, stalking toward me at a languid pace. The closer he gets, the louder my heart beats, and when my gaze drops to the bulge in his pants, I launch off the couch, making a break for the stairs. Excitement and anticipation flood through me like a drug, and my lips curve into a grin as I hear Kade and Lex coming after me. We're matched in speed now, so running from them is a lot more effective, which makes this game all the more fun.

"She never learns, does she?" Lex says to Kade as I dart into the primary bedroom. "We're always going to catch her."

Kade laughs. "She enjoys being chased as much as we enjoy chasing her." They appear in the doorway, while I stand on the far side of the room. "Isn't that right?" he asks me with a devilish grin.

I lick my lips, feigning indifference as I shrug.

Lex and Kade exchange an amused glance before they come at me from both sides. I shoot forward, aiming for the door to the hall, but Gabriel blocks it, stepping into the bedroom and making me back up—right into Atlas's chest.

Fuck, when did he get in here?

Gabriel cocks his head, watching me with a darkness in his eyes I don't see very often. The sight steals my breath, making the hair on the back of my neck stand straight.

"Is this what you want, angel? All of us coming after you?"

I catch my bottom lip between my teeth, unable to look away from his gaze. I nod slowly, my stomach clenched with nerves and desire.

Atlas grabs the back of my neck and pulls me against his chest, his lips finding the sensitive spot below my ear. "You have no idea what you're in for," he warns in a low voice, his lips tracing the shell of my ear, making me shiver.

Kade appears in front of me, smirking wickedly. It's the smirk I've seen him use to invoke fear, but I'm so fucking turned on, I'm practically vibrating with barely contained energy. "She's about to find out," he says in a smooth voice, grabbing the bottom of my shirt and lifting it over my head. Instead of lowering my arms back to my sides, Atlas grabs them from behind me and locks them behind his neck.

"Keep them there," he orders, nipping my earlobe and making me gasp softly.

Gabriel crosses the room to where Lex stands, watching intently.

Kade unclasps my bra from the front, his hungry gaze dropping to my chest as my breasts spill free. He drags his fingers slowly up my stomach, tracing a line back and forth between my breasts before finally cupping them in his hands, pinching my nipples between his fingers, shooting heat straight to my core.

I suck in a breath. "Yes," I breathe, letting my head fall back against Atlas's chest. And when Kade lowers his mouth to my breast, swirling his tongue around the nipple before sucking it between his lips, I nearly whimper at the intense sensations rippling through me. Holy shit, no one told me that becoming a vampire would heighten my pleasure. I feel as if I could come just from Kade's attention to my breasts.

Without thinking, I try to move my hands and push him lower, to where I desperately want his tongue, but Atlas grabs my wrists, tutting his tongue. I growl in response, and Kade chuckles against my skin, shooting sparks of pleasure through me. He pulls his mouth off my breast and seals his lips over mine, kissing me deeply until my head spins and my heart is hammering against my ribcage.

Between one moment and the next, he lifts me off the floor, and I instinctively wrap my legs around him. My back hits the giant mattress, and before I have a second to breathe, Lex grabs one wrist, while Atlas grabs the other. My bra ended up on the floor somewhere, and Kade adds to it, tugging his shirt over his head and kicking off his shoes and socks. He crawls onto the bed next to me, leaning over and kissing from my belly button to my collarbone. I tug on my wrists, but Lex and Atlas hold firm as they both kick off their shoes as well, sitting on either side of the bed just above my head.

When Kade reaches my throat, he kisses the pounding pulse there, swirling his tongue over my skin before teasing me with his fangs. My core throbs with need, and I tilt my head, baring my neck to him. Without hesitation, he sinks his fangs into me, and I moan. It doesn't hurt, not even for a second like it used to. Pleasure floods through me at the pull of Kade taking my blood, sending heat between my legs, and I press my thighs together, squirming beneath him.

Gabriel wraps his fingers around my ankles and spreads my legs open, trailing his hand higher and higher until he brushes my core, making me buck my hips. He doesn't waste any time, curling his fingers into the waistband of my leggings and tugging them down to my ankles, then dropping them onto the floor.

My chest rises and falls quickly as Gabriel's fingers inch closer to where I want them. Kade pulls his fangs from my neck and kisses me there, and I make a sound somewhere between a growl and a moan when Gabriel spears me with two fingers, using his thumb to work my clit in hard, fast circles, stealing my breath.

"Yes," I pant. I turn my head to look at Lex and find him stroking himself with his free hand, the head of his cock glistening with moisture. I missed the part where he got naked, but I can't take my eyes off him now.

Something unspoken passes between us, and I lean forward as he shifts closer. Kade turns his attention to Atlas, while I lower my lips to Lex's cock, licking along the slit before dragging my tongue down his shaft. He pulls in an uneven breath, biting his lip as he tips his head back and closes his eyes. I move back up his shaft, circling the head of his cock before taking it into my mouth as deep as I can go. He hits the back of my throat, and I hold him there, sucking gently and reveling in the way he groans for me. I moan deeply when Gabriel curls his fingers inside my pussy, which sends vibrations through Lex's cock, and the muscles in his thighs clench.

"Fuck," he growls, "you feel so good."

I pull back, alternating the pressure of my lips against him to drive him wild. Energy crackles through me, and I feel as if my entire body is filled with rampant electricity that could spark and explode at any given moment. Everything is heightened tenfold—the touches and sounds, the sensations and emotions... It's incredible and over-whelming and I never want it to stop.

Kade is palming Atlas through his pants, making him grit his teeth and hold my wrist tighter, gripping the sheets in his other hand until his knuckles are white. He lets go of my wrist for a split second, only to lace his fingers through mine. For someone so used to having control, seeing Atlas on the receiving end is, well, really fucking hot. Kade pops the button on his pants and tugs the zipper down before freeing Atlas's cock. He pumps his hand up and down, his eyes bouncing between Atlas and me as he alternates speed and pressure, making Atlas drop his head back and groan. The sight of it sends heat through me, and sweat dots my brow as I suck harder on Lex's shaft.

Gabriel leans down and sucks my clit into his mouth, adding a third finger and thrusting into me hard and fast. My stomach clenches and my thighs shake, and I pick up speed, attending to Lex's erection. His grip on my wrist tightens, which is my only warning before he grunts, shooting his release against the back of my throat. I swallow, pulling back just as an orgasm slams into me, and I cry out, bucking my hips against Gabriel's face and clenching around his fingers. He gives me a minute as I ride the delicious aftershocks, then pulls his fingers out, licking them clean and offering me a satisfied grin.

Lex pulls his cock out of my mouth and leans forward, using his thumb to wipe my lips. I catch it with my teeth, and his eyes flash with lust. I suck the digit into my mouth, swirling my tongue on the pad of his thumb before he pulls it out.

"Fuck," Atlas groans, squeezing my hand as he finds his release, coming into Kade's hand. Kade grabs Lex's shirt off the ground, using it to clean his hand while Atlas tucks himself back into his pants.

Lex growls at him. "Bastard."

"When have you ever done laundry?" Kade shoots back, tossing the shirt back onto the floor, and Lex flips him off in response.

Gabriel crawls over me, snaring my gaze as he lowers his mouth to mine, kissing me deeply. I taste myself on his lips, making my pulse race, and when I feel the head of his cock at my entrance, I kiss him harder, moaning into his mouth when he pushes inside me in one smooth thrust. He reaches between us, strumming my clit in time with his thrusts, alternating between slow and deep, hard and fast. My head is spinning and my heart is trying to beat out of my chest. And when he flips us over, guiding me up to ride him, he hits a deeper spot, making my pussy clench around him.

I bite my lip, my head thrown back as I hold onto his shoulders to keep my balance. I lift my hips slowly, then drop down, impaling myself on Gabriel's hard cock, making him groan. His fingers dig into my hips as Lex and Atlas move closer and run their hands up my stomach until they reach my breasts. They tease and massage them, pinching my nipples and making me gasp as I attempt to catch my breath while continuing to ride Gabriel's cock, and then they just sit back and watch. It shouldn't be as hot as it is, but having those silver eyes locked on me while I'm being impaled by Gabriel is probably the most erotic thing I've experienced.

Kade gets out of the bed for a minute, coming back and kneeling behind me, resting his hands on my hips, guiding them up and down Gabriel's shaft. The walls of my pussy tighten around him, and he groans, his hands gripping the pillows at his head.

I tense when Kade's grip on my hip disappears and he squirts something I immediately identify as lube into his hand. There's a low rumble in his throat as he works it into his cock, and then I feel him at my back. "Kade," I breathe, my thoughts scattering.

He leans in, pressing his chest against my back, and his lips find my ear, nipping the lobe. "I enjoy stretching you here." He guides the head of his cock to my puckered, tight hole, and my pulse pounds beneath my skin. My orgasm is building quickly as Gabriel thrusts his hips up, slamming his throbbing length into my pussy once, twice, three more times until he comes, announcing his release with a deep groan. He holds still inside me, his cock twitching as my walls throb around him.

Inch by inch, Kade fills my ass with his cock until he's fully sheathed, and I can barely breathe. I'm so full, and when Gabriel reaches between us and plays with my clit, I completely fall apart, coming hard and squeezing both cocks inside me. I collapse onto Gabriel's chest as Kade thrusts into my ass at a speed that would likely kill a human, until he too reaches climax, grunting deeply as his fingers leave marks on my hips.

I feel like a shell of a person, absolutely spent and filled with pleasure that I can't think of moving from this bed for a good while.

Gabriel and Kade pull out of me, making me shiver and feel weirdly empty. It takes a good five minutes for my breathing to return to a somewhat normal pace, and in that time, the guys get dressed and sit around me on the bed.

"Do you want us to stay with you?" Kade asks.

"If you don't mind, I think I'll spend tonight by myself. I appreciate everything you've done to make sure I'm okay, but I just need a minute to catch my breath."

"Of course, angel," Gabriel says with an understanding smile. He leans down and kisses me softly. "Sleep well." He slides off the bed and slips out of the room.

Lex snags my chin and kisses me long and slow, pushing his tongue into my mouth before pulling back and shooting me a wink. "See you in the morning."

I turn toward Kade, lifting my hand to his cheek and drawing him in to slant my mouth over his. Our kiss is short and sweet, and he drops another quick one against my forehead before sliding off the bed.

Atlas lingers after the others have left the room, watching me with an expression I can't quite decipher, and it's making me squirmy.

I lean back against the headboard and arch a brow at him. "What is it?"

"I'm trying to figure it out."

I shake my head. "I don't follow. Figure out what?"

He closes the distance between us, sitting on the edge of the bed and gripping my chin between his thumb and finger. "Of all the outcomes we could have ended up with from that damn blood oath, I can't figure out how we were so incredibly lucky as to find you."

My eyes widen, and I'm leaning in too fast to say anything before our lips collide. The kiss starts slow and quickly builds, deepening into a fiery exchange of power. Where he pushes, I pull; we move together perfectly in sync, our hearts pounding as if they're trying to escape their cages and be closer.

We're both breathing heavily when we break apart. His lips return to mine, lingering there as he whispers, "Good night."

In the blink of an eye, he's gone, leaving me trying to catch my breath as I stare at the delicate floral design on the duvet covering my legs. I press my hand against my chest, waiting for my heart to return to a normal pace before I slide fully under the covers. I stare at the ceiling, going over the events from the last few days. It all feels like a fever dream—some of it incredible, but a lot of it a nightmare.

I toss and turn for an hour, trying desperately to get comfortable, but sleep refuses to come. I'm too wired, and my thoughts are racing, trampling one another and keeping me awake.

Pushing my hearing outward to the other bedrooms, the sounds of the guys' steady breathing reaches me, and I sigh. At least they're getting some rest. Which is good, considering I couldn't do what I'm about to if they were awake.

I slip out of bed and find my phone at the bottom of my duffle bag, opening a new text to Brighton. I chew the inside of my cheek as I stare at the screen, my heart beating in my throat as I type out a short message.

I need to see you tonight. Alone.

Five minutes go by as I force myself to sit on the end of the bed instead of pacing the room so I don't make any unnecessary noise and risk waking the others. Because what I'm about to do really isn't going to go over well.

My phone buzzes in my hand and my heart races as I read her response.

Lincoln Memorial in an hour?

I quickly type back, *Yes.*

Tiptoeing around the bedroom, I change into jeans and a T-shirt, shrugging on a jacket before I pull on and tie up my Docs. I slide my phone into my back pocket and open the bedroom door slowly, praying the hinges don't make a sound. A few seconds that feel like hours later, the door is open wide enough for me to slip through into the hallway. I close the door behind me, cringing when it makes a soft *click*.

I make it three steps toward the staircase before I freeze, immediately sensing the vampire ahead of me in the dark.

"What is it," Atlas says in a low voice, stepping into the hallway, "you think you're doing?"

I zip up my sweater, exhaling a sigh. "I want to see her, Atlas."

"Right." He nods. "And what part of absolutely the fuck not didn't you understand earlier?"

Anger rises in my chest, and I cross my arms. "Oh, I understood it perfectly fine. What, did you all think distracting me with a few orgasms would make me forget about my best friend?"

He steps forward, and I suspect he'd look a lot more menacing if I couldn't see clearly in the dark now. "You are one of us now, and she's one of them. Do the math, Calla."

"So, what? We're going to kill her too?" I snap at him.

"If it comes to her or one of us, yes, without hesitation." His voice is firm and there's a fire raging in his eyes that makes my heart beat faster.

Part of me gets it—his intense response—I understand why he's angry. He sees what I'm doing as idiotic, putting my life at risk unnecessarily to help Brighton. I recognize the danger, I'm not ignorant to the risks. They've been making my head spin since I decided to text her. Brighton is one of the most important people to me and has been for years. I couldn't forgive myself if I just let her continue down this path she doesn't want just because she's scared. I'm scared too; I need my best friend as much as she needs me. So I have to take the chance. In this case, I believe taking the risk is necessary. But it's painfully clear Atlas doesn't agree.

"You'll glamour me to stay here if I try to leave?" I ask in a tight voice.

"I truly hope you don't force me to do that, but yes, I will."

The urge to scream builds in my chest, making it harder to breathe. I glare at him a few beats longer before shoving past him with a snarl and going back to my bedroom, slamming the door as I fight back tears.

Dropping onto the end of the bed, I pull my phone out and open the text conversation with Brighton.

Can't make it tonight. I'm sorry.

What? I'm already on my way there. What's going on? Where are you?

I bite my lip, my fingers hovering over the screen. I can't tell her where we are and I'm sure as hell not going to tell her I'm a vampire over text, so I keep that to myself.

It's too dangerous right now, Bri. Just lay low for as long as you can and we'll figure this out.

She immediately tries to call me, but I reject it. If I hear her voice, I'm going to break.

Calla, what the fuck does that mean?! What am I supposed to do?

I'm sorry. I need to figure things out. I promise I'm trying to get you out of this mess. I'll be in touch as soon as I can.

With that, I turn my phone off and shove it in the drawer beside the bed, nearly choking on the lump in my throat.

I shift up the bed until my back hits the pile of pillows at the headboard and stare at the closed door as tears fill my eyes. I haven't felt like a prisoner with the guys in a while, but I sure as hell do right now.

FOURTEEN

ATLAS

The tension in the house this morning is palpable.

I let the others know about Calla trying to sneak out to meet up with Brighton last night, and she doesn't say a word to any of us when she gets up and comes downstairs, not even Gabriel when he hands her a cup of coffee. She immediately sets it on the counter and goes back upstairs, turning on the shower in the en suite.

"We'll need to deal with that," Gabriel says, sitting at the dining room table, sipping from his cup of coffee.

Kade and Lex exchange a look and make an excuse to leave the house in search of clothes and food for our stay here.

"Hmm." I pinch the bridge of my nose, frowning at the pressure behind my eyes. I thought we were past *keeping* Calla, but when she's determined to do something so idiotically dangerous, it's difficult to give her the freedom she's wanted since we showed up at her apartment all those weeks ago.

There's a knock at the door, and Gabriel gets up to answer it before I can. "That's Marcel. Let's put a pin in this for now."

They exchange pleasantries at the door and then walk into the dining room, bringing with them the scent of citrus and leather—a combination I've come to associate with our informant—and the faint scent of several different blood types.

Marcel nods at me, setting a cooler on the table. "This should hold you guys over for a while. Let me know when you need more, and I'll make sure it gets here."

"Thank you, Marcel," I say.

He runs his hand through his golden hair, pushing it out of his face before dropping into the chair adjacent to where I'm sitting at the head of the table. "I'm going to cut to the chase because we don't exactly have time for anything else."

"That works for us," Gabriel says, sitting back in the chair in front of his coffee.

"I received word early this morning that something is coming down the pipeline from the Department of Defense to several local law enforcement departments.

I nod. "I'm assuming you know the news."

"Starting at midnight, there will be a curfew put in place due to the spike of what they're calling 'gang-related attacks.' Unless given government clearance, all citizens must remain in their homes between the hours of eleven at night and five in the morning."

"Whose side are they on?" Gabriel asks. "They're getting the people off the streets, but for what reason? To help clear them for the hunters? To protect us from exposure?"

"We have local law enforcement," I comment, "but I can't say for sure at this moment about the higher levels of government." I exchange a glance with Gabriel. "That depends on if my father followed through with his plan to get rid of some people who he deemed untrustworthy."

Gabriel takes the lead in filling Marcel in on the added pressure from my—from Simon and Lenora.

"He wants to kill the senators who may be aligned with the hunters?"

I nod. "He demanded I take care of it."

Concern fills Marcel's gaze, and he looks between me and Gabriel. "What does that mean?"

"It means nothing, Marcel. I will protect my people as best as I can. What I will not do is kill people who do not deserve it."

Gabriel sets his mug on the table, tapping his thumb against the rim. "Perhaps we can do things differently this time," he suggests, looking my way. "You wanted to separate yourself from your parents, from the way they do things, and maybe now is the perfect time to take a stand and make that differentiation."

"Differently how?" Marcel asks.

"Let's say we attempt to stop the war between hunters and vampires instead of diving into the front lines."

"That would never work," Marcel says. "They despise our very existence. Even if we've done nothing inherently wrong, to them, the fact that we're breathing is crime enough worth killing us over."

"Some of them believe that, sure."

I lean back in my chair, closing my eyes briefly as a sigh passes my lips. "I see where you're going with this and I don't like it."

Gabriel chuckles softly. "Neither do I, really, but I do think it's worth considering. Otherwise, we do things the old way, and a lot more blood is shed—on both sides."

"Considering it is one thing," Marcel comments, "but putting it into action is a completely different situation. How would we even go about proposing..." He trails off, shaking his head. "I don't know, a ceasefire?"

"It's something we would need to discuss at length, weighing the pros and cons, potential outcomes, and risks. I'm not saying it's something we need to dive into immediately; however, I think we need to put it on the table for discussion. This is a war that has gone on for centuries, and while our species has always come out on top, if there's something we can do to stop the fighting, it could save a lot of lives. And I think that's important."

I thrust my hand through my hair, scratching the back of my head. He's not wrong, and I commend him for his view on the situation. We've lived in a war zone for so long, I think a part of me has gotten used to it in such a way that picturing a world without it seems difficult. Certainly not as difficult as attempting to put an end to the war with the hunters, but a challenge nonetheless.

Calla chooses that moment to rejoin us, wearing the same matching bra and leggings set from our training session. Her hair is tied in a towel and her cheeks are pink. She glances around the table, pausing on Marcel, and offers a subtle wave as her eyes drop to the cooler and her jaw clenches.

Marcel follows her gaze and smiles politely, opening the cooler and pushing it toward her. "Help yourself," he offers.

"Thanks," she says, the discomfort in her voice easy to pick up. She grabs a blood bag and pulls out a chair, dropping into it. "I think I should be part of this conversation."

I lift my brows. "No one was trying to keep you out of it, Calla. You're the one who went back upstairs."

Her eyes narrow, and she tears open the blood bag, lifting it to her lips.

"I can get you a—"

"Don't bother," she says, cutting off Gabriel's offer.

"It'll taste better warm," Marcel comments mildly.

She turns her unimpressed expression toward him. "I'm not really looking to enjoy it. It's a necessity, that's all."

He blinks at her. "How long have you been a vampire?"

She pulls the blood bag away from her lips, swallowing, then considers it for a moment. "A few days," she answers finally. "Why does that matter?"

He shakes his head. "I'm just surprised. Most new vampires enjoy the feed if not become consumed by it."

Her brows tug closer together. "Yeah, well, that's not really an option for me. I think we should talk about this potential new solution or whatever it is you want to call it. You want to work with the hunters now."

A muscle ticks along my jaw. Her tone is grinding on my nerves and I'm fighting the urge to grab her by the arm and pull her out of the room. She can be pissed about last night all she wants, but the attitude she's bringing to the table is not going to help, and I refuse to put up with it.

"I've been thinking," Gabriel says, "if there's any chance we can not necessarily work with the hunters but come to something of an arrangement wherein we only feed on willing humans and blood bags, of course."

"Willing humans?" Calla cuts in, arching a brow at him.

"Yes," he says, "feeders who offer themselves without glamour and are compensated for doing so."

She wrinkles her nose. "That seems, I don't know, wrong?"

"More wrong than vampires attacking people on the street?" I ask.

She scowls at me. "No, of course not. I just... Fine. Say that works. Why would the hunters agree to it? It's something that's happening anyway, and they want to stop it."

"I considered that," Gabriel says, "which is why I've also been thinking about how we could help them. There needs to be an exchange. If they feel they're not getting anything out of this potential deal, there is no way they will agree to it."

Calla nods. "What are we going to offer them?"

My gaze is bouncing back and forth between Gabriel and Calla like a fucking ping pong ball, and it's giving me a headache.

"I think, if we offer to help the hunters ensure the safety of the humans, they will at least consider a limited scope partnership of sorts. There are still going to be vampires who refuse to behave appropriately, to feed on willing humans, and to protect the secrets of our species. If we propose to assist the hunters to eliminate those vampires, perhaps they might be more willing to not try to kill *us*."

Calla sits back, crossing her arms over her chest, digesting Gabriel's words.

I go over them in my head as well, going through the hundreds of potential scenarios. "These are solid ideas, Gabe," I tell him. "My concern is how many vampires will agree to it. I know a lot who won't. And if the hunters don't agree, it won't work."

Gabriel nods. "I understand that, which is why we need to put out feelers to see if we can make this work and then go to the hunters with our proposal."

My eyes slide to Calla, and she's staring down at the table. "Do you have anything you'd like to add?" I ask her.

She lifts her head, meeting my gaze, and shrugs. "I think it's a good idea," she finally says. "I'm sure Lex and Kade will agree. Though I assume they're not the vampires you're concerned about getting on board with your plan for peace."

I shake my head. "There are a lot of vampires who view humans as a lesser species. They're slower, they're weaker, they die easily..."

"Okay, I know I'm not human anymore, but I still take offense to that," she grumbles.

My lips twitch. "It's just the facts, Calla. I'm not being an ass here. You've met Simon and Lenora. What do you think they would say if we brought this to them?"

Her lips curl into a snarl. "That would be a monumental waste of time. I think they're the type of vampires we should be protecting humans from, quite honestly."

"That's fair," I tell her. "But because of their position in our world, they have a lot of vampires who look up to them and who have the same ideations. Those vampires will not think twice about this and they will not agree to controlled feedings and protecting humans."

"That's ridiculous. They should want to protect their food source."

"There's no shortage of humans," Gabriel chimes in.

"What are we supposed to do about the vampires who won't agree to this?"

I shrug. "I suppose we let the hunters do their job."

She sits back again, falling silent.

Gabriel turns to Marcel. "Can you put some feelers out to see what the communities around you think about this? Keep it quiet. If we can't get the numbers, this is going to be over before it starts."

"Of course," he says, rising from his chair. "If you need anything else, you know how to reach me."

Gabriel walks him to the door, leaving me alone with Calla.

"You're still upset with me about last night."

Her chest rises and falls as she sighs. "Actually, Atlas, I am fucking pissed. After everything we've all been through, I refuse to be a prisoner again. If that's what you want me to be—"

"No," I cut in, "but when you're trying to do something that is going to get you killed, you're damn right I'm going to stop you."

She shakes her head. "You don't know that's what was going to happen, and it's not your call to make. How is me trying to connect with Brighton any different than you guys meeting up with the hunters to try to create peace? It doesn't make sense."

Irritation tickles the back of my neck, and I clench and unclench my jaw before I say, "The difference is that you were sneaking out to meet her by yourself in the middle of the night when you had no idea if she was the one you were actually meeting or if she was going to show up alone. Had I not stopped you and you'd met with her, it could have been fine; however, it could have also been an ambush and you would be dead—for good this time. Do you understand that?"

Her lashes lower as her gaze drops to the table. "I don't need to be lectured," she says in a tight voice.

"And I don't wish to lecture you, so stop acting like a moron."

Her gaze snaps up to mine. "Fuck you, Atlas."

Gabriel walks back into the dining room and immediately sighs, clearly sensing the tension. "I just got a message from Lex. They're on their way back from Target with supplies."

"Great," I grind out, getting up from the table. If I don't walk away now, things are only going to escalate, and getting into a shouting match with the vampire I just sired is not how I'd like to spend my Friday afternoon.

FIFTEEN

CALLA

After yesterday's argument with Atlas, I've reserved myself to stay holed up in my bedroom except for the brief occasions I slip downstairs to grab a blood bag, timing it strategically to ensure I don't run into him.

The cravings have been hard since I woke up this morning. They're stronger than they've been, and I imagine it's because my emotions are all over the place.

My muscles are itching for a run, but there doesn't seem to be any workout equipment in this place, and the odds of being let out the front door without an escort are slim. And that really doesn't help my mood.

The guys leave me alone for the most part. Gabriel pokes his head into my room at one point and brings me an iced caramel latte from my favorite café near campus, but he doesn't push me to talk about anything. There's nothing new to say at this point, anyway. They all know what happened the other night, why I'm pissed, and they can continue treating me like a caged animal if it means leaving me alone. I'll get over my anger eventually—hell, there's even a part of me that understands why Atlas responded the way he did—but I'm still going to simmer with it for now.

I find some ridiculously stupid cartoon marathon on TV and lie on my stomach in bed, watching it until I doze off sometime late in the afternoon.

When I blink my eyes open, my gums are throbbing and my throat feels like sandpaper. I groan, which doesn't help the rawness, and curse when it hits me that I'm not alone in my bed.

"Hey, sleepy head," Lex purrs, grinning at me with his head propped on a pillow.

"What the fuck, Lex," I grumble around a yawn, sitting up. "What do you want?"

"Geez, you can put the fangs away," he says in a teasing tone.

I poke one with my tongue and frown. I hadn't even realized they were out. "Shit," I whisper, mainly to myself, though he would have heard it.

"You're hungry." It's not a question.

I thrust my fingers through my hair, pressing them into my scalp in an attempt to ease the pressure building there. It feels like the headaches I used to get with abrupt weather changes. "Were you watching me sleep like a weirdo?"

"And if I was?" he shoots me a wink. "Oh, relax. I was watching, uh, whatever the fuck that is." He gestures toward the TV on the wall across from the bed.

"Right, and you couldn't watch TV downstairs?"

Those silver eyes narrow slightly. "I don't much like grumpy Calla. Any idea when she's going to return the Calla we all love?"

I pause, my heart stuttering at that last word. I shove past it and say, "Maybe once you all stop doing shit that makes it feel like we're moving backward. I may not be locked in a room, but I am most definitely a prisoner here. Again."

Lex juts his lower lip out in a pout. "Only because you want to run away and do something that could potentially get you killed."

I cross my arms, shifting to face him on the bed. "The same could be said for what Gabriel and Atlas are planning with the hunters," I point out. "I don't want to keep talking in circles, which is why I've kept to myself today. There's no sense wasting my energy shouting at a brick wall, so I'm just going to hang out in here until I don't feel like ripping Atlas's head off, which I can't do anyway thanks to the whole sire thing."

He laughs softly. "You're so well-adjusted for a newbie vampire. It keeps throwing me off."

I arch a brow at him. "Uh, thanks? I think."

Lex nods. "Yes, Calla, that is a compliment. Now, get up. You're going to need to be a lot perkier for where we're going."

My brows knit. "What are you talking about? You're crazy if you think Atlas is going to let me leave right now."

His eyes shimmer with mischief. "Hmm, then it's a good thing he isn't here." He slides off the bed and heads for the door. "Hurry up. We're leaving in five."

"Lex, wait. Where—"

"Five minutes," he calls out, already walking down the hallway.

I groan, forcing myself out of bed. I'm not exactly in the mood for one of Lex's field trips, but if it'll get me out of this house, I suppose I shouldn't complain.

I leave my hair pinned up in a claw clip and get changed into black jean shorts and an emerald silk shirt with thin straps and lace along the V-neck, then shove my feet into my trusted Docs before heading downstairs. Lex is already waiting by the door.

"Gorgeous, as always," he says, stepping closer. He reaches for the clip in my hair, pulling it out and tossing it on the bench by the door. My dark brown waves tumble free, spilling down my chest, and smell of the rose shampoo I used earlier. "Hmm, that's even better."

I roll my eyes but can't help the smile tugging at my lips. "Are you going to tell me where we're going?"

He opens the front door, sweeping his arm out for me to walk ahead. It's dark outside and the temperature has dropped a bit, but I don't find myself bothered by the coolness. There's a car idling at the curb, and Lex closes the front door, sliding his fingers through mine as we walk toward the waiting vehicle. "I'm taking you to my favorite club, but we have to hurry up because this damn curfew is really putting a damper on the Washington nightlife."

I dig my heels into the pavement. "Are you sure that's a good idea?" My chest immediately tightens at the thought of being in a room filled with humans.

He moves in front of me. "You'll do just fine. Plus, it's a popular place for willing feeders, so if you're feeling peckish..." He trails off, shooting me a wink.

My skin tingles with anxiety, and I press my lips together. "I'll only go if you promise me you won't let me hurt anyone."

He grasps my chin with his other hand, looking into my eyes. "I've got you, Calla."

If I believe nothing else, I know that to be true.

"Okay," I finally say, and we walk the rest of the way to the car, Lex opening the door to the backseat for me to slide in. He gets in after me, closing the door, and we're off.

Fifteen minutes later, the car drops us off outside a black brick building with a line going down several blocks and music blasting from inside.

I start toward the end of the line, and Lex catches my elbow, guiding me to the front. "Lex—"

"Good evening, Mr. Bishop," the thick-armed bouncer says to Lex. He smells of drug store cologne and also a little like pizza. His sandy blond hair is cropped close and he has the brightest blue eyes. *They're contacts*, I realize after extended inspection. Evidently, he's a vampire who got the memo to hide his silver eyes.

"How's it going, Ethan?" His hand falls away from my elbow and rests against the small of my back.

"Very well, sir."

Sir?

Lex nods. "Glad to hear it." He tips his head toward me. "This is Calla. She's with me."

Ethan nods, offering me a smile. "Nice to meet you, Calla."

"Likewise," I say automatically.

"My guys will take care of you inside," he assures me. "Have a great night, you two."

I smile at Ethan, and Lex says, "Oh, we very much plan to."

Lex ushers me inside, and I'm instantly transported to this whole other world of music, flashing lights, and moving bodies—both human and vampire. The smells I'm expecting—booze, perfume and cologne, pot, and body odor—are stronger than I'm used to. I wrinkle my nose as we move through the crowded room toward the circular bar in the middle. Heads turn our way as we pass, and I move closer to Lex.

"You own this place, don't you?" I don't shout over the music, knowing he'll hear me.

He shoots me a wink as we approach the bar, where he motions for the bartender. I recognize her immediately as the woman who tattooed Lex a couple of months ago.

"Scarlett's a bartender too?"

"She works here one or two nights a week. And she prefers the title mixologist," he says in an amused tone, turning his attention toward her. "Hey, Scar."

"Long time no see," she says in greeting. "What are you guys having tonight?"

"Whiskey sour, please," I tell her.

Lex shrugs. "Same for me. Thanks."

Scarlett nods and turns away to make our drinks, while Lex slides his arm around my waist and tugs me against his side, pressing a kiss to the side of my head.

"What exactly do you have in mind for tonight?" I ask.

He peers down at me, the flashing lights making his eyes appear brighter. "Fun," he says with a teasing gasp. "A novel concept, I know."

I bite my lip as it tries to curl into a grin. "Huh. Yeah, I think I've heard of that."

He laughs, dipping his head until his lips brush my ear. "We're surrounded by people, and all I can think about is getting you alone and ravishing your gorgeous body."

My skin flushes with warmth, and I close my eyes, letting myself get lost in the vibrating bass of the music around us. I lean into Lex, and we move together, ending up on the dance floor with his lips against my neck, our drinks completely forgotten.

Lex pulls my back against his chest as we move in sync, his mouth teasing the skin below my ear as his hands roam my body, sliding down my sides. He digs his fingers into my thighs, grinding me against him, and my breath hitches at the feel of his cock straining against his pants.

My heart slams against my ribcage and heat pools low in my belly. Lex swirls his tongue, licking, kissing, sucking my neck and making my skin tingle. My nipples harden through my top, and I chew my bottom lip, pressing my thighs together as we sway to Delacey's *Cruel Intentions*. My core is throbbing, begging to be touched, and when Lex's fangs scrape my skin, my own slide down from my gums, and I moan, turning to face him at a speed so fast the room blurs. I slam my lips against his, breathing him in as I shove my tongue into his mouth and slide my fingers into his hair, gripping it as I kiss him hard. He growls into my mouth, holding me firmly against him, his hands cupping my ass.

We're lost in each other when I nick my tongue on his fang, and he makes a sound at the back of his throat, something between a groan and a hungry snarl. I taste my own blood, and it flips a switch in me. He pulls back, and we're both breathing heavily.

"If we don't stop—"

"I don't want to stop," I breathe, pulling him back to my mouth.

Lex kisses me violently for a fleeting moment before grabbing my jaw and breaking contact. "Come with me." His hand finds mine, and our fingers lace together.

I follow him through the club, my entire body pulsing with heat and hunger, a desperate need to sate the ache between my thighs and in my gums. "Lex, I need—"

"I know exactly what you need," he assures me, pulling me through the crowd and down a dark hallway. He pushes open the set of double doors at the end of the hallway, and we walk into what looks like a private lounge. There's a much smaller bar with no one behind it, and a massive black brick fireplace across from the doorway, with black velvet couches facing each other and a black marble table between them.

Lex slams the doors shut, muffling the music volume, and backs me up against them. He grabs my wrists, lifting them above my head and pinning me against the door. His mouth descends on mine once more, and I gladly give myself over to the wicked sensations flooding my body. Every part of me needs him right now, and I have no reservations in showing him that.

"Fuck," he growls against my lips. "My cock is rock hard for you."

"Hmm..." I kiss the corner of his mouth. "I guess now would be a good time to let you know I'm not wearing any panties."

He leans back to look at me, and his pupils are blown wide, his eyes filled with desire. "You're going to be the death of me."

My lips curve into a grin. "At least you'll enjoy it."

"That," he murmurs, licking his lips, "is very true."

"Lex?" I whisper, my pulse pounding beneath my flushed skin.

"Hmm?"

"I want you to fuck me against this door until I'm screaming."

He stares at me with a mix of disbelief and awe, and then his mouth is on me. He kisses me hard, dragging his mouth along my jaw and across my collarbone. He makes quick work of popping the button on my shorts and tugging them down to my ankles. He growls hungrily as the smell of my arousal fills the space between us. My face fills with warmth, but I don't have time to feel embarrassed, because his fingers sink into the heat between my legs, thrusting into me and teasing my clit.

"Yes," I breathe, tipping my head back.

He frees my wrists and pulls his fingers out of my pussy. "I need to be inside you before my cock explodes."

I fumble with the zipper on his pants, my fingers shaking with anticipation, and he chuckles softly, his head bent as he watches me struggle. I scowl at the zipper before finally getting it, and slide my fingers into his boxers, pulling his cock free. I pump my hand up and down his shaft a few times before Lex grabs my hips and lifts me up, slamming me back against the doors. I catch myself on his shoulders and suck in a sharp breath when his cock presses against my clit.

"I've been thinking about burying my cock in you all fucking day," he says in a low voice thick with arousal.

The muscles in my stomach clench as moisture gathers between my legs. *Holy shit. I'm literally dripping for this man.*

Lex positions himself at my entrance, then pushes into me at full speed, hitting a spot so deep I nearly come right there. My pussy squeezes him as I hang onto him, drawing his mouth back to mine. He swallows my moans as he slams into me, rattling the door on its hinges behind us. My breasts tingle, and as much as I'm loving this one-on-one time with Lex, I wish one of the others were here to give them some attention.

Lex helps keep me upright with one hand as he continues his relentless thrusts, and wraps his other hand around my neck, breaking our kiss. "You feel so good wrapped around my cock. I want to keep you right here forever."

"Yes," I agree, closing my eyes and pulling my bottom lip between my teeth.

Lex squeezes my throat until my eyes pop open. "Eyes on me. I'm going to watch you fall apart on my cock and then I'm going to bend you over the couch and take you from behind." He increases his speed, and everything in me tightens before I explode, coming hard and crying out his name in pure desperation. "That's it," he purrs. "You come so beautifully for me."

Sweat dots my brow, and I hang onto Lex for dear life as he pulls his cock almost all the way out before slamming back into me. He buries himself deep in my pussy over and over, until I'm panting. The sound of his groans fill the room as he reaches his own climax, and my pussy clenches around him, throbbing with pleasure so intense I whimper, overcome by another orgasm.

"Look at you," he murmurs, tucking my hair behind my ear. "So fucking gorgeous." He slowly pulls out of me and sets me down. My knees shake, but he doesn't let go, so I'm not worried about falling on my ass.

I slide my fingers along his jaw, cupping the side of his neck, still catching my breath as I look into his eyes. "I love you," I tell him, unable to contain the smile on my lips. It goes without saying at this point, but the words feel good to speak aloud. Especially seeing the way his eyes widen and the blush that fills his cheeks. "You look so surprised," I tease him.

His lips curl into a grin, and he leans in, pressing his forehead into mine. "To hear you say it," he clarifies. "I love you more than I ever thought possible to love another person."

"What about the others?" I ask in a teasing tone.

His expression fills with amusement. "You know what I mean, and don't pretend you don't. They are as much my family as you are."

My chest tightens at that, though not painfully. It makes me think of my mom and dad back in New York and how everything that's happened has come to this moment. "Do you ever think about what your life would be if Atlas hadn't turned you?"

"Well, I'd be dead, so no."

I smack his chest. "You know what I mean."

Lex chuckles softly. "Sorry. Couldn't resist. But sincerely, I don't. Despite how difficult it was at the start, my life was made so much better by becoming a vampire. Even more so after meeting you." He slants his mouth over mine, kissing me slow and deep, and my body responds immediately, coming back to life under his touch.

Apparently, becoming a vampire does wonders for your libido—at least in my case.

I lose myself in him once more. We can't get close enough, can't kiss long enough to satisfy my craving for him. I quickly decide that I can spend all night in this room with Lex, so long as he doesn't stop touching me.

And then the club fills with terror-filled screams.

We break apart, and my eyes widen with panic, my heart lurching in my chest.

"Son of a bitch," Lex growls, tucking himself back into his pants and zipping them up.

I'm already tugging my shorts back on. "Wha—"

"Hunters."

My stomach drops as the smell of blood reaches me and the shrieks of agony close in on me from down the hall. Fear fills my veins with ice, and I back away from the door. "Atlas is going to kill us," I mutter, gritting my teeth as a new fear slams into me. *What if Brighton is with the hunters?* My heart lurches in my chest, slamming against my ribcage, and I turn my wide-eyed gaze to Lex.

"Let's make it out of here alive and then we can worry about that," he says in a tight voice. He grabs me, tugging me back as the doors fly inward and break off their hinges.

The room floods with hunters, and the pure hatred on their faces makes my lips pull back in a snarl as my fangs extend fully. I scan the room in a matter of seconds; Brighton isn't with this group. It's a tiny victory, considering we've still been ambushed by hunters, but I can't help being slightly relieved because I still have absolutely no idea how I'm going to face my best friend as a vampire.

"I want you to run the first chance you get," Lex hollers, taking on two hunters, narrowly dodging a dagger flying through the air toward him. It slams into the wall, and Lex growls in the faces of the hunters around him.

"No fucking way I'm leaving you," I shoot back, ducking before a hunter can get his meaty arms around me. I pop back up behind him and push him into the nearest wall. With my new inhuman strength, that force knocks him out cold, and he crumples to the floor.

I really, *really* don't want to kill anyone, but if it comes down to them or me, *I will not hesitate.* I hear Atlas's voice in my head telling me those words, and as much as I'm dreading having to face him after this, I really hope I get the chance to.

Lex and I end up fighting back-to-back. We fall into a decent rhythm of dodging attacks and going on the offensive. He is far less reluctant to kill the hunters than I am, snapping necks every which way, but somehow one hunter still manages to get past our defenses.

She slams a dagger into Lex's stomach, and he growls in pain. I'm moving without thought, grabbing her by the hair and yanking her head back before sinking my fangs into her throat. I drink viciously, too fast for her to even attempt to break free, and shove her lifeless body toward another oncoming hunter. The woman cries out, clearly having known the other one—whose blood is dripping down my chin.

Lex yanks the dagger out, pulling his arm back and letting it fly. It impales another hunter in the throat, and he reaches for it, unable to pull it out as blood pours from the wound.

We advance on three more hunters, and Lex sinks his fangs into one while I slam the others' heads together, wincing when their skulls crack on impact. *Shit.*

Lex pulls back from the one he's feeding on and drops her to the floor carelessly. "We need to go before more show up," he grounds out, grabbing my arm and hauling me toward the doorway.

I pull out of his grasp and almost stumble over the body of a very dead hunter in the process. "Okay! I can walk, Lex."

Sounds of fighting and death are still coming from the club, but he doesn't turn in that direction. Instead, he opens the door adjacent to where we came from that leads to another, shorter hallway. There's a red EXIT sign above a solid metal door at the end of this hallway, and Lex shoves it open.

I'm immediately blasted by cool, night air, which is a relief to my heated skin. "What about Scarlett?" I ask, breathing heavily as we walk down an alley until the sounds from inside grow quieter.

"She's human. They won't hurt her. Plus, she has a gun behind the bar and is a pro at Krav Maga."

"Holy shit," I mutter. "I want to be her when I grow up."

Lex laughs, though it's not his usual easygoing one that I've become rather fond of, and I understand why. Tonight was a complete shit show. And it really doesn't bode well for any sort of negotiations we might be trying to plan with the hunters.

The house is quiet when we walk through the front door, but the hair on the back of my neck is standing straight up.

We make it two steps inside before Atlas is there, slamming the door shut with pure fury etched into his sharp features.

Lex and I exchange a quick glance before he sighs. "Here we go."

In my many decades on this earth, I cannot recall ever being so unreservedly furious.

Feeling this way toward two of the most important people to me makes it significantly worse.

Lex and Calla are covered in blood—some of it theirs, most of it not. They're completely disheveled but otherwise appear to be okay. Because they got fucking lucky.

Lex has the sense to look apologetic as our eyes meet, and the icy glare I shoot him makes him drop his gaze almost immediately.

"I will deal with you later," I growl at him, grabbing Calla by the arm and dragging her down the hallway.

I throw open the bedroom door and shove her inside, storming in after her and slamming the door behind me. I close my hands into fists at my sides to keep myself from grabbing her by the throat and slamming her against the wall. "Do you have any idea how incredibly stupid what you did tonight was?"

Her heart is hammering in her chest, her eyes a mixture of panic and anger. There's dried blood on her chin, and I can see the tips of her fangs when she opens her mouth to scowl at me. "First of all," she says, "tonight wasn't even my idea, and even if it was, I'm an adult. And last I checked, you're not my dad."

A muscle ticks along my jaw as I tower over her. "I want to know every single detail of what happened."

She stares at me a moment, then sighs heavily. "Seriously? It was an ambush, Atlas. What more do you want me to say?"

"How many did you kill?"

She shakes her head, lowering her lashes as her gaze falls from mine. "A few."

There's a part of me that wants to pull her into my arms and comfort her, but I can't bring myself to. I grab her chin, forcing her gaze to mine. "It was you or them, right?"

"Yes," she answers in a tight voice.

"Then forget about it." It's as close as I can get to comforting her when the anger in my chest still burns so hot. "If you ever do something like that again—"

"What?" she snaps, cutting me off. "What are you going to do? Lock me up? Lock Lex up?"

I lean in, lowering my voice. "If that's what it takes to ensure you don't go out and get yourself killed, you're damn right I will."

She shoves my hand away from her face, baring her fangs as she says, "You do that, and I can't speak for Lex, but I won't forgive you."

"This isn't a game, Calla. This is real. This is war."

She throws her hands up, shaking her head. "I understand that, but staying cooped up in a house and being afraid to go outside is not *living,* and considering you just extended my life for literally eternity, I refuse to live that way. So, if that's your plan, I'm out."

My eyebrows lift, and I press my lips into a tight line, letting the silence linger between us for several beats. "That's not..." I trail off, shaking my head. "Of course, that's not my plan. None of this has been my plan. And I'm not saying it's forever, but we have a lot of shit to figure out before we can go gallivanting around nightclubs without the risk of being daggered."

She continues glaring at me. "Oh, please. You're just jealous you didn't get to go out and have fun tonight."

I open my mouth to respond, but the anger that is tightening around my chest makes it impossible to speak.

"You know," she continues, "despite being scared for my life tonight, I also had fun. We danced, got lost in the music and each other, and when Lex pulled me away from the crowd into an empty room and fucked me against the door—"

"Enough," I growl, advancing toward her. Her pulse races as I grab her by the throat and pull her to me.

"What are you going to do?" she challenges.

I shake my head, my jaw clenched so tight my gums throb in protest. And then I slam my mouth against hers, taking her lips in a bruising kiss as my fingers squeeze her throat.

I back her up until she hits the end of the bed, falling onto it, and I pin her to the mattress as my cock hardens in my pants and I drag my mouth along her jaw.

She kisses me back just as violently, our hearts pounding in sync as she reaches for my shirt, tugging it off over my head and throwing it behind me.

I tear the front of her shirt open and drop my mouth to her breasts, sucking hard on her skin and making her gasp. I slide my hand down her stomach and into her shorts, growling against her skin when I realize she's not wearing any panties. I don't hesitate, plunging two fingers deep inside her, reveling in the way she clenches around me, and use my thumb to stimulate her clit as her breathing hitches and she moans deeply, her throat vibrating against my fingers still wrapped around it.

"Atlas," she breathes, and it goes straight to my cock.

I pull back and unbutton my pants, freeing myself from the confines of my clothes. I shift off the bed, discarding my pants before crawling back over her and settling between her thighs. I don't give her any warning before I slam into her, and she cries out, the sound a mix of shock and pleasure. I pound into her, rolling my hips and hitting deep inside her pussy, groaning as she squeezes me. I brace myself with one hand against the mattress, wrapping my other back around her throat, forcing her to look at me as I dominate her body.

"You drive me fucking crazy," I growl, stealing her mouth without giving her a chance to respond.

She bites my lip hard enough to draw blood, lifting her hips and meeting my thrusts. The coppery taste sparking over my tastebuds spurs me on, and I push my tongue past her lips, flicking it along the roof of her mouth as we fight for control over the kiss. I grip her throat tighter until she yields to me, and lust floods through my veins as my breathing picks up.

Her mouth breaks from mine. "I'm going to come," she pants, chest heaving.

I slow my thrusts, licking the erratic pulse at her throat. "After tonight, I shouldn't let you."

She tenses. "I swear to everything holy, Atlas, if you leave me like this—"

I roll my hips, thrusting deeper, and hold still inside her as our hearts pound. If I had stronger willpower, I would bring her to the very edge and leave her there. But my release is too close to deny, so I pull nearly all the way out before slamming back into her, sinking my fangs into her shoulder as I force her to take all of me over and over until she's crying out, clenching around me and coming hard. I follow her over the edge, my muscles tightening near-painfully, and I swallow a mouthful of her blood, growling as the monster inside me relishes her taste, even as a vampire.

I lick the blood from her shoulder as we remain joined for the shiver-inducing aftershocks of our climaxes.

"What are we doing?"

I chuckle darkly. "I thought you'd be familiar with this by now, Calla. I'm not sure if I should be insulted or—"

She punches me in the shoulder. "That's not what I mean, and you know it. What are we doing about the hunters?"

I pause. "My cock is still buried inside you, and *that's* what you're thinking about? Now I really am offended."

She shoves me away, and I pull out of her. "Atlas," she grumbles, "I'm serious."

I drag a hand through my messy hair and sigh heavily, dropping onto my back next to her and staring at the ceiling. "I received another call from New York tonight as a *courtesy*." The word tastes bitter on my tongue. "According to a messenger from Simon and Lenora, they are making plans to eradicate the hunters as quickly as possible. It's something they've done more than once before, but it's been a very long time since the last generation was wiped out."

Calla sits up, pulling the covers around her as she stares at me with a horrified expression. "They being who?"

I sit up next, leaning against the headboard, and look at her. "A lot of very old, very powerful vampires. Unfortunately, my parents aren't the only vampires who are—"

"Psychotic?" she offers in a venom-filled voice, and I don't blame her in the least. Her hatred for them is completely understandable and valid. She shakes her head. "I know you don't like Brighton and certainly don't trust her, but that doesn't mean I will sit back and let her die. She's still my friend and there's a loyalty there I can't and won't ignore."

I hesitate before nodding. "And if she's in too deep with the hunters because of what happened to her mother?" I ask. "What then?"

Calla frowns, dropping her gaze to the bedsheet she's pulling through her fingers. "I know you think I have blinders on when it comes to her, but I have considered the possibility." She lifts her head and meets my gaze again. "Can we please just cross that bridge if we have to?"

"I suppose," I say, lacing my fingers together behind my head. "This really cuts into our timeline to gauge a potential ceasefire with the hunters."

Calla nods. "It'll divide the vampires, choosing to go to war and wipe out the hunters or deciding to work alongside them to protect both sides."

Closing my eyes, my lips turn down at the dull pounding in my temples. "It won't be easy," I say, "there are going to be a lot of vampires who choose what they know. Bloodshed and killing come naturally to most. Taking a risk and working with the enemy is a huge ask. One many will refuse to even consider."

"You're right," she murmurs, "but I believe we still need to try."

I open my eyes and sigh. "Yeah."

She reaches over and slides her fingers along my cheek, turning my face toward her. "It's going to be okay," she says, her eyes flicking between mine.

I drag my tongue over my bottom lip, wetting it. "The certainty in your voice makes me want to reassure you that's true, but this is a centuries old fight."

Calla nods thoughtfully, holding my gaze as she drops her hand back to the bed. "Okay. So, we fight for something new. If we're going to risk our lives, it should be for something that'll make a positive change, right?"

I stare at her silently for a long moment. For someone so young, her optimism and determination is, while understandably naive, really quite incredible.

It's no wonder we're all in love with her.

"You can say it, you know," she says with a little twitch of her lips, and when I arch a brow at her, she adds, "You can admit I'm right. The world won't implode."

I chuckle softly, sliding out of the bed and getting dressed before heading for the door.

"Where are you going?"

I turn back to her. "I need to speak with Lex."

"Atlas," she says with a frown.

"Don't start," I warn her.

She sighs heavily, putting her hands up in defeat. "Fine, but if you don't scold him the same way you did me, he's going to be very disappointed."

SEVENTEEN

The days are passing painfully slowly, and considering this new place doesn't have any workout equipment, I resort to basic bodyweight exercises on the lawn in the backyard. I still manage to work up a sweat, which is the goal. That, and a distraction from waiting to hear back from the groups of vampires Marcel's been contacting to see if a meeting with the hunters is even a possibility.

I'm blasting Valerie Broussard's *Killer* in my wireless earbuds on my second set of pushups when the music cuts out to an incoming call. I sit cross-legged on the grass and grab my phone, answering the call to the Bluetooth function of my earbuds when I see my mom's number on the screen.

"Hey, Mom," I say, uncapping my water bottle and taking a long drink before tossing it next to me.

"Calla, oh I'm so happy you answered. I've been thinking about you lots." The relief in her voice makes my chest swell. I want to see her so badly. I think I'm confident enough to know I won't hurt her or my dad, but now that simply walking outside without sunglasses or colored contacts puts a nationwide target on my back, visiting them needs to be pushed to the back burner. I won't put them at risk because I miss them. Until it's safe to go, I'll have to deal with phone calls and video chats.

"How are you?" I ask. She's pretty much back to normal after the accident, but I still feel the need to check, to make sure.

"I'm doing just fine, honey. I called to ask *you* that."

"I'm okay," I say automatically.

"And how are you really?" she asks in that tone of hers that makes it impossible to lie, even over the phone. It must be a mom thing.

I press my lips together, then blow out a breath. "Uh, well, it's been an adjustment for sure, but... I don't think it's as hard as I was worried it would be."

"Really?"

I smile at the return of her relieved voice. "Yeah. Lex even said I was a better vampire than him because I didn't kill my first feed."

She laughs, but it sounds forced and awkward.

I cringe, pressing my fingers to my temple. "Oh god, I'm sorry. I shouldn't have told you. You definitely don't need to hear about that stuff."

"No, no," she says, sounding slightly more normal. "You should be able to tell me anything and everything you want, Calla. I'll get used to this, I promise."

I laugh softly, smiling though she can't see it through the phone. "Okay, but still, I'll keep the vampire talk to a minimum." I pick at the strands of grass, pulling them out of the ground and tossing them aside idly.

"You sound happy," she comments, and I can hear a smile in her voice. "I know it hasn't been that long, but I miss my daughter. Will you visit soon?"

My throat constricts, and I swallow past the lump forming there. There are some things I will not share with my mom—the war between the vampires and the hunters is one of them. She's never been one to watch the news, either, so I'm hoping she hasn't seen any of the broadcasts about vampires. Something tells me I would've heard about it if she had.

"Calla?"

"Yes. Sorry," I force out, then clear my throat before I add, "Of course, I'll visit as soon as I can, Mom. I miss you guys."

"I won't keep you, but let's chat soon."

"Sounds good. I love you."

"I love you," she echoes before we disconnect.

With a deep sigh, I force myself off the ground and head inside, not really feeling the workout anymore.

After a quick shower, I get dressed into yoga pants and one of my cozy university hoodies—forgoing a bra and panties—then head downstairs to get a blood bag.

The cravings come and go, but when they come, they're like crashing waves strong enough to pull me under. My gums are raw today, and I'm not sure if that's normal, but it's really freaking irritating.

My stride falters halfway down the hall when I pick up sounds from the bedroom closest to the top of the stairs. I immediately recognize Lex's groan and Kade's responding chuckle. Heat flares in my cheeks, and I instantly feel bad for listening. But then I'm walking the rest of the way to the door and reaching for the handle because the only thing that could be hotter than listening is *watching*.

There's no chance they haven't heard me outside the bedroom door, so I open it wide enough to slip inside, closing it behind me. My eyes land on where they are in the bed. Lex has Kade pinned to the mattress, taking him from behind.

Kade turns his head on the pillow, and his eyes slam into me. His gaze is filled with lust, his pupils blown, and a smirk curls his lips. "Come to join us, or are you just going to watch?" he asks.

Lex chuckles, looking at me over his shoulder as he continues thrusting into Kade's ass.

Heat pools low in my belly, and I press my thighs together as my core throbs with desire. Part of me wants to get in between them, but the other part is curious to stand by and watch as they bring each other to climax.

I shift closer to the bed as Lex grips Kade's hips, driving into him at inhuman speed, his thighs tensing a moment before he groans, stiffening as he comes.

A second later, Kade flips them over, and I see a flash of his hard cock before it slams into Lex's ass.

Holy shit. I can't stop myself from dragging my hands under my sweater and pinching my nipples as I watch them. I bite my lip as my nipples harden and the heat between my thighs turns into an ache. I let my other hand slide past the waistband of my pants and tease my entrance, keeping my eyes locked on the bed in front of me.

"Fuck," Kade growls, "I can smell your arousal from here."

His words urge me to push two fingers inside myself, using my thumb to simulate my clit as I close my eyes and moan. I focus on the sounds of our combined breathing, the short gasps and groans of pleasure coming from the guys, as my breath hitches, and I speed up my fingers, finding new levels of pleasure at how fast I can move them inside me.

Lex announces his orgasm with a roar, gripping the sheets on either side of him until his knuckles are white.

Kade pulls out of him and appears in front of me in the blink of an eye as I continue fingering myself. "I'm tempted to let you finish, but I am too selfish." He grabs me by the hips and throws me onto the bed next to Lex, who immediately grips my chin, turning my face to his and sealing his mouth over mine as Kade moves between my thighs, dropping his mouth to my core.

Lex swallows my moan as Kade devours me, sucking my clit into his mouth and swirling his tongue around it until I see stars. He thrusts his tongue deep inside me, flicking it against the sensitive walls of my pussy until I clench around him, coming hard. He sucks my clit until my hips jerk off the bed, then moves his lips to my thigh, and I yelp against Lex's lips when Kade sinks his fangs into the sensitive flesh there.

The pull of blood leaving my body only adds to the pleasure I'm feeling as I break the kiss with Lex and find the pulse at his throat, letting my fangs extend to their full length before biting into his flesh.

He groans softly, holding onto me and tipping his head back to give me better access.

The sensations from drinking Lex's blood while Kade takes mine is incredible. It's overwhelming and leaves me dizzy with bloodlust and pleasure like I've never felt before, and if I wasn't already lying down, I'm sure I would've collapsed at this moment.

Kade pulls back, licking his lips at the same time I do, and he smirks at me as Lex sighs with pleasure.

"Well," I say in a quiet voice, "that was unexpected."

"Hmm," Kade agrees, "though the best things usually are."

After we get cleaned up and dressed, I slip downstairs to the kitchen to find something to eat. My stomach's grumbling but my gums hurt so bad I can barely think of anything besides the blood bags in the fridge.

Drinking from Lex was hot as fuck, but it did nothing to sate the cravings of human blood I now have to live with.

I pour the contents of one blood bag into a mug and stick it in the microwave before grabbing things to prepare a chopped salad. I'm sure if I asked Gabriel, he'd be more than happy to make me something fancier, but I like knowing that I can still do these things on my own.

I'm sipping on the blood as I slice some grilled chicken when Atlas walks into the room, the stoic expression I've come to naturally associate with him on his face.

"What's going on?" I ask him, trying to keep my tone casual and light.

He leans against the counter opposite me, crossing his arms over his chest, watching me work for a few moments before lifting his gaze to mine. "What we talked about last night..." He starts and immediately has my full attention. "I'm willing to forge a different path than the one Simon and Lenora have pushed me down my entire life. We're going to try to work with the hunters in an attempt to build a bridge of peace between us, but I'm going to need your help."

I drop the knife onto the cutting board and stare at him, my eyes widening. *I can't believe he just said that.* I move at vamp speed, throwing my arms around him in a tight hug.

His pulse pounds in his throat, and I can hear the way it quickens as his heart beats faster. A giggle slips through my lips, and he responds by holding me tighter, tipping my chin up and sealing his mouth over mine in a fiery kiss. Our tongues dance, but this time, it's not a battle for control. It's slow, explorative, and nice. Something I certainly wasn't expecting from him.

Hooting sounds behind us, and I immediately recognize Lex's voice as I pull away from Atlas, my cheeks burning as if he caught us doing something we shouldn't be.

After I finish lunch—and Lex eats half of my salad—the five of us sit around the coffee table in the living room with Fallon and Jace on the phone.

Gabriel filled them in on what we're going to attempt, and while they're in New York City, they wanted to be a part of the conversation and have offered to come to whatever meeting as backup for us.

I sit on the couch, my knee bouncing as I try to focus on what's being said. And as much as I want to be part of the discussions, I can't help feeling overwhelmed by the whole situation. It feels as if someone is sitting on my chest. Pulling in a breath is becoming more and more difficult.

I need air.

I get up and leave the living room, stepping outside to the patio in the backyard. Pulling my phone out of the pocket of my hoodie, I type a quick text to Tessa, and her response is almost immediate.

Hey! Good to hear from you. How are you adjusting to life as a vampire?

I groan, shaking my head, and type back, *I reached out to distract myself from that, so I want to hear about YOUR life.*

Instead of responding by text, Tessa calls me.

I answer, laughing softly. "Hey."

"We need to get together and drink until our problems are funny."

"Deal," I say immediately. "Where should I meet you?"

Tessa sighs. "I wish I could get on a plane right now and come hang with you. I'd even deal with the guys just to be able to spend some time with you and be away from this place for a minute."

My lips turn down. "I wish you were here. Things here are getting more complicated by the day."

"What do you mean?"

"For starters, Lex and I went to a club the other night, and it got raided by hunters."

She sucks in a breath. "Holy shit. Are you okay?"

"We're totally fine. I mean, Atlas had a hissy fit, but what else is new? It just doesn't bode well when we're trying to figure out if there's a possibility that we could broker peace with them."

"Wow, that sounds intense."

"Yep," I drag out the word, running my fingers through my hair as I walk back and forth across the patio.

"Keep me posted. We need to meet up once the dust settles. You know I'm here for you but I don't get involved with vampire business. Not when I can help it."

I press my lips together, my stomach sinking a little. I don't know if part of me was hoping that she'd offer to come help, but this fight isn't hers and she was already a huge help when it came to Selene. "Yeah, of course. I understand. So, you got my update. Do you want to talk about what's going on at your end?"

There are several beats of silence before she offers a humorless laugh. "I'm sort of caught in the middle of two guys, and that's, uh, putting it mildly."

I stop pacing for a moment. "Why get caught in the middle when you can have both?"

Tessa groans. "I have no idea. Handling one of them is tricky enough, but the other..." She trails off. "I don't know. It would be a lot easier to explain if you knew them. Hell, I still feel like *I'm* getting to know them some days. One of them, I trust with my life, but I can't... I mean, people would lose their shit if they knew about us."

"Why's that?"

"He's older and holds a position of power here."

"Sounds hot," I say. "So what? We like powerful men. Is that a crime?"

"Not a crime, per se, but it's against the rules."

My brows scrunch together. "Wait, really?" I'm missing something. I must be.

"Hmm, yeah. He's also sort of a mentor at the academy."

Realization hits me, and I can't help but laugh. "Hot for teacher, huh?" I tease.

Tessa groans. "It's not funny!"

"Sorry. I'm sorry. You're right. That sounds intense."

She sighs. "That's one word for it."

I tap my fingers against my thigh, getting momentarily distracted by the sound of a bird singing in the line of trees along the back of the yard. The tune is pitchy and annoying and it's filling my head like nails on a chalkboard, making me cringe. I manage to pull my attention away and focus on the sound of Tessa's breathing through the phone. Which, sure, it's a little weird, but it's a better alternative than climbing into the tree and ripping the head off that damn bird. "Tell me about the other guy."

"He is the worst person I've ever met and I'm pretty sure I hate him."

"Sounds romantic," I remark dryly.

"I told you it was complicated." There's a knock on her end, and she sighs again. "I should get that. We'll chat soon, though."

"Of course. I need to hear more about these guys. I'll have to meet them when I visit you this summer," I tell her.

"I look forward to it and I hope everything goes well with the hunters. It'd be monumental if vampires and humans stopped trying to kill each other all the time."

"Yeah," I say, "that would be ideal."

After we say our goodbyes and end the call, I slide my phone back into my pocket, tipping my head back to enjoy the lingering warmth against my face.

I plop down into one of the lounge chairs on the patio and enjoy the soft pink and orange sunset.

The back door opens, and Gabriel slips out, taking the chair next to me. I glance over at him and smile.

He returns it, his eyes bouncing between mine. "I came to check on you," he says.

"Thanks, Gabe. I know I should be in there and I want to be a part of the conversation. I just, um, had a bit of a panic attack."

He nods thoughtfully. "That's understandable. You're going through a lot and should take as much time as you need to adjust to all the changes happening in your life."

I consider that, and part of me is appreciative of him offering me time to adjust, but I also can't forget Atlas saying he'd need me to help with the hunters. More than that, I *want* to help.

"You've handled everything with such grace," Gabriel continues, moving from his lounge chair to perch on the edge of mine. I immediately shift over to make room for him, sliding my fingers through his.

"I'm trying my best," I say in a quiet voice. "There's a lot that still worries me, though."

His thumb moves back and forth over the top of my hand. "Do you want to talk about it?"

I tip my head back to look at him. "Is it okay if I say no?"

He smiles warmly, using his other hand to brush the hair away from my face, tucking it behind my ear. "If that's what you want. And just know, I only want to help you. To make you feel safe and loved."

My chest swells and my lips curl into a faint grin. "Aw, Gabriel, are you saying you love me?"

He dips his face closer, sliding his finger along my jaw before curling it around my chin. "Of course, I love you, Calla."

Before I can say it back, his lips brush mine, kissing me softly, once, twice, three times. I tug him closer, wrapping my arms around his neck. I close my eyes as our lips move together, and my pulse thumps in my throat as Gabriel slides his hand up my thigh. He flicks his tongue along my lips until they part for him, and our tongues dance, our hearts beating faster as we lose ourselves in each other.

Gabriel kisses me until my head spins. He pulls his mouth away from mine, moving across my jaw toward my neck, peppering kissing along my heated skin.

"Please," I say in a thick voice, "touch me."

"Are you sure?" he murmurs.

"I love you," I say in response, "and I want you." Even more than when I was human, if that's possible.

He leans back and looks into my eyes, offering me a smile that nearly takes my breath away. It's so filled with love and certainty, and it wipes away any fear I have over saying those three words.

His mouth descends on mine once more and his hand slides further up my thigh, curling into the waistband of my yoga pants. I grin at the jump in his pulse when he realizes I'm not wearing anything underneath, and I moan against his lips as his fingers brush my folds, teasing my entrance before moving upward and circling my clit lightly. I push my hips out, wanting him inside me, but he moves his fingers away from where I desperately want them and keeps teasing me.

"Gabriel," I grumble, breaking our kiss, "if you don't do something, *I'm* going to."

He chuckles softly. "Patience," he murmurs, "we have forever now, remember?"

I scowl halfheartedly. "Yeah, but that doesn't mean you have to drive me absolutely insane before you let me come."

"You know I'll take care of you."

It's not a question, but I nod anyway. There isn't a doubt in my mind of that.

"Good." He plunges a single digit inside me, making me suck in a sharp breath as he starts massaging my pussy walls. His thumb works my clit, alternating speed and pressure before he adds a second finger inside me.

"Yes," I moan, "right there."

He hits the same spot over and over, driving me wild as my heart tries to break through my ribcage and beat out of my chest.

"Oh, fuck," I breathe, pulling my bottom lip between my teeth in an attempt to quiet my moans.

"Don't hold back on me, angel." He adds another finger, circling my clit harder and faster, biting my shoulder without breaking the skin.

I ride his fingers, moaning unreservedly as stars explode behind my eyes and I come hard, my pussy clenching around his fingers, soaking them with my release.

"That's it," he purrs, continuing his thrusts as I grip the armrests of the lounge chair. He slowly pulls out of me, making the muscles in my thighs shake, and I shiver in response. I watch with utter rapture as he lifts his fingers to his mouth, licking them clean.

When I reach for the drawstring on his sweatpants, he catches my hand, bringing it to his lips, and kisses my knuckles.

"What about you?" I ask, feeling a little neglectful. He gave me a toe-curling orgasm using just his fingers—I feel like I should return the favor.

He cups my cheek in his palm, smiling down at me before pressing a kiss to my forehead. "Like I said, we have forever now. I'm not in any rush."

"How are you even real?" I say under my breath as we get up and head back inside. His only response is a soft laugh.

Gabriel leaves me in the hallway to go start on dinner, and I can't stop smiling... until I walk into the living room, and Atlas grabs me by the elbow and pushes me against the wall, caging me in. "Did the whole of Washington need to hear you come?"

My smile morphs into a smirk, electricity zipping through my veins as he glares at me, his pulse uneven. I tilt my head to the side slightly. "Jealousy isn't an attractive look on you, my sire."

His eyes narrow. "I hope you plan to get some rest tonight, because we'll be up at five o'clock tomorrow morning."

Arching a brow at him, I ask, "For what purpose, exactly? Does supernatural world peace need to be brokered at the ass crack of dawn for some reason?"

His lips twitch briefly. "If you think I'm letting you anywhere near those hunters without more training, you are sorely mistaken."

I blink at him. "Fine, but there isn't anywhere to train here." The backyard worked for the basic stuff I was doing yesterday, but it's not big enough to practice fighting, which is what I'm assuming he's concerned about.

Atlas nods. "I have a place."

I lean against the wall, rolling my eyes. "Of course, you do."

He stares at me several seconds longer, flicking his tongue over his bottom lip. Just when I think he's going to lean in and slant his mouth over mine, he pulls back and starts walking away. "Five o'clock," he repeats without looking back.

EIGHTEEN

ATLAS

As warned, I slip into Calla's room two minutes before five. She's still fast asleep, curled on her side with one arm hugging the pillow under her head and the other resting against the mattress. Her breathing is even, calm. Her face is relaxed and without tension—exactly as it should be. She shouldn't be stressed with the dangers and politics of our world. But it's her world too now.

It's one minute to five, and I fully intend to watch her, drinking in her beautifully serene features for the next sixty seconds before waking her up. Because I don't see that serenity lasting once I drag her ass out of that bed at what she would refer to as *an ungodly hour*.

Without flicking the light on, I walk around the room, approaching the bed from the side her back is facing. I lean over, pulling her hair over her shoulder as I perch on the thick duvet cover. My fingers trail over her cheek, caressing her soft skin, and I have to shove away the part of me that wants to pull her into my arms and bury us both under the covers to ignore the rest of the world.

"Atlas," she murmurs, still mostly asleep, her eyes closed.

My fingers freeze against her cheek. "Time to get up." I trace my thumb back and forth across her cheekbone.

"No," she whines as she rolls onto her back, blinking her eyes open and squinting at me. "I'm still sleeping."

I pull my hand back, watching her face. "I told you it would be an early morning."

"I thought you were just being an ass."

I shrug, standing from the bed. "Think whatever you want, but you better be downstairs in five minutes, or I'll be back and won't be nearly as nice." I don't wait for a response before leaving the bedroom, though I do catch the low curse she grumbles as I walk through the doorway.

Four minutes and thirty-seven seconds later, I'm standing in the foyer with my arms crossed over my chest, smirking softly as Calla trudges down the stairs, tying her hair up and glowering at me. She's wearing a pair of black leggings and running shoes paired with what I believe is one of Kade's old T-shirts with the sleeves and sides cut out, exposing the black sports bra she's wearing underneath.

"Twenty-three seconds to spare," I remark in a dry tone. "I'm impressed."

Her eyes narrow, and she says, "This is sire abuse. It has to be."

A chuckle slips past my lips before I press them together, and the others laugh from the living room where they were waiting for our girl to get her ass out of bed.

Gabriel gets up first, grabbing the travel mug off the coffee table, and walks into the hall, offering it to Calla. "It's an Americano. I figured you could use the caffeine."

"You're officially my favorite," she says, taking the mug and hugging it to her chest as if it's her most prized possession.

Kade and Lex join us in the foyer, the latter rolling his eyes. "Please, anyone can make coffee. Not everyone can make you—"

"Don't start," I cut in. "She needs to stay focused on training this morning."

"Boring," Kade singsongs, sliding past Lex and throwing his arm around Calla's shoulder, kissing the side of her head. "Good morning."

She leans into him, sighing with annoyance aimed very clearly at me. "Maybe it would be if it wasn't still pitch-black outside."

I ignore the quip and walk out the front door, leaving Gabriel to lock it behind us as we pile into the vehicle.

It's a twenty-minute drive to the fitness club, and I peer in the rearview to find Calla dozing off against Lex's shoulder. The corner of my mouth tugs up, and I slam on the breaks after making sure there's no one behind us.

Calla startles, yelping in surprise and whipping her head around. "What the fuck?" She meets my gaze in the mirror and scowls. "Bastard."

"Just making sure everyone's awake and alert," I say in a level voice, switching my foot back to the gas and speeding up again.

She grabs her mug from the cup holder beside her, evidently choosing to drink her Americano instead of responding to me.

I use the spare key the owner, Dom, gave me years ago, and unlock the garage door entrance, pushing it up to reveal the commercial garage turned fitness club. It's been closed to the public for months, so Dom invited us to use it.

"Whoa," Calla murmurs, wandering around the second we're inside. "This place is cool."

I close the door behind us, not needing any outside attention to what we're doing. "Warm up." I direct that order at Calla, and she arches a brow at me.

"Maybe *you* should warm up," she replies, and there's a clear challenge in her voice.

One I'm all too happy to accept.

I move across the room and snatch the coffee mug out of her hands, tossing it into the kitchenette sink nearby. It clatters against the stainless steel, and Calla's heart lurches in her chest. I back her up against the wall, caging her in.

She catches me off guard, slamming her knee into my stomach with newly amplified speed and strength, knocking me back a few steps as I grunt in more surprise than pain. She advances without giving me a second to recover, her fist flying toward my face. I duck in just enough time to avoid it connecting with my jaw and grab her upper arm, pulling her back against my chest as I wrap my arm around her neck in a chokehold.

"Okay, I guess we're not warming up," Kade comments mildly, amusement lacing his tone, and Lex chuckles. The two of them begin sparring as Gabriel walks over to where Calla is struggling to break free of my grasp. Despite her newfound strength, I still have decades on her. Without the element of surprise, she doesn't have much of a chance against me. And if she genuinely wanted to bring me harm, which I don't believe she does—even after hauling her out of bed this morning—because I sired her, she'll never be able to.

Calla slams her elbow into my ribs over and over, gritting her teeth until her molars grind, and growls deep in her throat. "You've made your point," she says under her breath, digging her fingers into my skin as she attempts to pry my arm away from her neck.

I let her go, turning her around to face me. "You're stronger," I tell her, "which is good. Your previous training will also lend you a hand."

She arches a brow at me, then her eyes narrow. "Why do I feel like there's a 'but' in there somewhere?"

"I think he's trying to compliment you, angel," Gabriel says, leaning against the wall near us with one ankle crossed over the other. Gabriel has never been one for fighting—not since he escaped Selene's clutches. He tends to leave the violence to Lex or Kade—or both, depending on the situation.

"Oh. Thanks."

Instead of responding, I attack again, coming at her from the side and taking her down onto the mats. Calla grits her teeth, her sharp silver eyes narrowed at me as I trap her wrists above her head. She immediately bucks her hips, knocking me to the side and slamming her foot into my ribs. I grunt, releasing her wrists, and she gets up in a blur of movement.

Kade moves in next, and I get off the mats, watching their technique closely. He launches at her from behind, but she hears him coming and whips around, throwing her arm out and catching him in the chest. He goes down hard, and she drops to the mats with him, kneeing him in the stomach and wrapping her fingers around his throat. Both their hearts are pounding, and despite his position, Kade is grinning like a child on Christmas morning.

Lex joins the fight, snaking an arm around Calla's waist and hauling her off Kade. She slams her head back, and it cracks against his jaw. He curses, letting go of her, and she whirls on him, kicking his legs out with a grunt. Her breathing is heavy and sweat dots her brow, but she isn't giving up. Our girl is strong and resilient, and I expect nothing less from her.

I glance toward where Gabriel is observing the match. He meets my gaze, and I nod at him to join the training. He inclines his head slightly and pushes away from the wall, stalking forward as Lex jumps up from the floor. The three of them converge on Calla, and her gaze bounces between them.

"Seriously?" she breathes, still trying to catch her breath as she inches away from them. "Three against one? That's hardly fair."

"Focus," I snap at her.

Gabriel shoots forward first, grabbing Calla by the shoulders. She growls in his face, her pulse pounding as she focuses her energy on defending herself against his attack. Shoving against his chest, she manages to put a bit of distance between them before taking a swing at his face. He catches her fist at the last moment and pushes her back—right into Lex's chest. He wraps both arms around her like a cage, holding her arms against her sides, and lifts her off the floor when she tries to pull away. She throws her head back, and Lex barely manages to avoid taking it square in the face. He drops her, and she slams her elbow back into his ribcage, making him grunt. Kade barks out a laugh, retreating toward the mini-fridge, and grabs a bottle of water, downing half of it.

Before the others can make another attempt, I close in on her, snaring her attention immediately.

"Are we done?" she asks, glancing at Gabriel and Lex before returning her gaze to me. "I need a shower."

"In a minute." I'm fairly satisfied with what I've seen. I wasn't expecting her to be able to fight off all of us at once, but what she managed to do did impress me. "What do you do when a hunter gets behind you?"

She swallows, licking her lips as her chest continues rising and falling quickly. "I'd start by—"

"Wrong," I cut her off, stopping only once I'm a single breath away from her. "You don't *let* a hunter get behind you."

Calla scowls, propping her hands on her hips. "Don't ask me questions if you're not going to give me a chance to answer them."

I ignore the attitude in her voice. "The opponents you could be up against are mostly human. They are trained to kill vampires, but they don't share our preternatural speed and strength. So as long as you stay focused on your surroundings and don't allow yourself to be caught by surprise, you'll have the upper hand."

Her brows tug closer as she digests what I've said. "You said *mostly* human." She shakes her head. "Do you think I'll be up against other vampires?"

"It's something we can't rule out," Gabriel chimes in. "If things work out positively with the hunters, there will be some angry vampires, and we can't determine with complete certainty what they'll do in retaliation."

"Super," she deadpans. "Either way, we're facing a battle."

"Yes," I answer honestly. "Would you rather side with the vampires and wipe out the hunters, or try to reconcile with the hunters and take the chance of making enemies in our world?"

"Why are you asking me as if it's *my* choice?"

I cross my arms, shrugging. "It's not. I'm just curious."

She doesn't know it yet, but the decision has already been made. I spoke to Scott Ellis after Calla fell asleep last night, and after a very long, very tense conversation, he reluctantly agreed to meet with us in a neutral spot to discuss our... *relationship* moving forward.

"You know what I think. I've made it quite clear. We need to try to figure things out with the hunters. That path has the least amount of senseless fighting and casualties. There's always going to be a black sheep in every group of people—human, vampire, or otherwise."

"Otherwise?" Kade calls out, ducking under Lex's arm before he can grab him.

Calla shrugs. "Figure I shouldn't rule anything out at this point. Vampires and witches exist, so I'm going to assume other supernaturals do too."

Gabriel and I exchange a brief look.

She's not wrong, but this isn't a conversation for today.

"Let's see how the meeting goes and we'll take it from there," Gabriel says.

Calla turns her gaze toward him. "Why does it sound like you've already *arranged* a meeting?"

"We have," I answer. "A very circumstantial one."

Her heart beats faster, and she wets her lips before saying, "That was fast. How many vampires did Marcel contact that will agree to work with us and meet with the hunters?"

Kade and Lex take a break from attacking each other and join us, breathing heavily with sweat dampening their hair.

"Marcel is still in the process of contacting people, but he's gotten mixed feedback so far. A lot of the younger vampires are more open to it, but as we suspected, the older ones prefer the way things are and are more likely to side with the vampires planning to eradicate the hunters.

"As you know, Fallon and Jase will stand with us, and besides, this meeting isn't for all of us to sit around a campfire and hold hands. I don't want a lot of people there on either side." The *in case things go sideways* goes without saying.

"When is the meeting?" she asks, focusing on me again.

"Tomorrow night. So, you better be prepared to train again tomorrow morning, because there's no way you'll be coming with us if I'm not fully confident you're ready."

"What the hell?" she says in a confused tone, shaking her head. "Didn't I just prove myself to you?"

"What happens if someone gets hurt and bleeds?" Lex offers. "Are you going to be able to fight with the smell of blood in the air?"

Her jaw clenches, and she shoots an icy glare at him. "I don't know. Let's stab you and see how well I can focus."

None of us bother mentioning that human blood would have an entirely different effect. She knows it by now.

"If you can't keep your cool in here with us, how can we know you'll be able to handle being at this meeting?" Kade points out.

"I can handle it," she says firmly. "Why are you guys pushing me? Haven't I proven myself enough times?"

Gabriel regards her thoughtfully. "We're just worried about you, angel. This could be the start of a very positive thing for us and the human population as well, but it also has the potential to be—"

"A bloodbath," she cuts in. "I know that. But I want this just as badly as you do. All I'm asking is for you to see that and believe in me. I can handle this." The determination in her voice grabs my attention, and I can't stop staring at her.

We need to give her more credit.

I need to give her more credit.

She survived us coming into her life and stealing her away from it, then she survived becoming a vampire.

Calla is quite possibly the strongest person I've met in my many decades on this earth—and she deserves to know it.

She sucks in a soft breath, her eyes landing on me and her pulse racing. Realization colors her delicate features, and her lips slowly curl into a smile.

"What is it?" Kade asks, arching a brow at her.

She bites down on her bottom lip, her eyes bouncing between mine as if she's waiting for me to speak.

"Is this some weird sire thing?" Kade asks Lex, who likely is feeling some of what is happening between Calla and me right now, though certainly not to the degree we are.

"You could say that," Lex answers him, while I keep my eyes trained on Calla. There's a bright shimmer of hope in her eyes that makes my chest tighten.

She glances around the circle we've made in the center of the garage, pursing her lips for a moment. "I should call Brighton. If she's going to be involved with this, she needs to know what's coming down the pipeline. She doesn't know I'm a vampire yet, and I want to be the one to tell her. I'd rather do it in person instead of over the phone, but I'm not sure there's time."

"Absolutely not," I say immediately. "You're not seeing her ahead of any meeting we have with the hunters." Before she can run her mouth at me, I continue, "You need to be more cautious from here on out, Calla. Being too trusting during anything with regards to the hunters is dangerous. Do you understand me?"

"Do you want to keep talking down to me as if I'm a child?" she shoots back. "Of course, I understand that. But we have to be somewhat trusting; otherwise, this isn't going to work, and then what the hell was the point?" She crosses her arms. "You told me you needed my help with this, so you'd better fucking listen to what I have to say and fully consider it before you stand there and act like you know better than me just because you've been around the sun a million times." Her pulse is ticking faster by the time she finishes speaking, her chest rising and falling unevenly.

Lex whistles under his breath and the others remain silent.

I stare at her, her gaze unwavering as those silver eyes hold mine. "Fine," I finally say in a tight voice, because nothing about this feels comfortable. I'm used to being in complete control, and this... this is very new. "We'll try it your way."

NINETEEN

CALLA

Sleep refuses to pull me under. I toss and turn for well over an hour, and I'm not the only one who isn't able to find rest.

Atlas and Gabriel are sitting in the backyard shortly after two in the morning, speaking in hushed tones, but I hear every word clearly—and I really wish I don't.

They don't have high hopes for the meeting—Atlas especially. He wants to ensure we're prepared for a fight if that's what we're walking into; however, Gabriel is far more optimistic that we can have a productive discussion. He's always the most level-headed of our group, it seems.

"It's in their best interests as much as it's in ours," he says to Atlas as I press myself against the wall beside the window so they can't see me from below. I peer down at the T-shirt I stole from Kade a while ago. It's an old Pink Floyd tour shirt that nearly reaches my knees, making it the perfect sleep shirt.

"We'll see," is Atlas's only response.

Gabriel sighs heavily. "We should try to get some sleep. Kade's been snoring for over an hour and Lex was half asleep through dinner." There's a brief pause. "And Calla's been hanging onto our every word and should get to sleep as well."

My stomach drops, heat filling my cheeks as I dive into the bed, hauling the covers over me, and turn onto my side, hugging my pillow to my cheek.

They share a short laugh as my pulse pounds after getting caught. Rookie mistake. *Of course,* they knew I was listening.

I close my eyes, focusing on leveling my breathing. The patio door opens and closes before footsteps come up the stairs. I hold my breath as one set of footsteps slows outside my bedroom.

"Goodnight, angel," Gabriel says from the other side of the closed door.

I press my lips together, smiling faintly. "Night."

He walks away, and a few moments later, his bedroom door shuts.

I roll onto my back and open my eyes, staring at the plain white ceiling as I play over potential scenarios for tomorrow in my head.

Atlas comes up the stairs and doesn't bother knocking before slipping into my room, closing the door behind him. "You should be asleep."

"So should you," I reply, watching him walk closer, and sit up, resting my back against the pile of pillows at the headboard.

The corner of his mouth tugs up ever so slightly as he keeps his eyes locked with mine and sits on the bed. The urge to reach for him floods my system, and I bite the inside of my cheek, gripping the sheets to keep my hands to myself. I'm still frustrated with him over what happened at the fitness club, and I'm not going to let that go just because part of me craves comfort from the vampire who made me. It's fucking complicated and certainly something I wasn't expecting when I decided it would be Atlas who'd turn me.

"What are you doing awake?" he asks, dropping his chin, his hair falling forward into his face.

"Oh, you know, enjoying a little late-night overthinking sprinkled with fear of the unknown and some general dread over our circumstances. Just the usual."

"Calla."

"Atlas," I level.

"Drop the bravado. You can't hide anything from me and you're above acting indifferent to the things happening around you."

My eyes narrow slightly as the throbbing in my gums grows increasingly more irritating. "What do you want me to say?"

"You could start with the truth," he offers, shifting closer.

"The truth," I echo with a humorless laugh. "You already know everything I'm feeling, so I don't see much sense in vocalizing it."

He shrugs. "Sometimes saying things aloud helps. If it's something you're worried about, talking about it takes away the power it holds over you in the fear it causes."

I arch a brow at him. "Do you have a psych degree I don't know about?"

"No. But living as long as I have has taught me a thing or two."

I drop my gaze to my lap, tapping my fingers against my thighs. "Do you ever get tired of it?"

"Living forever?"

I nod without looking at him.

"Not in a long while. You created quite the rift in all of our lives. I imagine as did we in yours." He places his hand over mine. "I can't see what the future holds for all of us, but with you around, I can be sure of at least one thing—it won't be boring."

Pressing my lips together against a reluctant smile, I turn my hand over and lace my fingers through his.

He shifts closer, sitting next to me against the headboard with his legs stretched out in front of him on top of the covers.

"And what about tomorrow?" I ask.

"Tomorrow," he says with a sigh, "could go a few different ways." He turns his face toward me. "But I need you to promise me you won't hesitate to fight—and kill if necessary—any hunters."

I can't help but frown. "If it's them or me, I promise."

His gaze lingers for a moment before he nods. "Thank you."

I exhale a heavy breath, rubbing my eyes with the hand that isn't holding his.

"Do you want me to help you fall asleep?" he offers in a soft voice.

"No," I say, shaking my head for added measure, "that isn't fair. You don't have anyone that can do that for you."

Atlas tilts his head to the side, his eyes roaming my face. "I'm not worried about me." His concern for me may not be evident in his expression, but there's a tingle in my chest that tells me it's there. It's a new sensation that I'm still getting used to—being able to *feel* Atlas in different ways that deepen our connection past what I share with the others.

I roll my eyes, dragging my thumb back and forth across the back of his hand. "Of course you're not, but *I* am." I move into his lap, still holding his hand and using the other to push his hair back. "Maybe we can help each other," I murmur, leaning down and resting my forehead against his. I lick my lips, the corner of my mouth curling at the quickening of his pulse. That has to be one of my favorite things about being a vampire I've discovered so far—hearing how I affect the guys after months of them knowing how they affect me.

Atlas tips his head back. "Are you trying to distract me with seduction?"

I lean back a little. "Is there something wrong with that?"

I'm granted one of his rare grins as he shakes his head. "Just checking."

Shifting in his lap, I bear down, grinding myself against him. "Yeah? Are you sure?"

He grips my hips, flashing his fangs as he hardens against me. "Careful," he warns, desire flaring to life in his gaze. "You want to keep teasing? Because that isn't a game you'll win."

My stomach tightens as my core throbs with need. I want him to take me with his tongue and fingers and cock. As much as his high-handed behavior pisses me off often, tonight I *want* him to take control. I want to turn off my brain, stop thinking, and just get lost in him.

"Kiss me," I murmur, pressing my chest to his.

His mouth slants over mine without hesitation, capturing my lips in a slow, sensual kiss that makes me tingle all the way to my toes.

I tangle my fingers in his hair as he moves my hips in his lap, igniting a fiery desire to immediately do away with the clothing that separates our skin from touching.

Atlas slides his hands under my shirt, pushing it up my thighs, exposing my black lace panties before continuing upward, my breath hitching as his fingers inch closer to my breasts. They ache for attention, my nipples stiffening against the material of my shirt before he even reaches them. I gasp softly into his mouth when his thumbs brush across the hardened peaks, shifting in his lap as pleasure and heat shoot straight to my core, dampening my panties. Atlas pushes his hips forward, the bulge in his black sweatpants grinding against my entrance through the thin material.

I break the kiss and lean forward to grab the hem of his shirt, tugging it up until he has to pull his hands out of my shirt so I can get it off the rest of the way. He immediately returns his attention to my breasts, using one hand to alternate between them, massaging and teasing, while his other slides down my stomach toward the apex of my thighs. My pulse ticks faster the closer he gets, and I suck in a sharp breath when his fingers brush my folds. He pushes his thumb against my clit, teasing me before sliding his fingers inside my panties, making my stomach muscles tighten.

Instead of pulling them down, Atlas rips the lace clean off me, dropping the torn bits onto the mattress as his gaze hones in on my core.

Heat floods my cheeks and chest, and I reach for the drawstring on his pants, tugging them to bring him closer, then slide my hand past the waistband, gripping his thick length in my fist and pulling it free. I pump my hand up and down his shaft, reveling in the way his heart pounds in his chest, matching mine.

He hisses out a breath, pinching my nipple between his thumb and finger at the same moment he slides two fingers inside me.

"Fuck," I moan and match his pace, pumping his cock as his fingers thrust in and out of my pussy.

It quickly becomes an unspoken challenge to make the other lose control first. Atlas curls his fingers, rubbing the spot deep inside me that makes my head spin with pleasure.

I increase both the speed and pressure of my thrusts, using my thumb to tease the thick head of his cock, making him curse under his breath, his chest rising and falling faster as his pulse trips over itself.

A haze of lust fills my head, making it feel light enough to float away, and I spread my legs wider, needing to feel more of him. His thumb circles my clit hard and fast, and he's pulsing his fingers so quickly inside me they feel like a vibrator.

"God, yes," I breathe, thrusting my hips to push him deeper.

"I am no god," he growls.

"You're right," I shoot back, "you're the fucking devil."

"Hmm... and I'll worship your body just the way you like." Atlas pulls out of me and grips my wrist, forcing me to release his cock before he flips us over, pinning me to the mattress. He traps my wrists above my head in one of his hands. Without warning, he slams into me, stealing the air from my lungs. He swallows my surprised moan, kissing me hard until I'm dizzy and my pulse is pounding beneath my skin. Reaching between us, his fingers find my clit and work it until it's so sensitive my thighs are shaking. I'm racing toward release and there's no way in hell I'm going to hold back in an attempt to make him come first. I'm too fucking close and everything he's doing feels too fucking good.

Come for me.

His voice fills my thoughts and grips my body. I don't have a second to process that or try to understand how his voice got into my head as my muscles tighten and pleasure floods through me like a tsunami. My pussy clenches around his cock, soaking it with my release as I come hard, announcing my climax with a loud, breathy moan.

Atlas continues thrusting into me, wringing moans and whimpers each time he's fully sheathed in me. A few more thrusts, and he grunts deeply, his cock throbbing inside me as his orgasm hits hard, and he drops his mouth to mine, sealing us together in a consuming kiss that could go on forever without any complaint from me.

I shiver with the aftershocks of my orgasm, my toes curling and my skin tingling as he slowly pulls out of me, dropping down next to me on the bed. My body is warm and tingling with pleasure as I fight to keep my eyes open. "You know," I murmur, my eyelids drooping, heavy with exhaustion as I snuggle closer to him, "this is something I can't see myself ever getting tired of."

The five of us are silent the entire drive to the meeting place the following evening. We're all drinking from the blood bags Lex packed in a cooler to ensure we're at our strongest should that be necessary.

The spot Atlas and Scott agreed to meet is a conservation area near the outskirts of the city that's currently closed to the public. Fallon and Jase are meeting us there, along with Marcel and his close team of six other vampires, according to Gabriel.

My knee bounces nervously as I stare out the windshield from the passenger seat. Atlas is behind the wheel, while the others are in the back.

"You remember what I said last night?" Atlas says in a low voice as he flicks the blinker and turns off the main road onto the county highway. There are massive open fields on one side and a forest on the other.

I force my knee to stop moving. "Yes."

"Let's hope it doesn't come to that, but if it does—"

"I know," I cut in, my voice level.

"Good."

Gravel crunches under us as Atlas pulls onto another, far narrower road. It twists and turns for several miles before we slow to a stop in what appears to be a makeshift parking lot.

There's another SUV with tinted windows parked across the gravel lot, and the second Atlas puts the vehicle in park, the doors to the other car open, and Fallon and Jase hop out, walking toward us.

Gabriel gets out, greeting them with hugs, while Kade and Lex linger a few feet away.

I stay in the vehicle a bit longer with Atlas before sighing. "Now or never, I guess."

Atlas leans across the center console, gripping my chin and turning my face toward him. He kisses me hard and fast. "Don't do anything stupid," he says after pulling back, then lowers his voice. "Please."

"Love you too," I say back, getting out of the SUV and walking across the lot to meet up with the others. I give Fallon and Jase a quick smile and wave.

"Welcome to the fang family," Jase says with a grin.

I laugh somewhat awkwardly. "Thanks."

Another car pulls into the lot, and my heart beats faster before Gabriel leans over and says, "That's Marcel."

He parks next to us and gets out, followed by six other vampires—three men and three women—that I've never seen before.

Once we're all together, Atlas nods toward a break in the trees. "There's a clearing on the other side of those trees," he says. "Scott will be waiting there with his second-in-command and a few members of the organization."

My thoughts immediately go to Brighton and if she'll be among them. We move quickly, passing through the thick forest, the smell of pine and damp soil heavy in the air as the sunset filters through the trees.

The moment our group steps into the clearing, I scan the faces of each person flanking Scott. A pang of relief flickers through me when I realize Brighton isn't here.

We stop about twenty feet from them, and Atlas is the first to speak. "I think this meeting is long overdue."

"That is debatable," Scott answers.

"Well, you're here," Kade chimes in, "which means you've come to your senses and realized that the only way you survive this is to agree to our terms."

Atlas shoots him a dark look, which Kade merely shrugs at.

Perfect. We're off to a great start.

Scott's brows lift as he glances at the hunter on his left, then his right, before addressing us once more. "Is that what it means?" He reaches around and pulls a dagger from a holder in his belt, and my pulse immediately jumps, my focus narrowing on the weapon—one of the only things that can kill me now.

"You are disappointedly predictable," Atlas says to Scott, his jaw set tight before he sighs. His heart is beating slightly faster than normal, which immediately puts me on high alert, my sharp gaze scanning our surroundings.

Several more hunters inch into the clearing, keeping close to the tree line as they grip the weapons in their hands tightly, their faces filled mostly with anger and hatred. Some look as young, if not younger than me, and of them, fear is reflected in the faces of a few.

Scott's expression remains stoic, impassive. "What you think you can offer is not enough." His voice is gravelly and filled with utter hatred.

Pressure fills my chest and dizziness threatens to overtake me as I stand with the vampires I've come to love and realize the hunters under Scott's leadership will never agree to our proposal. Which means we've walked into an ambush.

Everything happens in blurs of movement, though seemingly in slow motion. Chaos erupts in the clearing, and the hunters charge toward us. We are severely outnumbered, which was our second mistake. I suppose trusting the word of a man hellbent on killing us was the first.

The vampires fan out, and the blood starts flowing seconds later. We may be outnumbered by hunters but we have the speed and strength they lack.

When a pair of hunters come at me, I back up a few steps before I stop, shaking my head, and remind myself they're the ones who should be afraid of me.

"You don't want to do this," I say in a level tone, hoping they somehow magically decide to turn in another direction.

What an awful moment to realize the guys haven't taught me glamour yet.

"Oh, we really fucking do," the younger guy says, sneering at me as he adjusts his grip on his dagger. The guy next to him nods in agreement.

I swallow, my heart beating like the wings of a hummingbird in my chest. "I don't want to kill you. I don't want to hurt you." I back up a few more steps as they continue to advance. "That's why we're here. I don't know what Scott told you, but—"

It comes out of nowhere. A body slams into me, knocking me to the side, and I stumble over the uneven ground, whipping around with my fangs extended to their full length and come face-to-face with Brighton.

Her eyes are filled with horror and pain as she shakes her head. "N-no."

My stomach plummets. "Bri—"

"*No.*" Her eyes are glassy with unshed tears and her jaw is clenched tightly. Exhaustion, anger, and confusion darken her features, but she doesn't back down. My gaze drops to the dagger she holds in her dominant hand.

"Please, I... This wasn't... Please let me explain." Desperation makes my voice pitchy, and I hate it. I hate this whole thing.

She gasps, her eyes widening seconds before two hunters attack me from behind. One grabs a fistful of my hair, yanking me backward. Sharp pain lances across my scalp, and I snarl, throwing my arm back to catch the guy in the face with my elbow, breaking his nose with a satisfying *crunch*. Blood pours from his nostrils, and my throat burns at the sight, my gums throbbing. *Sink your fangs into him. Drink him dry and end his suffering.*

I recoil, not sure where the hell that came from. That isn't me—that *can't* be me. But it was my voice.

Another small group of hunters circles me in the few seconds I was caught in my own head, and my pulse spikes with panic. More so over the thought of having to kill them than *them* killing *me.*

A black-haired female hunter moves in front of me, managing to clip my jaw with her fist. It doesn't hurt as much as it catches me off guard, and before I can shove her away or disarm her, I feel movement behind me and turn just in time to catch the sharp end of a dagger in my shoulder. A growl tears from my throat, and I pull the dagger out by the hilt, jamming into the side of the woman's neck who stabbed me before she has the sense to move away. Her eyes bug out of her head, and she gasps, choking on her own blood as she sinks to her knees and collapses on the ground, her eyes going vacant in seconds.

"Calla." Brighton's voice makes me turn back toward her. Big mistake. Four new hunters are right there, grabbing me by the arms. I snarl, gnashing my fangs in their faces as I manage to fight a couple of them off, though not before one lands a solid punch to my gut and another takes a shot at my chest with his dagger and gets me in the side.

Screams of pain and anger echo through the clearing as the fight rages on, and not having even a second to take a look around and make sure my guys are okay has me wired.

I yank the dagger out and drop it on the grass, blinking down at it, my stomach churning at the sight of it covered in my blood.

Another hunter grabs me from behind before I can dart out of reach, and she jabs something into my side that immediately fills my veins with fire. My knees give out and hit the ground, my muscles seizing tightly as I gasp for breath.

That bitch just tased me with a goddamn cattle prod. Something that would likely kill a human and is making it difficult to focus as I scream at my legs to work, to move me away from the hunters closing in on me.

Fuck, fuck, fuck.

I cry out for Atlas—at least, I think I do.

Sounds are muffled and my vision is going in and out, refusing to focus.

A heavy boot connects with my chest, knocking me back flat against the cold ground.

I blink hard, willing my vision to clear so I can at least attempt to fight off my attackers until someone steps in to help me.

When Brighton's face appears over me, blocking out the sunset in the sky above, my stomach clenches with nausea.

Oh no. Please, no.

She crouches beside me, her expression filled with anger and pain, and when she pulls a dagger out from behind her, everything in me seizes with fear and dread.

The orchestra of fighting around me starts to come back and the familiar sounds of the guys' shouting is like a punch in the gut. They're trying to get to me, but there are too many hunters holding them back, and it even looks as if a few of Marcel's guys have been taken out.

"Pl-please," I croak, tears leaking out the sides of my eyes as I blink up at her.

She shakes her head, a sheen of sweat covering her forehead. She clenches her jaw as her chin quivers and her pulse becomes even more erratic, her heart pounding in her chest. *She doesn't want to do this.* She doesn't want to be here as much as I don't want to be here.

I try to get up, but the woman with the cattle prod is back, slamming the hilt of it into the side of my head before shooting another shockwave through me near my ribs. Seconds later, I barely make out Brighton's dagger-wielding arm lifting in the air.

"Brighton, don't!" Atlas snarls.

White-hot pain flares through me, searing my veins with para-lyzing agony. The world around me narrows. My stomach drops, my throat constricting too tight to breathe as the weight of realization slams into me like a freight train, making my eyes burn with tears. Betrayal and heartbreak rip through me, sharp as the dagger sticking out of my chest.

My best friend is going to kill me.

RAPTURED BY ETERNITY

CHAPTER

ONE

CALLA

I've already died once this month. I really don't want to do it again.

Everything is moving in slow motion around me. Voices are muffled and the music of battle is distorted as fire licks through my chest, searing me to the marrow with white-hot pain. My heart pounds violently, screaming at me as if I didn't already know I'm in real danger of not making it out of this alive. Darkness creeps along the edges of my vision, threatening to pull me under, and I'm so tired and cold, I can't fight it much longer.

"You... missed," I croak, barely clinging to consciousness as a chill from the damp ground seeps into my bones, wracking me with violent shivers.

"I know," she cries, tears soaking her cheeks. Her expression is twisted into a mix of anguish and shock as she continues to stare at me, her face getting blurrier by the second.

The last darkened, distorted image I see is of a tattooed arm covered with vines and thorns and roses hauling Brighton off me before the darkness swallows me whole.

CHAPTER

TWO

ATLAS

The stench of blood burns my nostrils. My gums throb despite my fangs already being extended to their full length, and my pulse is a wicked, uncontrollable jackhammer beneath my heated skin.

Two words make me nearly fall to my knees.

You missed.

Relief floods through me at a dizzying pace, and I grit my teeth against the sensation, charging forward in a blur. Pain ebbs through me, mirroring only faintly what Calla is experiencing. It pushes me to move faster, desperate to take that agony away.

Lex beats me to her, grabbing Brighton around the waist and hauling her away from Calla.

I drop to Calla's side, cupping her cheeks in my hands. "Keep your eyes open," I demand, shifting my attention to the dagger sticking out of her chest. The slight tremor in my voice makes me grit my teeth. *She's going to be fine.* "I'm going to pull this out now," I tell her. "You can't heal with the white ash in your system."

Kade growls from somewhere behind me moments before two more hunter bodies hit the ground with lifeless *thuds*. I spare him a glance and find blood dripping from his mouth and covering the front of his shirt. His eyes are blazing with rage as they flit between the hunters and where Calla is on the ground.

Gabriel is fighting his own group of hunters, though they seem more scared than determined to kill him.

Fucking hell, how young are they?

I shake my head and grip the dagger, pulling it from Calla's chest in one swift movement. She tenses, sucking in a breath, but even that is subdued. We need to get her out of here and fed so she'll heal.

"Gabe," I holler, and he's at my side instantly, covering me as I scoop Calla up, cradling her against my chest. She groans uncomfortably, her brows scrunching together and her eyelids fluttering. "I know," I murmur to her, "just hang on."

"Bri..." she whispers.

"Lex is taking care of her."

Her eyes fly open, fear darkening her silver irises. "N-no."

I frown at her, walking along the tree line to avoid what's left of the fight. Many of the hunters are dead or have fled—including Scott. *Fuck.* "He won't hurt her." *Not yet.* There isn't time now to deliver the level of pain that human deserves for nearly killing what's ours.

Calla relaxes in my arms, her eyes falling shut once more, as if that moment of panic stole the little energy she had left.

Fallon and Jase catch up to us halfway to where we left the vehicles. They appear ruffled and dirty—with blood and dirt—but are otherwise unharmed. Marcel, alongside a few of his vampires and Kade, are still in the clearing, either killing or chasing away the remaining hunters.

"Safe to say that was an epic fail," Fallon mutters, shoving her hands into her windbreaker.

"Fal," Jase says under his breath, shaking his head.

Gabriel frowns, keeping his eyes on Calla, as if he's afraid to look away. "Let's just get out of here and regroup, then we can discuss everything." He stays close to Calla, his forehead creased with concern and his heart beating unsteadily as he watches her. He doesn't ask to take her from me—he knows there's not a chance in hell of me letting her go right now, even to him.

We get back to the car, and I lay Calla across the backseats, brushing the hair out of her face. "You still with us?"

She grumbles incoherently.

My lips twitch. "You did good out there."

"Yeah," she says in a hoarse voice, "until I got stabbed."

I run my thumb along her bottom lip, bringing a bit of color back into her cheeks. "Happens to the best of us," I offer, referring to the time she got me with the letter opener in my office.

Not long after, Kade comes through the break in the trees. Marcel and the other vampires are several paces behind him, also covered in blood and dirt.

"Well, that could've gone better," Kade nearly growls, coming to a stop outside the vehicle. "How's our girl?" Worry has replaced some of the anger, making him appear younger.

"Alive, but she needs blood, so let's save the conversation for later." Kade nods, moving around the car to confirm Calla's condition himself, and I look to Marcel. "You good?"

He nods. "We lost a couple good ones, though."

"It shouldn't have gone down that way. I'm sorry."

Marcel offers a soft sigh and shrugs. "We knew it was a possibility." He glances around the small group gathered around the vehicles. "Let's chat tomorrow?"

I nod, gripping and squeezing his shoulder. "Thank you, Marcel."

He dips his chin before turning away. His team piles into their respective vehicles, while Fallon and Jase hug Gabriel before heading for theirs.

Gabriel climbs into the backseat with Calla, carefully shifting her into his lap and cradling her to him. He meets my gaze in the mirror when I get behind the wheel. "Lex?"

"Stole one of the hunters' cars and took Brighton back to the house."

Kade takes the front passenger seat, slamming his door shut. "Let's get the fuck out of here."

Gabriel carries Calla into the house and gently sets her on the couch, propping her head up with a cushion, while Kade disappears into the kitchen. He returns a moment later with a blood bag in each hand.

"We need to decide what to do with the Ellis girl," he says with a scowl on his mouth; he's not attempting to mask his hatred for Brighton, and I can't say I blame him.

I swipe one of the blood bags, tearing it open, and crouch before Calla, gripping her chin and tipping her head back before bringing it to her lips. Her nostrils flare at the sharp, copper scent, and she purses her lips enough for me to pour the liquid down her throat, small amounts at a time. A few minutes pass this way, until her heart beats harder, steadier, and her lips close around the blood bag. Calla starts drinking on her own, sucking down the blood as color returns to her face. She quickly empties the first bag, and I toss it onto the coffee table behind me. When I turn back, her eyes are open, and she's reaching for the second bag, stealing it from my grip and tearing into it herself.

"Easy," I tell her. "You'll end up vomiting if you drink too quickly."

A soft sound of annoyance rumbles through her, but she slows her pace, sitting up as her eyes bounce around the room, softening when they reach Gabriel, who is standing close by.

"Now that we know Calla isn't going to die again, we need to address the human in the other room."

"Kade," Gabriel starts.

"Personally," Kade continues, "I'd like to rip her to shreds and send the pieces to Scott one by one. Starting with her heart."

Calla pulls the blood bag away from her lips for a moment to offer a stern, "No." Then she finishes the blood, tossing the empty bag next to the first. She frowns, prodding her gums with her finger and sighing. "I need more. My throat is still on fire and my skin is itching like crazy." She gets up, swaying a little. I'm there in an instant, steadying her.

Before any of us can tell her that was the last of our stash in the house, Lex comes down the hallway with a pale-faced Brighton nearly cowering behind him.

"Perfect timing," Kade says, charging forward and grabbing Brighton. He drags her toward where I'm standing with Calla, and the human wails in fear, tears streaming down her cheeks as she begs Kade to let her go.

Calla pulls away from me, growling deep in her throat. "Stop it, Kade," she snaps.

Kade rolls his eyes and lets go of Brighton, who immediately sinks to her knees and continues crying.

"Come on," Lex says to him, nodding toward the door. "We'll pick up some more blood bags."

With a heavy sigh, Kade stomps away, following Lex out the door.

Gabriel moves toward Brighton slowly, while I focus my attention on Calla. Her breathing has gone shallow, her eyes narrowed on Brighton—specifically the bleeding cut above her eye. She licks her lips, swallowing hard as she breathes through her nose. A shudder ripples through her, and the sound of her molars grinding makes me frown.

"Hold on to me," she says so low there's no chance Brighton picked it up.

"Calla," I murmur, shifting closer at the uneven tone of her voice.

"I don't want to hurt her," she says through her teeth, though the look of pure, animalistic hunger on her face says otherwise.

I slide my arm around her waist. "And you won't."

Her heart pounds in her chest. "If you let go, I'm going to tear into her throat and drain her blood."

Brighton sucks in a shallow breath, her eyes filling with tears as she stares at us. "Calla... I—"

"You don't talk," I snap, and her face goes white as she presses her lips closed and sits in silence. My grip tightens on Calla. "Listen to me. You're not going to hurt her." I press my lips below her ear, then say softly, "The hunger is lying to you. Killing Brighton won't feel good, Calla, it will only hurt you. Don't give in. Fight it."

Her chest rises and falls quickly and her voice cracks when she forces out, "I'm trying." She's gripping my arm so tightly, her fingernails have sliced into my skin. And fuck if that doesn't turn me on.

"I know." I smooth my hand over her hair. "You're doing good. I'm going to let you go in a moment and I want you to walk into the other room and wait for Lex and Kade to come back with more blood. Can you do that for me?"

Her nostrils flare as she drags in a shallow breath. "I... I think so."

"You can," I assure her.

"You're not glamouring me," she whispers, her grip falling away from my arm.

"No."

She tears her gaze away from Brighton, meeting mine, her eyes wide and desperate. "Maybe you should?"

My lips curl into a faint smile. "I don't think so. You can do this."

Calla stares at me for several beats, clenching and unclenching her fists at her sides. "Okay," she finally says.

I free her from my grasp, stepping back and glancing at Gabriel over the top of Calla's head. He nods at me before turning his attention to Calla. We watch her closely as she puts one foot in front of the other, then moves in a blur, leaving the room. Seconds later, a door slams shut, leaving Brighton alone with Gabriel and me.

"Get up," I snap at her, waiting for her to scramble to her feet, her eyes looking anywhere but at me. Rage flares to life in my chest, burning so hot, I hiss out a breath, my fangs extending as I step forward.

"Atlas," Gabriel says in a firm voice. He spoke one word—my name—but it said much more. He's reminding me I didn't stop Calla from killing Brighton just to end her life myself, despite very much desiring it at this moment.

Gabriel stands against the wall, his eyes on Brighton. "You're going to tell us everything you know about the hunters, what your father is planning, and why the hell you tried to kill your best friend."

Brighton takes a minute to collect herself, sniffling and pushing her hair away from her face.

I nod toward the couch. "Sit."

She crosses the room and does as she's told, eyeing the empty blood bags on the coffee table. Gabriel follows her, sitting in the armchair across from the couch, while I remain standing. Brighton folds her hands in her lap, her knee bouncing in time with her erratic heartbeat.

"Start talking," I say in a forced level voice. We'll likely get more out of her if she's not completely terrified. Though I suppose we could always glamour her...

She takes a deep breath. "I... um. I'm not sure where to start." A tear slips down her cheek, and she doesn't wipe it away. "I don't know what information you already have about my family."

"Start with what happened after your mother died," Gabriel says; his voice isn't soft, but it's not unkind either.

Her jaw clenches. "After a vampire killed her, you mean."

"Yes."

"I never wanted to be a hunter. This was never supposed to happen. The moment I..." Her voice breaks. She swallows and tries again. "The moment I stabbed Calla with that dagger, I saw how fucked up things had become."

I cross my arms over my chest. "It took you almost killing someone you supposedly care about to realize that?"

Her eyes fill with tears again, and I fight the urge to roll my eyes. "N-no, of course not," she insists. "I didn't even know Calla was a— That you made her one of you."

"And now that you know?" Gabriel asks, a muscle ticking in his jaw. His restraint is much stronger than mine these days.

She turns her attention to him. "I want to help. I mean, I want what you want, and I think there are other hunters who'd be willing to work together like you were trying to coordinate with my father."

Arching a brow, I say, "You want to work with the same creatures that killed your mother?"

Brighton frowns. "I'd rather you didn't put it that way."

"Why should we believe you?" I challenge. "What could you possibly say that would make it even remotely possible to trust you?"

She nods slowly. "For the record, I don't trust you."

I laugh humorlessly. "I'm devastated. And you're really not making a strong case. It's going to take a hell of a lot for you to prove yourself, *especially* after what you did to Calla. If it were up to me, I'd have let Kade play with you until he got bored and tore you apart."

Her lips part in a silent gasp as she stares at me in horror. "But you won't," she says in a quiet voice, "for the same reason you made sure she didn't attack me. Because you love her and you know it would hurt her."

"True," I say in a lower voice, "but I suggest you do not mistake that for a free pass to behave dangerously. Because if you put Calla in harm's way again, if you threaten her safety in any way—"

"All I want is for her to forgive me," she cuts in, her pulse racing. "I'll do whatever it takes to make that possible. To make sure she doesn't hate me forever."

I press my lips together, considering her words. Having Scott's daughter on our side—so long as she *is* on our side—could work in our favor. Especially if she can talk other hunters into joining us as well. I sure as hell don't trust the human, but this plan for peace among the vampires and hunters is too important to ignore this opportunity.

Brighton's gaze bounces between Gabriel and me. "Look, I know I messed up. What I did to Calla, I... I don't have a reasonable explanation besides not expecting to see her there, like that, and the endless hours of training I've endured kicked in automatically."

"Which is exactly what we're going up against in trying to get the hunters to stop daggering every vampire they see," Gabriel says, his voice much calmer than mine.

She nods. "I was in shock and I made a mistake. You don't know how thankful I am that my aim was off. If I had..." Her voice trails off, and she clears her throat. "I'm in this. Whatever happens, I'm in this. And I'll do whatever it takes to prove that to you."

"Fine," I finally say, but before I can add more, something along the lines of, *but you're not going to like what that entails,* Lex and Kade stroll back through the door. Lex is carrying a small cooler, which he takes into the kitchen and pops open, pulling out a blood bag. After pouring the contents into a glass, he puts it in the microwave.

Kade chuckles. "You really think she's going to give a shit what temperature we serve it to her at right now?" His eyes shift toward us in the other room. "What are we doing with her?" he asks. "Maybe we should leave it up to Calla."

The microwave goes off, and Lex takes the glass out, nudging Kade toward the bedroom, where I can hear Calla pacing the floor, waiting for the blood. The two of them go to her, while Gabriel and I stay in the living room with Brighton.

My phone vibrates, and I pull it out, reading the message and cursing inwardly. I glance up briefly, exhaling a slow breath in hopes the others don't notice the dip in my pulse as dread fills my chest. Lex and Kade are occupied with Calla, but I catch the concern in Gabriel's eyes. I school my features and read the message again.

Son, I trust things are going well. Your mother and I look forward to meeting the awakened Ms. Montgomery soon. I hope our next meeting will be more pleasant than the last. I'll have one of the staff arrange a dinner gathering promptly.

Well, fuck.

Blood sloshes around in my stomach, dulling the burn in my throat as I finish the glass Lex and Kade brought me. I'm finally able to retract my fangs and breathe a little easier now that the voice of hunger has quieted.

"Thanks for taking care of me," I say, glancing between them and managing a small smile.

"Always," Lex says, offering me a wink.

I set the glass on the bedside table and stand, stretching a little, relieved to feel somewhat normal. Considering our circumstances as of late, that's nothing short of a miracle.

"Do you want to take a few minutes and clean up a bit?" Kade asks.

I glance down at myself and frown. I'm still covered in dirt and blood, and I don't smell too great either.

"Come on," Lex says, taking my hand and pulling me gently toward the bathroom attached to the bedroom.

"Wait." I dig my heels into the carpet and try to push my hearing out to listen to what's going on with Brighton.

"She's fine," Kade says, looking bored. "Gabriel will make sure Atlas doesn't rip her head off her shoulders."

I purse my lips, considering that. Kade is right, but I still want to see for myself that she's okay.

Okay? The girl who stabbed you? That's what you're worried about? Pathetic.

I grit my teeth, shoving away the voice at the back of my head, mostly because it's right. Brighton tried to kill me; she's a hunter now and she can't be trusted. As gut-wrenching as that truth is, I can't ignore it. Because it's not just my life at risk but the vampires I've come to love too. "Fine," I finally say, letting them guide me into the bathroom. The tile is cool on my bare feet, and I quickly tug my shirt and pants off, dropping them on the vanity, while Kade turns on the water in the massive glass shower. There are several rainfall shower heads, and the room slowly fills with a warm haze, fogging the mirror over the vanity.

I grab my toothbrush and squirt a good amount of fresh mint toothpaste on it before shoving it in my mouth, watching Lex through the mirror as he pulls his shirt off, walking up behind me. My gaze follows the vines and roses wound around his arm until he presses his chest against my back, dipping his head to kiss my shoulder.

After rinsing my mouth out, I turn and drape my arms around his neck, resting my forehead against his.

"How are you doing?" he murmurs, dropping his hands to my hips and brushing his thumbs back and forth across my skin, making it tingle as warmth gathers between my legs.

"Never better," I reply sarcastically.

He pulls back, shaking his head with a soft chuckle.

Kade chimes in, "Liar, liar, pants on—Oh. You already took them off."

I turn my gaze to him, and my throat dries up when I see the hunger in his eyes. Before I can say anything, Lex steps back and tugs off his pants, leaving Kade the only one of us dressed.

"Well then," he says with a grin, his liquid silver gaze bouncing between Lex and me. "Allow me to catch up." In a blur of movement, he adds his clothes to the pile on the vanity and snakes an arm around my waist, hauling me against his chest. My breath catches when his cock presses between my legs, and I grab his shoulders to steady myself. He lifts me, and I wrap my legs around him as he walks toward the shower, Lex following close behind.

The hot spray of water hits my back, and I sigh as Kade sets me down. I run my hands over my face, scrubbing at my skin, while Lex grabs the bottle of lavender body wash, pouring it into his hand before stepping closer, and starts massaging it into my shoulders. The shower fills with the calming scent, and I lean into him, my eyelids feeling heavier by the second. Kade grabs a puffy loofah and trails it along my arm, cleaning the dirt and blood, then moves across my collarbone to the other arm before pressing it between my breasts. He circles each one slowly, thoroughly, a teasing light in his eyes that has my lips curling into a soft grin. Lex's hands move down my back, kneading and massaging all the way to my ass. He gives each cheek a slap, and I suck in a breath, more out of surprise than pain. Kade chuckles in front of me, setting the loofah aside and using his hands to cover my breasts, rolling my nipples between his fingers.

"Kade," I sigh his name, arching my back to push my breasts into his hands.

"How are you feeling now?" he asks, his eyes flicking between mine.

"That depends on what the two of you plan to do with me," I answer as heat fills my cheeks and a not-so-subtle throbbing starts between my thighs.

Lex drops his mouth to my neck, kissing and flicking his tongue against the delicate skin just below my ear. "We're going to take care of our girl." His lips tickle the shell of my ear before his fangs scrape along my shoulder.

"I'm lucky you're both so good at sharing," I murmur, reaching for Kade, my lips in search of his. Lex moves with me, staying at my back as his cock presses between my ass cheeks. Kade groans against my lips, dropping his hands to my hips and digging his fingers into my skin. The growl that rumbles through him shoots heat straight to my core, and when he grinds himself against me, I moan into his mouth, my pulse kicking up. Kade nips my bottom lip, pressing his cock to my clit and circling it agonizingly slowly, while Lex continues to tease my ass.

I break away from Kade's lips to catch my breath and shoot Lex a look. "You're not getting in there without some serious foreplay."

A dangerous glint fills his eyes. "Challenge accepted."

"No," I mutter, "that wasn't... Never mind."

Kade snags my chin, turning my attention back to him. "You trust us, don't you?"

I arch a brow at him. "I think that really depends on the scenario we're discussing."

He rolls his eyes, but he's also grinning at me. *Talk about mixed messages.* "We've got you. You trust that." He's not asking, so I don't respond right away. "Let me rephrase," he continues. "You know we'll make you come so fucking hard your legs will give out and you'll see whatever deity you choose to pray to."

"Someone's full of themselves."

"You will be soon too," Lex says in my ear.

"You did not just say that," I grumble, though I can't stop the shiver that zips up my spine when he nips my earlobe.

"Oh, he definitely did," Kade confirms, tugging me closer and trails his fingers along my thigh, dipping into the heat at my center. He drags a single digit along my slit while holding my gaze. "Tell me, would you rather I fuck you with my fingers or my tongue before I fill you with my cock?"

My throat goes dry. I lick my lips, my chest rising and falling quicker now. "And if I want both?"

"Needy today, are you?"

"Yes," I answer plainly, "and you're going to take care of me."

He presses his thumb against my clit, leaning in until his nose brushes mine, and murmurs, "Until forever ends."

I suck in a shallow breath, my chest swelling at his words, then moan when he slides two fingers inside my pussy, curling them while circling my clit with his thumb. Lex kisses my back, massaging my shoulders while Kade continues moving his fingers inside me, reaching deeper and deeper, hitting the spot that makes my head spin. He seals my mouth with his, pushing his tongue inside and grazing mine. I close my eyes, giving into the sensations, and just let go—of everything. Nothing besides us at this moment exists. It's heaven; blissful and everything I could ever want.

Pressure builds at my core, and my breathing quickens. Kade breaks our kiss, resting his forehead against mine. "I feel you pulsing around my fingers," he grounds out, his cheeks a soft pink. "I'm rock fucking hard."

I pull my bottom lip between my teeth, panting quietly. "I'm so close," I breathe.

"Let go," Lex purrs, reaching around from behind and cupping my breasts, rolling my nipples between his fingers. "Let go and come."

"Fuck," I moan, my muscles tightening and my pussy clenching around Kade's thrusting fingers. I soak them with my release, moaning deeply as my climax hits like a wave of ecstasy.

"That's a good girl." Lex kisses my neck. "You come so prettily for us."

Fucking hell.

Heat ripples through me as I ride the delicious aftershocks, and I barely have a second to catch my breath before Kade pulls his fingers out and turns me around to face Lex, who steals my mouth and thrusts his cock into me. I gasp into his mouth, and he grips my hips, lifting me and pressing me against the tile as he holds still deep inside me. My inner walls pulse around him, still sensitive from my first orgasm. Lex holds me up with ease, pulling out slightly before slamming back inside. His lips leave mine and land between my neck and shoulder, his fangs sinking into my skin. A strangled noise—an odd mix of shock and pleasure—escapes my lips, and my eyes fly open to find Kade standing under the water, pumping his hand up and down his hard shaft.

The pull of blood leaving my body and into Lex's while he fills me with his cock is like nothing else. My head swims with lust and heat, my heart hammering in my chest as I hold Kade's dark gaze. He tips his head back against the opposite wall, picking up speed at the same time Lex does.

"Fuck," Kade grunts. "I want you to come with me."

I nod, reaching between my body and Lex's to play with my clit while he slams into me over and over, bringing me to the precipice of pleasure and then launching me over the edge.

"Yes," I cry out, clenching around him and coming hard. "Yes, yes, yes. Don't stop. I want you to come too."

Lex pulls his fangs out of my shoulder and kisses me hard. I taste my blood on his lips, moaning deeply as he tenses, a groan tearing from his throat. Kade follows seconds later, and the sounds of our collective pleasure fills the steamy room.

Once the remnants of orgasmic bliss wears off, we rinse ourselves clean and get out of the shower. Kade wraps a towel around me before tying one around his waist and tossing another at Lex.

The guys leave me in the bedroom to get dressed. After tugging on a pair of jeans and a maroon sweater, I make my way back to the living room, feeling overall better about being close to Brighton without wanting to tear her throat out. Trusting her, though, is a different challenge altogether. I don't want to think my best friend—if I can even call her that anymore—could go through with killing me, but I'd be incredibly naïve to rule it out in an attempt to avoid the sharp sting of betrayal.

Lex and Kade meet me in the hallway, and the three of us walk into the living room together, earning a disapproving look from Atlas.

Kade snorts, throwing his arm around me. "We were taking care of our girl. Don't be jealous."

Atlas rolls his eyes but says nothing.

My eyes land on where Brighton is sitting on the couch. I duck under Kade's arm, moving away from him and toward her, my stride hesitant, cautious. I'm not about to let myself end up on the pointed end of a dagger again.

She stands, her eyes locked on me. They aren't filled with fear this time, but her posture is still rigid, unsure. I don't blame her for that, considering she's the only human in a room full of vampires—including one she stabbed in the chest.

"Hi," I finally say, standing at least six feet from her.

She presses her lips together for a moment. "That's what I was going to say."

I inhale a steadying breath, then exhale a sigh. "Things are really fucked up, Bri."

She nods, plucking at the hem of her shirt. "I told them I wanted to help."

I blink at her. "You did?"

Another nod.

My brows tug closer, and I frown, flicking a glance toward Gabriel. I want to believe Brighton but I also can't disregard what happened in that clearing. Someone who I used to trust with my life made the choice to almost end it. Scared or not, Brighton stabbing me with a white ash dagger isn't something I—and certainly not the other vampires in the room—am fine with pretending didn't happen.

"When I saw you there," she starts, her heart beating fast in her chest, "it caught me off guard. Seeing you as a vampire... I wasn't prepared for that."

"I didn't want you to find out that way," I tell her. "Honestly, I was just as shocked to see you there. Maybe that was naïve of me, but I wanted to believe you wouldn't join the hunters."

Her gaze falls. "It's a long story."

"Is it?" Kade cuts in, his tone mocking.

Brighton ignores him. "You know I never wanted to become a hunter." Her tear-filled gaze returns to mine. "Same as how I *thought* you didn't want to become a vampire."

I open my mouth, then close it and nod. "That... is also a long story."

"Neither of you have any concept of the word long," Kade mutters, leaving the room. Lex chuckles under his breath and drops onto the couch, keeping an eye on Brighton and me.

Brighton takes a step closer, and I can't help it. I stiffen. If she notices, she doesn't show it. "Like I told Atlas and Gabriel, I will do whatever it takes to make things right with you, Calla. You're..." Her voice catches. "You're still my best friend, and I'm here for you. No matter the circumstances. Even... even though you drink blood now."

My eyes narrow slightly, the knot in my stomach twisting tighter. "Are you sure? Because 'whatever it takes' might be something you're not okay with."

She swallows hard, and I wait for the uptick of her pulse to reveal she's lying, but it remains unchanged as she says, "I meant what I said."

I nod, glancing to where Atlas is leaning in the doorway to the dining room, then to where Gabriel is sitting in the armchair across from the couch. I turn back to Brighton. "We need to come to an agreement with the hunters—a treaty to protect both humans and vampires alike from being hunted."

"Right. That was the reason behind the meeting that turned into a battle."

"Because your father is a moron," Lex comments from the couch.

Atlas pushes away from the doorway and walks over to stand next to me. Something in me—call it instinct or some weirdly ingrained need to be close to my sire—makes me lean toward him... and suddenly, I wish we were alone. Need vibrates through me, and I have to make a physical effort to push it down and focus.

"You need to realize that if your father won't get on board, he'll need to be dealt with, alongside anyone he's convinced to follow him." Atlas's voice is firm.

Brighton can no longer keep the tears from falling down her cheeks. She cries quietly, reading the underlying message of Atlas's words: her father is going to die.

Kade chooses that moment to reenter the room with a glass of blood in his hand. "Yeah, and Papa Ellis already fucked us over once. We're not about to give him an opportunity to do it again."

"So what?" Brighton says in a low voice, "You won't give him a chance to consider this treaty? You're just going to kill him without even—"

"Yes," Kade cuts in sharply. "We're going to kill him before he can try to kill all of us. Again."

Brighton's pulse is racing, her breathing uneven as she presses her lips together, her chin quivering. She looks as if she's trying desperately not to cry, and there's a severely conflicted part of me fighting the urge to comfort her, which only intensifies the pressure in my chest and unease in my stomach. Because I don't trust her—I can't—and it's killing me. Her father wants not only to kill people I love, but me as well. He'll never agree to a treaty between the vampires and hunters, which leaves few options on what to do with him.

"Can we detain him while we discuss other options?" I ask, glancing between the guys, ignoring the hopeful look in Bri's eyes. I don't *want* to take away her last living parent, but if it comes down to him or us... Scott is dead.

"Absolutely not," Kade says immediately.

"Yeah, no. We're very picky about who we kidnap," Lex adds, shooting me a wink, which I deflect with a *not the time* glare.

Gabriel and Atlas exchange a look before the latter turns his attention to Brighton. "I've known your father for many years, Brighton. Longer than you've been alive. He won't change his mind about vampires."

Brighton bites down on her lower lip as it trembles, her eyes shining with fresh tears. And despite Brighton stabbing me—barely missing my heart—seeing her like this feels like a dagger in the chest all over again.

FOUR

GABRIEL

Calla's expression is filled with barely masked pain. Her gaze jumps between Brighton and the rest of us, her forehead creased and her heart rate uneven. She's torn, wanting to be there for her friend but being aware of the dangers associated with doing so. I can sense the distrust lingering between them—mostly from Calla, and for good reason.

She swallows, wiping her hand across her mouth. "I... need a minute."

Brighton sucks in a shallow breath when Calla moves at a speed too quick for her eyes to track, disappearing from the room in a blur. Kade and Lex frown, while Atlas's expression remains impassive. With a sigh, I leave the room as well, because something tells me Calla—while she doesn't want to be in here anymore—doesn't want to be alone.

I find her on the front porch, sitting on the outdoor couch with her legs tucked under her and her arms wrapped around herself.

She glances toward me as the front door clicks shut and bites her lip. She's trying not to cry.

"Oh, angel," I murmur, walking over and sitting next to her, guiding her against my side.

She drops her head to my shoulder and inhales shakily. "I'm sorry."

"You don't need to apologize," I assure her. "I understand that conversation was upsetting."

Calla sighs. "Brighton has been my best friend since I moved to

Washington, and now... I look at her and I don't know if I can trust her. She wasn't supposed to get tangled up in the hunters. She wasn't supposed to be in that clearing."

I run my hand over her hair. "Do you believe she's being truthful about wanting to help?"

There's a stretch of silence before Calla says, "I want to believe it, Gabe, I really do. Part of me wants to have her glamoured to make sure she's telling the truth, but then I remember the way being glamoured made me feel and I..." She trails off, sighing. "I don't want to fear my best friend."

I cradle her head against my shoulder. "If it makes you feel better, I believe she wants to help."

Calla lifts her head and meets my gaze. "Why?"

"The pain you're feeling—the uncertainty and fear of losing someone you care about—she's feeling it too."

She nods slowly, her eyes watering. "I feel so fucking helpless."

"I understand." I run my hand up and down her back and press a kiss against the side of her head. "Why don't we take a breather? Get out of here for an hour?"

"And go where? Scott probably has patrols out searching for us and Brighton. Isn't it too dangerous to leave?"

I smile. "Probably. But we won't be long and we'll be careful." I stand from the couch and offer her my hand.

She presses her lips together for a moment before taking it, lacing her fingers through mine. "I hope you're prepared for the wrath of Atlas when he finds out we've left."

I chuckle softly, pulling my sunglasses out of my jacket pocket and slipping them over my eyes. I hand Calla her pair that I swiped on my way outside, and we walk down the steps.

"Do you have a plan?" she asks.

I shrug. "Not entirely. What do you think about a walk along the water?"

She smiles, and the sight warms my chest and makes me pull her closer to my side as we walk. It's been a very long time since I've felt this way about someone, and I know with great certainty there isn't anything I wouldn't do for her.

The breeze off the water is cool, so I shrug off my jacket and drape it over Calla's shoulders, taking her hand again. She squeezes mine, sending me a soft grin. As a vampire, she likely isn't as cold as she'd be as a human, but it's clear she appreciates the gesture.

"Do you want to talk about anything?" I ask her when we let a few joggers pass us.

"Like what?" she asks, arching a brow.

"The future," I offer, "what you want out of life, how you're adjusting to being a vampire."

She chokes on a breathy laugh. "Those are some heavy topics for a walk that was supposed to make me feel better, Gabe."

"We don't have to talk about those things. We can talk about whatever you want or nothing at all."

Calla shakes her head. "I don't mind talking to you. Honestly, it's probably better than keeping everything inside."

I nod in agreement. "Do you want to go back to school?"

"Yes," she answers quickly. "I need to graduate, though I know in the grand scheme of things and with everything going on, it may not seem all that important."

I stop walking and move in front of her, using my free hand to cup her cheek. "If it's important to you, it's important to all of us."

Her eyes flick between mine as her cheeks tinge with pink. She leans in, resting her forehead against mine, and closes her eyes. "You know, when the four of you showed up at my apartment and swept me away from everything I knew, I thought my life was over. I couldn't imagine how I'd be able to live with you all, to tolerate being stuck with a bunch of vampires who had some supernatural claim to me." She takes a deep breath, letting it out in a soft sigh that makes my lips tingle with the desire to kiss her as I close my eyes, and she continues, "And then you all went and made me fall in love with you."

I tip her head back and slant my mouth over hers, kissing her deeply as our hearts pound in sync. "Say it again," I murmur against her lips.

She lets go of my hand and grabs the front of my shirt with both hands, pulling me flush against her. "I love you," she whispers, "so fucking much it's hard to breathe sometimes."

I kiss her again, harder this time, pushing my fingers into her hair and cradling the back of her head. "I will love you as long as I'm still breathing. Even after that. I will love you in this life and whatever comes next."

"Fuck," she says with a soft laugh. "You're making it really hard not to jump on you right now."

"I wouldn't complain." Neither would my cock, which is growing harder by the second. "Though that might invite attention we don't want."

"Yeah, I guess having sex in public is kind of the opposite to keeping a low profile."

I chuckle, kissing her forehead before pulling back and taking her hand again.

We walk in silence for a few minutes before I ask, "What do you think you'll want to do once you graduate?"

"Hmm…" She seems to consider that for a moment. "I want to help people. I recognize that could be a little tricky now that I'll have to fight the urge to bite them, but still."

"There's quite a lot you could do with a sociology degree," I comment.

She nods. "That's true. I've considered social work, though that would probably require more education and certification."

"Whatever you need, we'll make sure you have it."

"That's not—I wasn't asking for anything."

A smile curves my lips upward, and I squeeze her hand again. "Everything we have is yours, Calla. That includes money, contacts, resources—everything."

She presses her lips together. "Um, okay. Then I guess I'd like to follow that path, maybe work for an adoption agency or education system to help young people."

"You would be excellent at that."

Her cheeks flush, and she looks at me. "You think so?"

"Those kids will be lucky to have you."

She lowers her gaze, her lips curling upward. "Thanks."

"Of course," I say with a smile before shifting the topic of conversation. "How do you feel about seeing your parents? I'm sure they're eager for you to visit."

Her pace slows, and I follow suit. "I'm…" She sighs. "I want to see them. I just… I'm scared of hurting them. And even knowing you guys would never let that happen, I'm still terrified they're going to hate me now."

"Those feelings are completely valid," I tell her in a gentle voice as we continue along the waterfront. "Though I have to say, I truly believe they could never hate you. Atlas, Lex, Kade, and me? Absolutely. But never you."

Calla offers me a watery smile. "Thank you for saying that."

I nod. "And there's no rush, angel. You can visit them whenever you're ready."

She nods. "Maybe once we've come to an agreement with the hunters? I'd rather that not be a concern when I see them. If they never have to know about the hunters, I'd much prefer it that way."

"I get that. Let's hope that day comes sooner than later." The seemingly ever-present pit in my stomach throbs, and I fight back a cringe, not wanting to add to the upset Calla's going through. We're all on edge when it comes to things with the hunters. We want this to work while also being painfully aware there's a high probability it won't. At least while Scott Ellis has influence over the hunters and Atlas's parents rule the vampires. And there only seems to really be one way to handle both situations...

Calla and I return to the house almost an hour later, our cheeks pink and our hair windswept.

She pulls my jacket off her shoulders as we walk up the porch steps and hands it back to me. "Thanks."

"Anytime."

"I meant for the walk. And the jacket too, I guess."

I smile at her. "I know."

We walk inside, and Calla goes into high alert immediately. She must've noticed the absence of a human heartbeat; Brighton isn't here. She rips off her sunglasses on her way into the living room, and I follow.

Lex and Kade are chatting on the couch, while Atlas is in the armchair I'd been sitting in earlier, reading something on his phone.

"Where is Brighton?" Calla asks, her heart beating faster.

Atlas glances up and sets his phone on the armrest. He looks at me before turning his narrowed gaze on Calla. "Where were *you*?"

She crosses her arms over her chest, stepping forward. "Answer my question, Atlas." A tinge of panic laces her voice; she's worried they hurt Brighton.

Atlas rises from the chair, closing the distance between them, while

Kade and Lex exchange a look and get up as well. Before Atlas can speak again, Kade says, "Calla, she's fine."

She isn't convinced. "Where *is* she?"

"With Marcel," Atlas answers in a hard voice.

"He picked her up a few minutes ago," Lex adds. "She'll stay with him at a safe house until we decide what needs to be done. And before you ask where the safe house is, none of us know."

Calla blinks at him, then shakes her head, turning toward me. "Did you know this was happening? Is that why you took me away?"

I frown, the pit in my stomach growing even heavier at the anger and hurt in her eyes. *Shit*. We should have trusted she'd be able to handle sending Brighton away. "I'm sorry, angel."

She swallows hard, blinking back tears. "You went behind my back and did this..." Shaking her head again, she adds in a low voice, "I thought we were a team. I thought..." She trails off, her jaw clenching tight.

"This isn't forever," Kade chimes in, walking closer to Calla. He reaches into his pocket and pulls out a flip phone. By the looks of it, it's a burner. Kade offers it to her. "There's one number programmed," he says. "You can speak to Brighton safely this way. It can't be traced."

She stares at the phone in his palm for several beats before snatching it up and leaving the room in a blur. Seconds later, a door slams shut.

"Super," Lex mutters dryly. "That went really well."

FIVE

I don't want to be upset with the only people I have in my life at the moment, and yet, here I am. I'm tired of this dance with them; I thought we were past it.

I trust the guys to know how to handle things in this world I've only just become part of, and certainly trust them to keep me safe—there's no question about that.

And it's not that they decided to send Brighton away—when I sit back and look at the bigger picture, it absolutely makes sense. It's that they did it without telling me. They didn't trust me, and *that* is what I'm struggling to get past.

As much as I would rather sulk in here for the rest of the day, we don't have time for that. Too many things are up in the air. So I tuck my hurt into a tiny ball and shove it down.

I walk back to the living room and find Kade sprawled across the couch. I don't bother pushing my hearing out to find the others, instead I ask him where everyone is.

He pulls away the arm that's covering his eyes and blinks at me a few times. "Oh," he says, "I guess I fell asleep. I think Atlas is out back. Not sure about Gabe and Lex."

I huff out a sigh, crossing my arms over my chest.

"Jeez," he says. "Sorry, I didn't realize it was my turn to vampsit."

I shake my head at his awful attempt at comedy. "I think it's time I learned how to glamour. God knows it would have come in handy during that fight. Maybe I could have avoided getting stabbed by my best friend."

Kade sits up, running his hand through his hair. "Are you asking me specifically?" A faint grin plays on his lips. "Because I like to think of myself as one of the more skilled vampires when it comes to glamour. Certainly more so than Lex. Maybe even Gabe."

I shake my head. "I don't really care. This isn't a competition, I just need to learn."

"Look no further. I'm the perfect mentor."

Lex chooses that moment to walk in the room and snorts, throwing his arm around my shoulders. "I don't know what he's telling you he's good at, but he's lying."

"Hey," Kade says, catching Lex's attention, "Fuck you."

"What's happening now?" Gabriel asks, walking into the room with a steaming cup of coffee in his hand.

With a sigh, I turn my attention to him and say, "I was just telling Kade that I need to learn glamour, and he graciously offered to teach me."

Gabriel's gaze shifts from me to Kade then back again. "All right. This is probably something we should have taught you right off the bat. I'll grab Atlas."

"I don't need all of you to teach me one thing."

Gabriel takes a sip of his coffee. "He's going to want to be a part of this."

"Well, we don't always get what we want, do we?" There's an edge to my voice that I don't like, especially directed at Gabriel.

"Too bad," Atlas says, strutting into the room. His hair is damp with sweat and his cheeks are flushed. He grabs the hem of his shirt, lifting it to wipe the sweat off his brow, and my eyes drop to the slice of abs exposed. I curse the warmth that fills my chest and much lower, and force myself to refocus on the task at hand.

"Perhaps we should share our techniques with you one by one and you can see what resonates with you the most. What you find the easiest to work with and what feels best to you."

"The idea of having control over another person doesn't feel right to me at all, but I get what you're saying. Kade, since you so kindly offered your services, why don't you go first?"

Kade grins. "Good choice." He stands, walking closer to me. "I can't glamour you anymore but I'm going to pretend like I can."

I nod, letting my arms fall to my sides.

"Because I'm not a special vampire like your sire over there, I have to use eye contact to connect to a human's mind." His gaze meets mine and holds, his silver irises swirling subtly. I've been glamoured by Kade before, the night we met, and his eyes looked the same. Except this time, I don't feel the loss of control over my body. "Typically, I would feel the connection snap into place about now. It's like turning on headlights on a dark road."

"Often the human will make a soft noise at the back of their throat," Lex chimes in from somewhere behind me. "It could be a sound of shock, or fear, or even relief. And most times, their eyes get this deliciously vacant look..." He trails off, and I keep my eyes on Kade, trying to focus on one thing at a time.

"Then what?" I ask, my pulse ticking faster.

"Once the connection is made, I can say whatever I want to the human, and they will obey."

My lips turn down, unease swirling in my chest. "That's it?" It sounds too easy. Something so potentially detrimental should require more effort.

Kade nods, his eyes returning to their normal mix of slate gray and silver. "Yeppers."

"My turn," Lex announces, snaking an arm around my waist and pulling me around and toward him.

I untangle myself from him with a glare. "How does your... technique differ from Kade's?"

He purses his lips, seeming to consider that for a moment. "Kade waits until the connection forms," he finally says. "I make my demands immediately."

I arch a brow. "And what if you end up not being able to glamour someone? Isn't that risky?"

Lex shrugs. "Maybe. But it hasn't happened yet."

"Uh, okay. Still, I don't think I'm going to do it your way." The thought of trying to tell someone to do whatever I want before I know if I'll actually be able to control them freaks me out. Honestly, the entire practice of glamour does.

Kade snorts from behind me, and Lex flips him off before turning his attention back to me.

"Suit yourself," he says with a shrug, then goes to sit on the couch, kicking his feet up on the coffee table.

I turn to Gabriel. "What about you?"

"I take a more gentle approach."

"How shocking," Lex mutters, but Gabriel doesn't offer him a response. His answer doesn't surprise me in the least. Despite being a vampire—for all intents and purposes, a predator—Gabriel is one of the most gentle people I've met. Save for a few occasions...

"I find humans far more susceptible to influence when they are open and trusting. Sure, you can scare them and force them into compliance, but I find it easier when their guard is already down."

"So what? You just woo them with your charm and then attack them with glamour?"

He pauses, a hint of amusement flickering in his eyes. "I suppose so, yes."

Gabriel's technique sounds the best to me so far. The least invasive, though that's impossible to avoid completely when you're messing with someone's mind.

I look toward my sire, who has glamoured me on more than one occasion, and who has it the easiest, in my opinion. "And we all know you can control people with a simple touch, so I don't think there's any sense in hearing about this from you."

Atlas leans in the doorway separating the living and dining rooms. "You and I will train once we're done here," is all he says in response.

Before I can say anything, Lex says, "Why don't we take a little field trip and find someone so she can practice?"

"She won't know if she can do it until she tries," Kade adds.

"Is that something you want to do?" Gabriel asks.

"Not really," I say without hesitation, "but I understand that it's important for me to learn." I sigh. "Where are we going to—"

"On it," Lex cuts in, heading for the front door.

"Wait," I call after him. "You can't just grab someone off the street!"

He turns back to me, grinning like a cat. "Sure I can." Shooting me a wink, he adds, "I was just going to walk next door and borrow a neighbor."

"That's not... This isn't like asking to borrow a cup of sugar, Lex."

He cocks his head. "Who's asking?" He disappears from the room before a response can form on my lips, and the front door closes a few seconds later.

"No one will get hurt," Gabriel assures me, shifting close enough to touch my shoulder.

I turn my face to look at his hand. I want to push it away, to turn my nose up at it, because I'm still upset, but I'm also in a very vulnerable place right now. The support and reassurance... I need as much as I can get.

"You wanted to learn," Atlas says in a level tone.

I don't bother voicing a response. He's right.

My pulse ticks faster in the three minutes it takes for Lex to return with a guy with shaggy brown hair and hazel eyes, dressed in a gray Georgetown University hoodie, jeans, and... Crocs. Well, that's a stylistic choice. He can't be much older than me, I realize as Lex nudges him toward me.

"Hi," he says, offering a nervous smile, his cheeks flushing.

"Hey." My gaze flits to the pulse at his throat, and my mouth waters.

No. He's not here for me to feed.

I swallow hard, cringing inwardly at the burn in my throat, my gums throbbing uncomfortably. "Thank you for helping me."

The guy nods.

I lick the dryness from my lips and focus my gaze on him. His hazel eyes—mostly brown but with some flickers of green depending on the way the light touches them—dart around the room.

"Push your will toward him," Gabriel says in a calm voice. "Your will is to become his."

"Think about what you want from him while you're saying it," Kade adds.

I take a deep breath. Let it out. Then step forward and lock eyes with the guy. Granted, he doesn't try to move or look away, so this exercise is *very* basic. I consider what I want him to do. Figuring I better keep it simple to start, I picture him lifting his left foot off the floor to show off his interesting choice in footwear. Next, I vocalize it. "I want—"

"Don't bother with that," Lex interrupts.

"Fine," I grumble without breaking eye contact with the human. "Lift your right leg." My voice is low and smooth, and my eyes widen when his glaze over and he does what I said. "Drop it back to the floor," I say next, and he does. I exhale a heavy breath as if I'd been holding it. "Now what?" I ask my group of mentors.

"Try something a little more complex," Kade instructs.

I glance at him over my shoulder. "Like?"

He crosses his arms over his chest. "Like something he really wouldn't want to do."

I frown at that. "I don't—"

"Do it," Atlas says.

I open my mouth to shoot him a snarky reply, then stop myself. Despite the lingering annoyance, a voice deep in the back of my mind reminds me the guys are doing this to help me. I asked them to teach me glamour—this is part of it.

Atlas must see something in my expression, because he nods, his expression morphing into something more calculated as he watches me like a teacher observing a student.

Turning my attention back to the human who has planted his foot back on the ground now—evidently breaking eye contact severs the glamour—I snare his gaze once more. I lick my lips, inhaling through my nose as I slow my breathing and focus on pushing my will toward him. "Wrap your fingers around your throat." My voice is soft and warm like honey, which makes me shiver at the severity of my words.

The human's forehead creases slightly, as if he's trying to fight the urge to do as I say. I repeat the direction, using a little more force. Slowly, he lifts his hand, his fingers shaking and his jaw set tight. His chest rises and falls faster as his pulse races, and he wraps his fingers around his throat.

My own heart is trying to beat free from my rib cage. I hesitate for several seconds before I force out, "Squeeze."

His eyes go wide as his fingers tighten around his throat. Thirty seconds in, his face is a deep red and covered in a sheen of sweat. "Pl-please," he wheezes.

"Harder," I say through my teeth, my eyes stinging with tears. I hate this. I hate this so fucking much.

The human's face is purple now, his eyes going bloodshot and his pulse growing weaker. He's going to pass out any second.

I feel someone at my back just as I say, "Stop."

He tears his hand away from his throat, and when I blink a few times to sever the glamour, he doubles over, choking hard and desperately sucking in air.

Gabriel moves in to help him up and walks him out of the room, while I turn to the others.

"How was that?"

"Something about you torturing him made me rock fucking hard," Lex says.

My eyes widen, and I grumble, "You are so twisted."

He shoots me a wink and saunters out of the room toward the kitchen.

I arch a brow at Kade, waiting for him to comment.

He shrugs. "Not bad. Not as good as me, but it'll do." With that, he follows Lex, leaving me alone with Atlas.

"You did fine," he says, walking closer.

I press my lips together, nodding. Part of me wants to step away, to stop him from closing the distance between us. I swallow hard, my eyes dropping to his mouth and my pulse racing when his lips curl into a faint smirk. My gaze snaps back up to his. Those silver irises are flickering with amusement that makes my cheeks fill with heat. Looking away now would only make things worse, so I force myself to hold his gaze.

"What?" I grumble.

"You tell me," he says, stepping closer again. His breath stirs the hair at my temple.

My eyes narrow. "I'm still mad at you."

"You can be angry and aroused at the same time."

I cross my arms over my chest and instinctively shift back when my arm brushes his shirt. "I can also control myself."

Atlas cocks his head to the side, dragging his tongue over his bottom lip. "You sure?" His gaze trails the length of me, setting my body on fire and halting the breath in my lungs.

"Yep," I force out, my pulse thrumming beneath my skin.

He moves quicker than I can, wrapping his fingers around my throat and backing me into the wall. My heart slams against my rib cage, and I suck in a breath, my eyes flying to his. The throbbing between my thighs goes straight to my head, and heat pools low in my belly, making my skin tingle with the desire—the raw and unbridled *need*—to be touched.

Atlas leans in until his nose grazes the side of my head. "Good," he says into my ear. "Fight me off."

"What?" I breathe, the gravelly sound of his voice making my clit throb harder.

His grip on my throat tightens. "You heard me."

I shake my head as much as I can. "I'm not in the mood, Atlas."

He barks out a humorless laugh. "I beg to differ, considering I can smell your arousal and know without even touching you that your panties are soaked." His voice hardens. "Fight me."

"Fuck me," I shoot back in a defiant tone.

He leans back to look me in the eyes, shaking his head as his grip on my throat loosens. "So fucking stubborn."

I tear his hand away, catching my breath. "Thanks. I get it from my sire."

"Cute," he deadpans, snagging my chin. "You need to keep up with your training. Just because you're a vampire—"

"Doesn't mean I'm invincible," I cut in, slapping his hand away. "I'm aware."

"Prove it."

I arch a brow at him. "What are you, twelve?"

"I'm not messing around, Calla. And we're not leaving this room until you do."

"So you'd like to turn the living room furniture into firewood? Because if we fight, that's what's going to happen."

"You're awfully confident," he muses in a lighter voice.

I shove him backward so I can move away from the wall. "You should take that as a compliment, considering you're the one who taught me a lot of my fighting skills."

Atlas advances, reaching for me, and I narrowly avoid him, ducking under his arm and popping up behind him. I slam my foot into his back, and he collides with the wall at a speed that cracks the drywall. He recovers in seconds, shaking the dust out of his hair as he inspects the damage to the wall. "Hmm. Perhaps we should take this outside."

"You think?" I remark dryly.

Gabriel walks through the front door, glancing between us, then sighs. "Don't you think Calla has had enough excitement for today?" he offers Atlas.

I press my lips together to fight a smile before I can remind myself that I'm mad at Gabriel too. "Calla," I say pointedly, "has had enough excitement to last a lifetime, what with blood oaths and vampirism and all." My eyes widen as the words leave my lips, an idea hitting me so fast, I suck in a breath, my chest tightening.

Gabriel's expression fills with concern, and Atlas moves in front of me. "What just happened?" he asks, searching my face for an explanation.

"I..." I shake my head, already knowing how they're going to respond to my potentially fatal idea.

"Calla," Atlas says firmly, grabbing my shoulders. Gabriel moves to stand beside him, watching me carefully.

"The blood oath," I finally say.

Atlas shakes his head. "What about it?"

"What if we can use it? Not ours, obviously, but the idea of it."

Atlas and Gabriel share a glance, and the latter says, "I don't follow."

"What if we form a blood oath between me and Brighton? Link us so that whatever happens to one happens to the other. Maybe it will make Scott more willing to agree to negotiate peace with the vampires if it'll keep his daughter safe." Is it a foolproof plan? Absolutely not. Tying myself to Brighton by blood is risky—not to mention manipulative as hell—but we're running out of options that'll allow Brighton to keep her only living parent *living*. Not that I find myself all that concerned for Scott's wellbeing, considering he's tried to kill us all and turn Brighton against me. I'd just as quickly rip his throat out myself for all he's done, but Brighton... I don't think I can do that to her, even if it's difficult to get past what *she* did to *me*. And if connecting us makes it easier for me to trust—or at the very least understand—Brighton's motives, maybe this weight in my chest will feel a little lighter.

Atlas lets go of me and takes a step back, considering it for a moment. "It's not the worst idea, but I'm not sure Brighton's life is enough to stop Scott from hunting vampires—you included, even if it means losing his daughter."

My stomach twists painfully. I don't want to believe it but I'm also no longer so naive to ignore the possibility that Atlas is right. Despite that, it's still something we should try, which means we're going to need magic. "I'll reach out to Tessa and see if there's a witch in the area who can help." I'd be more comfortable having Tessa do the spell herself but I also know how much she doesn't enjoy being pulled into vampire business and I respect that. I can't expect her to come running every time us vampires need something.

Atlas sighs. "You're not going to let this go, are you?"

I offer him a look.

"Of course not." He turns to Gabriel, who shrugs.

"It's worth a shot. It won't put Calla in any more danger than we're already all in, so I'm on board."

"Don't we get a say?" Lex says as he and Kade return to the living room.

"Nope," I announce. "This is my decision. It's happening, so deal with it."

They exchange a look, and Kade's lips twitch. "That's our girl."

"Damn right it is," Lex agrees.

Atlas clears his throat, capturing everyone's attention. "While we're all here, we need to discuss something else."

My stomach sinks. I have a feeling I know where this is going and I don't want to hear it.

"What is it?" Kade asks, leaning against the back of the couch, while Lex flops onto it, taking a massive bite out of the sandwich I'm only now realizing he's holding.

"Simon and Lenora are... *requesting* an audience with us—Calla specifically."

I can't help it, I stiffen. Nausea tears through me like a vicious, unforgiving wave, and the room suddenly feels much smaller. I clench my jaw, forcing the bile in my throat down.

Atlas focuses on me. "I'm sorry," he says in a low voice, as if we're the only two in the room.

The fear wrapping itself around my chest quickly burns into a fierce anger. Not toward my sire but on his behalf. He deserves so much better than the *family* he was born into. My hands ball into fists at my sides, and I shake my head. "We'll deal with it," I force out. "Along with how they're going to play into the potential agreement with the hunters, because there's no way that won't be an issue."

Kade curses under his breath at the same moment a dark look passes over Atlas's face. "They are even less likely to agree to any peace treaty than Scott Ellis is."

I nod slowly, almost too afraid to ask the question that is likely on all of our minds: "What does that mean for us?"

He inhales deeply, blowing it out before he says, "It could very possibly mean another war—this one between the vampires."

CHAPTER

SIX

CALLA

The minute I'm behind the closed door, I flip open the burner phone and select the only number on the contact list. It rings twice before the line connects.

"Brighton," I say in a hesitant voice.

"It's me." Her voice is quiet. "Are you, um, okay?"

I blow out a breath and rake my fingers through my hair. "As okay as I can be right now. Marcel's being nice to you?"

She laughs, and I blink in surprise despite her not being able to see me. "Yeah, you don't have to worry about that. I'm fine, and if this is the way it has to be to make sure whatever needs to happen happens, it's okay."

I press my lips together for a moment. "They didn't glamour you, did they?"

"Calla, no. Seriously. If you think about it, this makes sense. And they said this would be a short-term solution, anyway."

"It might be shorter term than you think. I had an idea that could help the situation."

"I'm all ears," she says.

"So you know how the guys and I... How they came into my life, because of my ancestors."

"Yeah," she says hesitantly.

"Well, back then, a witch performed a spell that joined them with the Montgomery's firstborn. Fast forward to now, obviously it wasn't

816

me, but the idea of connecting lifeforms made me think about our situation."

There's a beat of silence, and then: "You want to connect lifeforms?"

"Yes," I answer, "yours and mine."

"What?" she squeaks. "Are you sure this is what we have to do?"

I frown at the irritation prickling along the back of my neck. "No, I'm not sure, but it's one of very few options we have, Brighton."

"Okay." Fear leaks into her voice through that one word. "The whole magic thing freaks me out, but... if this will help you trust me again, I'll do it."

"It's not about that," I say automatically. *Not completely*. "I think if you and I enter a blood oath that connects us, it'll protect us both—mainly from your father—and I'm not entirely sure how blood oath magic would work because I'm immortal now. It could protect you from harm."

"And you think by linking your life to mine, it'll stop my dad from trying to kill you?"

"Nothing means more to him than you do," I answer.

"Right." A muffled sniffle sounds through the phone, and my chest tightens. "I want to believe that," she tells me, "but I'm not sure it's true. I know my dad loves me, but this mission—the hunters protecting the world from vampires—I think it's a lot bigger than his relationship to me."

I pace back and forth, clenching my fist at my side. "We don't have to do this if you don't want to. We can find another way. It's—"

"No," she cuts in. "If you believe this will help, I want to do it. Plus, if that means they don't have to keep me stowed away in some safe house, even better. But it's not going to be permanent, right?"

"Definitely not."

"And how does it work exactly?"

"It'll differ from the connection I had with the guys, but I think the magic will be similar. We'll have more information once I get in touch with the witch who will help. I'll keep you posted. I'm assuming Marcel is listening to this conversation so I'll also remind him to take care of you or I will kick his ass."

"I've already said I'll do it, and I will, but I have, like, a million and one questions." *Understandable. I have a few of my own.* "And everything is fine here..." She offers a faint laugh. "Marcel is smiling from the kitchen at your ass-kicking comment. He's making pancakes."

Pancakes? As though they're friends having a casual brunch? I should be glad he's taking care of her and she's okay being with him, but part of me is uneasy about it.

It takes a couple days for Tessa to get back in touch after my initial contact about the situation.

Nothing about this sounds fun. I'm really sorry and I wish there was more I could do from here. Let me ask around and see who's in the D.C. area that can help you with the spell. Are you sure you want to link yourself to a human?

I chew my lower lip, reading her response from the end of my bed where I've been sitting for the last half hour trying to talk myself down from a panic attack. I can't stop thinking about having to see Atlas's parents again, which has spun me into a whirlwind of dread and anxiety.

Yes. We are quickly running out of options here, Tessa. I don't want anyone else to get hurt, and if this can help convince Brighton's dad to at least give the treaty a chance, it's worth the risk.

Her response comes a few minutes later.

Okay. I'll get back to you as soon as I have info.

Thank you. I owe you a drink.

I'm going to hold you to that. Visit soon! Until then, take care of yourself.

You too, I write back before tossing my phone beside me. I let out a sigh and fall back against the mattress. My breathing is still too shallow, so I close my eyes and force myself to focus on each breath. Five seconds to inhale, five seconds to hold, five seconds to exhale. I repeat the exercise until my breathing is somewhat normal.

I feel his presence before I open my eyes. "You're lurking."

Atlas leans in the doorway. "You took off earlier. I'm not lurking, I'm checking in."

"I'm fine," I say automatically, sitting up and scooting forward until my feet touch the floor at the end of the bed.

He pushes away from the doorframe and walks into the room. "Want to try again?"

"Not really."

He nods. "Have you forgiven us yet?"

I blow out a breath, staring at my hands in my lap. "Not really."

Atlas stops in front of me, cupping my chin in his hand and tilting my head up to meet his gaze. "What will it take?"

My lips part as my chest tightens. "I... don't know." *Maybe don't keep shit from me anymore?* That should be a given, though. And considering they're going to have to take me to Brighton now anyway, that's a pointless request. But being angry at people you care about is exhausting; I don't want to do it anymore. So maybe I'll forgive them—not for *them* but for me.

"I won't stand here and justify what we did." His thumb runs along my jaw. "You know it had to be done even if you don't like it."

My jaw clenches, and I think over several responses. "I care less about what you did and more that you kept it from me."

"You need to trust us." Atlas sighs, dropping his hand from my face. "Brighton is safe. Nothing we did put her in danger. The same can't be said for your plan with this blood oath."

I gloss over the 'you need to trust us' bit, because he knows damn well I do. I bite my tongue against what I want to say: *what about your trust in* me? Instead, I respond to his comment about the blood oath, narrowing my eyes as he steps back and I stand. "It's our best option."

"I disagree."

"I don't care." I close the distance between us in a heartbeat. "You want me to forgive you for going behind my back? How about having it now?"

His eyes dance across my face. "You'd like me to support a plan that puts you in danger?"

My brows tug together as I stare at him. My voice is lower when I say, "I'm in danger either way."

His facade cracks as he shakes his head, dropping his chin. "If anything happens to you—"

Something in me breaks, obliterating my anger toward him. I cup his cheeks in my hands and lift his head until he's looking at me. The vulnerability in his eyes makes my lungs burn, and I swallow hard. "I'm going to fight with everything I have to make sure that nothing happens to any of us. We're stronger when we're fighting together, and I wouldn't choose anyone else to be by my side." I search his eyes, willing him to find comfort in my words. "Because I did, you know. Choose you. And I will continue to choose you—until forever ends."

His mouth is on mine in a second, kissing me, devouring me. I slide my fingers into his hair, tugging at the ends as his mouth moves against mine in a bruising, passionate kiss that sets my soul on fire. His hands drop to my hips, and he pulls me flush against him. Our hearts pound in sync, slamming against our chests as if they're trying to reach each other.

When Atlas pulls back to give us both a moment to catch our breaths, his lips are swollen and his cheeks are flushed. I fucking love that I did that to him. I have an instinctual desire to lay claim to him in every way physically possible, and it both excites and terrifies me because I've never felt something so... *primal* before. I chalk it up to yet another vampire sire thing and smile at him as he pushes the hair away from my face, tucking it behind my ear. His eyes are glimmering with something faintly familiar but not familiar enough to keep me from asking, "Why are you looking at me like that?"

Atlas flashes me one of his rare smiles. It's full and genuine and sends my heart racing once more. "You terrify me, Calla Montgomery."

I blink at him, frowning briefly. "I..." I have no idea how to respond, because *what the fuck does that even mean?*

He chuckles, sliding his hands along either side of my neck and tipping my head up with his thumbs along my jaw. "Perhaps that wasn't the best way to phrase it." He dips his face, skimming his nose along mine. Inhaling a slow breath, he murmurs, "I love you with all that I am. So entirely that if by some devastating stroke of fate you were no longer part of my reality... there would be a part of me that would cease to exist."

Tears prick my eyes. "You... you can't say stuff like that to me." My chest feels as if it's about to explode, and I can't bear the thought of Atlas not being in my life. It's not a sire thing, and I know that because I feel the same about Gabriel, Kade, and Lex—even when they annoy the hell out of me.

Atlas brushes away the tear that slips down my cheek. "If you can make potentially dangerous decisions that scare the hell out of me, you can stand to listen to me tell you how I feel." He kisses me before I can respond, only pulling away once I'm breathless and my heart is pounding—his very intention, I'm sure. I shoot him a knowing look, to which he flashes a grin at me, and my god, he looks like an angel when he smiles.

I exhale a heavy breath. "You can let the others know Tessa is getting in contact with a witch here to help us with the blood oath spell. We'll have to let Marcel know when it's time to bring Brighton back."

He rakes his fingers through his hair, scratching the back of his neck, then exhales through his nose. "All right."

A few hours later, the five of us are sitting at the back of The Hamilton waiting for Tessa's contact to show up. She's already twenty minutes late, so things aren't off to a great start.

"Are we sure this witch is even coming?" Kade grumbles from behind the bar menu.

I nod. "Tessa wouldn't screw us over."

"I'm not convinced of that," Lex says, glancing down at his phone. "Marcel's in the parking lot."

My head immediately turns to the window, looking for Brighton. I don't want to be nervous to see her, but tension unfurls in my chest, the spot where she stabbed me with that dagger tingling uncomfortably. The wound is completely healed, and yet, I still feel it like a haunted memory.

When the two of them walk through the front door, I stay where I am in the booth and examine her cautiously before turning my gaze to Marcel, who nods at me as they approach.

"Thanks for keeping Brighton safe," I tell him.

His gaze shifts from me to Brighton. "It was my pleasure," he says.

My eyes narrow slightly, glancing between them. The soft flush of her cheeks has my brows lifting. Her eyes flit toward me and her blush deepens.

"Are we, uh, ready to do this?" she asks.

"Yeah," I say, shooting her a questioning look, which she shakes her head at as we approach the table where the guys are waiting.

I end up sandwiched between Gabriel and Brighton with Marcel on her other side and Atlas, Kade, and Lex on the other side of the booth. It's certainly cozy; being this close to Brighton has never made me feel so on edge before, and I'm desperately hoping this oath will ease some of that crackling anxiety living in my nerves.

Brighton glances toward the bar menu Kade is still idly flipping through. "Oh, we're drinking. Good." Her knee is bouncing under the table and her voice shakes slightly.

Marcel chuckles, and I catch him placing his hand on Brighton's knee, his thumb rubbing back and forth as if he's trying to calm her.

Something is clearly going on there, and I'm itching to ask, but it's definitely not the time or place for that conversation. Regardless, I'm happy she has someone; I trust Marcel, and the longer I watch the two of them together, the more I like it. So long as Brighton can get past his fangs and thirst for blood. And if she can get past it for him, that gives me hope for our friendship... Once I get past her almost murdering me.

"What time is this meeting supposed to start?" Brighton asks.

"Thirty minutes ago," Kade says in a clearly unimpressed tone, lifting a hand to wave over a waiter.

"Oh." She frowns. "Sorry we were late."

"Don't worry about it," I chime in. "Kade's just in a mood and doesn't think Tessa's contact is going to show."

Brighton nods. "And if they don't?"

Before I can answer, the waiter approaches the table with a tablet in his hand. "What can I get for you?" he asks in a polite tone.

"Old fashioned," Kade answers.

"Just water for me, please," I say.

Brighton arches a brow at me. "You're not drinking?"

"Not yet." I lower my voice. "I want to get through this meeting first."

"Right." She sighs, looking at the waiter. "Water with lemon, please."

Marcel, Gabriel, and Atlas all order whiskey neats, and Lex... Lex orders a peach bellini, specifically asking for a paper umbrella, because *of course* he does.

"Apologies, sir, we don't serve peach bellinis here. I can, however, recommend the white sangria, which will have similar flavors."

Lex purses his lips. "Fine, fine. Where'd we land on the umbrella?"

"Lex," Atlas mutters from beside him before telling the waiter, "That will be all, thank you."

The poor guy looks utterly at a loss and hurries away from the table, while I make a mental note to tip him generously.

The drinks come shortly thereafter, and nearly forty minutes late, a woman who appears to be about as old as my mom walks up to our table, locking eyes with me immediately. She's wearing minimal makeup and has light brown hair twisted into a fishtail braid over her shoulder. There are faint smile lines around her mouth and eyes, aging her more than the stylish purple blouse and dark jeans she's dressed in. "Calla."

I nod, taking a sip of my water. "You must be—"

"Gwen." She glances around the table before settling her vibrant green eyes on Brighton. "One human surrounded by vampires. Brave girl."

"Brave *hunter*," Lex corrects, and there's an edge to his voice.

I shoot him a dark look across the table, then return my gaze to Gwen. "Thank you for coming. I'm not sure how much Tessa told you, but—"

"She told me all I needed to know." She takes a chair from an empty table and sticks it at the end of the booth, sitting and clasping her hands in front of her. Each of her fingers is decorated with a unique, glimmering ring. "You'd like to do this here?"

"We've glamoured everyone here to ignore us besides one waiter, who we'll take care of before we leave," Gabriel explains. There aren't that many people in the restaurant now anyway, but it was a precaution the guys insisted on, especially considering none of us are wearing contacts and many people saw the newscast about vampires.

Gwen nods. "Calla and..."

"Brighton," she quickly offers her name.

"Calla and Brighton will need to consume each other's blood while I perform the spell."

Unease fills my stomach, and Brighton's face pales. I offer her a reassuring smile. "It'll be over quickly."

Her entire body is tense, but she nods, visibly cringing. "And if I throw up, will that mess with the spell?"

"For the love of—" Lex starts under his breath, but I kick him in the shin to cut him off.

"I can glamour you," I offer. "I've been working on it and I think I'm pretty good. It'll help you through this." I glance toward Gwen. "Is that okay, or will it affect the magic?"

"I'd rather the human not be under the influence of any glamour. The spell will work better if both parties are fully in control of themselves. There needs to be no question of the validity of the oath."

I press my lips together, stealing a look across the table. I can't tell for sure, but I think Gwen is taking a shot at us based on the last oath I thought I was tangled up in. "Right. How much did Tessa tell you about us exactly?"

Her lips twitch briefly in response.

"Okay then. Let's get this over with."

"Wait," Brighton blurts in a panicked tone. "How long will this last?"

The witch blinks at her. "Until the spell is undone."

"And if one of us gets hurt or..."

"Dies?" Gwen offers, then answers, "Whatever happens to one happens to both."

Brighton's pulse is a jackhammer beneath her skin, her eyes darting between Gwen, me, and Marcel. "Does linking me to a vampire mean I'll need to drink blood?" Her voice trembles, and I get the urge to reach across the table and take her hand, because despite what she did, I do care about her, and seeing her so scared and unsure makes me feel awful.

Gwen chuckles. "No. I wouldn't complete the spell if that was a possibility. No human should have to suffer the grotesque bloodlust vampires seem to thrive off these days." The distaste is clear in her voice.

I bite the inside of my cheek, waiting for one of the guys to bark something crude or threatening at her, but they all remain silent.

"O-okay," Brighton finally says, then echoes my last comment. "Let's get this over with."

Gwen has us shift around the booth so Brighton and I are sitting at the end of each side. She closes her eyes and starts whispering under her breath. When she holds her hands out to each of us, Brighton and I place our hands in hers. A spark of energy floods through me, and I tense momentarily before my body adjusts. Brighton's eyes are wide and her heart pounds in her chest. I hold her gaze, hopefully showing her we're in this together.

"It's time," Gwen says, keeping her eyes shut, and tightens her grip on our hands. "You must drink each other's blood to complete the spell and seal the oath."

Kade slides his empty glass across the table as I bite my wrist, wincing as my fangs easily slice through the skin. I hold my wrist over the glass, filling it halfway with blood before sealing the wound with my tongue. I push the glass toward Brighton, and her jaw clenches.

"Oh god..." Her chest rises and falls fast, her gaze darting around the room as if she's looking for a way to escape.

"Hey." I pull her attention back to me. "It's okay. We're almost done. This is the last step, then we can drink and pretend this didn't happen." I have a feeling it's going to be difficult to pretend when we're linked, but I keep that to myself. She's probably thinking the same thing.

Brighton takes a deep breath and straightens, pressing her back flat against the booth cushion. "Okay." She picks up the knife next to her.

"Whoa, no." Marcel plucks the knife from her grasp and sets it on his other side. "You don't want to do that. Way too messy."

She frowns at him. "Are you offering then?"

His brows lift, and he glances my way for a moment before returning his attention to Brighton. "If you're comfortable with that."

Instead of responding, she pushes her sleeve up to her elbow and clenches her hand into a fist, placing it on the table.

Marcel takes her wrist gently and lifts it to his mouth. He holds her gaze as he sinks his fangs into her skin. She sucks in a sharp breath, her brows knitting as she presses her lips together, and he pulls back a second later, his jaw clenched tightly.

I lean over the table as Brighton offers me her wrist, the coppery scent of her blood making my gums throb. It takes more focus than I'd like to admit to keep my fangs from extending, but I manage it. I wrap my fingers around her wrist and guide it to my lips as she lifts the glass with my blood to hers.

Gwen continues the spell as Brighton closes her eyes and starts drinking. I keep mine open and close my lips around Marcel's puncture marks. Brighton's blood explodes on my tastebuds, and I force myself to drink slowly, pulling her wrist away the moment she finishes drinking my blood.

Gwen finishes the spell and lets go of our hands. Brighton wipes her lips with the napkin in front of her, then immediately downs half a glass of water. I offer her a smile, and she shoots me a weak thumbs-up, finishing the water before setting the glass back on the table.

"Is it done?" she asks Gwen.

The witch nods. "It's done."

Nothing feels immediately different, but there's a weight in my chest and a tingling at the back of my neck that tells me it worked. Brighton's life and mine are connected.

"Thank you," I tell her. "Whatever we owe you—"

She arches a dark brow at me. "I don't want your money."

"Uh, okay. What do you want?"

"A favor." She stands, pushing her chair back. "Not now, but I will collect when the time comes." With that, she walks away from our table and disappears through the restaurant.

"Now we owe a debt to a witch?" Kade mutters. "That's fucking great."

I ignore him and glance across the table Brighton. "How are you feeling?"

She frowns. "I'm not sure. A little nauseous?"

"That's understandable. How about that drink?"

"Honestly, I think I just need a nap."

"Right, yeah, of course. We can go back to the house and..." I trail off when she breaks eye contact with me. "Brighton?"

She looks at me again. "My things are still at Marcel's—the safe house, I mean. Maybe I should just crash there tonight, and we can meet up tomorrow?"

"Are you sure?"

Brighton nods. "As long as it's cool with Marcel."

Lex snorts. "Pretty sure it's more than *cool* with him."

Brighton's pulse jumps, her cheeks and chest flushing pink as she looks at me while sliding out of the booth. I get up too, and she wraps me in a tight hug without warning. "See you soon."

I stiffen immediately, my pulse leaping. It takes several beats to force my muscles to relax. *She isn't going to hurt you again*, I chant over and over until my breathing returns close to normal, and I echo, "See you soon."

Marcel whispers something to Gabriel too quick for me to catch, then guides Brighton toward the front of the restaurant. I watch them go, and my brows shoot up my forehead at the spark of excitement that zips through *me* when Marcel's hand rests at the small of Brighton's back.

This is going to be interesting...

When we get back to the house, I retreat to the bathroom and turn on the shower as hot as it will go. Now that I've had time to sit with the fact that Brighton and I are linked, along with my friend's blood sloshing around in my stomach, I feel quite uneasy about it. I'm hoping the feeling will pass knowing there's an added level of protection for me as well as her. Still, I scrub my skin with the lavender body wash until it's red and tingling, and spend extra time shampooing and conditioning my hair for no other reason besides not wanting to get out of the shower.

I stand under the hot spray of water until it becomes lukewarm and my fingers are wrinkly. Finally, I get out and wrap myself in a robe before padding into the bedroom and sitting on the end of the bed. I stare at the window as the sky changes colors and the sun starts to set.

I hear his approach before there's a knock on the door, and Lex pokes his head inside the room.

"Can I come in?"

"Might as well. You're already halfway."

A flicker of a frown curves his lips before he slips inside and closes the door. "How are you feeling?" he asks, approaching at an easy pace and stopping only a foot away.

"I don't really know," I answer honestly. "I just hope this works."

"We all do," he agrees. "Can I get you anything?"

"What are you trying to—"

"I just want to take care of you," he says before I can finish my sentence. "I know things are rocky between us, and that's our own fault, but I fucking hate it. I hate you being mad at me."

I drop my chin and exhale a soft sigh. "Yeah, it hasn't been fun for me either, Lex." Not to mention it feels slightly moot, considering I'm now linked with the person they sent away. They still chose not to trust me knowing the plan before putting it into action, and even when I think I'll be able to let it go, there's an annoying sting of pain when I think about it.

He steps closer, his legs touching my knees, and snags my chin as he crouches and kisses my forehead. "Let me make you forget about everything for a little while," he offers, and my skin flushes hotly.

I press my lips together, the pounding of my heart mirroring the throbbing between my legs, and I find myself nodding.

His mouth seals over mine, warm and soft, and our lips explore each other's as he tangles his fingers in my wet hair. Cradling the back of my neck, he deepens the kiss, gliding his tongue past my lips and grazing it against mine. Everything in me tingles with warmth, and all I want to do is pull him closer. But a part of me doesn't want to rush this, so I let Lex take the lead. He slides his hand into the front of my robe, untying the drawstring and letting it fall open. His eyes devour my body, his gaze filled with hunger and lust, and I can see the tips of his fangs when he pulls away. "You are the most stunning creature I've ever laid eyes on," he professes, kissing me again. He trails his lips along my jaw, down my throat, across my collarbones. And then he drags his mouth across my chest, kissing each of my breasts and flicking his tongue against my nipples until they harden into stiff peaks. My breathing shallows and the need to have him between my legs intensifies, so I push him lower. He drops to his knees at the end of the bed, sliding his hands up my bare thighs and spreading my legs open. He presses a gentle kiss just above where I desperately want him, then the inside of each of my thighs, heading toward my feet.

I grumble, which sounds more like a pathetic moan.

Lex chuckles against my skin, pausing with lips hovering over my core. "Am I not giving you what you want?"

I stare at him between my legs, narrowing my eyes. "You know exactly what I want."

He nods. "Maybe I just like to hear you say it."

"You need reassurance you're doing a good job getting me off?"

He shrugs, grinning softly. "Maybe I do."

"Or maybe he just needs a little help." Both our heads turn toward the door and find Kade walking into the room. He kicks the door shut behind him, smirking at us as if he just found us doing something we shouldn't be.

"And I assume you're the help?" I ask in a cheeky tone.

"Only you would be so lucky," he says, walking closer. He tugs his shirt off over his head and moves faster than I can, using his shirt to tie my wrists above my head and securing them to the headboard.

"What the hell is this?"

He offers me a fanged smirk. "Lex is taking care of you. *I'm* having fun."

Before I can respond, Lex drags his tongue along my slit, sucking my clit into his mouth and swirling his tongue around it hard and fast. I choke on a moan, growling when I can't pull my hands free. Granted, I'm not trying very hard, and with my new vampiric strength, I could shred Kade's shirt to ribbons. But if I'm honest, giving up control is really fucking hot.

When Lex plunges his tongue inside me, sending my head spinning and heat rushing to my core, my thoughts scatter. I grip the headboard as Lex pins my hips to the mattress, devouring me so completely my world narrows on the wickedly delicious sensations whipping through me.

Kade unbuckles his belt, popping the button on his jeans and tugging the zipper down. I turn my head toward him as he frees his cock, and I try to reach for it, momentarily forgetting that my wrists are bound by his shirt. He grins, pumping his hand up and down his length until moisture beads along the tip and his heart is beating faster.

I lick my lips, pulling the bottom one between my teeth. My eyes are locked on his movements and my thighs tighten around Lex's head when his tongue hits a sensitive spot. He presses his thumb against my clit, circling it lightly, teasing me while Kade holds my attention.

"Untie me," I tell him.

"Hmm... I don't think so."

I arch a brow, my breathing growing shallower as my heart pounds in my chest, my pleasure reaching new heights as the tongue inside me increases speed and pressure. "Untie me so I can make you feel how Lex is making me feel."

Kade pauses, flicking a glance toward the vampire between my legs before returning his gaze to me. "I think I'd much rather fuck that mouth of yours."

In the space of a heartbeat, his mouth is on mine, kissing me hard and pushing his tongue past my lips. I kiss him back, moaning as Lex brings me closer to orgasm. Kade straddles me, taking over for Lex in holding me down, and braces himself over me using the headboard. This puts his cock directly in front of my face, which has me licking my lips in anticipation. He fists his thick length, pumping it a few times before dragging it along my lips until I part them. I take him into my mouth slowly, inch by inch, until the head of his cock bumps the back of my throat. Closing my lips around him, I moan from Lex's ministrations, which sends vibrations through Kade's cock. The wood of the headboard creaks as Kade grips it tighter, sucking in a breath. I drag my tongue along the underside of his length as he pulls it out of my mouth, only to thrust it back in seconds later. I suck hard, changing pressure until his breathy grunts fill the room. Pressure builds between my thighs lightning-fast, and then my pussy is clenching around Lex's tongue, soaking it with my release. My moans push Kade over the edge, and his thigh muscles go taunt, my only warning before he groans, spilling his release into my mouth. I swallow the warmth down my throat, licking the rest from my lips as he pulls out of me. He shifts lower, holding himself over me with his hands pressed into the pillows at my head, while his lips brush my forehead, my nose, my jaw, then tease the hammering pulse at my throat.

I shiver as Lex pulls back, licking me clean and pressing a gentle kiss against the overly sensitive bundle of nerves at my core.

"I think you can take more," Kade murmurs, flicking his tongue against the skin below my ear.

I'm still catching my breath when I say, "Are you going to keep me tied up?"

He pulls back to look at me. "That depends. Are you going to behave?"

I tilt my head to the side and steal a glance at Lex, who is undressing with a faint smirk on his lips as he tosses his clothes onto the chaise next to the window. Kade grips my chin and forces my gaze back to his. "Probably not," I answer with a tone of defiance.

Kade smiles. "There's your answer then." He drops onto the mattress beside me as Lex crawls onto the bed, grabbing my knees and spreading my legs wide open. His cock is hard, the tip already glistening with evidence of his arousal, which makes my pulse race. He positions himself at my entrance, holding my gaze as he pushes only the tip inside.

"Do you want to come again?" he asks in a low voice, his eyes dark with lust.

I nod, my inner walls pulsing with the need to have him deeper.

He pulls out completely, and I bite back a disapproving growl. "Ask for it," he instructs.

Kade leans in close, his lips brushing my neck before his fangs scrape my skin. "Ask for it," he whispers darkly, "or I'll make you beg for it." He slides his fingers along the underside of my breasts and pinches my nipple hard, making me suck in a sharp breath.

"Make me come," I tell Lex.

He tuts his tongue, shaking his head. "That's not very polite."

This time, I growl aloud, tugging on my restraints. They tear easily, freeing me from the headboard, but Kade is there immediately, wrapping his fingers around my wrists and holding my arms above my head.

"Ah, ah, ah," he says with a grin.

I try to fight him off, but even with my heightened strength, Kade is a much older vampire than I am. It's going to take more energy than I have to overpower him, and by the amused glint in his eyes, he fucking knows it.

Lex dips his cock back inside, moving agonizingly slowly. "Let's try this again, shall we?"

My eyes narrow, but I can suppress the shiver that zips through me when Kade lowers his mouth back to my neck as if he's about to sink his fangs into me. "Please," I say in a low voice, "I need you to make me come."

"Do you?" Lex asks, pushing in deeper. "How badly?"

I open my mouth to snap a crude remark at him, and Kade chooses that moment to bite me. His fangs are deep in my neck between one second and the next, stealing my breath and making my pussy clench around Lex's cock. Turns out, it doesn't matter that I'm a vampire. Being bitten is still, if not more, euphoric. My eyes roll back and my lips part in a moan as I tilt my head, giving him better access. Lex pushes the rest of the way into me, and I see fucking stars. He plays my clit like an instrument, timing his thrusts so perfectly, I'm barreling toward climax in minutes. That paired with the sensation of blood being pulled from me, has me panting, the muscles in my stomach coiling tighter by the second.

Kade pulls his fangs out of me, licking his lips and freeing my wrists, and the world spins when Lex pulls out and flips me over. I don't have a moment to register what happened before Kade hauls my body over his and sinks his cock into me to the hilt. I grab the headboard and roll my hips, biting my lip as sweat dots my brow.

Lex shifts behind me, running his hands along my back and grabbing my hips, pushing me down. I'm flush against Kade's chest, my nipples hard and tingling, and I tense when Lex's cock presses against the puckered hole at my ass.

He chuckles, leaning down and kissing my shoulder. "Relax for me. We both know you enjoy this."

I inhale a deep breath as Kade reaches between us to play with my clit, holding still inside me. Slowly, my muscles unclench.

"That's it," Lex murmurs, pushing his cock into me at an easy pace. It slides in easy enough, but I'm gripping him like a vice.

I hold my breath, hanging on Kade's shoulders tightly. "Fuck," I grunt, gritting my teeth.

"Easy," Kade murmurs, circling my clit and kissing my jaw. "Breathe."

You'd think this would get easier, but it still feels uncomfortably close to the first time one of them stretched me there. "Kiss me," I force out, and he complies instantly, stealing my mouth with his. Our lips move together, and he thrusts up, pushing Lex deeper into my ass. I hang onto him for dear life, moaning against his lips as he and Lex both thrust into me at alternating times and speeds. My head is spinning and I think there must be some moment when I stop breathing altogether.

Everything in me is on fire. There's a sheen of sweat covering my body, and my heart slams against my chest as my muscles seize, clenching around the cocks inside of me. I break away from Kade's mouth, crying out my release as an insanely powerful climax tears through me.

Lex grunts, digging his fingers into my hips as he picks up speed and continues thrusting. I collapse onto Kade's chest as he groans, finding his release, and Lex does the same only seconds later. He pulls out of me and drops onto the bed beside us. I lift my hips enough for Kade to pull out, then end up sandwiched between them, my entire body spent and throbbing with aftershocks.

I'm not sure how much time passes before Kade says, "We should get in the shower. The hunters called another meeting. It's in an hour."

832

Thirty minutes later, we're in the car. Atlas and Gabriel are up front, while I'm stuck in the back with Kade and Lex.

"Someone want to fill me in on this meeting?" I called Brighton on the burner phone; she and Marcel are coming, so I suppose we're going to find out how effective my blood oath idea is.

Gabriel turns in his seat and looks at me. "Marcel made contact with Scott and allowed him to speak with Brighton. After she convinced her father we didn't take her captive, he demanded to see her."

"What does this mean for us?" I ask.

"Brighton had the sense to use this opportunity to attempt another discussion between the vampires and hunters—on a much smaller scale and in public as an added layer of protection for both sides. She, with Marcel's guidance, filled Scott in on the peace treaty idea."

I blink in surprise. "She did? So now what?"

"We're meeting Scott, and likely an entourage of hunters, at that café you and the human love so much," Kade chimes in, glancing out the window as we round the corner on the street of our destination.

I frown. "Great, so if this goes downhill and something happens, we'll never be able to go there again."

Lex huffs out a laugh. "I think there's more to be concerned about than that."

I say nothing, because as much as I'd like to argue that, he's not wrong.

We find parking and walk toward the café. I spot Marcel's car along the way, and my heart beats a little faster knowing Brighton's already here. The point of the spell Gwen did was to protect Brighton, but I'd much rather not have her involved at all. Same as I'm sure the guys would prefer to sideline me, though I think they know better than to try that at this point.

I zip up my windbreaker and take a deep breath.

"Hunters are here," Gabriel announces in a voice so low my previously human senses wouldn't have picked it up.

Atlas opens the door to the café, and we file inside. I'm the last to step through the door before Atlas, who lets it close behind him.

There are only a few other patrons, and my eyes immediately land on the large circular table at the back of the room, where Marcel and Brighton are surrounded by at least half a dozen unfamiliar faces —except one.

I stalk forward, only making it a few steps before Atlas catches my arm. "Let go—"

"Take it easy," he warns. "We need to be careful here."

I clench my jaw but force a nod, and he releases me.

Everyone stands as we approach the table, and I immediately go to Brighton to make sure she's okay. I don't doubt Marcel, but even this has to be outside his wheelhouse.

"Hey," she says in a low voice, wrapping her arm around me in an awkward half-hug that, at the very least, doesn't catch me completely off guard this time.

"You okay?" I check, searching her eyes as she nods. Her pulse is uneven, and she keeps chewing her bottom lip.

I turn to Scott, who is, unsurprisingly, glaring at me. "Nice to see you too, Mr. Ellis," I offer dryly.

He shakes his head, his lips curling with disgust. "I am only here to ensure the safety of my daughter, monster."

"Dad," Brighton says, her eyes glassy with unshed tears and a frown on her lips.

"It's okay," I tell her, sensing Atlas and Gabriel shifting closer. The hunters who came with Scott don't move, but their eyes are sharp and focused on the two of us. "He's not going to hurt me."

"I should kill you," he nearly snarls.

"And kill your own daughter in the process? That's cold."

Scott whips around to face Brighton. "What the hell is she talking about?" he demands.

Brighton shakes her head. "I'm sorry, Dad. I... You need to listen to them."

"Answer the question, Brighton."

She quickly brushes away the tear that slips down her cheek. "Calla and I... We're linked. You can't hurt her without hurting me."

His face blanches and then goes red with rage. He charges toward her, and Marcel immediately moves to stand between them. Scott has a dagger in his hand in seconds.

So much for safety in a public place...

"Dad, stop!" Brighton cries, attempting to step around Marcel. "Please! It doesn't have to be like this."

Everyone—vampires and hunters alike—is on high alert, focused and ready to dive into a fight. The hunters have their dominant hands on their dagger holders.

My gums throb painfully, and I'm barely able to keep my fangs concealed. Baring them really won't help the situation.

Get ready, Atlas's voice echoes through my head.

My eyes widen and snap toward him. This is the second time he's been able to communicate with me like this, and we haven't explored it. Now obviously isn't the time, but we'll need to figure it out at some point.

In my peripheral, Gabriel is quickly and quietly going around to the few human patrons and glamouring them to leave and forget being here. He returns to our group a minute later once the café has cleared out and the front door is locked.

"We didn't come here to fight," Atlas announces, commanding attention from both sides. "I'm going to ask that you hear me out. Listen with an open mind and set aside our differences for at least the duration of this meeting. What we are proposing could save a lot of lives—yours included."

"Vampires are dangerous and cannot be trusted—simple as that," Scott interrupts, his words filled with venom. "And just how many vampires would even agree to this treaty? There are plenty of your kind who couldn't care less about human safety. They hunt and kill for sport."

"I could say the same for your kind," Gabriel chimes in calmly. "Some hunters may kill vampires with the motive of protecting humans. That isn't to say there aren't also some hunters who choose to hunt vampires for sport with no regard for the consequences of that."

One hunter with a permanent scowl shrugs. "Either way, humans are being protected."

"Not all vampires pose a risk to humans," I snap at him, wincing at the throbbing in my gums, which is growing stronger every minute we're here. In hindsight, I probably should've had a blood bag on the drive over.

"As long as vampires require blood to survive, their mere existence is a risk," Scott shoots back, which has a couple of the other hunters nodding in agreement. And when he grips the hilt of his dagger tighter, the rest of the hunters grab theirs, moving around the table to flank their leader.

"We don't want to fight," Gabriel says, addressing the hunters, "and just because he does, doesn't mean you have to."

"Enough!" Scott bellows.

And then everything erupts into chaos.

Gabriel ducks in just enough time to avoid a flying dagger aimed for his chest, while Atlas and Lex attempt to block me from the oncoming hunters. Kade snarls, baring his fangs at them, and gets into it with the bulkiest one of the group.

As a team of three hunters charges toward us, my heart lurches. They have their eyes locked on Atlas, probably figuring he's the most powerful of our group and stupidly thinking they can eliminate him from the fight. The curvy blond hunter reaches for the holster at her thigh, her hate-filled features twisting with disgust. I launch forward and slam my foot into her chest before she can wield her dagger at my sire. She goes flying backward into the table she was sitting at not too long ago, groaning in pain when she hits the floor. There's a gash across her cheek, dripping blood down her face.

I lick my lips, the dull burning in my throat magnified by the throbbing in my gums. I force my gaze away from the red staining the front of her shirt now and look toward Atlas, a rush of adrenaline zipping through my veins. "You're welcome," I say, surprised at the cockiness in my voice. God, I sound like Kade or Lex.

His lips twitch for a moment before he snaps, "Focus."

I give him a middle finger salute, then canvas the room again. These hunters are different. At least, some of them are. They don't seem to *want* to fight. A few of them keep looking to Scott, for direction maybe, I'm not sure. What I am sure of is he's trying to move toward Brighton, which is not about to happen.

I dodge a feeble attempt at an attack from one hunter, knocking him aside with no genuine effort, and appear in front of Scott, effectively blocking his path to his daughter.

"Get out of my way, Calla," he says, his cheeks flushed with anger and his heart beating rapidly.

"Oh, I'm Calla now? What happened to *monster*?" I taunt, and I can't help myself, I flash my fangs at him. I shouldn't have, not when we're trying to keep things peaceful, but being called a monster seems to have sliced deeper than Brighton's dagger did.

Scott moves faster than I expect, and I only avoid the sharp end of his dagger because Gabriel grabs me from behind and hauls me back.

Brighton rushes over, putting herself between me and Scott. Her heart is racing and her sweat-dampened hair sticks to the side of her neck, where her pulse is pounding like a drum. The monster Scott referred to me as rears her ugly head, salivating as she recalls what Brighton's blood tastes like.

Gabriel tugs me back, his grip firm around my upper arm as Brighton faces her father.

"Stop fighting," she tells him, and despite her racing pulse, her voice doesn't waver. "Dad, *please*."

My gaze flits around the room in a matter of seconds. The hunter I threw across the room is back up, fighting Kade with flushed cheeks and shallow breaths as she struggles to keep up with his speed and strength despite the vigorous training hunters go through. And that's with him showing restraint; he could have killed her three times over by now, but we're trying to *avoid* killing anyone.

Another hunter is circling Lex as he fights off two others, grinning with his fangs on full display as if he's enjoying this, which he probably is. One hunter—an older-looking guy with slicked back hair and a brown leather jacket—takes a shot at Lex's face, grazing his cheek with a dagger. Lex hisses in annoyance and backhands the guy so hard the grotesque *crunch* of his nose breaking reaches me, and I cringe. He collapses, dropping his dagger and howling in pain as he cups his hand over his nose. Blood pours from it, spilling through his fingers and making my throat burn, but I force my attention forward, knowing Lex can handle that.

Scott frowns at Brighton. "Oh, sweetheart. I thought you understood the importance of what we do."

"Understood?" she echoes, shaking her head. "How could I when you won't even hear them out? This treaty could save so many lives."

He inhales a shaky breath, then sighs, shaking his head as sadness fills his gaze. "Please know that having to do this breaks my heart."

Brighton blinks in confusion, her pulse ticking faster as fear shallows her breaths. "Wh-what are you... What does that mean?"

Scott's eyes shift to me, and the hatred in their depths makes my blood run cold.

We were wrong. He doesn't care that Brighton and I are linked. *He's going to kill me.*

Gabriel moves before I can, slamming his fist into the side of Scott's face and knocking him to the side. Atlas and Kade are at my side in the time it takes me to blink, while Lex's growl fills the room and he makes quick work of subduing the hunters opposing him.

Scott tries to catch his balance as he stumbles around a few steps, but before he can, Kade zeroes in on him, whipping his elbow out and catching him in the jaw, snapping his head back. My breath catches as

Scott's eyes roll into the back of his head and he collapses onto the floor.

Brighton screams, and Marcel is there in an instant, pulling her away as she tries to go to her dad.

"Get her out of here," I holler at him.

His eyes meet mine, and he nods, snaking an arm around Brighton's waist and hauling her toward the door as she continues to scream and fight him, tears streaming down her face.

Once she's gone, my attention goes to where Lex is advancing on a hunter that I hadn't noticed before. She must have snuck in while my focus was on Scott. Her eyes are wide, filled with panic as they bounce around the room and get stuck on where Scott is lying unconscious but alive.

I cross the room in a matter of seconds, stepping over two knocked-out hunters slumped against each other, and blocking Lex's path. "Stop."

He arches a brow. "What are you doing?"

"She isn't trying to fight." I turn to face her. "Why are you here?"

The hunter, who I'd guess is only a few years older than me, swallows hard and clears her throat before speaking. "The treaty. Peace between the hunters and vampires... I want that."

"You do?"

She nods, tucking a bit of dark red hair that escaped her bun away from her face. "I was raised by hunters. From the time I was thirteen, I was learning about vampires. By fifteen, I was training to kill them." She reaches for the dagger secured to her thigh, and my back straightens as I prepare to fight her. So imagine my surprise when she pulls the dagger out and tosses it on the floor with a heavy sigh. "I don't want to do it anymore. I've seen and met vampires who don't hunt humans, who don't pose a threat to our survival. Scott and some others either can't or refuse to see that, but that isn't the case for a lot of us."

I scan the room again. One hunter—the male Kade was fighting—is dead, while four, including Scott and a few others, are unconscious. That leaves the one in front of me and another who is being held by Lex and Kade. He appears relatively calm, leading me to believe he's here for the same reason we are.

"How is this going to work?" he asks, glancing at Kade then Lex. "You guys don't have to keep holding onto me. Don't get me wrong, I don't mind, but you should know, it isn't necessary."

The female hunter walks toward them, and I follow her, kicking the dagger across the room—just in case.

"What's your name?" I ask as we approach him.

"James." He offers me his hand once the guys let go of him. "Hopefully nice to meet you, Calla."

"Right." I shake his hand, then turn to the female hunter. "I didn't catch your name."

"Sera," she says, and we shake hands.

I manage a smile. "The two who left were Marcel and Brighton, who you probably know already." I point to each of the guys and offer their names as we all cross the room and meet in the middle.

"Why don't we sit down?" Gabriel suggests.

The seven of us pick a new table and take our seats. I'm in between Atlas and Gabriel, and my eyes keep going to Scott, making sure he's still out. We likely don't have much time.

"How exactly do you see this working?" James asks.

"The treaty vampires will agree to hunt the rogue vampires alongside the hunters to ensure the protection of humankind," Atlas explains.

"And in exchange," I say, "the hunters agree not to hunt us."

"It'll take some time to organize things, get the word out to everyone, that sort of thing," Sera points out.

Lex nods. "That's right. And we're very aware there are bound to be individuals from both sides who will flat out refuse to be part of this." He glances toward the bodies on the floor. "As they've exhibited for us today."

Sera nods, looking to Atlas. "I happen to know what bloodline you belong to. The York clan isn't only well known in vampire circles. What do they think of this?"

"You let me handle that," Atlas says in a dangerously calm voice, and I press my lips together, trying not to frown at the tension rippling through him. My fingers itch to reach for my sire, but I fold my hands in my lap under the table to keep them to myself.

"This will take some time," Gabriel says, "but we're glad you're willing to work through the logistics with us."

James nods. "We're happy to take it on. The hunters have been at war with the vampires for too long."

"And we know the history," Sera adds. "Any other way we look at it, we're on the losing side."

Gabriel drums his fingers on the table. "We should set another meeting in a month to reconvene after we've gotten word to as many people in our respective communities as possible."

Sera nods. "James and I will do our best to get things moving on our end."

The hunters stand, and we follow suit. They head for the door but stop near Scott and the other hunter, who is groaning softly, evidently coming to.

"What about them?" Sera asks. "Are you going to kill them?"

"No," Gabriel answers. "We'll glamour the woman and send her home."

"And Scott?" James asks.

"We're still figuring that one out," Kade supplies.

Seemingly satisfied with that, James and Sera walk out of the café together, leaving us with the two semi-conscious hunters.

I lean against the counter, surveying the room, and exhale a heavy sigh. Things are moving in what feels like the right direction, but the pit in my stomach leads me to believe everything is about to get more complicated before anything gets better.

CHAPTER

EIGHT

ATLAS

My grip on the steering wheel has my knuckles white. I can feel Calla watching me from the passenger seat but I keep my eyes on the road, grinding my molars at the sound of the human heartbeat in the backseat.

Kade healed the other hunter, glamouring her before sending her on her way before we left the café... with Scott fucking Ellis in tow.

"What the hell are we going to do with him?" Lex mutters, and I glance at him in the rearview mirror. He's glaring at the human who is now fully awake and heavily glamoured to keep quiet. He's slouched against the back window as if drugged, and honestly, I couldn't care less.

My vote is to kill the bastard.

"I want the opportunity to talk to Brighton before we decide anything," Calla says.

Gabriel nods. "Marcel took her back to our rental."

We're silent for the rest of the drive, pulling into the driveway well after midnight, which is probably a good thing, considering that Kade and Lex are practically carrying Scott into the house.

Calla disappears the moment we're inside, coming into the living room where we've all gathered with a small white bottle and a glass of water. She opens the bottle and shakes out a couple pills, offering them to Scott along with the water. Her expression is blank when she says, "I'm sure you have one hell of a headache."

841

He says nothing but takes the pills, swallowing them before downing the entire glass of water.

It takes every ounce of control I have not to break his jaw with my fist for treating Calla with such disrespect even when she's showing him kindness. Kindness he sure as hell doesn't deserve after the way he spoke to her. And considering he had clearly decided to kill her and sacrifice his daughter, I don't see how he deserves anything now besides a slow and painful death.

Maybe I need to take a walk.

Brighton is sitting on the couch next to the chair the guys dropped Scott into. Marcel is sitting next to her, stealing glances her way every minute. He's never been one to hide his affection for anyone, and Brighton is no exception. Though they haven't known each other long, he cares for her. It worries me—add it to the list—the thought of him being hurt by whatever might come from this war with the hunters and Brighton's involvement. But as much as the lot of us—save for Calla—didn't want the human around, she's part of this now, and being connected to Calla means we're going to protect her like our own.

Calla sits on the coffee table in front of Brighton, taking her friend's hands in hers. "Do you want to go for a chat?"

Her eyes are rimmed in red and puffy; she's likely been crying since Marcel dragged her out of the café. "You didn't kill him," she whispers in a broken voice.

Calla shakes her head. "But we need to talk about how to handle this."

"Get away from my daughter," Scott snarls.

Before I can step in, Calla whips toward him and says, "Shut the fuck up."

His eyes glaze over and his lips press together.

I exchange a glance with Gabriel; safe to say we're equally impressed by our girl. She picked up glamour quicker than many.

She turns her attention back to Brighton. "What do *you* want to do?"

Fresh tears fill her eyes and roll down her cheeks. "I... I don't..." Her voice cracks and she sniffles. She shakes her head. "I don't know," she finally whispers. "But if he continues down this path of hatred toward vampires, it's going to get him killed."

Calla nods. "What if we wipe his memories?"

Brighton's eyes widen, and she pulls her hands away from Calla's, wiping the tears from her cheeks. "Of wanting to kill vampires?"

"Of *everything* to do with vampires," Calla explains.

"I'm sure he has a second in command," Lex says. "They'll just take his place."

"That's a different issue." Calla briefly glances at him. "Doing this will eliminate the conflict of interest we have with the hunters' leader, hopefully making the peace treaty easier."

Brighton clears her throat, then says, "He grew up in Chicago, and we still have family there. If you're going to erase his memories of the supernatural world, I think he should go there where people know him as Scott instead head of the vampire hunters."

I consider that for a moment. It's not the worst plan. The last thing any of us vampires want is to give Scott a happy ending, considering he's hellbent on ending *us*, but time isn't on our side these days, so this will have to do. And we're not really doing this for Scott, anyway. We're doing it so Calla doesn't have to live with taking Brighton's only living parent away. "All right." I look at Marcel, and he's already standing.

"I'll make the arrangements," he says, pulling his phone out and lifting it to his ear as he walks out of the room.

Calla takes Marcel's spot on the couch next to Brighton. "I know you want to help with the treaty between the hunters and the vampires, but no one will judge you if you want to go with your dad. I know none of this was what you wanted, or what your mom wanted for you. You got caught in the middle of something you never should have had to deal with."

Brighton looks toward Calla, her bottom lip quivering as if she's about to burst into tears. Again. "I don't know," she says in a low voice, biting the inside of her cheek. "My dad grew up there, but I've only been a few times to visit family and, I mean, my life is here. I don't want to think about having to change schools..." Brighton rakes her free hand through her hair and sighs heavily. "And, uh, after what he said... part of me doesn't see him as my dad anymore. I'm not sure when the switch flipped, but at some point, I stopped being his daughter." She swallows hard, shaking her head as if she's willing herself not to cry any more. "I want to stay here," she says as Marcel walks back into the room. There's a light in his eyes having heard her deciding to stay that I note. Brighton wasn't under his charge for very long, but it's clear, I think to the rest of us, they've grown closer or at least have some sort of understanding.

"Okay," Calla says, hesitating for a moment Brighton likely doesn't even notice, and pulls her into a hug. "Then we'll figure this out." She explains to Brighton what went down after Marcel took her away from a café and asks how familiar she is with James and Sera.

Brighton purses her lips in thought. "I've seen them at a few hunter meetings, but they kept to themselves. Maybe this is why. Maybe they never wanted to follow my dad."

Calla shrugs. "I'm not sure, but my gut says to trust them. In this, they want what we want."

Marcel takes one of the empty chairs, his attention locked on his phone as Calla glances between Brighton and me.

"We're addressing one of the bigger issues we're facing," she says, "but what about the whole being outed to the public as vampires?"

Marcel glances up from his phone. "I'm handling that."

She arches a brow at him. "Care to explain?"

"As you may or may not know, much of the government has been infiltrated by the supernatural. A lot of vampires hold high-up positions on all levels of government. There's going to be a press release in a couple days that explains to the public that there is a new drug-related disease making people hallucinate and attack each other, which should explain away the whole vampire thing. The government will assure the public they are safe and the threat has been neutralized, confirming they have no reason to believe the existence of actual vampires."

"We're really going to blame this on some sort of acid trip?"

"Essentially," Marcel remarks dryly. "It's a bit more complex than that but it'll get the job done. Nothing like this has happened before, at least not on the same scale we've seen with social media." Marcel glances at his phone for a moment before continuing. "That being said, we've had instances of exposure to the public and we've been able to work through it every time—this occurrence will be no different. I assure you, there is no need for concern. My team has it handled, and considering what we've got going on here, this isn't something you need to add to your list of concerns."

Calla's gaze sweeps over the rest of us, seemingly waiting for us to voice *our* concern, but we've all known Marcel long enough. When he says something is being handled, we have zero doubts.

"So what are we supposed to do?" she asks.

"Until the next meeting with the hunters, we'll be contacting groups of vampires," Gabriel says.

"The goal is obviously to get as many on board with the peace treaty as possible, which will also inadvertently warn those against it of the consequences of preying on humans for sport," Kade adds.

"I've got the Washington clans covered," Marcel announces.

I exhale a heavy breath, which does nothing to ease the pit in my stomach or the dread coiling in my chest. "Looks like we're going to New York."

We leave for New York a few days later after Scott is successfully glamoured and relocated to Chicago. Brighton opted to stay in Washington, and Marcel offered to take her back to her apartment and monitor her while we're away.

The closer we get to the city, the bigger the knot in my stomach grows. I was too nauseous to eat anything this morning, and I barely got through half a blood bag before I had to stop.

Lex falls asleep in the backseat, while Kade and Gabriel chat softly about the groups of vampires they've been in contact with in Michigan and Portland. Most of them seem open to the treaty idea, which is promising, though it does little to ease the upset in my stomach. Because we still have to face some of the worst, most powerful vampires—Atlas's parents.

And because that's not enough, I've decided to stop putting off a meeting with my own parents, so we're heading there first. There's no chance I'll hurt them—the guys won't let that happen—but panic still trickles through me with each breath. Because what if they see me and it shocks them so much they want me to leave? Knowing I'm a vampire and seeing me as one are two very different things. I don't want to think that could happen, that my parents would turn their backs on me now, after everything, but I can't seem to rule out the possibility either.

Gabriel leans forward, resting his chin on the corner of my seat.

"Close your eyes and take a breath, angel. Everything is going to be okay."

"I know," I force out, despite the building pressure in my chest.

"Close your eyes," he repeats gently, and this time I do as he says. "Breathe in through your nose slowly. There you go. Hold it a few more seconds. Now let it out through your mouth. Slowly," he repeats.

I exhale, controlling my breath even as it shakes a little, and after a handful more deep breaths, I'm feeling slightly better. "Thanks, Gabe," I murmur.

"Anytime." He squeezes my shoulder, and I reach and place my hand over his for a moment before letting go so he can sit back.

I stare out the windshield, watching different cars pass as an attempt to distract myself. I jump when Atlas reaches across the console that separates us and places his hand palm up on my thigh. I wet my lips, glancing down at it before looking at his face. He keeps his eyes on the road as I slide my fingers through his, closing my eyes again, and immediately feel grounded.

I go through Gabriel's breathing exercises a few more times, while Atlas brushes his thumb over the back of my hand. Eventually, I doze off, which is a minor relief from the anxiety frying my nerves these days.

A hand brushes my cheek, and I blink my eyes open, squinting at the brightness for a few seconds before I realize we're parked at the curb of my parent's house.

My stomach clenches with intense nerves, and Atlas's fingers still against my cheek. "Breathe," he says in a low voice. "You're ready for this. Nothing bad is going to happen, and we're all here for you."

I cover his hand, holding it against my cheek as I pull in a deep breath, allowing myself to soak up this rare moment of softness from him. And then I pull away and get out of the car, walking toward the house.

I grew up here, but it still feels necessary to knock. Not that we need an invitation to get inside, but this gives me another few seconds to prepare before—

The door swings open, and my mom's eyes widen when they land on me. She knew we were coming, though I suppose seeing me with silver eyes is a bit of a shock.

"Hey, Mom," I say in a soft tone and force a smile. "It's good to see you."

She stands in the doorway, just staring at me for several beats before she shifts away a step. Her heart is hammering in her chest and her eyes are glassy as she holds back tears. "Oh, wow," she finally says. "Those eyes are really quite something."

I press my lips together, unsure how to respond to that. They freaked me out at first too. "Yeah."

She blinks and seemingly snaps out of whatever daze she was stuck in. "Your dad and I are glad you're here." Her words don't match the hesitance in her tone or her stiff stance, as if she's going to bolt any second.

A lump quickly forms in my throat, and I swallow hard. "Me too."

"Come in." She ushers us inside, moving to the other side of the entryway and effectively putting a healthy distance between herself and the vampires—including me. "Your dad is just whipping up something for lunch on the barbecue. It's the first he's pulled it out since last summer, so uh, you're in for a treat."

"Or a dead raccoon," I say with a faint grin, recalling a backyard dinner we had several years ago where Dad opened the grill and found a decomposing raccoon.

Mom grimaces through a somewhat awkward, forced-sounding laugh. "Oh, yes. That poor thing." She continues to keep some distance between us as we walk down the hall toward the kitchen, and I pretend not to notice. *I wish I hadn't noticed.*

The guys follow, and my eyes land on the spread prepared for us. There are too many dishes to count, between salads and desserts and burgers, there's enough here to feed at least twice as many people.

"Fuck yeah," Lex says too quietly for my mom to pick up.

The back door opens, and Dad steps inside with a plate full of cooked burger patties and a few hot dogs.

"You guys didn't have to go to all this trouble," I say instead of a proper greeting to my dad.

He sets the plate down, and his eyes lock on mine. "Of course we did." He finds it in himself to manage a smile in my direction. "It's... good to see you, sweetheart."

"You too, Dad."

My chest swells; this meeting I was so anxious about isn't a complete disaster so far. Mom is struggling with this, but she's trying. They both are.

"Well," Dad says, glancing toward the guys before returning his attention to me. "Should we eat?"

"Absolutely." Now that my stomach isn't entirely tied in knots, it's quick to grumble. All the delicious smells wafting through the room are only intensifying my hunger—for human food this time. It's a pleasant change from the bloodlust I'm still growing accustomed to.

Everyone fills their plates before taking a spot around the dining room table. This scene isn't one I could've imagined when picturing what my future would look like, but my heart is full, and despite the dark cloud of hunter and York family drama looming... I'm happy.

"So, things are going well?" Mom asks, taking a sip of her drink.

I stab into my potato salad, shoving a pile into my mouth and nodding. Once I swallow, I say, "Things are definitely different from what I thought they'd be." I keep my eyes on my mom while everyone else's are on me. "There's a lot I'm still learning in this new life, plenty of obstacles unique to the world I'm now part of, but it, uh... it feels right. Like it's always been my world in some way." I haven't thought about it like that before, but it's true. My human life seems so far away even though I'm aware not much time has passed since I turned. I suppose my perception of time has changed in the weeks after I became immortal.

Mom and Dad exchange a look before Dad reaches across the table and takes my hand, squeezing it. "So long as you're happy and safe, that's all we could ever want for you, Calla."

I offer him a watery smile, willing myself not to cry at the table. "You don't have to worry about that," I assure him, looking then to my mom. "You never need to worry about that."

Dad nods, sitting back in his seat. "So, any plans for the future?" he asks.

I laugh. "Uh, yeah, kind of. I'm going to finish school, probably not this year as planned, but before the end of next year. I still want to help people, and there's a great community outreach program a few of the professors at school are starting that I'd really like to be part of."

"That sounds wonderful," Mom says, sounding relieved. I can't imagine everything that's been going through her head since I decided to become a vampire, and I certainly don't fault her for being concerned about my future.

I nod, smiling. "Besides that, I'm taking things day by day. The idea of living forever is still pretty daunting, so I find it easier to keep my head on straight when I'm not looking too far ahead."

"Of course," Dad agrees, "that's understandable."

"Calla has adjusted exceptionally well," Gabriel chimes in.

I can't help the blush that spreads across my cheeks.

"She makes the rest of us look bad," Lex adds with a wink in my direction.

"Well," Dad says, looking a little uncomfortable addressing the other vampires in the room, "I suppose that's good."

"Do you have any questions?" I ask my parents. "If I can't answer them, odds are, one of these guys can."

Mom's expression morphs into something slightly more reserved. "Oh." She glances at my dad. "I'm not sure we've really thought of anything specific."

"That's okay," I rush to say. "I didn't mean to put you guys on the spot. You don't have to ask anything right now, just know that you can whenever you want to."

Her shoulders relax a little, and she nods. "Are you planning to... I mean, do you need a place to stay? I don't think you mentioned how long you'd be in the city."

"I think we have a room at a hotel nearby, but thank you. I didn't want to impose or—"

"Impose? Calla, this is your home."

I appreciate the intention behind her words, but this house hasn't been my home for some time. "Thanks, Mom," I say anyway. "I would feel more comfortable at the hotel. This has been great. Really. You have no idea. I was so worried about seeing you guys after, you know, and it couldn't have gone better. I just don't want to push our luck."

Mom's brows tug together, her lips pressing into a thin line, then she nods. "We understand," she says after a brief glance at my dad. "This has been really nice, and I hope you'll visit more."

Relief blooms in my chest, and I offer her a genuine smile. "Yes, I promise."

After the meal, saying goodbye to my parents is harder than I was expecting. Knowing what we'll be facing over the next few days, weeks, months, however long it takes—and also having kept them completely out of it—makes this farewell feel different. More important in some scary way. That has me hugging them tightly as we part ways at the front door.

"Keep us posted on everything," Dad says, taking a moment to glance at the guys. "Take care of her. Please."

"Of course," Gabriel tells him.

My breath halts when Dad offers Gabriel his hand. They shake firmly, nodding at each other, before Dad repeats the gesture with each of the guys. Holy shit. I was *not* expecting that.

Mom keeps her hands to herself but offers a genuine, warm smile to the lot of us before I walk with the guys down the driveway and climb into the back of the Escalade. I wipe the tears from my cheeks before anyone can see; there are so many emotions at war in my chest at the moment, I can't be sure which is causing me to cry. I swallow past the lump in my throat as we pull away from the curb and stare out the window the entire drive to the hotel.

Following the guys from the check-in desk to the bank of elevators, I'm unable to really appreciate how fancy this place is. I expect nothing less from them by now, but it's unfortunate I don't even feel as though I'm in a place to appreciate it. I did notice, however, the bar in the lobby, which I set my sights on, planning to return once I've freshened up.

After a quick shower, I change into plain black leggings and a light blue sweater, tugging on my Docs before swiping the room key off the marble coffee table in the sitting area.

"Where do you think you're going?" Kade says, glancing up from his phone where he's sitting in the wingback chair near the coffee table.

"I don't know about you guys, but I need a drink."

"Cheers to that," Lex says, strutting into the room from the second bedroom. He throws his arm around my shoulders and starts walking toward the door, semi-dragging me with him.

I glance over my shoulder. "Are you guys coming or are you going to hang out up here while we have fun without you?"

Atlas and Gabriel exchange a glance, while Kade is already getting up and walking toward us with a faint smile. Gabriel follows suit, and I set my gaze on Atlas.

"Well, sire," I say in a teasing voice, "are you going to be the only one not having fun?"

He shoots me a look as he rises from his chair and stalks toward us. "Behave," he says in a low voice.

I lean up on my tiptoes when he gets close and press a kiss to his cheek. "Always."

The elevator ride back up to our room after a couple hours in the lobby bar feels unexplainably amusing, and I can't stop giggling at nothing. Lex and Kade are also laughing while the other two watch us with barely reserved amusement.

"You're a little drunk," Kade says in a light voice, poking my nose.

I slap his hand away. Or at least try to, but I'm about ten seconds too late. "*You're* a little drunk," I accuse, giggling some more.

The elevator dings, and we spill out into the hallway, heading for our suite with Atlas leading our group.

I barrel toward him and leap onto his back, reaching over his shoulder and trying to snag the room key from his hand. "Let me do it. Let me do it. Let me do it."

Between one heartbeat and the next, he throws me off his back, pinning me to the wall, and my breath halts.

"Uh-oh," Lex sings from behind Atlas.

He holds me against the wall, his hands gripping my shoulders and his eyes dark with lust.

"That wasn't very nice," I whisper, my pulse pounding beneath my skin.

"When have I ever done or said anything that makes you believe I am?"

I open my mouth to respond, then close it and pout. "Well, when you put it like that..."

He leans in until his nose touches mine. "Have you had enough tonight?" he asks in a low voice.

"Enough?" I echo in confusion.

Those dark silver eyes bounce between mine, searching. "I want to know how far I can push you."

Warmth spreads through me, pooling low in my belly, and the muscles in my thighs tighten, urging me to press them together. "Push me as far as you want," I say, my lips barely brushing his. "Launch me over a fucking cliff, I don't care."

He pulls in a shallow breath, tutting his tongue softly. "You have no idea what you're saying."

"Fuck you. I do so, and you can't scare me away," I insist. "Not anymore."

His lips touch mine again. "Good."

"If you guys want to fight or fuck in the hallway, that's totally cool. But the security cameras will certainly get a show," Kade says, pulling out his own room key and stepping toward our suite. "I don't know about anyone else, but I'm going to go take a shower and pass out. Wake me up when you solve all our problems."

Lex follows him, and after hesitating a few moments longer, Gabriel does too, leaving Atlas and I alone in the hallway as the suite door clicks shut.

I drag my eyes over Atlas's face, committing every bit to memory, and sigh. "I guess he has a point."

His lips twitch. "You waited for him to leave to say that. He'll be so disappointed."

"He'll never know," I say back, pushing against his chest to leave, but he strengthens his hold, pinning me to the wall still.

"I'm not done with you."

My body comes alive at his words. Every nerve ending waiting to be touched. I tip my head back against the wall, peering into his eyes. "What are you going to do?" I ask in a hushed voice.

He cocks his head to the side, watching me. "I haven't quite decided yet."

"Cool, so I guess we'll just stand here until you do then."

He shrugs. "Or you could try to fight me, but we both know you won't win."

"I don't know that," I point out defiantly. "If I remember correctly, I was getting pretty close to being able to kick your ass as a human, so don't discount my abilities now. Otherwise, you're kind of insulting yourself."

Amusement flickers to life in his gaze as his thumbs press into my shoulders and he leans in again. "Go for it, Calla."

"Well, it's no fun when you're expecting it," I grumble, and instead of trying to fight him, I lift my hand and press it against his chest, sliding my fingers down until they reach the hem of his shirt, then make quick work of unbuckling his belt and unbuttoning his pants.

He glances around, spotting the camera, and repositions himself to block its view of us before his eyes settle on me again, blazing with barely contained lust. "I'm going to let go of you because I want you on your knees."

My cheeks flush hotly and my throat goes dry, though the idea has me all kinds of excited. Nevertheless, I murmur, "And if I say no?"

He smirks. "You won't."

"Maybe I will," I shoot back as he drops his hands to his sides. The throbbing between my legs wants to make a liar out of me.

Atlas leans in until his lips are at my ear. "I'll tell you what. If you can stand there and honestly tell me you're not soaked through your panties right now, I'll walk away."

My breath catches in my throat. I could lie, but we both know damn well that he's right. I narrow my eyes slightly. "Maybe you should get on your knees then."

The smile he offers me is slow, and it does funny things to my stomach. "I'll take care of you later. You don't need to worry about that."

I exhale through my nose, my heart pounding like thunder in my chest, and slowly sink to my knees in front of him. I reach for the zipper on his pants, tugging it down before pulling his cock free. It bobs proudly, hard and thick in front of my face, and my mouth waters as the scent of his arousal overtakes me. I lean forward, dragging my tongue along the tip and tasting the moisture already gathered there. Warmth floods my chest when he pulls in a shuddering breath, because even though I may have taken his direction, I'm in control here.

I swirl my tongue around him a few times before closing my lips around his shaft, slowly taking him into my mouth, inch by inch, until he bumps the back of my throat. I close my eyes, but Atlas bends and grips my chin.

"Eyes on me." His voice is gravelly, and my eyes fly open at his command, the throbbing between my thighs becoming more pronounced. "Good girl." He slides his fingers into my hair, gripping the back of my head as I pull back, scraping my teeth along his cock. I suck him into my mouth again, alternating my speed and the pressure of my lips around his throbbing length. His grip on my hair tightens as I hum softly. I continue bobbing my head up and down his cock, taking him to the hilt with each pull of my lips and using my hands to work the base before massaging his balls.

His lips part as he groans, holding my gaze as his brows draw together. The muscles in his thighs tighten, his cock throbbing against my tongue in the seconds before his release fills my mouth. "Swallow it," he growls, his head tipped back and his grunts filling the hallway.

Fucking hell, if anyone comes out of their room right now...

I do as he says, swallowing as much of the saltiness as I can without choking. A bit spills out, dripping down my chin and as he pulls out of my mouth, dragging the head of his cock over my lips and painting them with his release. I lick them clean, earning a wicked smirk from my sire as both our hearts beat faster in our chests.

After helping me to my feet and tucking himself back into his pants, he offers me his hand.

"What now?" I ask, sliding my fingers through his.

Atlas tugs me against him, pressing his lips to the side of my head as we walk to our suite. "Now," he murmurs, "the real fun begins."

I'm never the first one awake, but after sleeping like shit last night, I don't bother staying in bed. The clock on the nightstand taunts me with those stupid fucking neon red numbers. As if the dark sky outside the suite's floor to ceiling windows weren't obvious enough; it's barely after four.

Glancing over to find Lex still fast asleep—the lucky bastard—I throw the sheets back and haul my ass out of bed. After a very lonely shower, I grab Gabriel's tablet off the coffee table in the sitting area and head down to the hotel lobby. I'm relieved to find the café just opening for the morning and grab an Americano before I find a chair near the window and get comfortable.

As much as we all need to be focused on working with the hunters —and getting vampires *on board* to work with the hunters, I haven't been able to stop thinking about our home in Washington. Marcel took care of renting it out for us to ensure we could keep the property but not have it sit empty for however long it took before it was safe to return. There's a hopeful, potentially misguided part of me that believes that time is close.

I shoot Marcel a message requesting the information on the current tenants and sip my drink, glancing around the hotel lobby at the few humans coming and going with luggage and to-go cups of coffee.

An email notification dings about half an hour later, and I open it, reading through Marcel's response.

Kade,

Here's the info you requested:

Tenants are Lily and Steven Marcus. They are in their late twenties, from Georgia, moved to D.C. for Steven's job, and are expecting their first child in the fall. Rent is paid in full and on time.

My jaw clenches as I read the message, because fuck. Of course they are the perfect tenants and are just starting their lives together.

Marcel also included phone numbers and email addresses for both of them. I could reach out... buy them off to leave. Or we could just show up, glamour them to leave, and take it back. But I can already see the disapproving looks from Gabe and Calla.

"Uh-oh," Lex says, dropping into the wingback chair across from me. "That look is ominous."

I glance over at him, setting my cup on the small table between us. "What are you doing up?"

He shrugs. "It's after five. Plus, I woke up, and you weren't around so I figured I should make sure you weren't getting into trouble."

"That's bullshit, and you know it. If I was getting into trouble, you wouldn't stop me, you'd join me."

He takes a drink from his own cup, grinning softly as he sets it down. "Well, yeah, most likely." His eyes hold mine, calculating. "What are you up to?"

I drop my gaze to the tablet in my lap. "I'm getting our home back."

"I'm in," Lex says immediately.

"It's not that simple." I explain the situation, letting him read Marcel's message.

He hands me back the tablet. "So fucking what? That place is ours."

"I know, I know. But we can't just kick these people out."

"You want to wait until their lease is up?" he asks.

I shake my head. "I think we should make them an offer."

He arches a brow. "Glamouring them would be a hell of a lot easier."

"I'm aware," I mutter. "I'm thinking we have Marcel find them an alternative place to stay and cover moving expenses. And as further incentive to end their lease early, we can offer to take care of any medical bills until their child is born."

Lex stares at me. "Should we set up a college fund for the kid too? Fuck, Kade, this isn't a charity."

I roll my eyes, leaning back in the chair. "It's the right thing to do. We're disrupting their lives—"

"To get *ours* back," he cuts in. "Why do you care so damn much?"

"It's the right thing to do," I repeat. Beyond that, there's a part of me that wishes I could have what those twenty-something, soon-to-be parents do. Plus, it's what Calla would do. If she ever asks about it, I want to give an answer that will make her happy. "Are you with me or not?"

He exhales a heavy sigh. "Fine. I'm in. Are we going to tell the others about your spontaneous act of kindness?"

"No, I want to make it a surprise. Marcel will make arrangements with the tenants and the cleaning crew to get the place ready for us, but I want to see the looks on the others' faces when we get to go home."

Lex's lips curl into a smirk. "You're getting soft in your old age."

I flip him off, drinking the rest of my Americano before typing a message back to Marcel to fill him in on the plan.

The tablet chimes a few minutes later.

There are ways to end a lease early without offering all the extra compensation you mentioned. I'll call you shortly to discuss.

I show Lex the message, and he shrugs.

"Gabriel usually deals with the legal stuff."

"You own property," I comment. "You should know about this *stuff.*"

"What do you want to do then?"

It's my turn to shrug. "We should still offer them everything." I shoot Marcel a quick reply to reiterate our position, and he assures me he'll handle it. I set the tablet on the table and sigh, my eyes already stinging with exhaustion, and the day has barely started.

"Well done," Lex comments mildly. "You've done your good deed for the day—hell, the year." He shoots me a wink, leaning back in his chair. "I'll be glad to get back to that place."

"It's home," I agree.

Lex nods. "I keep thinking about the future, despite all the annoying dark clouds above us. The storm will pass, and we'll get back to building our lives."

"They are certainly going to be more interesting with Calla around."

"Especially now that she can keep up with us," he adds with a smirk.

I chuckle softly. "No kidding. I don't think any of us could have foreseen this. How deeply she's changed all of us for the better."

"And how amazingly she's adjusted to our world, to being one of us."

Talking about Calla makes me wish I was still tucked into bed with her, wrapped in my arms. Or with my head between her lovely thighs bringing her all the pleasure she can take—and then some. Her transformation into a vampire has been wildly impressive. She's taken everything in stride, and while she isn't without the common struggles our kind face, she handles them exceptionally well. She's like the poster child for a perfect vampire. If I didn't love her so damn much, it would likely be annoying.

Lex must see something in my eyes, because his lips curl into a grin, though he doesn't comment on it. Instead he asks, "What do you think we'll do once this treaty business is dealt with? Once we get back to whatever *normal* is for us?"

I shrug. "Calla's going to finish school. Gabe will probably go back to work for the government in some capacity. You and Atlas will do whatever the fuck it is you do that makes money, and I... I don't have a fucking clue." I'm surprised to find that it doesn't really bother me. Before Calla joined us, I'd earned more than enough from modeling gigs, but I'm not sure I want to continue down that path. It all seems... inconsequential at this point.

"We should take her somewhere she's never been. When everything is over, we'll have more than enough of a reason to celebrate being alive and together."

I immediately picture the five of us naked on a private beach, drunk on champagne and each other.

"I'm in," I say without hesitation.

The streets of New York are quiet. Quiet for the city anyway. Though considering it's barely six in the morning on a Saturday, it's to be expected.

Kade and I go for a walk, chatting about nothing in particular as we make our way toward the blood donation clinic, using the shipping entrance around the back of the commercial building to sneak inside.

We fill a small cooler with blood bags; we're in and out in five minutes, heading back to the hotel as the air warms up for the day.

"Are you sure you don't want to tell them about the house?" I ask Kade on the elevator ride to our suite.

He glances up, shaking his head. "If we run into any problems, I'll consider it. Otherwise, I think it'll be a nice surprise. We've all been so focused on the hunters and trying to work with them, I think we all need this."

"You'll get no argument from me."

Kade swipes the key card when we get back to the room, and we walk inside to find the others awake, sitting in the living room area of the suite. Gabriel and Calla are snuggled up on the couch, while Atlas is reading something on his phone from the armchair across from them.

"We brought breakfast," Kade announces, lifting the cooler bag. He opens it, tossing blood bags toward the others. Before one comes launching at my face, I grab it out of the air, shooting him an annoyed look, which he only grins at. I head toward the kitchenette to pour it into a mug and heat it in the microwave. Glancing over my shoulder, my gaze lands on where Calla's sitting on the couch, frowning as she tears into the blood bag and drinks it without bothering to heat it up.

Atlas leaves his on the coffee table and continues scowling at his phone.

"What's with the face?" Calla asks him.

Atlas glances up from his phone, looking at each of us before he says, "Simon and Lenora are demanding an audience immediately."

An hour later, we're in the car, heading toward the last place any of us want to go.

When we arrive, a member of the York's staff meets us at the door. It never seems to be the same person. In the time I've known Atlas, his family has been notorious for going through employees. They don't fire them, and they don't quit. They're likely eaten for dinner.

This human is a young man, probably in his mid-twenties, with shaggy black hair and tired blue eyes. He has bite marks in different stages of healing on his skin, and while it looks as if he's attempted to hide them with clothing and concealer in some spots, I don't think any of us miss them.

"Welcome," he says in a polite voice. "Please follow me. Mr. and Mrs. York are waiting in the sitting room."

We follow the human through the house, as though all of us don't already know where we're going, Calla being the only one who actually doesn't. Considering the rest of us have been here too many times to count over the decades—unfortunately—we know this place as well as our own.

The sitting room is the Yorks' formal space for socializing. I've attended many events here, the high-ceiling room, decorated differently each time.

The human opens the double doors and steps aside, revealing the room with floor to ceiling windows along one wall covered by heavy red velvet drapes and dark brown leather furniture in the middle of the room. The focal point is certainly the massive black stone fireplace, where flames crackle and fill the room with a warm glow. Lenora and Simon rise from the couch and glide across the room to meet us.

"My son," she greets, wrapping her arms around Atlas in a brief embrace before kissing his cheek. "I am so happy to see you."

Atlas offers a curt nod. "Mother," he says, stepping away from her to stand beside Calla—an intentional move on his part. He offers the same nod to his father, whose eyes barely land on his son for a second before moving to Calla.

The rest of us step into the room, watching the two of them and waiting for someone to speak. Calla stays silent, her lips pressed together and her body angled toward our sire.

"Miss Montgomery, how lovely of you to join us." The double meaning in his words isn't lost on any of us.

Still, she says nothing.

"Oh no, do not tell me you are shy all of a sudden."

"No," she says in a tight voice, "I just don't like you." Her eyes widen briefly, as if she's surprised by her own words.

Atlas's posture stiffens, and I'm sure he's cursing inwardly, whereas I'm trying my hardest not to laugh. I didn't think I could love her any more.

Lenora scoffs sharply. "You watch your mouth."

Calla's eyes flit toward her, and she frowns. "You wanted to see me as a vampire. Well, here I am. Becoming this didn't change my personality, and I won't apologize for that."

"Calla," Atlas says lowly, and she ignores him.

"So if that's all, maybe we should put everyone out of their misery now, go our separate ways, and pretend this meeting never happened?"

Lenora turns her attention from Calla, focusing again on Atlas. "Explain to me why I've been hearing rumblings of a treaty with the hunters."

Simon places his hand on her shoulder, looking at each of us before saying to Atlas, "We do not need to tell you how utterly ridiculous and impossible that would be. Why don't you confirm our sources are mistaken, and we can clear this whole thing up?"

"They aren't mistaken," Gabriel chimes in calmly, because it's Gabe, and he's always been the patient and reasonable one.

"That is nonsense," Lenora says. "As creatures at the top of the food chain, we do not yield to lesser species."

"Perhaps we should sit down and discuss this fully before any conclusions are met," Gabriel offers, maintaining his level tone.

I have to give him credit; I'm biting my tongue so hard I'm surprised it hasn't sliced off, and every time Simon's gaze shifts toward Calla, the tension in my chest grows more pronounced. The rest of the guys are on edge as well. I'm ready to rip out his throat if he tries to touch her.

"Of course," Lenora says, "let's sit."

We walk over to the couches near the fireplace. Calla ends up sandwiched between Atlas and Gabriel, while Kade and I flank them, sitting on each end. Lenora and Simon take the couch opposite us, Lenora's eyes locked on Atlas, while Simon continues staring at Calla. He's not even trying to be subtle about it.

"You need to shut down whatever this treaty is," Simon says, sparing a glance at the rest of us.

"We expect you to handle this," Lenora adds. It goes without saying, her version of *handle* means to eradicate the hunters. Simon and Lenora have no desire for peace with them, and it's clear they think we're ridiculous to consider it a viable solution.

The tension in my chest is not only my own but Atlas's as well—it rolls off him in waves. We all figured the Yorks wouldn't be on board with the plan to work with the hunters initially, but to take this stance... That was not something we were entirely prepared for.

"You'd prefer to repeat history time and time again? We've been here before and we'll be here again so long as you remain stuck in your ways of jumping to violence to get what you want." Atlas's voice is much calmer than mine would be, and I sincerely commend my sire for keeping his cool.

"This is not a discussion we will be continuing." Simon's voice is firm. "This is how it is, and you *will* get on board, son."

"Hunters aren't the only ones dying," Atlas shoots back. "The longer we fight with them, the more of ours are wiped out too. Ones that are just trying to live normal lives and have to do so in fear of being hunted for what they are, even when their existence doesn't necessarily pose a risk to anyone."

Lenora sighs as if she's bored with this entire discussion, which makes me grit my teeth, wanting to snap at her. That woman has always been infuriatingly flippant about human lives. "Atlas," she says, disappointment clear in her voice. "I truly expected more from you."

"Why?" Kade cuts in. "Because he's considering something besides mass slaughter as a solution to a centuries-old problem?"

Simon chuckles. "It is not a problem when we come out on top every time."

Kade starts to move, but Gabriel grabs him, pulling him back down.

Simon growls low in his throat. "Enough."

"No," Atlas snarls, getting to his feet. "I refuse to play by your rules any longer. It's about time the vampires have someone looking out for their future in the long term."

Simon stands in a blur, snarling back in Atlas's face. "Watch yourself."

Atlas ignores him and grabs Calla's hand as she stands, and the rest of us follow suit, heading for the door.

"Atlas," Lenora calls out in a shrill voice. "If you walk out that door, you can consider yourself an enemy of this family."

Atlas stops, twisting around and barking out a harsh, humorless laugh. "Family," he spits, shaking his head. "You have no idea what that word means."

Lenora bristles. "Leave now, and you will have no power or protection under the York name any longer."

Calla's eyes widen, locking on Atlas. He holds a stoic expression, crossing his arms over his chest, where his heart is beating only slightly faster than normal.

"If you truly believe I need that—or anything from you—you are sorely mistaken, Lenora."

Her cheeks flush, her silver gaze sharpening with anger. "Don't do this," she warns as Simon grabs her hand.

Atlas lets his arms fall back to his sides and turns around, motioning us toward the front door. We move as one, our footsteps echoing off the marble floors.

"You will regret this defiance, Atlas," Lenora vows as we make a hasty exit. The cold tone of her voice and the weight of the threat behind it sends a shiver through me.

We step outside, and Atlas exhales a heavy breath, a muscle feathering along his jaw and darkness clouding his features.

"I think that went well," I mutter dryly as the Yorks' front door slams shut behind us.

TWELVE

CALLA

We got back to Washington a few days ago, and in the time we've been home, the guys have been making calls and sending messages to everyone they know. It feels as if we're campaigning for senator and our rental property has become our headquarters.

Atlas has been reserved since our return, even for him. He isn't sleeping, I can tell that much by the darkness under his eyes and the way he's left his stubble unshaved for two days now.

He disappeared into his office first thing this morning and hasn't come out since, so I heat up a glass of blood and bring it to him. Knocking softly, I wait a few seconds before slipping inside and closing the door. Atlas is sitting at his desk and glances up as I approach. He's dressed casually in a navy V-neck and black slacks, and his hair is messy, falling into his face and tousled as if he's thrusted his hand through it many times over.

"I brought lunch," I say, setting the glass on his desk.

He holds my gaze. "Thank you."

I bite the inside of my cheek, uncertainty filling me as I try to come up with the words I'm looking for.

Atlas sighs, leaning back a bit in his chair. "Calla—"

"I'm worried about you." The words rush out of me.

"I know," he murmurs.

"Right. Well... what can I do?" I walk around his desk to the side he's sitting and perch on the corner. "You shouldn't hide in here when there's a living room full of people who care about you. Your *family*."

He closes the laptop in front of him and turns his chair so he's facing me. "I needed some space. Some time to myself."

I nod in understanding, because I've been there more times than I'd care to admit. "I just wanted to make sure you ate. I'll go—"

His hand lands on my thigh, and he rolls his chair closer. "Don't."

I press my lips together, the heat of his hand searing right through my leggings and shooting tingles straight to my core. "Are you sure?" I ask softly, my eyes dancing across his face.

Atlas stands, towering over me, and slides his hand higher, tracing his thumb dangerously close to the throbbing between my legs. "Unless you'd like to," he offers in a gravelly voice.

I shake my head, lifting my hands to cup his cheeks. "I'm here for you. Whatever you need."

His jaw clenches against my palms, his gaze darkening with hunger. He leans forward until his forehead touches mine. "Hmm..." His other hand brushes the inside of my thigh before he slowly spreads my legs open, stepping between them. My breath catches in my throat, and I drop my hands to his shoulders, my pulse skyrocketing when his finger traces over my center.

"Atlas," I whisper, my eyes fluttering shut, "kiss me."

His lips come crashing down on mine, claiming me with a fiery kiss that sends my heart racing. A moan slips through my lips when he presses his thumb against my clit, and he swallows the sound, kissing me harder as heat pools low in my belly. His hand moves until he's able to slide it under the waistband of my leggings. The moment his fingers slip past my folds, my hips buck off the desk, heat filling my cheeks. His lips leave mine only to trail along my jaw and nibble on my neck, while he slides two fingers into my pussy, curling them at just the right spot.

"Yes," I breathe, tipping my head to give him better access. His fangs scrape against the delicate skin just below my ear, and I shiver, pressing my lips together and keeping my eyes closed to feel the sensations he's wringing from me on a deeper level.

He kisses my pounding pulse, circling my clit with his thumb as he pumps his fingers in and out of me. My breathing gets shallower as he picks up speed, the muscles in my stomach tightening as I race toward the edge of pleasure.

I bite my lip until I can't take any more and moan his name.

And then he stops.

I growl as he pulls his fingers out, my eyes flying open. I glare at him, panting, and he smirks. Before I can curse at him, he pushes me back on his desk and tugs my leggings off, leaving them in a pile on the floor.

"Holy fuck," I mumble, lifting my arms as he grabs the hem of my shirt and pulls it off over my head, dropping it next to my leggings and leaving me in nothing but a light blue lace bra.

Atlas's gaze roams over me, lighting my body on fire as my pussy throbs with need. He slides his hand up my chest and pushes me back until I'm lying across his desk with my legs hanging off the edge. He leans over me and kisses my collarbone, then above each of my breasts before his lips trail down my stomach. Grabbing my thighs, he spreads them open and presses a soft kiss against my clit. I suck in an unsteady breath, my eyes locked on him as he sinks to his knees between my legs and leans in until his tongue flicks along my slit. I press my lips together, my thighs shaking as he holds them open, baring me to him. My head falls back against the desk when Atlas sucks my clit into his mouth, swirling his tongue around it hard and fast until I'm panting, reaching for something—*anything*—to grip onto and subsequently knocking a bunch of stuff off his desk.

He chuckles against me, shooting vibrations to my core, and the muscles in my thighs tighten. Heat flows through me, flushing my cheeks and chest as if I've been drinking all morning, and I moan deeply when he uses his thumbs to spread my folds open and thrusts his tongue into me. I slam my hands against his desk, bucking my hips and breathing heavily. He quickly slides his arm over my hips, trapping me there while he devours me, his tongue moving inhumanly fast, massaging my inner walls as they pulse around him like a heartbeat. He closes his lips around me, sucking hard, and moaning against me.

I cry out and I think I moan his name once more as my muscles tighten and an orgasm slams into me, stealing my breath and making my head spin. His tongue keeps moving, lapping up my release until the sensations become too much, and I grab a fistful of his hair to make him stop the torment. There's a sheen of sweat covering my forehead and my heart is pounding so hard I can feel it in my throat.

Atlas leans back and licks his lips before smirking faintly. He stands and offers me his hand, helping me to sit up when I take it. "I thoroughly enjoy making you moan my name," he purrs.

"Safe to say I enjoy it too," I shoot back, grinning softly as I bask in the lingering aftershocks of my orgasm, my core still tingling with oversensitivity.

He slides his fingers along my jaw, wrapping them around the side of my neck and tipping my head back with his thumb under my chin. His eyes search mine, and I'm a little relieved to see some of the darkness has faded from his—at least for now.

So I'm not entirely sure why I open my mouth.

"I guess now would be a bad time to tell you I booked a flight to Oregon to visit Tessa."

He blinks at me. "When did you do that?"

I hesitate before answering, "On our way back from New York. I know it probably isn't the best time, but..." I trail off when Atlas steps back, but he doesn't say anything immediately. The brief silence is deafening. I sigh, sliding off his desk and retrieving my clothes. I'm pulling my leggings back on as the door to his office flies open and Lex comes in.

"Absolutely fucking not," he says, clearly having heard my travel plans.

"Non-refundable ticket," I say as I finish getting dressed. "Sorry."

"Calla—" Atlas starts.

"This is my choice," I cut him off, keeping a level tone. "The decision has been made. I'm going."

A muscle ticks along his jaw, and I prepare myself for him to fight me. So imagine my surprise when he nods.

"What the fuck?" Lex grumbles.

"Would you relax, please?" I say. "I'm going to visit Tessa, not hang out with the mafia."

Gabriel makes a quiet entrance into the office, with Kade on his tail. "Valor Academy is a safe place," Gabe comments, seemingly for Lex's benefit, before saying to me, "I'm sure Tessa is looking forward to your visit."

Lex shoots him an annoyed look before turning to Kade, who just shrugs, evidently choosing to stay out of it. With a heavy sigh, Lex turns his attention back to me. "How long are you going for?"

"Only a few days considering all that's going on here. Think you can survive without me for that long?"

"No," he says seriously, "I'm very needy."

"We know," Kade chimes in.

"Perhaps we should all go," Gabriel says. "I was planning on speaking with the headmaster there to fill her in about the treaty. An in-person meeting would be better."

"I... You guys want to come?" My brows knit. I was looking forward to this being a solo trip, but I suppose I shouldn't complain. The treaty is what's important right now. Plus, I'll still get to hang out with Tessa, and this way, I won't have to feel guilty about taking a trip while we're still working on peace with the hunters if Gabriel is going to use the trip as an opportunity to spread the word about the treaty. At least, that's what I'm telling myself.

"Don't worry," Kade chimes in with an amused tone, "we won't ruin your trip with your new witchy friend."

I roll my eyes, glancing between Lex and Atlas before addressing all of them. "If you guys promise not to interfere with what we're doing, I won't fight you on this."

"That's a first," Lex remarks dryly, shooting me a wink.

I flip him off while smiling sweetly. "My flight leaves tomorrow morning at nine, and Tessa was going to pick me up at the airport."

"We'll fly together and rent a car when we land," Gabriel says. "The academy is a little under an hour from the Portland airport. You can let Tessa know she doesn't have to pick you up."

I nod hesitantly. "I was planning to stay in Tessa's dorm at the academy. Where will you guys be?"

"Where do you want us?" Lex asks, barely containing a grin.

Gabriel ignores Lex. "There are guest cabins on the academy's property," he explains. "I'll arrange for us to stay in one."

"Okay," I say, glancing around a little awkwardly. "I guess we better pack."

I retreat to my bedroom, throwing clothes and toiletries into a duffel bag. I'm not going for that long so I'm not too concerned about what I'm bringing.

Stepping into the bathroom to take a quick shower, I stop dead in my tracks when I find Atlas leaning against the vanity. I thought I sensed his presence, but being in such close quarters, I kind of feel him all the time. I press my lips together, frowning at his ability to still catch me off guard. "What... are you doing?"

"You and I haven't been apart, not at any great distance, since I sired you," he says, pushing away from the vanity and closing the distance between us.

"Okay?" I frown in confusion.

"Had you left for Oregon and I stayed here, you would have felt that. That won't happen now, but I figured you should still know."

My brows tug closer. "I would have *felt* it? What does that mean?"

He tilts his head to the side, his eyes searching mine. "It could be difficult for both of us—the physical distance."

"That's a little ironic, considering I thought you hated me for a while at the beginning."

His lips twitch briefly. "I just want you to be aware of what different things you could feel being away. It's not permanent, and the more time that passes, the less you'll notice it. You can talk to Gabriel or Kade about it, but Lex hasn't been away from me for any great length of time since I turned him."

"Okay," I say, dragging out the word. "That's good to know, I guess."

"There's a chance Brighton will feel something similar with you being linked to her now. Does she know you're going?"

"Yeah, I let her know. Do you think... I mean, will it hurt? I'm not concerned about me, but Bri—"

"Will be fine. I'm not an expert in magic, but she'll likely feel like something is missing but unable to put her finger on it. That emptiness is you being gone. So perhaps it's a good thing. A little reminder of what she almost caused."

I frown at the way his voice hardens. Instead of responding to that, I say, "She and Marcel seem to get along well."

"You noticed that too," he muses.

I nod. "I think it's good for both of them."

He nods but adds nothing else.

"If that was everything, I'd kind of like to take a shower."

"Hmm. I wasn't the one who invited us on your trip, but I might invite myself to *that*."

His words bring heat to my cheeks, and I step in closer. "I would not be entirely opposed to that."

A glint of amusement fills his eyes. "No?" he checks, dragging his tongue along his bottom lip as his hands drop to my hips, and he tugs me against him. A quick gasp escapes me when he presses his cock to the heat gathering between my legs.

"I seriously need to shower," I tell him.

"Uh-huh," he says, leaning in and sealing his mouth over mine. He kisses me deeply, pushing his tongue into my mouth and grazing it along mine as I grip the front of his shirt, gathering it up and tugging it over his head when he breaks the kiss. I drop it on the floor and add my clothes to the pile.

We undress in a matter of seconds, blurs of movement until all of our clothes are in a pile and we're standing naked in front of each other.

I walk over to the shower and turn it on. Seconds later, Atlas spins me around and steals my lips again, pressing me against the outer glass of the shower, my nipples stiffening against his chest. His lips swallow my moan, and he reaches between us, pressing his thumb to my clit, circling it teasingly until my breathing quickens, my chest rising and falling fast against his.

"Shower," I say against his lips, and he chuckles in response, guiding us to the side and opening the glass door without breaking the kiss.

The hot spray of water cascades over us, and still, his lips never leave mine. His teasing thumb becomes more incessant, circling my clit harder and faster. I gasp when he plunges two fingers into me, scissoring them to massage my inner walls, then curling them deep inside to hit the spot he knows will drive me wild. I reach for his cock, pumping up and down the already hard length, alternating speed and pressure as he groans deep in his throat.

Steam fills the room, the sounds of our labored breathing and breathy moans joining it. Tension builds low in my stomach, the muscles in my thighs tightening as Atlas brings me closer to the height of pleasure.

I reach back to massage his balls, and he stiffens against me before slamming me into the shower wall, thrusting his fingers harder as his lips pull away from mine. I see a flash of his fangs before he buries them in my throat. I cry out with a mix of pleasure and pain as my pussy clenches around his fingers and I come hard while he drinks from me. My head spins and I have to stop rubbing him and grab onto his shoulders so I don't collapse as pleasure overtakes me. As I come down slowly from the high of my orgasm, my body tingling from the aftershocks, I slump against the wall, counting on him to hold me up.

He retracts his fangs from my neck, licking his lips, and the sight of my blood dripping down his chin sends another wave of warmth through me.

I lean forward and kiss him, tasting myself on his lips, which makes my gums throb. I wrap my fingers back around his cock, pumping hard and fast as he flattens his palms against the wall behind me.

"Fuck, Calla." He groans, and my lips curl against his. I increase my speed and pressure slightly as the muscles in his abdomen tighten, then slow right down moments before pushing him over the edge. He growls against my lips, slamming his hand against the wall, and I move my lips away from his, trailing them along his sharp jaw as my fangs poke through my gums. Without hesitation, I sink them into his shoulder, returning the speed and pressure to my hand as it moves over him. He grunts deeply, and it only takes a few more pumps of my hand before he shoots his release into it, cursing my name as he climaxes.

I drink deeply, the taste of his blood making my core throb, and then pull away, licking my lips. He grabs my chin and kisses me quickly before spinning me around and pressing my front against the cool tile. Our hard breathing fills the space between us, and I press my palms flat against the wall.

"I need you inside me," I breathe.

"I know," he growls back, taking his cock in his hand and pumping it a few times before pressing it between my ass cheeks.

I shoot him a glare, to which he smirks at, then rolls his hips and slams his cock into my wet pussy. I suck in a sharp breath, then exhale a moan. He holds still inside me, pressing his lips to the side of my neck, his breath tickling my skin. And then he starts moving, thrusting into me slowly at first, then at full speed, filling me to the hilt. I clench around him, my breasts pressing to the shower wall, and slip my hand between my legs to play with my clit as Atlas continues to pound into me, our heart's beating against our rib cages.

It's still a fairly new connection, to be able to hear how quickly his pulse races simultaneously with mine. The entire experience of being with him is heightened by our connection and the improvements to all of my senses. It's still overwhelming at times, but right now, it's everything I need.

Atlas kisses my neck, his steady thrusts making me pant breathlessly—until he pulls out of me.

"What the fu—"

He turns me around to face him, sliding back into me in one smooth thrust. "I want to watch you fall apart so beautifully for me." He bends slightly, his hand gliding up the back of my thigh before lifting it and pushing himself deeper into my pussy.

"Atlas, please," I beg, grabbing his face and drawing his lips back to mine. Our kiss is fiery and all-consuming.

His thrusts are slow and deep, turning me absolutely ravenous. My heartbeat is thunder in my chest, and the heat of the shower paired with Atlas knowing exactly how to use my body has my head spinning.

I break the kiss to suck in a breath, my pussy tightening around his cock. "Fuck, I'm so close. Please... don't stop."

"Hang on to me," he says in a deep voice filled with arousal. I comply instantly, and he rolls his hips, picking up the speed of his thrusts and pounding into me as he reaches between our heated bodies and finds my throbbing clit. He strums it with expert precision, and pleasure floods through me as I lose myself in him, coming hard and squeezing his cock.

Atlas growls, stealing my lips; his kiss is hungry, demanding, and I give myself over to it without a fight. His thrusts are unrelenting, and his fingers continue moving over my clit even as I whimper against his lips. My legs threaten to give out as he pounds into me over and over, until finally, he makes a strangled sound deep in his throat and comes hard, throwing his head back and breaking the kiss.

I collapse against him as he pulls his cock out of me, and he catches me around the waist, holding me against him under the warm spray of water. "I'll never tire of this," I murmur as he runs his hand up and down my back. My core throbs faintly with the aftershocks of one of the most intense orgasms I've experienced, and I'm not sure I have the energy to shower anymore.

"Never means forever, and forever is a long time," he says, his eyes softening as he holds my gaze.

I smile at him, lifting my hand to his face, and trace his bottom lip with my thumb. "Not long enough."

I slept terribly last night. Between the tossing and turning and the nightmares of Lenora and Simon sinking their fangs into me when I drifted off, I didn't get any actual rest.

I pry my eyes open shortly after six, the sky still dark outside the bedroom window. I roll over and reach for my phone, squinting at the screen as I read the message from Tessa.

Can't wait to see you! Have a safe flight.

I sit up, leaning against the headboard and send a quick reply.

Slight change of plans. The guys are coming with me. Gabriel is meeting with your headmaster about the vampire/hunter treaty, so we're flying together and renting a car when we land.

Her response comes a couple minutes later.

Okay. I'll just see you when you get here then?

They won't disrupt our visit, I promise! Looking forward to getting a taste of your world and hearing more about your suitors. 😉 *See you soon!*

There's a soft knock at the door before Gabriel sticks his head inside. "Morning, angel. We need to leave soon."

I set my phone on the bedside table and push the blankets off, swinging my feet over the side. "So you guys got on the flight?"

He approaches me with a steaming cup of coffee and holds it out to me. "It was fully booked. I put us all on a different one an hour later."

"Oh. Okay." I take the mug from him. "Thanks."

Gabriel nods, scanning my face. "You doing okay?" he asks in a soft voice laced with concern.

I take a sip of the coffee, shrugging. "Sure. Just tired. Worried about everything the rest of you are."

Understanding fills his expression and he steps closer, reaching for me and brushing his knuckles across my cheek before he bends and kisses my head. "We'll be in the living room when you're ready."

I nod, gulping down another mouthful of coffee, praying it'll pour some life into my veins. "I'll be down in a few."

After Gabriel leaves, I get up and shuffle into the bathroom to get ready, grabbing a comfy pair of navy sweatpants and a plain black hoodie to wear on the plane.

I haul my suitcase downstairs and leave it at the front door with the others, walking into the living room to find the guys waiting for me.

"All set?" Gabriel asks from the chair next to the unlit fireplace.

I nod. "Let's do this."

THIRTEEN

CALLA

Gabriel booked business class tickets, so after breezing through security, we take advantage of the lounge while we await boarding.

Lex and Kade hit up the breakfast bar, piling their plates with enough eggs, bacon, and hash browns for an entire family. Atlas stands near the observation window, sipping a coffee, while Gabriel types away on the tablet in his lap, nursing a cup of espresso.

I sit next to Kade, stealing a piece of bacon from his plate and nibbling on it. My stomach is filled with nervous excitement to see Tessa and be somewhere new. As apprehensive as I was about the guys joining me, I'm glad to not be going alone.

"Did you guys leave any food for other people?" I ask in an amused tone, though, to be fair, we are currently the only ones in the lounge.

Lex shrugs, shoving a forkful of eggs into his mouth, and grins at me.

I roll my eyes, shaking my head. I get up and wander around the lounge, looking at the different art prints hanging on the walls.

"Are you excited to see the little witch?" Kade asks from behind me.

I keep my back to him, letting my eyes roam over the forest land-scape in the painting before me. "Of course. It'll be a nice distraction from things for a little while."

He steps closer, the heat of his chest against my back. His lips are at my ear when he speaks next. "If you're looking for a distraction, all you had to do was ask."

I close my eyes despite myself, pressing my lips together as my body instinctively leans toward him. "Are you trying to seduce me in an airport lounge?"

"That depends," he murmurs, snaking his arm around my waist and caging me against him. "Is it working?"

Heat floods through me, filling my cheeks and pooling low in my stomach. "Hmm... maybe."

Kade moves the hair away from my neck, teasing me with his lips against my skin. "Maybe?" he echoes, kissing my racing pulse. His arm tightens around my waist as his other hand slides up the inside of my thigh inching closer to the need growing between my legs. "I love the way you light up under my touch." His words send a shiver through me, and I turn my head enough to catch his lips with mine, kissing him hard. He groans against my lips and curls his fingers into the waist-band of my sweatpants, sliding his hand into my panties. A startled sound escapes my lips when he pushes a single digit past my folds, massaging my inner walls slowly. I try to grind against his hand, my hips pushing against his hold on me, and he chuckles against my lips, pressing his thumb to my clit.

I break the kiss, gasping, "Fuck." My head falls back against his chest, and I writhe against him, my knees threatening to buckle as he quickens his pace and slides a second finger into my pussy. "Kade, please."

"You can hold on a little longer," he taunts lowly, curling his fingers deep inside me as he circles my clit with his thumb.

I growl at him, my stomach tightening as pleasure floods through me. I slam my hand into the wall next to the painting, grabbing Kade's arm around my waist as my pussy clenches around his invading digits. He doesn't slow down as he adds another finger, stretching me deli-ciously, and bites the side of my neck, sucking gently without breaking the skin.

The tension between my legs reaches its peak, and I moan deeply as I climax, coming hard around his fingers and grinding against him. My heart pounds in my chest, reverberating in my ears as I ride the waves of pleasure flooding through me. Kade slowly pulls his fingers out, teasing my clit until I dig my fingernails into his arm at the sensory overload. He chuckles, dragging his tongue along my neck before pulling away. I turn and lean against the wall, watching in rapture as he lifts his fingers to his lips and licks the evidence of my release off each one, holding my gaze with a glimmer of lust in his.

I open my mouth, but before I can speak, the intercom announces priority boarding for our flight is open. My gaze drops to the bulge in Kade's pants, and my lips twitch. "Think you can make it six hours?"

His eyes narrow slightly. "I think the fuck not."

"Let's go," Gabriel calls from across the lounge, sliding his tablet into his duffle bag.

Kade grumbles something under his breath, too low for even my heightened hearing to catch, and crosses the room as I follow him, pressing my lips together against a laugh threatening to spill free.

I spend most of the flight barely paying attention to the true crime documentary I put on the screen in front of me, dozing in and out of restless sleep with Lex sitting in the seat next to me, watching my screen instead of his. I offer him a headphone at one point so we can both listen, and he takes it, sliding his fingers through mine and tracing his thumb back and forth across the top of my hand. His touch lulls me to sleep as I listen to the story of a mother killing her son's fiancée the night before their wedding.

Lex nudges me awake sometime later, grinning softly. "We're getting ready to land. Think you want to wake up now?"

I mumble a nonsensical response, still half asleep.

After we land and stop at the car rental counter, we hit the road. Half an hour later, we pull off the main road and keep driving until there are no buildings, just greenery in sight. The closer we get, the heavier the forest is on both sides of the road, until Atlas slows, turning at a barely noticeable break in the trees. We drive through another forested area for a few minutes and then the academy comes into view.

My lips part in a silent gasp. "Holy shit. She lives in a castle."

We stop at a massive wrought iron gate with an intricate decorative arch at the top that appears like vines surrounding a 'V' and an 'A' etched into the deep gold plaque in the middle. Marble pillars with oil lamps affixed to them stand on either side of the gate, with tall wrought iron fencing running around, I imagine, the entire academy. There are guards stationed on either side, and the one closest to the driver's side approaches the car as Atlas hits the button to roll down the window.

"A vehicle of vampires can't be a good thing," the guard who looks to be around my father's age says with narrowed eyes.

"Your headmaster is expecting us," Atlas replies in a level voice.

The guard nods stiffly, then motions for the other one to open the gate. It slowly swings inward without a sound, and we drive through. The academy grows bigger the closer we get, its dark red brick exterior at least six stories high.

Atlas pulls the car around a large circular fountain and slows to a stop in front of wide stone steps that lead to the oak double doors. Tall glass windows fill a lot of the front view, which makes me think the natural light inside must be stunning.

I quickly text Tessa that we're here, then unbuckle, getting out and inhaling deeply. The air is refreshing after being stuck in a plane and car for hours.

Kade grabs my suitcase out of the back, and as I finish thanking him, Tessa slips outside and bounds down the steps, her lips breaking into a huge grin as she rushes toward me and wraps me in a tight hug, squealing softly.

"I can't believe you're here," she says, her pulse ticking steadily. "I know we've talked about it a bunch and you sent me your flight info and whatnot." She sucks in a breath. "I'm sorry, I'm rambling. I just... I'm really glad you're here."

I laugh, hugging her back. "Me too, Tess," I tell her, giving her a squeeze before we break apart. I give her a quick once-over, immediately feeling like a slob in my sweatpants and hoodie with my hair thrown into a bun.

Lex clears his throat dramatically. "What? No warm welcome for us?"

Tessa rolls her bright emerald eyes before plastering a blatantly fake smile on her lips and turning toward him as I fight a grin. "So glad you guys decided to crash Calla's trip. Can't you tell how happy I am that you're here?" She turns back to me. "Now then. Want a tour?"

"Damn right I do. But first, there's somewhere I can get a coffee, right?"

She laughs. "I got you. There's a café I love on the other side of the main building. We can grab lunch there too, if you're hungry."

My stomach grumbles to remind me I was too anxious to eat anything for breakfast before my flight. "That sounds amazing."

Tessa grabs my suitcase. "We can drop this at my dorm on the way. Say goodbye to your girl," she tells the guys. "I'm kidnapping her for the next three days."

Lex gasps, turning his gaze on me. "Hey. I thought that was our thing."

"Ha ha." I walk over and give him a hug, jabbing him in the ribs.

He laughs, bending to kiss me on the cheek. "Have fun. Don't miss me too much."

"Touché."

"Already do." He shoots me a wink as I pull away and move to hug Kade.

"Sorry for leaving you like that at the airport," I say in a teasing voice, my lips brushing his ear.

He wraps an arm around me, hauling me against him. "And then you didn't even join me in the bathroom on the plane. So inconsiderate," he jokes.

I shake my head at him, moving toward Gabriel, who immediately offers me a warm smile and reaches to tuck a bit of hair that escaped my bun behind my ear. "Enjoy your time with Tessa. We'll be around if you need anything."

I nod, wrapping my arms around his middle and hugging him tightly. "Thanks, Gabe."

Atlas fixes me with an annoyingly unreadable stare as I close the distance between us. I arch a brow at him. "You good?"

He holds his hand out, then draws me against his chest when I take it, dropping his lips to my ear. "Be careful," he says in a low voice. He kisses the side of my head as he pulls back. "And have fun."

I blink at him in surprise, then remember to nod, smiling softly. "I will."

Tessa and I climb the steps to the academy's front doors, and she opens one for us to walk inside.

"I can't get over how beautiful this place is," I gush as we step into a foyer with creaky wood floors and warm-toned walls. The space is filled with light coming from several fixtures hanging from the ceilings and walls. This place fits the dark academia aesthetic to a T. It smells faintly of paper and leather and candle wax. It's nothing like my university campus or the guys' house, but I absolutely love it.

"You have stars in your eyes," Tessa says amusedly, nudging me with her elbow.

"Sorry, this place is just..." I trail off, taking everything in. From the vaulted ceilings to the dark wood stairs ahead that lead to a landing with twin staircases on either side and an enormous chandelier casting everything in soft, golden light. "Wow," I finally say.

"Yeah. I had a similar reaction once I got over the initial shock of the reason I was brought here."

I nod slowly, enraptured by everything as we walk up to the second level, then down a long hallway with a deep red afghan rug running along the floor and oil paintings hung on the walls in between the closed doors. Everything appears to be made of wood or concrete, making me think this place has been around longer that I have.

People pass from all different directions, casting us glances of curiosity and indignation. I avert my gaze, and the buzz of activity fills my ears along with the pounding of hearts and blood pulsing through bodies, which I try very hard to ignore. The dull burning in my throat and throbbing in my gums makes that rather challenging though.

Tessa leads me up to a door at the end of the hallway on the fourth floor, where she presses her hand to a panel, and the door clicks open.

"Okay, that's pretty cool. You don't have to worry about losing keys."

She tosses me a quick grin over her shoulder, pushing the door open to let us inside. Her dorm is a simple room with a bed, dresser, desk, and reading nook built into a window overlooking more forest. She's decorated with twinkling fairy lights, candles, and a fluffy rug, making the small space feel incredibly cozy.

"This place is beautiful," I tell her, leaving my suitcase against the wall next to the door and walking toward the window. There are a few other buildings that look similar to the one we're in, as well as outdoor seating and lots of grassy areas that back onto the thick forest line of trees.

She peers around the room, dropping onto the end of the bed, and offers me a smile. "Thanks."

After that pit stop, she takes me to the café, where I scarf down a ham and cheese croissant. I take a sip of my vanilla latte and clasp my hands together on the small table in front of me. "Okay, tell me everything."

She laughs softly, taking a drink of her iced coffee. "You just got here. I'm going to let you experience some of the academy before I quote, unquote *tell you everything*."

"Uh, okay. I don't know if I should be intrigued or scared."

She shrugs, grinning faintly. "Hmm... probably a bit of both."

"Good to know," I say dryly.

A small smile plays on her lips for a moment. "What's going on in Washington?" she asks. She's clearly not ready to talk about her stuff yet, so I concede for now.

I blow out a breath. *What a loaded question.* "Well, that depends on where you want me to start." I tap my finger against the rim of my mug. "I saw my parents."

"How did that go?"

"Really well, actually." I laugh. "It was a little uncomfortable to start, but the entire visit went better than I expected. We also had to see Atlas's parents. They're not exactly happy with us. With this whole hunter treaty thing…" I sigh. "They are so stuck in their archaic ways of ruling by making everybody fear them."

Tessa frowns. "So basically, they can't get their heads out of their asses long enough to consider that this could be a positive alternative to—"

"Essentially killing all the hunters, yeah. Which they seem to have done in the past. Eradicate them for a number of years before they come back again and again. As one of the newest members of team immortal, repeating history like that, sounds awful, honestly."

She nods. "No kidding. And I'm sure having your bestie's family involved has made things even more complicated. How is it being linked?"

I purse my lips. The physical distance between us at the moment has made the connection go quiet; I don't feel her like I did when the connection was forged, but something tells me I would know if something was wrong. "It's actually helped me. After the ambush that ended with a dagger in my chest at her hand, the whole trust piece was hard."

Tessa nods again. "I can see why her not being able to hurt you without hurting herself would be reassuring."

"I want to believe that she wouldn't hurt me again, regardless." I sigh. "I'm still working through it." I force a smile, finishing my latte and setting the empty mug on my plate. "Needless to say, I'm happy to be visiting you. Plus, I've been dying to see your magical academy of yours."

"I see that sparkle in your eyes." There's a lilt of amusement in her voice. "It's not Hogwarts, sorry to disappoint."

"That's cool, I never read *Harry Potter*."

She snorts. "Neither did I, but everybody knows what Hogwarts is."

"Yeah," I say with a laugh. "Anyway, this place is seriously cool. Are you able to come and go as you please?" I ask. "You visited me a couple times, but those were extraordinary circumstances."

She nods. "I'm able to leave whenever I want now. When I first got here I couldn't, though I tried several times to sneak out." When my brows shoot up, she glances over at me, chuckling softly. "Yeah." She drags out the word. "I was freaked."

"Hey, no judgment from me. I also tried escaping my fate. We are most definitely kindred spirits. Anyway, are people going to be weirded out or pissed off that you have a vampire staying in your room? I know witches don't approve of us." If the front gate guards are any indication, we aren't exactly welcome here.

She purses her lips. "There are some vampires who live here. Ones that practice magic as well. So, while some witches aren't fans of fangs, you and the guys will be fine."

"You know, that's not very reassuring, but thanks?" It comes out as more of a question.

Tessa smiles. "And you don't need to worry. The cafeteria serves blood."

I try to mask my relief with a smile of my own as we get up and discard our dishes at the counter before heading toward the door.

"Why don't we explore the grounds a bit?" she suggests as we leave the café. "Oh, and I have a few friends I'd love for you to meet." She walks away without looking to see if I'm following. I hurry to catch up; this is probably the last place I want to get lost in.

"Okay," I say, keeping stride next to her. "Time to spill everything going on with you."

She inhales deeply, then sighs. "Do you want the long version or the CliffsNotes?"

I bump her shoulder with mine. "Everything means everything, Tess. We've got time."

She runs her fingers through her hair as we keep walking, following a gravel path along what appears to be the back of the main academy building. "Well, you know a little about why I'm here."

I nod. "I remember you telling me you didn't know anything about your magic until the night you caused the fire and Selene stepped in to bring you here."

"Right. When I first got here, it was more than challenging—adapting, learning, *accepting* everything they were telling me."

"But you're still here," I say. "Because you want to be?"

"Yeah," she answers. "I can leave at any time, I just don't know that I want to. There's nowhere else I want to go at this point. That, and there are things keeping me here."

My brows lift and my eyes roam over her face, waiting for her to elaborate.

"I, uh, fell for the witch who helped me when I got here."

I can't help but smile. "That makes sense. You were probably feeling pretty lost. And he was someone who gave you guidance and helped you through what I imagine was one of the hardest things you've ever experienced."

"Yeah, but it wasn't just that. He makes me feel things... When he looks at me, the world just completely falls away. It's intense and wildly complicated."

"Look who you're talking to," I offer.

"Right. There's a bit of an age difference, and he's one of Valor's mentors."

"Ohhh," I say, dragging out the word as the realization hits me. "So, you're hot for teacher, huh?"

She cringes, shaking her head. "God, please don't put it like that."

My lips twitch. "I seem to remember there being two guys. Who's the other one?"

She groans, thrusting her fingers through her hair. "Liam. He's..." She trails off as if she's trying to find the words and eventually sighs. "I don't really know how to explain him. He took me by surprise, and I'm still trying to figure things out when it comes to him."

"That's okay, you know," I tell her. "You don't have to have it all figured out. And I'm not going to stand here and tell you that you have to choose. That would be a little hypocritical of me."

She stops walking, glancing out toward the back of the academy grounds, frowning. "To make matters even more complicated, they hate each other. Like, with a fiery passion."

"But they both care about you," I say.

She presses her lips together, her cheeks flushing. "Yeah. There lies the complication."

"Okay," I say, clapping my hands together. "I don't have any answers or helpful suggestions you haven't already thought of, so I say we just get drunk and forget all about them. You can forget about your problems here, and I can forget about my problems in Washington, and we'll just have a good time."

Some of the tension releases from her shoulders, and she laughs. "You have no idea how good that sounds."

I open my mouth to respond, but the words get caught in my throat as perhaps the most attractive person I've ever seen—and I live with four fucking male models—starts toward us. He has golden blond hair cropped short on the sides and slightly longer on top and he's wearing an olive green V-neck under a black leather jacket and jeans with a pair of worn black boots. "Holy shit," I say under my breath, turning to Tessa as her pulse kicks up. "If I wasn't already tangled up with my fair share of vampires..."

The guy smirks, flashing brilliant white teeth and a razor-sharp pair of fangs. "I like your friend, Tess."

"Unreal," I mutter under my breath, shooting Tessa a raised-brow look.

She shakes her head, exhaling what sort of sounds like a laugh. "Calla, meet Liam. Liam, Calla."

"Ah, the newbie vamp." Liam sticks his hand out.

I nod, hesitantly reaching out to shake his hand. "Nice to meet you."

His eyes shift to Tessa, and I notice the dip in her heartbeat before it picks up, which means Liam caught it too. His lips curl into a grin that reminds me of Kade: dangerous.

I pull my hand back. "Should we keep going? I'm sure there is a ton more for you to show me."

She nods quickly. "Yeah." Turning to Liam, she adds, "See you."

"Count on it," he says in a velvet-smooth voice before he disappears in a blur of movement. The second he's gone, I slap Tessa in the arm.

"Ow! What was that for?"

"You didn't tell me he was fucking gorgeous," I nearly shout at her.

She rolls her eyes at me. "Because your mates are real hard to look at," she remarks dryly.

"Yeah, yeah," I flick my wrist. "Oh my god, now you have to tell me *everything*. Have you slept with him?"

Her cheeks turn red. "That's not... I don't..." She groans, scrubbing her hands down her face.

"Ha!" I laugh. "I knew it. Lucky girl. He looks like he'd know what to do."

Tessa presses her lips together, her pulse racing beneath her skin, but voices no response. She doesn't have to.

This is nice—it feels *normal*. Walking around, talking about guys. It's the perfect distraction, a much-needed break from dealing with the supernatural shitstorm I'll be facing with the guys too soon enough.

FOURTEEN

CALLA

Our time in Oregon passes in a blur. Tessa and I go hiking through the forest, shopping in the small town close to the academy, and exploring the grounds. I meet a few of her friends, and we tag along to a bonfire one night.

After our run-in with Liam, I'm hoping even more to meet the other guy vying for Tessa's heart, though considering she said he's a mentor, it makes sense why we didn't cross paths.

To my surprise, I didn't see the guys once from the time Tessa and I left them at the front doors until I left her dorm the morning of our flight back to Washington.

They are waiting for me with the rental car where I left them a few days ago. Tessa walks with me, wrapping me in a tight hug.

"Keep in touch, yeah?" she says.

"Of course. You too." I squeeze her before pulling back. "And don't worry," I add in a lower voice, "you'll figure everything out."

She presses her lips together, smiling faintly. "Thanks, Calla."

I throw her one more smile before heading toward the car idling at the bottom of the front steps.

Lex is the first one to grab me, wrapping his arms around me in a bear hug and kissing the top of my head. "I've made the executive deci-sion that you're not allowed to spend any more than twenty-four hours away from us." He's grinning at me, but something tells me his words are completely serious.

I roll my eyes. "We were on the same property the entire time."

Lex finally lets me go, and I have about two seconds to recover before Kade tugs me into his arms, nearly knocking the air out of my lungs as he squeezes me. When he leans back, he kisses me hard on the mouth until my head spins, and I pull away to catch my breath.

Gabriel stands near the car, smiling at me as Kade takes my suitcase to load it into the back. I walk over to greet Gabriel, wrapping my arms around his neck and pressing my cheek against his chest as his arms come around my waist.

"Morning, angel," he says in my ear, and I close my eyes for a moment, smiling.

"Hey, you," I murmur back.

I walk around the car to get in on the other side, and Atlas gets out of the driver's seat, blocking my path. Without a word, he holds out his hand, and I take it, letting him draw me in. He lifts his other hand to my face, brushing his knuckles across my cheek before sliding his fingers into my hair.

"Hi," I whisper.

A faint smile tugs at his lips. "Hi. Did you have a good time?" he asks.

I nod, leaning into him. "We had a lot of fun."

He brushes his lips against my forehead before opening the door to the backseat for me to climb in.

Kade and Lex get in the back with me, while Gabriel takes the passenger seat, and Atlas slides behind the wheel again.

Tessa waves from the front steps of the academy as we drive away, and just before she's out of sight, I catch a dark-haired guy join her, making my lips crack into a grin.

"So, what did you get up to these last few days?" Kade asks from the seat behind me.

I turn my attention to him, making a mental note to text Tessa about the guy later. "It was interesting, being surrounded by other supernaturals but people who are still different from me."

Gabriel turns, looking at me over his shoulder. "The witches didn't give you any trouble, did they?"

I smile at him. "No, and Tessa would've had my back if anyone tried anything."

"Tessa?" Lex says, shaking his head. "I'd be worried for any sorry son of a bitch who tried to take *you* on."

I laugh softly. "I'm going to take that as a compliment, because I think that's what you were getting at."

He shoots me a wink in response.

"How did it go with the headmaster?" I ask Gabriel.

"Quite well. We met with her and several council members—which are essentially representatives for the witches," he explains. "They are apprehensive but hopeful and will fully support the treaty, so long as they aren't required to be part of it."

I nod along. "Okay then. That's fine, right?"

"It's nothing we didn't expect. Witches and vampires haven't seen eye to eye for a very long time. It's certainly not as volatile a relationship as the vampires and hunters, but the witches rarely go out of their way to be involved with us."

"Right," I murmur back, glancing out the window as we get closer to the interstate.

Kade props his chin on the edge of my seat, blowing air on my neck until I shiver and turn enough to look at him.

I lean back against the headrest. "What do you want?" I grumble, but my annoyance is half-hearted at best.

"I hope you got some rest while you stayed with the witch, because I am very much looking forward to getting reacquainted with every inch of your body."

My throat goes dry and I struggle to swallow past it, keeping my composure. "Can you wait until we get home?" I ask, my tone rather dry.

"If I say no?" His eyes flick between mine, his liquid silver gaze filled with lust. Before I can answer, he reaches forward and unbuckles my belt, pulling me into the backseat. I yelp in surprise, grabbing for him so I don't fall off the seat or smack my head against the window.

"Fuck. Seriously, Kade?"

"Tell me you weren't thinking the same thing," he shoots back.

"I..." I snap my mouth shut. "Whatever," I grumble.

"Oh, come on." He slides his hand up my thigh, wrapping it around my hip, and tugs me closer to him. His other hand slides up my arm to cup the side of my neck and tips my head back. "I don't enjoy being away from you," he says in a low voice, resting his forehead against mine.

I lick my lips, leaning into him a little more and sliding my hands up his chest to feel his heart beating steadily against my palm. "I'm right here."

His lips find mine, slow and gentle at first, but it's not long before our kiss turns fiery, desperate. Kade slides his hand up my shirt and massages my breast, using his thumb to flick my nipple into a hardened bud. My clit throbs intensely, having gone days without release; my body remembers his touch, and it sets me on fire almost instantly.

I grab his wrist, guiding his hand to the waistband of my leggings, and his lips curve into a smirk against mine. A hint is all he needs, and he takes control, sliding his fingers inside my panties and circling my clit at an agonizingly slow speed as his middle finger traces back and forth along my slit.

I pull back from his lips, panting from both the movement of his fingers and from his kiss. "Yes," I breathe.

"Fuck, I've missed this," he growls in a low voice, keeping his forehead pressed against mine.

I nod in agreement. I don't think I realized just how much I missed being with them until this moment. "I want you inside me now."

Without hesitation, he pushes two fingers into my pussy, curling them deep and hitting just the right spot to make me moan. I ride his fingers, grinding against him as pressure builds quickly between my thighs. My inner walls throb around his invading digits, and he thrusts them into me at a speed that makes me lightheaded, and I'm clinging to him in minutes. I roll my hips, pushing him in deeper, and grab his face, stealing his lips with mine and putting everything I have into the kiss. His pulse jackhammers and his cock hardens against me, shooting liquid heat through me. His fingers find my clit once more, and he pulls his lips away from mine, pressing them to the side of my neck, kissing and sucking, swirling his tongue over my skin. My head lolls to the side, and I catch Atlas's dark gaze in the rearview mirror. They hold a promise of pleasure—and maybe a bit of pain, which, paired with Kade's touch, has me vibrating with excitement.

"Faster," I breathe. "Please. I need to come."

Lex chuckles from the seat in front of us. "Three days, and you've got all this pent up—"

"Shut up," I growl at him, and my pussy clenches around Kade's fingers. "Fuck, I'm close."

His fangs scrape my throat, shooting a shiver through me as he slides a third finger up inside me, strumming my clit at a pressure that has me crying out and coming hard, soaking his fingers with my release.

I float down from my orgasm, my breathing slowing as I cling to Kade's shirt, wrinkling the front of it in my grip.

"Welcome back," he says against my ear, nipping the lobe. I shiver as he pulls his fingers out of me and licks each of them clean, smirking at my expression.

I want more.

My body is greedy after being away from my men, but we're almost at the airport now, and the last thing I want is to get into something I can't finish. So I climb off Kade's lap and return to my seat, my breathing returning to a normal speed as I rest my head back and sigh contently.

After an uneventful flight, which I mostly sleep through, we arrive back at our rental house in Washington.

Part of me is expecting Atlas to take his turn with me after the way his eyes held mine with such promise back at the academy, and I'd be lying if I said I'm not a little disappointed when he takes a call the minute we walk in the door.

Lex carries my suitcase into the house while I wander into the kitchen in search of coffee. The faint throbbing in my gums is a timely reminder I should also drink some blood.

While I was away, Tessa made sure I had what I needed, but even surrounded by witches who were part vampire and also drank blood, I was uneasy about doing it in front of anyone. So I never had as much as I probably should have.

I snatch a blood bag out of the fridge drawer and pop the cap, bringing it to my lips and sucking down a few mouthfuls. Any lingering tension in my muscles melts away as the blood fills my stomach, and I turn on the coffee maker while I work on the blood bag.

Gabriel joins me in the kitchen a minute later. His hands in the pockets of his jeans, he leans against the counter, watching me with a small smile on his lips.

"Coffee?" I ask.

"If you're making it," he says lightly, and I pull down two mugs from the cupboard above the machine.

"Any updates you want to fill me in on with the hunters?"

He pulls his hands out of his pockets and crosses his arms over his chest casually. "We just got home, angel. We don't need to get into it right this minute."

"Okay, well now I think we do, because you not wanting to tell me makes me think there's bad news."

Gabriel laughs softly. "No bad news. We've contacted several groups of vampires in the area and all over North America. The consensus is overall positive. Of course, some are hesitant, and others are downright refusing to take part in any talks, which we expected."

"Right." I nod, scooping the coffee grounds into the machine. I fill the tank with water and turn it on, waiting as it rumbles to life. "So what do we do now?"

"Hmm..." He hums, letting his hands fall to his sides as he walks over to stand in front of me. "I've spent every night you were gone thinking about you. Dreaming about you. Missing you." His words bring heat to my cheeks, and I smile.

"I missed you too."

He lifts his hand and tucks my hair behind my ear before leaning in and pressing his lips against my forehead. His heart beats a little faster in his chest, and my eyes drop to the bulge in his pants, which immediately has parts of my body on alert. I grab the front of his shirt and pull him firmly against me, guiding his lips to mine and kissing him. Pushing my hips forward, I deepen in the kiss, gliding my tongue over his bottom lip until he opens to me, and I push inside, grazing my tongue against his. His hands drop to my hips, gripping them firmly, and he lifts me onto the counter without breaking the kiss. He makes an indistinct sound at the back of his throat, something akin to a growl that has my pulse jackhammering.

"Forget the coffee," I mutter against his lips, and he nods, lifting me off the counter. I wrap my legs around him, and he carries me out of the kitchen. In a matter of seconds, we're in his bedroom, and he kicks the door shut behind us before laying me down on his bed. The soft silk sheets slide under me as I scoot toward the headboard, but Gabriel grabs my ankles and pulls me back to the end of the bed where he kneels before me, running his hands up my thighs and curling his fingers into the waistband of my leggings, dragging them down with my panties and leaving me bare to him. My heart beats faster as I realize what his intentions are, and I suck in a quick breath when he presses his lips just above my clit.

"I want to bury myself inside you," he says in a thick voice. "But first, I need to taste you."

I grip the sheets on either side of me, making a strangled noise of pleasure when he plunges his tongue deep inside me. He sucks hard, using his fingers to stimulate my clit as his tongue dives in and out at a steady rhythm that has me panting in record time.

"Oh my—Yes, right there. Right fucking there."

His lips curl against me, and he pulls back just a little, dragging his tongue along my inner walls and moaning deeply to send vibrations through me.

I cry out as an orgasm crashes through me like a violent, unforgiving wave. Only seconds pass between the time Gabriel pulls his tongue out of me, kicks off his pants and hovers over me, his copper hair falling into his face. I reach up and push it back; it's grown longer, and I kind of like the look on him.

He grips his thick length in his hand, pumping it as moisture beads on the tip. "I've thought about this every moment since you walked away from us at Valor," he murmurs, dipping his face and kissing me softly as he lines the head of his cock up with my entrance. I'm trembling beneath him, anticipation clinging to me when he slams into me with one steady thrust, stealing my lips and my breath. I gasp into his mouth, and he swallows the sounds of my pleasure as he rolls his hips, reaching even deeper inside me. He slams into my pussy harder than he ever has, and his hands grip my wrists, pinning them above my head as he moves over me.

Gabriel's lips devour mine as his cock hits the deepest part of me, launching me toward another powerful climax. I turn my head to break the kiss, panting, and his lips find the most sensitive spot just below my ear. He sucks gently on my neck as his thrusts pick up speed once more, and everything in me clenches tightly as I come around his cock. He continues to thrust into me until the muscles in his thighs tighten, and he grunts into my neck, shooting his release deep inside me as he comes.

We're both breathing heavily as he pulls out and collapses onto the bed, pulling me into his arms and covering us both with the heavy duvet. I curl against his side, resting my cheek against his chest and running my fingers through his hair as our hearts beat near in sync.

"That was intense," I murmur.

"Are you okay?" he checks in a soft voice, concern flickering in his eyes.

"Intense in a good way, Gabe. You don't need to worry about me."

He slides his fingers along my jaw, curling one around my chin and turning my face to his. His lips brush over mine, his eyes filled with adoration.

It's unexplainable how much fear that look brings me, knowing there's a possibility in a matter of days, we could lose it all.

FIFTEEN

CALLA

The following day, we leave the house shortly before noon to meet with some vampires in the area. Most of which, I'm told, are already on board with the plan, but some of them need a little more encouragement. Others want more information to fully commit to what we're asking of them. Which, considering the alternative, it doesn't seem to me like there's room for any question, but I've been a vampire for, like, ten seconds, so I suppose I'm not the best person to speak on the topic.

We drive to what appears to be a ranch on the outskirts of Arlington. Pulling off the main road, the tires of the Escalade crunch over a gravel winding road that eventually leads to a modern-looking farmhouse.

"Who lives here?" I ask.

"Friend of a friend," Atlas answers vaguely, and I arch a brow at him from the passenger seat. To Lex's disappointment, I called shotgun the minute we walked out of the house back in Washington.

"Oh."

"We've all connected with many people over the years, Calla, which you'll learn more for yourself soon enough."

"Okay," I say, shrugging.

We get out of the car, walking toward the house, and I frown briefly, glancing toward my sire.

"There are humans here."

It's not a question, but he nods. "Feeders. A meeting with a bunch of vampires requires them." He lowers his voice. "Some vampires refuse to drink from blood bags."

My eyebrows tug together. "That could make this treaty a lot more complicated."

"Yes, well, nothing about it is *un*complicated at this point." He pauses, clearly sensing my unease. "Try to remember that even if some vampires will only drink from the vein, it doesn't mean they're attacking or hurting anyone."

I press my lips together and nod in response. We climb the wooden steps onto the porch, and Gabriel knocks on the all-glass front door. Moments later, a woman with white blond hair and silver eyes opens it, smiling at our group. She is absolutely stunning, and I hate that I immediately feel self-conscious. As much as I try to tamp it down, I don't want to look at this woman for any extended period. She, however, seems keen on eye fucking each of the guys in greeting, which makes my jaw clench. I shove my hands into my pockets to keep them from curling into fists, because how ridiculous is that? I won't stand here and—

"Welcome. I'm so glad you accepted my invitation to host your summit at my estate."

Atlas nods politely. "We appreciate the offer, Delia."

"Please come in. You're one of the first groups to arrive, and we have plenty of food." Her eyes slide to me. "You're new," she comments mildly.

I force myself to look at her and smile. "I guess," is all I say.

Kade chuckles from behind me, and I fight the urge to whip around and glare at him. We step inside, and Lex closes the door behind us. The woman—Delia, apparently—leads us down a wide hallway with ornate archways on either side, one leading to what appears to be a parlor with several seating areas and an enormous stone fireplace that's crackling with flames, filling the room with warmth. The room on the other side of the hallway is a formal dining room, and I immediately realize the people sitting at the long dark wood table are human. *The feeders.*

"Is anyone hungry now?" Delia asks, gesturing to the room of humans.

"No, thank you," Gabriel says.

"Very well. They're here whenever you'd like them." She continues into the parlor where there are five groups of vampires chatting amongst themselves. "Make yourselves at home and get started whenever you're ready. Please let me know if you need anything." The woman touches Atlas's arm, and a low growl rumbles through my throat before I can stop myself.

Atlas's lips twitch, and I immediately take a step back as the woman glances at me and removes her hand from him.

Don't attack her, don't attack her, don't attack her. She's way older than I am, and I will have my ass handed to me. I chant the words in my head, locking away the dangerously territorial side of myself I'm still very new to.

"Are you going to behave?" Lex teases in my ear.

"Fuck off," I grumble, walking over to where a bar is set up. I pour myself a healthy glass of champagne, my eyes widening briefly at the label on the bottle. Perhaps I shouldn't be surprised that vampires are dropping thousands on several bottles of champagne, and I'm sure as hell not going to complain about it. I take a sip and close my eyes, taking this tiny semblance of enjoyment, because shit is likely about to hit the fan.

"Take it easy." Atlas's voice is low, and he's standing at my back.

I down the rest of the glass, leaving it on the table, and turn to walk back to the rest of the guys.

Atlas snatches my wrist, holding me in place. "Do you need a minute?"

"I'm fine," I say automatically, irritation prickling along my neck. I'm not even entirely sure the cause of it, which makes it even more annoying. Some of it is the result of the gorgeous woman making eyes at the guys, but I think the stress of this meeting is only adding to it. As much as I want this treaty to be successful, I don't particularly want to be here right now.

"Calla."

"Atlas," I level.

His eyes flick between mine, and he lowers his voice even further, murmuring, "I love you." He snakes an arm around my waist and pulls me against him, sealing his lips over mine. It's over as quickly as it happened, and Atlas says in my ear, "Let's get this over with and go home, okay?"

I nod, clenching and unclenching my hands at my sides. Exhaling a deep breath, I slide away from my sire and rejoin the others, smiling faintly at Gabriel when he offers me a concerned glance.

Over the next half hour, about a dozen more vampires arrive, including Fallon and Jase, who greet our group before mingling with the others. The parlor is filled with the buzz of mild conversation coming from different groups. My gums throb at the smell of human blood that permeates the air. Of course I didn't expect the other vampires to abstain from the all-you-can-eat human buffet in the other room, but I also didn't expect for it to affect me this much. I chalk it up to being on edge already and do my best to ignore the burn in my throat.

"Thank you for coming," Atlas says, standing in front of the fireplace. I'm directly to his right, with Gabriel on my other side. Lex and Kade stand on Atlas's other side—we're a complete unit. Powerful. *Unbreakable.*

At least, that's what I keep telling myself. It's that or get caught in a doom spiral thinking about everything that could go wrong.

"I hope it's safe to say the reason you've attended this meeting is that you believe what we're trying to do will be beneficial for all parties involved. A treaty with the hunters could very well lead to the end of constantly worrying about being hunted every time you walk outside —hell, even in your own home."

"The idea of peace between species who've been taught to hate each other forever seems too good to be true, York," a bulky guy with messy black curls and a sharp fashion sense says. His tone isn't accusatory, and his expression is that of concern.

Atlas nods. "Of course, it does. I'm not saying it's going to be an easy undertaking or that we won't have to fight for it." He chuckles humorlessly. "Quite the opposite, in fact. We'll likely have to fight *harder* to make this work."

"Nothing worth having comes easy," another vampire says, and some of the crowd nods in agreement, while others have their arms crossed and their silver eyes are filled with doubt.

Unease swirls in my gut, but I keep a neutral expression. We won't win everyone over, especially those already convinced our plan is impossible. Hopefully, though, most of those people didn't bother attending this meeting.

"I want to get on board," an older looking woman says, glancing around the room before returning her gaze to us. "These are the conversations we should have in order to protect the future of our kind."

"What are your reservations, if you don't mind sharing?" Gabriel asks.

The woman looks from Gabriel to Atlas. "I'd like to know what your parents think of this idea to work with the hunters."

Atlas doesn't miss a beat, though I'm holding my breath. "Simon and Lenora are opposed to the treaty," he answers honestly. "As many of you know, they have been around for a very long time. They've seen the rise and fall of hunters more than once and believe they will fall again. Their plan is to do what has been done in the past and eradicate them. It's an option, of course, but I don't think I need to explain that it's merely a temporary fix. We could get rid of them for a century now, only to have to repeat history time and time again." His eyes scan the room carefully, surveying the audience. "Or we can try something different. Something that will save more lives now and in the future."

There is some murmuring near the back of the crowd, and several vampires walk out.

"I'm sorry," another more mature vampire says, stepping forward to address Atlas. "I can appreciate what you're trying to achieve with the treaty, son, but your parents have been at this a long time. How can we know you're up to protecting us as they have?"

"Yeah," someone shouts from the back of the room. "What makes you think you can handle the pressure when your parents have always protected you along with us from the dangers of our world?"

A few others shake their heads and move in a blur out of the room before Atlas even has a chance to respond.

My stomach sinks, though I'm not surprised, and a quick glance at the others tells me they're not concerned with the people who left. The reality is, we don't want them here if they're not fully on board. I understand it, though, not wanting to be part of something they can't be sure will work to ensure their safety.

"For starters, my parents have taught me most of what I know, for better or worse. I've grown up accustomed to the pressure some of you are concerned I may not be able to handle. Besides, I'm not the only one standing here. With every vampire who chooses to stand with us, we have a better shot at making this work. I'm not asking you to look up to me as if I'm my parents—frankly, I'd rather you didn't. What I *am* asking is that you stand with your family, your friends, the others in this room who want the same future for our kind that you do, otherwise you wouldn't be here."

Even with the group of vampires who left, there are at least two dozen in the room, and I believe these are the ones who already want to help or can be convinced that getting on board to work with the hunters is the right thing to do. Then if we're able to protect humans and vampires alike from each other, we'll all be able to live better lives.

"All that said, if anyone else would like to leave," Atlas announces, "please feel free to do so. We aren't here to force anyone's hand, and something of this magnitude and importance will take being on board fully to work. The hunters are having similar conversations to what we're having here today, and I'm sure their outcome will be much like ours. Some of them will refuse to consider working with us, while others—some I've personally met—will see this as a positive opportunity."

"Say the rest of us here agree to this treaty. What happens next?"

Atlas takes the question with a nod. "We've nominated representatives from both sides of the aisle. If you have any concerns, they are your first point of contact. Once this meeting and the meeting the hunters are having is concluded, the representatives will discuss a joint meeting to hammer out the details."

"Didn't we try that once before?" someone asks, and he's not wrong. Both times we've tried to meet with the hunters while Scott was still in charge, we were met with violence.

"Again, I'm not saying this plan is without flaws or risk," Atlas says, "but at some point, something has to change. And so, I'm willing to take the risk. I'm asking you to do the same or leave. It's that simple and that complicated."

"What are the consequences for those who refuse to abide by this treaty?"

Lex speaks up, giving Atlas a break. "Part of the agreement with the hunters is to help keep the vampires in line, ensuring to the best of our ability that humankind is in a better position against being fed on unwillingly than they currently are."

"So we're to kill our own?" someone barks. "That's absurd!"

"No one said kill," Lex shoots back, an edge to his voice. "Protecting one doesn't always mean killing the other. If you can't save a human without killing the vampire attacking them, it sounds like you need to get some training in."

"Which we are happy to coordinate," Gabriel adds smoothly.

That shuts the vampire up pretty quickly.

A few others think they're sneaking out of the room, but it's pretty obvious when all of us have heightened senses. I frown briefly when my eyes land on Delia across the parlor, and the pit in my stomach grows. The hungry look in her eyes as she watches Atlas address the room makes me want to claw them right out of her face. Which, of course, would be counterintuitive to the reason we're here, so I swallow my pettiness and suck it up. She can look at him—at any of them—all she wants. I'm the only one going home with them, because they. Are. *Mine*.

"I don't care about the risks," another vampire shouts. "Because you're fucking right. Something needs to change. I'm tired of living in fear, waiting for a moment in time where the hunters are temporarily not a threat."

"I'll be honest, I've followed the lead of your parents for a long time, Atlas," the woman who spoke up previously says. "But I see a lot of promise in you. Your leadership skills are powerful, and I'd very much like to align myself with what you're working to achieve."

"Thank you," he says. "I intend to prove myself to each of you, to whatever degree necessary for you to trust that I have your best interests in mind when making decisions that will affect all of us. Because I, like you, am tired of this war between us and the hunters. In simple terms, it's unnecessary. Once we agree to help protect humans from vampires not abiding by the agreement to only feed on the willing, and the hunters agree not to attack vampires without proving they are a legitimate threat, our quality of life will improve exponentially."

"It's beneficial for the hunters as well," Gabriel adds, "which is why we're optimistic we can make this work. There will certainly be growing pains, and we'll end up learning a lot as we go along, but this is the start of something important, something good for everyone— and we hope you feel the same."

The buzz of conversation following the meeting seems to be mostly positive. The pit in my stomach has lessened, but scanning the room full of vampires, I suddenly feel like a kid on the first day of school. These are supposed to be my people now, but I'm not sure how to interact with them. I should make the rounds and introduce myself. Do some of them already know who I am because of how well known the guys are? The thought makes my cheeks flush, and then I can't stop dwelling on what these people possibly think of me. Thus starts the doom spiral.

"Are you ready to go?"

I whip around and slap my hand against my chest to find Lex and Kade standing there. "*Fuck*." I exhale a startled breath and let my hand fall back to my side.

"Geez, Cal," Kade says. "Didn't think we could sneak up on you anymore."

"I was, uh… lost in thought." I frown, staring between the two of them. "Sorry, did you ask me something?"

They exchange a quick glance before Lex says, "Are you ready to leave?"

"Oh. Yes, please." I look around the room, which has started to empty as vampires trickle out, either to feed or head home. "I mean, are you sure we shouldn't stay until everyone is gone?"

Kade shrugs. "Atlas and Gabe are in the hall chatting with Delia and a few others about hosting the next meeting here, but it sounds like they're just wrapping up."

That stupid flare of territorial jealousy rears its ugly head, and I walk out of the parlor into the hallway between one second and the next. I find where Atlas and Gabriel are standing and head toward them. Lex and Kade catch up to me, linking their arms through mine and guiding me toward the front door.

"Hey—"

"Lovely to see you, Delia," Kade calls over his shoulder.

They half-carry me outside, and I don't bother fighting them until we reach the Escalade.

"Was that necessary?" I bark when they let me go.

"Yep," they say in unison.

I roll my eyes. "When we get back to the house—"

"What?" Kade says, getting close to my face and effectively trapping me between his chest and the vehicle. "What are you going to do?" There's a challenge in his eyes that makes me momentarily forget everything else going on around us. My gaze drops to his mouth, and his lips twist into a smirk, making my heart beat a little faster. "Hmm, that's what I thought." The arrogance in his voice calls to something in me, but before I can get out a snarky remark, Atlas and Gabriel walk up to us.

"Time to go," Gabriel says, wrapping his fingers around Kade's shoulder and pulling him away from me. "You two can play when we get back to the house."

Kade's eyes glitter with the promise of that, and I'm squeezing my thighs together before I can stop myself. He flicks his tongue across his bottom lip, a slight predatory look coming over him that makes my breath catch. Kade's always been a bit of a wildcard, and even as a vampire, I find myself drawn to the darkest parts of him.

I'm about to slide away from him to get into the car when he mouths two simple words that set my body ablaze.

You're mine.

The drive back to our rental house is less than half an hour, but the looks Kade continues giving me only feed the heat spreading through me like a wildfire.

I squeeze my legs together and force my attention to focus out the window, watching the scenery as we return to the city.

We arrive a short eternity later, and the five of us climb out of the Escalade. Gabriel takes a call, lingering on the front porch, while the rest of us head inside.

Lex kicks off his combat boots, leaving them near the door and yawns dramatically. "I think I'm going to take a nap." His eyes shift to me. "Care to join?"

I shake my head and add, "Not tired." Heading into the kitchen, I ignore the gazes searing into my back as Kade and Atlas both watch me walk away from them. I can't look at them right now, not without seeing Delia and her flirtatious looks and eye-fucking. I grit my teeth, clenching my hands into fists until my nails bite into my palms. I exhale a frustrated breath and open the fridge in search of the only thing that will ease the burning in my throat. I grab a blood bag, closing the door and sucking in a breath when I find Atlas standing there. *Shit, I am really not paying attention to things today.*

"You're coiled like a snake," he says in a low voice, stepping in front of me so my back hits the fridge.

"I'm fine," I shoot back, refusing to meet his gaze.

He plucks the blood bag from my hand, tossing it on the counter. He steps in closer, bracing one hand on the fridge while he slides the other up my arm. "I see you."

"Well, I'm standing right in front of you," I mutter.

His responding chuckle stirs the hair at my temple as he dips his face closer to me, snagging my chin and forcing my gaze to his. "You want to talk about why you're so pissed? We did well today."

"Yeah, I'm sure you loved having the gorgeous vampire practically drooling all over you." The words fall from my lips before I have the sense to clamp my jaw shut.

Atlas blinks at me, then his lips curl into a knowing grin as he slides his finger along my jaw. "Hmm, I understand now."

My eyes narrow. "You do not—"

"She made you jealous." His eyes twinkle with amusement.

Heat flares through me, flushing my cheeks and chest, and pools low in my stomach. I'm fully prepared to lie and deny, but I nod instead. No sense in hiding it now. I grab the front of Atlas's shirt, gripping it until my knuckles go white and tug him as close as I can. "I don't appreciate someone thinking they can have what's mine."

Lust fills his gaze, darkening the silver of his irises. "Fucking hell," he growls, and his mouth slams into mine, swallowing my groan as he presses himself flush against me. I push my fingers into his hair, gripping it tightly as he drops his hands to my hips and digs his fingers into my skin. We battle for control, and this time, I'm not giving in. I'm fucking claiming my sire, now and forever.

"*Mine*," I breathe against his lips, my heart slamming against the cage of my ribs.

"Yes," he agrees, sliding his hands around and cupping my ass before lifting me easily without breaking the kiss. I wrap my legs around him, tilting my head to deepen the kiss as our lips fight to dominate each other. I nip his bottom lip before pulling it into my mouth, and a growl rumbles through Atlas's chest as he carries me into the bedroom I've been sleeping in. He kicks the door shut behind us, and it rattles on its hinges from the force, making my pulse race, anticipation skating over my skin and sending a shiver along my spine. My breasts tingle, my nipples hardening into pebbles as they rub against the fabric of my bra, pressed firmly against Atlas's chest.

He makes no effort to be gentle as he throws me onto the bed, and I suck in a deep breath, greedily refilling my lungs after our fiery kiss from the kitchen. In the space of a heartbeat, Atlas climbs over me, grabbing the waistband of my pants and tugging them along with my panties to my ankles, then drops them onto the floor. He slides his hands up my legs, wrapping them around my thighs before spreading them open. The cool air makes my core tingle and Atlas's hunger-filled gaze has a heady mix of desire and need overtaking me in seconds.

Instead of going where I desperately need him right away, his eyes trail up the length of me, and he moves in, lifting my shirt up and over my head, tossing it blindly over his shoulder. He licks his lips, and in one swift movement, rips my bra clean off.

I gasp softly, my chest rising and falling quicker as he takes me in.

His eyes darken, lust and something much more complex filling them. He pulls his shirt off with one hand, adding it to the pile of clothes on the floor, and crawls over me, sealing his lips over mine. He devours me slowly, thoroughly, until my head is spinning and I'm reaching for him desperately. His mouth leaves mine, trailing along my jaw to my throat, where he lingers on my pulse, flicking his tongue against it. My breath catches, my heart racing at the sound of his beating faster. His lips are featherlight along my collarbones before moving lower, and the first pass of his tongue over my nipple has me arching my back, trying to push my breast into the warmth of his mouth. He gives me what I want, sucking me into his mouth and swirling his tongue around my nipple as he uses his other hand to work my other breast.

"Mmm," I moan, running my fingers through his soft hair and closing my eyes.

He presses his lower half into me, making my core throb as he teases me with his cock straining against his pants. I'm torn between wanting him to take his time with every inch of me and wanting him to take me with his cock right fucking now.

Atlas pulls back, releasing my nipple with a soft *pop*, and shoots me a dark smirk. His gaze paired with the way he keeps pressing against my throbbing core flips something primal in me. I move at vampiric speed, flipping us over and straddling him. His smirk morphs into a downright wicked grin as he rests his arms behind his head against the pillows and watches me curiously. He hisses out a breath when I move lower, grinding against his erection through his pants. I press my palms against his bare chest, holding him there and balancing myself as I circle my hips.

"Fuck, Calla," he grounds out.

"That's the idea," I murmur sweetly before sliding off him only to tug his pants off before straddling him again in seconds. His cock stands proud, long and thick, with moisture already beading at the head. My mouth waters, and I lick my lips, making him groan beneath me.

Atlas shakes his head, his gaze locked on mine. "We are the luckiest bastards on this godforsaken earth," he says in a voice thick with arousal.

"Fucking right we are." Kade's voice comes from the door, and I look over my shoulder to find him leaning in the doorway. I hadn't heard him open the door, though I'd been a little preoccupied by the vampire under me. Kade saunters into the room, leaving the door open and moving closer to the bed. "Mind if this lucky bastard joins?"

The corner of my mouth tugs up, and I arch a brow. "Since when do you ask for permission to do what you want?"

He shrugs, stopping at the foot of the bed, where he reaches for me, pulling my hair over my shoulder and dropping his mouth to my heated skin.

I open my mouth, but the words die on my lips, a strangled sound of surprise and pleasure falling from them when Atlas's thumb finds my clit. He strums it idly before circling it slowly, and moisture gathers between my legs.

Without a single word passing between any of us, Kade lifts my hips, angling me over Atlas's cock, and kisses my shoulder blade as I lower onto my sire's thick length. I moan deeply as he stretches me at this angle, my head falling back.

"Fuck, that's hot," Kade says, sliding his hands around me and cupping my breasts in his palms, squeezing and massaging them.

I pull my bottom lip between my teeth, my pussy pulsing around Atlas as I slowly seat myself on him completely. He growls when I circle my hips and hold him inside. I lift inch by delicious inch, but before I can lower myself onto him again, he thrusts his hips up, filling me again. I gasp, nearly collapsing onto his chest, but Kade holds me upright, pinching my nipples as Atlas works my clit harder and faster.

"Fuck," I cry out, breathing heavily and grinding my hips against him as his cock rubs along my inner walls, making my core throb harder.

Kade's touch disappears for a moment, and when he returns, the heat of his skin radiates against me. A quick look at him confirms what I thought; he's as naked as the rest of us now. He moves onto the bed and leans in to kiss the side of my neck, teasing me with his tongue and fangs as he sucks and nibbles playfully. What I really want is for him to—

His fangs sink into my throat, and I let out a deep moan, clenching around Atlas's cock.

"Yes," I breathe, whimpering softly.

Kade fists his cock in one hand and runs the other down my back, making my skin tingle as he gets to my ass. I jump a little when he cracks a hand against my ass cheek, and he pulls his fangs out as his finger circles my tight, puckered entrance.

Atlas makes a sound of barely there restraint when I start moving up and down his throbbing length. Each time he fills me, heat rushes through my veins, pushing me closer to release. And with his fingers working my clit and Kade teasing me from behind—

"I'm close," I pant, picking up my pace.

Kade pushes a finger into my ass, holding it there while Atlas slams up into me, circling my clit hard and fast.

"Yes, yes, yes," I chant, throwing my head back and closing my eyes as I ride Atlas, bouncing hard on his cock.

"Come for us, gorgeous," Kade orders in my ear, his own breathing heavy as he works his cock, pumping fast.

"Yes," I moan, the muscles in my thighs tightening as my pussy clenches around Atlas's cock, milking it as an orgasm tears through me. I cry out as pleasure overtakes me, and I more than willingly give myself over to it.

"Fuck," Atlas grunts, following me over the edge to his own release, fisting the sheets with his free hand, the other still moving over my clit.

Kade twists his finger in my ass, making my pussy tighten again, and Atlas growls in response. I lift off him, still vibrating with after-shocks as I collapse onto his chest, listening to the rapid beat of his heart, mixed with Kade's sounds of pleasure as he works himself to orgasm, shooting his release onto the sheets next to me. He flops down near the end of the bed, grinning at both of us, lust still glimmering in his gaze.

"Feel better?" Atlas asks, running his fingers up and down my arms.

I scowl, but it's weak. "So long as we're on the same page." I glance between him and Kade. "The four of you are as much mine as I am yours, and should anyone try to come between us, I will not hesitate to end them."

Kade's pupils dilate, and Atlas's fingers wrap around my arm. "Understood," the former vampire murmurs, looking all-too pleased about it.

You have all of me. Atlas's voice caresses my innermost thoughts, bringing heat to my cheeks.

I'm still not used to him being in my head like that, but it's some-thing I've come to enjoy, the connection to him is like nothing I've ever experienced.

The same can be said for each of the guys—and I will protect that at all costs.

SIXTEEN

GABRIEL

We're nearing the end of June; the days are longer, but it feels as though we're running out of time. Time to make this treaty work before Atlas's parents step in and obliterate all the work we've put into bringing this agreement between the vampires and hunters to fruition.

Marcel, along with Fallon, Jase, and several others we trust have been working tirelessly, connecting with more vampires across the states. Some meetings have gone better than others; regardless, with the number of vampires who have given us their support, the ones who outright refused don't come close to measuring up. It's clear our kind is ready for a change, and for a lot of them, they haven't seen one in centuries.

Now it's time to bring both sides together and put that change into action.

The meeting we are having today with the hunters is on neutral territory, a country club in Maryland where, ironically, a few hunters *and* vampires have memberships. Enough that we could shut the club down for the day to ensure no humans stumbled into something they shouldn't.

Atlas drives, as usual, while I sit next to him in the passenger seat. Lex and Kade are behind us, with Calla, Brighton, and Marcel in the very back. The girls chat about Calla's trip to Oregon and Brighton's new role advocating for the hunters who want to work with the vampires, while Marcel remains silent, listening and smiling here and there during their conversation. He has barely taken his eyes off Brighton, and as uncertain as the rest of us were about her initially, I'm pleased for Marcel. There's no question about how smitten he is with her, and the way her cheeks flush when she catches him looking at her makes me think it's not one-sided.

We arrive at the club shortly thereafter, climbing out of the Escalade and making our way inside. I thought we were making good time, but even early, we're not the first ones to arrive.

Fallon and Jase approach, nursing to-go cups of coffee by the smell of it. I'm a little surprised, albeit thankful, they didn't bring flasks of blood to 'spike' their drinks. I hug each of them before Calla greets them with a smile that I find myself unable to look away from. She's absolutely radiant, our girl, even when she's vibrating with nervous energy. I rest my hand against the small of her back, the tightness in my chest easing some when her pulse slows to a more normal pace.

Brighton walks over to the group of half a dozen hunters, greeting them by name before waving us over. We're all on high alert as we cross the room, and Brighton introduces each of the hunters to us and us to them.

I smile warmly, ensuring to make eye contact with each of them, though I'm very aware they're all carrying. They've made no effort to conceal their daggers.

"How many bloodsuckers are we expecting?" the short redhead who Brighton called Isla asks, her hazel eyes narrowed slightly. She can't be much older than Calla and Brighton.

Marcel steps up next to Brighton. "Nearly fifty," he answers. "Brighton let us know that about the same number of hunters should be in attendance."

Isla nods, and I notice Calla watching her with furrowed brows.

"Do you go to Georgetown?" Calla asks her. "You look so familiar."

She turns her attention to Calla and nods. "We've had a few classes together, though I'm pretty sure the last time we saw each other you were human."

Calla smiles. "Right. It's... I want to say it's good to see you again, but these are, uh, interesting circumstances."

"We're all here for the right reasons," Isla points out, the tension in her shoulders easing a little. "So, it's good to see you again too."

The rest of the hunters don't bother trying to make conversation, though neither do we.

Calla and I take a lap around the room, and she grits her teeth against a growl when her gaze turns to the doorway the exact moment Delia arrives, greeting Atlas with an all-too friendly embrace. I press my lips together, resting my hand at the small of her back to draw her attention away from the vampire. She grumbles under her breath as we keep walking.

Over the next half hour, the room fills with vampires and hunters—including James and Sera, who we met during Scott's final attempt at overthrowing us.

There's a clear divide straight down the middle of the room, but the people here want change. They want to work together. It's just a matter of hammering out the details to make it possible, which is why we're all here. Despite that, the tension is palpable—thick and uncomfortable, stuffy like being stuck on a long haul flight with a full plane of strangers.

Atlas steps onto the raised stage at the front of the room, and the chattering dies down in seconds. "Thank you, everyone, for coming today and for being part of something important to all of us. This is the beginning of a mutually beneficial relationship between our kinds and protecting humans and vampires alike."

No one responds. There are a lot of suspicious and untrusting glares being shot in both directions. We're off to a tense start; no one trusts each other, and both sides are waiting for the other to attack, it seems.

Brighton, Marcel, and Isla join Atlas on the stage, and Brighton says, "For this to work, the hunters must kill only those vampires who pose an obvious risk to humankind or to the secrecy of the paranormal. This effectively eliminates hunting any random vampire you may come across. Simply put, if they aren't bringing harm to a human, leave them be."

Marcel speaks next. "The vampires must feed only on willing humans—and not through glamour—or from blood bags. We will also assist the hunters in protecting the humans from vampires who choose to still attack for any reason, whether it be to feed against the human's will or for sport."

"If you're standing in this room," Atlas says, "you agree to abide by these rules. Leave now if you cannot do that." His voice is clear, firm. It leaves no room for debate or rebuttal.

Everyone stays. Some share glances filled with uncertainty, but no one leaves.

"Good," Atlas says a moment later. "We have selected three vampire representatives and three hunter representatives to assist with any concerns you have moving forward."

Isla clears her throat. "The hunters have chosen Brighton Ellis, Hudson Steele, and myself."

Atlas nods, and Marcel says, "The vampires have chosen Atlas York, Rachel Royce, and myself."

I've interacted with Rachel on several occasions over the decades; she's the type of person who gets along with everyone, which is the reason she was nominated. She's also a born vampire like Atlas, though she's younger than him by a long shot. With dark hair and clothing, she exudes class and maturity as she stands with a group of vampires from New York, where she lives as well, and offers a confident smile, fangs and all.

Both sides' representatives join the others on stage, and slowly, the divide between our kinds starts to close.

"We've prepared an agreement in writing," Marcel announces. "Both vampire and hunter representatives have reviewed it and are prepared to sign today. If anyone in attendance would like to review the agreement for themselves, we are happy to provide a copy. While only three people from each group will sign, this agreement belongs to everyone."

"Everyone?" a deep voice filled with venom barks. "That's a load of shit. 'Everyone' implies there aren't people opposed to your treaty."

The crowd parts, revealing the man who spoke up.

Calla sucks in a sharp breath. "What the fuck?" she breathes, and Brighton rushes to her side. "Is that—?"

"My uncle Jack," Brighton answers in a low voice, her face pale and her heartbeat erratic.

He's the spitting image of Scott Ellis, though perhaps a handful of years older. He holds the same malice in his gaze as he glares at us.

Atlas crosses the room with Kade and Lex flanking him. "You are not welcome if you're choosing to disrupt the peace we're building here."

"Peace?" he echoes bitterly and offers a harsh laugh. "With vampires?" Jack shakes his head, shoving his hand into his jacket and pulling out a dagger. "You're selling everyone here a fucking lie!"

Growls vibrate the walls and many of us look around to see how others are reacting. Several hunters have their daggers in their hands now, but they don't look as if they're about to wield them. Everyone is on high alert, tense and waiting.

"Jack, please," Brighton begs, stepping in between her uncle and Atlas.

Jack's gaze falls on his niece, and his upper lip curls in disgust. "You... What you're doing here, what you did to your father. You are a disgrace, you little bitch."

A few gasps filter through the room, and between one moment and the next, Marcel shoots past me in a blur, snarling as he lunges for Jack, driving his fist into the hunter's face.

Brighton screams as Jack bellows in pain, cupping his broken nose with one hand and swings his dagger with the other, catching Marcel in the side. Four other hunters push through the crowd with their daggers raised and move toward Jack. Vampires and hunters alike close in, shooting each other untrusting glares.

"Enough," Atlas commands, his voice ringing clear through the entire room.

Jack glances at the hunters on either side of him, blood gushing from his nose and staining the front of his shirt. He nods at them once, and I stiffen. It wasn't a nod of concession.

They turn away from Jack and lunge toward the crowd, grabbing for the first vampires they can get their hands on, swinging their dagger-wielding arms at any target close enough.

We're all moving at once; screams of anger and pain fill the room as vampires and hunters alike are torn between attacking and helping one another.

Lex and Kade take hold of Jack, dragging him out of the room, while Atlas and Calla stand back to back, their gazes sharp and their jaws set tight as they evaluate the scene. We don't want to attack, to feed into the violence, but we must protect ourselves and each other.

Fallon and Jase track down the hunters who stood with Jack and disarm them fairly quickly, not hesitating to use glamour to get them out of here.

Isla and Hudson dive into the fray, blocking a group of hunters from moving toward a group of vampires.

"Remember why we're here," Isla urges them, holding her hands up as if she believes she can calm the storm with gentle hand movements. "Don't let everything we've worked for be taken away by a man with a desire for power he's never tasted."

While they work to talk down the hunters, Marcel and Rachel move through the smaller groups of vampires.

"I shouldn't have snapped," Marcel admits. "To be fair, it had little to do with that jackass—no pun intended—being a hunter and all to do with how he spoke to Brighton."

Hudson glances over at Marcel, frowning briefly before turning back to the hunters. "We can still make this work," he says in a smooth voice. "We *need* to make this work. Everyone will be much safer once we do."

Ever so slowly, the tension releases from the room. Not all, but most of it. The representatives return to the stage, and Atlas steps forward.

"We knew this would not be easy. There will be bumps in the road even after the agreement is signed today. Don't let this bump destroy what we've all worked for and what we all want."

Many look to another, gauging reactions to his words, uncertainty filling the gazes of hunters and vampires alike.

"Sign the agreement!" someone shouts from the back of the room. "I'm ready for this nightmare to be over."

Atlas nods curtly. "We share your sentiment." He glances down the line of representatives, then turns his attention back to the crowd, his gaze lingering briefly on where Calla stands with her arm around Brighton, whose eyes are rimmed in red. "If there are no further objections, we will begin."

The room falls completely silent, save for the tune of nervous heartbeats and breathing. The seconds tick by, and Atlas waits a full minute before nodding again.

Isla steps forward next. "We were about to offer the opportunity to anyone here to read the agreement before any of us sign, so let's start there."

We pass along a tablet with the agreement, and a couple dozen people read it. The buzz of conversation fills the room once more as the representatives on the stage wait patiently for anyone who wants to read it to do so.

When the time comes, I pull the paper copy of the agreement out of a manila folder and step onto the stage while Lex and Kade carry a small table up for everyone to sign on. Setting the legal size paper down, I hand each vampire and hunter on stage a ballpoint pen before turning to Hudson, a built blond hunter with vibrant blue eyes. "Your dagger, please."

He hesitates for only a moment before pulling it from his light denim jacket and holding it out to me.

"Thank you." I set the dagger on the table for each representative to seal their signature with blood, binding the agreement completely.

I step off the stage and stand next to Calla, resting my hand against the small of her back hoping to calm her nerves. She shoots me a quick smile, but there's nothing real about it.

It only takes minutes for everyone to sign at the bottom of the paper. Atlas seals his signature first, plucking the dagger up and pricking his finger without hesitation.

Calla stiffens as her sire lets the blood drip from his finger onto the page before handing the dagger to Rachel to do the same. The process repeats until each representative has sealed their signature with their blood, and the agreement is complete.

I lean in and speak softly into Calla's ear. "It's done. Breathe, angel."

She nods robotically. "I didn't expect the blood to bother me."

I glance sideways at her and find her fangs fully extended. "It's okay," I murmur reassuringly. "This is overwhelming for all of us. We'll be out of here soon."

"Okay," is all she says, keeping her eyes trained on the stage.

"With that," Atlas announces in a deep voice, "the vampires and hunters have agreed to a treaty of peace. To working together to ensure the survival of both species. Anyone who tries to disrupt this peace will be dealt with according to the terms of the agreement. This meeting is officially over. We invite you to join us quarterly to check in and ensure things are still working, but until then, I'd like to thank you all once again for attending. This is the beginning of a brighter future for all of us."

I certainly wasn't expecting the room to erupt into cheers and applause, so even I'm slightly taken aback when it does. Calla's eyes widen, scanning the room as her heart beats faster, but slowly, her lips curl into a smile. Mine do the same, something akin to hope blossoming in my chest like it hasn't in a very long time.

We wait for the club to clear out before leaving. Marcel ends up catching a ride with another group of vampires, and Brighton leaves with Hudson after an extended goodbye hug with Calla.

"She likes them both," Calla says to me as the hunters' car drives away. "I don't have any details—I mean, she hasn't told me anything yet—but I could feel it."

I peer over at her, arching a brow. "Both... Ah. Hudson and Marcel." And Calla can sense Brighton's feelings on a deeper level since the witch linked them.

Calla nods, cringing briefly. "Because *that's* not complicated, right?"

"Brighton is a smart young woman," I say. "In the last couple of months, she has matured a great deal. I'm sure she'll figure it out, and she's very lucky to have a friend like you to confide in."

She cracks a smile. "Yeah. Thanks, Gabe."

The five of us climb into the Escalade, and Lex steals the front passenger seat, while I slide into the far back so Calla and Kade can sit in the middle seats. Within minutes on the road, Calla is asleep, breathing steadily. I smile, leaning forward and smoothing my hand over her hair while she sleeps. As much as I want to pull her into my arms, I leave her be so I don't disturb her rest.

When we pull into the driveway of the rental house, Kade gets out first, and I use his door to exit before walking around the car to open Calla's side. She stirs a little, and I unbuckle her, scooping her into my arms and carrying her into the house. Kade walks ahead of us, opening the door, while Lex and Atlas follow behind. Calla murmurs something indecipherable against my chest, and I hold her a little tighter.

"Shh," I whisper to her. "We're home now." I carry her into the bedroom, setting her gently on the bed before pulling off her shoes and covering her with the duvet. With a soft sigh, I kick off my own shoes and slide in next to her. Exhaustion like I haven't felt in a while clings to my muscles. Today was a win, there's no doubt about that, but the tension we've all felt has left everyone needing a long, uninterrupted sleep.

I rest my head against Calla's pillow and gently pull her to my chest, draping my arm over her waist and holding her to me. She makes a soft sound before rolling over to face me and resting her cheek over my heart. She inhales then exhales contentedly. My body relaxes for the first time in days, and before long, I drift off. The darkness pulls me under, and I'm grateful for it.

SEVENTEEN

CALLA

I wake up tangled in limbs. I pry my eyes open to the daylight streaming in the windows and find myself pressed up against Gabriel. A smile curls my lips, and I snuggle closer, closing my eyes again.

"Morning, angel," he says, his lips pressed against the side of my head.

"Mmm," I grumble back, keeping my face buried in his chest. "What time is it?"

"A little after ten," he answers, smoothing his hand over my hair. "You can go back to sleep, but I need to get up."

I exhale a heavy sigh and pull back a little to look him in the eyes. "No, the others are probably up, and we didn't really get to chat about yesterday when we got home."

Gabriel nods and slides his legs over the side of the bed, standing and offering me his hand. I scoot over to the side where he slept and entwine my fingers with his, letting him help me off the bed. We walk downstairs hand in hand and find the others sitting in the living room. Lex and Kade are on the couch watching some trashy reality show, while Atlas is sitting in the chair across the coffee table from them. He's typing rapidly on his phone, concentration etched into his face, but he glances up when we walk into the room.

"Morning," I say.

Kade grabs the TV remote and turns down the volume. "Welcome back to the land of the living," he says with a faint smirk.

I roll my eyes and ask, "Is there coffee?"

"There will be once you make it," Lex says, shooting me a wink.

I offer him a sweet smile and flip him off before walking into the kitchen and turning on the machine. Once the coffee is brewed, I pour myself and Gabriel cups and carry them back into the living room, holding a mug out to him. He murmurs a quick 'thank you', and we share the other chair, Gabriel perching on the armrest.

"We have something to announce," Kade says, glancing around the room.

I arch a brow, and my gaze flits toward Atlas, but he looks as confused as I feel. Evidently he has no idea what Kade is talking about either. I look up at Gabriel, who shrugs, then turn my gaze back to Kade. "Oh god. What did you guys do?" I ask dryly, taking a sip of my coffee. It fills my stomach with warmth, and I cradle the mug in my hands as if it's my most prized possession.

Kade and Lex exchange a subtle grin. "We're moving today."

I shake my head. "What are you talking about? We haven't been here that long."

"Sorry," Kade adds, "I should have clarified. We're going *home* today."

My chest tightens, and I'm acutely aware that the tension there isn't just my own but Atlas's as well. My pulse ticks faster, my gaze bouncing around the room at all the guys. "Are you saying... Do we have the house back?"

Lex nods. "We made a deal with the current tenants. They moved out yesterday. Marcel has a team cleaning everything right now, so we'll be able to go back in a few hours."

Tears prick my eyes, and I'm surprised at my reaction, considering at one point I felt that house was my own personal prison. As fancy as it was; I was still stuck there. But it quickly became a lot more and a place that I was sad to leave. I knew it killed the others as well, especially Atlas being the one who designed the entire thing.

Gabriel's hand rests against my shoulder, and he smiles at Kade and Lex. "Well done," he says. "I think we all needed good news like this."

I smile as well, looking toward my sire. There is still skepticism in his eyes, but even his lips curl into a faint grin. I can feel the excitement sparking from him, and when his eyes meet mine, there's recognition there; he knows I'm feeling what he's feeling.

"Well," Lex says, pulling our attention back to him, "let's get fucking packing and get the hell out of this dump."

"Okay," I say dryly. "This place is very nice."

He shrugs. "It's a dump compared to our home, Calla."

I roll my eyes but stay silent. I'm not gonna fight with him over this. Today is a good day. Today, we're going home.

Gabriel, Lex, and Kade disappear, likely to shove what few belongings we have here into a suitcase, leaving Atlas and I alone in the living room. I walk over to where he's still sitting near the fireplace, and he watches me, tipping his head back to hold my gaze as I get closer.

"What are you thinking about?" I murmur, stopping in front of the chair, my legs just brushing his.

He moves lightning-fast, gripping my hips and tugging me into his lap. "That I'm ready to go home," he says in a low voice, his fingers brushing the sliver of my stomach where my shirt lifted as I fell into the chair. "That I'm ready to take my girl home."

A grin tugs at my lips as warmth rises in my cheeks. "Yeah? I'm very much looking forward to getting our gym back." I can't help but think of the training sessions we've shared—there and other far less fancy places—and how they usually end with us tearing each other's clothes off.

His lips twitch, those brilliant silver eyes of his glimmering with amusement. "Hmm... I bet you are." He leans forward, resting his forehead against mine as his grip on my hips tightens. "I'm very much looking forward to teaching you many, many new things."

Heat flushes through my body, making my pulse race, and I lick the dryness from my lips as I meet his gaze. "It's a good thing we have forever."

Pulling up to the front of the house, the level of barely subdued excitement in the car has me pressing my lips together against a smile. The exterior is unchanged, of course, and suddenly it feels as if we never left. The glass and dark wood and pristine landscaping—the familiarity has me itching to get inside.

Atlas pulls the Escalade into the paved driveway, parking in front of the wood-paneled garage door.

"The tenants left the opener on the kitchen counter," Kade comments as Atlas kills the engine and pockets the keys.

We get out of the car and climb the cement steps to the front door, where Gabriel pulls a key out of his jacket pocket and unlocks the door. We file inside, having left our bags in the car to bring in once we've had a chance to see the place, and the door clicks shut behind us.

I immediately feel at home in the open-concept space. I've missed the floor-to-ceiling windows at the back of the house, the pool with its water glittering in the midday sunlight, even the purposely mismatched pieces of custom-made furniture surrounding the glass coffee table. It's still stacked with books, as if we never left.

Everything smells freshly cleaned, the faint scent of lemons lingering in the air, similar to the day the guys brought me here. I remember it as though it was yesterday when it was nearly four months ago.

A lot has happened in that relatively short amount of time, but I'm not sure I'd change any of it. Our story isn't the most common, but ordinary is boring.

We all wander around, reacquainting ourselves with the house. Lex drops into one of the olive green chairs in the living room, glancing around and sighing happily.

I cross the room into the kitchen, running my hand along one of the marble slab islands. Warmth fills my chest at the memory of Lex kissing me for the first time pressed against the island, and I chew my bottom lip, turning toward the dark wood cabinets and double oven. The dining room beside the kitchen snags my attention, and I smile at the vase of fresh white orchids.

"I asked Marcel to bring those," Kade says, stepping up beside me.

I turn toward him, smiling wider. "Thank you."

A faint smirk curls his lips. "I have to be honest, though. Right now, I want to shove that vase off the table and lay you on it."

I laugh softly as my cheeks flush. "Or we could just..." I trail off, taking the vase from the dining room table and setting it on the counter in the kitchen before returning to Kade's side.

"Now you've ruined the moment." His eyes drop to my mouth as he steps closer, moving in front of me.

"Yeah?" I murmur, leaning into him. "That's too bad. I guess I'll just have to go see what the others are—"

His lips are on mine before I can finish my sentence. I grab the front of his shirt, pulling him flush against me, and he grips my hips, digging his fingers into my skin. He devours me completely, making my head spin as he pushes his tongue into my mouth, grazing it along mine. Our hearts beat faster, threatening to break free of our rib cages, and I slide my hands up his chest and into his hair, gripping the ends tightly as I deepen the kiss. The throbbing between my legs intensifies as he presses his lower half into me, growling low in the back of his throat. He lifts me up, setting me on the edge of the table without breaking the kiss.

Our lips move together, perfectly in sync, and desire zips through my veins like electricity. I cling to him, needing him closer, and gasp against his lips when he reaches between us and presses his thumb against my clit.

"Kade," I breathe against his lips.

"I know," he murmurs, finally breaking the kiss. He grabs the waistband of my leggings and tugs them along with my panties down to my ankles in one go, and then my bare ass is on the table. My chest rises and falls quickly, and I don't have a moment to catch my breath before Kade slides his hands up my thighs, spreading them open and baring my center to him. His pupils dilate as he stares between my legs and lowers his mouth, pressing soft kisses to the inside of each of my thighs before licking the length of my slit.

I press my lips together, dropping my head back as I brace myself with my hands on the table behind me. I exhale a shallow breath, and Kade chuckles softly, swirling his tongue around my clit as he enters me with two fingers, massaging my inner walls as they flutter around his invading digits.

"Lift your hips," he instructs in a thick voice, and when I do, he sinks a third finger into me, curling them deep and hitting the spot that makes me writhe against the table in seconds. "Good girl," he purrs, picking up speed. He lowers his mouth back between my legs, and I cry out when he flicks his tongue against my clit then sucks it into his mouth. Kade times the thrusts of his fingers with the sucking of my clit perfectly. My breathing quickens and my thighs tremble, squeezing his head as my pussy clenches around his fingers, soaking them with my release as the sounds of my pleasure fill the room.

Lex appears over Kade's shoulder, tutting his tongue. "That didn't take long."

Kade pulls his fingers out of me as my body continues to pulse with the aftershocks of my orgasm and chuckles at Lex. "You're just jealous you didn't get her first."

"Nah, because now she's all warmed up for me." He shoots me a wink that makes my chest flush with heat as I slide off the table and retrieve my leggings. "Put those back on," he warns, "and I'll tear them clean off you."

I press my lips together, my eyes flicking between his. He's being completely serious. "We just got home," I point out. "Don't you think we should bring our stuff inside and get settled in?"

Lex cocks his head to the side. "If that's what you're thinking about right now, Kade didn't do a very good job."

"I beg to differ," Kade grumbles, snatching my leggings away. "Maybe we should tie you up, hmm?"

Parts of me like that suggestion way too much. "Maybe I should tie *you* up," I shoot back, very aware that I'm naked from the waist down, while they're both still fully dressed.

"You could try," he offers, closing the distance between us in the space of a heartbeat. "But I'm still older and stronger than you, as is Lex. I think we both know who would win." He smirks at the jump in my pulse. "Though that seems to be exactly what you want."

"Shall we see if the others would like to join?" Lex chimes in, then follows up with, "Never mind. Atlas is on the phone in his office."

Gabriel comes down the hallway and into the room then, glancing between each of us. The hunger in his gaze when it lands on me makes my mind up in an instant.

"Perfect timing, Gabe," Kade says with a mischievous grin. "We—"

I make a break for it while they're distracted, moving across the room in a second. I'm not fast enough, though. Gabriel catches me around the waist, hauling me against his chest.

"Angel," he purrs in my ear, sending a shiver straight through me and making my clit pulse.

"Couldn't let me have this one, huh?" I say, but the annoyance in my tone is half-hearted.

He chuckles softly and presses a kiss to my cheek. "I won't apologize, because it wouldn't be genuine, but I will make it up to you." He scoops me up and the room blurs around me as we move down the hall into the bedroom I stayed in when we were living here before.

Lex and Kade are a second behind us, kicking the door shut as Gabriel sets me on my feet, backing me up until I hit the end of the bed. He pulls my shirt off over my head, dropping it on the floor beside him before sliding his fingers under the straps of my bra, dragging them off my shoulders.

Stepping in closer, he dips his face and presses his lips against my collarbone as he reaches around and unclasps the hooks on my bra, pulling the straps the rest of the way off and adding the bra to the pile with my shirt.

"This is hardly fair," I grumble. "You're all still dressed."

"Hmm," Kade hums, prowling closer as his eyes roam over my exposed skin. "I don't recall ever claiming to be fair." He glances at Lex. "You?"

"Nope," he says, popping the 'p' and licking his lips.

Gabriel snags my attention again, pulling his shirt over his head and tossing it toward Lex. "Better?" he asks, grinning softly.

My eyes drop to his hard abs, to the indents on either side of his hips, and the patch of hair leading to the bulge in his pants. "I'm certainly not going to complain," I say with a grin.

"You tell us how you want to do this, angel."

My eyes widen slightly and my gaze flits to the others behind him. "Oh, um..." I hesitate. "I don't know."

He trails his fingers along my jaw and tips my head back so our eyes meet. "Tell us what your body wants."

"Or don't," Kade says, shooting a grin at me as he nudges Gabriel out of the way. "We'll find out soon enough." He pushes me onto the bed and traps my wrists above my head, sliding his other hand down my chest between my breasts. "Do you want Gabriel's cock in your pussy?" he asks in a low voice.

"Yes," I say, my breathing becoming shallow as his fingers inch closer to where he brought me to climax not ten minutes ago on the dining room table.

"And Lex? Where would you like him? Perhaps in that gorgeous ass of yours?" My pulse kicks up at the thought of taking Lex back there while my pussy is filled with Gabriel. Kade smirks at me. "I'm going to take that as a resounding 'fuck yes'." He shifts off of me, keeping my hands above my head.

Gabriel takes Kade's spot after removing his jeans and adding them to the growing pile of clothes on the floor. He crawls over me, pressing a soft kiss to my lips before his fingers find my clit, strumming it expertly as my breath catches in my throat. "Are you ready for me?" he asks gently, using one hand to pump his cock until moisture beads on the tip. I nod quickly, and he seals his lips over mine as he rolls his hips and slams into me, swallowing the desperate moan that rips from my throat. His thrusts are slow and steady to start as his mouth devours mine, and Kade reaches down to tease my breasts, rolling the nipples into hardened buds.

I've lost track of Lex until Gabriel rolls me onto my side, keeping his cock buried deep inside me and picking up the speed of his fingers on my clit. I feel Lex at my back and then he's squirting lube into his hand and working it on his cock. He drags the head up and down between my ass cheeks, applying pressure slowly, and despite the handful of other times we've done this, I can't help the stiffening of my muscles as he pushes into my ass, My pussy grips Gabriel's cock tighter and his lips move from mine to my jaw, feathering kisses along it. "Breathe, angel," he says calmly. "You need to relax. Let him in."

I pull in a slow, shaky breath before forcing my muscles to relax as Kade pinches my nipples and Lex grips my hips, pushing deeper into me.

"There you go," he says into my ear. "Good girl."

I exhale a short breath and turn my head to find Kade has added his pants to the pile of clothes on the floor and is stroking himself as he watches the other two filling me completely. Heat rushes through me in waves, and I lick my lips, wanting to feel Kade's cock inside me too.

His eyes meet mine and darken with lust as he moves closer, and I lean toward him, dragging my tongue along the head of his cock. He sucks in a breath, pushing his cock past my lips to the back of my throat. My heart hammers in my chest as Gabriel and Lex thrust in and out of me. I suck Kade's throbbing length, alternating my speed and pressure until he's biting his lip and throwing his head back with a grunt, his release spilling into my mouth. I swallow as much as I can, moaning loudly as I come hard and my pussy clenches around Gabriel's cock, milking it and pushing him closer to release. A few more quickened thrusts, and he climaxes as well, gripping the sheets on either side of me as his thigh muscles strain. He holds still inside of me, playing with my clit as his lips trail along my neck, kissing and sucking the sensitive skin there.

Lex continues to work his cock in my ass over and over, picking up speed until I feel as if I'm going to pass out. I squeeze my eyes shut as Kade pulls his cock out of my mouth, and Lex's groan fills the room. He bites down on my shoulder, his fangs breaking the skin as he pulls out of my ass and spills his release onto my back.

The room is filled with the heavy aroma of sex and my blood. We all collapse onto the bed, breathing unevenly for a few minutes.

Gabriel speaks first. "I'm going to run you a bath." He kisses my cheek and slides off the bed. The three of us admire his ass as he walks toward the bathroom, and I rake my fingers through my hair as my breath returns to a normal pace.

A few minutes later, the rest of us join Gabriel in the bathroom. It's filled with steam, warmth, and the relaxing scents of eucalyptus and mint. Kade helps me into the tub, and I sigh happily as I sink lower into the hot, bubbly water.

Lex grabs a fluffy loofah from the vanity drawer and walks over, kneeling in front of the tub. He dips his hand into the water, soaking the loofah, and starts working the soapy water into my shoulders. Kade settles in near the end of the tub and reaches under the water, running his hands along my feet before wrapping his fingers around one and starts massaging it.

I rest my head against the plush towel and close my eyes, allowing myself to simply enjoy this pure bliss.

Gabriel's hands start working the tension out of my shoulders, while Lex continues using the loofah on me, and Kade switches feet.

I could fall asleep like this. I'm on a cloud of pleasure and relaxation, and I never want to leave.

I'm in such a haze, I don't hear Atlas walk into the room.

"I'm in my office for an hour, and the four of you are already up to things." He chuckles, shaking his head. "I suppose I shouldn't be surprised."

I pry my eyes open and peer over at where he's leaning in the doorway, one ankle crossed over the other and his arms folded across his chest.

"Everything okay?" Kade asks, still massaging my foot.

Atlas's eyes stay locked on mine, and his silver gaze darkens as he drags his tongue over his bottom lip. "It will be." He stalks toward the tub, his bare feet padding soundlessly on the tile, and my heart hammers in my chest, my stomach dipping when my eyes drop to the very obvious bulge in his pants.

Kade sets my foot back into the water as Lex offers me his hand. My mouth goes dry, and I'm still stuck in Atlas's gaze as I take Lex's hand, allowing him to help me stand. Water sloshes around the tub and drips down me as the air hardens my nipples into tight buds. I press my lips together, heat flaring through me under the gaze of all of my men.

Atlas takes his time, his gaze devouring me from head to toe. My cheeks are burning by the time his eyes return to mine.

"Fucking hell, you look like you're about to fall to your knees in worship of her," Lex says.

Atlas's eyes darken as if he's genuinely considering it. "Are you done in there? Because I'm a patient man, but I don't think I can wait much longer."

I step out of the tub, letting go of Lex's hand and moving toward Atlas as I drip water on the floor. Licking the dryness from my lips, I stare up at him. "Hmm, you know, I think I might just go to bed." I fake a yawn and stretch a little, enjoying the way his eyes narrow. My stomach swirls with heat, desire and excitement mixing in a heady combination as I walk past him.

A deep growl sounds behind me a second before Atlas grabs the back of my neck, pulling me against his chest. I suck in a breath, the room spinning as he whirls me around, and his lips come crashing down on mine. He isn't giving me a chance to breathe, his mouth hard and demanding.

My head spins as I kiss him back fervently, thrusting my fingers through his hair and gripping it tightly as his hands slide down my sides to my hips and lift me. I wrap my legs around him, moaning into his mouth when his erection presses against the throbbing at my core. He moves so fast my hair is blown around my face, and between one moment and the next, Atlas throws me onto the bed, pinning my arms above my head with one hand. He hovers over me, breathing heavily, his dark gaze boring into mine as I fight to catch my breath. I tug on my wrists, but he isn't letting go.

He smirks darkly, pushing his knee between my legs as he lowers his face, skimming his nose along mine. "Is this what you had in mind?"

I purse my lips, my heart beating like the wings of a hummingbird in my chest. "Well, I was thinking more like passing out watching Netflix, but I suppose this will do."

His lips twitch, his grip on my wrists tightening. "Tell me what you want," he demands in a low voice that sends a shiver through me. His lips barely brush mine, and every inch of my body is aching for him.

I tilt my chin up, dragging my tongue along his bottom lip as I press my thighs together, trapping his leg between them. "I want you to make me come with your tongue inside me and then I want you to fuck me with your cock until I can't see straight." Without warning, I kiss him hard. "Is that what *you* had in mind?"

Before Atlas can respond, Kade walks into the room, chuckling as the others follow him, but my gaze remains locked on my sire. Gabriel and Lex slide onto the bed on either side of me and each take one of my wrists from Atlas's grip. He pulls back, standing momentarily, and I catch sight of Kade lingering near the end of the bed, licking his lips as his gaze wanders the length of my body on full display.

My eyes flick back to Atlas when he drops his pants onto the floor and my mouth goes dry at the sight of his cock, long and thick, and my pulse races as he moves closer. He grabs my ankles and tugs me down the mattress before bending my legs and spreading them wide.

Arousal floods through me as he sinks to his knees at the end of the bed and leans in. His breath tickles the inside of my thighs, and my breath catches at the first pass of his tongue over my clit. I want to reach for him, to push his face between my thighs until he takes me into his mouth, but Lex and Gabriel won't release my wrists.

Lex bends, lowering his lips to my ear. "Beg him."

My eyes pop wide as heat fills my cheeks, and I squeak, "What?"

"You heard me. Beg him to fuck you with his tongue."

I turn my gaze to the vampire between my legs as he slides his hands under my ass, lifting me toward him and kissing the delicate skin along my thigh. I swallow hard. "Atlas," I murmur, "please."

"Mmm..." His tongue swirls against my skin, making me squirm. "Please what?"

I hiss out a breath. "Please put your mouth on me. I need to feel your lips around my clit and your tongue deep inside me. *Please.*" Desperation creeps into my voice, and I'm only a little shocked that it heightens my arousal—especially when Atlas instantly obliges. He closes his lips around my clit, sucking it firmly and circling it with his tongue.

"Ahh," I moan, bucking my hips and tugging on my wrists.

Lex shifts on the bed, sliding his arm over my hips and trapping them against the mattress as he leans over me and sucks my breast into his mouth. Gabriel quickly takes the cue and does the same to my other breast, and I close my eyes, already writhing with pleasure as the three guys tease me with their mouths.

Atlas releases my clit, dragging his tongue along my slit, and chuckles softly. "You're so fucking wet for me. My cock will glide into you beautifully."

I close my eyes, throwing my head back against the pillows Gabriel moved to support me, and bite my bottom lip as Atlas pushes his tongue deep into my pussy. He drags it along my inner walls, teasing and massaging as my head spins and sounds of desperation and pleasure fall from my lips.

I'm barreling close to release in seconds, my body overwhelmed by the intense stimulation, and when Atlas's tongue moves faster and he slides his fingers over my clit, strumming it like the perfect instrument, I come undone with a loud moan, my thighs clenching around his head while my pussy walls pulse and squeeze.

Gabriel and Lex pull back, leaving my breasts warm and tingling, and when I try to stretch my legs out, Atlas grabs them, holding me open to him. My eyes drop to his cock, and I tug on my wrists once more.

"Let me go," I grumble at the vampires holding them. I meet Atlas's gaze. "I want to touch you."

Fire burns in his gaze, and he merely glances between the others, and they release me immediately.

Licking my lips, I sit up enough to reach for Atlas's cock, brushing my fingers over the bulbous head already glistening with moisture. I push my thumb through it, rubbing it into the sensitive skin there before pumping my fist along his shaft a few times as he grits his teeth, breathing shallowly. I catch Kade's eyes over Atlas's shoulder and can't help but smirk at the lust in his gaze as he watches me stroking my sire's cock.

Atlas growls deep in his throat, then shoves me back against the mattress. He leans over me, pressing his cock against my clit before dragging it along my slit, teasing my entrance.

"Yes," I breathe, completely focused on him now. "Please," I beg and spread my legs wider for him. The corner of his mouth kicks up as the hunger in his gaze threatens to swallow me whole.

He hovers over me again, stealing my mouth in a searing kiss, and slams his cock into my pussy until he's fully sheathed inside me. I cry out at the invasion, my pussy clenching around him and my pulse pounding so hard it's in my throat. Atlas rolls his hips, somehow pushing himself even deeper as his lips move against mine. His tongue darts out, teasing my lips, coaxing them to open before he pushes into my mouth. He slams his cock into me over and over, our bodies slapping together as our hearts beat rapidly and in sync.

I am completely overwhelmed by sensations and emotions as I close my eyes and give myself over to everything flooding through me at once. My thigh muscles clench, and I wrap my legs around Atlas, digging my heels into his ass to hold him deep inside me. Either Lex or

Gabriel reaches between us and circles my clit, shooting another burst of pleasure through me as my legs tremble. I break our kiss, gulping in a breath before exhaling a deep moan, hanging onto Atlas's shoulders as he pounds into me.

"Come for me," he growls. "Let go and give me everything." His words grip me, and everything in me tightens. His thrusts become harder, faster, all-consuming, and I can't hold on any longer. My fingernails dig into his skin as I lift my hips, meeting every thrust, and the sounds of our labored breathing and arousal fill the room. Between one thrust and the next, Atlas wraps his fingers around my throat and squeezes firmly. His cock hits a particularly sensitive spot deep inside me over and over, each time his grip on my throat tightening, until my head is spinning.

Everything in me tightens, and I make a strangled sound of pure ecstasy as my orgasm slams into me with the weight of a freight train. My pussy clenches around Atlas's cock, soaking it with my release, and he doesn't stop slamming into me. He fucks me hard and fast, throwing his head back with a loud grunt as he climaxes, spilling into me as the walls of my pussy throb around him.

I'm catching my breath as he pulls out of me, making me shiver with aftershocks. My skin is tingling, and I am completely spent, ready to pass the fuck out.

Gabriel and Lex both lean toward me, kissing each of my cheeks, while Kade grins at me from the chair close to the bed.

Atlas snags my chin, turning my attention back to him. He kisses me so tenderly it steals the breath from my lungs, then leans back and smiles at me, murmuring, "Welcome home."

EIGHTEEN

Over the next week, we get settled back into the house and a somewhat normal routine. I even return to school, taking summer classes to catch up. It's nice having something to occupy my time that has nothing to do with vampires or hunters or treaties or anything supernatural. Something that helps me get closer to the future I've always wanted to build for myself, and being able to pursue that when I truly didn't think it was going to be possible has made the reality of living forever a little more bearable.

I'm bouncing with excitement as I quickly finish half a glass of microwaved blood and then head for the garage. Even that, drinking blood to survive, has started to feel somewhat normal.

"Where are you off to with such an obnoxious grin?" Lex says, stepping into my path.

"I have brunch with Brighton and then I'm heading to class."

"Look at you being all normal." He shoots me a wink and quickly presses a kiss to my cheek. "Have fun."

I smile at him before walking into the garage and grabbing the set of keys to the black BMW. It's the least fancy of the vehicles in here, which makes me feel a bit more comfortable about driving it.

It takes me a few loops around the block to find parking, but I'm only a couple minutes late by the time I step inside the café.

Brighton waves at me from a table near the back, and I make my way over. She gets up as I approach, and we hug before sitting down. I glance around the café before I settle my gaze on her. She smiles, and I return it. A few seconds pass before she exhales a laugh. "This feels kind of weird, doesn't it?"

"Doing something normal? Yeah."

"It's good, though," she says.

I nod. "Right. So how are things?"

"They're good. I'm back at my apartment now and my dad seems to be settling into his new life in Chicago really well. There aren't too many hunters who are upset with his abrupt decision to retire early."

"That's good," I tell her, "and how are *you* doing?"

"Good. You know, just trying to focus back on school like I know you're doing, which is awesome. I've been meeting with the hunters to keep tabs on things but I'm not actively hunting, which, thank god, because I'm pretty lousy at it."

My lips curl into a faint grin. "And have you been in touch with Marcel at all?"

She gives me a knowing look. "Very subtle, Cal."

"What? I'm curious. You're telling me nothing happened in the time that you were with him? I'm not blind. It was pretty obvious. There's something going on between you two."

She sighs, thrusting her fingers through her hair. "I don't even know. We've talked a bit since I moved back to my apartment but it's been mostly formal stuff about the treaty and working together."

"Did something happen when you guys were staying together?"

She presses her lips together, a soft pink blush filling her cheeks. "We kissed once."

"So the truth comes out," I tease.

She buries her face in her hands and groans. "I don't know what to do. I didn't think that... I mean..." She stumbles over her words, and I press my lips together against a smile.

"Liking him," I say, "there's nothing wrong with it, Bri."

"I know, but how would it look if a representative for the hunters started something with a vampire?"

I arch a brow at her. "In theory, it should make the treaty stronger. Showing just how well both sides can work together."

"Yeah, I don't know if they'd see it that way. At least, some of them."

"Okay. What do *you* want?" I ask.

"I don't entirely know," she says in a quieter voice. "There's also this other guy..."

"Hudson?" I offer.

Brighton nods. "I've known him forever, and he's been there for me since my dad went away, differently than Marcel has. Hudson's been a hunter—been part of that world his entire life, so he just gets it on a different level. His parents were also hunters—apparently it ran in his family." She sighs. "I don't know, it's—"

"Complicated?"

She frowns. "That feels like a gross simplification, but yeah."

"You'll figure it out." I reach across the table and squeeze her hands.

"And you know I'm here for you, whatever you need, no matter what."

"Yeah, thanks. Right back at you." She smiles as the waitress brings over a French press filled with coffee and a couple mugs along with a dish of cream.

"Thank you," we both say before she walks away.

"What's new with you?" Brighton asks, pouring us each a mug full of coffee. The rich aroma hits my senses, and I inhale deeply, enjoying the way it makes me feel all warm and fuzzy like nothing else. I may be the only vampire to need blood *and* coffee to survive.

I take a small sip, cradling the mug in my hands before answering Brighton. "I have a lot of schoolwork to catch up on. And obviously this treaty isn't a one and done situation, so we'll be working on that for the foreseeable future. I'd also love to plan a trip somewhere warm for Christmas. I know it's still almost six months away, but—" My voice cuts off when someone pulls a chair up to our table and sits down. In an instant, my chest tightens as I turn toward the newcomer, and my blood runs cold when my eyes meet those of Lenora York.

My gaze flicks toward Brighton, and I pray my eyes convey the danger of the woman sitting at our table. She could slaughter every single person in the café in a matter of seconds and not think twice about it, besides if she got blood on her deep purple pantsuit.

Brighton dips her chin in a subtle nod, and a sliver of relief fills my chest. She knows she needs to leave. But before she can get up, Lenora grabs her wrist and snaps the bone. My eyes pop wide as Brighton screams, her face going white as a sheet, and her eyes fill with a mix of pain and disbelief. Everyone in the café looks over, and my heart pounds in my chest, my teeth gritted as my own broken wrist heals.

Lenora either doesn't notice or doesn't care that we're connected. She turns to me, her expression calm, almost bored, and says, "You are going to change my son's mind about this little arrangement you have created with the hunters." She offers a small smile to Brighton, who looks seconds away from passing out as she cradles her broken wrist to her chest, silent tears rolling down her cheeks. "Or your human friend will pay the price with a very painful, very drawn out death."

Fury flares to life in my chest, sending my pulse racing as I glare at the vampire who forced me to become one. "Go to hell," I snap at her.

Lenora smiles and reaches across the table, quick as a snake, gripping my chin in an unforgiving hold and digging her nails into my skin. "Stupid girl," she snarls. "Get up and follow me out of this disgusting place. Bring the human with you."

Horror fills me as Lenora's glamour settles into my consciousness and my body moves on its own. I try to resist it, but the weight of her glamour is far too heavy. Confusion floods through me as I reach for Brighton, sliding my hand along her back and guiding her toward the door. Halfway there, realization hits me like a ton of bricks in the gut. Lenora must be able to glamour me because Atlas is part of her bloodline, which gives her the same power over me that her son has.

Fuck. This isn't good.

The three of us walk toward the exit as the other patrons stare at us with varying looks of concern, confusion, and even annoyance for disturbing them. A heavy pit fills my stomach as fear clamps down on my chest, and I continue moving against my will, dragging Brighton into the depths of hell with me.

My fist collides with the punching bag hanging from the ceiling, the force rattling the heavy iron chains. Sweat rolls down my bare back and drips from the ends of my hair. I shove it out of my face and hit the bag once more, reveling in the discomfort that flares across my knuckles. My heart pounds in my chest as I pull back to hit the bag another time when nausea fills my stomach, and I grit my teeth.

Something is wrong.

Seconds later, Lex's boots pound against the wood as he flies up the stairs, his brows drawn together and a frown etched into his face as he bursts into the gym.

I swallow hard, forcing down the bile in my throat. "You felt that too?"

He nods grimly.

In minutes, we're all standing in the living room. I'm dialing Calla's number, while Gabriel tries to get a hold of Marcel. Lex tries Brighton's phone, but it goes straight to voicemail.

"What the fuck could've happened?" Kade barks at no one in particular as he stalks back and forth across the living room, his nostrils flaring. "We *just* signed that treaty..." He shakes his head and stops pacing, gripping the back of the couch until his knuckles go white. "It could be hunter retaliation."

"I think we need to take a minute and consider all possibilities,"

Gabriel says in a level voice, though the concern in his eyes is clear.

I nod stiffly, shoving my fingers through my hair, exhaling a heavy breath. "We shouldn't have let her go."

"If we tried to keep her locked up in here forever, do you really think that would slide?" Lex offers.

I take several seconds, my mind racing with all the possibilities of what could happen and what we should do. There's a pit in my stomach—I think Lex feels it too—telling me we know what most likely happened to Calla. He meets my gaze, frowning briefly.

"Care to loop the rest of us in?" Kade asks, glancing between us.

"I think Simon and Lenora are behind whatever this is. They were adamant about the treaty not moving forward and made it very clear that making it happen would have consequences."

Gabriel scratches along his jaw. "We need to be absolutely sure before we act on any suspicions." He pulls out his phone. "Give me a few minutes to make some calls, touch base with the representatives for both sides so we can rule out hunter involvement."

"Fine," I mutter.

While Gabriel does that, I disappear into my room and take the quickest shower of my existence, listening to each brief call he makes, being assured by the representatives for the hunters that they had nothing to do with whatever has happened to Calla and Brighton. My stomach twists painfully, dread coiling tight and making me feel so fucking nauseous I nearly vomit in the shower.

Guilt weighs heavily on my shoulders. Whatever happens to Calla is on me. I should have known better than to let her go out alone. But she wouldn't have stayed here, even if we'd asked, and to use glamour on her now... it doesn't feel right.

After scrubbing a towel over my hair to dry it, I get dressed and return to the living room. "We need to contact every vampire we know who is firmly on our side and in an agreement of working with the hunters."

"Perhaps we should also ask the hunters for help," Gabriel suggests. "One of their own has been taken. This is exactly the situation the treaty is supposed to protect against."

Lex and Kade nod in agreement, and I finally do as well.

We all get on our phones and start making calls. Gabriel starts with Marcel, whose anger echoes through the phone clear as day. There's certainly no mistaking his feelings for Brighton now. He offers to get in touch with the hunter representatives, Hudson and Isla, assuring us he'd be ready to dive into action as soon as we make the call.

Lex gets a hold of Rachel, while Kade reaches out to Delia. I stand against the wall, watching them make calls and gather our allies. I can't move. My heart stutters in my chest, my brow dotted with sweat.

If anything happens to Calla—if we lose her...

I close my eyes, hearing the tail end of Gabriel's conversation with Fallon and Jase, who immediately agree to come and back us up.

Over the next twenty minutes, the guys make more calls, send texts, and get in touch with anyone and everyone who can help.

Gabriel hangs up from talking to Marcel for the second time. "The hunters have agreed to help. They'll send in as many as we need."

"Good," I say. "And the vampires?"

Lex takes a moment to meet my gaze. "Some of them are a little reserved. They don't necessarily want to go up against your parents."

My jaw clenches. "I can't blame them for that," I say in a tight voice. As angry as the news makes me, I can't expect any vampire to risk their lives for one I sired. She's *my* responsibility. And if it weren't for my psychotic parents who took it upon themselves to kidnap her and Brighton, we wouldn't be in this fucked up mess.

"We're one hundred percent sure this is Simon and Lenora?" Kade checks.

The pit in my stomach is confirmation enough. "It's them," I say in a flat voice.

He nods. "Marcel is on his way with several groups of vampires, but it's going to take them some time."

"I'm not waiting," I growl.

"We figured as much," Lex says.

Kade stands, slamming his hands together. "I don't know about you guys, but I am so ready to spill some ancient vampire blood."

Gabriel's lips are set in a thin line. "We may need a more concrete plan than that, Kade."

As much as I agree with him, there isn't time. The longer we stand here doing nothing, the longer Calla is trapped in the presence of my psychotic mother who is hellbent on teaching me a lesson for defying her demands.

"If we get there before any of the others, I say we bust down the door and kill everyone in sight," Lex offers grimly.

The vicious monster inside me rattles its cage, excited by that. "Simon and Lenora are to be left for me," I say in a low voice.

"And how are we going to kill born vampires that are centuries older than all of us?" Kade asks, the shadows of darkness creeping over his features and his jaw set tight. He's thinking about the violence we'll be forced to tap into as much as I am.

"You remember what it felt like to go after the hunters who killed your sister," I comment in a level voice and don't wait for him to respond; it isn't a question. "Simon and Lenora won't expect us to take them on, to crack ourselves open and let our demons free to hunt and kill anything in the path to our girl. I am prepared, and I believe you all are as well, to let go of any shred of humanity we cling to most days, and embrace the brutal, unforgiving beasts that live inside each of us."

The others nod firmly, and without another word, we walk into the garage, heading toward the Escalade. Before I can get behind the wheel, Gabriel plucks the keys from my hand and gives me a stern look. I haven't felt this on edge in a very long time, and the others know it, so I don't fight them. I get into the passenger seat and pull out my phone to keep in constant contact with Marcel as we head for New York City. He's already there alongside several groups of vampires and at least a dozen hunters, with more on the way.

Gabriel grips the wheel hard as we tear out of the garage and up the incline of our driveway, the tires squealing before they grip the road.

Kade whistles under his breath. "Let's go get our girl back."

TWENTY

CALLA

In the back of a black town car, we speed down the streets of Washington with Lenora sitting in the seat across from us. She stares out the window with an indecipherable expression, as if we're not even here.

Brighton's pulse is erratic and her breathing is shallow. I want to reassure her that everything's going to be okay, but I'm struggling to keep myself in check. *I don't know* if everything *is* going to be okay.

"You need to drink my blood," I say to her in a gentle tone as she cradles her broken wrist to her chest.

"What?" she squeaks. "No, I can't... That's—"

"Brighton." My voice is firm. "I don't want to force you to do anything, but you need this to heal. Please don't make me glamour you." The thought of using mind control on her makes me sick, but I'm not going to let her sit here in pain.

Her bottom lip trembles as she stares at me with tears in her eyes. Finally, she nods.

Lenora makes no move to stop me, so I take a deep breath and let my fangs extend to their full length before biting into my palm. I wince at the second of sharp pain, then lift my hand to Brighton's lips. She grimaces, taking a deep breath before opening her mouth. I tip her head back and pour my blood down her throat. She swallows, making a quiet sound of protest and squeezing her eyes shut. Slowly, she lets her wrist rest in her lap.

"Better?" I ask, examining it.

"Yeah," she whispers hoarsely, her complexion slightly more normal than it was a few minutes ago. "Thanks."

My chest tightens as the guilt bears down on my shoulders. "Please don't thank me. You're in this mess because of me, and I... I can't tell you how incredibly sorry I am."

She sniffles. "Let's just get through whatever the fuck this is and then maybe we can call it even and start rebuilding our friendship." She tries desperately to lighten the mood. "I'm thinking you bringing me on that sunny vacation this Christmas should do the trick."

I laugh, but it comes out uneven and sounds forced. "Deal."

Ten minutes later, we pull into an airstrip, and the driver parks the car in front of a private plane. He gets out and opens the door on Lenora's side. She gets out, and I grab Brighton's hand.

"I'm sorry," I say in a voice thick with tears.

She nods. "I'm sorry too." Her eyes are glassy as she fights to hold back her own tears. "She's going to kill us, isn't she?"

I shake my head. "We're no good to her dead. Just follow my lead," I say, though I have no idea what I'm doing at this point. *Whatever it takes to stay alive*, a stubborn voice at the back of my head says, and I cling to it.

The driver opens our door, and I squeeze Brighton's hand before getting out. She follows, and we walk toward the plane, climbing the stairs.

Lenora takes a seat near the middle, crossing one leg over the other, flippant as always. "You may as well get comfortable, girls. Nothing is going to happen for now."

Brighton I sit near the back of the plane on a couch. She has her hands folded in her lap as her knee bounces anxiously. We take off a few minutes later, and a stewardess comes by, offering drinks and snacks. I blink at her, flicking a glance toward Lenora before looking back at the human, who evidently doesn't know we're here against our will or has been glamoured not to care. I turn to Brighton. "Do you want anything?"

"Besides getting the hell off this plane? Not really."

I nod in agreement but order us each a glass of bourbon. "It'll help with the nerves," I whisper to Brighton, and she nods, staring forward blankly.

The flight passes uneventfully, besides the growing pit in my stomach and the tension in my chest. I have a feeling Atlas already knows something has happened to me, but that doesn't mean he'll make it in time to stop whatever his mother is planning.

After we land and get into another town car, I'm mildly surprised when we pull up out front of the York estate. It seems too obvious, like this is the first place the guys are going to check. I can't help but think that's Lenora's arrogance at play… Or maybe she *wants* them to come, to think they can rescue us, only for her to rip my heart out in front of them. My stomach plummets at the thought, and I shove it away. Crafting scenarios and trying to figure out Lenora's angle won't help us out of here.

The panic on Brighton's face as we walk into the entryway makes my jaw clench. I want to protect her, to put her behind me and block her from anything bad, but even as a vampire, I have little power here. Not against ancient born vampires like Lenora and Simon.

The latter vampire sweeps into the room with a pleasant smile on his face that twists the knots in my stomach tighter. "Miss Montgomery, lovely to see you again."

I blink at him, clenching my hands into fists at my sides so he can't see the way they shake. "I don't think it is. Whatever you're planning, I won't have any part in it."

Lenora sighs, clearly irritated with my unwillingness to blindly follow them. Much like her son was when we met, she isn't used to or fond of people refusing her.

"That is too bad," Simon says with a frown. His eyes move to Brighton, and her lips part in a silent gasp. He narrows his eyes at her before his lips twist into a subtle smile. "You were right, my love," he says to Lenora. "They are joined."

"Not for long. Is Terrence here?"

Simon nods. "Waiting in the parlor."

"Excellent. Ladies," she says to us, "let's not keep him waiting."

My snarky remark dies on my tongue when a faint whimper escapes Brighton's lips. "It's okay," I tell her. "Take a deep breath." She swallows hard, and I grab her hand as we follow Lenora into the parlor, where a guy around our age with blond hair tied into a knot at the base of his neck sits near the fireplace.

He stands when we walk in the room, smiling warmly at Lenora, and I know we're screwed. Lenora greets him with a kiss on each cheek, before turning to us. "Terrence here is a witch. He's going to take care of the little blood oath the two of you ignorantly created."

"No," I say instantly, tugging Brighton back.

Lenora chuckles humorlessly. "My dear, that wasn't an offer or a suggestion. Sit down and keep your mouth shut."

I'm not sure what kind of magic this guy practices, but the process for undoing the blood oath is the most painful thing I've ever experienced. It feels as if he's ripping a part of my soul out of my body. My skin is on fire, my fangs slice through my gums, and I pant as sweat dots my brow.

Brighton's reaction is similar. She cries, tears and sweat rolling down her face, and goes so pale, I'm worried she's going to pass out.

I grip her hand tightly, and we cling to each other until the pain finally ebbs away, and Brighton slumps back against the couch, wheezing.

Terrence leaves as soon as the link is broken.

"Hmm," Lenora says, lowering herself onto the couch across from us and folding her hands in her lap. "That looked unpleasant."

"Fuck you," I snarl at her before turning my attention to Brighton, wiping the tears from her cheeks as her eyelids flutter.

"There is no need for crudeness, Calla. I was simply expressing concern over your wellbeing. You're not looking so good, my dear. Perhaps you should feed?"

"I'm fine," I say through my teeth.

Lenora clicks her tongue, stealing my attention, and the minute our eyes lock, panic fills me like ice in my veins. "You need to feed." she says, and my entire body goes rigid as the power in her glamour steals over me.

My eyes widen, and I fight to break her hold on me, but it's useless. "Don't," I force out. "Don't do this."

She cocks her head to the side, her lips twisting into a cruel smile. "There's a perfectly good human right there, Calla. You need to feed," she repeats the words, and they settle into my consciousness.

I need to feed.

My entire body trembles as I slowly turn back to where Brighton is nearly passed out on the couch, her head tipped back against the cushions and her throat exposed. I swallow hard, trying with everything I have to fight, but I'm not strong enough to resist Lenora's glamour. I lean in, opening my mouth wide, and sink my fangs into Brighton's throat. Her blood explodes on my tastebuds, and I swallow mouthfuls, filling my stomach with warmth and my veins with energy. I squeeze my eyes shut, my heart pounding against my rib cage, and terror grips me as the sound of Brighton's heartbeat slows to a dangerous pace. I'm still feeding, drinking more than I should.

If I can't stop myself soon, I'm going to kill my best friend.

But I can't stop. I drink deeper, swallowing more and more of her blood.

"That's enough, Calla."

I pull away as if I've been burned, scrambling off the couch and hitting my tailbone hard on the floor as Brighton's blood spills down my chin, and I stare at her in horror. She's barely alive, and I... I did that to her. I wipe the back of my hand over my mouth as hot tears spring to my eyes and swallow down the bile rising in my throat.

"See, don't you feel much better now?" Lenora taunts.

My head turns slowly toward her, and I bare my fangs as I snarl, "I'm going to kill you."

She sighs. "I don't think so. Besides, think of all the fun we could have if you just opened your mind a bit and realized that our way of living is what you truly desire."

"You are fucking psychotic." I get to my feet, and she stands, folding her hands behind her back.

"I do hope you will change your mind soon," she says before leaving the room.

Moments after Lenora is gone, four vampires storm the room, grabbing both Brighton and me, and drag us back into the main entryway. As hard as I fight, these vampires are clearly older than I am. Brighton is no longer conscious, and I scream when they pull us in different directions, but it doesn't do any good.

In less than a minute, I'm shoved into a room with the door shut and locked. I immediately slam my fists against it until they're red and the skin is raw. My heart pounds against my chest as my mind whirls with all the possibilities of what's happening on the other side of the door. Finally, I turn around and take in the space I'm locked in. It's a simple bedroom but there are no windows. The only thing in the room is a bed and a lamp sitting next to it on a small dresser. Across the room is a small bathroom. I step inside and tap my fingernail against the mirror. It's not glass, which means I can't smash it to use as a weapon.

I stalk back into the bedroom and drop onto the end of the bed, pushing my hearing out to try to pick up on anything, but I'm met with nothing but deafening silence.

I lose track of time as the ringing in my ears becomes almost unbearable. It could be hours, it could be days.

I slip in and out of restless sleep, staring at the ceiling. My head turns toward the door every time I think I hear a bit of sound.

At some point, the door flies open, and I immediately get to my feet, standing defensively.

Simon stands in the doorway, giving me a once-over and frowning briefly.

"What the fu—" My voice cuts off when I hear Brighton scream, and I take off, shoving past Simon and into the hallway. I follow the sounds of Brighton's agony-filled whimpers. My hand flies to my mouth as I gasp in horror at the scene I stumble onto. Brighton is being held up by chains attached to the ceiling in a room I haven't been in before. It looks like a ballroom, with ornate chandeliers hanging from the ceiling and shiny marble floors, which are now spattered with Brighton's blood.

My fangs extend instinctively, and I barrel toward the vampires closest to Brighton. Lenora snaps her fingers, and they move away from her. I stop short, whipping my head toward the ancient vampire. "What the fuck are you doing? How is this going to help anything? If this is your idea of trying to convince me to—"

"I don't much care. I'm growing very impatient with your childish behavior, Calla. You know nothing of this world, and frankly, I don't have the time to teach you. Go ahead, heal your friend."

Without hesitation, I approach Brighton, and she lifts her chin. Recognition fills her eyes, and then the tears come.

"Hey, it's okay. You're okay," I whisper over and over. I hold her gaze and focus on making my will hers. "You don't need to be afraid," I say, and the weight of my glamour settles over her shoulders. "Don't be scared. Everything's going to be okay." My voice shakes a little as I speak, and I bite the same spot on my palm as I did in the car, holding it to her lips and healing her. The gashes on her face and chest stitch themselves shut as my blood works through her system, while the dark circles under her eyes fade and her breathing evens out.

"C-Calla, w-what's happening?" she asks in a weak voice.

"Don't worry," I say, struggling to hold my glamour on her through the tears in my own eyes. "I'm going to fix this," I promise her.

One of the other vampires pulls me away, shoving me toward Lenora.

"Thank you," she says mildly.

I shake my head in confusion. "I don't—" Before I can get the words out, Brighton screams again. Looking back, I find the vampires sinking their fangs into her wrists. One of them grips her throat, cutting off her air as she struggles against them, pulling on the chains. I immediately move forward, but Lenora grabs my wrist holding me back, her grip unbreakable. My head whips around, and I stare at her incredulously. "What the hell are you doing?" I demand, my voice trembling with sheer panic.

"Don't you see, Calla? This is what happens when you try to cross me." She backhands me so hard I collapse onto the floor, blood filling my mouth. I spit it out as dizziness floods through me and force myself to my feet. I'm not going to let her hurt Brighton any more.

I advance in a blur of movement, throwing my fist out and catching her in the jaw, but it barely fazes her. A look of annoyance crosses her sharp features, and I duck just in time to avoid her fist coming toward my face. She disappears from in front of me, and then her foot slams into my back, knocking me across the room. I collide with the wall and grunt as pain flares up the side of my body. If I was still human, that move likely would have shattered the bones in that half of my body. I push the hair away from my face and steady my stance once more, storming toward her with my teeth bared, but the sound of Brighton's whimper catches me off guard, and I turn toward her for a moment too long.

Lenora slams into me, digging her nails deep and slashing them across my throat. I gasp as white-hot pain slices through me, and my blood spills over her fingers. She slams my head back against the floor, cracking the marble, and my vision blurs, darkening around the edges. Lenora offers a disappointed frown before standing. She walks over to Brighton, and I struggle, trying to get up and stop her, but all the strength in my body is gone.

I can't move.

All I can do is watch as Lenora grabs the back of Brighton's head, yanking it to the side, and sinks her fangs into her throat.

TWENTY-ONE

ATLAS

"Do you really think they took them to the estate?" Lex asks from the backseat.

"Yes," I say in a flat voice. "My parents aren't concerned about us finding them. In fact, I'm sure that's exactly what they want." To use Calla to force my hand to do their bidding, because it's always been like that. They've always had me under their thumb, for as long as I can remember. But that ends today. I am fully prepared to do whatever it takes to get Calla back and ensure they're never able to hurt her again. To hurt *us* again.

I can't be sure when Calla and Brighton were taken. They'd gone for brunch midday, but we weren't expecting Calla home for hours after that, considering she was going to school. It was supposed to be her first class.

All that to say, they're already hours ahead of us. We would have taken a plane, but flying commercial would have taken twice as long, and the private airstrip we've used in the past was having staffing shortages. They couldn't get us on a plane until tomorrow, so driving the four and a half hours was our best option.

Calla is still alive. I'd feel it in my chest if she wasn't. But that doesn't mean she isn't suffering at the hands of the monsters who raised me, and that feels like a white ash dagger to my heart, knowing that, for the next three hours, there's absolutely nothing I can do about it.

"Do you want to send Marcel in before we get there?" Kade asks. "He says he's ready whenever you want to give the order."

I look over to Gabriel, who glances at me briefly before returning his attention to the road. "I don't know," I ground out. "As much as I want our guys in there as soon as possible, the thought of sending them in without us being there... If something goes wrong..."

"I'll tell them to wait."

I clench my hands into fists, my fingernails digging into the flesh of my palm and slicing it open.

"Take a breath, Atlas," Gabriel says calmly from next to me.

I take his direction, inhaling through my nose and exhaling through my mouth several times, but it does nothing to ease the tension in my muscles or the dread that's making a home in the pit of my stomach.

We make it into the city in just under four hours thanks to Gabriel's impressive driving. He ignored the speed limit the entire way, but when you have glamour to count on in case of getting pulled over, there's a little more room for bending the rules.

"I'm sharing our location with Marcel," Lex says, "so we're all heading toward the estate at the same time."

"Good." I stare out the windshield as my pulse ticks faster the closer we get. "When we get in there, show no mercy," I say. "If anyone tries to hurt any of us or get in our way, kill them—no hesitation. Vampire or human, I do not care."

"And your parents?" Gabriel asks, picking up speed to change lanes and exit the interstate. "You're sure you want—"

I don't miss a beat. "Leave them to me."

No one speaks for several minutes as we drive toward the outskirts of the city. Buildings thin out the further we get from Manhattan, replaced by more greenery and several massive homes.

"Marcel is behind us," Kade announces as we pull onto the road that leads to the estate. "And Jase and Fallon are in the car behind him with a few other vampires."

"Send them in first," Gabriel says. "We'll follow and find Calla and Brighton, while the others fight whatever guards Simon and Lenora have protecting them." He glances at me for confirmation, and I nod in response.

"They're going to have more guards than usual," I comment. They know we're coming, there's no doubt in my mind about that. But we have them outnumbered. Between the vampires and the hunters—and the rage simmering in my veins just waiting for an opportunity to explode—they don't stand a fucking chance.

We speed up the winding drive, the wheels of the Escalade kicking up gravel. Gabriel pulls up and hits the brakes in front of the house I grew up in. Car doors slam as vampires and hunters alike spill out and storm toward the house. Some are familiar, ones we've met and worked with to create the treaty, including the representatives both sides elected. I notice Fallon and Jase alongside Marcel's people, and unbuckle my belt, blowing out an agitated breath.

"How long do we wait?" Kade asks.

The sounds of fighting spill out of the house seconds later. The sharp coppery scent of blood fills the air and makes my gums throb. I'm usually more in control of the bloodlust, but I'm not even attempting to rein it in—not today.

Three more vehicles show up, and hunters jump out, sprinting toward the house.

"Give them a minute," Gabriel says as a dozen more vampires and hunters converge on the estate.

The seconds tick by. Lex and Kade unbuckle their belts, their hearts beating faster as the anticipation builds.

Gabriel unbuckles his seatbelt last.

Thirty more seconds pass.

"Now," I order in a sharp voice, already reaching for the door handle.

We move as one, storming into the house without hesitation. Chaos consumes us immediately. There is blood spattered and bodies scattered all over the entryway floor. Both vampires and hunters fight together against Simon and Lenora's guards; all the human staff are dead or hiding, but their employers are nowhere to be seen.

"Split up," I bark at the others, my pulse pounding in my ears. "I'll take this floor. Kade and Lex, upstairs. Gabriel, there's a staircase near the back that leads—"

"On it." He's moving before the sentence is out of my mouth. Kade and Lex are gone too, and I stalk toward the parlor, stepping over several bodies in my path. One of my parents' senior guards snaps the neck of a hunter and tosses her aside before storming toward me.

"You stupid boy," he snarls. "Your parents have worked tirelessly for over a century to—"

"Save the lecture, Rufus," I say, my barely existing patience running very thin. "You want to fight me? Fine. But you won't win."

Anger radiates from him, and he snaps forward, lunging for my throat with his fangs bared. I drop to my haunches and kick out, knocking his legs out from under him. I grab him by the throat and slam him hard into the marble floor before sinking my fangs into him and ripping out his throat. I spit his flesh and blood onto the floor and grab the white ash dagger from the lifeless grip of the hunter he killed, slamming it into his chest, straight through the bastard's heart. He was always too arrogant for his own good.

I stand, wiping my mouth with the back of my hand and walking away from his corpse toward the parlor—only to find it empty. I'm heading toward the ballroom—because, yes, Simon and Lenora York are that fucking obnoxious—but I stop dead in my tracks when the sound of Calla's earsplitting scream reaches me.

I'm moving in an instant, closing the distance between me and the gut-wrenching sounds coming from the woman I love. I launch myself at the doors to the formal dining room, and they snap off their hinges, clattering to the floor as I storm inside.

Calla is sitting at the head of the long table, her face pale and her eyes filled with pain. They land on me immediately and widen, filling with tears, but she doesn't move. Blood stains the front of her shirt and is caked on her throat as if it has been cut, but her vampiric healing would've worked to mend it quickly. It only takes a second for my eyes to drop to where her hands are pressed flat against the table, pinned there by white ash daggers. Her eyes are dark and it looks as if she hasn't fed in far too long, which fills me with a renewed sense of rage as my eyes land on my father, then my mother who sits next to Calla at the table. They are sipping blood out of crystal wine glasses as if their house is not the scene of a war.

"Welcome home, son," Lenora says, and the hair on the back of my neck stands straight as I growl low in my throat.

I snarl, "Never call me that again."

"Enough of the theatrics, Atlas. This game of yours has gone on long enough. It's time to end it."

Despite the anger warring in my chest, I freeze. I'm surprised to find it difficult to swallow, to take a normal breath. My mother's voice is devoid of any emotion. This woman, while having given birth to me, doesn't care that what she's doing is hurting me. In fact, there's a glint of amusement in her silver gaze that slices right through me.

She is my family by blood, but Lenora York cares for me as much as she does any number of the lifeless bodies of her staff piling up in her entryway. And that knocks the air out of my lungs in a way far more vicious than I could have expected.

Any love I ever held for my mother dies at that moment, pain exploding in my chest as my heart cleaves in two.

I grit my teeth and hold her gaze; she doesn't notice the shift in me; the pain lancing through my limbs so violently nearly brings me to my knees. Forcing a deep breath, I steel myself and school my expression, stepping forward as Lex and Kade fly through the doorway. They growl deeply when they spot Calla, moving to her side in the blink of an eye, while I turn my gaze from Lenora to my father.

"I couldn't agree more." I launch myself at Simon, knocking him out of the chair, and take him to the ground. He bares his fangs at me, flipping us over and slamming me into the ground. He sinks his fangs into my shoulder, and I lift my knee, catching him in the groin. My father growls, pulling back, and I clip him hard in the jaw with my elbow. Flipping us over once more and wrapping my fingers around his throat, I squeeze as hard as I can, but he throws me off and launches me across the room.

I collide with the wall, knocking off an ornate mirror, and it shatters around me, covering the floor in reflective pieces of glass. My pulse jackhammers as I climb to my feet, taking in the scene before converging on Lenora, pieces of the mirror crunching under my boots. Even as I stalk toward her with pure anger and hatred in my eyes, she looks disinterested at the entire display. Not as if her life might actually be at risk, but as if this entire thing is nothing but a mere inconvenience to her.

"Atlas, look out!" Calla screams.

I turn a moment too late as Simon crashes into me, slamming me into the wall. He grabs me by the throat and his eyes lock on mine. "You can still make this right," he growls in my face.

"What do you think I'm trying to do?" I spit back at him, noticing Marcel and Delia slipping into the room from my peripheral. They move along the wall, going unnoticed by my parents, likely only because they are so focused on what I'm desperately trying to do.

"You want to make a name for yourself? Fine. But this is not the way to do it."

"I beg to differ." I slam my forehead against his, and he stumbles back. My vision blurs for a moment before it rights itself, and I kick out with all my strength, catching Simon in the stomach. He doubles over, and I advance, slamming my knee into his face. I'm rewarded with a satisfying *crunch* as blood spurts from his broken nose. He growls in fury, reaching for me, but Gabriel comes at him from the side, having snuck into the room from the employee entrance in the kitchen. He grabs Simon in a headlock, holding him and tossing me a white ash dagger.

Before I have the chance to use it, Simon rears his head back, smashing it into Gabriel's face. He hollers in pain as blood drips from his mouth, releasing my father, who whirls on him, wrapping his hand around Gabriel's throat. Gabriel gasps for air, his eyes widening, and Lex and Kade move in on him while Marcel and Delia grab my mother. Lex drives his fist into Simon's face while Kade grabs his arm, snapping the bone to make him free Gabriel. They each grab one of Simon's arms, gritting their teeth as they use every ounce of strength they have to hold him.

Breathing heavily still, Gabriel moves to Simon's back, wrapping his arm around my father's throat in another headlock, and snarls, "Do it now, or we lose this shot." The *and it's the only one we're going to get* goes without saying.

I grip the white ash dagger until it bites into my skin, stepping forward, my feet heavy as concrete.

"Atlas," Lenora screams, attempting to break free, and Marcel and Delia barely manage to hold her. "Don't you dare!"

I turn and look at her for a single heartbeat—and then I plunge the dagger into my father's heart.

Gabriel snaps Simon's neck before he drops him to the floor, and I back away slowly, my heart hammering in my chest. My eyes immediately seek out Calla, who is watching with wide eyes and tears rolling silently down her cheeks.

Gabriel goes to her, pulling the daggers out of her hands and helping her stand, while I prowl toward Lenora. Marcel and Delia struggle to hold her, and Lex and Kade intervene just in time, doubling their efforts to overpower her. They're doing relatively well holding their own against her, but she still has decades on them.

I cross the room at an unhurried pace, and Lenora refuses to meet my gaze as she tries to break free of the four vampires holding her. Her eyes dart toward where her husband lay motionless on the floor across the room with a dagger sticking out of his chest. She sucks in a horrified breath, her gaze finally snapping to me. "What have you done?" she snarls, her fangs fully extended.

"No," I say, and my voice cracks on that single word. I shake my head slowly, holding her gaze so she can see the devastation and heartbreak in mine. "*You* did this. But don't worry, you'll join Simon soon enough and none of it will matter."

She screams, throwing the vampires off her in a fit of pure rage and coming toward me in a hurricane of fury.

I shoot my arm out, grabbing her by the throat and throwing her against the wall, shattering the art piece hung there. The glass falls to the floor along with Lenora, the shards slicing into her skin but healing seconds later.

She breathes heavily and pulls herself to her feet, her eyes filled with hatred as she stares at me. "Atlas," she says, and there's a desperation in her voice that almost makes me smile. "This doesn't have to end this way. Listen to me, I've only ever wanted what's best for you. Those hunters, you can't trust them. They'll turn on you in a second. The only way to protect our kind is to eliminate the threats against them."

"You know what? On that, you and I agree." I bolt forward, grabbing her hair and wrapping it around my hand as I tug her head back and plunge my hand into her chest, wrapping my fingers around her heart. Her eyes bulge out of her face, her mouth opening in a perfect 'O' as she gasps for breath. Her heart pounds in my palm as I squeeze it harder before ripping it out of her chest. Lenora's eyes roll into the back of her head, and I snap her neck before dropping her body to the floor, letting her warm heart roll off the tips of my fingers and fall next to her unmoving body.

Everything happens in slow motion after that. I walk toward Calla, cupping her cheeks in my hands and studying her face.

"Hi," she says through her tears.

I swallow past the lump in my throat, ignoring the burning in my own eyes. "Hi."

"Where's Brighton? Is she okay?" The desperation in her voice makes my chest tighten.

I glance toward Kade and Lex, and the former says, "She's with Marcel. We'll go check on her now." They leave the room, and Gabriel watches us a moment longer before following them out, murmuring something about checking on Fallon and Jase.

A moment later, Calla and I are alone in the room with the bodies of my parents. Calla's eyes are stuck on Lenora's body; she's looking right through me.

"Calla," I say in a low voice, but it doesn't seem to register. I grip her shoulders gently. "Calla, look at me." I allow an ounce of glamour into my words, and her eyes flick to mine. "You're in shock."

She blinks at me. "I am?" she asks. "You just... you just killed your parents, Atlas," she all but whispers. "How are you *not?*"

I sigh softly. "Are you okay?"

She considers it for a moment before nodding. "I am now."

"Then I'm okay."

She grabs the front of my bloodied shirt and tugs me forward, leaning up on her tiptoes and slanting her mouth over mine. I close my eyes, wrapping my arms around her waist and lifting her up, pressing her back into the wall as I kiss her with everything left in me. She wraps her legs around me, deepening the kiss as her tongue flicks along my bottom lip, seeking entrance. I open to her, and her tongue darts inside, dragging along the roof of my mouth and grazing mine as her heart pounds against her chest.

I break the kiss, dragging my lips along her jaw until I find the soft skin just below her ear. I swirl my tongue there, scraping my fangs against her skin and reveling in the delicious sounds she makes in response.

"We shouldn't do this here," she breathes, though considering she's also grinding against my hardening cock, I'm getting mixed messages.

I inhale deeply, losing myself in her scent. Beyond the blood and sweat, the faint scent of lavender and vanilla lingers. "Do you want me to stop?" I ask, my lips brushing her throat.

Her thighs tighten around me. "Please, no."

I spin her around and walk toward the table, keeping one arm securely around her, and use the other to sweep everything off the surface. Laying her down, I crawl over her, stealing her lips as my hand glides down her chest, sliding past the waistband of her pants and into her panties.

"Fuck," I growl against her lips, my cock twitching. "You're already soaked."

"Just for you," she purrs.

Holy hell. This woman is going to be my undoing.

"I won't be gentle," I warn her, nipping her earlobe.

She shivers under me and grabs my face, turning my gaze to meet hers. "I don't want you to."

I slide off the table and quickly tug down my pants, freeing my throbbing cock. I step forward and curl my fingers into the waistband of Calla's leggings, pulling them down with her panties and leaving her bare for me. Without hesitation, I run my hands up her thighs, spreading her legs and leaning in to drag my tongue along her folds.

She sucks in a shallow breath, and her hips launch off the table.

I clamp my arm across them, pinning her to the table as I continue teasing her with my tongue, gliding it up and down her slit before circling her clit and sucking it into my mouth.

"Atlas," she whimpers, and the sound goes straight to my cock, which is already beading with moisture.

I slide my hand under her shirt, moving between her legs. I fill my palm with her breast, squeezing it hard as I line my cock up with her entrance. Her chest rises and falls quickly, anticipation crackling through her like a live wire, and I can't hold back a second longer. I thrust into her pussy with one smooth motion, filling her to the hilt and holding myself above her. Her mouth opens in a silent gasp, and I smirk at her before slamming my mouth against hers. She reaches for me, burying her fingers in my hair and tugging me on top of her. I have to pull my hand out of her shirt to brace myself on the table, rolling my hips and thrusting harder. Her pussy clenches around me, and she turns her face, breaking the kiss and gasping for breath. I reach between us and find her clit, circling it hard and fast as she moans beneath me. My gums throb seconds before my fangs extend, and Calla's pulse races, her own fangs poking through. As desperate as the monster in me wants to sink my fangs into her, she's in no shape to lose any more blood. I hold my cock still inside her for a moment, focusing on teasing her clit, and she grinds her hips against me. And when I pick up the pace of my thrusts once more, leaning over her, she grabs the front of my shirt and tugs me closer, sinking her fangs into my neck. My cock throbs deep inside her, the pull of my blood leaving me and filling her, pushing me closer to climax.

"Fuck," I groan. "I'm going to come and I want you with me."

She moans against my neck, drinking deeply.

I pound my cock into her pussy as deep as I can go, bumping her cervix, and stimulate her clit until she clenches around me. Heat fills my lower half, surging to my cock, and my balls tighten. I grunt as my orgasm slams into me and I come inside Calla's pussy as it clenches around me, milking me hard as she pulls away from my neck, crying out with pleasure and announcing her own climax. She licks my blood from her lips and kisses me hard, her inner walls fluttering with the aftershocks of her orgasm.

Slowly, I pull out of her, grabbing one of the linen napkins left on the table, and clean us both up before offering her my hand to help her down. She slides her fingers through mine and hops off the table. We find our pants and get dressed before I wrap my arm around her and walk away from my parents for the last time.

TWENTY-TWO

CALLA

Everything hurts. Having sex with Atlas on a table after having the shit beaten out of me and being starved might not have been the best move, but we both needed it.

My nostrils flare as we get close to the doorway. Blood fills the air along with... fire?

"Do you smell that?"

Atlas peers down at me and nods. "They've started a fire to dispose of the bodies and make sure the vampires are absolutely dead."

My stomach sinks a little at that. "Right."

We step into the massive entryway, and I frown at the blood-soaked floors. Someone has cleared the bodies out, which I'm grateful for not having to see, but the amount of blood tells me enough. A lot of people are dead.

"Hey." Atlas squeezes my hip. "Stay with me."

I nod automatically before my attention moves toward the staircase leading to the second level, where Marcel and Hudson are helping Brighton to our level. She's trying to walk on her own but is clearly struggling.

I slip away from Atlas and hurry toward them, wrapping her in a gentle hug. "I'm so sorry," I cry.

"I'm fine," she insists.

I pull back, sniffling. "But—"

"Nope. Look at me, I've never been better."

Marcel presses his lips together against a smile but stays silent, and Hudson glances off to the side.

"Right. Okay, well let's get out of here, yeah?"

"Please," she says, nodding, and the guys help her forward as we all head for the front door. "Oh, and I'm thinking Barcelona."

"Huh?" I ask, wrapping my arm around Atlas's waist.

"For Christmas vacation." She grins. "You owe me, remember?"

I find myself laughing for what feels like the first time in forever. "Right, of course. I'm looking forward to it."

Stepping outside, my eyes scan the crowd of vampires and hunters. They are all in varying stages of battle torn, but otherwise in decent shape. Gabriel is standing with Fallon and Jase and a couple of hunters, while Lex and Kade are chatting with Isla and several more hunters.

As awful as the entire ordeal with Lenora and Simon was, one positive thing came out of it. It seems to have solidified the peace treaty between the vampire and hunters. It's at least brought us all one step closer to living civilly in the future, which is really any of us can ask for.

After hugging Brighton one more time, she climbs into Marcel's car. He's assured us he'll take care of her and get her back to Washington as soon as she's feeling up to par to travel. They get a subtle side-eye from Hudson before he gets into a vehicle with a bunch of hunters heading to Washington. That's definitely another conversation Brighton and I need to have once everything returns to normal—whatever that is going to be.

One by one, the cars leave the driveway until it's just us left, standing in front of the York estate as it burns. Windows shatter and dark, thick smoke fills the air as flames lick every inch of that godforsaken place.

"Marcel is already in contact with the local authorities. They'll handle covering this up and make sure no one asks any questions," Kade says.

"Good," Atlas says, exhaling a heavy breath as his shoulders slump with relief. "I guess that's it."

The guys move to stand around me, and my gaze meets each of theirs. I smile, feeling at peace for the first time in far too long.

"Take me home?"

EPILOGUE
CALLA

Two months later...

There are four vampires in my living room.

The space is pitch-black, but I can see everything almost as clear as if it were daylight. Everything is the same as when I lived here before that fateful night the same vampires came to steal me away.

Kade and Lex perch on the couch, while Gabriel leans against the exposed brick wall, with his arms crossed over his chest.

"Don't run." Atlas's voice caresses me, taunting and teasing all at once.

I can't help the grin that curls my lips as I whirl around and make a break for the door, yanking it open and moving at heightened speed toward the bank of elevators at the end of the hall. My heart pounds in my chest, a laugh getting caught in my throat as I slam my fist against the elevator button and step inside, calling for the lobby as the doors slide shut.

Instead of getting off at the sixth floor, which is exactly what they're expecting me to do, I ride to the lobby. I push off the wall when it arrives with a soft *ding*, grinning to myself as I step into the lobby and claim my victory. I walk across the room, my signature Docs echoing faintly on the polished floor with each step as I make my way outside. The warm September air brushes my skin as I shove my hand into my pocket and retrieve the keys to Atlas's Escalade, which is parked a couple blocks away. Wasting no time, I jog down the sidewalk and round the front of the car, sliding behind the wheel and starting the engine.

I pull away from the curb, grinning from ear to ear and feeling like a kid on Christmas morning.

Ten seconds later, a call comes through the bluetooth on the vehicle with Kade's name, and I have to force back the laughter as I answer it.

"Atlas told you not to run," he says.

"That sounds like his problem," I say, my voice tinged with amusement. "I won this time."

He whistles softly. "I mean, you kind of cheated. That's not exactly fair."

I laugh. "I don't recall ever claiming to be fair." I echo the words he's said to me before without giving him an opportunity to respond. "Enjoy your walk," I say sweetly. "It's a lovely night." I disconnect the call and head home to wait for my men.

Since the events that went down at the York estate, we've made a point of keeping things light and fun as often as possible. Despite the overall positive response to Atlas taking over as the leader of the York dynasty, some of the vampires were outraged at him for killing his parents. On the flip side, many were relieved to finally be free of the cold-hearted leaders that were Lenora and Simon.

We're still learning every day on how best to work with the hunters. There are still bumps here and there, but after working together to bring Brighton and me home, there's been a significant shift. Vampires and hunters are spending time together casually, creating relationships that extend past the treaty we created to keep the peace between both sides. There is still more work to be done, but things are moving in the right direction.

As for me, I'm still figuring things out day by day. I caught up on classes over the summer, so I'm heading into my final year of school before I graduate in the spring and can start making a difference in the lives of people outside the supernatural world.

I approach our house, clicking the garage door opener, and smile as I pull into the driveway. Warmth fills my chest, and I take a deep breath as I get out of the car and head inside to the rest of my forever.

THE END

Keep reading for *A Very Crimson Christmas*, an exclusive Christmas
short story!

CHRISTMAS DAY

here is nothing more peaceful than a midday nap, slightly buzzed on mimosas from breakfast, with soft Christmas music playing and snow falling outside.

I blink my eyes open, stretching out where I fell asleep on the couch, and yawn. Pushing my hearing out past the soft sound of Brooke Annibale's cover of *O Come, O Come Emmanuel*, I pick up on Kade and Lex playing a video game on the lower level—a gift from Marcel, given to them at last night's dinner party. Atlas is taking out whatever emotions he's feeling on the punching bag in the gym, and Gabriel is making our kitchen smell like heaven.

Pulling myself off the couch, I run my fingers through my hair and smooth the frizz at the back as I make my way into the kitchen.

Gabriel is at the sink, humming to the song under his breath, and I can't help the curl of my lips. I pad across the room and wrap my arms around his middle, pressing my cheek against his back. I inhale deeply, sighing contentedly. "Hmm... What are you making that smells so damn good?"

He chuckles softly. "Turkey is in the oven with the stuffing."

"What are you doing now? Can I help?"

He turns to face me, and I keep my arms around him. "I'm going to start on dessert—a chocolate peppermint yule log. You're welcome to help." He leans down, pressing his lips to my forehead and sending tingles of warmth through me.

"I'd like that."

He grins before pulling away and walking across the kitchen to the pantry. He pulls out an apron and returns, wrapping it around my waist and tying it snuggly. "How's that?" he murmurs, his lips at my ear.

I'd rather you take off *my clothes.* "Perfect, thanks."

We get set up on the kitchen island, which is covered with mixing bowls and measuring cups, as well as all the ingredients to make the dessert.

Thirty minutes later, I've made a complete mess, but the cake is in the oven and the icing is prepared in a bowl, ready to be spread across it.

I swipe my finger through the icing and lift it to my lips. I close my eyes, moaning at the sweet peppermint flavor as I suck it off my finger.

"Angel," Gabriel says, his voice raspy.

I open my eyes to find him standing so close his breath tickles my cheek. Gabriel catches my wrist, bringing my finger to his lips and closing them around it. His tongue darts out, sliding along the digit as he holds my gaze and steals my breath. I pull my finger out of his mouth and bring my lips to his, kissing him lightly until his hands drop to my hips and tug me closer. He claims my mouth, deepening the kiss as a groan rumbles through his chest. Pressing me against the counter, he drags his mouth away from mine, kissing along my jaw until he reaches my ear. I inhale sharply when he sucks my earlobe into his mouth, nipping it playfully. Heat shoots straight to my core, where it throbs with need.

"How much time do we have until everything is ready?" I breathe, gripping the front of his shirt to hold him against me.

He pulls back enough to say, "Not enough for me to take my time with you, which is a damn shame." He kisses the pulse at my throat.

"Agreed," I say with a sigh. "I guess you'll just have to fuck me against the counter then."

The corner of his mouth kicks up as his eyes flick between mine. "Yeah? Is that what you want?"

I slide my hands up his chest and into his hair, gripping the ends as I lean in until my nose brushes his. "I want you inside me." I lick my lips, going on my tiptoes and pressing my mouth just barely to his. "Please."

The hitch in his breath makes my heart race. To know I have the same effect on him as he has on me is a heady sensation, to which I want to cling. He pushes my sweater up, shooting tingles through me as his fingers skim over my skin and slip past the waistband of my pants. I close my eyes as our lips meld together and moan as he teases my entrance, dragging his finger back and forth along my slit. I push my hips out, and he presses his thumb against my clit, making a whimper escape my lips. The ache between my thighs is growing more intense with each moment, and the more he teases me, the stronger the urge becomes to take control of what I want.

I reach between us and pop the button on his pants, yanking the zipper down. Pulling his cock free, I pump my hand along the hard shaft as Gabriel hisses out a short breath. I grin in response and kiss him hard, picking up the speed of my hand.

"Angel," he breathes against my lips.

"Fuck me." The throbbing at my core is the only thing I can focus on currently, and Gabriel is nothing if not accommodating.

He curls his fingers into the waistband of my pants and tugs them down until they fall to my ankles. I quickly step out and kick them aside before Gabriel lifts me onto the counter. A soft laugh spills from my lips at my bare ass being on the counter we were just cooking on. That laugh quickly morphs into a desperate moan as Gabriel lines the head of his cock up with my entrance. I grab his shoulder with one hand and lean back, bracing myself on the counter with my other hand and arching my back as he thrusts into me completely. He fills me, burying himself in my pussy to the hilt. I clench around him, my inner walls pulsing at the delicious friction. He holds still inside me until I'm squirming on the counter, trying to get him to move. He grips the counter with one hand and buries the other in my hair, cradling the back of my neck as our lips find each other's once more. He pulls almost all the way out before rolling his hips and slamming into me again and again until our hearts are pounding and my head is spinning.

I break our kiss with a breathless, "Fuck. Yes."

"There?" he asks, thrusting harder.

"Mmm! Right there," I gasp, digging my fingers into his shoulder.

He reaches between us and teases my clit as he increases the speed of his thrusts. My pussy tightens around his cock, the muscles in my thighs clenching as he pushes me closer to release.

"Pl-please," I beg, my gums throbbing as my fangs threaten to extend, "don't stop."

"I'm right here, angel," he says, resting his forehead against mine as he continues thrusting. His cock hits a particularly sensitive spot deep inside me, and I cry out. He focuses there, hitting that spot over and over. "Come for me," he says in a voice thick with arousal, and that's all it takes to set me off. Everything clenches as warmth explodes through me, and I come hard around his cock, milking it with every thrust. "That's it," he says, thrusting harder, his movements becoming shorter and faster. "Stay right there. Keep coming with me now." Two more thrusts, and he grunts deeply, reaching his own climax and spilling his release inside me.

A shiver runs through me as he stills and pulls out, and a trickle of warmth seeps out of me and down my thigh.

"Stay there," he murmurs. "I'm going to get you cleaned up."

"I'm not moving anywhere at the moment," I say with a breathy laugh, my pulse still a jackhammer beneath my heated skin. I wipe the sweat from my brow and pull my hair back with the scrunchie from around my wrist as Gabriel watches me. He flashes me a grin before disappearing in a blur, only to reappear a moment later with a warm, damp washcloth in his hand. He runs it up each of my thighs, my skin near-vibrating under his touch. I suck in a soft breath when he swipes it gently across my core, still overly sensitive and tingling with the aftershocks of my orgasm.

"You know," I say, letting him help me off the counter, "I really enjoy spending time in the kitchen with you."

<hr>

After finishing in the kitchen—in more ways than one—I slip away to my bedroom to call Brighton, wishing her a Merry Christmas and catching up for a few minutes as I tug on the pair of fuzzy socks that I found in my stocking this morning before a call from my parents comes in. I chat with them for a while; this is the first Christmas I haven't spent with them in, well, ever. It's been a little weird, but we're having dinner with them tomorrow, so it's not as if I'm completely missing out.

Once I'm off the phone, I head for the office to find a book to stick my nose in until dinner. I'm running my fingers along the spines when the hair on the back of my neck sticks up. The sound of his approach reaches my ears before he speaks.

"We're going to play a game."

Those words send my pulse racing and a shiver skating across my skin despite the heavy knit sweater I tugged on this morning. I lick the dryness from my lips and meet Lex's hunger-filled silver gaze. "Is this one of those times it's better if I don't ask for details?"

A deep chuckle comes from behind me, and my heart trips over itself. Kade steps beside me, his eyes sparkling with amusement. "You'll enjoy this," he assures me.

"You guys always say that," I grumble, glancing between them with slightly narrowed eyes. I can't begin to guess what they might have in store for me, which, admittedly, is part of the fun.

"And we're always right," Lex points out, shooting me a wink.

"I..." The argument is lost on my tongue. He's not wrong. "Fine. What are we doing?"

Kade exchanges a glance with Lex before giving me a once-over. "You'll need to change."

My brows lift, and I glance down at my ensemble of sweats and fuzzy socks. "Gabriel didn't have a problem with it," I argue, not wanting to change out of my comfy and warm attire.

Lex snorts. "Well, we won't be baking dessert like you did with Saint Gabriel."

I exhale a sigh, glancing toward the front window where fat snowflakes fall from the sky. As much as I dislike winter, at least the sun is shining, making the snow sparkle on the ground.

"You want me to chase you up the stairs?" Kade offers with a wicked smirk.

My body lights up at his words, warmth swirling around my stomach and the bundle of nerves between my thighs tingling. "I can manage on my own," I say, despite my physical response.

His eyes flick between mine, his smirk growing as he steps in front of me, effectively blocking my view of Lex. "I don't know that I believe you."

"That sounds like a you problem," I mutter, my pulse jumping under his darkening gaze. He hasn't touched me yet, and my body is already vibrating with energy.

Kade drags his tongue over his bottom lip. "How about I make it a *you* problem?" he taunts, lifting his hand to my face, capturing a piece of my hair and twirling it around his finger.

This all feels eerily similar to the night they broke into my apartment and stole me away from my old life. A heady mix of apprehension and excitement tightens my chest, and I pull my bottom lip between my teeth to muffle my soft gasp. *This is the game.*

I swallow before saying, "I'm as fast as you are now."

Kade cocks his head to the side, watching me like a predator would their prey, but instead of scaring me, it only makes me crave him more.

"Hmm, I beg to differ," Lex says from behind Kade. "And I'm going to enjoy proving that very much."

Without warning, I bolt. My fucking socks slide on the hardwood as I round the corner into the hallway, and my hip smacks into the railing to the stairs. I curse and slow momentarily, but even a second is too long. An arm snakes around my waist and hauls me back against a hard chest. Immediately, I slam my elbow back, satisfaction rushing through me like a drug when I'm freed. I take the stairs two at a time, not giving myself any time to catch my breath. *I refuse to lose this game.* I need to get out of the house... and it won't be the first time I've broken out of it. Granted, I wasn't on the second floor, but still. If being a vampire has gifted me nothing else, at least I can jump out of a window to make a getaway—even if it is a game.

I dart into the first bedroom, slamming the door shut and immediately moving the heavy chest of drawers in front of it. My heart is trying to break free of my ribcage, but I can't help the grin spread across my lips. This is *fun*.

Moving across the bedroom in a blur, I open the window, and the cold air feels like heaven on my flushed cheeks. After quickly scouring the room, I find a pair of too-big boots and tug them on, tying the laces as tight as they'll go before I climb onto the windowsill and leap from the second level. I land easily in the gathering snow and chuckle to myself. That was such a rush.

I choke on that laugh when slow clapping sounds at my side. I whip around and come face to face with my sire. *Fucking hell.*

Atlas steps forward, snow clinging to his dark hair and a smirk that would make the devil nervous on his lips. "Calla," he purrs.

I huff out a breath despite the racing of my heart and throbbing between my legs. "This feels a little too much like history repeating," I comment mildly, crossing my arms over my chest.

"You at least made it off the property last time. And as a human. I have to say, I'm a little disappointed." The amusement in his tone makes me scowl.

"I don't suppose you'll take my side on this one?"

He tips his head to the side but offers no response.

"Of course not," I mutter, adjusting my stance in preparation to fight him. He arches a questioning brow, and I shrug. "Gabriel wanted to bake dessert, Lex and Kade wanted to play a fucked-up game of cat and mouse, and you... I'm not actually sure what you want."

Atlas steps closer, those mesmerizing silver eyes searching mine. "Oh, but you do."

"To kick my ass in the snow?" I offer, only half kidding.

His lips twitch. "I don't want to fight you."

"No?"

"Not today," he amends.

"A day off from training? I think I'd rather have a fancy necklace or an expensive car if I'm honest, but I suppose I'll take what I can get. So what? You want to build a snowman, or...?"

He appears in front of me and snags my chin in a firm grip that makes the breath halt in my lungs. My gaze gets stuck on the hint of his fangs I can see, and it's slightly alarming how badly I want him to sink his teeth into me. A deep growl rumbles through him, and he steps in before his lips slam into mine, violent and all-consuming. He steals the breath from me unapologetically, and I am more than willing. I grab the front of his shirt and pull him closer, kissing him with enough fervor I no longer feel the chill in the air. My body is ablaze with desire and need, and if he keeps kissing me like this, I'm not sure we'll make it back inside before either—or both—of us is naked. He pushes me back until I collide with the building's exterior. His hands drop to my hips, pinning me there, and my pulse jackhammers when he presses his lower half into me, teasing me with his cock.

"Atlas," I breathe against his lips.

He kisses the corner of my mouth, resting his forehead against mine. "What I want to do to you..."

"Do it," I practically beg.

His chuckle stirs the hair at my temple. "Right here?"

"I don't care." My chest rises and falls fast against his, my nipples tingling with the stimulation against my sweater.

His nostrils flare, and he murmurs, "I can tell."

I catch my bottom lip between my teeth and chew it, running my hands up his chest. "What do you want to do to me?"

He doesn't miss a beat. "Worship you. Punish you. Fuck you within an inch of your life." He uses his thumb to pull my lip free from my teeth.

"Says the man who made me immortal."

Atlas lowers his voice, tracing the shell of my ear with his lips. "Precisely, my little vampire."

Neither of us moves when we hear Lex and Kade approach from the front of the house. Hell, I'm surprised it took them this long... Though they've been good at occupying each other for as long as I've known them.

"You ruined the game," Lex says with a pout.

I glance around Atlas at him. "You better be talking to our sire. He was the one who got in my way."

Lex sighs. "I had this whole thing planned where we'd take you back to your old apartment and—"

"Hang on." I slide away from Atlas and approach Lex and Kade. "You still have that place?"

He shrugs. "It's a smart investment."

"Yeah, maybe when you have actual tenants living there," Kade chimes in dryly, then turns to me. "He's made a challenge, seemingly with himself, to make you come on every surface of that place."

My body flushes with heat, and I press my lips together as I attempt to ignore the throbbing at my core. "I, uh..." I rake my fingers through my hair, stealing a glance at Atlas, who remains silent. Kade looks as if he's trying not to burst into laughter. "Can't we just do that here?"

Lex stares at me for a moment, and the second it takes for his lips to curl into a grin is the only warning I get before he shoots forward and scoops me up, hauling me over his shoulder and trudging back toward the house as I yelp in surprise. Kade moves past us in a blur, leaving the front door open, and I lift my head enough to see Atlas following, a faint glimmer of amusement in his eyes.

The house is warm, filled with the sweet scents of apple and cinnamon. Gabriel is still tinkering around in the kitchen, and the soft piano melody of *O Holy Night* sounds throughout the main floor.

Lex carries me into the formal living room, which we've turned into a Christmas wonderland with a giant, gold-themed tree and matching stockings for each of us lining the mantel above a crackling fire.

Between one moment and the next, Lex lays me on the couch. The warmth of the fire touches my cheeks, and I can't help the smile curling my lips as Lex crawls over me, kissing my jaw. I turn my head, giving him better access to my neck, and my eyes flutter shut when his lips find the sensitive spot behind my ear. My breath hitches as he presses his lower half into me, teasing my entrance with his cock. I immediately want to incinerate the clothing that keeps him from filling me. I lift my hips to grind against him, and he groans against my neck.

"You drive me wild, you know that?"

I lick my lips, turning my head to look into his eyes. His pupils are blown, his gaze filled with desire. "Then do something about it," I challenge, lifting my hand to push back the hair that fell into his face.

He smirks, flashing his fangs, and it's incredible how much that still affects me when I have them myself. "Oh, I very much intend to." He pins me to the couch with his legs on either side of my hips, then slides his hand under my sweater and finds my breasts, massaging them and teasing my nipples until I'm squirming beneath him. His hand moves lower, his fingers skimming along my belly button and slipping under the waistband of my leggings. He sucks in a breath, then exhales a soft chuckle. "No panties. Merry Christmas to me."

I roll my eyes, but whatever remark I had gets lost on my lips when his thumb brushes over my clit. "Mmm," I hum, closing my eyes and grabbing the front of his shirt, pulling him close enough to seal my lips over his.

He slides two fingers into my pussy, already wet from my encounter with Atlas outside. I moan against his mouth as he works his fingers inside me, massaging my inner walls and hitting the spot he knows will drive me over the edge within minutes. His lips leave mine, kissing slowly along my jaw as he teases my clit with his thumb, circling it gently while he scissors his fingers, curling them deep inside my heat.

I pant, struggling to tug off my sweater, then drop it on the floor. Without hesitation, Lex lowers himself on top of me, picking up the speed of his fingers and closing his lips around my nipple. Using his free hand, he kneads my other breast, sending heat straight to my core and making my skin feel all tingly and warm. I arch my back, pushing my breasts into his hand and mouth as I writhe beneath him, closing my eyes and giving myself over to the pleasure he's wringing from me.

"You're throbbing against my fingers," he breathes against my skin. "Are you going to soak them?"

I bite my lip, stifling another moan. "Hmm." My hips grind against him in an attempt to push him deeper, and I gasp sharply as my climax slams into me like a freight train. My pussy clenches around his invading digits, indeed soaking them with my release, and I cry out as Lex sinks his fangs into the flesh of my breast. I grind against his fingers, thrusting my hips up as my body rides the waves of my orgasm. Lex pulls away and kisses me hard; I taste my blood on his lips, and my pussy throbs harder around his still-moving fingers.

"Enough, enough," I beg in a high-pitched voice, overstimulated and struggling to catch my breath. My body is on fire, crackling with such an intense level of pleasure, my vision blurs momentarily.

Lex stops moving and holds his fingers still inside me. "Enough?" he coos, chuckling softly. "Oh no. We're just getting started."

My heart trips over itself at the promise in his words. He knows just how to use my body to provide the highest amount of pleasure humanly... er, inhumanly possible.

Lex kisses down the length of my stomach, swirling his tongue around my belly button before delving lower, settling between my legs. He shifts onto the couch and slides his hands up my legs, spreading them and guiding them over his shoulders before kissing his way closer to my core. My clit is throbbing, still sensitive from my last orgasm, and the muscles in my thighs are trembling. Anticipation crackles through me like a live wire, and the first gentle touch of Lex's tongue on my clit makes me press my lips together against a whimper. It vibrates in the back of my throat, and I close my eyes, chewing my bottom lip.

"I'll never get tired of your sweet taste," Lex purrs from between my thighs, bringing heat to my cheeks as it gathers once more low in my belly. I'm not sure if it's being with the guys that has made my libido so ravenous and if becoming a vampire heightened that as well, but I'm already ready for him. I grip his hair, pushing him back to my pussy, and moan when his tongue pushes through my folds, lapping up what's left of my release and massaging my inner walls. When he sucks hard and moans, shooting vibrations through me, I see fucking stars. My eyes shoot open and widen at what they land on.

Kade is standing in front of the fireplace... with nothing but a giant red bow tied around his cock.

My moan turns into a choked laugh.

Lex pulls back. "You know, laughing while my tongue is inside you doesn't do great things for my confidence."

"Sorry," I rush to say, "I'm sorry." I nod behind him, and he twists around to look.

"Fucking hell," he says, laughing as well. "You are the gift that keeps on giving."

Kade's lips split into a wide grin. "Mind if I join in the festivities?"

I arch a brow at him. "That depends on where you plan on putting that thing." I gesture toward the bow.

Kade struts over, his grin still fully in place. "Well, I had planned on using it to tie you up like a mistletoe."

Shaking my head, I say, "I don't even know what that means." When Lex drags his tongue over my clit, stealing my attention again, I suck in a sharp breath.

"Well," Kade says, stopping in front of the couch with the bow near eye level. "Unwrap your present."

I shoot him a look. "You did not just say that."

"Don't ruin my fun. Play along."

I hesitate, feeling utterly ridiculous for a moment... until Lex plunges his tongue back inside me. I press my lips together against a moan and reach for the bow tied around Kade's cock, gently undoing it and letting the ribbon fall to the floor. I take his length in my hand, pumping up and down slowly as he props his hands on his hips and tips his head back, pulling in a breath. I can hear the increase in his pulse, and it only intensifies the excitement running through me like a shot of pure energy. Moisture beads on the head of his cock, and I lean over enough to press my tongue against it, tasting him before closing my mouth around his throbbing erection. His breathing shallows and his eyes land on me, filled with lust and his pupils blown. I hold his gaze as I take more of him into my mouth until he hits the back of my throat. I suck gently, pulling back, my tongue dragging along the underside of him, and continue that motion over and over until his heart is pounding and he's gritting his teeth. Meanwhile, Lex pulls back just enough to swirl his tongue around my clit, making my head spin and my body fill with heat. Without warning, he pushes two fingers into my pussy, curling them at just the right angle to hit my G-spot, and I moan around Kade's cock. The muscles in his thighs tense, and he groans deeply before shooting his release into the back of my throat. I swallow it down, sucking hard as I massage his balls with my hand, and he grabs the couch to steady himself as he pulls out of my mouth. Breathing heavily, he lowers his mouth to mine, kissing me hard as Lex continues thrusting his fingers in and out of me until my pussy clenches around them, soaking his digits with my release. I shiver as he pulls his fingers out, and Kade moves away just in time for me to see Lex lick his fingers clean and stand.

Kade offers me his hand, and I let him help me off the couch. I'm too late to notice he has the ribbon in his hand. I turn away, only to come face to face with a smirking Lex. In the space of a heartbeat, Kade has the ribbon wrapped tightly around my wrists, securing them together.

"You know I could easily shred this, right?" I grumble at him over my shoulder.

His eyes narrow slightly, and he whips me around to face him. "Sure, but you won't because this game is as much fun for you as it is for us."

I'm certainly not in a position to argue with that.

He tugs me forward, and I follow, stopping when he lifts my arms above my head, attaching the ribbon to the pull-up bar in the doorway between the living room and hallway. "I love how multifunctional this thing is," he says with a wicked grin, trailing his fingers across my collarbones and in between my breasts, all the way down to my navel. My skin tingles under his touch and my core is still throbbing from Lex's ministrations. I'm not sure how much more I can handle, but I have a feeling I'm about to find out.

Kade stands in front of me in the hallway, and Lex disappears from behind me for a brief moment. The sound of him rummaging around in a drawer has my brows lifting, but the heat of his chest against my back returns before I can question what he's doing.

Lex uncaps something behind me, and I immediately get a whiff of peppermint before he reaches over my shoulder and pours oil down my chest.

Kade steps closer, trailing his hands up my stomach and around my breasts, then massages the oil into my skin. My breath hitches as my skin starts to heat and tingle, and I press my lips together, my eyes widening as they meet his. Amusement flickers in his gaze as the corner of his mouth tips up, and Lex grips my hips from behind, massaging more of the oil there before sliding around to my ass and kneading my cheeks with his palms.

"Holy shit," I say in a low voice.

"You like that?" Lex says in my ear.

"It feels amazing," I say, my eyes fluttering shut. I tense briefly when Lex's finger slides between my ass cheeks, nuzzling into the puckered opening there.

"You're always so resistant," he purrs, his lips tracing the shell of my ear.

"Yeah, well, you've had decades to get used to having somebody stick something in your ass. This is still pretty new to me."

Kade chuckles and snags my chin as the oil drips down my stomach. "And you fucking love it."

The tingling intensifies, and a wave of desire ripples through me. I arch my back, pushing my breasts closer to Kade, who quickly takes the hint, focusing back on massaging the oil into my skin before dropping his mouth to my nipple and sucking it hard, swirling his tongue around it as he teases and pinches the other with his fingers. My heart slams against my ribcage as Lex slowly pushes one finger into my ass up to his knuckle and twists it while reaching around with his other hand and finding my clit.

"Oh my god," I breathe, tipping my head back. Everything heightens tenfold, and it's more than just my enhanced supernatural senses. Between the oil and the overstimulation, my body is vibrating. I didn't think I had another orgasm in me, but as Kade continues attending to my hardened nipples and Lex adds a second finger into my ass, circling my clit faster, my breathing picks up, and I race closer to the edge of release once more.

"Don't come yet," Lex growls in my ear.

"If you keep touching me like that, I'm going to," I shoot back at him, my chest rising and falling quickly with each shallow breath.

Kade hums, shooting vibrations through my breasts, and pinches my other nipple hard. I whimper, my eyes widening as I sense Atlas's presence. Seconds later, he walks past as if nothing is going on. He pauses, then backtracks, leaning against the wall opposite the doorway. His eyes roam the length of me, on display for him, then lock on mine, his lips curving faintly as he watches the others play my body with such intimate skill, I fall over the edge, climaxing hard.

There's a moment of concern that I'm going to black out as pleasure swallows me whole, but I don't care. I give myself over to the otherworldly sensations, unashamed of the sounds coming from my lips as I ride my orgasm to completion, panting. I can't help the full body twitch when Lex pulls his fingers out of my ass, and he chuckles in my ear before kissing the side of my head and slapping my ass.

Kade straightens and grins at me, reaching for the ribbon to untie it.

"Leave her there," Atlas says in a deep voice.

Something akin to panic with a conflicting sliver of excitement takes hold of me as his gaze darkens and he pushes away from the wall, coming closer.

Kade slips past me into the bedroom, retrieving his pants, then he and Lex leave me alone with my sire.

Atlas's eyes roam my face, a glint of curiosity in their silver depths, as if he's waiting for me to say something. I keep my lips pressed together, waiting for him to do the same. He offers a soft chuckle, closing the remaining distance between us and sliding his fingers along the side of my neck, using his thumb to tilt my chin up. He leans in until I can feel his breath on my cheek and then murmurs a simple, "Hi."

My lips part as heat rushes to my cheeks, and I'm suddenly somehow more aware of the fact I am literally baring myself to him. It shouldn't make a difference that he's fully clothed, but being like this, on display as his eyes devour me, makes a part of me want to run away. The look in his eyes tells me if I were to try, he would only catch me anyway, and I'd be lying if I said that didn't make a twisted part of me want to do it a bit more. The curve of his lips makes me think he can read that on my face clear as day. "Hi," I whisper.

He cocks his head to the side. "Comfortable?"

I bite the inside of my cheek for a moment. "Honestly, my fingers are almost numb, and I feel seconds away from collapsing so I could use a hand and a shot of espresso, if you're offering."

I've never seen Atlas as the caretaking type—that's more Gabriel's thing—but something in his gaze softens, and he reaches up and tears the ribbon, freeing my wrists. I sigh in relief, rubbing where the ribbon chafed my skin. "My hero," I remark dryly, leaning into him and resting my hands on his shoulders. My breasts press against his chest, and he makes a low sound in the back of his throat, his grip on my neck tightening just a little.

My gaze drops to his lips. "What," I ask in a soft voice, "are you going to do with me?"

He lowers his lips to my ear. "I'll do whatever I please with you, and you'll let me."

I close my eyes against the shiver that runs through me, and my breath catches in my throat. I swallow past the dryness there, searching for a response, but it doesn't come fast enough.

Atlas sweeps me off my feet, and I yelp in surprise as he cradles me to his chest and walks down the hall toward his bedroom. Instead of depositing me on the bed like I was expecting, he carries me into the bathroom, setting me on the marble vanity before he walks over to the giant clawfoot tub in the middle of the room, turning it on and dumping in what smells like eucalyptus bubble bath and Epsom salts.

He walks back to me as the water fills the tub and the room with steam, and my brows tug together. The corner of his mouth kicks up. "Why are you looking at me like that?" he asks.

"I don't..." I trail off, shaking my head. "Sorry, I just—This isn't—"

"What you were expecting?" he offers.

"Right," I say, averting my gaze.

He steps between my legs, cupping my cheeks in his hands, his thumbs brushing over my face as his eyes search mine. "This is new for me too, Calla," he admits, pausing before he adds, "I'm not entirely sure if this change came from bonding us when I turned you, but I feel the need to not only protect but take care of you, differently from other feelings I had before you became a vampire."

My eyes widen; I can't help it. I'm surprised by his admission. Probably not as surprised as he was to come to this realization, but still. My lips slowly curl into a grin, because what can I say? The thought of Atlas wanting to take care of me is really fucking nice. "Okay," I say softly. "The feeling's mutual, though for me it isn't so different from before. I mean, besides you scaring the absolute shit out of me sometimes, I still wanted to be near you. You siring me has seemed to magnify that urge, but it's certainly not unwelcome."

He dips his face closer, resting his forehead against mine. "Good to know," he says in a deep voice, and I can hear the smile in his tone. His lips brush mine slowly, softly, and his hands slide down my neck to my shoulders, massaging them.

I sigh against his lips as he works the knots out of my muscles, and despite the exhaustion clinging to them, desire sparks to life deep in my belly, making my core throb.

Atlas chuckles against my lips, and the heat flushing my skin isn't from embarrassment, not anymore. I'm no longer ashamed that my body responds to my men as it does. Even when my brain thinks I've had enough, my body knows what it wants and what it needs.

He steps back, breaking the kiss, and moves across the room in a blur, turning off the water just as it finishes filling up the tub, and returns to me in the blink of an eye. "Take your time," he says, his eyes flicking between mine. "I'm going to go see if Gabriel needs help in the kitchen."

"I'm naked, and you're leaving?"

Atlas smirks. "I'm giving you a chance to recover. Because after dinner, you're all mine." He presses a chaste kiss to my lips before leaving the room.

I slide off the vanity and tie my hair into a messy bun on the top of my head before padding across the cool marble floor to the tub. Dipping my toe in, I check the temperature before stepping in and sliding down until I'm almost fully submerged. With a deep sigh, I close my eyes and relax as the bath melts away the tension in my muscles.

I'm not sure how much time passes. I stay in the bath until the water is more room temperature than hot, then I force myself to get out. I pull on a plush navy robe as the sounds of the guys setting the table in the dining room reaches me. Christmas music plays throughout the main floor, and the savory smells from the kitchen are filling the house, making my stomach grumble.

After dressing in a silk black tank top and bright red blazer with high-waisted dress pants, I take my hair down, combing my fingers through it as I make my way toward the dining room.

Atlas and Gabriel are sitting at the heads of the table, while Lex and Kade each take one side, leaving the spot adjacent to Atlas open for me. They all stand when I walk into the room, and my chest swells with warmth as my lips curl into a smile.

"Everything smells and looks amazing," I say, turning my attention to Gabriel. "Thank you for putting so much effort into all of this."

"My pleasure, angel." He steps in closer and kisses my cheek.

We all sit down; I take my seat next to Kade, and he reaches over and squeezes my knee, grinning softly. When I turn my gaze to Lex across the table, he shoots me a wink, before reaching for the dish of mashed potatoes. As the music plays softly in the background, the five of us fill our plates with turkey, stuffing, steamed vegetables, and potatoes. On one side of my plate is a glass of blood and on the other is a flute of champagne. Once we're done dishing our food, Atlas lifts his champagne flute, and the rest of us follow suit.

"It's been one hell of a year," he says, "but there is no one else I'd rather spend it with than those sitting here tonight."

Everyone nods in agreement, and I lick my lips before saying, "This isn't the Christmas I pictured myself having. After you all came into my life, I didn't think I'd *want* to celebrate anything." I glance around the table at the vampires, who, in less than a year, have become the most important people in my life, and a smile forms on my lips. "I can't tell you how glad I am to have been wrong about that." I hold my champagne flute in front of me. "So, cheers." The sound of glasses clinking together fills the air as the room glows with golden light from the chandelier above. "And Merry Christmas."

Join my mailing list at https://www.authorjacarter.com/newsletter-sign-up to be the first to know about new books and get access to reader exclusives!

Join J.A. Carter on Patreon at www.patreon.com/authorjacarter for exclusive access to signed paperbacks, bonus content, early cover reveals and book releases, plus so much more!

Follow J.A. Carter on Instagram and TikTok (@authorjacarter) to stay up to date with all of the things!

Join J.A. Carter's Reader Lounge on Facebook for first looks and exclusives!

www.ingramcontent.com/pod-product-compliance
Lightning Source LLC
Chambersburg PA
CBHW020344220726
48290CB00014B/1001